'I—don't know,' Anthea said slowly.

What *did* she say? Could she spend two weeks in Charles's company without ending up completely besotted with him? And what would that bring her? Nothing but black misery. He'd been honest with her.

His eyes were fixed on her, and it seemed that he was following at least part of her train of thought.

'I admit I'm being entirely selfish,' he said. 'I should very much enjoy your company. But of course if you're looking for a——'

'A sexual romp? I'm not,' Anthea said coolly.

Another book you will enjoy
by MARJORIE LEWTY

LIGHTNING STRIKE

April in Paris was a chance not to be turned down, even if Lissa was to spend two weeks working alongside her irascible boss, Hugh Winchester. What she didn't anticipate was how quickly her feelings for him would change. Not that he must ever find out, of course...

DEEP WATER

BY

MARJORIE LEWTY

MILLS & BOON LIMITED
ETON HOUSE 18-24 PARADISE ROAD
RICHMOND SURREY TW9 1SR

First published in Great Britain 1991
by Mills & Boon Limited

This edition 1992

ISBN 0 263 77304 3

Set in Times Roman 10½ on 12 pt.
91-9202-51731 C

Made and printed in Great Britain

CHAPTER ONE

SHE was sitting in the transit lounge of Miami airport when she saw him again. It was five years ago, but she recognised him at once.

He was leaning against a pillar, a tall, dark, faintly-bored-looking man, probably in his mid-thirties. He held a newspaper in his hand, but she didn't think he was reading it. Every now and again he'd look up, frowning, at the departures board, then his glance would pass without interest over the occupants of the rows of seats. Once it passed over her, but it didn't pause for an instant. Why should it? He wouldn't recognise the pale, tired-looking girl in the smart taupe travelling suit as the shy seventeen-year-old he'd befriended at a wedding party five years ago.

Charles, she thought. She'd never heard his other name and she hadn't wanted to enquire.

Charles. It suited him. Suited his tall, spare, muscular frame in its expensively tailored dark suit. He'd worn a white dinner jacket that other evening and that had seemed swooningly romantic to her then. What a naïve child she must have been!

Now, in this airport lounge halfway across the world, she stared at him and to her amazement felt a faint stirring low inside her. A hangover from five years ago? Or merely a frank female reaction to a man whose sexual magnetism was so immediately evident? His black hair had threads of white over the ears now, she saw, which gave him an even more distinguished appearance. A captain of industry, no doubt about that. Five years ago that wouldn't have worried her, but now it would. Geoffrey was a financial wizard, as were all his friends, and she had had more than enough of financial wizards in the last few months.

She amused herself by wondering how the man standing by the pillar would react if she went up to him and said, 'Hello, Charles—remember me? I'm Anthea Lloyd—we met at my sister Pamela's wedding party in London, ages ago.'

He would, she thought, be polite and hide his dismay and boredom. He was too kind to give her a brush-off. She remembered his kindness that night of the party. He hadn't *had* to rescue a shy young girl, lost among the sophisticated friends of her elder sister and her new brother-in-law.

Suddenly she felt her body brace itself to rise from the seat—as if some outside force were pulling her towards him. Then she saw him fold his newspaper, thrust it impatiently into a litter bin and become lost to view as he strode off through the crowd towards the information desk. She sank back into her seat, rather devastated to find that she was trembling all over. A few minutes later, when she boarded her plane to Grand Cayman, her knees still felt weak. But that, she told herself, was because she really was tired out. Nothing to do with a memory of a teenage crush.

The flight from Heathrow to Miami had seemed endless, but now there was only about another hour to go. She laid her head back and looked down at the dark blue of the sea below and tried to feel thrilled and excited that she would soon be having a luxury holiday on a luxury island.

She *would* be thrilled and excited when she got there and saw Pamela again, after nearly two years. But just now all she felt was a dragging tiredness.

She wrenched her thoughts away from the traumas of the last months and centred them on the here and now.

How odd that she should see Charles again after all this time! Even odder that she should recognise him without any doubt in her mind. It was ages since she'd given him a thought, but now she found the memory coming back to her, vivid and detailed, of that strange little meeting five years ago at Pamela's wedding party.

Five years ago... Anthea closed her eyes and drifted into a half-sleep, lulled by the distant throb of the engines. And then she was back in that riverside apartment in London. She was seventeen and she was wearing a pink jersey dress which she'd designed and made herself. It had long, fitted sleeves, a soft, flutey skirt and a wide belt with a silver clasp, and she'd been rather pleased with it—until she saw the clothes the other women were wearing. Now she was feeling awkward and self-conscious among a roomful of smart and sophisticated strangers.

Pamela and Guy had left for their honeymoon an hour ago, but the party in Guy's London apartment was dragging on. There was plenty of food and drink left and the guests had evidently decided to make an evening of it.

She stood alone beside the long window opening on to the balcony, and her palms were beginning to feel damp with nerves. She didn't know any of the other guests and they weren't taking any notice of her.

Her father had been spirited away to another room by Guy's father, presumably to get some peace.

In the long, elegant drawing-room, someone put on a record and, as the September light began to fade, the room was soon full of gyrating couples.

Presently she slipped out on to the balcony and leant on the railings, watching the dusk settling mistily over the Thames and the river-boats gliding silently along. It was all rather beautiful, she thought with pleasure, the air cool on her cheeks. Lovely to get away from the noise and heat inside the room. She could stay here until Daddy came to fetch her. She was rather glad that her stepmother had had one of her migraines and hadn't come to London for the wedding. Neither she nor Pamela had much in common with their father's new wife.

She didn't hear the man come up behind her until he spoke. 'Why all alone out here?' he said, and his voice was deep and quizzical, like the voices of the heroes in the Regency romances she loved.

She glanced sideways and upwards, but couldn't see his face clearly. It was easier not to feel shy when she didn't have to meet the politely bored expression on the faces of Guy's city friends.

'Because I'm a wallflower,' she answered, adding with a grin, 'If you're familiar with the term. And because I like it out here.'

He moved forward and stood beside her, his tall body a dark shadow against the paling sky. His head was close to hers as he rested his forearms on the rail. 'I like it here too,' he said. 'And I rather like wall-flowers. They bloom in May and herald the summer, and they smell nice.' He leaned towards her. 'Mmm—you smell nice too.'

Her stomach lurched. What was this—was he going to kiss her? Suddenly she felt very young and inexperienced. It wasn't because she'd never been kissed, but this man was in a different league from the boys at tennis club dances, and she guessed that his kisses would be different too. She felt a *frisson* of something that might be fear in the pit of her stomach. When he drew away again she felt relief—or could it be disappointment?

'Who are you—what's your real name, little wallflower?' he said. 'Heavens, that sounds like something from Gilbert and Sullivan.'

She laughed, suddenly relaxed. 'I know.' She sang softly, '"I'm called Little Buttercup, dear little Buttercup, though I could never tell why..."'

'Very nice,' he said. '*Pinafore*, isn't it? We share an enthusiasm, do we?'

'I love Gilbert and Sullivan,' she replied eagerly. 'I've got all the records.' She added a little sadly, 'They were my mother's—all old LPs.'

'Not very fashionable. Don't you go in for pop or rock or whatever the latest thing is?' he asked, not with superior amusement but almost as if he wanted to know.

'Oh, those too—a few,' she admitted.

'But you haven't told me who you are and why you're here,' he said.

'I'm merely the bride's kid sister. Nobody, really.'

He swung round with his back to the railings, so that the light from the room fell full on his face. Her heart skipped a beat. He was so dark and—not exactly handsome, but—somehow *exciting*. Just meeting the gleam of his eyes beneath their lowered lids made her feel very odd inside in a way she'd never felt before.

'Oh, no,' he said softly. 'Not "merely". And certainly not "nobody". Even in this light I can see that you're going to break a lot of male hearts very soon.'

'Me?' she croaked, overcome. 'You're just being kind, aren't you?'

He chuckled, a sound deep in his throat. 'Oh, I'm always reasonably kind, I hope, to little children and dumb animals, but you don't come into either category, so you must believe that I'm being truthful. You're very lovely, and that's a beautiful dress you're wearing. Is one allowed to kiss the bride's sister?'

He leaned down and kissed her gently on the lips. His hair brushed her forehead and her heart gave a great throb and bounced about crazily. When he drew away she put a hand up to her throat in case he should see the way the bodice of her pink jersey dress was straining against her breasts.

This immediate awareness of a strange man was new and overwhelming. But of course he wasn't like any man she'd ever met before—ever even seen, for that matter. He was as different from the boys she knew as—as a jungle leopard from a domestic tabby. He was dark—and dangerous—and utterly devastating.

'Come and sit down and tell me about yourself,' he said, and drew her to a wooden seat beside the wall. 'I take it you've left school? What next?'

'I'm starting at college soon, here in London,' she told him, 'studying fashion design.'

He nodded. 'And you live at home?'

'My home's in the Midlands, but I'm going to share a flat in London with two other girls.' Suddenly she found herself talking easily, telling him about her widower father's having married again recently, and about her stepmother, who didn't fancy having a grown-up stepdaughter around the house. 'I suppose you can understand that, really,' she said rather wistfully. And about her sister Pamela, six years older, who had just got married and was so amazingly beautiful...

'But, of course, you know Pamela,' she said, suddenly becoming self-conscious again.

'Not really—Guy is a colleague of my sister's husband at the bank.' He laughed. He had a gorgeous, deep laugh, and it sent little shivers down her back. 'I'm gate-crashing the party, actually.'

The music changed to a slow, smoochy beat. Inside the room the lights were dimmed. Couples clung together, rocking on the spot or moving languidly like figures in a film dream-sequence.

The man turned towards the open door into the drawing-room. He's leaving me, Anthea thought, and felt as if she were slipping into a great black hole.

But he held out a hand to her. 'Come and dance with me, little wallflower,' he said, and she went into his arms as if it was the most natural thing in the world to be pressed against him, to move with him to the heavy beat of the music, her head against his shoulder, her body soft and pliant, and a slow warmth creeping all over her.

'Charles!'

A vision in glittery white, smooth and perfumed, came between them in the dim light, sliding one arm possessively round the man's neck. 'Darling, I'm so sorry I couldn't make the start of the party, but I thought you might still be here. Have you had enough—shall we go back to my flat?' The light voice dropped huskily on the last words.

'Cherry, my sweet!' They were kissing now, at length, like lovers.

She ought to have expected it; she should have known he had a girl—probably lots of girls. But the shattering of the dream was so sudden, so brutal. Shivering, she turned and began to grope her way towards the door. She must find her father—tell him she wanted to leave. But the close mass of swaying bodies barred her way.

Charles's arm shot out and caught her.

'We were dancing,' he said. 'Remember?' He added, to the girl in white, 'Wait in the car for me, sweetheart; I'll be with you soon.'

The girl he'd called Cherry—or was it *chérie*?—laughed lightly. 'OK, I'll leave you to your duty-dance, darling. But don't be long.'

This was the worst of all—to be looked upon as a duty. 'Please . . .' she stammered as his arms closed round her again. 'You don't have to—it was kind of you but . . . but really I'm OK. I must go and find my father.'

'Really?' His voice was faintly teasing.

'Yes, really.' She drew away and felt as if she was going to burst into tears. 'Thank you for taking pity on me,' she muttered, not looking at him, and pushed her way desperately between the clinging couples into the hall . . .

Gradually the scene faded. Anthea was back again in the plane, and her eyes were full of tears. She was aware of the beat of the engines and the smiling stewardess beside her with a tray of coffee.

She blinked at the girl stupidly. 'Oh, thank you. Yes, coffee, please.'

She laid her head back against the seat, part of her mind still back in that other scene, five years ago, marvelling that the sight of the man called Charles should have recalled that small episode in such detail. But perhaps it wasn't so strange. At the time she had engraved it on her memory—on her heart. She hadn't allowed herself to forget Charles. She'd thought about him all through the two years at college. She'd come across a photograph of him in a glossy magazine, taken in a group at some millionaire's house-party, and had cut it out, isolating him from the surrounding people, and hung it on the wall of her bedroom. The names were under the photograph, but the print was too blurred to decipher. She was rather glad. He was . . . just Charles.

Whereas the other girls had had pin-ups of pop stars and racing drivers, she had had Charles. Her pin-up. And, although she'd giggled at the absurdity of it, she'd allowed herself to fantasise over him now and then. He'd seemed to her youthful idealism like the perfect man, and she'd endowed him with all the qualities she especially liked: humour, kindness, generosity, broad-mindedness—he had the lot, as well as being tall and gorgeous to look at. And even now, after all this time, she remembered how his brief, friendly kiss had jolted her into a knowledge of her own sexuality.

Five years ago! And the magnetism was still there. She had almost made a fool of herself in the airport lounge. Ah, well, ships that pass in the night, she thought, with a rueful smile for the romantic girl she'd been at seventeen. She was hardly likely to encounter her pin-up again. She gazed through the plane's window at the blue sea below and turned her thoughts to the happiness of seeing Pamela, and to the holiday ahead.

That night, in her sister's luxury condo on Seven Mile Beach in Grand Cayman, Anthea slept round the clock. Jet lag, plus the after-effects of a dose of flu, plus the worries and disasters of the last two months, had left her feeling like a washed-out rag. She hadn't realised how tired she'd been. Sleep was what she needed most.

She opened her eyes and closed them again quickly. Just lately, waking up had been something she'd put off as long as possible. There'd been no promise of a glad new day when she'd awakened to the dismal January light that had seeped in through the window of her London flat.

But now something was different. Filtered sunlight was caressing her eyelids; a warm, scented breeze was fanning her cheeks; a softly-sprung mattress was moulding itself seductively to her slim body.

Cautiously she opened her eyes again and lifted herself up on to one elbow. The bedroom was a dream. White slatted blinds at the wide window let through narrow bars of sunshine, falling across the sleek ivory furniture, the pale green carpet, the silky multi-coloured bedspread that covered her to the waist. Through a half-open door she could see the pale green fitments of a connecting shower-room.

A smile began to pull at the corners of her mouth. Of course—the Caribbean! To be exact, the Cayman Islands, that paradise of the rich and successful. Anthea wasn't rich, or successful, but Pamela was both, and that was how she had come to be here.

The door opened a crack and then swung fully open, and her sister came in, a white wrap drifting round her, her wonderful golden hair loose around her beautiful face—the face that, until her marriage, had appeared on the covers of most of the glossy magazines in the Western world. She was smiling, and carrying a small tray.

'Thea—you're awake at last, my poppet. You've had a lovely sleep—how are you feeling now? You were absolutely all in when you arrived yesterday. I tucked you up in bed straight away.'

Anthea pulled herself up against the pillows, smiling and stretching her arms above her head. 'I'm in heaven, of course, so I feel marvellous.'

Pamela came across the room, put down the tray to give Anthea a hug, and sat on the side of the bed. Six months of pregnancy hadn't changed her dazzling beauty—only, it seemed, added to the dazzle.

She studied Anthea's pale face, frowning slightly. 'Darling, it's marvellous to have you here. But you really have been taking a beating, haven't you? Sweetie, you look rotten. What's been happening? I've been marooned here in the Caymans without news of you. You haven't written for ages—not since you wrote to tell me about that awful fire at the warehouse and losing all your stock.'

There was no doubt about the two girls' being sisters. But Anthea had sometimes thought that if Pamela could be viewed in Technicolor then she herself might be a sepia edition. Her own hair was as fine and lustrous, but, whereas Pamela's was a rich corn-gold, hers was the brown of autumn beech leaves. Pamela's eyes were dazzling blue; Anthea's were a darker blue, shading to violet. Pamela's cheeks were tanned by the Caribbean sun to a pale biscuit colour. Anthea's had the pallor of England in late January.

It was just as well, Anthea thought wryly, that she had never wanted to compete. Pamela's ambitions hadn't been hers, although she loved her sister dearly.

'*Marooned*, Pam?' she scoffed. 'In this fabulous luxury condo...' she waved a hand round the bedroom '...with an adoring husband and a baby on the way, and sun and sea and sand all around? Marooned! Don't give me that!'

Pamela pulled a face. 'OK, I take back the "marooned". But you haven't answered my question. What goes on?'

Anthea shrugged. 'Oh, a dose of flu last month. Pressure of work. There's been such a lot to attend to since the fire—dealing with customers, writing dozens of letters, all the insurance to sort out and so on.' She hesitated, biting her lip and looking away. 'Geoffrey's exit from the scene. The last two items not unconnected, I may say.'

Her elder sister put in quickly, 'Oh, you poor darling, I'm so sorry. But I must admit I always thought Geoffrey Derningham was a bit of a creep. What happened?'

'He—sort of lost interest when the business folded, after the fire. When I was successful and had time to dress up and make him proud to take me out among his well-heeled friends, everything was marvellous. But after the fire I was worried, and I suppose I got a bit bothered and dismal, and he didn't want to know. When everything went up in smoke our romance did too.'

She was silent for a moment, then she firmed her lips. 'Best thing, really. If he wasn't prepared to back me up when things went wrong *before* we were married, what chance would there have been for us afterwards?'

Pamela sighed and shook her head affectionately. 'It's been a wretched break for you, poppet. I worry about you, you know. You always seem to be working too hard to have any fun. I seem to have so much and you've got——'

'Don't say I've got nothing,' Anthea put in quickly. 'It was a horrid blow about the fire, but it was just as bad for all the others who had studios and work-rooms in the warehouse. I'll find somewhere else and start again—and there's still plenty of time for fun; I'm not over the hill yet—I'm only twenty-two. But don't let's talk about me any more—how about you? You look blooming, Pam. Impending motherhood certainly suits you.'

'Yes, doesn't it? Everything's fine; Junior's coming along a treat.' Pamela's smile was radiant. 'I can recommend pregnancy—it makes you feel so beautifully important. Everyone makes a fuss of you. And now we're together again, which makes everything lovely.' She leaned over and kissed Anthea's cheek impulsively, and a breath of French perfume wafted on the warm air. 'I've missed my little sister.'

Then she drew back and studied Anthea's pale face thoughtfully, frowning a little. 'But I wish *you* were having a better time, Thea. All that work—setting up the business and then——'

'Don't let's talk about it,' Anthea put in quickly. 'I want to forget it; it was just one of those things.'

Pamela nodded seriously. 'You lost a lot, did you? You must have done.'

'Everything went. My new electronic knitting machines, every last bit of yarn, more than twenty finished garments. Everything.'

'Oh, gosh, that's bad.' Pamela shook her head. 'Look, if there's anything that Guy and I can do...'

Anthea held up a hand. 'Thanks, Pam, but I'll get the insurance money—eventually. Anyway, I couldn't accept any more. Paying my fare to come out here was a lovely birthday present, and I'm going to make the most of my stay and go home fighting fit.'

Pamela shook her head. 'You shouldn't have to fight. What you need is a nice rich husband to do your fighting for you.'

'Like yours?' Anthea's violet-blue eyes twinkled.

'You could do worse,' her sister said smugly. 'I'll have to find one for you while you're here.'

'Don't you dare, bossy boots! I'll find a husband for myself—if I decide I want one, that is. I'm not sure that I do.'

Not after Geoffrey. She'd been in love with Geoffrey and when he'd walked out on her it had hurt badly. It wasn't an experience she wanted to repeat.

Pamela stood up and put the tray on her sister's knees. 'Now eat your brunch like a good girl, and then we'll have a lovely lazy afternoon until Guy comes home from the bank. That OK?'

'Fine! And, Pam...'

'Mmm?'

'Thanks for everything,' Anthea said. She grinned. 'I love you. Just so long as you don't go trying to find a rich husband for me! Promise.'

Pamela looked at her and walked across to the door. Anthea knew that look of old. It meant that her sister was planning to get her own way about something.

'Promise!' Anthea wailed.

Pamela turned, pulled a face at her, and closed the door.

CHAPTER TWO

'GLAD you're here?' Pamela's voice came lazily from the green canvas lounger next to Anthea's. In the late afternoon they had the area round the private pool to themselves.

Anthea opened her eyes behind their dark sunglasses. 'Mmm—this is pure paradise.'

She let her gaze move over the scene. The three dazzling white condo buildings, each with two duplex apartments, were grouped round curving driveways. Low-growing shrubs, starred with tiny pink flowers, dotted the grass borders. In the swimming pool turquoise water glittered in the sunshine. Ahead, the feathery fronds of the casuarina trees fringing the beach formed an archway, through which she could see a rim of fine white sand leading down to a murmuring sea whose colour changed from palest green to deep, deep blue on the horizon. As she looked, the multi-coloured stripes of a tall pointed sail glided silently past. It was like looking at a brilliantly lit theatre stage.

'It really is heavenly here—just as good as you've always told me,' Anthea said dreamily. 'I don't know how you'll be able to bear to leave when the time comes.'

Pamela stretched her arms above her head and yawned. 'Oh, I don't know. We've been here for two years and one gets tired of anything in time. Sometimes I quite yearn for grimy old London and the theatres and the shops and all our friends. Not that there aren't some nice people around here too. And here's one of them—Nancy Jamieson. She and Bill were at my wedding—remember them?'

'No, I don't think I do.' Anthea's memories of the people at her sister's wedding had all faded—except for one: a tall, dark, fabulous man who had kissed her on a balcony overlooking the river.

'Bill and Nancy haven't been here long,' Pamela went on. 'Bill's in the bank with Guy. They're the nicest folk.' She lifted an arm. 'Nancy—over here!'

The woman who came towards them, smiling cheerfully, was considerably older than Pamela, forty-ish probably. She wore a jazzy beach-dress that barely covered an ample, almost matronish figure, and her dark hair was cut in a straight fringe across her forehead.

'Pamela—the very person I wanted to see.' She plonked herself down into the hammock chair next to Pamela's. 'Phew! I haven't adjusted to the climate yet. But what I wanted to say was: are you and Guy dining anywhere special tonight? If not, will you join our table at the Coconut Tree and help Bill and me to amuse my baby brother, who's descended upon us for the diving—rather unexpectedly?'

'Yes, of course, we'd love to.'

Anthea's heart sank a little; she'd hoped for a quiet evening and an early bedtime. But Pamela sounded genuinely enthusiastic. Pamela had always been a party girl. 'Never refuse an invitation,' had been her motto from schooldays; 'you never know what might turn up.'

'We'll be three,' Pamela added. 'Not just Guy and me. This is Anthea, my sister from London. Anthea, meet Nancy Jamieson. Nancy and Bill are in the club—bank people.'

Nancy leaned across and took Anthea's hand in a firm grip. 'Great! You two young things will be able to find lots to chat about and leave the old buffers to their boring shop talk.'

'Shop talk?' Pamela squeaked indignantly.

'Well, it is, isn't it?' Nancy grinned, pulling herself out of her chair with a grunt. 'Guy and Bill, deep into putting the financial world to rights, and you and I discussing baby clothes. Now I must go and see how my poor young brother is getting along. I left him on his own while I went into the town to get my hair done, and he's rather in the dumps just now.' She grimaced. 'Trouble in his love-life, I guess, although he's pretty clam-like about it. Doesn't say much. Ah, well—the miseries of youth! See you both tonight.' She gave them a cheery salute and strode away purposefully towards the middle block of the condo apartments.

Anthea slid her sister a dark look. 'You jumped at that invitation, didn't you? I wouldn't by any chance be right in suspecting that some wheels are turning in that busy little brain of yours, would I? You wouldn't be having thoughts about a certain young man whose love-life has gone wrong and who needs cheering up?'

Pamela put on an innocent look. 'You mean the bit about the "two young things" that Nancy suggested? No, cross my heart, love, I didn't even know the young brother had arrived. Nancy told me she has a young brother who works in the City, in London, but I don't think I've ever met him. It may be fun for you to have someone to play tennis with, or go diving. You'll have to learn to dive, you know.

You can't have a Caymans holiday without inspecting the underwater scene. The colours! It's absolutely amazing. If Nancy's young brother has come for the diving he'll be able to give you a few lessons.'

Anthea smiled. Pam was off again—making plans, producing young men, just as she had done in London before Guy was moved to the Caymans. She wasn't capable of scheming and interfering—of course she wasn't. She simply wanted Anthea to find the right man, as she herself had done. What she didn't realise was that Anthea wasn't likely to find the right man among the set that Pamela and Guy moved in. Guy was a sweetie, and he and Pam adored each other, but life in the fast financial lane wasn't for Anthea. She looked for a lot more in a man than a knack for making a great deal of money. She'd thought she'd found it in Geoffrey. She'd been mistaken, and she certainly didn't want to try again for a long time. But it might be agreeable to have someone to play tennis with—and possibly to dive with, if it wasn't too difficult to learn, and if Nancy's brother was willing to teach her.

'OK, I'll look the young man over,' she said with mock loftiness. 'But if he's nursing a broken heart he doesn't sound very good company.'

Her sister laughed mischievously. 'You, my sweet, are just the right antidote for a broken heart. You wait and see. Now, you've had enough sun for your first time. You have to be very careful here—something about the ultra-violet light's being especially strong. Let's go in and have a drink all ready for Guy when he gets back from the bank, shall we? He'll be home soon.'

She swung one leg out of the hammock chair and groaned. 'Help me up, there's a nice child. There are *some* disadvantages in producing an infant—I'm beginning to feel like a barrel.'

Anthea stood up and held out both her hands. As she heaved Pamela to her feet, she said, 'Pam, have you told Nancy about me—you know, about losing the stuff in the fire and all that?'

'No, love. I didn't think you'd want it spread around.'

They walked arm in arm together towards the condo building. 'Thanks, that was tactful,' Anthea said. 'I don't want anyone but you and Guy to know. And I want to forget all about it for the time I'm here.'

Pamela nodded emphatically. 'Very sensible. We'll make sure you do.'

'Welcome to the Coconut Tree.' Pamela led Anthea into the restaurant later that evening. 'Romantic, don't you think?'

Guy had gone ahead to enquire about the table booked by his friend Bill. He came back to the two girls now. 'They haven't arrived yet, but our table's on the deck outside. Will that do for you, sweetheart? You wouldn't rather be inside?' He put a protective arm round his wife's waist, which was already starting to swell, and bestowed a frankly adoring look on her.

'Perfect for me!' Pamela returned the look with her beautiful limpid smile.

Watching the two of them, Anthea thought that they made the best argument she knew for the married state. More than five years and they were as much in love as ever.

Guy turned to her, quirking an eyebrow. 'I'm honoured to be escorting the two most beautiful ladies in the room.' He sketched a little bow.

Pamela chuckled as they followed him to where a waiter stood, indicating their table. 'Isn't Guy beautifully old-fashioned? He says such lovely things—and really means them.'

'Guy's a dear,' Anthea said, watching the back of her tall, upright brother-in-law in his rather formal attire of black trousers and white shirt. His fair hair was neatly brushed, and he walked with a stride that seemed to indicate that he was at home in the world and pleased with his place in it. 'And he's right about you anyway, Pam. You look gorgeous in that caftan.'

Pamela swished the folds of the loose, flowery garment. 'So useful when one's size is increasing daily! They're made locally and they have a huge selection in one of the shops in George Town. You'll have to indulge in one while you're here. But, to return the compliment, you look pretty good yourself, Thea, love. Is that top one of your own designs? I love the colours—the blue and green and the silver threads running through.'

Anthea nodded. 'Designed and made by my own fair hand—just before tragedy struck.' She tried to sound wry and jokey about it but it wasn't easy. 'I don't usually wear things I've made myself, but this had a small error in the pattern and I couldn't put it into stock. Lucky really, or it would have gone the way of all the rest—up in smoke.'

Pamela squeezed her arm in silent sympathy as they caught up with Guy and were installed at their table by a smiling dark-skinned waiter.

Anthea looked round and sighed with pleasure. If anything could heal the nasty wounds which had come her way recently, this holiday must surely be it. The evening was deliciously warm and the smell of succulent seafood mingled with that of the tall palm trees that overhung the sides of the deck. Almost immediately below, a line of white waves broke lazily on the sand, and beyond lay the darkness of the ocean under a black sky thick with stars. A white-suited quintet was playing Caribbean music on a dais in the corner, behind a bank of crimson and yellow flowers set among trailing greenery.

The tables round the central dance-floor were beginning to fill up, one or two couples were already dancing enthusiastically, and there was an atmosphere of laughter and light-hearted chatter. Anthea sat back, feeling relaxed and happy for the first time for weeks. Oh, yes, she could put her woes behind her and enjoy her stay here.

The waiter was hovering. Guy ordered drinks and said they would wait until their friends arrived to give the main order.

'Here they are now.' Pamela raised an arm in greeting. 'Trust Nancy to be punctual! And—oh, my goodness!'

'What?' enquired Guy, lifting his head from the menu.

Pamela gave a stifled laugh. 'Just—some baby brother!'

Anthea looked round to where Nancy Jamieson, in a blue and white candy-striped dress, was coming towards them across the wide deck. Beside her, her husband was short and spare, with thinning sandy hair and gold-rimmed glasses. And behind them walked the man who had to be Nancy's 'baby brother'.

Anthea felt her mouth go dry and her stomach clench uncomfortably. She had the strangest feeling that somewhere at the very back of her mind she had known all the time that it would be Charles. He must have decided to come on a later plane from Miami.

She watched him stride across the deck, and it seemed as if he was walking straight towards *her*. She almost expected him to come up and greet her. She felt a smile of welcome begin to stretch her mouth—the kind of smile you give to a friend you've known for years.

The little group had reached the table now. 'Sorry we're a bit late,' Nancy was saying in her blithe way. 'Pamela, do you know my brother, Charles Ravenscroft? I think he came to your wedding party with us, but I can't quite remember.'

Pamela laughed her silvery laugh. 'I can't remember a thing about it. Isn't it a shame? Your wedding-day is supposed to be the greatest day of your life, and you're so nervous that afterwards it's all a blur! Hello, Charles——' she held out her hand '—nice to meet you now, anyway. I'm sure you know Guy, don't you? Nancy said you're a City chap. And this is my young sister, Anthea.'

Anthea's smile had become fixed. Her hand went out automatically. 'Hello,' she murmured. It was absurd, this feeling of tension. What did she expect? Of course he wouldn't remember her; he had probably never seen her face clearly that night on the balcony—and after the glamorous girl in white had appeared he wouldn't have looked at *her*, even though he'd been courteous enough to offer to finish their dance.

His hand touched hers briefly. 'Hello,' he said. His glance passed over her without recognition or interest—just as it had done in the airport lounge.

He turned to his sister. 'Where do you want me to sit, Nan?' He couldn't have made it plainer—short of absolute rudeness—that he didn't in the least want to be here.

Nancy introduced her husband Bill to Anthea, and then she fussed round, organising the seating. 'No, Pamela—Guy's going to entertain *me* tonight, aren't you, Guy?' She fluttered her eyelashes under the straight, dark fringe, mock-flirtatious. 'And Bill, you can practise your charm on Pamela. Anthea, you sit here—so that you can look out at the ocean. And Charles next to you.'

When Nancy had got them all settled to her satisfaction, drinks had been brought to the table, and the ordering had been done, Bill Jamieson said jovially, 'Well, this is very pleasant—our little party has expanded delightfully.' He raised his glass. 'Here's wishing you a super holiday, Anthea. And Charles too, of course.'

'Thank you,' Anthea said. Her throat was stiff and her mouth was dry, and she was ridiculously conscious of the man sitting next to her, dark and silent. This wouldn't do at all, she berated herself. She wasn't a teenager any longer, having love-sick fantasies about a marvellous man whose photograph was pinned up on her bedroom wall. She would be cool and poised, reminding herself that she had been the owner of a successful business until fate had stepped in and spoiled it.

The obvious thing to do was to remind him that they had met before. Put the situation on a casual footing, where it belonged. She turned towards him. 'Didn't we meet five years ago at Pamela's wedding? I seem to remember...'

She took a quick glance up at his dark, grim face. The change in him from the man she remembered was shocking. The mouth was drawn into bitter lines, the dark eyes sombre, hooded, faintly bored. But, most important of all, although it didn't show overtly, she sensed a deep, corrosive anger.

He took a long swig of wine and reached for the bottle to refill his glass, even before the waiter could do it for him. 'Did we?' he said laconically. He turned his head the merest fraction. 'I'm afraid my memory doesn't go back as far as that,' he drawled.

If he had intended a snub then he could hardly have done better. Anthea felt as if she'd been punched in the stomach. Certainly she wasn't going to remind him, with chapter and verse, of their brief earlier meeting, and risk being snubbed again. Neither was she going to submit tamely to such a deliberate put-down.

Her eyes narrowed. Her soft lips curled. 'Mr Darcy, I presume?' She had to take for granted that he was familiar with Jane Austen's haughty, arrogant hero in *Pride and Prejudice*.

Of course he was. From the corner of her eye she saw him blink and jerk his head towards her, lips parted, as if she had touched a sensitive nerve.

Too late, my friend, she thought with a small sense of triumph, and smiled at Bill Jamieson, sitting on her other side. 'Do tell me all about your new assignment,' she said sweetly. 'Are you both looking forward to your stay in this paradise island?'

Bill Jamieson's eyes twinkled behind their gold-rimmed glasses. 'I hear good reports of it,' he said. 'It seems to be famous for two things—money and diving, in that order. I understand that there are more than three hundred wrecks to be investigated around the coast. And there are certainly more than three hundred banks here!'

Everyone laughed—except, of course, Charles Ravenscroft, who looked incapable of laughter, Anthea noted. The talk became general. Guy and Pamela were both eager to quiz their friends about London and all that was going on there. 'We'll feel like country cousins when we get back,' Pamela declared.

Bill and Guy had lots to talk about, mostly bank gossip. Nancy was anxious to have Pamela's tips about getting the best out of the shops in Grand Cayman. She was careful to include Anthea in the conversation—with a smile or a remark. Charles, for his part, lapsed into silence, eating very little of the succulent seafood dish that was served to them, and drinking freely of the fruity white wine.

As coffee was served, the jangling beat of the music changed to a slow rhythm. Guy took his wife's hand. 'Come on, sweetheart, this is something you can tackle if we take it gently.'

Pamela agreed with a laugh, and they moved on to the dance-floor. Nancy and Bill followed, Nancy opening her eyes wide in an encouraging backward glance towards her brother as they went.

Charles was left with the choice of being abominably rude—or asking Anthea to dance. For a moment or two they sat there together. Like a couple of waxworks, Anthea thought, and had a job to stop herself giggling.

You couldn't take Charles seriously, and she wasn't going to. She looked straight ahead of her and murmured, 'As I remember, Mr Darcy didn't consider any of the ladies worthy to lead on to the dance-floor. No doubt you wish to continue acting in character.'

He grunted angrily, 'I don't like being needled.' There was a silence. And then he growled roughly, 'Do you want to dance?'

'I always want to dance,' she said brightly, 'if my partner is up to my standard, *and* if I'm asked courteously.'

He got to his feet, frowning, and gripped her wrist, almost pushing her past the tables and on to the dance-floor. Both his arms went round her waist, pulling her hard against him as if he wanted to punish her—and perhaps he did. There was nowhere for her own arms to go but round his neck, and she put them there.

He was a superb dancer—as she remembered well. They moved as one person, her steps following his effortlessly. He might be behaving disgustingly but at least he couldn't change the way he moved his body—rhythmically, subtly, fitting them both to the languorous beat of the music.

Dancing under the stars! Anthea thought dreamily. Oh, it was wonderful! She could go on like this forever! Her head reached to his chin and she laid it against the thin stuff of his shirt, feeling the warmth from him spreading all over her, revelling in the dangerous *frissons* of delight that ran along her nerves.

He drew her even closer, and suddenly she was aware that he was aroused. Anger did that to a man, didn't it? she thought dizzily, and he was very, very angry. Should she draw away prudishly?

She found she was totally unable to move out of his close embrace. It was shaming the way she felt waves of sheer lust rippling in her stomach. Her arms tightened round his neck, and she knew that if they'd been alone in some solitary place she would have invited his kisses—and much, much more.

The music stopped. For a moment longer he held her; then he drew away and, with a hand at the small of her back, guided her towards their table.

The other two couples were coming back, laughing and talking. Anthea caught Pamela's eyes dancing mischievously and saw the message in them. Well done, Thea, she seemed to be saying. Carry on with the good work!

They sat down, and Charles reached for the bottle of wine and filled his glass. He drained it at a gulp, and sat frowning straight ahead of him. Just as Anthea was making herself believe that she had imagined what had just taken place between them, he turned to her and rapped out, 'I'm trying to remember. Did we really meet at that wedding party?'

It was fiendishly difficult to meet his eyes with a cool, slightly puzzled look, but somehow she managed it. At all costs she mustn't let him guess how that dance had disturbed her. 'Oh—that! I'm not sure, really. At first I thought I remembered you, but there were so many people there. I might have been mistaken.'

Guy and Pamela were getting ready to leave, and she got to her feet. Guy said, 'Pamela needs her early nights, but you stay on by all means, Anthea, if you like. Bill will drive you back.'

'Oh, no, thanks,' she said hastily. 'I'll come along with you. I need an early night too. I'm not quite over my jet lag yet.'

Nancy pulled a face. 'End of party! But I'm sure you're both right. We'll get along too, shall we, Bill? Are you ready, Charles?'

He shrugged. 'I'll walk back. Don't wait up for me. We'll settle up later for the dinner, Bill.' And, with a curt nod towards the party in general, he turned and walked away.

Nancy watched the tall form threading its way between the tables without a backward glance, and sighed. 'Poor old dear! He's taking it hard.'

Taking what hard? Anthea wondered. Had he lost a girlfriend—a mistress? A wife, perhaps? She wondered if Nancy had confided in Pamela. But whatever the circumstances it was quite unforgivable to behave as he had done. Boorish—rude—ill-mannered. Whatever had happened to the wonderful man she'd developed an adolescent crush on five years ago? He wouldn't be anyone's pin-up now. Or would he? She remembered with a little shiver how she'd felt when he'd held her in his arms on the dance-floor. Just sex, she told herself. And not particularly admirable with a man who was behaving like that. Forget it.

'Coming, Thea?' Suddenly she was aware that Guy and Pamela were waiting for her. Hastily she followed them out to the car.

It was a very short drive to the condo, where the two families had their apartments next door to each other. Their cars pulled up side by side in the car park.

They all agreed that it had been a delightful evening, and nobody mentioned Charles. Nancy said, 'We may as well make the most of our time before the doors of the bank close on poor Bill when he starts work properly. How about a four at tennis tomorrow morning? Us two against Charles and Anthea? And poor Pam can sit and cheer us on. You do play, don't you, Anthea?'

Pamela put in quickly, 'Anthea's first-class. Coming up to county standard.'

Anthea demurred. 'That was years ago. I haven't played for ages. I don't think I could...' She really didn't want to encounter Charles again so soon.

'Rubbish,' Pamela said briskly. 'Of course you could. What time, Nancy?'

It was arranged that they should meet on the court belonging to the condo complex at ten. 'Before it gets really hot,' Nancy added. 'Good—we'll look forward to it.'

In the apartment Guy announced that he had some work to do and settled down at his desk in the big living-room, a whisky beside him. Pamela planted a kiss on top of his head and said, 'Me for bed. You too, Thea? Let's brew up a cuppa and depart there, shall we?'

The kitchen was a dream: gleaming white, small and compact, with every up-to-the-minute gadget built in.

'I'll make the tea,' Anthea offered. 'Just show me where things are, then I can lend a hand while I'm here. It'll be a joy to work in a kitchen like this. You go and get into bed and I'll bring it up to you.'

Ten minutes later Pamela was installed in the big double bed, a froth of pale blue georgette round her shoulders, her golden hair loose around her face. As Anthea put the tray down on the bedside table and sank into a basket-chair near the bed, Pamela said rather too casually, 'Well, what did you think of the "baby brother"? Rather gorgeous, isn't he?'

'Looks count for very little,' said Anthea crisply, bending her head over the teapot, 'when their owner is such a double-dyed pain in the neck.'

Pamela chuckled. 'He did look rather grim, didn't he? Crossed in love, poor dear. I expect he'll perk up in a day or two. Good dancer, is he? I thought the two of you looked rather marvellous together.' She took the cup that Anthea handed her with a sideways glance.

'Oh, he can dance OK,' Anthea said with a shrug, glad of the shaded light as she felt a wave of heat surge into her cheeks.

She'd always confided in Pamela, but now she found to her surprise that she didn't want to talk to her about Charles, about how they had met at the wedding and what had happened. She snuggled back into her chair. 'Oh, isn't this *nice*? Being together—like old times! Now, I want to hear all about the baby. I can't wait to become an aunt. Have you decided what to call him—her?'

They drank their tea companionably, and the conversation, diverted into safe channels, lasted until Anthea began to yawn.

'Off to bed with you,' Pamela ordered. 'I'm taking you in hand, my girl. You need plenty of fresh air and sunshine and sleep. Juliana will bring your breakfast up in the morning—she's my household treasure. Comes in for a couple of hours each day, and is willing to oblige in the evening if required. Goodnight, love.' She held out her arms, and Anthea went into them and was soundly hugged.

She felt like a little girl again as she went off to her bedroom, taking the tea-tray to the kitchen on her way. As she undressed she thought about Pamela and how marvellous she had been when Mummy had died. Pamela had been sixteen and already a beauty, with her corn-gold hair and vivid blue eyes. She'd had dozens of boys after her, but she'd always found time for the heartbroken, ten-year-old Anthea, who, in turn, had adored her elder sister, clung to her, and turned to her for advice and comfort as she would have turned to her mother.

Pamela hadn't changed: still serene, still kind, still thinking the best of everyone and making excuses for them. Look how she'd jumped to make excuses for the utterly inexcusable conduct of Charles this evening.

Charles! But she didn't want to think about Charles. She *wouldn't* think about Charles. Charles had turned out to be the biggest disappointment of her life.

'Poor dear' Pamela had called him. Poor dear, indeed! Being crossed in love didn't have to make you an insufferable boor. She'd been crossed in love herself, hadn't she? But she wasn't taking it out on everyone around.

Anthea turned out the light and padded across to the window. What a magic place this was! The moon had just risen and was streaking the darkness of the ocean with silver. From here she could see over the tops of the casuarina trees right down to the beach.

And there, at the margin of the tide, she saw a tall figure walking slowly, head bent. Even from this distance, she knew it was Charles.

There was something forlorn about that solitary figure, and just for a second Anthea felt a tug of pity.

Then she whirled round and closed the curtains with a snap. Why should she pity the man, for heaven's sake? You couldn't feel sorry for someone who was so patently sorry for himself.

And yet it wasn't quite like that. She remembered sensing the anger buried deep inside him.

Oh, well, it hadn't anything to do with her, and the less she saw of Charles Ravenscroft the better. If she could get out of the tennis game tomorrow without being unfriendly to his pleasant sister Nancy, then she would. She'd come here for a quiet, restful holiday, not to be made the butt of a man with an outsized chip on his shoulder.

But, as she slid under the light silky duvet, she heaved a long sigh before she settled down to sleep. It felt like a kind of betrayal to discover that your idol had feet of clay.

CHAPTER THREE

ANTHEA awoke next morning to the sound of the curtains' being swished back and the sight of a dark-skinned girl with a scarlet bow in her black hair standing beside the bed, beaming down at her.

'Good morning, miss. I'm Juliana and I've brought your breakfast.' The soft voice had a faint lilt to it, and the smile was delightfully friendly.

Anthea pulled herself up in the bed and smiled back. 'Hello, Juliana. Well, this *is* a treat,' she said, as the girl deposited a breakfast-tray upon her knees. 'I don't have anyone back at home to bring me breakfast in bed. It looks delicious.' She gazed with unashamed greed at the crisp rolls and butter, the preserves in little crystal dishes. A ripe peach reposed on another dish and a silver pot of coffee wafted its fragrance over the room.

Juliana nodded enthusiastically, and the red bow bobbed up and down. 'Enjoy your meal.' With the standard pleasantry, she smiled again and departed.

Anthea certainly did enjoy her meal, but she didn't linger over it. There was something she had to arrange with Pamela as soon as possible.

She showered, pulled a thin wrap over her panties and bra, brushed her silky light-brown hair and went looking for her sister. The sound of a vacuum cleaner led her to the long, sunny living-room, where Juliana told her that the master had had breakfast and left for the bank, and the missus was still in bed.

Master . . . missus—how delightfully old-fashioned, Anthea thought, tapping at the bedroom door.

'Come in, Thea. Good morning. I'm being lazy.' Pamela put down a copy of *The Times* on the bed. 'One good thing about living out of the world is that when you read all the bad news it's out of date and much too late to start worrying about. How are you, love? Sleep well?'

'Marvellously. And I've had a super breakfast. I like your treasure Juliana; she's a sweetie.'

'Yes, isn't she? The islanders are the nicest people; I've always got on very well with them.'

Pamela would get on very well with anybody. She just wanted everyone to be happy and did her best to see that it happened. Which made it rather difficult for Anthea to say what she had come to say.

She perched on the bottom of the bed. 'About this game of tennis . . .' she began doubtfully.

'Yes, it was a brainwave of Nancy's to suggest it. Nothing like some hard exercise to chase away the blues. Billy and Nancy are a good pair—I've seen them play—and you and the "baby brother" should team up well together.' The blue eyes glinted with mischief. 'I've got a suspicion that Nancy's putting great store by you as a healer of hearts, Thea, love.'

This had to stop—*now*. Anthea could almost see a trap closing on her. And she was sure that Charles wouldn't want to be in the trap any more than she did. 'Look, Pam,' she began firmly, 'I'm really not keen on being a healer of hearts. I wasn't at all impressed with the man last night; in fact I thought he was absolutely the end—so rude and aloof. He made no effort to hide the fact that he didn't want to be with us.'

Pamela reached out and touched Anthea's hand. 'Oh, I don't think he really meant it, love. He was just in a bad mood. You have to make allowances.'

'Do you? Well, I'm not sure I want to. And I certainly don't want to partner him at tennis. Anyway, I haven't got a tennis dress with me.'

'A bikini?'

'Not on your life!' The thought of Charles Ravenscroft's insolent gaze passing over her near-naked body made the blood rush into her cheeks.

Pamela was laughing openly now. 'Goodness, the man *has* got under your skin, hasn't he?'

'I just hate his type,' Anthea said rather grumpily.

Pamela was easing herself out of bed. 'Well, give him another chance, there's a dear. Nancy would be so disappointed if you called it off. I've got a natty little tennis number you can wear.' She opened the wardrobe and flicked along the rail, selecting a mini-dress of white silky material, finely pleated, with pale blue hand-embroidery round the low neck. 'Here you are—this'll fit beautifully.' She pulled a wry face. 'Some day it may even fit me again. *And*——' she rummaged in a drawer and pulled out a pair of frilly white lace knickers '—here you are, centre court style! Now, get yourself ready, there's a dear, and we'll go down and meet the others.'

Anthea sighed and took the garments. 'Do you always get your own way?'

'Only when I'm right.' Pamela wrinkled her pretty nose and shooed her sister off.

In her own room Anthea slipped into the white dress and zipped it up the back. It was *extremely* short. She certainly couldn't wear it with the panties she had on.

Reluctantly she took them off and thrust her long, slim legs into the frilly knickers.

At home, when she'd had time to play tennis recently, she'd gone in for much more businesslike attire—usually shorts and a cotton shirt. This luxuriously expensive garb wasn't her style at all. She twisted before the long mirror, letting her silky brown hair flop against her neck. Yesterday's sunbathing session had turned her skin just a touch brown—about the colour of a rich tea biscuit, sufficient to contrast with the pure white of the dress. Not bad, she thought reluctantly, not bad at all. She looked more like Pamela than she had ever done before.

Ah, well, here I come—the healer of hearts. And I hope you're in a better temper this morning, Charles!

The two girls went down at ten o'clock to find Nancy alone outside the front entrance to the condo. 'Hello, good morning—isn't it a marvellous day?' she greeted them cheerfully. 'Charles went out for a stroll; he'll be back in a minute—ah, here he is now.'

Her brother sauntered up from the beach towards them, swinging a racket loosely in his left hand. Anthea could see at a glance that he wasn't relishing this game of tennis any more than she was herself. But she had to admit that he looked heart-stoppingly gorgeous in very brief navy shorts and a white knitted cotton vest. Working behind a desk in the City couldn't provide that healthy tan, those whipcord muscles in his legs and arms. But of course he could afford winter holidays in the sun, like this one.

'Good morning, Charles. Ready for the fray?' Pamela carolled.

He managed a grunted, 'Morning,' and then, flicking his racket against his heel and looking at nobody in particular, 'Shall we go, then?' He didn't actually add 'and get it over as quickly as possible', but he was quite obviously thinking it.

Nancy said, 'Afraid there's been a slight change of plans. Poor old Billy's just had a call from the bank and they want him in there this morning—something to do with his new office. He went off a few minutes ago—grumbling like mad. He said to offer his apologies, Anthea, and we'll have to put off the doubles until another day.'

'Oh, that's quite OK,' Anthea murmured, but she thought her words were drowned by Charles's brisk,

'Right! If I'm not wanted I'll get along to the dive-shop, then. Put this inside for me, Nan.' He held the racket out to her.

'Hey, steady on.' Nancy was laughing, but there was more than a touch of the elder sister in her voice. 'You and Anthea can have a set of singles. Go along, the two of you, and Pamela and I will come and watch in a few minutes.' She turned to Pamela. 'I found the magazine I was telling you about, Pamela—the one with the pattern for a dear little matinée jacket. I'd just love to knit it for you if you'd like it. Come along in and I'll show it to you.'

She linked her arm with Pamela's and led her back to the open door. 'Have a good game, you two,' she called over her shoulder.

Anthea almost followed them, but a small devil inside her made her stay where she was beside Charles, and say brightly, 'Shall we go, then? Will you show me where the court is?'

She made herself glance up at his face. He looked just as angry as he had done last evening when his sister had manoeuvred him on to the dance-floor.

'Do you really want to play tennis?' he said ungraciously.

Rude brute, Anthea thought; she wasn't going to let him get away with it. 'Of course,' she said, looking surprised. 'I thought that was your sister's suggestion.'

'Another of her little tricks,' he muttered under his breath. 'Come on, then.' He strode away at a great pace along the path, which led round the buildings to a green cement tennis court. There was a thatched hut at one end where pink bougainvillaea rioted. Low-growing trees around the court provided partial shade, and, here and there between the trees, glimpses of the sea flashed vivid blue in the sunshine.

'Isn't it a lovely day?' Anthea tossed out the social cliché in hope, but got no response whatever. Charles went into the hut and came out with a handful of balls, which he dumped on to the court. Then he felt in his pocket for a coin and tossed it. 'Heads,' said Anthea.

Heads it was. 'I'll take this side, you can serve,' she said, glancing doubtfully at him. Was the whole game to be played in an atmosphere of glacial silence?

He picked up a couple of balls and patted them across the net to her with a contemptuous flick of the wrist. She returned them without difficulty and realised that it wouldn't take long for her to get into form again. Charles probably played very well—she couldn't judge from the patronising way he was behaving—but she felt sure she could give him a game, allowing for the fact that a good man player would always beat a good woman player.

She went back to the baseline and tried a few services, while he stood looking bored.

She felt her temper surfacing. The man was insufferable. She gathered the loose balls together and sent them back to his end of the court. 'Go on, then—serve, if you've quite finished play-acting.' She glared at him fiercely and stalked back to the baseline.

When she turned to receive service and saw the anger in his face she had a moment of doubt. She remembered the steely note in his voice last evening when he had said, 'I don't like being needled.' Golly, she thought, now I've got under his skin.

There was a brief moment when he flung the ball high, coiling his body, and even from this distance she could see the power in the man, the tension under perfect control like a great steel spring.

Then he served.

It wasn't merely a hard service. It was a calculatedly vicious service. The ball that came scorching over the net straight at her might have been sent down by Becker to McEnroe at a critical moment in a Wimbledon final. As a service from a man to a girl in a friendly match it was quite unforgivably aggressive, even dangerous.

Some instinct of self-preservation made Anthea throw up her racket before her face. By a pure fluke the ball made contact—the force of it jerking her back on her heels—and dropped dead on the opposite side of the net. If she had intended to play the shot it would have ranked as a superb stop-volley.

The man at the other end of the court didn't move to return the shot. He stood quite still on the service-line and stared at the ball rolling across the green surface of the court, as if he couldn't believe what had happened.

There were two chairs beside the left-hand net-post. Furious, Anthea walked over and sat down on one of them, rubbing her palm, which was stinging from the impact of his shot, and uncomfortably aware that her legs were trembling. She couldn't have felt more upset if she'd been mugged.

That, of course, was the last game of tennis she would play with Mr Charles Ravenscroft. Short and—certainly not sweet.

After a time he came slowly across the court and sat down on the chair beside her in a heavy silence, elbows on knees, head bent.

Anthea edged as far away from him as possible. She was beginning to recover her cool now. 'You know, there must be better ways,' she said, her voice dripping with irony. 'You could try poisoning my wine, or pushing me over a cliff.'

He raised his head and the dark face was haggard. 'What can I say?'

She examined the strings of her racket. 'You might start by saying you're sorry. Then you might offer to have Pamela's racket restrung. The poor thing isn't quite up to your standard.'

He ran a hand through his dark hair. 'OK, I *am* sorry. It was bloody ill-mannered, boorish, crass. I really don't know...'

'What came over you? It was obvious—you wanted to murder someone. But, as you really don't know me at all, I can hardly think you intended me to be the victim. Or did you?' She looked at him with interest.

'Don't be ridiculous,' he muttered.

She leaned her chin on the top of the racket handle, and gazed thoughtfully at a brightly plumaged bird pecking in the grass under the trees. 'It may not be so ridiculous. I have a suspicion that your sister Nancy is doing her best to foist me off on you as a holiday playmate, and that the idea is—to put it politely—unacceptable to you. You've made that quite clear from the start, as the politicians say. Well, for your information, *my* sister seems to have the same idea, and it doesn't appeal to me any more than it appeals to you.'

'It doesn't?' He sounded genuinely surprised.

'No, it certainly doesn't. You're the last person I'd want to spend my time with. So, now we both know where we stand, we shall know what to do about it.' She stood up and turned away from him.

'Hang on a bit.' His hand shot out and gripped her wrist, and Anthea came to a sudden stop. His touch was hard and dry, and the sensation that ran up her arm was quite unmistakable. Sexual magnetism, she thought; that's all it is. Well, she knew the man was magnetic, didn't she? You've only got to look at him. Ignore it.

'Sit down,' he rapped out, and she found herself obeying. Not, of course, because he had told her to, but because she was mildly interested to hear what he had to say.

'You're quite right,' he said. 'My sister has this pathetic idea that because she has a satisfactory marriage herself it's possible and desirable for everyone else to have one. Recently, since my—since a relationship came to an end, Nancy has been producing a string of nubile young girls to tempt my appetite and mend my broken heart.' His voice was hatefully cynical. 'I'm afraid it always works in reverse. I'm just not prepared to get involved. So I must warn you straight away, Miss—er—Anthea. At the risk of being ill-mannered once again, I must tell you that, as far as I'm concerned, there's nothing doing.'

Anthea turned her head slowly towards him, her eyes widening in disbelief. Then she burst into uncontrollable laughter.

'Am I funny?' he demanded, outraged.

'No, not funny,' she choked. 'Just disgustingly pompous. Didn't you hear what I said—that I don't relish your company?' She regarded the scowling black brows with mild interest. 'Are you always like this? Isn't it rather tiring to keep yourself in such a beastly mood all the time?'

He shot her a nasty look. 'What are you trying to do, Little Miss Sunshine? Can't you understand that there are times in a man's life when it's bloody irritating to be cheered up?'

'Quite,' she said crisply, and stood up again. 'Now, if you'll excuse me——'

He was on his feet too, barring her way. 'I thought we were supposed to be playing tennis. We'll be in the doghouse with our respective sisters if they don't find us here, enjoying ourselves. I've apologised for my earlier lapse and I promise it won't happen again, so what about it?'

She looked up uncertainly and thought she caught the merest gleam of amusement in the liquid dark eyes, but of course she might have been mistaken.

To her intense annoyance her own eyes refused to hold his and she looked away in confusion. 'Very well,' she said stiffly and marched back to her end of the court. 'Your service, wasn't it?'

After what had happened, she half expected him to put on a patronising show of pat-ball. Instead he sent down a medium-paced service which she returned without difficulty. A brisk rally followed, lasting until Anthea managed to finish it with an accurate backhand drive.

Charles was smiling grimly when he came up to the net to retrieve a loose ball. 'It's like that, is it? OK, we'll see.'

She'd surprised him. She'd even made him smile—well, sort of smile. It was quite amazing what a pleasant glow that gave her as she walked back to receive his next service.

Anthea loved tennis, and what followed was quite the most exciting game she had ever played. She was out of practice, but for some reason the sight of the tall figure of the man on the other side of the net challenged her to lift her game, and quite soon she found herself flying around the court, driving and volleying and smashing, just the way she had done when she'd played in the first team at college.

Charles paid her the compliment of giving her no quarter, except that he kept his enormous strength in leash.

He won the set, of course, but Anthea was delighted to have taken three games from him, and, when she finally collapsed on to the seat at the side of the court, she was breathing hard and feeling fitter than she'd done for weeks past.

She said, 'I enjoyed that.'

He didn't sit down beside her. 'You play very well,' he said formally.

He stood looking down at her, frowning slightly, as if there was something he was trying to say. And suddenly she saw how five years had aged him. There were deep lines on his wide forehead, dark hollows under his eyes, and his face was thinner.

He went on staring at her. All the anger had drained out of him, perhaps with the physical effort of the game, and she saw a deep sadness in his face. 'I wish...' he muttered. He touched her shoulder briefly. 'I didn't mean to be so foul to you... I...' He gave a start and drew himself up. 'I must go,' he said in quite a different tone. 'Perhaps you'll excuse me?'

She watched him walk away, racket under his arm, dark head bent, the sunshine turning his strong arms and legs to deep gold. When he reached the thatched hut he stopped and looked back over his shoulder, and she saw that he was still frowning. Then he walked round the side of the hut and was gone.

Anthea stared at the place where he had disappeared from view, her eyes widening. In those last few moments she had seen the Charles she remembered. She almost expected him to come back, smiling that slow, sleepy smile that she had thrilled to every time she'd stood adoring the Charles of her pin-up photograph.

Then, very slowly, the little thatched hut smothered in bougainvillaea turned upside down and floated before her eyes in a smudgy haze of pink before it righted itself again even more slowly. Her insides began to churn with an almost painful sensuousness. She sagged back against the hard wooden rail of the seat and closed her eyes.

Something earth-shaking and utterly appalling had just become clear to her. The old magnetic attraction that she had felt five years ago for this man was still as strong as ever.

She touched her shoulder where his hand had rested, and a wave of love and compassion shook her to the depths of her being. He had been terribly hurt and she wanted quite desperately to comfort him. She felt a violent hate for the woman who had had the power to change him into the bitter, cynical man he was now.

She had no idea how long she sat there. It might have been minutes or hours. But then she was vaguely conscious of a voice coming from somewhere behind her.

'Hi there!' it said. 'Are you OK?'

Anthea blinked towards the place the voice had come from, and was hazily aware of a very tall, lanky young man pushing aside an overlap in the stop-netting just behind her.

'Sorry if I woke you up. Mind if I join you?' He sat down beside her. 'Peter Jordan,' he introduced himself. 'Looking for a quiet game of tennis. Have I struck lucky, Miss...?'

Anthea stared at him stupidly. 'Lloyd,' she murmured. 'Anthea Lloyd.'

'How about it, then, Anthea? Will you give me a game?'

She stared at him blankly—he might have been a stranger from another planet. She dragged herself back from a distant place where she had been floating in a dream about Charles confiding in her, telling her that what he needed was a girl who understood him and truly loved him.

'A game...?' she muttered vaguely.

This was ridiculous—she *must* pull herself together. She gave herself a little shake, aware that the young man was waiting for her answer. Forcing herself to concentrate on him, she saw that he had floppy, nondescript hair, and was wearing jazzy Bermuda shorts and a T-shirt with a lobster on the front. She murmured, 'I'm sorry, I must have dozed off—I'm not quite awake yet.'

'I promise to lose if you play with me,' he said cheerfully. 'I make a habit of it. I'm not very good,' he added with humorous resignation.

'Oh, I'm sure you are,' she murmured. What was he talking about?

'I'm not—scout's honour! You're looking at the world's worst sportsman, the one who's crazy about sport. Tennis, golf, football, marbles, shove ha'penny, tiddly-winks, kiss-in-the-ring—I love 'em all and I'm a no-hoper at every one. Except the last one, maybe.' He slid her a meaningful glance.

Oh, lord, not that! The last thing she needed was to be landed with a flirtatious young man. She got to her feet, and just then she caught a glint of red out of the corner of her eye and turned to see Nancy coming towards them from the direction of the hut. Even from this distance, the bewildered dismay on her face was obvious.

'Where's Charles?' she hissed as she got near enough.

Anthea joined her, doing her best to appear unconcerned. 'He went off somewhere; he didn't say where he was going.'

'Oh, that's too bad of him,' his sister said crossly. 'He really is the limit—I'm so sorry, Anthea.'

'It didn't matter a bit,' Anthea lied. 'Do you two know each other?' she asked, as Peter Jordan came up beside her.

But Nancy didn't stay to chat. 'I'll see where Charles has got to,' she said, biting her lip in annoyance, and strode off, her scarlet sun-dress slapping against her ample thighs.

Anthea turned in the opposite direction, murmuring an excuse about being too hot to play. She *had* to get away by herself.

But Peter Jordan wasn't to be dismissed so easily. He walked beside her, chatting brightly. To Anthea it sounded like a radio that wasn't quite tuned in, a voice going on and on. '...arrived last week...holiday with the parents...something in the bank in London...a flat in Hampstead with two other guys...

'How about you, Anthea?' he shot at her suddenly.

'Me?' She blinked. She'd only taken in about a quarter of what he'd been saying. 'Oh, I'm staying with my sister Pamela and my brother-in-law.'

'Guy Stokes-Neville? Yes, I know them. Guy works with my dad. Pamela's a real beauty, isn't she?' He cast a frankly admiring glance down at her. 'It runs in the family, of course.'

They had arrived at the pool-side by now. Pamela was lying in a green recliner, a huge straw hat pulled forward to shade her eyes. If she was surprised to see Anthea appearing with Peter Jordan instead of Charles, she didn't show it. 'Hello, you two. I'm being lazy. Have you been energetic enough to play tennis?'

'Hello, Mrs Stokes-Neville.' Peter's tone was just a touch deferential. He had nice manners—not like some, Anthea thought darkly. 'Anthea found it rather too hot for a game—which she certainly would have won,' he added wryly.

'Poor Peter!' Pamela gave him her creamy smile. 'Never mind, you'll start winning all before you one day.' She evidently knew about Peter's avowed hopelessness at games.

There was a squeal of, 'Peter!' from the far end of the pool, where several sun-bronzed bodies were disporting themselves, and a curvaceous girl approached at a fast crawl and hung on to the side. 'Pete—come along in! I'm waiting to win against you over five lengths.' Tendrils of wet red hair were plastered becomingly over an attractive small face, and two perfect rows of white teeth glistened in the sunshine as the girl laughed up at him invitingly.

Peter grimaced comically at Anthea. 'You see? I'm always relied on to lose. OK, Babs, be with you in a jiffy.' He loped off towards the condo.

Pamela looked up at Anthea curiously. 'What goes? Nancy went off to watch you and Charles playing tennis.'

'She was much too late.' Anthea rummaged in her beach-bag for her dark glasses. 'The set was over very quickly. Charles slaughtered me.'

Pamela patted the empty chair beside her. 'Come and relax, then, and get over it.'

Anthea stepped backwards hastily. 'No, I—I think I'll go in. I'm just longing for a shower.'

'Why not put on a swim-suit and dive in the pool?' Pamela suggested.

'I—I'd rather go inside,' Anthea said lamely. 'It's a bit too hot for me out here.'

Her sister sat up, regarding her anxiously. 'You're OK, love? You haven't overdone it on your first day?'

'I'm fine—fine. Just hot. See you later,' she murmured, and escaped across the grass. She felt confused and upset, and she needed time to think before she encountered Pam's questioning gaze again.

Upstairs in her room, she sank into a chair beside the big open window. The sun was warm on her arms and legs. A breeze bearing a delicate scent of flowers touched her cheeks. The sound of shrieks and splashes came from the pool as if from a long, long way away.

She'd been shocked by the sudden strength of her feelings out there on the tennis court. Didn't they say that pity was akin to love? And Charles had looked so desperately unhappy. She had had a wild desire to stroke his dark hair—to comfort him. She had had to stop herself from jumping up and running after him.

What idiocy! she thought now. She could well imagine the scathing look he would have given her.

She'd be completely crazy to start mooning over a man who had showed plainly that he didn't want her company. Even his slight apology had seemed to be dragged out of him.

And as for finding the Charles she remembered underneath the armour of cynicism and bitterness—what hope was there of that? She wasn't the kind of girl who could 'foist herself', as he had so elegantly described it, on a man who didn't want her. Let him go off on his own and brood if that was what he wanted. *She* was going to enjoy her holiday on this paradise island.

Goodness only knew what she was going to find waiting for her when she got back to London; it wasn't going to be easy to start all over again. So she must be bounding with health and high spirits and ready to tackle anything. She certainly mustn't return as a pale and pathetic lovelorn creature.

She didn't even have to decide to keep away from Charles. He had shown quite plainly that he wanted to keep away from her. So that made everything much simpler, didn't it?

Before she could find any flaws in this sensible conclusion, she got up and showered, changed into a cheerful yellow sun-dress, and went down to have lunch with Pamela.

CHAPTER FOUR

'WHAT is it between you and Charles Ravenscroft?' Pamela's lovely face was alive with curiosity as she pushed a cup of coffee across the table to Anthea. 'There's *something*, I can tell. You looked positively shattered when you came along with Peter Jordan. Don't tell me you'd had words with Charles. You haven't taken an instant dislike to the man, have you?'

The sisters were lunching together in the long, cool living-room, shaded by the canopy that covered the veranda outside, where bunches of green grapes hung from the slatted-wood roof.

It was just as well, Anthea thought, that she was ready for Pamela's good-natured quizzing. She said wryly, '*He* seems to have taken an instant dislike to *me*.' That was near enough to the truth to put Pamela off the scent.

'Hm, it didn't look like that when you were dancing together last night.' Pamela sighed gustily. 'He's so gorgeous, isn't he? And you looked so lovely together.'

Anthea concentrated on peeling a ripe pear. 'Pam, dear, don't start imagining things. And don't try to pair me off with Charles Ravenscroft. I'm sure he isn't in a mood just now to be paired off with anyone—which really couldn't concern me less.'

She felt a twinge of guilt. In the old days she had always confided anything and everything to Pamela—had never had any secrets from her. But the idea of opening her heart to anyone about Charles filled her with a kind of panic.

Pamela said thoughtfully, 'His sister Nancy absolutely idolises him. She's talked to me about him for hours—how kind he is, how generous, what fun he can be.'

'Hmm,' put in Anthea with dark scepticism.

'And he must have a very good brain,' Pamela went on imperturbably. 'He and a friend have built up a successful financial business in London, and it's going from strength to strength, Nancy says.' Pamela turned her limpid blue eyes on Anthea. 'You don't want to judge him too quickly, love. Most men act up one way or another after a break-up with a girl. He's just taken it badly, that's all—he'll get over it. I'm sure if you got to know him better——'

'Pamela!' Anthea laughed shakily. 'Stop it this minute. It's clear that Charles isn't interested in girls just now. In fact, I think he's trying to get away on his own.'

'Mmm, well, it looks as if he wasn't trying quite hard enough,' Pamela said. 'Look at that.'

Through the window Anthea saw the tall figure of Charles striding along the path from the beach. He had taken off his shirt and looped it over his arm, and his broad chest glistened in the sunlight, the muscles rippling with health. Beside him, her arm linked with his, was the girl who had hailed Peter in the swimming pool—Babs, he'd called her. Her hair had dried into a fiery, frizzy cloud round her piquant little face, and her kelly-green bikini barely covered any of her slim brown body. She was laughing up into Charles's face, nestling close to him, and he was bending his dark head down to hers. They looked like a man and a girl revelling in the holiday atmosphere together.

Anthea felt jealous, as though a thin steel blade were piercing through her, and for a moment she thought she was going to be sick. She pressed a hand against her stomach, leaning forward so that Pamela wouldn't notice.

But Pamela was gazing out of the window with interest. 'It's Barbara Raikes—her father's manager of one of the big international companies with an office in George Town. She's been here for a week or so—I think she's a student at one of the American colleges. She's been going around with Peter Jordan. She's rather stunning, don't you think?'

Anthea swallowed hard. She said, 'Yes—very. I expect she's Charles's type. Now don't let's talk any more about him. I want to hear about you—all about the baby and everything . . .'

Her sister needed no encouragement, and Anthea drew a breath of relief. She had managed to get through that bad moment rather well, she congratulated herself. Seeing Charles unexpectedly like that—and with another girl—had given her a sharp twinge, but of course it was bound to happen in a place like this, so full of pretty girls. Next time it would be easier.

After lunch Pamela announced that she was going up to her room. She had to rest most of the afternoon, she told Anthea. 'I don't mind; I find I'm being delightfully lazy at this stage. Probably when Junior arrives I'll be made to pay for it. Sleepless nights—isn't that the price for having a baby?' She didn't look at all apprehensive.

Anthea gave her an affectionate glance. 'If he—she—inherits your temperament, Sis, I don't think you need worry. You must have been a really placid baby.'

'Mummy always said I wasn't any trouble.' Pamela's beautiful eyes clouded. 'Isn't it a shame she had to die? She was such a lovely person, and it would have been such fun to have had her with us still.' She was silent for a moment, then she said, 'How's it going with Janice? Do you see much of Daddy—and her?'

'Not more than I can help,' Anthea told her wryly. 'I rang Daddy to tell him about the fire. He said he was sorry, but I don't think it meant much to him. We're miles apart really. Janice invited me for Christmas, not very enthusiastically, but I declined with thanks. I thought—then—that I'd be spending Christmas with Geoffrey.'

Pamela said gently, 'You poor child—you've had to go through all this on your own. You know, you really *do* need a nice, kind, understanding husband.' She was only half joking.

Anthea held up a hand, laughing. 'No more of that—I value my independence. Now, off with you to have your rest.'

When Pamela had departed Anthea searched the bookcase, found a mystery novel she hadn't read and stretched out in a hammock chair on the veranda.

She had discovered some time ago that giving herself suggestions went some way to stopping worries scurrying round her brain like ants. Now she opened her book and muttered, 'You are *not* going to start thinking about Charles and that girl. You are not going to think about Charles at all—it would be a complete waste of your holiday time. You are going to read your book and get involved in the plot . . .'

Fortunately it was a mystery that had the quality of gripping from the very first paragraph. After an hour she was deep in chapter three and already making a shrewd guess about the identity of the murderer.

'Hello there—not asleep again, are you?' Peter Jordan's light voice roused her from her concentration.

She lifted her head as he came towards her across the veranda, looking fresh and groomed in white shorts and a sleeveless blue vest. 'No, wide awake.' She smiled at him, thinking he was a perfect example of the boy next door. So very different from Charles and his dark-eyed, sultry sophistication. 'Tracking down a murderer,' she added hastily. Why couldn't she put that man out of her mind?

Peter came nearer and glanced at the title of her book. 'Ruth Rendell—my favourite. I read that one last week. The wife of the garage man——'

'Don't tell me!' Anthea squealed in alarm. Peter was a nice boy but sadly lacking in subtlety.

'Sorry!' His fair cheeks flushed. 'I'm always putting my big foot in it.'

'Rubbish, of course you're not.' Anthea felt rather sorry for him. 'Where are you off to?' she asked him brightly.

'Going for a dive,' he told her. 'I had a lesson yesterday and it's grabbed me. The underwater scene is absolutely fabulous.' He eyed her shyly. 'Like to come along and have a go?'

Anthea hesitated. 'Is it difficult?'

'Dead easy,' he told her. 'I got the hang of it in no time at all. I'll teach you,' he added, confidence rising. 'You'll be safe with me, I promise. You can hire the gear at the dive-shop—that's what I did. How about it?' He grinned hopefully at her.

'What do I wear?' she said.

'Exactly what you're wearing.' He eyed her citrus-coloured bikini and the soft curves inside it with obvious admiration. 'You look smashing.'

Anthea got out of her chair, and marked the place in her book. 'I'll leave a note for Pamela, saying where I've gone.'

She went up to her bedroom, slipped on a green polyester-cotton dress over her bikini, picked up a towel and her handbag, and scribbled a note to Pamela, which she left on the table in the dining-room.

Then she joined Peter, and five minutes later they were bowling along the dusty road in his small hired car. 'There are lots of dive-shops in Grand Cayman,' he told her, 'some of them very pukka and attached to the big hotels. Joe's is one of the smaller ones but it's reckoned to be very good. He's well known to be an expert, no doubt about that.'

'Did he teach you?' Anthea enquired idly.

'Oh, no, he has several instructors working for him. I didn't even see him yesterday. As a beginner I didn't rate a lesson from the great man.' Peter grinned his deprecating grin. 'Here we are.'

The dive-shop was immediately behind and above the beach—a long wooden building with an open-air annexe beside it in the shade of the tall palm trees. The annexe obviously served as a coffee-bar and ice-cream parlour, and most of the white tables were occupied.

Anthea began to follow Peter into the shop, when a voice behind her said, 'Where are you off to?'

Her heart gave an uncomfortable jolt as she turned to see Charles behind her, not looking at all amiable.

'Peter's going to teach me to dive,' Anthea said sweetly. Peter had turned back and she sketched an introduction.

'Hi,' said Peter, holding out a large paw.

The handclasp was very brief. 'You have an instructor's certificate, of course?' Charles said brusquely.

Charles must be over six feet tall, Anthea thought, and Peter topped that by three or four inches; but he was only about half the width across the shoulders. They made an odd-looking pair as they stood eyeing each other suspiciously.

'Instructor's certificate? Well, no,' Peter said. 'We're only going cruising around. I had a lesson yesterday and I know the drill.' He seemed to stiffen his long backbone. 'What's it to do with you, anyway?' he demanded belligerently.

Charles's hooded glance raked the younger man from head to foot. 'If you're not qualified to teach a beginner you've no right to take Anthea out. I suggest you limit your activities to paddling in the shallows.'

Peter's fair cheeks were crimson. 'We'll see about that in the shop. Come on, Anthea, let's find out about hiring some gear for you.'

He marched into the dive-shop and Anthea, without another glance at Charles, followed him.

Inside there was a curious mixture of smells—wood and rubber and salt. Light coming in from a high window showed all the paraphernalia of diving. Anthea recognised some of it—the masks, the curved tubes, the fins. All these she had seen on TV, when divers, surrounded by shoals of fish, glided effortlessly through the water or pried into beautiful coral caves and wrecked ships.

Peter strode up to the counter, where a tough-looking man, with skin burnt to a mahogany colour, was reading a newspaper.

'Er—good afternoon,' Peter began. 'I hired some gear yesterday afternoon and had a lesson—I don't think I saw you.'

The man raised his head. 'No—I was out with the boat.'

'I'd like to hire the same again, and for this young lady too. I enjoyed it so much I'd like to get her started.' His face was rather flushed, and Anthea wondered if he was as confident as he sounded, or if Charles's words had shaken him.

The man subjected Peter to the same scrutiny that Charles had turned upon him. 'You're wanting an instructor? 'Fraid there's no one in just now.'

'Oh, I wasn't thinking of a lesson. I'm sure I picked up enough to pass on my—er—expertise.' Peter laughed a little self-consciously.

The man shook his head. 'Sorry, mate, we don't hire diving gear to beginners going out alone. Too dangerous.'

Peter looked as if he might be going to argue. 'I only propose to keep this side of the reef...' he began, but the man was still shaking his head.

A cool voice from behind them said, 'It's OK, Joe. I'll go out with them.'

The man grinned over Anthea's shoulder. 'Hello, Charlie; well—that's a different matter.' He prised himself slowly out of his chair and strolled round the counter, waving a rugged arm. 'Help yourself.'

Charles lounged across the cluttered shop towards a stand where face-masks hung from hooks. 'You look after the gentleman, Joe, and I'll fix the lady up. We'll stick to snorkelling for a start.'

Peter walked up to him, using his slightly superior height to make a show of looking down on Charles's dark head. 'Look here...' he began huffily.

Charles's eyes met his blandly. 'Yes?'

Peter hesitated—and was lost. 'Oh, have it your own way, then. You take Anthea out—I'll remove myself.' He turned. 'Sorry, Anthea.'

She had a horrid feeling that he was going to cry.

'No, don't go, Peter—I'll come with you,' she said. 'I'm not all that keen on diving. We could play tennis or—or something.' She felt desperately sorry for the young man. But Peter had turned and almost run out of the shop.

She took a couple of steps after him, but Charles's hand came out and closed over her arm. 'Let him go,' he said quietly. 'He'll get over it. We all have to learn.'

She glared at him. 'You needn't have been so—so quelling. You hurt his feelings badly—he's sensitive.' The dark eyes met hers and again she saw the bitterness in them.

'He isn't the only one,' he said flatly. Then, in a different tone, 'Now, how about having your first diving lesson? You may as well, now you're here. Joe has all the best gear in the island, haven't you, Joe?'

Joe grinned and lifted one thumb. 'If you say so, Charlie-boy.'

Anthea said coolly, 'May I take it that you have your instructor's certificate, Mr Ravenscroft?'

'As it happens, I have.'

The dark eyes glittered into hers as Joe guffawed loudly. 'He's the best, miss. You'll be safe with Charlie.'

Anthea was torn. She very much wanted to learn to dive and she didn't doubt that Charles would be an excellent teacher. If she accepted his offer it would seem like deferring tamely to his high-handed treatment of poor Peter. But her sense of fairness had to admit that he was probably right.

'Well? Made up your mind?' He was looming over her, thumbs stuck nonchalantly in the waistband of his navy shorts.

'Why do you want to waste your time teaching a beginner?' she said, looking out through the door to where a lesson was going on: several heads in masks were bobbing about in a small pool, their owners taking orders from a thin man—evidently an instructor.

'They're having a lesson out there,' she added. 'I could learn like that, couldn't I?'

'You could, of course. But it would be much quicker one to one. It's a straight offer—take it or leave it.'

Anthea had a short argument with her sensible self. It would be prudent to refuse. Dimly, she could sense danger ahead if she tangled with this man. But she did, very much, want to learn to dive.

'Well?' he asked impatiently.

'Thank you,' she said, 'I'd like to accept your offer.'

'Right!' he said matter-of-factly.

Suddenly Anthea had a mischievous urge to break through his aloofness. She slanted a glance up at him under her long curving lashes. 'That is,' she said, 'so long as it isn't your intention to drown me.'

He started as if she had struck him, his face as black as thunder. 'What the hell . . .?' Then, very gradually, his frown cleared. His long, sensitive mouth twitched at the corners, his lids lowered into the sleepy smile that Anthea remembered from five years ago.

'I . . . see. Well, I give you my word that your safety will be my first consideration,' he said with mock solemnity. 'Does that reassure you?'

His hand had closed on her upper arm as he'd led her towards the stands at the side of the shop. The touch of his fingers on her skin was doing strange things to her breathing. This man was dangerous to her peace of mind—she shouldn't be meekly agreeing to his invitation. She should be running away from him as fast as possible. Instead she heard herself saying, 'I'll hold you to that.'

She looked up into the dark sleepy eyes and they didn't move from hers. It seemed to her that the dive-shop with all its stacks of equipment faded away and there were just the two of them with an unspoken question hanging between them.

At last Charles shook his head puzzledly. 'I wish I could . . . Oh, well, never mind. Come along and I'll fit you with a mask. As I said, we'll stick to snorkelling for your first lesson. If you like we can progress to scuba later on.'

Anthea shook her head helplessly. 'Explain, please. I come from Birmingham—about as far away from the sea as you can get in England. I learned to swim on holidays in Cornwall when I was small, but diving is a closed book to me.'

'I see. Briefly, snorkelling is staying more or less on the surface of the water—although you can take brief trips downwards when you get confidence and if you're good at holding your breath. The mask is worn so that your eyes can work in their normal medium of air instead of underwater, and the snorkel tube allows you to breathe through it while swimming on the surface with your face submerged. Snorkelling is a good way of getting started. Once you experience the thrill of seeing what goes on underwater you very soon want to go deeper and deeper—which you can when you progress to scuba diving. That's when you carry your own supply of air in a cylinder on your back. Get the idea? Now, we'll fit you with a mask. It's very important to get a good fit so that it makes a proper seal against your face.'

Anthea had been watching Charles's face as he spoke, seeing how the strain and bitterness had ebbed away as he'd become engrossed in something that interested him.

Standing still while he selected a mask for her presented its own problems. His fingers, busy against her cheeks and pushing her hair away from her forehead, were sending little messages along her nerves. When he was finally satisfied he let his hand drift down to her neck and linger there long enough to make the gesture deliberate. His dark eyes, seen through the glass window in the mask, looked strangely intent.

'There,' he said. 'That feel comfortable?'

Anthea swallowed. It felt wonderful. Suddenly she ached for his hand to travel lower, to touch her body in all sorts of intimate places. 'Y-yes—fine,' she muttered.

'Good.' He removed the mask, speedy and businesslike again. 'This snorkel tube should do, and these fins. Just slip off your sandals and try them.'

Her knees felt curiously weak as she stood on her left foot to pull the sandal from the right one. She wobbled and reached to the counter nearby to steady herself. But Charles was there before her, a hand round her waist.

She pulled away with a jerk. 'I can manage, thanks.'

He removed his hand at once but she sensed, rather than saw, that he had noticed her reaction. Damn him, she thought, does he imagine I want to flirt with him? But I just hope he keeps his hands off me, because when he touches me I begin to melt.

She thrust her feet into the fins and he stooped to examine the fit and pronounced it satisfactory.

'All in order, Joe; we'll hire this little lot. Stick it on my bill, will you? I'll pick up my own gear from the locker on the way out, OK?'

Joe handed over a key. 'Help yourself, Charlie. Good diving.' He grinned appreciatively at Anthea.

Outside the shop Charles paused and looked around. Apart from the learners in the enclosed tank there were perhaps half a dozen people sitting at white tables in the annexe, and three or four couples sunbathing on the sand. A few snorkel tubes rose from the water like little periscopes as swimmers finned in leisurely fashion a short distance out from the edge of the tide. Further out a sailboard toppled slowly over, depositing its passenger into the water.

'Place is like Piccadilly Circus,' Charles said with disgust. 'Come on, we'll look for somewhere less cluttered.'

He loaded the gear into an open black Suzuki, and as Anthea climbed in beside him she said, 'Joe's quite a character, isn't he?'

'One of the best. As tough as they come. He came here from Australia—used to have a diving school near the Great Barrier Reef. He taught me all I know about diving out there.'

He didn't volunteer any more information and Anthea stole a glance at his stern profile as he waited for a bus to pass before pulling out into the road. She tried to think of something to say, but could only come up with, Oh, did you live in Australia? which was about as trite as you could get. So she said nothing.

When they were out on the road he said, keeping his eyes straight ahead, 'I'd better warn you—I don't indulge in nostalgia.' He must be a mind-reader.

That was her answer, then. OK, Mr Prickly Charles, I won't bore you with small talk. I'm not very good at small talk myself; I'd rather have large talk. She giggled at the idea, and he slanted her a suspicious glance but didn't deign to enquire what the joke was, and the rest of the short journey was undertaken in silence.

Anthea had expected that the drive would be more or less the same distance that Peter had driven on his way to the dive-shop, but the car passed the entrance to the condos and went on and on.

When Charles finally drew into a small clearing beside the road and parked the car, she said, 'Where are we? We seem to have come miles.'

He was unloading the gear from the back seat. 'About seven miles, to be exact—the length of the Seven Mile Beach.'

'The beach is seven *miles* long?'

'That's right.' He turned his mouth down at the corners as he quoted, '"Seven miles of dazzling white,

white sand,'' the tourist brochures are fond of reminding one. But for once they're not exaggerating.'

He gave her the two pairs of fins to carry and hitched the rest of the gear, together with a rug, over one shoulder. 'Come and see for yourself.' He led the way through a clearing bordered by palm trees and a profusion of wide-leafed shrubs.

When they came out on to the beach Anthea drew in a breath of delight. Miles of shimmering white sand stretching in both directions, backed by luxurious hotels and condo apartments—none more than treetop high—almost hidden from sight behind clumps of pines and feathery bushes. Uncluttered, uncrowded—the few people in sight were mostly in the sea.

She turned to Charles, who was spreading a rug in the shade of the bushes and unloading the diving gear. 'Paradise island, indeed!' she breathed. 'You know it—you've been here before?'

His face became expressionless. 'Oh, yes, I've been here before,' he said curtly. 'Now, you strip off and then we'll get geared up.'

She'd walked straight into that—he'd warned her that he didn't go in for nostalgia and she supposed that meant no questions about the past. But the snub hurt all the same.

Her fingers trembled as she undid the buttons of her sun-dress. Charles divested himself of shorts and shirt, disclosing narrow black swimming trunks which showed his masculine shape beneath so explicitly that Anthea looked away quickly.

Charles had no such delicacy. 'Very nice!' he said with a grin, his eyes moving over her curves, barely concealed by the citrus-yellow bikini.

She was surprised by the flirtatious tone of the remark. Up to now he hadn't shown any sign of wishing to flirt with her. He'd either been furious—or sarcastic, or arrogant, or, on that one occasion, curiously dejected. A lighter approach would make a nice change.

'Thank you,' she said and smiled at him.

The grin left his face as if it had been wiped off. He picked up her mask. 'See if you can get yourself into this,' he said shortly.

Anthea's spirits sank. Suddenly it seemed as if the sun had gone in. Clumsily she struggled to get the face-mask adjusted.

'Here—let me do it.' He eased the straps over her head and this time she noticed that his hands did not linger on her cheeks.

'OK, let's get going, then,' he said finally, picking up the two pairs of fins and starting off towards the sea, not waiting for her. Anthea stumbled after him, her feet sinking into the fine, warm sand. It was stupid to allow the man to have such a maddening effect on her, sending her spirits up and down like a crazy thermometer. She was beginning to wish she'd insisted on having her first lesson from one of Joe's instructors.

At the edge of the tide they stopped to fix the fins on their feet. 'Right,' barked Charles—rather like a drill-instructor, Anthea thought. 'Now the snorkel—fit the flange between your lips and gums and bite lightly on the two lugs. Breathe easily and naturally. We're just going to drift across the surface to get you accustomed to the finning movement and the feeling of keeping your face underwater. OK?'

Anthea nodded. She hadn't expected to feel so nervous; her insides were quaking. Then Charles took her hand firmly in his and they paddled together through the shallows, and suddenly all her nervousness left her. She was safe with him; he wouldn't let anything go wrong for her.

The water received her like a warm caress. She found herself following Charles's instructions automatically, letting her face dip into the sparkling, clear water, holding on to his hand as she imitated the slow, lazy finning movement of his strong legs.

At first she was hardly conscious of anything but the gentle gliding movement through the silky water. Then she realised that she had been keeping her eyes closed. When she opened them, the scene that appeared below was a magic fairyland.

Of course she'd seen films of the underwater world, but seeing it at first hand, through the amazing clarity of the sun-flecked water, was an entirely different matter. The forest of coral seemed so close, the shapes and colours so washed and fresh—sprouting tubes and crusted boulders and delicate spreading horns like those of some sea elk or reindeer. And the colours! Floating veils of weed in pinks and blues and greens around and between which tiny rainbow-coloured fish, striped and spotted, darted and wheeled as if intent on some secret and important business of their own.

Her hand was still held in Charles's hand and as they moved lazily through the water, finning in unison together, Anthea felt dreamily that they were sharing a wonderful experience and she wanted it to go on and on. But all too soon she felt a pressure on her arm, indicating that she should lift her head out of the water, as he did himself.

He removed his mouthpiece, and she followed suit. 'How's it going?' he asked, and she felt as if she herself were glowing all over with delight as she smiled at him.

'Marvellous! Unbelievable! Can we go on?' She wriggled her fins underwater as if she were one of the eager, purposeful small fish down there.

'Managing the breathing OK?' he asked, and she nodded impatiently. 'Right—we'll have another session,' he said. 'Take it easy.'

The second time was even better than the first. Anthea was confident now, well into the rhythm of the thing. She was fascinated by the way the fish disappeared into the little caves and inlets in the coral. Charles was not holding her hand now and she swam slowly beside him at her own pace.

Suddenly she spotted a large coral growth shaped like a shell, dimpled and pale blue, lying on the seabed. Its curved lower edge was raised slightly, forming the mouth of a dark cave, from which the face of a large fish peered out impassively as if viewing its own watery world. Anthea was captivated. She *had* to get a closer sight of this entrancing creature, which seemed to her fancy to be inviting her to examine his home. Impulsively she twisted her body and pushed downwards, finning as hard as she could.

She wasn't clear what happened next. She was conscious that the fish in the coral cave was much further down than she had thought. She pushed harder, automatically gulping in her breath. The next moment she was wildly churning up the water in an effort to get back to the surface. Her chest felt as if it were bursting.

What happened next had the quality of a nightmare. She was being dragged up to the surface and on to the sand; then the face-mask was off and the water was everywhere—blinding her, deafening her, pressing on her chest. She fought wildly for breath, retching and gulping as her head was pressed down and somebody—something—was thumping her back. She could hear horrible noises and knew it was her—she was dying. The thumping on her back got harder; a voice was shouting something but she couldn't make out the words.

Then, miraculously, she could breathe. She drew in a deep scratchy breath that hurt her chest and made a horrible noise in her throat. Another—and another—she *wasn't* going to die. She began to cry weakly.

Charles was kneeling beside her, his arm holding her. 'Better?' His voice sounded grim, angry.

She nodded, gasping in the warm, life-saving air, the tears pouring down her cheeks. Then she was scooped into his arms and he was carrying her back up the beach. It was wonderful to be held safe and close to the strong, warm body after the bleak moment of fear. She pressed closer, burying her cheek in the springy damp hair on his chest, listening to the loud beating of his heart. She wanted him to hold her like this for a long, long time.

He deposited her on the rug and wrapped a towel round her. Then he stood and looked down at her, frowning. She peered up at him miserably through her wet straggle of hair. 'What did I do wrong?'

'Just about everything,' he said unhelpfully. 'But let that pass. Now you stay here while I go along to the nearest hotel and rustle up a hot drink of some kind. Don't move,' he added fiercely.

As if she would! She watched him stride away across the sand and her eyes were wet still—but with tears of humiliation. It had been such a marvellous experience and she had made a fool of herself, and now Charles would certainly not bother with her again.

She bit her lip to stop it quivering, shocked to realise just how much that mattered to her.

CHAPTER FIVE

By the time Charles returned Anthea had pulled herself together. She had thrown the towel aside and stretched out on the rug. Her bikini was already dry in the hot afternoon sun, and her hair was drying rapidly too, spread out in a honey-brown tangle. Everything must be back to normal as soon as possible. No more panic. No more tears. No more clinging on to Charles. If he intended to drive her back to the condo and wash his hands of her—so be it, she thought, stiffening her pride.

He held out a plastic mug to her. 'It's not exactly five-star service but the kitchen staff were off duty for their afternoon break, and I had to persuade the receptionist to produce this. Drink up—it's the best possible antidote to shock.'

The sweet tea tasted good, washing away the taste of salt water that clung around her mouth. And there was a dash of something stronger in it, brandy probably. 'Thank you,' she said.

He lowered himself to the rug beside her and sat leaning back against the trunk of one of the tall palm trees that fringed the beach, his long legs thrust out before him. 'How are you feeling?' he said.

She glanced cautiously at him, trying to gauge his mood, but his face was expressionless.

'I'm fine,' she said. 'Thanks to you. Merely feeling ashamed of myself. I'm sorry to have behaved so idiotically.'

His long mouth pulled at the corners. 'We seem destined to apologise to each other.'

'What? Oh, you mean——'

'I mean we both appear to act on impulse now and again, and then regret it.'

'Two impulsive people!' she giggled. There must have been more brandy in the tea than she had realised. 'Sounds like the title of a song.'

'I can't admit to any excuse for my deplorable behaviour on the tennis court,' he said. 'What's *your* story?'

Anthea was beginning to get her confidence back. 'There was this fish . . .' she began, and she told him about the large fish peering at her from the opening to his coral cave. 'I didn't think,' she admitted. 'I just wanted to get down closer—to have a good look at him, and—and then I found I'd run out of breath and . . .'

He nodded. 'OK, I get the picture. I take a certain amount of responsibility. I should have explained to you the technique of breath-holding dives before we started. But I didn't expect you to start a love-affair with a fish.' He was smiling openly now, and Anthea grinned back at him, feeling a little light-headed because he wasn't angry, or dismissive, or patronising.

She finished the last drops of tea and put the mug down. 'Can we go in again now?'

He frowned, shaking his head. 'Oh, I don't think so. You've had a shock—you're not up to it.'

'Oh, I am, I am,' she wailed. 'I have to, don't you see? Don't you think it's better to—to start again straight away when you've had a set-back? Such as falling off your bike—you get on and try again straight away. If you don't you're left with the memory of failure.'

He was looking at her curiously, dark eyes hooded. 'Quite the psychologist, Miss Lloyd!'

'Heavens, no. It's just common sense.' She knelt up and reached for her face-mask. *'Please.'* She made a small gesture of pleading.

She wasn't prepared for what happened next. He stretched out and took her hand in a firm grip and pulled her down on the rug beside him.

'OK, you win,' he said. 'We *will* go in again, but not just yet. There are one or two things I want to say to you first.' His eyes narrowed in the lazy smile that pulled at her heart-strings. 'Are you sitting comfortably? No, you're not.' His arm went round her waist in a friendly way, pulling her against him.

For a moment she stiffened, then the touch of his hand on her midriff, the strength of his arm enclosing her, sent such a sensation of heady delight tingling through her that she relaxed weakly against him with a small sigh.

'That's more friendly,' he smiled.

He seemed quite content to sit there, holding her, and Anthea was content too—more than content: she was blissful. At last, this was the Charles she remembered, the hero of her youthful fantasies.

After a time he leaned his chin on the top of her head and said thoughtfully, 'You know, something you said just now hit me with a clang.'

Anthea murmured dreamily, 'Something I said?' and nestled a little closer. This was just the beginning, she thought. Very soon he's going to kiss me and then . . .

'Mmm—about getting on your bike again when you fall off. I had a bad tumble myself a short time ago, and instead of getting back on I sat by the roadside bristling at everyone who came near me, rubbing my wounds and feeling bloody sorry for myself. And, incidentally, sending my poor sister Nancy round the bend.'

Yes, the real Charles *was* still there, the man she'd idealised so long ago. She felt a leap of pleasure. It was as though she were meeting an old friend and finding he hadn't changed at all.

He went on thoughtfully, 'My sister is rather a special person and she has what she thinks of as my happiness and best interests at heart. For reasons which we won't go into, she thinks it would be good for me to get involved with a nice girl, to which end she's been applying herself for the past few weeks—first in London and now here. And nearly sending *me* round the bend,' he added drily, 'as you might have noticed.'

'Surely you——' Anthea began, but he held up a hand.

'Yes, I know, I could tell her what to do with her little plans, but I'd have to be fairly brutal to have any effect on Nancy. Once she's made up her mind to something it's not easy to shift her. And being brutal to Nancy doesn't appeal to me at all. For one thing I'm very, very fond of her. For another, she's trying valiantly just now to recover from the worst disappointment of her life. Losing a first, longed-for baby when you're over forty must be . . . well . . .' He spread out his hands, at a loss for a word.

'How wretched for her; I'm sorry,' Anthea said.

There was another pause. Where was all this leading? she wondered. If it was leading anywhere, that was.

'You see my difficulty?' he said. 'Nancy won't give up. I'm no psychologist but I imagine she may be concentrating all her disappointed maternal feelings on me. She'll be producing nubile young girls for me, like that red-headed siren Barbara she sent after me this morning when all I wanted to do was to get off on my own.' He groaned. 'God, how she chattered.'

Anthea said slowly, 'Was it Nancy who arranged for you to stop me from going diving with Peter?'

He quirked a dark eyebrow. 'Quick on the uptake, aren't you? I have to admit it was. It seems she was standing at her window and overheard your conversation with that young idiot, Peter. She—er—suggested I should come after the two of you and keep an eye on what was going on.'

'Really?' Anthea said distantly. 'I'm very sorry to have inconvenienced you and taken up your time.' She drew away from him and started to towel her hair vigorously.

'Don't be silly,' he said smoothly. 'On this occasion she didn't have to push me. I judged that caution was necessary. Nancy had gathered that the boy was a novice diver, and you can't be too careful. It's possible for accidents to happen, even when swimming or snorkelling—as you found out for yourself just now when you had your love-affair with the fish. Which brings me to what I was going to say. If you want to start an affair with anything—or anybody—while you're here, why not with me?'

For the second time in half an hour all the breath was knocked out of Anthea's body. She turned her head and goggled at him, but his eyes were closed.

'Joke?' she said.

'Not really.' He opened his eyes a fraction and they glittered in the sunshine like lines of jet under the heavy lids. 'How long are you here for?' He shot the question at her.

Taken off guard, she said, 'I plan to stay a fortnight or so.'

'A fortnight,' Charles mused. 'The same for me. That fits in splendidly.'

'Look,' Anthea said, dropping the towel and fumbling in her bag for a comb. 'I haven't the remotest idea what you're talking about. Or maybe I have.' She slid him a glance. It seemed out of character and totally contrary to everything that had happened, but if he really was making her a proposition she wanted nothing to do with it. It was too soon, too casual—oh, definitely no. 'If it's what I think it may be, the answer's no.'

He laughed aloud and it was the first time she'd heard him laugh—since that time five years ago. It was a good sound, deep and full-throated. 'You know, Anthea, I'm beginning to like you; I think we could be friends. And I doubt if I've ever said that to a girl before. No, as a matter of fact it *isn't* what you're thinking—and I know what that is. I'm not suggesting a sexual romp; just now I'm strictly celibate.' The hint of bitterness was back in his voice, but only for a moment.

He went on a little more quickly, 'I was merely suggesting a holiday friendship—destined like all holiday friendships to be a thing of the present. No past, no future, a fortnight of pleasure picked out of time. I thought we might find things to do together. We could explore the island, play tennis, go dancing. And I could teach you to dive—I'd like that. I promise to make you an expert in scuba by the end of a fortnight. What do you say?'

'I—don't know,' she said slowly.

What *did* she say? Could she spend two weeks in Charles's company without ending up completely besotted with him? And what would that bring her? Nothing but black misery. He'd been honest with her. He liked her—as a friend—but it was patently clear that some woman had dealt him an almost mortal blow quite recently. She—Anthea—would be a convenience. To let his sister think he had fallen for her would save him the hassle of having all these 'nubile young girls', as he called them, produced for him.

His eyes were fixed on her, and it seemed that he was following at least part of her train of thought.

'I admit I'm being entirely selfish,' he said. 'I should very much enjoy your company. But of course if you're looking for a——'

'A sexual romp? I'm not,' she said coolly.

'A man back in London?' he queried, tilting his head to one side.

'No, not any more.' She saw his lips firm and knew that he'd understood the message.

'Well, then, what about it?'

The questioning dark eyes seemed to be sending little trickles of electricity down her backbone. 'I . . .' she murmured uncertainly. Then slowly her mouth widened into a smile and her violet-blue eyes danced. 'I'd very much like to learn to dive,' she said.

He gave her an exuberant hug. 'Well said; I'll see that you do.' He got to his feet, picked up their snorkelling gear in one hand and pulled her up with the other. 'On your bike, girl.' His laughter rang out and was carried away by the breeze.

Running down the beach to the sea, hand in hand with him, Anthea suddenly felt a wild, surging happiness. There was just this moment, with the white sand warm to her feet, and the turquoise sea beckoning ahead, and this man beside her, her hand in his. As for the future, it could take care of itself.

'Happy now?' Charles asked quizzically, as they piled the diving gear into the back of his hired car an hour later.

Anthea collapsed into the passenger-seat with a long sigh. 'Blissful!' She raised shining eyes to his as he climbed in beside her. 'I was all right the second time, wasn't I?'

He let his glance travel over her flushed cheeks and settle on her lips, parted over even teeth as creamy white as peeled almonds. Then, for a fleeting second, they moved lower to the tender swell of her breasts under the green cotton dress. 'More than all right,' he said, a shade huskily, and turned the key in the ignition.

She said, 'I think I've found my natural habitat, as a Pisces girl—in the sea, of course. I could have gone on forever.' She slid him a wary glance. 'Or do you think star signs are all rubbish?'

He backed the car round and turned on to the road. 'At least I know what *my* star sign is.'

'Oh, let me guess.' Anthea sat back in the corner of her seat and subjected him to intense concentration. How lovely to have an excuse to do just that!

The strongly boned face, the autocratic nose, the sensual mouth—with just now a tolerant lift at the corners—the thick hair, drying into deep corrugations where he'd run his fingers through it. But most of all the eyes. Those hooded dark-as-night eyes. Magnetic. Hypnotic, almost.

She felt a deep shiver pass through her. You shouldn't tangle with a man who had eyes like that. You shouldn't agree to spend a 'platonic' fortnight with him. She remembered that violent moment on the tennis court when he'd let passion get the better of him. The man was a volcano—and if he erupted——

'Well? Made up your mind?' He slanted her an amused glance.

Anthea swallowed hard. 'Scorpio?' It had to be Scorpio.

He laughed aloud. 'Well, blow me down, the woman's a witch. How did you know?'

'Just a guess.' She wasn't going to admit to gobbling up magazine articles on the subject. Not until she knew him better, anyway. One thing she was remembering, and it was burning into her. That was that Pisces and Scorpio were marvellous together. She wouldn't mention that either.

She said quickly, 'When do I get my next lesson?'

'At the very first moment possible,' he told her. 'I have to see first if Nancy and Billy have anything arranged, but I'm darned sure Nancy will be ready to scrap any plans if she thinks you and I are going to get together. She'll be hearing wedding bells ringing loud and clear.' He chuckled as he swerved the car round a stationary bus.

Anthea stared straight ahead. 'It doesn't bother you at all that you're deceiving her? That she'll be disappointed when the charade is over at the end of a fortnight?'

She could sense the change in him, like frost settling over the clear surface of a pond. 'I don't look ahead as far as that,' he said shortly. 'And I'd suggest that you don't either.'

Of course—*no future*. He'd drawn the boundaries himself and she had to accept them or opt out altogether. She supposed it was kinder, really, to know the score from the start. She'd seen too many of her friends, back from romantic holiday affairs, waiting with painfully dying hope for letters and phone calls that didn't arrive.

She'd accept the reminder with good grace. 'OK,' she said cheerfully. 'Message received.'

He threw her a brief smile. 'Thanks, pal,' he said.

At least that seemed to cement the understanding between them—and the friendship too. It would have to be enough.

When they got back to the condo Charles left the car in the car park. 'I'll take the gear along to Joe's later,' he said. 'Everything has to be washed in fresh water and he has the facilities laid on. I've got a locker rented there and I'll put your stuff in with mine, OK?'

'Thanks.' She smiled warmly up at him. There was a good feeling about their sharing a locker. It meant that they were, in a way, a couple. Planning things, doing things together. How extraordinary that only two days ago Charles had been a distant memory, and now here he was beside her, and all the time he was becoming more like the Charles of her pin-up. Perhaps she hadn't been wrong about him, after all.

As they strolled round to the front of the building they saw Pamela and Nancy stretched out in basket chairs on the veranda. Charles threw an arm casually round Anthea's shoulder.

'May as well give the right signals.' He leant his dark head down to hers, whispering the words. She had an urge to rub her cheek against the rough masculine cheek so close to hers. Help! she thought. This wouldn't do at all. Friendship was all he had offered. She had to learn to think of him as—what? Not her type, not remotely sexy as far as she was concerned? Impossible, she decided wryly. The man was dynamite, so all she had to do was to be careful not to light the fuse.

Nancy beamed on them as they approached. 'Hello! And what have you two been up to?' she asked rather coyly.

They came to a halt in front of the veranda, still casually linked together. 'Charles has been giving me a lesson in snorkelling,' Anthea said. 'It was lovely, seeing all the coral and the fish and everything.' She stretched her arms above her head luxuriously.

Charles looked from Nancy to Pamela. 'She took to it like a mermaid,' he grinned. 'In fact, I think she must have been a mermaid in a previous incarnation.'

Anthea examined her neat ankles. 'No tail!' she remarked, and they all laughed.

The 'affair' was getting off to a good start, she thought, a nice, light-hearted atmosphere developing.

Nancy said, 'Guy and Bill have just arrived home. They're inside, fixing drinks.' She waved a hand over her shoulder.

'Splendid! I'll join them,' Charles said. 'What's yours, Thea?'

Thea! Wasn't it overdoing it a bit to coin a diminutive so soon? But she had to follow his lead, she supposed. 'Oh, something long and cool—and non-alcoholic,' she told him with a winning smile.

'Your wish is my command,' he grinned. Then he paused. 'That rings a bell. I seem to recall a poem in the *Golden Treasury*—a memory from my schooldays. It was called, "To Anthea, Who May Command Him Anything".'

OK, Anthea thought, if we're going to be whimsical I may as well join in. 'I must remember that.' She glanced up into the dark eyes, her own eyes dancing. 'It may be useful. Go and fix me a drink, slave.'

Charles went off to join the other two men and she sank into a chair. Nancy was looking the picture of satisfaction. Pamela, who hadn't spoken yet, was regarding Anthea's face with a slightly stunned expression.

She said, 'What happened to Peter? In your note you said . . .'

Anthea wrinkled her nose. 'Poor old Peter! He actually offered to teach me to dive when he'd only had one lesson himself. I didn't know how dangerous that might be. Fortunately Charles just happened to be at the dive-shop. He realised what was going on and took things in hand.'

She smiled innocently in Nancy's direction. 'Charles can be very masterful when he chooses, can't he? He said you can't be too careful where diving is concerned, and Peter took the hint and sort of—faded away. Then Charles very kindly offered to show me how to snorkel. And he's promised to give me my first lesson in scuba diving later on.' As an explanation that was pretty thin—positively skeletal, she thought with amusement.

'Oh! Oh, well, that's splendid,' Pamela said rather lamely, and Nancy exclaimed,

'Yes, isn't it? Charles is a real expert, Anthea. I'm sure you'll get on very well with him.' She smiled happily, sinking back in her chair as the men arrived with drinks.

Guy and Billy handed round the drinks and sat down together, continuing a conversation about currency regulations. Charles brought his drink and settled himself on the wooden floor of the veranda, at Anthea's feet, leaning against the rail.

He looked up at his sister. 'Did you have anything special in mind for tomorrow, Nan?'

Nancy leaned forward, wrapping her capable brown hands round her glass. 'This evening we're bidden to dine at Government House. Tomorrow—as Bill seems tied up at the bank already—Pamela and I had an idea that it would be nice if the four of us went out to see a bit of the island in the morning—perhaps take a picnic. That is, if you'd like to drive us?' She was watching Charles a little warily, perhaps remembering how he'd reacted to her previous plans for him. And no wonder, Anthea thought.

But Charles was all sweetness and light. 'Good idea,' he said heartily. 'We'd like that, wouldn't we, Thea? Then we could have our diving lesson later on in the day.'

'Splendid!' Nancy beamed her approval, and began busily to make arrangements with Pamela about the time to start and who should organise the picnic.

Anthea met Charles's eyes and raised her eyebrows a fraction. Wasn't Nancy the least bit surprised at his sudden U-turn from introvert to extrovert? But he met her look with a bland expression which seemed to imply that his sister was a simple soul—easy to fool.

Anthea stood up abruptly. 'I think I'll go in now.' She smiled with particular warmth at Nancy. 'Thank you so much for the drink, Nancy, and I'll look forward to seeing you tomorrow.'

Without another look at Charles she escaped along the veranda and into the apartment next door. She supposed Charles knew Nancy, and knew what he was doing, but his ploy suddenly seemed trivial and selfish and she didn't relish being part of it. Also, she had a sense of let-down. She'd begun to think that she'd found again the Charles of five years ago—the ideal Charles she'd built up into a paragon of all the virtues. Of course, the fact was that she didn't really know the first thing about the man.

Feeling confused and rather cross, she peeled off her dress and bikini and went into the shower-room.

Anthea had expected that Pamela would remark on the rather sudden change in temperature between herself and Charles, from chilly to temperate—even warm. But when she went down to the living-room later, fresh from her shower and prepared with replies to any questions her sister might shoot at her, she found Pamela stretched out on the sofa, looking pale and languid. Guy was pacing up and down uneasily, and it was obvious that all was not well.

Guy came straight to the point. 'We've got a problem, Anthea. Our doctor called to do a routine check this afternoon and he's a little worried.' He paused behind the sofa and put his hands on his wife's shoulders. 'Nothing serious, he thinks, but he wants Pamela to fly to the mainland for a minor adjustment to be made. Something that he would be happier to have done in a larger hospital.' Guy was the most unflappable of men, but Anthea could sense that he was troubled.

She could feel the blood leaving her cheeks. 'Pam, darling, how rotten for you,' she said, trying to keep the alarm out of her voice.

Pamela smiled reassuringly at her. 'Don't worry, love, I'll be fine, and Guy will be able to come with me. Now that Billy's here he can take over Guy's job while he's away. Isn't that splendid?'

'Yes—yes, of course,' Anthea said in a small voice, pushing away all the horrid pictures that were creeping into her mind. Pamela desperately ill. Pamela losing the baby. Oh, no, *please*, she thought. Pam had always been so radiant, so lucky, so happy. It mustn't all be spoilt now.

She swallowed. 'When will you go?'

'Tomorrow, I'm afraid. The doctor phoned just a few minutes ago. He wasn't sure at first and he wanted to consult a very senior man in a Miami hospital before he said definitely that I ought to go.' Pamela stretched out a hand and Anthea grasped it and sank down beside the sofa. 'Poor love, it'll mean leaving you on your own here for a few days. Will you mind terribly?'

'Oh, for goodness' sake . . .' Anthea expostulated, 'don't bother about me! I'll be fine.'

Pamela turned to her husband. 'Darling, hadn't you better look in next door to tell Bill the news before they leave for their dinner party?'

When Guy had gone Pamela squeezed Anthea's hand. 'Now, you mustn't worry, love. I'm going to be perfectly OK. And you mustn't be lonely while we're away. Nancy's the kindest soul; I'm sure she'll be only too happy to stand in for me. And——' the brilliant blue eyes smiled into the violet ones conspiratorially '—isn't it splendid that you and Charles are hitting it off so much better?'

Anthea could have groaned. Now it wasn't only Nancy who'd got the wrong idea. It was Pamela too who would be hearing wedding bells.

Damn Charles Ravenscroft and his stupid play-acting. For two pins she'd tell Pamela the truth. She'd...

But, looking into her sister's beautiful face, so genuinely pleased and happily expectant, she couldn't do it.

She lifted Pamela's hand and rubbed her cheek against it. 'Get quite better quickly, Pam, dear,' she said. 'That's the important thing. Now, let me set about getting the meal that Juliana left for us. You just stay where you are—you're not to do a thing.'

As she made for the kitchen she couldn't help thinking that both her life and Charles's seemed to be complicated—for the moment—by having such very nice elder sisters. She hoped that neither of them would be too unhappy when their hopes were dashed at the end of the fortnight.

For herself, she refused to contemplate the end of the fortnight. *No future*, he'd laid down as a rule of the game, and she mustn't forget that, even for a moment.

CHAPTER SIX

IN SPITE of her doubts of the previous day, Anthea was glad of Charles's company next morning on the trip to Owen Roberts Airport. He had offered a lift in his hire car and Guy had accepted gratefully. They agreed it would be better than relying on a taxi.

The Suzuki could only seat four in comfort so Nancy stayed behind to see them off, to kiss Pamela and wish her luck over and over again.

As he piled the luggage in the boot Charles murmured to Anthea, who was helping, 'Poor old Nan, she's remembering only too well how things went for her.'

'Oh, *don't*,' Anthea gasped. 'Not Pamela, too!'

'Of course not,' he told her firmly. 'This is quite different. Your sister will be fine—she's got youth and everything else going for her. This is only a minor matter—Guy explained it to me. Now don't worry, sweetheart.' He closed the lid of the boot with a slam.

Anthea was comforted. This was the Charles she remembered—kind, encouraging, understanding. And he had called her 'sweetheart'. It wasn't much, but it sounded almost lover-like, the way he said it.

At the airport he took charge while Guy, much more white-faced and dithery than Pamela herself, hovered rather ineffectually.

'Poor darling, he's got the jitters,' Pamela chuckled to Anthea as they kissed goodbye outside Customs.

'Heaven only knows how he'll be when I'm actually having the baby.'

She turned to Charles. 'It was very good of you to give us a lift, Charles. And you promise to look after my little sister while I'm away?'

'I promise,' Charles said solemnly and kissed the cheek she held out to him.

What was that—a Judas kiss? Anthea allowed the thought to surface before she thrust it away again to join in the general goodbyes and arrangements to phone with news and telephone numbers when Guy had found a hotel.

She was silent as she walked with Charles to the car. As he headed back to town he said briskly, 'Cheer up, Anthea. Look, the sun's shining. I tell you what we're going to do. We're going back to the condo to have lunch with Nancy. After that you can have a rest and get into your swim-suit. I'll go along to Joe's to collect the scuba gear and you'll have your first real dive—and flirt with the fish as much as you like. How's that for a programme?'

'Fine,' Anthea agreed, trying to sound enthusiastic. Charles was being kind, but her mind was occupied with Pamela and what was going to happen at the hospital. A 'minor adjustment' Guy had called it. She wished she knew exactly what that meant—but of course even if she had known it wouldn't have helped. And minor operations sometimes went wrong, and . . .

The day went on just as Charles had planned. Nancy was already treating Anthea as one of the family—which gave her a nasty feeling of guilt—and lunch was a cosy affair, with Charles and his sister teasing each other and doing their best, not very successfully, to bring Anthea into the conversation.

'Now you must go and have a good rest,' Nancy told Anthea in a motherly voice when lunch was over. 'Then Charles will take you diving. That'll do you all the good in the world—take your mind off things.' She gave Anthea a conspiratorial smile and a friendly little push towards the next-door apartment.

It was grillingly hot in the bedroom and Anthea switched on the overhead fan, drew the curtains, peeled off her clothes and sank on to the bed. What a muddle everything was, she thought; and then, but what if Charles was really interested in her, and not putting on an act for his sister's benefit? What would happen next? He would find some place where they could be alone and he would take her in his arms and... Further than that she dared not imagine.

She closed her eyes and burrowed deeper into the soft mattress, pulled a flimsy coverlet over her as far as her waist, gave a long, deep sigh and almost immediately was asleep.

It was the strangest dream. She was back in her London flat and she and Charles were sitting at the table opposite each other. Between them was a dish on which reposed a large fish with shining blue and green scales. It was quite raw. 'Eat it up,' Charles was saying masterfully, 'it will do you good,' and she was weeping and pleading,

'I can't—I can't, please don't make me.' Then Charles got furious and started to thump on the table with a spoon.

Anthea opened her eyes with a start and realised that the thumping sound was someone knocking at the door. 'All right, I'm coming,' she croaked, sitting up and looking around for a wrap.

The bedroom door opened and Charles's dark head appeared round it. 'I couldn't get any answer downstairs . . .' he began. Then, as his eyes rested on the picture that Anthea made, sitting up naked in bed, he came further inside, grinning wickedly. 'Very nice,' he murmured. 'Very nice indeed!'

'Go away this instant!' Anthea grabbed the coverlet and pulled it up to her chin. He hadn't seen much more than was revealed by the top half of a bikini, but there was something about a bedroom that made the situation ridiculous and embarrassing.

He was still grinning as he went out and half closed the door. 'I'll wait downstairs,' he called back. 'Don't be long.'

Completely awake now, Anthea dived out of bed and slammed the door. Five minutes later, with a pink cotton skirt and top covering her white swim-suit, her bright hair brushed hastily and her feet thrust into white espadrilles, she ran downstairs.

Charles was standing at the window opening on to the veranda. 'Sorry to barge in just now,' he said, not looking at all sorry. 'I'd been knocking at the front door and began to wonder if you were OK when I couldn't get any answer.'

'I was perfectly OK,' Anthea said stiffly. 'I merely dropped off to sleep and didn't hear you. There was no excuse for you to walk into my bedroom.'

His raised eyebrow told her what he thought of such prudishness. She couldn't very well admit the truth: that, although she hadn't expected him to leap on her when he saw her naked, it was somewhat deflating that he found her sex appeal a minus quantity. Or, rather, a joke, which was even worse.

Then all of a sudden she saw the funny side of it and began to giggle. 'As a matter of fact I was dreaming about you,' she said.

His eyes widened. 'Go on—tell me.'

'You were trying to make me eat a raw fish and when I wouldn't you began to bang on the table with a spoon. That must have been when you were banging on the door.'

Her dancing eyes invited him to see the joke. But he wasn't smiling. He was looking at her intently and rather oddly, a cloud of bewilderment passing over his face.

Then it cleared and he grinned slowly. 'You've got quite a thing about fish, haven't you?' he teased. 'Come on, let's go and search for some in their natural habitat. I've got all the necessary gear in the car.'

They went out on to the veranda. 'No need to lock up here—there aren't any thieves in the Caymans, unless you count the ones in the big banks. With apologies to our respective brothers-in-law, who wouldn't see the joke.'

As they got into the car Anthea said idly, 'You aren't in banking yourself, then? I took it for granted . . .'

The dark eyes raked her with cold deliberation. 'It's safer to take nothing for granted,' he said curtly, and she could almost hear the ice crackling in his voice.

When they were both seated he didn't start the car immediately. One hand on the key and the other gripping the wheel, he said, 'Suppose we keep our conversation limited to the present moment—as I think I suggested.'

She stared at his hand on the wheel. The knuckles were white with tension—or was it anger? Back to square one, she thought despondently. How could she ever get used to this Jekyll and Hyde individual? She drew herself up and said stiffly, 'Very well, but if I forget, and occasionally behave like a normal human being, you'll just have to remind me.'

He relaxed, sighing deeply. 'I'm sorry, Anthea. You deserve better. If you want to call it off...'

She went cold. She'd accepted his terms and she knew the risk, but there was always hope and she wasn't going to give up yet.

She managed a laugh. 'Call it off? Certainly not. What about my love-affair—with the fish?'

'Yes, there is that.' He joined in the laugh but neither her laugh nor his would have convinced a third party. 'Come on, then, let's write the next chapter in the Girl Meets Fish saga.' He started the car.

In the days that followed, Guy's phone messages were reassuring. Pamela had come through the 'minor adjustment' satisfactorily and she was well and cheerful—although ordered bed-rest in hospital for the time being. Relieved of anxiety, Anthea threw herself with all her new energy into the challenge of learning everything Charles could teach her about scuba diving.

At the end of the holiday she would go back to London, to the endless chores of finding new premises, buying new equipment, working on new designs. But all that was in another world and she refused to think about it.

Perhaps, in a way, she and Charles were a pair, both of them using this fortnight's holiday to dispel the traumas of the past. The difference was that he was making it plain that she didn't figure in his future, whereas she . . . she was daily feeling more and more disturbed by his physical presence.

But he made no move towards her. Even when they were with Nancy and Bill he never touched her. For Nancy's benefit they were supposed to be getting seriously interested in each other—that was the ploy. Then surely it would have been more convincing if Charles had delivered a casual hug or kiss now and then? But no, he kept his distance. Sadly she decided that he must be making quite sure that at the end of the fortnight there would be no messy emotional parting.

Each day they drove out to Charles's favourite quiet beach, and each day Anthea became more skilled in the techniques of scuba diving. Her underwater dives with Charles as partner were intoxicating. When she was confident enough they swam further out, beyond the reef that divided the turquoise lagoon from the darker, deeper sea beyond. Sitting on a coral reef under fifty feet of water, stroking sponges and playing hide-and-seek with exotic fish round the pink and green trumpets of coral, was definitely an other-world experience.

She was learning all the time—learning the names of the fish they met: yellowtail snappers, striped sergeant fish, delicate blue and silver butterfly fish, friendly angel fish. She was learning other things too—the underwater sign-language divers used to talk to each other, the techniques of descent and ascent, the drill in case of emergencies, the use of compass, depth gauge, and wrist-watch to record time spent underwater.

But of course they couldn't spend all the days diving and learning about diving. Some mornings they played tennis, at other times they went on what Charles called the 'tourist trail'.

Anthea tried to persuade Nancy to join them on their expeditions, but she always found some excuse. She had shopping to do, she was meeting Bill for lunch in town, she had to wait for the maid to arrive.

So Charles and Anthea went together. They wandered round George Town, which seemed to Anthea mainly composed of gleaming banks and offices, as well as smart and expensive shops. They duly visited the district called Hell, where a wooden walkway crossed the jagged black rocks that gave the place its name—and from where one could send cards post-marked 'Hell' to one's friends and relations, with facetious messages. One day they drove out to the unique turtle farm at West Bay. Their stay at the turtle farm was very brief because Anthea couldn't bear to look at all the fascinating creatures swimming happily in their watery homes, from tiny babies to fully grown adults, without visualising their inevitable end—their beautiful shells appearing as trinkets in gift-shop windows, and what was beneath their shells as tasty items on restaurant menus.

Charles teased her for being squeamish but she argued stoutly for her point of view. There were lots of things they argued about and many tastes they shared. He was a delightful companion, fun to be with, outgoing and yet—curiously remote.

Guy telephoned every morning before Anthea went out, and once Anthea was able to talk to Pamela herself. She was fine, she said, and longing to get home. How was everybody, and was Anthea managing to have a good holiday? And was Juliana turning up as arranged?

'Oh, fine, fine,' Anthea bubbled in reply to all the questions. She'd given Juliana a holiday, as her mother was ill. Nancy was being so kind and had insisted on Anthea's having dinner with them each evening. Bill had taken them all out one night to dinner at the Royal Palms—terribly posh! There was a suggestion that they might book for a trip in the submarine to see the underwater scene by night—it sounded fabulous!

'And how about Charles?' Pamela questioned, when Anthea had run through all her news without mentioning him. 'Are you two seeing much of each other? And do you like him any better? Don't hold out on me, love,' she pleaded, half laughing but unashamedly agog for news.

'Charles is teaching me to dive,' Anthea told her. 'He's an excellent teacher and we're getting along quite well. And that, sweet sister, is all there is to tell. So don't think any more about a rich husband for me, there's a dear. There's nothing doing in that direction.'

'Oh!' Pamela's disappointment travelled clearly along the telephone wire. 'Oh, well, you never know.'

I know, Anthea thought, as she said goodbye and put down the receiver. Only too well.

Each evening at dinner Charles regaled his sister and brother-in-law with Anthea's progress in scuba diving. He was delighted with his pupil, and Nancy was quite obviously delighted with the state of affairs.

'Charles is so much happier,' she confided to Anthea. 'You two nice people really do hit it off marvellously, don't you?'

Do we? Anthea wondered as she murmured some sort of response. What sort of 'hitting it off' was it when a man and a girl spent hours together every day without any personal conversations, without once touching each other? The worst of it was that she found herself longing more and more for him to touch her, letting her gaze dwell on his mouth, his hands, and being utterly unable to stop herself imagining how it would be to be in bed with him. What was this? It couldn't be love, not in just a few days—you couldn't count that teenage crush five years ago. So it must be plain lust, which thought did nothing for her self-esteem. To yearn for a man who never laid a finger on her was humiliating.

But Charles had made the rules. Friendship and companionship for two weeks, then—finish! And definitely no sex.

As the blue and gold days followed each other she felt she was living on borrowed time. The days were racing past much too quickly.

Eleven days of the fortnight gone—three days left.

Anthea groaned as she counted the shrinking hours. She had three days to—to what? To make him fall in love with her? Not a hope, she told herself dismally. And it was a waste of time kidding herself that it was merely lust she felt for the man. She was in love with him, deeply, painfully in love. The time dragged heavily when they were apart. Her insides squeezed up tight when she saw him coming towards her. She only came alive when they were together. She didn't know how she was going to continue to live when the fortnight was over.

* * *

'What about this, then?' Charles inspected the tiny rock-bound cove with approval. 'So there really *is* a deserted beach in Grand Cayman. Not just quiet, as the tourist adverts say, but definitely deserted.'

'Just in time—I couldn't walk another yard.' Anthea flopped down on the sand in the shade of a coconut palm, hugging her knees, which were encased in pink linen jeans to protect her legs from the intense heat of the afternoon sun and the possible attack by sand-flies. For the same reason she wore a loose long-sleeved top of pink lawn. She was browning nicely but she still had to be careful, and it was easier to cover herself up than to have to plaster sun-block cream all over her body as usual.

This morning had been occupied by the daily diving lesson and this afternoon Charles had suggested a change. They had driven up towards the north of the island and from then on Anthea had been quite lost. They had lunched, in a little restaurant with a thatched roof, off a superb seafood dish followed by ice-cream laced with tropical fruit. They had parked the car when the road ran out and then made their way slowly—very slowly—through a mini-jungle bordering a swamp forest. The trees, plants, crabs and exotic parrots were all part of the magic, and it hadn't seemed to matter that in places the swamp slopped over on to the path and they had had to proceed barefoot.

And then, suddenly, they had come upon this little cove, where the breeze off the ocean was cool and the waves creamy, and the leaves of the coconut palms rustled above them.

'I don't know about you,' Charles said lazily, 'but I'm going to have a kip.' He flung himself down and lay back on the soft sand, hands behind his head. 'Poke me if I snore.'

'You bet I will,' Anthea promised. That was the way it was with them—friendly, jokey. She might have been his much younger sister.

He was asleep almost immediately. Anthea lay back beside him, took off her sunglasses and closed her eyes, but sleep was a long way away. She was tinglingly aware of the long body of the man stretched out beside her. She moved a little further away but it was no better. It seemed that there was a magnetic current between them, drawing her towards him. She lifted herself on an elbow and let her eyes roam over him, over the strong-boned face, the dark hair, rumpled and clinging damply to his forehead, the thick lashes curving on to his cheek, the long, straight upper lip resting lightly on the full lower lip, the broad, square chin.

Her insides moved painfully. She loved him so very much. She wanted him with a desperation that shocked her. And she knew nothing about him. Nothing except a bit of gossip via Pamela about a broken love-affair. It must have been a deeply passionate, tragic affair to have made him choose a monk-like existence as he seemed to have done.

Her gaze travelled down his body, clad in a cotton vest and navy shorts that fitted tightly across his hips. Masculine, virile, powerful—those were the words that came into her mind. Yet they had spent hours together in this romantic sun-kissed island, and, except for that dance together when they'd dined with their respective families, and the time he'd hauled her out of the water on her first dive, he'd never even touched her—only when they were under the water together.

Any other man she'd met would at least have made a pass by now. Was he really heartbroken? Or was he married? But no; if he was married surely Nancy would know and wouldn't keep it a secret.

He had the dark skin that tanned quickly and easily, and in the shade of the trees his arms and legs were the colour of teak. Anthea couldn't tear her eyes away and her heart began to beat heavily.

Her arm moved without her willing it; she put her hand on his thigh and she drew in a long shaky breath as a wave of heat passed through her that had nothing to do with the sun.

The heavy lids lifted and he looked straight up into her bemused blue-violet eyes. 'Why don't you?' he said lazily.

She knew what he meant. It was an invitation but it was up to her—he wasn't going to make the first move. Slowly, never taking her eyes from his, she lowered her head and put her mouth on his.

For a long, frightening moment she thought he wasn't going to respond. Then his arms came up and drew her down beside him until their bodies were touching. His lips stroked hers gently backwards and forwards and she felt a rising tide of longing and opened her mouth... asking... needing. When she felt his tongue seeking hers a shudder of delight passed through her. She had never felt like this before—wanton, eager, aflame with desire. Her arms went round his neck, burying themselves in the thick hair, pulling him closer until he was lying half on top of her.

His tongue probed delicately, exploring the warm crevices of her mouth, savouring, tasting. His hands stroked her shoulders, her back, moving down over her hips, lightly, almost tentatively. There was no passion to match her own; he might have been an expert savouring a new wine, running it experimentally round his mouth.

A sob broke in her throat. 'Charles—Charles, darling,' she muttered. 'Please...' Her arms went round his waist pulling him down on to her.

Then everything changed. He was kissing her with crazy passion, breathing harshly, his hands fumbling for the zip of her jeans, his body, hard and aroused, moving on hers with a rhythm that shocked and thrilled her, setting up an ache in her loins that cried out for satisfaction. She heard a whimpering sound and hardly realised she was making it.

She couldn't believe it when he thrust himself away, rolling off her, gasping and fighting for control. Then, without a word, he got to his feet and staggered to the edge of the tide. She stared numbly, seeing him pull off shorts and shirt and plunge, naked, into the water. His arms gleamed brown above the turquoise of the lagoon as he struck out in a fast crawl for the line where waves were breaking over the reef.

Anthea was shaking all over. Her head felt like cotton wool, her limbs like jelly. All she was conscious of was humiliation like a great lump of lead inside her, so agonising that she could hardly bear it.

Time crawled by. If she could have got up and walked away from the beach she would have done so. But she doubted if her legs would bear her, and anyway she couldn't remember where the path was. Somewhere they had pushed their way through a thicket of bushes to reach this private cove but, looking round, she could see no opening.

Charles was a long way out from the beach now, swimming powerfully towards the open sea. Watching him, Anthea felt a tug of fear. He wasn't going to...he couldn't...

She wasn't thinking straight at all. All she remembered was the violence in him, the storm that had passed over him, turning him into a different man. A desperate man. Why? *Why?* she thought, but the only answer was that it was her fault; she had brought it on herself.

She fixed her eyes on the dark head that was now only a speck on the darker blue water beyond the reef, watched with a clench of fear in her stomach until she saw it coming nearer and knew he was swimming back to the cove.

When he stepped out of the water at the edge of the tide and stood very still, his body bronzed and perfect, he seemed to her like primitive man, glorying in his nakedness. Like Adam in his lonely garden—before Eve appeared to tempt him. She began to laugh helplessly, burying her face in her hands. And then, because she had first been stirred to the depths and afterwards scared out of her wits, the laughter turned to tears. She choked and gulped helplessly, the tears running through her fingers, her shoulders shaking.

'Anthea—stop it. Stop it this minute.' The words, barked out in the voice of a sergeant major, arrested her hysteria instantaneously. Without taking her hands from her face, she could see a pair of strong bronzed legs, dark hairs clinging wetly to them. She blinked the tears from her eyes and let her gaze travel further up, and saw that he'd pulled on his navy shorts. His vest lay in a crumpled heap where he'd flung it down on the sand.

He wrenched her hands from her face. 'What's the matter? Why the waterworks?' he asked irritably.

He had the nerve to ask her that just as if nothing had happened! She turned her head away. He was making her feel small and insignificant, looming above her. She wanted to spring to her feet and tell him what she thought of him, but she had no spring left in her and she was sure the words wouldn't come.

'Anthea—look at mc!' Hc was down on his haunches beside her now. His hand grasped her chin and turned her face roughly towards him. She put every ounce of effort she was capable of into stopping her mouth from shaking and meeting the accusing dark eyes squarely.

They stared at each other in silence. 'Look,' he said at last. 'It's not the end of the world because I kissed you.'

'Was that all it was?' she asked stonily.

He released her chin and slumped round until he was sitting beside her, staring bleakly out to sea. 'All right,' he said at last. 'I lost my head. I'm only human and my control isn't as good as I thought it was. If I alarmed you, I'm sorry,' he added stiffly, 'but I don't take all the responsibility, you know.'

Anthea lifted her chin a fraction. 'It seems that I'm only human too.'

He ignored that. 'I should never have started this game—it was a stupid thing to do.' He reached for a small stone and hurled it violently into the water. 'I told you—I warned you that I couldn't offer you a romantic holiday affair, with a spice of sex thrown in.' He turned towards her and his face was grim. 'In case you're getting any wrong ideas I may add that I'm *not* impotent, I'm *not* a health risk.' He bit out the words savagely. 'And I'm *not* going to get myself involved in any emotional entanglement.' He paused and added, 'That's the way things are.'

'OK, OK,' Anthea put in coldly. 'So I broke your precious rules. It won't happen again, I promise. Perhaps the less we see of each other for the next three days the better. Anyway, Pamela is coming home tomorrow. I told Nancy—did she tell you?'

'Yes, she did. I got the impression that Pamela, too, would be delighted to find that you and I are—to use Nancy's words—getting on so well together.' His mouth twisted hatefully. 'It seems that your sister Pamela has hopes for us too.'

Anthea dug up a handful of sand and let it trickle through her fingers. She sensed the violence seething just under the surface of Charles's words, and it frightened her. Somehow this conversation must be diverted into less dangerous channels.

She forced a brittle laugh. 'Pamela thinks I should find myself a rich husband—like hers.'

'I see. And does your sister think I would fit the bill?'

She didn't like the look in his eye. Did he know he was twisting a knife inside her? No, of course he didn't. 'Love' was a word that had never been mentioned between them.

But there was still pride. She shrugged. 'Well, I suppose she'd consider you about right. I'm sure you're absolutely stinking rich, aren't you? Oops—sorry! I'm not allowed to ask you that, am I?'

His expression hardened. 'No,' he said, 'you're not.' He got to his feet. 'Now, suppose we make our way back, and do our best to put this not very admirable episode behind us as if it hadn't happened?'

She scrambled up. 'Suits me,' she said in a carefully offhand tone.

As she followed him through the thick bank of prickly bush on to the path she saw that her arms were scratched and bleeding, but she didn't feel any pain. All the pain in the world seemed to be concentrated in her heart.

CHAPTER SEVEN

'SO PAMELA is coming home tomorrow.' Nancy smiled at Anthea over the rim of her coffee-cup. 'Won't it be lovely for you to have her back?'

'Lovely,' Anthea agreed enthusiastically. It *would* be lovely to see Pam again. It was the only good thing in an otherwise bleak prospect.

She had contemplated making some excuse to get out of joining Nancy, Bill and Charles for dinner at their usual restaurant, close to the condo. But Nancy had been worrying about the scratches on Anthea's arms and had insisted on giving first aid with antiseptics and bandages. If she'd pleaded a headache or some other minor symptom Nancy would have jumped to all sorts of dire conclusions about poisonous tropical plants, would have insisted on calling a doctor, would have treated her as an invalid and would have generally behaved like the kind, motherly soul she was.

So Anthea had decided that it was simpler to join them for dinner. Afterwards she would go straight back to Pamela's apartment, explaining that she wanted to have everything ready for Pamela's return. That would ensure that at no point in the evening would she risk being alone with Charles.

He had suggested putting this afternoon's episode behind them as if it hadn't happened, but it seemed that neither of them was capable of doing that. As they sat next to each other at the small restaurant table

Anthea felt the tension between them like an electric filament, ready to burn white-hot at the touch of a switch. He had been silent over the meal in spite of his sister's efforts to draw him out about the afternoon's expedition, and it had fallen to Anthea to describe the walk through the marshy jungle and the way they had finally found the little deserted cove.

She flicked a glance at Charles's dark unsmiling face as she talked. The very least he could have donc was to help her out, she thought crossly. He seemed to have reverted to the mood he'd been in when they'd all had dinner together that first night. The restaurant was full—mostly with bank staff and their families. Anthea let her gaze wander over the other tables, exchanging smiles with one or two people she had already met. Peter Jordan was there with a party—his parents presumably and several others, including the red-haired siren Barbara, who was chatting away vivaciously, telling some story, embellished by much waving of her hands and arms. Peter didn't seem to be listening. His long body was slumped over the table, fingers playing listlessly with his wine glass.

As he caught Anthea's glance he brightened and lifted a hand. Since the episode at the dive-shop she had encountered Peter several times. He had hopefully issued invitations—to play tennis, to go sailing, to drive round the island—and always Anthea had refused tactfully. Finally he seemed to have given up hope.

But this evening, annoyance with Charles put brilliance into her smile as she returned Peter's salute. She saw his immediate response. He straightened his long body, pushed back his flop of fair hair, stood up and loped across to their table.

'Good evening, Mrs Jamieson—Mr Jamieson.' He nodded vaguely towards Charles and flushed as his gaze moved to Anthea. 'I was wondering—Barbara and I are going on to the new night-club that's just opened along the beach . . .' He gestured across his shoulder. 'Would any of you care to join us? They've got a live band and there's dancing; it sounds as if it may be fun.'

Nancy beamed on the tall young man. 'I'm afraid Bill and I are too old-fogeyish for night-clubs, aren't we, darling?' She squeezed her husband's shoulder and he patted her hand, nodding urbanely, eyes twinkling behind their gold-rimmed glasses.

'But I'm sure Charles and Anthea would love to join you, wouldn't you, my children?' Nancy went on skittishly, but with a wary glance at Charles.

Anthea had a wicked urge to stir Charles out of his dark mood, or at least to challenge it. '*I* would,' she said brightly. 'How about you, Charles?'

To her amazement he agreed laconically, 'Why not?' He got to his feet. 'Come along, then, we'll join them.'

Oh, lord, what had she done? She'd have to dance with him, be held against him. And what effect would that have on her? If she was close to him she might have an overwhelming urge to press closer still. And then—if he thought she hadn't given up, that she was issuing another invitation to him? Oh, God, she couldn't bear it. To be slapped down once was enough.

She looked pleadingly towards Nancy, willing her to enquire about the scratches on her arms, to ask whether she was *sure* she felt like making a night of it. But Nancy was exchanging small talk with Peter about his parents, her dark eyes—so like Charles's—alive with animation below the straight-cut fringe.

'Go along, then, both of you, and have a lovely time. Bill and I will be fast asleep when you come in, Charles, but the door will be open.' Nancy cast a faintly coy glance towards her brother. To Anthea's fevered imagination she seemed to be saying that if he and Anthea chose to spend the night together while the apartment next door was conveniently empty of its owners, nobody would be asking any questions. Little did she know!

Anthea walked between Peter and Charles to the table where Barbara was already getting to her feet, her eyes resting greedily on Charles.

'Charles—you're coming with us? Brilliant!' She linked an arm with his. 'How marvellous—we're look-alikes.' She gurgled with laughter, indicating the minuscule caramel-coloured dress that seemed cleverly almost to disappear into her smooth, delicately browned skin, and then ran a finger slowly down the front of Charles's thin khaki shirt, her eyes dancing up to his, the tip of her tongue touching her lips.

He wouldn't stand for that sort of obviousness, surely? Anthea thought in disgust. But while he greeted the other members of the party briefly, he allowed the girl's arm to remain in his, and smiled down at her with apparent pleasure as they walked towards the exit door, leaving Anthea to follow with Peter. The night-club, he told her, was attached to one of the big hotels on Seven Mile Beach, only a couple of hundred yards from the restaurant where they'd been dining.

Outside, the sky was like black velvet, spattered with glittering diamond-clusters of stars. Lights from the hotels and apartment buildings gleamed through their protecting trees and shrubs on to the endless vista of white sand. Long, pencil-straight lines of waves turned over quietly, as if reluctant to disturb the peace.

'Not worth taking a car,' Peter said. 'Let's pull off our shoes and wade along with the crabs.' He sounded rather psyched up, Anthea thought, and wondered how much wine he'd drunk with dinner.

Barbara squealed, 'Oh, no, not crabs!' and clung on tightly to Charles.

'Silly girl, there aren't any crabs,' Charles told her, playfully tolerant. 'Come on, get those pretty little sandals off.' He had his arm round her waist and she raised her feet, one after the other, for him to remove her sandals, leaning against him, giggling that he was tickling her.

Anthea moved from the edge of the tide on to dry sand. She was not going to take part in such childish games. She glowered towards the two in front. 'I thought Barbara was with *you*,' she said to Peter, drawing away as she felt his arm encircle her waist.

'She was—until she found something better. So I'm afraid you'll have to put up with the discard, sweetie.' He chuckled as his arm came to rest more firmly round her waist.

Sweetie! That wasn't Peter's style. And when his face came close to hers she recoiled. He certainly *had* been going at the wine.

'Come on,' she said, striding out determinedly. 'Show me where this night-club is.' She couldn't help it if she let him see her lack of enthusiasm. That was how she felt. She'd been worrying about how she was going to respond to Charles in the intimate atmosphere of a night-club. She needn't have bothered, she thought viciously, glancing over her shoulder to where he was skipping in and out of the waves, with the red-head clinging to his arm and shrieking playfully.

Inevitably she and Peter reached the night-club first. He found a table by the window and ordered drinks from a gorgeous dark-skinned girl in a scarlet tunic with a white carnation in her hair. The whole room was decorated in scarlet and white and glowed like a gigantic jewel in the coloured lighting. On a dais near the bar a five-piece band was playing top-ten music and one or two couples were moving together on the postage-stamp dance-floor.

Barbara came rushing in, attractively breathless, green eyes dancing with fun, and flopped into a chair. 'Isn't this *brilliant*? Oh, look, Charles, they're going to do a floor-show. Come and sit by me.' She patted the chair next to her. 'Yes, I'd simply love a drink—just anything you'd like to choose.'

She didn't even glance at Peter. She had, as he had ruefully admitted, found something better.

Apparently Charles, too, had found something better, Anthea thought sourly. It was obvious that he was showing her that their little charade was over—she had spoilt it. But he needn't have been quite so obvious about it. In the disco lights that roved around the room and over the colourful gyrating bodies of the dancers in the floor-show she caught glimpses of Barbara and Charles like fleeting images in a pop video—Barbara rubbing her cheek like a kitten against Charles's silk khaki shirt, his arm round her shoulders, his dark head bent to hers.

Anthea gulped down her drink, trying to blot out the misery, and was hardly aware that Peter's arm was drawing her closer, that the bottle of wine he'd ordered was nearly empty and that his hand was straying down towards the hem of her skirt.

The floor-show ended, the band went off for their break, and disco music belted out. Barbara pulled Charles on to the floor and was soon jiving and twisting enticingly for his benefit, while he was content to move his body rhythmically to the beat without trying anything fancy. Anthea couldn't take her eyes off the two of them and a smouldering resentment burned inside her, somewhere between her throat and her stomach. Her head was starting to ache as the decibels from the loudspeakers boomed in her ears. Barbara was showing off, executing a complex dance movement, during which she managed to trip and fall, apparently by accident, into Charles's arms. Before he set her straight he dropped a kiss on her flaming red hair.

'Like to have a go?' Peter shouted over the noise. 'I'm not much good, but——'

'No, thanks,' Anthea shouted back hastily. 'I'd much rather stay here and watch.'

'Suits me.' His voice was slurred, and the hand at the hem of her skirt was groping its way upwards into more intimate territory.

'Please don't.' She grabbed his hand and removed it. It felt damp and limp. 'I—I'm awfully sorry, Peter, but I don't feel too good. Would you mind very much if I went back to the apartment?'

'Course not—come with you,' he said immediately.

'I'll be OK, really, if you'd like to stay,' she said. To get away on her own—away from the heat and the lights and the heavy beat of the music, and the sight of Charles with that girl—that was what she wanted. But Peter was basically a kind boy and she wouldn't hurt his feelings, so when he stood up rather unsteadily and held out his hand she went with him.

Outside, the air was cool and the sound of the shallow waves lapping against the sand was soothing. Anthea drew in a deep breath.

'Feeling better?' Peter's voice was steadier. Perhaps the fresh air had got to him too.

'Yes, thanks. I don't think night-clubs are quite my scene.'

'Not mine either,' he said rather glumly. 'I guess I'm an outdoor type.'

He linked his arm with hers. 'I hope I didn't . . . I wasn't . . .' he began awkwardly. 'I'd had too much wine.'

'Don't give it a thought,' Anthea assured him. She realised now that he was painfully shy and he'd been going through the motions of what he thought was expected of him. She felt an affection for him that was almost maternal. In a funny sort of way she understood what Nancy felt for Charles.

Charles! Charles was a very different matter. Charles wasn't shy—merely callous and self-absorbed and . . . and despicable!

'Tell me about your college,' she said to Peter. 'What games are you best at?'

Released from the necessity of putting on a macho act, Peter relaxed and chatted away about his hopes of getting into the second cricket eleven and taking up rowing next term.

At the front door of the condo he hesitated. 'Will you be OK on your own? Your sister's away, isn't she?'

'I'll be fine,' she assured him. 'The air's almost taken my headache away.'

He looked down at her from his great height. 'I'd hoped...' he began awkwardly. Then, 'It's that fellow Charles, isn't it? I've seen you about together and...'

She didn't pretend to misunderstand. Peter was a straightforward boy and he deserved a straightforward reply. 'No, it isn't Charles; it isn't anybody really,' she said, and added, 'There's someone back at home, you see.' That white lie seemed excusable.

She pushed the door open, but when Peter seemed rooted to the spot she said, 'I'll be going back to London in a couple of days, but I expect I'll see you before I leave. Thank you for looking after me this evening—I'm sorry I had to cut it short. Goodnight, Peter.' She reached a long way up and planted a kiss on his cheek.

'Oh...' It was too dark to see his face but she was sure he was blushing. 'Goodnight, Anthea. You're a—a marvellous sport,' he stammered.

She went in and closed the door, locking it. People seemed careless about locking their doors here, but somehow the act of turning the key was symbolic, as if she were finally shutting out the fruitless longing for Charles.

The thought of bed appalled her. She went up to the bedroom, pulled off her clothes and got into a flowery wrap of wild silk that Pamela had lent her. Downstairs again, she made a pot of tea and carried it to the sitting-room. Here she drew the curtains and switched on a reading lamp and picked up one of Pamela's paperback thrillers. It had a cover picture of a posy of lilies of the valley, beside which was a lethal-looking knife spattered with blood. She put the book down with a shudder. Extraordinary how a mild, sweet, loving woman like Pamela should be addicted to horror stories. You never really understood people, did you?

A loud banging on the door made her jump and catch her breath. The thought of blood-stained knives was still occupying her mind ghoulishly. She froze. Nobody she knew would bang like that—certainly not Nancy or Bill.

The banging stopped and then—oh, heavens!—heavy footsteps sounded on the veranda and impatient knocking on the window.

She got to her feet, her knees like putty, and sidled across the room. Tweaking the outer edge of the soft velvet curtain, she put one eye to the gap. A detective in a TV serial would have been proud of her, she thought hysterically.

Outside, in the starlight, Charles's large body was immediately recognisable. Gibbering with relief, Anthea pulled back the curtains and unlatched the sliding glass door.

He strode into the room, glowering into every corner. 'Where is he?' he barked.

Anthea collapsed on to the sofa. 'Where's who? What are you talking about? And how dare you come barging in like this?' she added as an afterthought.

'Where's that dressed-up drink of water? I'll——'

'If you're referring to Peter, he very kindly brought me home, said goodnight, and left.' Suddenly all the humiliation of the afternoon and evening came back in a rush. She sat up very straight and glared at him as he stood by the open window like an animal at bay. 'And what business is it of yours?' she said in a steely voice. 'You were too happily occupied yourself to notice what I was doing.'

'Not too occupied to notice he was mauling you about and you didn't seem to be objecting,' he said coldly.

'Don't tell me you were jealous,' she said, smiling frostily.

He slid the window shut and then came and sat down on the sofa beside her, not touching her.

'Jealous—good God, no. Why should I be jealous? I merely felt responsible for you; that's why I came after you—as soon as I could get rid of Barbara.'

She clasped her hands tightly together to stop them shaking. 'Well, now you see I'm not being raped, perhaps you'll leave?'

He drew in a deep breath, as if asking for patience. 'You don't have to be like that, Anthea. You know there's nothing . . . personal between us. We agreed on that, didn't we?'

'I seem to remember something of the sort,' she said distantly. 'I merely thought that, as we were invited together this evening, your behaviour to me was rather rude. Which wouldn't be particularly unusual,' she added pointedly.

He groaned. 'Look, let's get this straight. I told you I had no intention of starting a holiday affair. You agreed that you didn't want one either. That was why——'

'Why you suggested using me so that your sister wouldn't annoy you by producing "nubile young girls"—wasn't that the term?—to heal your broken heart?'

'I didn't mean to "use" you,' he said gruffly. 'I certainly didn't look at it like that. I just thought—we seemed to get along pretty well, and it would be a good idea to . . . spend time together, that was all.'

'A lovely platonic friendship?'

'Something like that.'

'No tiny twinge of desire? No soupçon of lust?'

'Dammit, Anthea, you know there was. That was pretty evident on the beach this afternoon. I'm a man and you're a very attractive girl. What happened showed me the way *your* mind was working but it didn't change *my* mind—I'm not going to involve myself in a holiday liaison.' He got up and strode to the window and stood looking out at the dark, star-strewn sky. 'Why do you think I fooled around with that moronic girl Barbara this evening? To show you beyond doubt that I had no intention of accepting your flattering invitation. At the risk of sounding brutal, I must repeat what I think I told you at the beginning of our acquaintance—there's nothing doing, my dear girl. Nothing has changed.'

My dear girl! It was too much! The pompous—insufferable... She wouldn't let him get away with that—he had to be cut down to size. He was going to pay, she fumed, for making her feel cheap and humiliated.

The way was ready to hand, if only she could carry it off. She summoned a pathetically twisted little smile to her lips. 'But what would you say if I told you that something *has* changed, Charles? That *I've* changed? That I'm tired of playing the game by your rules? If I told you I love you?'

He stood very still for a moment. Then, violently, he swung round, and the look of consternation on his face was beautifully satisfying. She'd really got him worried now. He came back to sit beside her. 'No, you *don't*, Anthea. Of course you don't.' He took her hand in a hard grip that crushed her fingers. 'It's just the—the sun and the sea——' he waved an arm '—and the palm trees and the flowers . . . all the romantic clichés—they've got to you, that's all. In a week you'll have forgotten I ever existed.' His voice rose in his frantic effort to convince her. He was almost shouting.

Now was the time to play another card. She drew her hand away. 'I don't think I will,' she said, shaking her head sadly. 'You see, I've loved you for five years.'

'What?' he roared.

He stared at her incredulously, eyes wide, searching her face, dark brows drawn together in a frown. Then his mouth fell open almost comically. 'Good God! Now I remember. It was at a wedding party. You were wearing a pink dress and we stood on a balcony looking at the river—and you told me you were going to study design . . .'

In spite of her anger a wave of delight washed over her. He hadn't forgotten—not altogether.

'What happened to your career?' He seemed interested, but she was certain he was only changing the subject.

'Oh, I enjoyed my time at college,' she told him. 'Afterwards I worked in a fashion design studio. A friend of mine had a knitting machine she couldn't get the hang of and she lent it to me. I got interested in knitwear design. I began to sell some of the garments I made. After a while I gave up my job and started on my own—I managed to get a work-room in a disused factory in the East End.'

'Clever girl,' he said admiringly. 'Go on.'

'I was lucky, I suppose. Soon I was selling to the big stores and later on abroad. Paris, Rome—it was tremendously exciting.'

And then it was all over—everything gone up in smoke. But she wasn't going to tell him that. Sympathy was the last thing she wanted from him.

'So—you're in the big time, and you've done it all by yourself. I like that.' He gave her his most charming smile. He must be congratulating himself that he was tactfully steering the conversation out of dangerous channels. But she had more surprises in store for him.

'It wasn't quite all by myself,' she said, giving him a sideways glance under her long lashes. 'I had help—a guide and mentor.'

'Some man?'

Her mouth quirked. She was almost enjoying the game she was playing now. 'Is that surprising? I thought he was the most wonderful man in the world. He was everything that I admired in a man——' she gave a long, gusty sigh '—strong and kind and understanding—and sexy, of course. I kept his photograph pinned up on the wall and I used to talk to him and ask his advice and tell him all the stupid things that had gone wrong. It was—sort of comforting when I was working alone.'

'And when you'd finished work I suppose the fellow was even more—er—comforting?' he said drily.

She shook her head. 'We-ell—no. You see, he was only a pin-up—someone I adored from afar, like a pop star, or a film hero. I only met him once.' She looked down at her hands, a demure smile touching her lips. 'It was at a wedding party. I was wearing a pink dress and we stood on a balcony, looking at the river.' She heard his quick intake of breath and made a slight pause for effect and then continued, 'I didn't know anybody and I was feeling gauche and awkward and he was kind to me. All the rest was a dream. I don't think girls dream much about wonderful men nowadays—or perhaps they still do—I don't know. But I was very young and very silly.'

She stood up and walked across to the table, leaning back against it, watching him, savouring her small triumph. The room was suddenly quiet. Only the continuous chirping noise of the night insects found its way through the closed window, and the distant sighing of the waves.

Then she heard him draw in a harsh breath as the whole truth dawned on him. He lifted his head and there was a haggard expression on his face that took her by surprise. 'Why didn't you tell me?' he said at last, and his voice grated on her raw nerves. 'I'd never for one moment have——'

'Walked into danger? Of course you wouldn't—you'd have run like a hare,' she said lightly. 'If you remember, I *did* tell you we'd met before and you looked right through me as if I didn't exist. Then, later on, at the tennis court you tried to annihilate me. I suppose I was a bit peeved. So when you came up with your grand scheme—*for your own convenience*—I thought it might be amusing to go along with it. When you've built up a fantasy picture of someone it's quite a temptation to find out how right—or wrong—you are. And, my goodness, was I wrong!'

His face hardened. He got up and stood in front of her and said very quietly, 'And that kiss on the beach this afternoon?'

'Oh—that!' She managed a laugh. 'I couldn't resist finding out how close to my fantasy the reality was.'

'And . . .?' There was a dangerous note in his voice now, but she chose to ignore it. She was goading him, she knew it, and excitement pulsed through her.

She shrugged. 'Four out of ten, perhaps.'

His eyes narrowed and she shrank from the dark fury she saw in them. His arms went round her, squeezing the breath from her body. 'Then let's see if I can improve my score,' he ground out between his teeth, before his mouth came down on hers.

CHAPTER EIGHT

ANTHEA flapped her arms wildly, trying to push against his chest. But there was no space to get her hands between their two bodies. She was so sure that he would repeat his performance of this afternoon on the beach—when, for a few terrifying moments, he had lost control and turned savage—that she put all her strength into the effort to twist out of his grasp. Quite useless. She was clamped to him as surely as if he'd bound them together with steel wire.

His lips were pressed hard against hers and she waited helplessly for the punishment he was going to inflict on her. Instead, he raised his mouth a fraction and she saw his eyes, close and out of focus. They looked like pools of dark water, and she could almost imagine he was smiling.

'You little wretch,' he murmured. 'What am I going to do with you?'

She wriggled against him. 'Let me go—please let me——'

His mouth closed over the last word. His mouth—soft and warm and unexpectedly gentle. Anthea felt her knees buckle as the slow, exploratory movement of his tongue round her lips set up a painful ache inside her. Without taking his mouth away, he edged her towards the sofa and lowered her down on to it. It was a wide sofa—plenty of room for two, and Charles took full advantage of that, pinning her down by flinging one leg over both of hers. When she felt his weight on her she gasped, 'No—no,' against his mouth.

'No what?' he mocked. 'You've had your fun, my sweet; now I'm going to have mine.'

Resting on one elbow, he rolled a little away and deftly undid the knot of the sash that held her filmy wrap closed. She grabbed at him as he pulled the fronts of the wrap apart, but he brushed her hand aside with the greatest of ease. Then she felt the cool air from the ceiling fan on her body, naked except for the lacy wisp of her panties. She heard his quick intake of breath. 'Lovely—much prettier without any covering.'

She was only too aware of the picture she must be presenting to him—her cheeks flushed, her breasts swelling, their peaks already hard and throbbing. A momentary consciousness of shame was swamped by the sensuous pleasure of being naked to the gaze of the man she loved.

Slowly, as if relishing the moment, he lowered his mouth to her breast and when his tongue stroked the nipples, one by one, her body jolted as if a powerful electric charge had been released into it. She sank back into the softness of the sofa, her head threshing on the cushion, moaning faintly as his lips closed tightly over one of the hard peaks, drawing it into his mouth. At the same time his hand was stroking her waist, moving over the rounded curves of her hips, her stomach, finding its way unerringly beneath the lacy bit of nothing that presented no barrier.

Wave after wave of heat ran through her as the exquisite torture went on. Nothing remotely like this had ever happened to her before. She had sometimes wondered what it would be like if he made love to her but that had been a thing of the imagination. This was real, entirely physical, every nerve contributing to the rising heat that burned through her.

She reached up and buried her fingers in the crisp hair at the nape of his neck, digging her nails convulsively into the damp skin there. She felt a deep shudder convulse him. Then, with a muttered curse, he rolled away from her and got to his feet, breathing fast. 'That's enough—more than enough,' he said roughly.

The shock of separation made her whimper. She felt a coldness, a loneliness, as if she had lost part of her own body. Then, slowly, she began to recover herself. She sat up, shivering, drawing the silk robe round her.

She felt his eyes on her but couldn't look up to meet them. She was burning with humiliation even while she shook with cold. All she wanted was to sink through the floor—to disappear completely. He had been calculating her response while she had been aroused to a point of frenzy. And he had known it, the brute; he had been watching her losing her mind, wallowing in passion, while he'd remained as unmoved as if he were—were tuning up a car engine.

He turned away and walked across the room, opening and closing doors in the built-in cupboard. She heard the noise of a cork's being pulled out, then he came back to her, holding out a tall glass. 'To cool you down,' he said, with a ghost of a smile.

The smile was the last straw. She took the glass, hurled the contents in his face, and threw the glass on the carpet. Then, to her utter mortification, she buried her head in the back of the sofa and burst into tears.

She covered her face with one hand, gulping and spluttering, while the other hand fumbled for the pocket in the gown she was wearing. In the pocket, by some merciful chance, was a wad of tissues. After she had choked away the tears she wiped her cheeks, dabbed her eyes and blew her nose hard. By then Charles would have left. There was no way he was going to stay and witness her abject performance. Men didn't have much patience with tears. She lifted her head cautiously to make sure he wasn't still there.

He was. He was leaning back in the easy chair next to the sofa, looking very much at home. He'd taken off his thin khaki shirt and it was lying in a sodden heap on the floor. In the subdued light from the reading lamp he looked bronzed and magnificent, the muscles rippling over his ribs and the dark shadow of hair streaking down to disappear at the belt of his jeans. I hate him, Anthea told herself. No, I don't, I'm crazy about him.

'Better now?' he enquired calmly.

She glared at him, saying nothing because she couldn't think of anything sufficiently hurtful to say.

'You know,' he went on calmly, 'I think we should call off the match at game-all. Another time, perhaps, we could play the deciding game of the set, but now's not the time.'

He leaned towards her, resting his forearms along his knees. 'Anthea, my dear,' he said urgently, 'let's not fight any more. Let's finish off the fortnight as friends—that way we'll have done something positive, however rocky it's been on the journey. I like you, I admire you tremendously. You're a lovely, warm, enchanting girl and if things had been different...'

He stopped, and for a moment the look of near-despair that she had seen before clouded his face. Then he brightened again. 'What do you say? Shall we call it quits?'

Let's finish the fortnight as friends. She pretended to consider it. She was starving and he was offering her a few crumbs of dry bread. He'd set her alight with his calculated lovemaking. What would it be like, she thought faintly, if it were real and not a sham? If he really wanted her as she wanted him? *Did he want her at all?* Or only when she made him angry? She remembered that time they had danced together on her first evening in the Caymans. He'd been angry then. And he'd certainly been angry on the beach this afternoon—angry with her for teasing him a little. Or had his response been nothing more than the act of a man desperately in need of a woman—any woman—who for a few moments could make him forget his real love—the unknown woman whose loss had poisoned his emotional life, leaving it barren and empty? She wished she knew.

'*Please*, Anthea.'

Two more days! Only one really, for tomorrow she would want to be with Pam when she got home. She wasn't sure that she could go on with the charade, not after all that had happened today. But if she refused it would be hideously difficult to explain to Nancy and to Pamela why they had quarrelled. If they parted as friends, when Charles left, the whole thing would just fade away and no questions asked—or not any that she couldn't tactfully evade.

She gave an almost imperceptible nod.

'Fine,' he said, treating her to a frank smile. 'No hard feelings? It's good to clear the air, don't you think?'

He'd got his own way—he was prepared to be charming. But *she* wasn't prepared to rake over any ashes. 'I'd like you to go now,' she said.

He got up immediately. 'Of course. How about tomorrow? You're expecting Pamela and Guy back, aren't you? Can I be of any assistancc—take you to meet them perhaps?' he offered courteously.

'No, thank you,' she said, stiffly polite. 'They couldn't say which flight they'd be on so they'll get a taxi from the airport.'

'Ah, yes. Well, let me know if I can help. And we must try to fit in our final dive before I leave, mustn't we?'

'Perhaps—if there's time. I have to see how Pam is.'

'Yes, of course,' he agreed smoothly. 'Well, good-night, Anthea.' He picked up his soggy khaki shirt and walked across the room. 'I expect we'll see each other some time tomorrow.' With a casual lift of his hand he departed the way he had come in—through the door on to the veranda.

Anthea leaned back and closed her eyes. That horrible, formal little exchange had left her feeling utterly deflated, like a burst balloon. She wasn't thinking; she wasn't really feeling either. She was just—empty.

After a time she got up and went to the kitchen for a cloth to dry the carpet as best as she could. She picked up the glass, which was unbroken, and carried it to the sink. Then she went upstairs to her bedroom. The moon had risen and the room was filled with white light and inky black shadows. After the heat of the day the air was blessedly cool with a little breeze wafting through the open window.

She stood beside the window, looking down to the sea where the moonlight threw squiggly ripples on the water. The endless stretch of sand gleamed silver as far as the eye could see. The palm trees sighed faintly and the cicadas put up their incessant shrill chirp. A perfect place, Anthea thought with detachment, but not the place to heal a broken heart. Charles hadn't managed it, and neither could she.

She closed the window and got into bed, lying on her back and staring at the ceiling. She'd go back to London as soon as she was reassured that Pamela didn't need her. The decision steadied her nerves. She felt a faint stir of enthusiasm for the task ahead—looking for a new work-room, getting started again on her designs, buying new machines. It was going to be a hard slog but she needed a demanding challenge if she was ever going to get Charles Ravenscroft out of her system.

She'd expected to lie awake for hours, but the decision to return to London had brought her a kind of peace and she fell asleep almost immediately.

The first thing Anthea heard when she wakened next morning was the hum of the vacuum downstairs. She pulled on her wrap and went down to find Juliana, wrapped in a red and white spotted apron, happily getting back into routine.

'My mother is better,' she told Anthea with her beautiful white smile. 'She tells me to go off to work again, so here I am. I give her half my wages, you see,' she added slyly.

Anthea laughed. 'I'm pleased to see you, Juliana. My sister and her husband are coming home today and I was going to do some cleaning myself. I'm afraid you'll find some dust around the place. I've been rather lazy.'

'Not lazy at all!' Juliana shook her dark head vehemently. 'You come for holiday, not to work yourself to frazzle. You have a good holiday?'

'Oh, yes, marvellous,' Anthea said, putting an ecstatic smile on her mouth. 'Who wouldn't in this heavenly place?'

Juliana nodded. 'I see you around with Mr Charles from next door.' She nodded sagely. 'Very good-looking man, that one!' The sloe-black eyes slid knowingly towards Anthea's.

'Yes—well—I'll go up and get dressed,' Anthea said hastily and escaped to her bedroom. Juliana worked for Nancy too, and no doubt would be asking some loaded questions when she got there. There was a villagey atmosphere in the condo and Juliana probably considered herself part of it.

By one o'clock the apartment was clean and polished, flowers were massed in every reasonably cool corner, and between them Anthea and Juliana had prepared a special native dish of conch and lobster which could stay in the fridge until required for supper.

'You like me to make you some lunch before I go?' Juliana offered, but Anthea thanked her and declined. She wasn't really hungry; perhaps being 'crossed in love' really did take your appetite away. Coffee was always welcome though, and when Juliana had left for her afternoon stint next door Anthea made coffee in Pamela's gleaming percolator and carried it out to the table on the veranda.

Five minutes later Nancy's head appeared round the woven grass screen that partly separated the two sections of the veranda. 'Do I smell coffee?'

'You certainly do. Come and join me—I'll get an extra mug.' Anthea welcomed her neighbour with pleasure.

During the time Pamela had been away Anthea had grown very fond of Charles's sister. Her apparent bluntness was actually an inability to put on an act. Her fussiness was a practical desire to help. She was a 'real' person, Anthea recognised, and there were all too few of them about. She understood, now, why Charles had jibbed against hurting her feelings when she had ingenuously tried to matchmake on his behalf. But understanding didn't help to make her feel any less guilty and uneasy about her own part in his little charade.

Nancy sank into a cane chair. She was wearing a brightly patterned sun-dress and she radiated good sense and good humour.

'Phew! I had to get away from Juliana; she makes me feel weak the way she buzzes round at ninety miles an hour. And talk! She talks the hind leg off a donkey, as my old granny used to say. Thanks, dear...' as Anthea passed a mug of coffee across the table. 'She likes to know everything that's happening to "her" folks—as she thinks of us, here in the condo. She's a good soul but it gets a bit much sometimes. This morning she wanted to know...' She paused and threw an apologetic glance towards Anthea. 'No—I mustn't embarrass you; I expect you can guess what I was going to say.'

Anthea sipped her coffee with a fair attempt at nonchalance. 'Yes, she was throwing hints around when she was here. She'd seen me with Charles, apparently. "Very good-looking man, that one."' She mimicked the girl's faint lilt with a grin.

Nancy sighed. 'Yes, I must say I agree, although he *is* my brother.' She was silent for a time and Anthea cast around desperately for something to say that would change the subject. But before she could think of anything, Nancy burst out impulsively, 'I've been worried about him, Anthea; I think you know that. Poor boy, he's been going through a very bad patch. A woman, of course—isn't it always some woman?' Her squarish good-natured face was suddenly venomous. 'Oh, she was beautiful, of course. The face of an angel and a heart of pure steel. The kind of woman that even the most intelligent of men make fools of themselves over.'

Nancy had been gripping her coffee-mug as if she would have liked to grip the neck of this unknown beauty who had ensnared her beloved brother. Now she put the mug down, her lips twisting apologetically. 'I expect you think I'm behaving like a possessive mama, but since we lost our parents when Charles was ten and I six years older—they were drowned in a sailing accident in Australia—I've felt a kind of...responsibility. Silly, I suppose, now we're both grown up, but when I think what Charles was like before that——' her mouth narrowed '—before that bitch Elsa got her claws into him, and the way it left him when it was all over, it makes me see red. Sometimes I was afraid...'

Suddenly the brown eyes were flooded with tears. Nancy sniffed and blew her nose. 'Sorry—I'm not usually a cry-baby. I don't know why I'm inflicting all this on you, my dear, except that you've been so good for Charles. He's gradually become more like his old self since he's known you. I shouldn't interfere, I know, but I must say it—you're so right for him. It's a shame he has to go back to London on Friday—a board meeting or something. But you'll be leaving for London yourself before very long?' she added hopefully. 'I expect you'll be meeting up there.'

'Maybe we shall,' Anthea said carefully. It was hateful having to deceive Nancy, for that was what it amounted to, but when Charles was back in London and Nancy was here in the Caymans this fortnight would fade into the past quite rapidly. Charles would get over his hurt in time and no doubt find another girl. But it wouldn't be *her*. Sadly she thought that she had come across him again at the worst possible time. Perhaps if they'd met later, when the wound had healed, perhaps . . . But that sort of thinking led nowhere. The time was now, and two weeks hadn't been long enough. The wound was still too raw for him to turn to a new love.

Nancy got to her feet. 'I'll be off, then. I'm getting the bus into town to meet Bill for lunch. Charles has gone out in the dive-boat with Joe this morning. I'll look forward to seeing Pamela—tomorrow, perhaps, when she's rested after the journey. Give her my love. Thanks for the coffee.'

She gave Anthea a faintly embarrassed smile. Probably she was regretting having lowered her guard, Anthea thought, watching the compact figure disappear round the grass screen. In spite of her friendly, open approach, there was a dignity, a strength about Nancy that didn't show on the surface.

When she had gone Anthea stayed sitting on the veranda, leaning her head back, her eyes closed against the bright sunlight that filtered through the canopy, thinking of what Nancy had told her about Charles. How little she knew of him! Their fortnight together had been such a strange time. Normally, a man and a girl getting to know each other would ask so many questions. Every little detail would be of vital interest. But Charles had been absolutely unapproachable. All she knew of him she'd just learned from Nancy: that they had lived in Australia when he was a boy; that their parents had been drowned; that he'd had a passionate love-affair with a girl called Elsa, which seemed to have wrecked his life. 'The kind of woman that...men make fools of themselves over.' Yes, it was all quite clear now; everything was clear, and she had never stood a chance with him.

The sun had attained its maximum heat and she felt the sweat breaking out on her forehead. The effort of trying to be sensible about everything had left her feeling nervy and unsettled. She must find something to do.

On an impulse she went back inside and rang up the airport to enquire the time of arrival of the next flight from Miami. Learning that it was due in just under half an hour, she phoned for a taxi. She'd meet the plane on the off-chance that Pamela and Guy would be on it.

She hadn't long to wait. In the arrivals hall she watched eagerly as the first passengers began to dribble through from Customs. Americans, bright as proverbial buttons, talking thirteen to the dozen, Europeans looking distinctly weary, with a long flight behind them. They came in couples, in parties, some looking around for taxis, others for friends expected to meet them.

Anthea's spirits drooped with disappointment as the crowd of arrivals began to thin out, with no sign of Pamela and Guy. The buzz of greetings faded as the lounge emptied. The last few stragglers emerged. A couple speaking German, with two exhausted-looking small boys. Two middle-aged ladies determinedly pushing trolleys. And then, walking alone and carrying only a weekend briefcase, a young woman who caught Anthea's eye immediately because of the contrast she presented with the crowd of holiday-makers.

Anthea's glance passed over the reed-thin figure in its black silk suit—which looked hideously expensive but quite unsuitable for arrival at a holiday hotel. One of the new breed of female business tycoons probably, Anthea thought without much interest. Then she caught a glimpse of the girl's face and felt a small shock. It was a beautiful face, a perfect oval, but in spite of the careful make-up the skin seemed pallid and the huge smoke-grey eyes stared straight ahead with an oddly haunted look. Even when she had passed, the memory of those strange eyes remained with Anthea as she waited with dwindling hope for Pamela and her husband to emerge, until there wasn't any point in waiting longer.

At the information office she was told that the only other flight from Miami was due to arrive at nine-thirty tonight. She calculated quickly. Another seven wasted hours when she might have been with Charles. She felt terrible. She should be thinking about Pam; instead she was trying to face the rest of her life without Charles and seeing only a long black tunnel of days.

Despondently she went back to the taxi she had booked to wait. 'Bribed' might have been a better word, because she had given the driver a hefty tip to ensure his compliance, in case Pamela was on the flight.

The taxi was still there on the forecourt—the only one remaining—and the girl in black was standing beside it, conducting a one-sided argument with the driver, who was leaning back, chewing gum and regarding her without much interest.

'Well, when will there be another cab?' Her voice was high-pitched and nervous and not at all in character with her sleek, groomed appearance.

Anthea approached the taxi and the driver reached out and opened the passenger door for her.

She smiled at him and turned to the girl. 'Like to share a cab into town? It's maddening to be left high and dry.'

'Thanks,' the girl muttered and climbed into the taxi.

Anthea followed and sat beside her. 'Where shall I tell him? I'm going beyond the town myself.'

'Oh—oh, anywhere.' Anthea noticed that her voice was unsteady and the white hands clasping her briefcase shook slightly.

The taxi trundled along the dusty road towards George Town. Anthea glanced at the girl beside her. She really was exquisite, her hair glossy as a raven's wing, her skin so fine and white and perfect, and those enormous grey eyes that Anthea had first noticed staring straight ahead with a fixed gaze.

They couldn't just sit here saying nothing. 'I came to meet my sister and her husband,' she said pleasantly, 'but they must have missed the plane.'

'Oh,' murmured the girl indifferently.

'You here on holiday?' Anthea tried.

The great grey eyes met hers and she experienced an odd shock. They were swimming in tears. The girl shook her head, swallowed back the tears and turned away again.

One didn't intrude on a stranger's troubles. There was silence until the taxi reached the town.

Anthea leaned forward. 'Please stop at the harbour,' she told the driver, and to the girl, 'You can reach most places from there. Will that suit you?'

The girl nodded wordlessly. When the car pulled up she fumbled in her bag, but Anthea touched her hand. It was icy cold. 'Please don't,' she said. 'I have to go on further in any case.'

'Thanks, then.' The girl climbed out and stood looking around uncertainly as the taxi moved away.

The driver turned his head with a smile. 'You goin' back home, miss?'

'Yes, please.' Anthea wondered briefly about the girl they had just left. But you couldn't worry long about strangers' troubles when you had plenty of your own.

At the condo she paid the driver and walked slowly from the car park. As she went she counted the hours that were left. 'I'll see you tomorrow,' Charles had said. And, 'We must . . . fit in our final dive before I leave.'

But Charles wasn't around today and now it looked as if she might not have any free time tomorrow. There was no way she could go off with Charles when

Pamela had just come home—even if he asked her to. Perhaps, she thought bleakly, it would be better that way, better that they wouldn't be alone together again. Their fortnight would end—fizzle out miserably. She felt black gloom settling round her, blotting out the sunshine.

Then she turned the corner and saw him coming to meet her and felt a sharp painful twinge behind her ribs.

'Wherc have you been? I've been waiting for you.' He took her arm and led her to the veranda. 'You OK? You look fagged.'

She sank into a chair. 'I'm fine—just hot. I've been to the airport to meet Pam and Guy but they weren't on the plane.'

'That's what I guessed. I've got a message for you. Pamela and Guy aren't coming back until tomorrow. Guy tried to ring you here and when there wasn't any reply he got through to our number. Nancy's out so I took the message. It's OK——' as Anthea shot up in her chair, eyes widening with alarm '—everything's fine. Pamela spoke to me herself.'

She relaxed with a sigh of relief, fanning her hot cheeks with her hand.

'You need a drink,' Charles said. 'Look, let me find something in Guy's drinks cupboard for you. What'll you have?'

'Something long and cool, please.' She watched him as he made for the door into the living-room. How brown his legs were, the dark hairs almost invisible against the skin, and how wide his shoulders under the white cotton vest! She thought in sudden panic, Oh, God, I love him. How am I going to live when he's gone?

'Here you are.' He put a tall glass into her hand as he sat down beside her. A grin touched the corners of his mouth. 'And for Pete's sake *drink* it this time, and don't hurl it in my face.'

She took a gulp of the ice-cold fruity drink. 'I'm sorry,' she muttered.

The grin turned into a laugh—a hearty guffaw. 'Don't let's start swapping apologies again—we'll never get to the end.' He peered down into her face. 'You *are* looking bushed. When did you last eat?'

She blinked foolishly. 'I had breakfast—I think.'

'Breakfast, you *think*!' he roared. 'And it's half-past three now. Don't you know you shouldn't skip meals just because you're in the tropics? And you're probably dehydrated too. Go on, finish your drink while I rustle up a sandwich for you.'

He got to his feet. 'As things have turned out we've got the rest of today to ourselves. Nancy and Bill won't be in until later, so we can make plans. We'll pick up our gear at Joe's, hire one of his inflatables and take it out beyond the reef. We can get into fairly deep water there—find a good drop-off. Diving from a boat's the one thing I haven't taught you. We must make our last dive together really memorable.'

She gave a mock shiver. 'You sound like the condemned man planning to eat a hearty breakfast.'

Suddenly the bleak, haggard look that she was beginning to recognise swept over his face. 'Don't say things like that,' he said sharply. He rested one hand on the table and the dark, sombre eyes stared down into hers. She could almost imagine he was memorising her face, but that was wishful thinking of course.

He straightened up. The moment was past. He said briskly, 'OK, you go and get changed. I'll raid the fridge and you can eat in the car. That way we won't waste any time.'

Anthea went upstairs, slipped quickly into the businesslike white swim-suit she wore for diving, and pulled a blue cover-up over it. There was a feeling of urgency now; she was no longer counting the days but the hours. Everything they did together would be for the last time so she must savour every minute. She mustn't allow herself to think of what would come after he had gone.

She peered in the mirror. Smile, she ordered sternly. Go on, smile.

It wasn't easy but she managed it, and before the smile faded from her lips she ran lightly downstairs to join Charles.

CHAPTER NINE

'WE'LL anchor here.' Charles switched off the engine and the small rubber dinghy rocked very gently in the water. He peered over the side. 'Should go down to twenty metres here—quite deep enough for a raw beginner.' He smiled lazily across at Anthea.

He was in his friendly, teasing mood. She liked that. This last time together must be happy—something to remember for years, perhaps forever.

She looked all around, trying to stack away every detail: the changing colours of the water from brilliant sapphire here beyond the line of the reef to glassy turquoise nearer the beach; a few dinghies with rainbow-striped sails; a white yacht moored offshore; a figure, dangling from a red and yellow parachute rising out of the water on a tow-line. The long strip of white sand was almost empty. At this time in the afternoon most of the visitors would be found lounging round their pools in the low-built hotels and clubs and condominiums that nestled behind the row of palm trees along the whole length of Seven Mile Beach. It was very quiet. The occasional scream of a seabird and the putt-putting of an outboard motor seemed to come from a long way away.

Out here, beyond the reef, there was only the smell of heat and sea and rubber, the silvery dazzle of sun on water—and Charles sitting across the boat from her, eyes narrowed against the sun, teeth white against bronzed cheeks. He looked so happy—he always did when he was on a diving expedition. Oh, God, I love him, she thought, and her heart squeezed up inside her.

She tipped her head back. 'Am I still a raw beginner? I thought I was making spectacular progress.'

He pursed his lips. 'I don't like the word spectacular. It has a hectic sound about it. Diving should be relaxed always, and over-confidence is the greatest hazard.'

'Oh,' breathed Anthea, feeling rather dashed.

'Having said which——' Charles smiled '—you are probably the best pupil I've ever had. You do what you're told, you don't jib at getting down to the sometimes boring theory. And you learn so quickly I'm positively amazed at how much you've remembered.'

Anthea chuckled. 'Thank you for those kind words.' She wouldn't tell him how many hours she had spent in bed poring over a book of Guy's she had found on scuba diving.

'And——' he continued, '—you're looking particularly lovely today, Anthea. You have five freckles on your delightful nose.'

She was glad the light was so strong that he wouldn't notice her blush.

'Now.' He was all businesslike again as he paid out the anchor-line. 'I've planned the dive—times and everything. You can leave that part to me. You know the underwater drill. Entering from the boat is the only new thing. I go first and wait for you on the surface. You sit on the tubes, check the water behind you, hold one hand over mask and demand valve, the other on the cylinder harness, tuck your head forwards. Relax and roll backwards over the side. You'll

bob up like a cork immediately. Signal OK to me and then we duck-dive together to get underwater, turn, and drop feet first. Remember to clear your ears as we go, and to breathe easily. Any questions?'

'No—sir,' she grinned.

'Am I a hard taskmaster, Anthea?' He met her eyes quizzically.

'We-ell,' she drawled, looking up questioningly into the pale blue of the sky. 'Let's just say——' she looked down again, '—the best. The very best.'

For a moment she thought he seemed taken aback. Had she given herself away—had she let the love she felt for him shine out of her eyes? Oh, please not, she thought; that would spoil everything. Friends they were—'buddies' in diving parlance—and friends they must remain until the end. That way there would be no room for bitterness or recriminations. 'Do we get ourselves kitted up now?' she asked practically, reaching for her pile of neatly stacked gear on the bottom of the boat.

Afterwards she was to remember how perfectly everything went at first—probably because she had absolute trust in Charles and obeyed his orders in every smallest detail. There was something wonderful and strange about dropping slowly hand-in-hand through crystal-clear water, bubbles rising above them to the sunlit surface, clouds of tiny coloured fish continually changing direction around them with a swish of a hundred tails.

And on the sea-bed there was the marvellous array of coral and sponges, brown and blue and gold, the waving green feathers of plants, the larger, lazier fish, that sometimes formed an interested audience, peering into their masks.

At this depth the light became dim and mysterious, but the visibility was still so good on the sea-bed that Charles now and then loosed his hold and allowed Anthea to roam free, although keeping very close. She finned in a sort of ecstatic trance, exploring, touching, encountering fish that she hadn't seen on their dives in shallower water. Many of them seemed quite tame. At one point she met a particularly friendly blue and gold angel fish which followed her like a pet dog waiting to be stroked. Anthea looked for Charles to share her delight with him.

That was when everything began to go wrong. He was about six feet away from her and as she signed to him to come closer she saw that he was signing back to her. Not the usual finger and thumb sign of 'OK', but the distress signal. Clenched fists waving to and fro urgently, then his cupped hand pointing to his mouthpiece.

The signal that meant, 'Out of air, assistance required immediately.'

For a split second icy terror ran through Anthea's every nerve. Then, immediately, she was completely calm. They had practised emergency ascents together during sessions in shallow water. But this wasn't a practice session, this was for real, and they were in deep water. If he'd been going to risk a free ascent he would have started up immediately. But he was waiting for her. He was relying on her help. His life depended on her.

Those thoughts flashed through her head in the time it took to reach him, to set in motion the drill that she had learned. Then some strength outside herself took over. She was cool, confident, automatic. Not a thought entered her head except those that told her exactly what she had to do.

Taking in two good breaths as she moved towards Charles, she grasped the strap of his harness, removed her mouthpiece and held it out to him with the air flowing. He took hold of one strap of her harness so that they were facing, and with the other hand guided the mouthpiece into his own mouth.

As he drew in several life-saving breaths she sent up a prayer of thanksgiving. It worked! She exhaled gently until he handed the mouthpiece back to her.

After a steady breathing-and-exchange rhythm was established she saw that Charles was in control again. 'Going up,' he signalled, and she replied with the 'OK' signal.

Face to face, holding each other by their harnesses, they rose steadily at the rate of the small bubbles above them, carrying out faithfully the one decompression stop which Charles had planned. Finally they were on the surface and she was drawing in wonderful, life-giving air, and the inflatable boat was only about ten metres away.

Anthea could never remember swimming to the boat or how she managed to pull herself in when she reached it.

The next thing she knew was that her harness and fins had been removed and she was sprawled on the bottom, that Charles had started the motor, and they were heading towards the land.

After that everything was hazy. She had done what she had to do and now shock was taking its toll. She was dimly aware of Charles's helping her out into shallow water and then of them both dragging the boat the last few yards on to the sand.

She was feeling very odd now, her body heavy as lead. But she mustn't give in. Charles was the one who might have drowned down there—she mustn't be the one to falter now. 'Shall I carry...?' she began, and suddenly keeled over on to the warm sand.

Charles was towering above her. 'I'll do the carrying round here,' he said, and picked her up easily.

It was so heavenly in his arms. She snuggled against him as he strode up the beach to the condo. How had they got here? she thought stupidly. They'd taken the boat out from the slipway outside the dive-shop. But it wasn't important. She turned her head a little into the damp warmth of his neck. His skin smelled delicious. She touched it delicately with her tongue and the salt burned her mouth.

He carried her straight upstairs, and lowered her on to the bed. She found she was shivering, which was absurd when it was stiflingly hot in the bedroom.

'Now you're going to rest,' Charles said. 'Let's get this swim-suit off.' He slipped the straps over her shoulders and, gripping the clinging stretch-fabric, began to ease it down.

'I can do it,' she gasped, trying to swing her legs to the floor.

'Lie down,' he ordered firmly, 'and don't be silly.' He pushed her back and gave the swim-suit one last tug. She felt it slipping over her stomach, her thighs, her legs.

'*That's* better.' He dropped the swim-suit on the floor and covered her with the duvet. 'Now you relax and don't dare to move. I'll go and make some nice hot tea. Always good recovery drill after the shock and tension of an emergency.' The dark eyes were looking down at her with—could it be tenderness? Or was she just imagining it?

'But—but what about you?' she stammered. 'It wasn't just me having the emergency—I feel such an idiot, flaking out like this.'

'Shut up, darling,' he said gently, and went out of the room.

She closed her eyes. He'd called her 'darling', and looked at her as if—as if...

By the time he came back with tea on a tray the shivering had stopped and she felt almost normal. Charles put the tray down and indicated his navy swimming trunks, which had a large slit up one side. 'Must have snagged them climbing into the boat. Do you think Guy would lend me some clobber? I don't want to risk going in next door in case Nancy's back and I have to start explaining.'

'Of course—help yourself. It's the room next to the bathroom.'

She would have to get something to cover herself. She couldn't sit up in bed to drink her tea showing her naked top half, and to pull up the duvet as protection would look ridiculous—especially as Charles had already seen all there was to see of her when he'd removed her swim-suit.

She slid out of bed and staggered towards the wardrobe. But her knees felt like elastic and she had to steady herself against the dressing-table, breathing hard.

'What are you doing? I told you to stay put.' Charles came up behind her and grabbed her round the waist. He had put on a pair of Guy's linen trousers and the stiffened material rubbed against her bare hips.

'I—I wanted to get my robe.' She nodded towards the wardrobe.

'I'll get it,' he said but didn't make any move, and his arm crept further round her waist until it rested under the swell of her breast. 'Nice,' he murmured and buried his mouth in the nape of her neck. She felt his tongue licking the skin below her hair, and her heart did a somersault.

'Salty—I like plenty of salt on my food,' he chuckled.

He was playing it light, so she must do the same. 'Too much salt's bad for you, didn't you know? Raises your blood-pressure.'

Suddenly he twisted her round until she was facing him. 'I don't need salt to do that,' he said softly and drew her against him, kissing her very gently.

'Charles—oh, Charles. I thought you were going to die!' She flung her arms round his neck and kissed him back with growing frenzy, pressing her body against his, thrilling to the growing hardness she encountered there. She was in his arms, where she wanted to be, and for a few mad moments she was going to forget the rules he'd made.

She felt him start to draw away and she clung even tighter. 'No,' he said shakily. 'It's not on, darling.'

'It is, oh, it *is*,' she pleaded. She'd never felt like this before—wanton and soft and swelling, and aflame with the intensity of a passion that had been growing and growing for all the days they'd spent together. Like a strong plant, pushing up out of the ground towards the sunlight.

Somehow they were lying on the bed and she could feel him trembling against her. 'It won't do,' he groaned. 'God, I want you too, my darling, but I've nothing to offer you. Nothing. *Nothing.*'

'It doesn't matter,' she sobbed. 'I don't care—I'd have a memory. Oh, *please*, Charles.'

She heard him mutter something that sounded like 'forgive', and then he was dragging feverishly at the zip of his trousers and his weight was on her and they were together, naked.

Once his control had finally broken he took all he wanted from her with hands and mouth, exploring every part of her eager body, every mound, every crevice, raising her to a point of frenzy where she writhed beneath him, her nails digging into the taut muscles of his shoulders, whimpering with a rising tension that was pain as well as pleasure. When he plunged into her she arched against him in a fierce response, holding her breath, moving with him in a wild climb to some undreamed-of peak, moaning in ecstasy as they reached that peak together and he gave a strangled, harsh cry and shuddered against her in an explosive consummation that made the bed rock beneath them.

It was over. That was Anthea's first coherent thought as he rolled off her and lay, panting, on the edge of the bed. It was over and it wouldn't happen again. It was as though she were hearing the tolling of a funeral bell. A choking sound that wasn't quite a laugh escaped her. Funny to compare what had just happened to a funeral.

Beside her, Charles muttered, 'Game, set and match—is that what you're thinking?'

She turned her head on the pillow and let her eyes feast on his face. Under the tan there was a flush high on his cheekbones. A lock of dark hair fell raggedly over his forehead and she stretched out and pushed it back gently, letting her hand linger on the damp, hot skin. 'It was you who turned it into a game, remember? But if it means I've won, then I suppose I should feel triumphant.'

'And you don't?' He grasped her hand and put it to his lips. 'What *do* you feel?'

She smiled dreamily. 'Satisfied. Replete. Sad.'

'Not regretful?'

'No, not regretful. If I won the match it was only because I cheated and broke the rules you'd laid down at the start. But I'm not sorry.'

There was a long pause. Then he swivelled round, his back to her, thrusting his legs into Guy's trousers. 'I've got to ask you this, Anthea. You took me by surprise when we were both—disturbed by what had just happened out there.' He gestured towards the window. 'Is it possible that you might have got yourself pregnant?'

She drew in a quick breath. He had hurt her so often that one more hurt didn't really matter. 'No, it isn't possible,' she said evenly, and heard his sigh of relief. She managed a small laugh. 'A girl doesn't come for a holiday on a tropical holiday island without some—protection.'

The look he gave her might have been ironic—she hoped it wasn't. 'So you *were* hoping for a holiday affair, with the usual trimmings. You told me——'

She sat up quickly, then realised she was still naked and made a quick dash for the wardrobe. Struggling into jeans and a cotton top, she said angrily, 'I was *not* hoping for a holiday affair. Sex was the last thing on my mind until . . .'

'Until?' he prompted quietly.

'Until I met my dream hero again.' She managed a silly little giggle. 'It was all *so* romantic. Just like in the novels.'

He crossed the room in a couple of strides and took her by both shoulders. As he studied her face she felt her smile fading under the scrutiny of those sombre black eyes.

'Was that all it was? Was it, Anthea?' He gave her a little shake. 'I want the truth.'

Their eyes locked and held. She said slowly, 'If you'd died down there, I shouldn't have wanted to go on living. I know it won't alter anything, but I may as well tell you.'

'Tell me—what?'

'That I love you,' she said simply.

She wriggled away from him. 'Look, the tea's gone cold,' she said in a high, brittle voice. 'How about that for a botched recovery drill? I'll go down and make some more; I think we both need it.'

Down in the kitchen she put the kettle on and stood leaning against the sink. She felt weak and shaky and she didn't know how she was going to face Charles again. For minutes there was no sound upstairs and then, just as the kettle boiled, she heard him coming down. He didn't join her in the kitchen and for a blank moment she wondered if he had walked straight out of the apartment, frightened out of his wits by her avowal of love.

But when she carried the tray into the living-room he was there, sitting on a corner of the sofa. He was wearing one of Guy's shirts—a short-sleeved cotton in a burnt orange colour.

'Very fetching! Just your colour!' Her mouth felt stiff but she managed a small smile.

He jumped up and took the tray from her, and she sat down in a chair by the window.

'Not there—here.' He put down the tray and gripped both her hands, pulling her up to sit beside him on the sofa. 'Your hands are cold,' he said. 'And this time you're going to drink the tea. You need it.' He poured out a cup and handed it to her, watching while she took a long gulp.

'That's better.' He followed suit, and between them they drank the pot dry. Anthea began to feel warm again, confidence creeping back to stiffen her spine. He'd asked for the truth and she'd given it to him, that was all. She didn't expect him to make any sudden U-turn, but there was no doubt that in the last half-hour things had changed between them. Colour crept into her cheeks as she remembered some of the ways they had changed.

He pushed the low table away and leaned back, not touching her. 'Now,' he said, 'we've carried out the proper recovery drill. Hot tea and relaxation. Especially relaxation.' He slid her an amused glance and her spirits shot up. He wasn't going to be stiff and awkward about her confession of love. He probably thought that she had been persuading herself that she was the kind of girl who wouldn't sleep with a man unless she'd convinced herself that she loved him. Oh, damn! It was all so complicated.

'I haven't thanked you,' he went on. 'I suppose you know that you may have saved my life.'

'I did what you taught me.' She made herself ask the question, 'What would have happened if I'd got it wrong?'

'I'd have made a free ascent. But from that depth it would have been—unpleasant.'

'And risky?'

He shrugged. 'Yes.'

She shivered, remembering that first moment of panic. She said, 'You sound so—sort of cool about it all. Weren't you even a bit scared?' Perhaps if she could break through the defensive wall he'd set up round himself—if she could get him to admit to an ordinary human frailty such as fear—perhaps then he'd unburden himself even more.

'Scared? The first moment when I breathed in and there was nothing there I was petrified. But I've been diving for a long time, Anthea, and accidents do sometimes happen. It helps to know what you have to do. I had to decide in a split second whether to start a free ascent straight away, or whether to wait and lose valuable time, trusting that you'd keep your head. I trusted—and you did. It was your first emergency and you handled it like a pro.' He smiled at her—a smile that seemed to trickle all over her body, warming every part of it.

His praise was very sweet to her, but not a single brick of the defences had loosened.

She swallowed a sigh. 'What went wrong—do you know?'

He shook his head. 'I'll have to examine the gear to find out. But——' he frowned to himself '—I have a horrible feeling that the fault was mine. I may not have checked my contents gauge carefully enough. Quite unforgivable if that's the case.' His mouth set in a grim line. 'In this game one can't afford to let one's concentration slip—whatever the excuse.'

He was looking at her as if she was in some way responsible, which was absurd, of course. In other circumstances that remark might have been flirtatious, but not now, and certainly not from Charles!

'Perhaps you'll find a fault in the equipment,' she said rather stiffly.

'Perhaps.' He stood up. 'Now, I'll go down and rescue the dinghy and take it back to Joe's. I can check in all the hired stuff—yours and mine. I shan't dive tomorrow—not without my "buddy"——' he slanted a quick grin at her which melted her brief annoyance '—and I'll be leaving early Friday morning. What shall I tell Joe about your hired gear? Will you be staying on?'

'I don't know—it depends on how Pamela is when she gets home tomorrow, and whether she needs me to stay longer. But I certainly won't be diving again. In any case, I'd have to be careful to leave a safe interval before flying, wouldn't I?'

There was something horribly final about this conversation. Everything was being tidied up, like shiny crumpled paper after a Christmas party. Tidied up and thrown away. No past—no future, he'd said. He'd made love to her because she had almost forced herself on him. No doubt he'd enjoyed it—certainly he'd appeared to—but, man-like, he would soon have forgotten all about it, and about her.

She got to her feet beside him. She felt more in control of herself when she was standing up. There was something she had to say and she couldn't think of the right words.

Finally she blurted out, 'It's the end of our fortnight and I want to...'

He took a step towards her and touched her mouth with his palm. 'No farewell speeches,' he said. 'You haven't got rid of me yet. Where would you like to go for dinner? Shall we dine in—or out? If it's up to me to decide I'd vote for eating here—am I invited?'

Reprieve—if only for a few hours! She wanted to dance and sing. Instead she dropped a mock curtsy. 'I should be honoured.'

'Good.' He lingered at the door. 'Anthea . . .'

'Yes?' She held her breath. There was something in his face; was the defensive wall cracking—ever so slightly?

'I—there are things I must tell you. I owe it to you,' he said bleakly. 'Later,' he added, and went out through the door on to the veranda.

She watched him run down the beach and push out the dinghy. She could almost sense the dammed-up energy in him as he heaved himself over the side and started up the motor. The dinghy headed out to sea and then turned sharply towards the south end of the beach, where Joe's shop was located. Charles raised a hand as if he knew she might be still there, watching. She waved back, although by now she would be out of sight to him.

She leaned against the window frame. She still had a few hours left. Dinner for two. Wine, candles, moonlight, the scent of flowers drifting in through the window, music—all the old romantic trappings. And why not, if it helped to get under his defences?

There was a skip in her step as she made her way to the kitchen to set about preparing a meal.

It was more than an hour before he came back. The meal was all ready in the kitchen—the conch and lobster dish prepared this morning, salad crisping in the fridge, a luscious-looking fruity concoction that Juliana had brought with her from one of the specialist shops in the town, crusty rolls and butter. Charles could choose the wine himself from Guy's store.

Anthea fussed round the table in the living-room, flicking an imaginary crumb off the snowy cloth, re-polishing the immaculately gleaming silver, touching the little posy of pink and white flowers she had gathered from the shrubs in the garden. Nature was co-operating by laying on a spectacular sunset. Outside the window the sky and sea were merged in a blaze of rose and apricot and salmon with streaks of palest sea-green and wispy veils of silvery grey.

She heard the sound of a car and her heart began to thud against her ribs. It might be Nancy and Bill coming home of course, but . . .

Charles's step sounded on the veranda and his size almost blotted out the sunset as he appeared at the window.

Looking at him, she was beset by an awful shyness. 'Hello, you're back,' she said, smiling foolishly.

He was smiling too, but his smile wasn't foolish at all; it was definitely purposeful. He came straight to her and took her in his arms and kissed her with lingering satisfaction. Immediately she knew that something had changed. The wall between them was coming down. When he lifted his mouth he held her away and looked down into her face. ' "Anthea, Who May Command Him Anything",' he quoted softly.

She swallowed past a huge lump in her throat. She couldn't believe that this was happening—there was a dream-like quality about it. But she mustn't take more for granted than he intended to imply. She looked up at him under her lashes. 'Is that true? Very well, then, how about starting by choosing a wine for us? Over there, slave.' She indicated the drinks cupboard.

He made a mock obeisance and crossed the room as she went into the kitchen. 'White or red?' he called through the doorway.

'What do you think? It's a fishy concoction with salad. That's all there was time for.' She wheeled the trolley in.

'Mm—looks delicious. White would be à la mode, I suppose, but I think we'll forget about being correct. Guy's got a very nice-looking *rosé* here. OK?'

'OK.' The smile seemed to be fixed on her mouth. She *hadn't* been imagining it before—the atmosphere between them had changed completely, become almost intimate. There was something satisfyingly domestic in the way Charles hunted for a gadget to remove the cork, in the way he drifted out to the kitchen to help her bring in the salad and mayonnaise and butter from the fridge, and sawed hunks from the crusty loaf. In the way he settled down at the table with an appreciative, 'Well, this is nice.'

'I looked in next door,' he told her, when they had helped themselves. 'Nancy and Bill are just back. I told them they could find me here if they wanted me—but I didn't encourage them to want me.' The grin he slipped to her was a promise and her heart missed a beat.

She said, 'What did Joe think—about . . .'

'About our slight contretemps?' His mouth twisted. 'Oh, Joe's a realist. So long as nobody needed urgent treatment for the bends—you know, decompression sickness—he didn't ask too many questions. But he knows—and he knows that I know—that it should never have happened. It was due to my own carelessness.'

He drained his glass and refilled it. 'But at least it brought me to my senses. I've been so bloody sorry for myself...' He shook his shoulders, as if he were shaking a burden from them. 'But let's leave all that for now and enjoy this moment and the splendid sunset the island's putting on for us.'

Anthea looked away from him through the window. The tall palm trees, silhouetted against the gaudy sunset, the lazy splash of waves and the thin song of a thousand insects. 'I'll remember all this when I get back to London,' she said. 'I'll be able to close my eyes and imagine myself back here.'

'You have to go back soon?'

'Oh, yes, very soon; there's my job waiting for me.'

He didn't know that there was no job waiting for her—he didn't know about the fire and the loss of all her stock and equipment. But now wasn't the time to talk about that. Perhaps later on she might. How wonderful it would be if they could really talk to each other, exchange confidences, break through the high wall he'd put up between them! She mustn't try to rush things; she had to wait. She said, 'It'll be lovely to have Pamela and Guy back in London again in a couple of months. I've missed them. Nancy and Bill will be the lucky ones—two years of this marvellous climate.'

Talk about their families took them through to the end of the meal. The sunset had given way quite suddenly to velvety darkness, but the stars hadn't yet appeared. Anthea closed the window against night insects and drew the curtains.

'That was a lovely meal—thank you,' Charles said as they settled down on the sofa with their coffee, having decided against brandy or liqueurs.

Anthea could find no reply. She seemed to hear the minutes ticking away in her head now. Had she been wrong in thinking that Charles intended to confide in her? He'd said, 'there are things I must tell you.' But perhaps he'd changed his mind.

The silence lengthened until she couldn't bear it any longer. 'You said——' she began.

'Anthea, I——' he said at the same moment, and they both laughed rather uneasily.

'Let me,' Charles said. 'I said earlier on that I owed you an explanation. At the beginning I laid down a lot of rules and you've been very sporting to accept them—I realise that it's not the usual thing to make rules about friendships.' His mouth tugged down at the corners.

'I was at the end of my tether when I arrived here. Just being with you has made life bearable. That sounds grudging, I know, but I'm trying to be honest.' He leaned forward, pressing his fingers against his forehead as if he was trying to push away a bad memory.

'You don't have to...' she began. She wanted to reach out to him, to tell him it didn't matter, whatever it was.

'Yes—listen,' he said jerkily. 'I must tell you about Mark. I want you to understand.'

'Mark?' Her eyes flew open wide.

'My cousin Mark,' he went on as if she hadn't spoken. 'When my parents were drowned we were staying with Mark's family in Australia. Afterwards, Nancy and I stayed on. Mark is an only child and his parents gave us a home. We were at school and university together. Mark and I were almost the same age—he was just a couple of years older. It was like having a twin brother—we shared everything. And when we grew up it was just the same—there was this strong bond. I'd have trusted him with my life—it was that kind of friendship.

'When the family moved back to England we had to decide what to do. It was taken for granted that whatever we did we'd do it together. I don't think either of us was wildly keen on any particular career, although we were both pretty good at maths. So when Nancy married Bill it seemed natural that Mark and I should go into the financial world too. We started our own company—with Bill's help—and we did well right from the start. Mark found he'd got a flair for handling people and for handling money. He was brilliant, I was——' he grimaced '—adequate. Life was exciting then. Parties, concerts, theatres, holidays, girlfriends. We worked hard and we played hard. I don't think we ever discussed it but it was sort of taken for granted that marriage wasn't an option that either of us contemplated.

'Then the inevitable happened: I met a girl—*the* girl. Her name was Elsa and she was quite the most beautiful thing I'd ever seen. I was crazy to get married straight away but she hung back—said she couldn't make up her mind to be what she called "tied down". Mark was away. His mother had died and his father had gone back to Australia. I couldn't wait for him to come back and meet Elsa.'

He said heavily, 'He came home, they met—and he took her from me.'

'Oh!' Anthea's soft murmur of sympathy was drawn out of her. There was so much she was beginning to understand. But she didn't think he was conscious of her at all now. He was living in the past.

His mouth was drawn into a bitter line. 'It was the stuff of which dozens of ham novels and plays have been written down the ages. That didn't make it any easier. I didn't . . .'

Suddenly he broke off. 'I think I'll have that brandy now, if Guy wouldn't mind.'

'Of course.' She leapt to her feet. 'I'll get it for you.' She went into the kitchen and brought glasses for them both. She was needing a drink too.

Charles was slumped back in the corner of the sofa. He looked desperately weary. She put the two glasses on the low table and went to the drinks cupboard. 'Water with your brandy?' she asked over her shoulder.

That was when the knock came on the front door—quick and urgent. Her first thought was Pam—something was wrong . . . the police . . . She ran to open it.

It was Nancy standing there. In the light that poured out from the hallway her face looked drawn, almost old. 'Anthea—is Charles . . .?'

He came out of the living-room. 'Hello, Nan—what's up?'

Nancy stared at him, not moving. 'Charles—Elsa is here. She's just come and she's asking to see you.'

Then, out of the shadows, another figure moved forward. A girl in a black suit with huge frightened grey eyes. The girl Anthea had shared a taxi with from the airport.

'Charles—I've been trying to pluck up courage to come. Oh, Charles!' Her voice quavered, broke, and tears blurred her eyes and poured down her cheeks. As he moved towards her she threw herself into his arms, sobbing.

'All right, it's all right,' he said, stroking her shining black hair. 'Come along; you can tell me what it's all about.'

Without a backward glance towards Nancy and Anthea standing together on the step, he led the girl away.

'I knew it,' Nancy spat out viciously. 'I knew that girl would come back and spoil everything. I'm going to get rid of her. I won't have her...' She stumped after the other two, antagonism in every line of her solid figure in its brightly patterned cocktail dress.

Anthea went slowly back inside the apartment and closed the door. In the living-room she poured out, very carefully, a small brandy and sat down, sipping it slowly. But the blood had turned to ice in her veins and it would take more than brandy to warm it.

Moving like a zombie, she went into the kitchen, washed up the supper dishes and left everything spotless. In the living-room she put the furniture straight and plumped up the cushions on the sofa. One of them was still warm, where Charles's head had rested.

She laid her cheek against it, burrowing down into the sofa like a hurt animal. A long time later, when the cold started to eat into her bones, she crawled upstairs to bed.

CHAPTER TEN

AT TEN o'clock next morning there was a loud knock at the door. Anthea, who had just got up after an almost sleepless night, was in the kitchen, wrapped in one of Pamela's silk shifts, making tea.

She pushed back her hair, her heart thumping. Charles? Had he come to apologise for walking out on her last night—or to say goodbye?

But it was Nancy who stood at the door. She wore a creased red skirt and top and she looked as tired as Anthea felt.

Anthea summoned up a smile. 'Come along in, Nancy. I'm afraid I overslept—I'm just making tea; will you join me or is it too soon after breakfast?' Her voice was wooden with the effort to pretend that nothing particular had happened last night.

It was a relief to find that Nancy wasn't even making the effort. 'I haven't had breakfast,' she said wearily. 'I haven't been to sleep at all.' She followed Anthea into the kitchen and sat on one of the high stools, watching her make tea. When they were both seated, with the pot between them on the counter, she said, 'Charles has gone.' She looked ready to weep but instead took a swig of the hot tea Anthea had pushed across to her.

'It was awful. We had the most frightful row. I've never...' her lip quivered '...never quarrelled with Charles before. Not seriously.'

Anthea had always thought of Nancy as a reserved woman, certainly not given to emotional outbursts, but now she had started the words poured out. 'When he said he was going off with that girl, I told him . . .' she took another gulp of tea '. . . I told him what a fool he was making of himself. I begged him not to go—to stay and think things over—b-but he told me to mind my own business and said I'd fouled things up for him too often with my—my interference, and . . . oh, all sorts of beastly things. I've never seen him look so—so distraught. I was on my own—Bill was out with one of the bank officials.' She shivered, remembering. 'I was scared out of my wits. I've never seen Charles like that.'

Anthea listened in silence. Her world had begun to tumble down round her last night. This was the final collapse, and it was worse even than she'd expected in her darkest sleepless moments.

'That girl just hung on to Charles, weeping crocodile tears, putting on a great dramatic act. She never left him for a moment while he threw his things into a bag and went off with her in the car.' Nancy's indignation flagged and she seemed to droop. 'He must be out of his mind after what happened before—the way she let him down,' she said miserably.

Anthea swallowed hard to make sure her voice would work. Then she said, 'Has he—have they left the island?'

Nancy nodded. 'He flung it at me as they were leaving—said they were going on the first flight out this morning. I don't know where they stayed last night,' she added flatly.

She jumped up. 'There's someone at our door,' she cried and ran out to the front.

Anthea followed slowly. A coloured boy was riding away on his bike and Nancy was unfolding a letter.

She stood like a statue in the sunshine, staring at the writing inside. Then, without a word, she handed the note to Anthea.

'Nancy, dear,' it read in what must be Charles's strong handwriting, but scribbled hurriedly in a page torn from a notebook, 'I had to go. Please forgive. I'll be in touch. Charles.'

Anthea handed the note back to Nancy, who was looking weak with relief. Whatever foolish things Charles might elect to do, Nancy would never lose him.

'I'm so glad for you,' Anthea said. 'Perhaps he'll be happy with her in the end.'

'Perhaps,' Nancy said doubtfully. She looked hard at Anthea, who was suddenly conscious that her eyes were puffy and her cheeks drawn. She said, 'I'm sorry, Anthea. Charles was right: I should never have interfered,' and the brown eyes were kind and perceptive.

Anthea smiled at her. 'I've had a lovely holiday,' she said firmly. 'Something to remember. And Pamela's coming back today.'

That was really all there was to say.

Pamela and Guy arrived by the afternoon flight and Anthea was at the airport to meet them.

As she waited at the barrier her thoughts went back to this very place, twenty-four hours earlier, when the girl in the black suit with the haunted grey eyes had walked alone through the crowd, looking lost and frightened. The girl whom Charles had loved and lost and found again. Perhaps it was better that it had ended as it had—so abruptly—between herself and Charles. The girl had the fragile beauty that drew men to her like bees to a dew-drenched flower. Even another girl had to accept that, if she was realistic. Sadly Anthea acknowledged that she could never have competed with a girl who looked like that.

'Anthea, sweetie—you're here, how lovely! I can't hug you, I'm too horribly fat!' Pamela's silvery voice broke through Anthea's unhappy thoughts. They kissed laughingly and with due care, and, as Anthea felt Pamela's petal-soft cheek against her own and was engulfed in a cloud of Pamela's special scent, a little of her misery lifted.

Guy followed with the luggage and kissed Anthea too. Guy always seemed delighted to see her—he was the nicest brother-in-law—but she got the impression that his greeting was specially enthusiastic today.

Later, back at the condo, when they had exchanged news and eaten the dainty tea prepared by Juliana before she had left that morning, Pamela went reluctantly upstairs to rest.

'Only for an hour,' she declared. 'I want to hear about all the fun and games you've been getting up to while we've been away.' She cast a knowing glance towards Anthea.

'*Two* hours, my love,' Guy told her firmly as he led her upstairs. 'Remember...'

'What the doctors said,' finished Pamela, pulling a face at him. 'OK, but Thea must come up and talk to me while I'm resting.'

When Guy came downstairs again his face was serious. He poured himself another cup of tea and came to the point immediately.

'Have you made any plans about going back to London, Anthea?'

'I thought—early next week,' she said. 'It's been a shame to miss so much time with you and Pamela,' she added, and wished she didn't have to feel a hypocrite, 'but I've got a lot waiting for me when I get back.'

He nodded. 'Yes, I appreciate that, but the fact is, Anthea——' he smoothed back his already smooth fair hair '—well, the fact is I'm going to take advantage of your kind heart and ask you to stay on until the baby arrives.'

Oh, no, was Anthea's first thought. To stay on here where everything reminded her of Charles—it would be agony. But something in Guy's words made her go suddenly cold. 'Pamela...' she said urgently. 'She's all right, isn't she?'

Guy's keen eyes were fixed steadily on her face. 'Don't be alarmed, Anthea,' he said, and she had a crazy idea that this was how he'd look across his vast desk at the bank and tell a customer that he might be going to lose millions of pounds. 'But, you see, Pamela's condition is not quite...' he searched for a word. 'The doctors aren't a hundred per cent satisfied. They think that probably all will go well and that the baby will put in an appearance at the proper time. On the other hand, there's a certain risk that he or she may be in too much of a hurry to enter this wicked world.' His smile didn't reach his eyes. 'And if that happens there may be—complications.'

Anthea bit her lip hard. 'She's not—not likely to be in danger?'

He looked away from her, fixing his eyes on the distant lagoon, just visible through the window. 'I won't let myself believe that,' he said bleakly.

'Does she know?'

He shook his head and she could see a muscle in his cheek working.

Anthea had always liked Guy but at that moment she felt closer to him than she had ever done before. She said, 'Of course I'll stay, and do anything I can to help.'

He turned to her. 'Thank you, Anthea. Just be your own cheerful, sensible self. That'll do more good than anything. And if there's any way I can help you when you get back to London, you must call on me.'

Cheerful. Sensible. It wasn't going to be easy.

'Thea!' Pamela's voice called from upstairs. 'Come and talk to me.'

Anthea's eyes met Guy's and they exchanged a small smile. 'Coming!' she called back.

Pamela was lying against lace-trimmed pillows, looking gorgeous in a filmy blue chiffon wrap. She patted the side of the bed. 'Now I want to hear all about everything. And by everything I mean Charles, of course.' She smiled teasingly.

'Charles?' Anthea sat down, opening her eyes wide. 'What about Charles? He's gone back to London.'

'Oh!' Pamela looked put out and puzzled.

They had to get this thing settled straight away. 'Look, Pam,' Anthea said firmly. 'Charles and I went around together while you were away. He taught me to scuba dive and it was fabulous. He's an interesting man—when you get to know him—but there isn't anything serious between us. As I said, he's gone back to London and I don't suppose we'll meet again, unless we bump into each other by accident. So don't go getting ideas, Pam.'

Pamela's huge blue eyes looked hurt. 'I thought—the way you spoke about him on the phone . . . I took it for granted that you . . . I'm sorry, Thea, darling, I didn't want to pry——' she bit her lip, pulled a lacy handkerchief from under the pillow and mopped her eyes '—being pregnant makes one very emotional.'

It was no good, Anthea thought. She couldn't be any help to Pamela if she started off by putting a whopping big lie between them. She sighed. 'OK, Pam, I'll come clean. I fell in love with the man, but it wasn't any good—he made that clear from the start. He was in love with someone else—and she turned up here yesterday. He went off with her last night. End of story.'

'Oh, Thea . . .' Pamela looked stricken. 'I'm so sorry. And here am I, selfish beast, weeping all over you.' She blew her nose hard. 'Do you want to talk about it?' she ventured.

Anthea shook her head. She was having a terrible battle with herself to hold back the tears. 'Let's leave it,' she whispered, and Pamela nodded understandingly.

In the days that followed Anthea sometimes thought that it would have been easier in London. London in February, cold and cheerless, would have matched her mood better than this glorious blue and gold paradise island.

At first the pain was like a hidden enemy: she never knew when it would strike, flooding her eyes with tears, so that she had to turn her head away, biting her lip savagely. But after a week it changed, eating deeper into her, until it was always there, a heavy lump of misery, somewhere between her throat and her stomach.

The very worst times were at night in bed. She had said to Charles, 'I should have a memory,' and it was only too true, but she hadn't reckoned on the anguish of remembering the feel of his mouth, the heavy weight of his limbs on her, the clean masculine smell of him.

She tried to be rational about it, reminded herself that she'd known all along that it would be futile to hope—but when you were in love you couldn't stop yourself hoping. Lying awake in the small hours of the morning, she imagined Charles's coming to find her, telling her that it was all a mistake, that he wasn't in love with Elsa any longer, that it was Anthea he really loved.

But in the brilliant light of day she had to accept the truth. He had gone out of her life and he wouldn't come back. She told herself that one morning she would wake up and find that she'd fallen out of love. She'd heard that it always happened. But as the days passed she was still waiting for it to happen.

Most of the time she spent with Pamela, sharing old memories, discussing Anthea's plans for starting up her business again, talking about the coming baby, carefully avoiding any mention of Charles.

They sat out on the veranda when the sun wasn't too hot. Sometimes Anthea swam in the pool while Pamela lay in one of the green loungers and chatted to bank acquaintances. Once or twice, when Pamela was resting in the afternoon, Anthea agreed to play tennis with Peter and found that his game was every bit as bad as he had promised her. But he was a nice boy, and he even made her laugh now and again.

Nancy was a frequent visitor. She seemed to have lost some of her sturdy energy these days; her voice was subdued and if she still held firm opinions about everything she kept them to herself. Anthea guessed that she, too, was fretting about Charles, although she never mentioned him.

Pamela noticed it. 'It's funny that Nancy never talks about Charles,' she said one day, as she and Anthea were having their morning walk round the condo grounds.

Anthea stooped to pick up a pebble from the grass. 'Oh, I don't think she approves of his girlfriend,' she said. She took Pamela's arm. 'Do you think Guy would run me into George Town tomorrow, while Juliana is here? I could buy a sketch-pad and some pencils and start jotting down a few new designs . . .'

'Of course; why didn't we think of it before?' Anthea heard the pleased relief in Pamela's voice and knew she was telling herself that Anthea was 'getting over it'.

But Anthea wasn't getting over it. Sometimes she felt she was two people—the cheerful lively girl who laughed and joked to keep Pamela's spirits up, and the other Anthea who was conscious always of the hard lump of misery gnawing away at her insides.

Two weeks dragged by. Three. Three and a half. Guy was looking more confident. 'I think we may have passed the danger point,' he told Anthea. 'Pamela has to go in for her check-up today; I'm keeping my fingers crossed.'

The appointment was for eleven o'clock and Guy was coming home to drive Pamela to the hospital.

After breakfast she said, 'I feel full of energy today—I'm going to make some ginger cookies, my speciality. We can have them for tea when I get back from the hospital.'

It was Juliana's day off and the two girls had the kitchen to themselves. 'They're so easy; you just stick everything in the pan together—butter, sugar, syrup—and when it's all melted you stir in the flour and ginger.' Standing at the electric cooker, Pamela gave a running commentary. 'Pass me down the flour from that cupboard, there's a dear.'

It was as Anthea was reaching up to the shelf that she heard Pamela give a little gasp. She turned to see her bending over, a hand pressed against her stomach.

After a minute or so she straightened up. 'I thought... I don't suppose it's anything.' She went on stirring.

But before the cookies were made she said quietly, 'I think you'd better ring Guy and ask him to come home. I'll just sit down for a while. And if you'd throw a few things in a bag for me, just in case...'

Anthea heard the car as she finished packing a bag for Pamela to take with her. She ran downstairs with it as Guy was helping Pamela into the car. Anthea got in beside her and held her hand on the drive to the hospital, marvelling at Pamela's pluck. The twinges were coming more frequently now, but in between she managed to joke.

'Six weeks early—the stupid little darling! Or perhaps it's me who can't count. Oh!' She drew in an urgent breath and clutched Anthea's hand tightly.

At the hospital Anthea kissed her before she was wheeled away, with Guy, looking very pale, walking beside the trolley. Then there was nothing to do but wait, and drink endless cups of tea, and try to keep her spirits up. When, hours later, she saw Guy coming towards her she jumped to her feet.

He was looking dazed. 'It's over,' he said. 'A little girl—they say a perfectly normal delivery and Pamela's OK, thank God. The baby's very, very tiny.' Suddenly his voice broke. 'Anthea, my dear, you can't imagine...' He put his arms round her and she felt the wetness on his cheek. How wonderful, she thought, to have a husband who loves you as much as that.

Anthea slept well that night for the first time for weeks, and next morning got up with a feeling that the heaviness inside her was lifting at last. Juliana was delighted about the baby and chattered away while she shared a coffee with Anthea in the kitchen. Later Anthea visited the hospital and saw Pamela, looking radiant, and later Guy took her to peep at little Elizabeth—named after Guy's mother—in her plastic tent, looking very tiny and helpless.

'They have to use all these tubes and things for a premature baby,' Guy assured her, very much the knowledgeable father, 'but they're pleased with her progress.' He sighed, gazing at his daughter. 'She's beautiful, isn't she?'

Anthea looked down at the tiny, helpless little human being with her wizened face, her minute hands and feet that looked as if they'd been put into a skin that was much too large for them, her scanty fuzz of nondescript hair, and squinting blue eyes, and she smiled with pure joy. 'Beautiful!' she breathed.

Pamela was to stay in hospital for a week and Guy spent most of his free time with her. The baby would be allowed home later, when she had put on the necessary weight. Anthea visited each day, and Nancy accompanied her on the third afternoon.

As they drove back to the condo in Nancy's little red Toyota Anthea remembered what Charles had told her about his sister's having lost her own baby, and was moved to admiration by the way she had responded so generously to Pamela's triumphant motherhood. She had been full of obviously sincere pleasure that Pamela had come through so well, and that the tiny Elizabeth was holding her own.

'It will be so lovely to have a new baby living next door until Pamela and Guy leave for the UK,' she said. She paused and flicked a glance at Anthea. 'Have you decided when you're leaving us?'

'Very soon,' Anthea said. 'Guy's arranging for a resident nurse for the first few weeks after the baby comes home, so there won't really be enough room for us all.'

There was a silence. Then Nancy said, keeping her eyes carefully on the road, 'I had a long letter from Charles today.'

'Oh, yes?' Anthea said brightly. 'How is he?'

'He seems much better. He talks about coming back to see us quite soon, possibly next week.'

Pain shot through Anthea like a sharp arrow. 'Oh, yes?' she murmured.

And bringing Elsa with him of course. She felt panic rise inside her, churning round sickeningly. She *must* leave before Charles came back. She started to plan feverishly. Tomorrow morning she'd go to the hospital and explain—Pamela would understand, bless her...she would ask Guy to book flights for her...perhaps she could leave tomorrow...she could at least get to Miami, even if she had to wait there for a flight to London. She was hardly conscious of arriving back at the condo and saying goodbye to Nancy with thanks for the lift.

'You're sure you won't come in and have dinner with us later on?' Nancy was saying, and somehow Anthea was managing to refuse regretfully, with the excuse that she had started work on some new designs and wanted to get on with them.

She went straight up to her own room, and sat down on the bed, shivering a little. It was ridiculous to feel like a trapped animal; she really must pull herself together. Charles wouldn't be here until next week at the earliest—that gave her three days to make arrangements and leave in a civilised manner, not run away like a scared rabbit.

Slowly, to calm herself down, she took out her travel-case and began to pack in some of the things she wouldn't be needing again. The sun-dresses, the bikinis, the swim-suits—everything reminded her of days with Charles, of things they had done together. The white one-piece swim-suit she'd worn that on their last dive when he'd carried her up the stairs after the accident, and laid her on the bed—just here—and she had begged him—yes, *begged* him to make love to her. Hot tears of humiliation, and loss, and wretchedness, burned at the back of her eyes.

There was a tap at the door and she sprang to her feet. Nancy, of course. She mustn't see her weeping. She made a dive for the adjoining shower-room and swilled her face with cold water, calling out, 'Come in, Nancy, I won't be a minute.'

Picking up a fleecy small towel she went back into the bedroom, wiping her face. 'I was just——' she began and then her knees went weak and she clutched the doorpost.

Charles was standing at the bottom of the bed. His face was pale under what remained of the tan, and thinner, almost gaunt; there were dark smudges under his eyes, and she saw the desperate tiredness there. He said, 'Nancy told me you were here,' and then he didn't seem to have anything else to say.

Anthea's hands were shaking so violently that thc towel dropped from her fingers on to the carpet. Charles stepped forward and picked it up, holding it out to her, and their hands touched.

'Oh, God,' he groaned, and somehow his arms were wrapped round her and he was kissing her with a terrible intensity, like a dying man in the desert who found water at last.

He said raggedly, 'I want to talk to you—can we go out somewhere? I don't find it easy to look at you standing in front of that bed, it——' there was a stark hunger in his face '—it puts ideas in my mind.'

Anthea was still reeling from that kiss. She allowed him to lead her down the stairs and across the condo grounds to the long stretch of white sand where the sea turned over in lazy ripples. The beach was almost empty in the early evening, only a few snorkellers swimming in the turquoise water. The sun was losing a little of its heat and a cool breeze touched Anthea's hot cheeks.

Charles took her hands in his and his eyes were like a dark flame. 'First of all, sweetheart, I can say now what I couldn't tell you before. You told me you loved me and you'll never know how much I longed to tell you the truth then. But now I can. I love you with all my heart, my darling girl, and if you can accept me with all the—er——' he smiled a little grimly '—the drawbacks I'll go into in due course, will you marry me very soon?'

Anthea found her voice at last. When a miracle happened you grabbed and hung on to it. She said faintly, 'Of course I will, tomorrow if you like. But—what about Elsa?'

'Elsa is past history,' he said.

'But——' Anthea began.

'No buts,' he said. 'What I thought was love bears no relation to what I feel for you. I longed for you every moment we were apart. I'm not even half alive when you're not with me. I don't know how I got through that dark time without you. I want us to be together for always.'

'I want it too,' she whispered. She put her arms round his neck and kissed him full on the mouth and felt the shiver that passed through him.

'I think we'd better walk,' he said. And, arms entwined, lovers now, they walked along the edge of the tide.

Charles said, 'I wrote to Nancy last week telling her everything, but the letter only reached her today. I was scared that you might have left and I was prepared to come after you to London at the crack of dawn tomorrow. I arrived here just before you and Nancy got back from the hospital. When Nancy told me about Pamela's baby and said that you were still here I think I rather overwhelmed the poor girl with my reaction. However, we won't go into that. What I want now is to finish the story I began that night when we were so rudely interrupted.'

Anthea nestled up to him, her head against his shoulder, glorying in the warmth of his body through his cotton shirt. 'You don't have to—not now,' she murmured dreamily.

'I think I do. I've put up so many barriers between us—I want to clear them away so that we can start our life together without any secrets from each other.'

Our life together. It sounded wonderful. Her eyes were misty with happiness.

'I told you about Mark and Elsa,' he began as they walked slowly along. 'For a time it was hell; I seemed to have lost them both. But after a while I managed to persuade myself that we could all still be friends.' He gave a bitter laugh. 'What a hope! They didn't want me—all that Elsa wanted was the high life, and Mark was besotted with her. So eventually I just bowed out. I know now what I didn't have any idea of at the time. Elsa demanded the lot and Mark tried to give it to her. He bought her clothes, diamonds, a villa in Majorca. God knows how much money he spent. He ran up debts that his income from our firm couldn't possibly have met. He gambled heavily and lost. Then he started to fiddle the accounts to cover his losses. We each of us had our own clients. The trouble was that he took the money out of the accounts of *my* clients, not his own.' He drew in a shaky breath. 'I still can't understand how he could do that to me. Not Mark.'

Anthea's heart twisted with pity for him. She reached up and touched his cheek. 'He was in love with her,' she said softly. 'They say that love is sometimes a kind of madness.'

He took her hand in a hard grip. 'Perhaps it is,' he said harshly. 'I loved Mark. Oh, not the sort of thing that still invites raised eyebrows these days. As a kid I loved him as a wonderful elder brother—hero-worshipped him, I suppose. He was dynamic, colourful, confident, popular—everything that I wanted to be myself. Even when Elsa left me for him I couldn't hate him.

'I kept myself busy and I had no idea what was going on . . . until Mark took Elsa on a luxury holiday to Acapulco—and they didn't come back. That was when it all started to come out. God! It was a ghastly time as the accountants and solicitors took over and unearthed the details one by one—all of them apparently pointing to my own guilt. Finally, when the situation became clear, a meeting of shareholders was called.

'I went out to Acapulco to see Mark, to plead with him to come back and help me to straighten things out.' He stopped for a moment and then went on, his face grim. 'I don't want to dwell on the next part. Mark had changed. He wasn't the Mark I knew. He looked me in the eye—and denied everything.'

He paused, and Anthea felt his body tense before he could bring himself to continue. 'I had a fortnight to put in before the shareholders' meeting. That was when I came here to the Caymans, to be with Nancy. I felt she was the one sane person in my world whom I could trust. But when I got here I couldn't bring myself to tell her about Mark. She thought that I was still depressed about losing Elsa. I let her think so. It wasn't true but it seemed the easiest way.' He laughed mirthlessly. 'Being Nancy, she tried to find a nice girl or two to take my mind off my troubles.'

Anthea said quietly, 'And that was when we met again.' So much was becoming clear. 'I think I can understand now how you must have been feeling.'

He bent his head and laid his mouth against her temple. 'There was something there between us right from the beginning, although I was so bloody awful to you.' He groaned. 'I had a terrible battle with my conscience. I knew I shouldn't involve you, but I couldn't help myself.' His arm tightened round her. 'You'll never know what you did for me, sweetheart. Just being with you in those two weeks restored me to a kind of sanity. Finally, I knew that what there was between us had to be put to the test. That last night I resolved to tell you everything and let you decide. Then—you know what happened.'

She nodded slowly. 'Your lost love came back to you.'

He gave a hollow laugh. 'It wasn't quite like that. She came to tell me that Mark was dead.'

'Oh, no!' Anthea pulled away from him, her eyes searching his face, wide with disbelief.

'Oh, yes,' he said heavily. 'I think he meant the Acapulco holiday to be a last glorious fling. When the money ran out he—took an overdose. Elsa couldn't cope and she turned to me for help. She found out from the London office where I was and got on a plane that same day. Eventually she arrived here with no money at all when she'd paid for her airline tickets. There was no time to make explanations—I had to go back with her straight away and take over. True to type, she didn't even wait for the funeral once the legal affairs were settled. She latched on to a Mexican millionaire staying at the hotel.' His voice was scathing.

'I thought...' whispered Anthea. 'I wish I'd known. Whatever happened, we'd have been together, to share it.'

'I was tempted,' he admitted. 'My God, I was tempted. I wanted to make sure of you. But I persuaded myself to do the decent thing. It wouldn't have been a very auspicious start to our married life if you'd had a husband in gaol.'

She felt the blood leave her cheeks. 'It wouldn't have come to that, surely?'

'It might well have done. It was a very nasty business—small investors defrauded. The courts don't look kindly on that kind of fiddle. Fortunately it didn't come to the fraud squad in the end. You see—it's difficult to talk about this, but you must know everything—Mark left a letter, admitting all he'd done, giving chapter and verse, absolving me. I threw in every last cent I had and the firm is being wound up. The shareholders came out of it reasonably well.

'There was a lot of clearing-up to do, but eventually my part was over and I could leave the rest in the hands of the accountant and the solicitors. My first thought was to get back to the Caymans and explain everything to Nancy and Bill and—most important—to find you again. It's been a hellish time since I left you, sweetheart. I can hardly believe that we're together and that I've found peace at last.' He drew her towards him and kissed her, a long, lingering kiss that made her whole body melt.

'You will marry me, my love?'

'Yes. Oh, yes, yes.' Stars shone in her eyes.

'Even though I'm practically skint and I've got to make a fresh start?'

'No problem. Fresh starts are exciting.'

'It shouldn't be too difficult,' he mused. 'I've got a lot of good friends. I think I may give the financial scene a miss this time.' He grinned. 'Do you need a manager for your thriving design business?'

She pulled a face. 'I'm afraid there isn't anything to manage.'

'No thriving design business?' he said in amazement. 'No sales to top stores? Paris? Rome?'

She shook her head. 'Not even a room to work in.' She told him about the fire and it didn't seem important any longer. 'All I've got is the insurance money on the equipment.'

'And you didn't tell me?'

She lifted her face to his. 'We've both been pretty cagey,' she smiled. 'But not any more.'

'No, by God,' he promised resolutely. 'From now on we work as a team—no secrets allowed.'

That was the cue to a long interval of bliss. When they finally managed to pull apart Anthea said, 'It'll be lovely to start afresh together.' Womanlike, she added, 'Where shall we live?'

He looked mysterious. 'We-ell, how do you fancy a cottage in Hampshire with a work-shop for you and an apple tree in the garden?'

'Mmm—lovely. What a wonderful dream,' she giggled.

'Dream nothing,' he said stoutly. 'It belongs to Nancy and Bill. They've offered it to me on a long lease while they're away from the UK.' He chuckled. 'This time I think I'll accept with thanks one of Nancy's little schemes on my behalf.'

Anthea shook her head incredulously. 'Heaven!' she breathed. She could see the apple tree quite clearly now. There was a pram beneath the branches. 'And Nancy *doesn't* scheme,' she added fiercely. 'She only wants to help. She's a dear and I'm very fond of her, and if it hadn't been for her we shouldn't have——'

He stopped the rest of her defence of his sister with a long, hard kiss. 'I'd have found you for myself; we were meant to be together. From the moment I walked out on to that balcony and saw a shy little girl in a pink dress my fate was sealed. But I'll allow Nancy a tiny bit of the credit. Come on, let's go back and tell her our news.'

The sun was setting and everything was bathed in a soft golden light. 'Just keep on saying you love me,' Charles demanded. 'Over and over again.'

She cuddled up against him as they sauntered back along the edge of the tide. 'I love you—love you—love you.' Her heart sang with happiness. 'From the moment you walked out on to that balcony...'

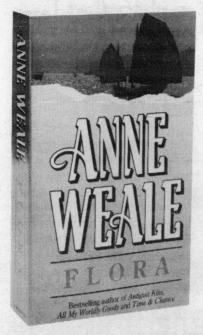

He leaned closer, his smile teasing, but as their eyes met the smile faded slowly.

Leonora lay hypnotised, unable to look away. She forgot her dream as she saw the blue eyes darken almost to black. She ran the tip of her tongue over her lips, heard the sharp hiss of Penry's intake of breath, then his head blotted out the light as his mouth met hers in a kiss which shot a jolt of electricity through every vein in her body.

She tore her mouth away, averting her burning face as Penry got unhurriedly to his feet.

'A mere kiss goodnight,' he said softly. 'It can't have been your first.'

Leonora forced herself to look at him. 'I—I don't know. I don't remember.' She blinked back tears fiercely. 'You may not believe me, but I honestly *don't* remember. Anything.'

Books you will enjoy
by CATHERINE GEORGE

UNLIKELY CUPID

Janus Stanhope was sure that Georgina was wrong for his brother Miles. Georgina was only helping Miles out by pretending to be his fiancée, but she couldn't tell the truth, which was a shame, because he turned out to be the man of her dreams. . .

BRAZILIAN ENCHANTMENT

When Kate arrived in Vila Nova to teach English, she certainly wasn't expecting the rude welcome of her imperious employer, Luis Vasconcelos. Then the little Brazilian mountain town started to work its magic—Kate would just have to avoid the demanding Vasconcelos. But that proved rather difficult. . .

LEADER OF THE PACK

The new managing director of Colcraft Holdings was set to take the place by storm—and Ellis with it. Ellis, for her part, was determined not to be swept away. . .

OUT OF THE STORM

BY

CATHERINE GEORGE

MILLS & BOON LIMITED
ETON HOUSE 18–24 PARADISE ROAD
RICHMOND SURREY TW9 1SR

All the characters in this book have no existence outside the imagination of the Author, and have no relation whatsoever to anyone bearing the same name or names. They are not even distantly inspired by any individual known or unknown to the Author, and all the incidents are pure invention.

First published in Great Britain 1991
by Mills & Boon Limited

This edition 1992

ISBN 0 263 77307 8

Set in 10 on 12 pt Linotron Times
91-9202-53974
Typeset in Great Britain by Centracet, Cambridge
Made and printed in Great Britain

CHAPTER ONE

THE process of waking up was painful. Both eyelids seemed weighted down. She decided to leave it for a while. Her head was throbbing so vilely that the effort was too much. And the weather outside sounded so bad that it seemed wise to stay as she was a little longer. The howling wind kept firing salvos of rain against the windows, but after a while she stirred reluctantly. Weather or no weather, if she was awake it must be time to get up. Steeling herself against the pain in her head, she forced her eyes open, then stared in horror and shut them quickly, her heart thumping. She lay rigid for a count of ten, eyes tightly closed, then very slowly opened them again.

It was no dream. The room was still there. It was small, with a sloping ceiling and a pair of windows set in deep embrasures. And she'd never seen it before in her life. She stared, teeth chattering, at white-painted walls, a heavy oak chest, the ornate brass-work of the bed. As she heaved herself up against the pillows she discovered she was wearing a man's shirt, extra-large and striped, and she'd never seen that before, either. She thrust back the bright patchwork quilt and levered herself to a sitting position, her feet dangling over the edge of the bed. She sat very still for a moment, the room revolving around her like a carousel as the pain in her head hammered to a crescendo then receded again to a just bearable throb. Slowly the mist in front of her eyes cleared. She breathed in slowly and regularly a few times, then got shakily to her feet.

This last proved more taxing than expected. The floor seemed to be heaving about beneath her feet like the deck of a ship. To reach a window she was obliged to cling to the brass footrail of the bed en route. This was no ordinary headache, she thought grimly. Seeing an upright chair stationed between the windows, she made a lunge for it and collapsed sideways on the rush seat to lean, exhausted, against the cold wall.

It was some time before she could gather her forces sufficiently to stand up and rest her hands on the chill white plaster of the window embrasure. As she peered through the double glass her blood ran cold. Not that there was much to see: only a stretch of close-cropped, undulating turf, broken here and there by protrusions of rock. And beyond that nothing but sullen grey sky and miles of stormy, heaving sea.

Panic surged up inside her, taking her breath away. She fought it, leaning on her clenched fists, her eyes closed until the wave of terror receded, leaving her limp and breathless. Where in heaven's name *was* this place—and what was she doing here?

She tensed, trembling. Heavy footsteps were mounting the stairs. She turned wildly, then staggered, her hands groping for the brass footrail of the bed. Her breath quickened painfully. She stared, hypnotised, as the heavy iron latch lifted, the door opened and a very tall man backed into the room, ducking his head to clear the lintel, his attention on the tray he was carrying. She received a fleeting impression of shaggy black hair and massive shoulders, then the tray was dumped down on the bedside table and she herself dumped in turn on the bed.

'You shouldn't be up.' The man tucked the quilt around her then straightened, eyeing her petrified face irritably. 'For heaven's sake! I don't bite.'

She shrank away in undisguised terror as he sat on the edge of the bed, reaching for her hand. She snatched it away, burrowing deeper beneath the covers.

His eyes glittered coldly. 'You're in no danger from me, I assure you.'

The voice was musical, with a slight cadence it was hard to pin down. And even in her present state of turmoil she could appreciate that he was a very handsome man, in a sombre, brooding sort of way. The cold eyes scrutinising her so impersonally were deep set beneath heavy black brows, and shadowed with fatigue. His mouth was wide and well cut, with a deeply indented upper lip, and a decidedly grim set to it, and there was something about him which kept her rigid with tension beneath the covers.

She cleared her throat experimentally. 'Where is this place, please?' She grimaced as her voice, unused for some time by the sound of it, came out in hoarse, rusty spurts. 'And who are you?'

'I was just about to ask the same of you,' he countered promptly. 'But before we go into all that tell me how you're feeling.' He leaned forward. 'Give me your hand, please.'

Her eyes narrowed in alarm. 'Why?'

'So I can feel your pulse,' he said impatiently. 'I'm a doctor, not a fortune-teller.'

Flushing, she extended her hand.

He held her wrist loosely between long, slim fingers, his eyes on his watch. 'How's your head?'

'It's aching. Badly.'

'Not surprising. You've had a nasty knock.' He looked up. 'Your pulse is racing—don't tell me you're *still* scared of me!'

She nodded dumbly. The movement lanced pain through her head and she gasped, her face contorted.

His hand tightened on hers for a moment.

'Your head will probably improve if I tell you where you are—and who I am,' he began conversationally. 'Answer one, we're on an island called Gullholm, just off the west coast of Wales. Answer two, my name is Penry Meredith Vaughan, by profession I'm a consultant physician, and I own the island.' He looked at her commandingly. 'Now return the compliment, please. Tell me who you are, young lady, and why the devil you're trespassing on my property.'

She gazed at him in horror. 'But that's *why* I'm so frightened, Dr Vaughan.' Her teeth caught in her trembling lower lip for a moment. 'I don't know. My mind's a blank.'

He rose to his feet, tall as a giant in the small room. 'You expect me to believe you have no idea how you got here?'

'I'm afraid I do.' She eyed him despairingly. 'I know it sounds far-fetched, but I—I don't know who I am, either. Not even my own name!'

Penry Vaughan studied her in brooding silence for a moment, then glanced at the forgotten tray on the bedside table. 'I've brought you some soup——'

'I couldn't eat anything,' she said with a shudder.

'If you don't eat,' he said grimly, 'you get no medication for that head, nor an account of how I found you.'

She struggled to sit up. 'Please——' she began, then clenched her teeth, perspiration standing out on her forehead as the vice-like pain gripped her skull. She subsided against the pillows, breathing shallowly until the spasm began to subside. 'All right,' she muttered at last.

Dr Penry Vaughan nodded in approval as he poured hot, fragrant liquid from an insulated flask into a mug. 'While you drink this I'll go downstairs and make tea and toast——'

'No toast!' she said hastily as she took the mug.

'As a house-guest you leave a lot to be desired, young woman,' he said cuttingly. 'The presence of a semi-invalid is something I neither invited nor desired, so please make it easier for both of us by giving as little trouble as possible.' He looked down his formidable nose. 'Drink that soup by the time I get back and possibly, just possibly, I'll give you a mild pain-killer. If not I'll leave you to your own devices until you see sense.'

She stared after him mutinously as he went from the room, willing him to bump his head as he went through the door, but to her disappointment Dr Penry Vaughan ducked his tall head with the grace and dexterity of long practice.

Alone again, she eyed the soup in her mug malevolently, convinced it would act as an emetic. For a moment she thought of staggering to the window again to throw the soup out, but decided against it. Not only was she too shaky on her feet, but by the sound of the storm raging outside anything thrown from the window would be hurled back in her face, courtesy of the wind. Gingerly she took a sip of the soup, surprised to find it was not only delicious but nothing to do with any can or packet. Dr Vaughan, it seemed, liked cooking. And instead of rebelling her stomach gave an appreciative little rumble. She sipped absently, so desperate to remember who she was and how she came to be here that the mug was empty before she realised it.

'Good,' said Penry Vaughan when he returned. He took the mug with an approving nod. 'I'm glad you decided to be sensible.'

'Thank you, Dr Vaughan. I'm sorry to be such a nuisance. I feel better already. I can be on my way soon. . .' She trailed away at his sardonic expression.

'On your way where?' He turned back to the tray to fill two cups. 'How do you like your tea?'

'Milk, no sugar, please——' Her eyes lit up as she took the cup from him. 'If I know that—which I do, somehow—surely I'll remember the rest pretty soon?'

'Quite possibly.' He handed her a plate containing four small triangles of toasted wholemeal bread, sparsely buttered. 'Now eat this while I tell you how I found you.'

Dr Penry Vaughan, she learned, had come to Gullholm for peace and solitude to get on with a series of articles. 'I needed a break from routine rather badly,' he said as he drew up a chair and sat down. 'A colleague advised a couple of weeks in the sun, away from it all.'

The girl in the bed glanced towards the windows involuntarily, as a vicious gust of wind drove rain against the windows like a fusillade of shot.

Penry Vaughan shrugged. 'Not much sun on Gullholm at this time of the year, I admit, but you can't beat it for peace and privacy. As a rule, anyway,' he added morosely.

She stiffened. 'My intrusion was involuntary, Dr Vaughan. I can't have meant to come here if it's private property.'

'I found you at first light this morning,' he said, getting up to take her half-empty plate. 'Good girl, I'll let you off the rest. Now drink some of the tea.'

She obeyed, then thanked Penry Vaughan gratefully as he handed her two tablets and a glass of water.

'These are pretty mild,' he said as she swallowed them down. 'But they should take the edge off the pain. Drink as much as you can, please.'

Once she was propped comfortably against the pillows Penry Vaughan sat down again and went on with his story. It was his habit to go for a run round his island every day before breakfast, and that morning, because rain was forecast for the rest of the day, he'd taken advantage of the brief spell of fine weather early on to gather up driftwood from the beach after his run. The shape of the island, he told her, was a rough figure-of-eight, with a narrow neck of land joining the two halves of landmass. The two inlets either side of the Neck were called Seal Haven to the westward, Atlantic side, and Lee Haven facing the Pembrokeshire coast.

'On Lee Beach there's a safe anchorage where I keep my old fishing boat,' said her host. 'But Seal Haven is a mass of rocks, with fierce currents boiling round them most of the time. And that, Madame X, is where I found you.'

As the promised rain swept in from the sea Penry had climbed the cliff path from Lee Haven with his bundle of driftwood, but as he reached the Neck a small patch of bright colour had caught his eye far below.

'Your scarf,' he told her. 'I jettisoned the wood, climbed down the path and there, neatly stashed away in a narrow inlet between the rocks, was my castaway, complete with gash on temple, soaked through, ice-cold to the touch and so deeply unconscious I thought at first you were dead.'

She shivered. 'But how on earth had I got there?'

'No idea. I was hoping you'd be able to tell *me* that.'

She slumped against the pillows, depressed. 'Well, I can't. I mean, it's not exactly swimming weather, is it?'

'Far from it. Nor, presumably, would you go swimming fully dressed with a small weekend bag slung over your shoulder.'

She stared at him. 'I came complete with luggage? Wasn't there something in the bag to say who I am?'

'I'm afraid not. It's a small nylon affair with some underwear and a spare sweater and that's about it. But you should be grateful to it,' he added. 'The bag may well have saved your life, first by doubling as a lifebelt, then by getting caught on a needle of rock in the inlet. Otherwise you'd have been swept away again.'

She hugged her arms across her chest convulsively under the bright patchwork quilt. 'Do you think I fell out of a boat?'

'It seems the most likely explanation.' He lounged back in the chair, a commanding figure, despite his ancient white fisherman's sweater and salt-stained jeans. 'But *what* boat? And where was it heading?'

She shook her head helplessly. 'I wish I knew!'

'I've contacted the coastguard and police by radio telephone. They should shed some light on the mystery once you're reported missing. As,' he assured her, 'you most certainly will be when you fail to turn up at whatever destination you were bound for.' He leaned forward to take her hand. 'No rings. Not that I expected any. You don't look old enough to be married.'

She pulled her hand away. 'How old is that?'

His face hardened. 'It depends. Marriage calls for a certain degree of maturity. Some people never achieve it.'

Ouch, she thought. A sore subject. 'I don't feel all that young,' she said tentatively. 'But you're a doctor. Can't you tell by my teeth, or something?'

His sudden smile transformed him to an astonishing degree, revealing the man behind the remote consultant. One who'd probably mowed the nurses down in his student days, too, she thought with a flash of insight. But the change was fleeting, the brooding mask in place again almost at once.

'Don't worry about it,' he advised, then searched in his pocket for a moment before holding out something which glittered in the palm of his hand. 'This was pinned to your sweater. Does it ring any bells?'

She examined the silver brooch eagerly. It was unusual. And, she knew beyond any doubt, it was hers. The workmanship was very fine, depicting a lioness and a vixen at ease together on what looked like a sleigh.

'Strange combination,' she said slowly, turning the brooch over in her hands. 'And why a sleigh, I wonder?'

'I don't think it's a sleigh. Turn it up on end.'

She did as he said, her eyes lighting up. 'Of course—it's a capital L!' She smiled for the first time, wincing as the pull of facial muscles reminded her she'd had a crack on the head. She reached up a hand to find a dressing near her hair-line. 'Was it much of a gash?'

'Too much to leave as it was. I put a couple of stitches in it while you were unconscious,' he said casually. 'You came to in the middle of it, unfortunately for you, but it gave me the opportunity to make a superficial examination.'

She frowned. 'You shone a light in my eyes!'

His eyes were suddenly intent. 'You remember?'

'Only vaguely.' Her mouth dropped. 'It's so frustrating—like having someone twitch a curtain aside then let it fall back again before I can see properly.' She swallowed. 'I felt a sharp pain and—and the light, blinding me. Like a fragment of a dream.' She sighed heavily. 'What a nuisance for you, having to stitch me up. I'm deeply indebted to you, one way and another, Dr Vaughan.'

'Nonsense,' he said briskly. 'I could hardly leave you in the condition I found you. Your clothes, by the way, are all drying on a rack in the kitchen.'

'Thank you,' she said politely, her sense of obligation increasing by the minute. She turned the brooch over in her hand. 'Since I was wearing this I assume it's mine. "L" for what, I wonder?'

'There's a lioness on the brooch,' he pointed out. 'It could stand for Leonie, or Leonora, perhaps. Ring any bells?'

She shook her head. 'Not really.'

'Nevertheless, my child, you must answer to something, if only for the time being.' He gave her a wry look. 'Not that you look remotely like a lioness—more like a half-drowned kitten.'

'I'll answer to anything you like,' she snapped, her eyes flashing, 'other than "my child"!'

One of his black brows rose tauntingly. 'Ah—the kitten has claws! Very well. If you're leaving the choice to me I vote for Leonora. Perhaps your father shared my taste for Beethoven.'

She shrugged. 'I don't, that's for sure.' Her eyes filled with sudden, angry tears. 'How in heaven's name do I know I don't like Beethoven, when I can't remember my own name?'

'Because you're suffering from amnesia, Leonora,' he said brusquely. 'A temporary loss of memory due to the blow on your head. You could wake up tomorrow with total recall. In the meantime, don't try to force it.' He got to his feet. 'I'm going to cook myself some lunch. Try to sleep. This afternoon, if you feel better, you can come downstairs.'

She felt a sudden violent disinclination for solitude. 'Can't I come now?'

'No.' He turned in the doorway. 'You've had a bad experience, Leonora. You're lucky to be alive. And because I took the trouble to save this life of yours I insist on seeing you recover properly and make full use of it. I'm a doctor, remember. So please follow my instructions. They're meant for the best.'

Leonora bit her lip in remorse. 'I'm sorry, Dr Vaughan. It must be a terrible drag having a patient foisted on you like this—a real busman's holiday.' She smiled diffidently. 'I haven't thanked you properly, either, for rescuing me from—from a watery grave. I'm very grateful. Truly.'

Penry Vaughan shrugged his formidable shoulders indifferently. 'Don't mention it. Now, if there's nothing more I can do for you for a while, I'll leave you to rest.'

'There is something,' she muttered, embarrassed. 'Could you point me in the direction of a bathroom please?'

'Of course. Sorry—I should have thought of that

before.' He returned to the bed, holding out his hands. 'Up you come.'

'If you'll just tell me where it is I can manage by myself, thank you.'

He frowned irritably. 'My dear child, is it possible you're embarrassed? Who do you think stripped your clothes off and put you to bed?'

Her face flamed. 'Nevertheless, Dr Vaughan, if it's all the same to you I'd still prefer to get to the bathroom under my own steam.'

'Oh, for——' He checked himself. 'All right. Have it your own way. The bathroom's just across the passage. But be careful. It's an old house, and the floor's uneven in places, so don't try exploring on your own just yet, please.'

'I wouldn't dream of trespassing,' she assured him stiffly.

'Don't talk nonsense,' he said impatiently. 'When you get back to bed try to sleep for a bit. I'll be up to see you later.'

Leonora watched him go with mixed feelings, not really sure she could make it to the bathroom alone, despite her fine words. If a visit there had been less pressing she'd have been very willing to cuddle down into the comfortable bed and let sleep blank out her problems for a while. It took her a long time to negotiate the journey to the small, functional bathroom across the passage, but in the end she accomplished it without incident. Then before she resumed her snail-slow progress back to bed she steeled herself to look in the mirror above the washbasin.

Her face was a great disappointment in more ways than one. Not only was it unremarkable and rather battered, it did nothing at all to jog her errant memory.

She had a lot of hair, but it was so tangled and matted it was impossible to determine the colour. And she was skinny. The shirt hung straight to her knees unimpeded much by feminine curves. No wonder Dr Vaughan had jeered at her maidenly modesty. She eyed herself with gloom. One of her eyes was passable; dark, and a rather pleasing almond shape. But the other was swollen and half closed, with a Technicolor bruise below it right down to her razor-sharp cheekbone. By some miracle her nose had escaped a battering. It was short and straight, which was more than could be said for her mouth, which was curvy and rather wider than it should have been for her ashen, wedge-shaped face.

Leonora shook her head sorrowfully at her reflection. 'What a scarecrow! All in all, my girl, you're lucky Dr Penry Meredith Vaughan didn't throw you back in the sea.'

CHAPTER TWO

WHEN Leonora woke again it was dark. Physically she felt much better. The pain in her head had dulled to a quite bearable ache, but her mind, she realised in panic, was still a blank. Her identity, her home, her family were still lost in the terrifying mist in her mind. And if she was missing from home why weren't her family moving heaven and earth to get her back? She beat down a gush of self-pity, knuckling away tears as she slid gingerly from the bed to make for the bathroom again. As she reached the door a tall, dark shape blocked out the light.

'You're awake,' said Penry Vaughan, and snapped on a switch, dazzling her.

Leonora blinked at him owlishly. 'You've got electricity?'

'My own generator.' He took a dressing-gown from the back of the door and held it for her. 'Put this on if you must wander about the house.'

'I was only venturing as far as the bathroom,' she said with dignity.

'I've put a spare toothbrush in there for you, but otherwise I can't offer you much in the way of beauty aids.'

'Pity. I could use some—badly.' She smiled ruefully. 'I plucked up enough courage to look in the mirror. But the toothbrush is welcome,' she added, then hesitated awkwardly. 'What would you like me to do afterwards? I can go back to bed and keep out of your way, if you prefer.'

'Don't talk nonsense!'

'Don't keep saying that!' she snapped, then flushed, embarrassed.

'I apologise.' He bowed slightly. 'I should be honoured to have your company at dinner, Miss Leonora X. Whenever you're ready to come downstairs give me a shout and I'll come and collect you. The staircase is a bit steep. The last thing you need is another concussion.'

'Is that what I had? Does concussion put the memory out of action?'

'Sometimes.' He opened the bathroom door for her. 'Now get a move on. No more questions until you're downstairs.'

Leonora eyed the bath longingly as she brushed her teeth. If there was a generator it seemed likely there was hot water. A sudden need for a bath overwhelmed her. As the bath filled she inspected the sparse supply of male toiletries, interested to find Penry Vaughan was not a man for sexy French fragrances. The only things on offer were a flask of shower-gel, a roll-on deodorant and a cake of soap, all from a chain of shops famous for herbal products.

The bath water was brownish, but wonderfully soothing to her quite remarkable display of bruises. She eyed her body wryly. Not a sight to inspire any man to raging lust, let alone a doctor. She had breasts after all, she noted; smallish, but quite respectable, but the rest of her was narrow, with angles outnumbering the curves. Her bruises stung badly as she anointed herself with gel, but the discomfort was a small price to pay for feeling clean again. After a moment's hesitation she lay back, plunging her head deep in the water before shampooing her hair with the gel, gasping as her wound smarted horribly. She sat up quickly, her head reeling for a moment. When it steadied she pulled out the bath plug and knelt to hold her protesting head under the running water from the tap. She endured the renewed pain stoically until the water ran clear, then turned off the taps and clambered from the bath, feeling very shaky, but wonderfully, blissfully clean.

Leonora wrapped herself in one of the large white bathtowels piled on a wicker stand, then, afraid to rub her hair, she swathed a towel turban-wise round her head and subsided on the chair, exhausted but triumphant. A few minutes later, when she'd got as far as wrapping herself in her host's dressing-gown, Penry Vaughan knocked loudly on the door.

'Are you all right in there, Leonora?' he called. 'You're taking a hell of a time.'

She opened the door, smiling guiltily. 'I'm fine. I hope you don't mind—I couldn't resist having a bath.'

Penry glared at her wet head. 'You weren't stupid enough to wash your hair?'

'I used some of your bath-gel——'

'Never mind the bloody bath-gel, it's your wound I'm worried about!' He cursed beneath his breath as he pushed her down, none too gently, on the chair. 'Let me take a look at it.'

He yanked open the bathroom cabinet and took out antiseptic and fresh dressings. She submitted meekly to his expert ministrations as he re-dressed the wound, giving her terse instructions to keep it dry from then on until the stitches were removed.

'I hope I haven't undone all your good work,' she

said repentantly, 'but I just couldn't exist a second longer without washing myself all over.'

'I sponged you down this morning, child. You weren't dirty!'

'I *felt* dirty.'

Penry gave her a fulminating glance, then shrugged. 'All right. But since you were silly enough to wash that mop I suggest you put a dry towel round your shoulders while we eat. No hairdryer.'

Leonora complied in smouldering silence, then followed the large figure of her host from the room. He paused as they reached the head of the stairs, eyeing her bare feet.

'I can't offer you anything in the way of shoes. Your own are still sodden. How about some socks?'

'Fine. Thank you.'

He led her back into the bedroom and sat her on the chair while he rummaged in the chest.

Leonora watched him in dismay. This was his bedroom, then. Which was pretty obvious, really. The bed was very large, which was only to be expected for someone of Dr Vaughan's heroic proportions. It had probably been the only one aired and ready for the unexpected guest this morning. She thanked him, subdued, as he handed her a pair of stretch-towelling socks.

'What's the matter?' he demanded. 'Not glamorous enough for you?'

'It's not that—I just realised I've put you out of your bedroom,' she muttered, pulling on the socks.

'It's not the only one in the house. There are three others, plus a sofa-bed downstairs. Mine happened to be the only one made up.'

'You're very kind.'

He put a finger under her chin and turned her face

up to his. 'You're wrong. Get that through your head right now, Leonora. You were a human being in desperate need of medical care. I'm a doctor. I supplied it. End of story. Don't invest me with qualities I don't possess.'

'Right.' She got to her feet, then tripped over the flapping toe of one of the socks.

Penry sighed, picked her up, and walked with her to the door.

'Please put me down, Dr Vaughan,' Leonora said with dignity. 'I can manage.'

'Oh, shut up and stop fussing,' he said forcibly, ducking neatly through the doorway. 'Tomorrow you can get around on your own once your clothes are dry.'

Leonora lay rigid in his arms, resentful of being carried about like a bundle of laundry. 'Tomorrow,' she said tartly, 'I hope to be away from here and on my way back to wherever I came from.'

Penry carried her carefully down a staircase which led straight into a large sitting-room. 'I doubt it. Even if your memory starts functioning by then the forecast is diabolical. March wind doth blow for some time to come, according to the coastguard, and believe me it blows hellish hard round Gullholm.'

Leonora digested this peace of news with mixed feelings as he set her on her feet. If he was right she had no alternative but to stay put. And since she had no idea where to go yet, even if she could get off the island, the only course possible was to take things a step at a time and try not to rail against a spiteful fate. Besides, she didn't feel so wonderful that she wanted a boat ride to the mainland just yet, even if it did mean staying shut up here with only this moody man for company. At least she now knew it was March.

She turned her attention to the room, which had obviously been three smaller rooms at one time. A wood-burning iron stove occupied the hearth of a big stone fireplace at one end. The rest of the room was crowded with shabby, comfortable chairs and sofas piled with cushions, small tables littered with electric table-lamps, oil lamps, candles in holders. There were shelves full of books and cassettes, a few water-colours on thc walls, a model sailing-ship in a big glass bottle on a side-table.

'This is lovely,' she said sincerely, and turned to smile up at Penry Vaughan.

'You like it?' he asked, surprised.

'I do. It's such a friendly room.'

'Unlike its owner, you mean.'

Leonora looked at him levelly. 'You said that, Dr Vaughan. Not me.'

He acknowledged the hit with a small bow. 'Right. Sit on the sofa nearest the stove. I'll bring in your dinner in a moment.'

'I'd offer to help,' she said apologetically, 'but I still feel a bit wobbly.'

'For pity's sake just sit there and try not to do anything silly for the time it takes me to fill two bowls with *cawl*.'

Leonora eyed him coldly. 'I didn't ask to get hit on the head—*or* to intrude on your private property, Dr Vaughan.'

'I'm referring to the shampooing session,' he said curtly, and strode towards a door at the far end.

The kitchen, I assume, thought Leonora, and swung her feet up on the sofa, chuckling at the ludicrously large socks. She spread her towel over a cushion so that she could lean her damp, aching head against it, then shivered as she listened to the howl of the wind outside. The rain had stopped, but the gale seemed to be gathering strength. The thought of crossing to the mainland, however near it was, brought a return of the panic she'd felt earlier. She clamped down on it hard, wishing passionately she could tear away the veil in her mind, see behind it to find out who she was and why she was cast away on Penry Vaughan's island. Someone, somewhere, must be worried to death about her. If only she could remember who it was. Who *she* was!

It was a relief when Penry returned with a tray containing two steaming bowls. He set it down on one of the small tables, then handed her a paper napkin, a spoon and a fork before giving her one of the bowls.

'*Cawl*,' he announced, then sat down with his own.

Leonora eyed her bowl warily. 'What is *cawl*?'

'A main dish soup made with lamb and root vegetables and leeks. Dumplings, too, when my mother's doing the cooking.' One eyebrow shout up. 'You look surprised. Is that because I can cook, or because I possess a mother, like other men?'

She smiled. 'Neither. You're so efficient it seems strange you haven't mastered the art of the dumpling. Even *I* know how to make those——' She stared at him, arrested. 'There I go again. My stupid mind knows I can make dumplings, so why on earth can't it tell me who I am?'

Penry continued with his meal, unmoved. 'It will, in time. Just be thankful your skull wasn't fractured. I can't X-ray it, of course, but I'm pretty sure you've suffered no more than a bad concussion. Once the wind drops I'll get you over to the mainland and get an X-ray done at St Mary's.'

'St Mary's?'

'It's a nursing home. I do a clinic there once a week.' He looked up from his bowl. 'What do you think of my cooking?'

'Wonderful!' She smiled. 'When I woke up this morning I felt like death. I never dreamed I'd actually be sitting up and taking nourishment so soon—*and* enjoying it.'

'The human body has amazing powers of recuperation.' His eyes travelled over her impersonally. 'There's not very much of you, but you're wiry, and you're young. You should be fine in a day or two.'

Leonora went on with her meal in silence until the bowl was half empty, then laid down her spoon. She looked across at her companion, whose gesture at dressing for dinner had been a newer, cleaner white sweater, and slightly less disreputable denims.

'But what will happen to me if I still can't remember who I am?' she asked forlornly. 'Or if no one reports me missing?'

Penry continued with his dinner with unimpaired appetite. 'You'll just have to stay with me, I suppose. I'm here for three weeks, barring accidents or terminal boredom. Until this weather changes you're marooned with me here, anyway. So let your mind rest. You'll regain your memory all the sooner. For the time being you've got bed, board, and a resident physician on hand. How many castaways can say that?'

She tried to smile. 'True. I just wish I didn't feel I was playing albatross to your Ancient Mariner.'

'Ah! The lady likes poetry.'

She thought for a moment. 'I don't know that I *like* it exactly. But I seem to remember the poem about the Ancient Mariner quite well.'

'You probably learned it at school, as I did.' He got

up to put their dishes on the tray. 'I draw the line at puddings, I'm afraid. There's plenty of cheese but at this time of night, with that headache, I don't advise it. You can't have coffee, either. Too much caffeine.'

'I'd like *something* to drink,' she said wistfully.

'Weak tea, then.'

Leonora lay listening to the wind while Penry Vaughan was in the kitchen. After a time she heard him talking to someone on the telephone, but, when he didn't reappear immediately, gathered that he had no news for her. Dejectedly she ran careful fingers through her hair, resigned to learn its colour was a light ash-brown.

'Why so down in the mouth?' asked her host, returning with a tea-tray. 'I thought I told you to stop worrying.'

'It's the colour of my hair.' She smiled crookedly. 'I was hoping for platinum-blonde, or red, but now it's dry I find it's plain old mouse.'

Penry cast an eye over her hair judicially. 'I wouldn't have said mouse, precisely. I told the police just now that you have very dark eyes and golden-brown hair.'

Leonora sat up, swinging her feet to the floor, biting her lip against the inevitable throb from her temple. 'What did they say?' she asked eagerly. 'Has anyone reported me missing yet?'

'Afraid not.' He handed her a cup. 'But it's early days. I only found you this morning, and reckoning by the tide you couldn't have been there long. Perhaps no one's missing from the Irish ferry, which rules out one line of inquiry.'

'Perhaps I fell out of a plane,' she said despondently.

'Out of the everywhere into the here!' He shook his head. 'I don't think so.'

Leonora sipped her tea in silence, watching him dispose of a large slice of cheese and several whole-wheat biscuits. There was, she conceded, a great deal of him to fill up. A large machine like Penry Vaughan's body must need a fair amount of fuel to keep it running efficiently.

He looked up to meet her eyes. 'I feel I should point out one other possibility, Leonora.'

Something in his tone put her on her guard. 'What's that?'

'There are quite a few islands around here. You could have been making for any one of them in a boat. And in all probability you weren't alone, which means that either you fell, or were swept, out of a boat someone else has landed safely somewhere.'

Her eyes lit up. 'Then they'll contact the police and the coastguard as you did, Dr Vaughan!'

He rubbed his chin. 'Possibly. But not everyone owns a radio telephone, or a way of contacting the shore. Which means this wind will have to die down a bit before they can return to the mainland.'

'So all I have to do is wait, then.'

'Don't get your hopes too high. Your companion might not have made it at all.'

Leonora paled. 'Did you have to say that?'

'I believe in facing facts.'

She digested the last, unwelcome fact in silence for some time. 'Will my own things be ready tomorrow?' she asked after a while.

'I'll bring them up in the morning after breakfast.'

'Dr Vaughan——'

'Let's dispense with the formalities, shall we? Since I can't address you as Miss Whatsit I don't see why you should keep to the "Doctor" bit—Penry will do.'

'It's an unusual name.'

'Not in Wales—means son of Henry. Until the English clamped down on the custom my forefathers all used the prefix "ap" in front of their names—the last king of South Wales, for instance, was Rhys ap Tewdwr. Needless to say, my father's name was Henry.' He smiled sardonically. 'Here endeth the history lesson.'

'Fascinating. Just like the Russian patronymics—though to me it sounds like a sort of spoken misprint—what's the matter?' she added, as he eyed her speculatively.

'I was just wondering what you do for a living.'

She shrugged. 'Who knows?' She thought for a moment, looking at her outspread hands. 'Perhaps I'm a chocolate moulder, or a poodle-clipper, or maybe I paint water-colours like those on the wall over there.'

'Lord, I hope not. They were perpetrated by my great-aunt Olwen, an eccentric lady with more enthusiasm than talent!'

She giggled, and he nodded approvingly.

'That's better. You're beginning to lighten up a bit. Is your head better?'

'Somewhat. It makes its presence felt now and then.' She smiled at him cajolingly. 'Could I have some more tablets before I go to bed?'

He shook his head. 'I'd rather you didn't, Leonora. Try to stick it out until tomorrow.'

She sighed. 'All right. Can I have a book to read, then?'

'I'm afraid it's no to that, too. Give your head a chance—count sheep if you can't get to sleep.'

She decided not to argue. 'Are there any sheep on Gullholm?'

'There used to be. This was a farmhouse once. A trawler-owning ancestor of mine bought the island, apparently convinced he could make a go of farming in a place surround by his beloved sea.'

'Was he Penry, too?'

He stretched his long frame comfortably in the deep leather chair as he explained that the gentleman in question was his mother's grandfather, a roistering old sea-dog by the name of Joshua Probert, more inclined to raising Cain than crops. The small-holding had failed to prosper due to the owner's propensity for fishing off Lee Haven, or drinking in the pub across the sound in Brides Haven.

'Since old Josh's time it's been used as a holiday retreat by various Proberts down the years,' he added, 'with some of the land let out for summer grazing to mainland farmers.'

'What happened in winter?'

'Ferreters used it in the past. These days I pay someone from Brides Haven to come over here at regular intervals to keep an eye on the place.'

Leonora was impressed. 'The island's your sole property?'

He nodded. 'My mother was an only child, so my grandfather Probert entailed Gullholm on me, which means I couldn't sell the place, even if I wanted to. He meant me to pass it on to my son.'

'How feudal!' She looked at him hesitantly. 'Do you *have* a son?'

His eyes went blank. 'No. I don't.'

'Sorry—didn't mean to be nosy.'

'Not at all,' he said politely. 'It's not classified information. I confess I did have a wife until recently, but, alas, no son—or daughter.'

Leonora felt a sharp pang of sympathy. The melancholy was explained. The poor man was here to get over a bereavement. 'I'm so sorry.'

A cynical gleam lit his eyes. 'Now what, I wonder, are you sorry for, Leonora?'

'Why—because you've lost your wife.'

'I didn't *lose* her, exactly. That smacks of carelessness, wouldn't you say?' His smile set her teeth on edge. 'Melanie merely lost interest in marriage to a busy consultant. She required a consort with more time—and money—to spend on her. The divorce became absolute not long ago,' he added abruptly, and got up. 'Would you like more tea?'

Leonora nodded dumbly, wishing the subject had never come up, as Penry Vaughan strode off to the kitchen. She gazed across the room at the door he kicked shut behind him, biting her lip. He must have loved the faithless Melanie very deeply to be so bitter over losing her. Tears welled in her eyes as she wondered about her loved ones. She must have a family, maybe even a boyfriend, all of them frantic, imagining her missing, even drowned. She slammed a mental door shut on the harrowing thought. What she must do was concentrate on getting her memory back so that she could get home to them as soon as humanly possible. The prospect of being marooned on Gullholm for days with a Heathcliff bereft of his Cathy gave her the creeps.

When Penry returned with her tea, looking withdrawn, as though he deeply regretted the mention of his wife, he put a plate of biscuits on the small table beside her. 'Eat a couple of those with the tea. You'll feel better.'

Leonora doubted that biscuits were much of a cure

for what ailed her, but she bit into one meekly, deciding that the best policy was to fall in with Penry Vaughan's wishes whenever possible, to keep the peace. He poured tea for her then retreated to his chair again with a glass of whisky.

'The weather forecast's pretty grim,' he said moodily. 'Gale-force ten in these parts soon, I'm afraid.'

'Pretty noisy already, isn't it?' She glanced nervously at the windows, wondering how they'd hold out against fiercer gusts than those already battering the house.

'Don't worry. There's secondary glazing everywhere. Keeps out the worst of it, and blankets the noise a bit too.' He smiled faintly. 'It's a good few decibels higher out of doors.'

Leonora shivered. 'Then I don't think I'll venture out for a stroll before bedtime.' She swallowed some tea hurriedly, then dropped the cup with a scream as the room was plunged into darkness.

'Are you all right?' demanded Penry urgently, shining a torch beam in her eyes.

'Yes—only I've broken your cup and spilled tea on your dressing-gown, she said breathlessly, running a hand down over the dampness on her chest. 'What's happened?'

'The confounded generator's on the blink again.' Penry struck a match and lit the oil lamp nearest Leonora, his face Mephistophelean over the flame as he replaced the glass chimney.

Leonora felt better instantly once there was light. She watched Penry moving round the room to light the other lamps, realising now why there was such a plentiful supply of non-electrical light sources everywhere.

'This happens a lot, I take it?' she asked. She bent

to pick up broken shards of china, gritting her teeth as her head protested.

'Too damned often for comfort,' he said irritably. 'The generator's old. I should replace it, but usually it only takes a bit of tinkering to get it going again. And to be honest I'm rather attached to it. I'm afraid I'll have to leave you to your own devices for a while.' He went to the shelves lining one wall and selected a handful of cassettes, then picked up a transistor radio. 'Would you like some music or a story for company while I wrestle with my old adversary? I keep a supply of batteries to save the blasted generator, so you might as well make use of them.'

Leonora received the offering with delight. 'Why, thank you, that's wonderful.' She scanned the selection of cassettes eagerly, then smiled up at him. 'No Beethoven?'

He shook his head. 'I remembered! And if you don't like any of those look for something else on the shelf, but try to move about as little as possible, please.'

'Yes, Doctor.'

'Are you being cheeky, by any chance?'

'I wouldn't dream of it,' she said demurely. 'I'll be good as gold, I promise. Besides, I've got Prunella Scales here, reading Jane Austen's *Emma*. I won't move a muscle until you're back.'

'My mother left that last time she was here. You share her taste in reading, obviously.'

Leonora looked up at him. 'Apparently so. It's like little bits of a jigsaw, isn't it?' Her mouth drooped. 'I just wish the complete picture would fall into place.'

'Now stop that!' he ordered. 'And mind you don't move until I get back.'

It was no hardship to obey. Lying on the sofa to

listen to her favourite story read with such consummate skill, Leonora shut out her worries and closed her ears to the howling wind while Penry went off to apply his healing skills to the rebellious generator.

Leonora lay with her eyes closed, so absorbed that Penry was obliged to turn off the radio to gain her attention. She sat up with a start, blinking, to find the room full of electric light again, and her host occupied in turning off the lamps, his face streaked with oil and his black hair wildly untidy, but with an air of triumph about him which she registered with some amusement.

'The patient recovered, I gather?'

He nodded with satisfaction. 'This time, at least. Every time it goes on the blink I wonder who'll win. So far I've come out on top, but one day the damn thing will expire just to spite me.'

'It didn't take you long!'

One eyebrow rose quizzically. 'It's an hour and ten minutes since I left you here with Jane Austen. A mere flash to you, but a long, hard grind out there in a freezing outhouse, young lady.'

She bit her lip. 'Was it really that long? I was so deep in the story I never noticed.'

'While I, on the other hand, was sweating blood to get the contraption going again in case you were frightened on your own in here!'

Leonora looked sceptical. 'Come off it, Dr Vaughan. I fancy you've been enjoying yourself just as much as I have.'

Penry smiled, shrugging, then looked down at his filthy sweater in distaste. 'I need a bath. Will you and Jane wait there for a while until I'm respectable again?'

Leonora, afraid he'd been about to order her to bed,

assented so rapturously that Penry eyed her in amusement as he crossed to the stairs.

'You're obviously feeling very much better tonight, Leonora.'

She thought about it. 'Yes—yes, I am. My head aches a bit, and I still feel battered, but if only my wretched memory would behave I'd soon be good as new.'

'Be thankful you're as good as you are, Leonora. You could have been drowned, remember.'

'Yes, Dr Vaughan,' she said, subdued. 'If it weren't for you I'd have been fish-food by now.'

'Stop that!' he ordered. 'Switch the tape on now, please, before I go upstairs.'

This time Leonora was allowed only a short session with *Emma* before Penry returned, damp about the head, but clean again in navy guernsey and tracksuit trousers, his bare feet in ancient espadrilles.

'Right, Leonora,' he said briskly. 'Time you were in bed.'

She switched off the tape, looking glum. 'Couldn't I stay down a bit longer, please?'

'You happen to be occupying the only sofa-bed in the room, young lady, and I need it——'

'Oh, but *I* could sleep down here,' she said instantly. 'You could have your bed back, and——'

'Nonsense.' He held out his hand. 'Come along. I want you safely upstairs in bed, not free to wander about down here, keeping me awake.'

Leonora eyed him resentfully, ignoring his hand as she took off the large borrowed socks. She stood up gingerly, relieved that the room stayed still. Her head gave a warning thump, but subsided almost at once to the now bearable ache. 'Very well,' she said grandly. 'But this time I go up under my own steam.'

'It really doesn't matter to me how you get upstairs,' he said indifferently as he followed behind her. 'Just as long as you get up there in one piece and stay put all night you can crawl up on your hands and knees for all I care.'

She preserved a dignified silence as she gathered up the trailing dressing-gown in one hand and kept the other on the rail attached to the wall on one side of the staircase. She mounted the uneven stairs with immense care, determined not to trip or fall, then turned as she reached the top. 'I shall be perfectly all right now, Dr Vaughan. Thank you for my dinner. Goodnight.'

He scrutinised her clinically. 'Right then, Leonora. Goodnight. If you need anything else in the night just call.'

She gave him a gracious little nod, determined to die first rather than do any such thing. Tomorrow, she assured herself, as she brushed her teeth, she would wake up with total recall of who she was and where she came from. All she had to do was get a good night's sleep. By morning perhaps the storm would have blown itself out, and the fog in her mind along with it.

When Leonora returned to the bedroom she found the bed turned down invitingly. A glass of water stood on the table beside the rose-shaded lamp, along with a torch and a candle and a box of matches in a pretty pottery holder. If the generator broke down in the middle of the night Penry had seen to it that she'd still be able to lighten her darkness. Unable to resist a look in the mirror, she gave a despairing sigh. Her hair, left to its own devices to dry, looked like the business end of a witch's broom. Hoping Penry Vaughan wouldn't mind if she borrowed his hairbrush, she set to work. It took some time, and no little resolution, before the tightly curling mass hung round her face tangle-free at last, and she could crawl wearily into bed.

Leonora leaned back thankfully against the piled pillows, listening to the wind, which howled around the house like a hundred banshees demanding entry. She lay motionless, utterly worn out by her exertions, yet at the same time ominously wide awake. She would put out the lamp in a little while, she promised herself. As soon as she felt actually drowsy she would turn it off. Drowsiness, however, was not forthcoming. She shifted a little against the pillows, wishing now she'd left her hair alone. Her head throbbed in rhythm with her bruises, yet she'd hardly noticed any of it downstairs. She sighed, feeling resentful towards Penry Vaughan for making her come up here. Which was unjust, she told herself firmly. If it weren't for Dr Penry Vaughan she might well be dead.

A tap on the door sounded above the wind. Leonora's eyebrows rose. Talk of the devil!

'Come in,' she called, surprised.

Penry Vaughan ducked his tall head through the doorway and moved to stand at the foot of the bed in the shadows beyond the arc of light from the small lamp. 'I saw the light under the door, and wondered if you'd like some company for the night.'

CHAPTER THREE

LEONORA gazed at him, heart hammering. She cleared her throat drily. 'I'm sure I'll drop off soon, Dr Vaughan. I must have slept too long this afternoon.'

He eyed her narrowly. 'What's the matter? You look petrified again.'

'Your knock startled me.'

'I'm surprised you heard it above this wind.' He bent to pick something up, then came round the side of the bed holding out the transistor. 'If you're wakeful I thought you might like company in the shape of *Emma*——' He stopped, his eyes narrowing as he saw the expression on her face. '*Now* what's the matter?'

Praying he couldn't see her agonised blush, Leonora smiled shakily. 'Nothing. It's very kind of you.'

Penry Vaughan's eyes lit with sudden, derisive comprehension. 'My dear little castaway,' he drawled, 'surely you didn't imagine I was offering *myself* as companion for the night? Ah—I can see you did.'

Burning with mortification, Leonora looked away, sliding lower beneath the quilt like an animal burrowing for cover as Penry sat on the edge of the bed.

'Leonora,' he commanded, 'look at me.'

Unwillingly she raised her eyes to his.

'How can I succeed in convincing you?' he demanded. 'When I said you had nothing to fear from me I meant it, young lady. I don't know just what kind of monster you imagine I am, but having my wicked way with a girl in your state of health is not precisely my style.'

'I'm sorry,' she got out after a painful silence. 'I misunderstood—which was very stupid. After all, I've seen myself in the mirror. You'd have to be pretty desperate to want—anything like that with someone who looks like me.'

'I wouldn't say that, exactly.' There was an unsettling gleam in his eye as he got up. 'You're very appealing, Leonora, black eye or not. Which doesn't mean I intend to leap into bed with you just because fate washed you up on my beach. And if you're imagining I pine for the delights of the conjugal bed now my wife's left me, you're a bit off-beam there, too. I was accustomed to a lonely bed long before she left me for someone else.' He checked himself, his face suddenly harsh. 'And why the hell I told you that I don't know. It's not something I want broadcast to the world.'

Indignation cancelled out any stray pang of compassion. Leonora eyed him angrily. 'Your marital problems don't interest me in the slightest, Dr Vaughan. Why would I want to talk about them to anyone else?' She sighed despairingly. 'At the moment I don't even *know* anyone else!'

Penry's harsh face softened a little. 'Be positive, Leonora. In the morning you'll probably wake to full recall. In the meantime listen to Jane Austen for a while, then try to sleep.'

She shifted her head restlessly against the pillows. 'I'll try. Thank you very much for bringing me the transistor—and I'm sorry, Dr Vaughan. For getting the wrong end of the stick, I mean. It was pretty far-fetched, really.'

He smiled slowly. 'Not that much, you know! But

you needn't lose any sleep over it, I promise—scout's honour.'

Leonora smiled faintly. 'Were you a boy scout?'

'No—too busy playing rugby. Were you a girl guide?' he countered swiftly.

'Oh, no, not my scene at all. . .' She halted, then blew out her cheeks. 'There I go again. Perhaps I'll do it by process of elimination; find out what I'm not bit by bit until I know who I am.'

'Go to sleep, child——' He checked himself, shrugging. 'Sorry, Leonora, but you look about twelve or so in this light.'

'Which is pretty clever of me, considering I feel so aged and infirm.' She smiled. 'Goodnight, Doctor.'

'Goodnight, Leonora.' He paused before ducking through the doorway. 'But remember, if you want anything just shout.'

She smiled non-comittally, then turned to the transistor, grateful for the wit and irony of Jane Austen. After an hour or so her eyes grew heavy and her yawns more frequent, and at last she stopped the tape at a suitable break. Hoping the generator could cope with one small lamp left on all night, she wriggled lower in the bed, pulled the covers over her ears, and fell asleep to the howl of the wind and the pounding of the waves on the rocks below.

Leonora woke in the night, gasping, her body drenched with perspiration. Still rigid with the horror of her nightmare, she heaved herself up in bed as the door flew open and Penry charged into the room at a run, his hair on end and his chest bare.

He took her by the shoulders, his eyes urgent. 'What's wrong? You were screaming your head off. Good lord, you're drenched, girl.' He went over to the chest, rummaging through it until he found a large white sweatshirt. 'I'll get a towel. Get back under the covers.'

Leonora fought for calm, her breath ripping through her chest as she clenched her teeth together to stop them chattering. Penry returned quickly with a warm, dry towel, which he draped round her shoulders as he took her wrist in his.

'I had—a nightmare,' she said jerkily.

'I gathered that! Quietly now, please.' He looked at his watch as he took her pulse. 'Hm. A bit rapid, but not unduly so under the circumstances.' He smiled encouragingly. 'Come on—off with that sodden thing. This sweatshirt will drown you, but it's warm and dry.'

Leonora's mouth set stubbornly.

'Did you hear?' he said impatiently. 'Get the damn thing off.'

'Turn your back, please.'

He stared at her in exasperation. 'Leonora, I'm a *doctor*——'

'I don't care. Turn your back. Please!'

Penry threw up his hands in surrender. 'I'll do better than that. I'll go downstairs and make you a hot drink.'

Leonora shuddered at the memory of her dream as she peeled the damp shirt over her throbbing head. She struggled into Penry's thick white sweatshirt, rolled the ludicrously long sleeves back, then began tidying the bed.

'Don't bother,' said Penry, coming in with an armful of bedding. He tossed her a blanket. 'Wrap yourself in that while I change the sheets.'

Leonora watched numbly as Penry, who had now added the navy guernsey to his tracksuit trousers, made the bed with a swiftness and dexterity any ward sister would have approved. When it was ready she got up, handing him the blanket as she slid wearily beneath the covers. Penry propped up the pillows behind her, then opened the bag he'd brought with him and took out a small torch.

'Right. Hold still now.' He held up his left forefinger in front of her. 'Keep watching that while I take a look.' He shone the slender beam into each eye in turn, then nodded. 'Pupil reaction satisfactory. How's the head?'

'Thumping,' she admitted. 'Not surprising after all that commotion.'

'Lie perfectly still for a while. I'll get these damp sheets out of the way then fetch that drink.' He paused in the doorway. 'Better now?'

'Yes.' It was the truth, Leonora realised, when she was alone. Her desperate, unreasoning terror had left her the moment Penry Vaughan hurtled through the door. She smiled faintly, wondering what he was like with his patients. Probably they got better rather than risk his wrath by doing otherwise.

'You're very clever not to bump your head just once now and then,' said Leonora hoarsely as Penry ducked through the doorway with a laden tray. She coughed drily. 'Listen to me! I'm croaking like a frog.'

'You've screamed yourself hoarse.' Penry handed Leonora a steaming mug, then hooked a large wicker chair near the bed and sat down. 'Right. Tell me what you were dreaming about,' he commanded.

She shuddered, then took a sip from her mug. 'This is nice,' she said evasively. 'What's in the milk?'

'Just sugar and a pinch of cinnamon.'

Leonora took a few more sips of the hot milk, then met his eyes. 'It didn't seem like a dream.'

'It sounded like a full-scale nightmare from downstairs.'

She breathed in deeply. 'I think my subconscious found a way of telling me a bit of what happened, Dr Vaughan.'

Penry leaned forward to take the mug from her. He put it down on the tray then captured her hand, suddenly very much the professional consultant. 'All right, Leonora, take your time. Was anyone else in the dream?'

'No. Only me.' She swallowed. 'I was in a dinghy—the kind you can use with an outboard engine.'

'Go on,' he said gently.

Her breathing quickened, her eyes dilating as they stared into his. 'The sea was very rough. I was soaked to the skin, my hands so cold I could hardly keep hold of the tiller. The wind rose and the dinghy was bucketing about like mad, then—then——'

Penry caught both her hands in his. 'Steady. What happened next?'

'The engine stopped. The dinghy spun like a top, a huge wave came at me, sweeping me overboard, and—and then I woke up.' She swallowed a sob of pure terror at the memory and Penry jumped up to sit beside her on the bed. He took her in his arms, holding her close in silence, the sheer size and warmth of him calming her very quickly.

'Sorry,' she muttered, pulling away. 'I didn't mean to fall apart like that.'

Penry stacked the pillows more comfortably behind her. 'You'll probably feel all the better for it. Drink up.' He returned to the chair, looking thoughtful. 'I think you're right. It's too relevant to be merely a dream. I think your subconscious decided to provide you with a sort of extract from the main story. It would certainly explain how you came to be washed up in Seal Haven.' He looked up. 'A good thing you were near Gullholm when the engine failed or you'd never have survived.'

Leonora nodded, shivering. 'I can't have been making for Gullholm, though, can I?'

'True. Only a fool would try to get here in a dinghy. I've got a chunky old fishing-boat myself, the type locals use for crabbing.'

She pulled the covers higher, feeling drained but oddly relaxed, as though the dream had relieved some of the pressure on her brain. 'If the dream is accurate——' She pulled a face. 'Something so realistic just has to be accurate! Anyway, it's a hint as to how I got here, if nothing else.' She eyed him apprehensively. 'Do you suppose I'll have a nightmare like that every night?'

'I've no idea. Try not to think about it,' he ordered, then added casually, 'Can you swim, Leonora?'

'Yes,' she said without thinking, then stared at him, shaking her head. 'I don't know how I know. But I do.'

He nodded. 'It probably saved your life.' He got up, stretching, his head endangering the overhead light. 'Right, Leonora. Do you think you can sleep now?'

She nodded, secretly doubting it very much. 'Yes, Dr Vaughan. Thank you. I'm sorry to be so much trouble.'

He smiled wryly. 'It relieves the monotony of my own company, if nothing else.' He paused in the doorway. 'By the way, was it daylight in your dream?'

Leonora thought for a moment. 'Yes. Yes, it was.' She looked at him questioningly. 'Why do you ask?'

'It means you couldn't have arrived in Seal Haven all that long before I found you. If you'd been there overnight it's unlikely you'd be alive to tell the tale.' He gave her a kindly nod. 'Now for heaven's sake get some sleep—and let me do the same!'

Leonora stared at the closed door forlornly, certain she'd lie awake for what was left of the night. After what seemed like only a doze she woke to daylight, the wind driving hail against the window with a force which threatened to break it. She reached over and turned out the light, sick with disappointment to find she was no wiser about her identity than the night before. She climbed wearily out of bed, consoling herself that her physical injuries, at least, were healing fast. She pulled on the red wool dressing-gown hastily, glad of its warmth as she tiptoed to the bathroom, doing her best not to wake Penry.

The confrontation with her reflection was encouraging. Both eyes were now wide open and reasonably bright. One, it was true, still sported a bruise which gave her a rather raffish air, but it was already fading. She was no raving beauty, she thought wryly, but at least she now looked human. Back in the bedroom, she brushed her hair gently, then got back into bed, uncertain what else to do until she knew Penry was up and about. She turned on the transistor very quietly, found a local radio station, and discovered, surprised, that it was nearly nine. Outside it looked more like twilight than early morning. She waited until the news summary at nine o'clock, but, when there was no mention of a missing female person, eyes dark, hair mouse, she returned to Jane Austen's *Emma* for consolation.

Shortly afterwards there was a perfunctory tap on

the door heralding Penry's practised juggling act with a laden tray as he ducked into the room. He eyed her closely as he set the tray down. 'Good morning, Leonora. I heard you up and about. How do you feel?'

'Better.' She smiled ruefully. 'At least my body does. My memory, wretched thing, is still playing truant. After my dream last night I had such hopes, too.'

Penry handed her a plate of steaming porridge. 'It'll come. Try not to worry. In the meantime eat that while it's hot. I've put a sprinkling of brown sugar and a dash of milk on it. OK?'

'Wonderful,' she said, tasting it. 'It's years since I had porridge—I think. I'd forgotten how good it is——' She stopped, grimacing. 'I wish that was all I'd forgotten!'

'Now then!' He checked the contents of the tray. 'Toast, butter, tea, milk. Anything else you'd like?'

'Absolutely not!' She smiled shyly. 'It's very good of you to bring me breakfast, Dr Vaughan——'

'Penry.'

'All right. Penry. But you shouldn't be waiting on me like this.'

'From now on I won't,' he assured her, on his way to the door. 'I'll bring your clothes up in a minute, then you can come downstairs. Not,' he added, with a wave at the rain-lashed window, 'that either of us is going anywhere in this. The shipping forecast said it should moderate later, so with luck I'll get you X-rayed tomorrow. We'll see.'

Leonora settled down to her breakfast in a better frame of mind than she would have believed possible the day before. Breakfast in bed was a luxury, that much was certain. In fact, she thought, crunching on a piece of toast, she was pretty sure breakfast didn't feature much at all in this unknown life of hers. She frowned as she remembered her dream. It had been so vivid it *seemed* real, yet had she really been idiot enough to set out on a rough sea in a mere dinghy?

'That's a very black frown,' commented Penry. He deposited a small pile of clothes on the end of the bed, then took her empty plate. 'Shall I pour some tea for you while you take a look through your things?'

'Yes, please.' Leonora examined the clothes eagerly. There were two pairs of jeans, one newish, one elderly, two chambray shirts, one pink and checked, the other plain light blue, plus a heavy navy wool sweater from the same chain store as the pretty cotton underwear. There was also, she saw with a slight flush, a peach silk camisole and French knickers. Three pairs of navy wool socks and a white-spotted red cotton scarf made up the total.

'Your shoes are downstairs, stuffed with paper—navy leather moccasin type. And you were wearing a ski-jacket, puffy navy thing. Probably supported you for a bit once you were in the water.' Penry handed her a cup of tea. 'Any of it ring a bell?'

'All of it.' She shrugged helplessly. 'I'm not sure about the silk things but the rest of it is mine, I know. But that's all I know. It's so frustrating!'

Penry collected the tray, looking thoughtful. 'In this dream of yours, did the dinghy have a name, by any chance?'

She shook her head, and winced sharply. 'I must remember not to do that!' She thought hard. 'It's all a bit blurred now anyway, but I was inside the boat during the dream. The name would be on the outside.'

'Merely a thought before I contact the coastguard and the police again.'

Leonora eyed him over her cup. 'Are you really going to tell them about the dream?'

'Yes. Any lead is worth following up.'

The moment Penry was through the door Leonora got out of bed, eager to see if the familiarity of the clothes would jog her memory. The cotton bra and briefs were a perfect fit, as were the pink shirt and the rather worn jeans, but there was no blinding flash of enlightenment once she had them on. Sighing, she pulled on socks and sweater, then knotted the scarf at her throat and secured one of the ends to her sweater with the silver lioness brooch so automatically that she paused, eyeing herself in the mirror. The little routine was second nature to her, evidently. She went on looking at herself, willing her reflection to start up some reaction in her brain, but with no success. She sighed as she tidied her hair, which hung to her shoulder-blades, curling tightly. Surely she didn't wear it loose like this?

Leonora made her bed then collected her cup and started downstairs, deeply thankful that she felt so much better than the day before. As she reached the foot of the narrow stair Penry emerged from the kitchen, his black eyebrows knitting together in a daunting frown at the sight of her.

'Hello.' She smiled at him warily. 'Have you got an old shoelace?'

His eyes dropped to the socks on her feet. 'Why do you need one?' he asked shortly.

She gestured at her hair. 'To tie this lot back. Whoever I am I'm in crying need of a haircut.'

'I'll see what I can do.'

Leonora stared at him blankly as he went into the

kitchen, wondering what she'd done to incur his displeasure again. Dr Penry Vaughan's brooding Celtic moods were a bit hard to take at times, to say the least. Scowling at his broad, white-sweatered back, she followed him into a room as neat and orderly as an operating theatre. Cupboards, surfaces, refrigerator, cooker, everything shone with pristine cleanliness, no clutter of any kind in sight beyond an electric kettle, a large cast-iron cookpot on the back of the wood-burning Aga. The only blots on the landscape were a pair of small shoes beside the Aga and a nylon ski-jacket airing on the back of a chair. Wondering if she dared risk sullying the gleaming sink, Leonora rinsed out her cup, then eyed the cupboards, wondering where to put it.

'In the cupboard on the right,' said Penry curtly as he searched through a drawer.

Leonora opened the cupboard and added the cup to a row of others, rather awed by the perfect symmetry of plates in orderly stacks according to size and function. When she turned round Penry was holding out a pair of unused white shoelaces.

'Will these do?'

'Perfectly. Thank you.' Leonora gave him a polite smile as she tied her hair securely at the nape of her neck. 'I don't suppose you were able to go for a run this morning in this weather?'

'No. I wasn't.'

She gestured to a half-open door beyond him. 'Is that a pantry?'

'It used to be. I've converted it into a study. The radio telephone's in there. And,' he added brusquely, 'I want it understood from the start that the study's off-limits to visitors.'

Leonora's chin lifted. 'Certainly, Dr Vaughan.'

'I should explain that I've got a deadline for the series of articles I'm writing. I fondly hoped the isolation of Gullholm would give me the requisite peace and quiet to meet it.'

'Instead of which you're landed with a nuisance like me!'

Penry Vaughan made no attempt to deny it. 'Since the situation is unavoidable I suggest that now you're better you make yourself as useful as possible, preparing meals and so on while I get on with my work. The moment the weather improves I'll take you over to the mainland and get that X-ray done. The sooner you recover your memory the better.'

Her mouth tightened. Anyone would think the loss was due to her own carelessness!

'I live for the moment,' she assured him coldly. 'In the meantime I'll earn my keep, don't worry.'

'Can you cook?'

'I believe so.'

He nodded briskly. 'Right. For lunch use the soup left in that pot. With a sandwich of some kind, that will do. While I go up for a bath you can take stock of the supplies I brought.'

'If I weren't here what would you have had for dinner?'

'Something easy. You needn't put yourself out too much.' He paused. 'But if you feel ill in any way, please say so. It's not my intention to jeopardise your recovery in any way.'

Leonora felt utterly flattened as he left her to go upstairs. What on earth was wrong? When he'd appeared with her breakfast Penry Vaughan had been reasonably friendly—and in the middle of the night he'd been kindness itself after her nightmare. But from the moment she'd come downstairs he'd been a different man. She cast a malevolent eye at the window as a squall of rain battered the glass, then began an inspection of supplies. It was no surprise to find enough food for a siege. The cupboards held tins and packages of every kind, even a box of fresh vegetables. The fridge was stocked with salad greens, several kinds of cheese, bacon, eggs, the remains of a cooked ham. A large porcelain crock contained several loaves of bread. Whether she could cook or not, thought Leonora drily, they were unlikely to starve.

Abandoning the kitchen, she wandered across the large living-room to the windows. A driving curtain of rain blotted out everything other than the sodden turf nearest the house, the view so depressing that she turned away with a shiver, drawn like a magnet to the books on the shelves. Penry Vaughan's family had diverse tastes, she found. There was something to suit everyone; Tolstoy, Hemingway and Hardy, thrillers and spy stories, historical novels, light romances. All tastes were catered for admirably. Leonora chose a brightly coloured paperback novel about the Crusades, and went over to the fireplace to curl up on the sofa. By the time Penry Vaughan came downstairs again she was deep in the adventures of a lady who had decided to dress as a boy to search for her lost crusading husband. She looked up with an absent smile.

'Shall I make some coffee?'

He nodded. 'Thank you. There's only instant, I'm afraid. I'll take it in when I make a start. I'll top up the stove here while you're in the kitchen.'

Couldn't he bear to stay in the same room? Huffily Leonora filled the kettle, made coffee, then took hers into the other room. 'I've left yours in the kitchen,' she said quietly, resuming her seat.

Penry straightened from his inspection of the stove. 'Thank you. This should be all right for hours now.'

She looked up at him diffidently. 'I don't suppose you've had time to ring the police for any news yet?'

'Of course. I'm just as eager as you to establish your identity,' he assured her with irony. 'I rang them first thing, but no one fitting your description has been reported missing anywhere in the entire country as yet. There were no reports of a dinghy washed up anywhere, either.'

Leonora turned away, her lips tight. 'I see. Thank you.' From the corner of her eye she saw him walk away, pause for a moment, then give an indifferent shrug as he went through the kitchen to his study. The door slammed shut behind him with a 'keep out' message she received with resentment. Penry Vaughan's irritation at being saddled with an unwelcome guest was understandable enough, but surely he could have let her know he'd spoken to the police!

Her animosity did her throbbing head no good at all. She laid her head back against a cushion, breathing in deeply and regularly to relax the tension in the back of her neck, but it was no use. Her mind kept wrestling with the problem of her identity, her imagination running riot as she pictured loved ones mad with anxiety about her. A particularly ferocious gust brought Leonora to her feet to roam about the room wishing passionately that the weather would improve. Not even her fear of setting foot in a boat again would keep her from making the crossing to the mainland the moment the trip to Brides Haven was feasible. Someone, somewhere out there just had to be searching for her.

Leonora pulled herself together after a while. This just wouldn't do, she told herself sternly. Then she paused, her attention caught by a canvas bag of knitting on one of the armchairs. The bag contained wool, needles and a pattern for a sweater obviously intended for Penry, by the measurements ringed in red. The design was complicated, with a serpentine pattern of dark blue and white with touches of black, and whoever was knitting it had completed only a few inches of ribbed welt.

I can knit, thought Leonora with a sudden flash of self-knowledge. One look at the intricate pattern was enough to tell her she could follow it with no trouble at all. She looked at the clock, frustrated to find it was only a little after eleven. Bearding the lion in his den just to ask about some knitting was a bad idea. She'd have to be patient until lunchtime, then soften up Penry Vaughan with a snack before she made her request.

Ten minutes before midday Leonora retired to the kitchen, tiptoeing past the closed study door. At first she tried to be as quiet as possible as she began preparations for lunch, but after a few minutes gave up and worked normally, deciding to impress the moody Dr Vaughan by making dumplings to top the soup. While they were steaming on top of the savoury liquid she whipped up a small quantity of French dressing, sprinkled it on shredded lettuce and tomato slices, then added grated cheese and made some sandwiches.

When two trays were ready she tapped on the study door.

'Yes?' barked her host.

'Your lunch, Dr Vaughan. Shall I bring it in?'

'I'll fetch it.' He emerged, closing the door firmly

behind him as he looked from Leonora to the kitchen counter. 'Thank you. I'll eat mine at my desk.'

Leonora bristled as she marched into the other room, realising she'd expected murmurs of appreciation to greet her offering. She had no objection to working for her keep, but if Penry Vaughan went on treating her as if she were some kind of serf she'd stick to plain, basic cooking from now on, she thought resentfully. As she began on her soup she tried to think of what possible sin she could have committed to change his attitude towards her. He hadn't been exactly jumping for joy to have her here in the first place, as she knew very well. But he'd shown definite signs of resigning himself to the situation—until her arrival downstairs after breakfast. She shrugged. There was nothing she could do about it, other than keep a low profile and stay well out of his way.

Leonora took her time over her lunch. When she went back to the kitchen Penry's tray stood on the counter, the plates satisfactorily empty. She cleared away, made coffee, then tapped on Penry's door, opening it warily as he called her in. He sat at a large desk covered with papers, journals, medical books, a portable typewriter pushed to one end. The radio transmitter, a surprisingly small, modern affair, occupied its own bracket on one wall, which was foot-thick whitewashed stone like the others, the chill only a little alleviated by the portable bottled-gas heater alongside the desk. Penry thrust his black hair back from his forehead, frowning as he looked up.

'Well?'

'Your coffee. Shall I bring it in?'

'Yes—please.'

Leonora collected the steaming mug and went into

the study, placing it carefully on the only unoccupied space on the desk.

'Thank you,' muttered her host, leafing impatiently through some notes.

Leonora braced herself. 'Dr Vaughan, would it disturb you if I listened to the transistor this afternoon?'

He looked up. 'No. If you keep the doors closed it won't make any difference to me.' He leaned back in his chair, looking at her. 'How's your head? Does reading make it ache?'

'A little. It would be easier to listen to a story for a while. But I feel much better today.' As she met the clinical look in Penry Vaughan's eyes she stiffened, the reason for his change of mood suddenly, mortifyingly, obvious. She drew herself up to her full height. 'Tell me the truth, please, Dr Vaughan. Do you by any chance think I'm faking?'

One eyebrow rose. 'Faking?'

'The amnesia. Ever since I came downstairs this morning you've been different, hostile. I've been racking my brains for what I could have done, then it struck me. You think my loss of memory is put on!'

'It had better not be,' he said cuttingly, then shrugged. 'I suppose you merit an explanation.' He swallowed some of the coffee, then eyed her moodily. 'I had no choice when it came to rescuing the helpless victim of an unknown accident. When I found you all my energies were directed towards mending, healing, reviving. You were the patient, I was the doctor. But today things are different. You look much better, less of a victim. To put it in basic terms, Leonora, you're no longer merely a patient in my eyes. You're a woman. Young and over-thin, it's true, but a woman just the same.'

Leonora stepped back involuntarily, her cheeks burning. 'I can't help that, Dr Vaughan!'

'True. But the fact remains that I retreated to Gullholm because it's the one place in my world *free* of the entire sex.' His eyes gleamed suddenly. 'Not that I'm a misogynist, Leonora. Far from it. Given time I'll no doubt revert to normal. But for the moment,' he added significantly, 'the fact remains that you're female, I'm male, and we're marooned here alone together—a dangerous situation, though none of my seeking.'

'Nor,' she said passionately, 'of mine! Oddly enough I didn't set out from wherever I come from to trespass on your island, or to lose my wretched memory. If I could leave right now I would!' Then she remembered her request, and forced herself to calm down. 'Dr Vaughan, who does the knitting belong to?'

He stared at her blankly. 'Knitting?'

'I found a bag with wool and a pattern for a sweater,' she explained.

'My mother must have left it here.'

'Do you think she'd mind if I went on with it?'

Penry Vaughan gave her a smile of genuine amusement. 'On the contrary, she'd probably be delighted. The pattern infuriated her, now I come to think of it. She abandoned it in disgust.'

Leonora made no attempt at an answering smile. 'Then may I carry on, please? I can knit while I listen.'

'If you're certain your head is up to it.'

'If it starts protesting I'll stop.'

As she went through the door he called her back,

eyeing her speculatively. 'You know you can knit, then, Leonora?'

'Yes. It's utterly maddening. Some things are crystal-clear, yet the rest keep lurking in the fog. By the way,' she added, 'what time would you like dinner?'

Penry Vaughan turned back to his work dismissively. 'I generally work until six-thirty. Give me an hour or so to unwind.'

'As you wish.'

He looked up. 'I forgot. It may cheer you up to learn that the weather forecast is promising. Tomorrow we should be able to get over to the mainland. Make a list of any supplies we need.'

Despite the disquieting exchange with her host Leonora felt rather more cheerful when she settled down with her knitting. Less apprehensive of the weather now she knew it was due to improve, she was glad of permission to use the transistor. Concentrating on *Emma* would help to keep her worries at bay for a little while. Then, just as she was about to press the switch to 'Play', it occurred to Leonora that Penry Vaughan's eyes weren't dark like her own, after all. At close quarters, meeting them across his desk just now, she'd discovered they were blue. A dark, smoky sort of colour, it was true, but very definitely blue.

CHAPTER FOUR

LEONORA found no difficulty in following the pattern which had defeated Mrs Vaughan. The design, the cover informed her, was inspired by ancient Viking jewellery, which explained the serpentine interweaving of the colours, and her brain and fingers co-ordinated over the task with such dexterity that Leonora had no doubt this was something she'd done often before.

It proved soothing. With her fingers busy and her mind occupied with the story it was late afternoon before the end of a tape brought Leonora back to earth with a start. Several inches of intricately patterned knitting hung from her needles, she saw with satisfaction, almost as if her fingers had worked independently while she listened. She went quietly into the kitchen to make tea, then knocked on the study door.

'Come in,' said Penry absently, looking up, yawning, as Leonora popped her head round the door.

'I thought you might like some tea, and a slice of the fruit-cake I found in a tin.'

He eased his shoulders. 'Sounds good.'

She deposited the tray on the desk, then took her own tea and a small piece of cake back to her former post, slotted a new tape into the machine for the next instalment of the story and settled down to enjoy the rest of the afternoon in peace.

'Isn't it time you had a rest?' enquired Penry Vaughan, startling her. At some stage Leonora had switched on the lamp beside her to see her knitting, but otherwise the room was in darkness.

Leonora stopped the tape. 'What time is it?'

'After six.' He went round the room drawing curtains and turning on lamps. 'Time you called it a day.' He stooped to replenish the stove then came to look at what she was doing as she finished off a row. 'Have you done all that this afternoon?' he asked, astonished.

'Oh, no. Your mother did the ribbing. I've only done the patterned bit.'

'Only!' As she finished he took the needle from her. 'This is extremely well done. You're obviously an expert.'

'I think I must be,' she agreed. 'The pattern seemed easy to me, anyway.'

He shook his head in surprise. 'My mother's knitted for all of us as far back as I can remember, but she acknowledged defeat on this one.'

Leonora stowed the knitting away carefully, then got up. 'Right. I'll go and make the sauce, then I'll have a bath while it's simmering if the generator's up to it.'

'Are you sure *you're* up to it?' he asked sharply. 'You look very pale.'

'My head's aching a bit, now you come to mention it, but I expect that's all the concentration,' she said cheerfully. 'I'll be fine after a bath.'

'Hang on a moment! I'll take a look at you first.' He went off to fetch his medical bag.

Once again Leonora was obliged to submit to light directed in her eyes, after which Penry Vaughan took her pulse and her blood-pressure before he was satisfied. 'I suppose you'll do,' he said grudgingly. 'But don't attempt anything too complicated for the meal. Bacon and eggs will do.'

'You can have that for breakfast. It's tagliatelle for supper. You've got some in the cupboard so I assume you like it,' she said, making for the kitchen.

Penry came to lean in the doorway, his eyes following her about as she took packets and tins from the cupboard, making her decidedly uneasy.

Leonora frowned over her shoulder. 'Your kitchen's small and so am I, Dr Vaughan, whereas you most definitely are not. I'll get on faster on my own.'

His eyes lit with an unsettling gleam as he brushed past her. 'I'll get some wood in for the stove, then. But once you've made this sauce of yours I suggest you have a bath and a rest before we eat. I want you fit and well as quickly as possible.'

'So do I!' Leonora snapped, then set to work at top speed while Penry was out chopping driftwood. In minutes she had garlic, onions, carrots and celery cooking together gently in olive oil. As she sieved the contents of two cans of tomatoes, Penry returned, sniffing the air.

'Great smell,' he said, pausing, the basket balanced easily on one hip.

'I forgot to ask if you like garlic, but there was some in with the vegetables so I took a chance,' she said, adding the tomato purée to the pot with care.

'I'm very fond of it, but until recently had to forgo the pleasure. My former wife disliked not only the taste of it herself but refused to come near me if *I* succumbed to its temptation.' Penry raised an eyebrow. 'The smell of your sauce is a two-fold comfort, Leonora. It points out advantages to my divorced state I hadn't thought of before.'

Leonora made no comment, determined to avoid personalities at all cost after his remarks earlier on.

'Dinner will be ready in an hour,' she informed him, and went up to run a bath.

She let herself down gingerly into the hot water, gritting her teeth as various bruises stung as they came in contact with the heat. The water cooled too quickly for her to stay long in the bath, but afterwards she lay fully dressed on the bed for a while, listening, her spirits rising as she realised that the wind had dropped at last. She could still hear the pounding of the waves on the rocks below, but felt lulled rather than threatened by the muffled boom, accepting it as an inescapable sound on an island surrounded by the Atlantic ocean.

When Leonora went downstairs she found Penry lounging in front of the fireplace listening to a newcast on the transistor. He jumped up as she joined him.

'I've rung the police, but nothing yet, I'm afraid. I don't know who you belong to, Leonora, but no one's anxious about you yet, obviously, so you'll just have to be patient.'

The sharp pang of disappointment seared her like a physical pain. 'I must belong to someone,' she said tartly to hide it. 'You'd think someone would have made enquiries about me by now.'

The smoky-blue eyes softened slightly. 'Probably you haven't been missed yet.'

'I suppose so. Thank you for ringing.' Leonora blinked hard as she forced a smile. 'I suppose I'll come to terms eventually with the blank in my mind. They say you get used to anything in time. Perhaps I won't like it when I find out who I am.'

'Of course you will,' he assured her, then looked down at himself in distaste. 'Sit down and listen to the radio for a bit while I go up and wash. I'll make up a bed in one of the other rooms tonight. This sofa wasn't designed for someone like me.'

She frowned. 'I wish you'd let me sleep in another bed. I don't need a big bed, and you do.'

He shook his head. 'I prefer not to risk further disorientation for you, Leonora. You stay where you are. The bed in the room next to you is perfectly adequate for me, I promise.'

Leonora wasn't at all sure she fancied the idea of Penry in the next room in the night. Now he'd brought the subject up it was very hard to forget that they were a man and woman isolated together miles from anywhere. Even harder to ignore the fact that her reluctant, brooding host was all male, with an attraction rendered more rather than less dangerous by his current attitude towards the female sex. Dr Penry Vaughan, she realised with deep misgiving, was pro tem the only other person in her entire world, and, like it or not, he was doomed to play Adam to her Eve until her memory deigned to function again.

But what if it never did? Leonora fought down a sudden rush of panic. It was only thirty-six hours since she'd been washed up on the island like a piece of flotsam, she reminded herself; early days to start bewailing her fate. She could hear Penry moving about upstairs as he made up the other bed. She jumped to her feet, suddenly in need of occupation, and went into the kitchen. She put a big pan of water to boil, ready for the pasta, then added canned mushrooms to the tomato sauce, which was giving off such a heavenly aroma that she felt hungry despite her inner turmoil.

Delivering a brief lecture on self-control, Leonora began frying bacon, cutting hunks of crusty bread, grating cheese, determined to keep so occupied that there was no attention to spare for the worries which seemed to be multiplying by the minute.

'Is it nearly ready?' said Penry, startling her.

Leonora whirled round, flushing as she found him watching her from the doorway. 'More or less. Shall I put the pasta on now?'

'Please do!' He leaned against the door-jamb, his hair brushing the lintel. 'I could eat a horse, Madame Chef.'

'No horse. You'll have to make do with bacon.' Cross to find her fingers transformed into thumbs by the watchful blue eyes, she added a spoonful of olive oil to the boiling water, then threw in the coils of pasta. 'Don't wander off, please,' she said, stirring busily. 'Once this is ready it must get to the plates quickly while it's hot.'

'I'm not going anywhere,' he said lazily. 'I'm perfectly happy where I am. Watching you.'

As a cure for clumsiness his statement was a failure. With such a disturbing audience of one, Leonora took far longer than intended to serve the meal. She was heartily glad when they were installed at last in front of the fire, trays on knees. Silence reigned for some time as they attacked the meal. Penry's plate was half empty before he said a word, other than grunts of pure appreciation.

'This is first-class, Leonora,' he said at last. 'It deserves some wine as an accompaniment, but I advise keeping off alcohol for a bit.'

'I don't drink very much, anyway,' she began, then paused, fork in hand. 'Ah. Another piece of the puzzle. Oh, Penry, I just wish the rest of it would fall into place!'

'It will.' His eyes gleamed. 'In the meantime I see

you've reverted to addressing me as Penry. This morning I was Dr Vaughan.'

'Mr Hyde, you mean,' she said tartly, twirling her fork round in the pasta. 'You were so horrible all of a sudden that formality seemed the order of the day.'

'I explained that.'

She flushed, her eyes falling. 'Let's forget all that—unless——'

'Unless what?'

'Unless you change back to Mr Hyde overnight and lump me in again with the rest of the female sex you're running away from.' The moment the words were out of her mouth Leonora could have kicked herself. His face took on the forbidding, sombre look which made her so uneasy.

'In actual fact I imagine it was myself I was trying to escape.' He shrugged violently, shaking off the thought as a dog shook water from its coat. 'But enough of that. I promise faithfully not to talk about it again. I'm normally quite an equable sort of guy, you know.'

She eyed him with scepticism. 'I'll take your word for it.'

'And when it comes to females I'd have a problem trying to escape them anyway,' he said, determinedly light. 'I've got far too many in my own family for starters. My father's no longer with us, unfortunately. He was a doctor too, a GP, and a damn good one. I miss him badly. But I still have my mother, three sisters, a sort of sister-in-law, and four nieces. Luckily the girls also managed to provide me with some nephews to balance it up a bit.'

Leonora sighed despondently. 'It's not fair! You're knee-deep in relatives, while I haven't a clue whether I possess any at all.'

'You'll soon find out.' Penry got up to take the trays. 'You look tired. *I'll* make coffee. I think I'll have some cheese to round the meal off. How about you? Would you like some cake, or a biscuit or something?'

'No, thanks. No room.'

'You should eat more. You could do with filling out a bit.'

'Ah, but would I fill out in the right places?' she said rashly, then bit her lip as Penry eyed the places in question with a deliberation which brought colour to her face. He went off to the kitchen, leaving Leonora apprehensive about the rest of the evening. To her surprise she enjoyed it very much, despite the fact that the only entertainment came from her host, who seemed bent on atoning for his earlier hostility by keeping her amused. Some of his anecdotes from his student days were hilariously funny, featuring enough females in them to convince his listener that he'd been the object of female adulation all his life until very recently.

This Melanie of his must have been a right madam, thought Leonora when Penry went off to get himself a glass of whisky. Penry Meredith Vaughan was a man of potent physical attraction, an attraction made doubly powerful by the formidable intellect behind it. He had to be brilliant, she thought, to be so well up in his profession at his age. His one big mistake seemed to have been his choice of wife.

'Would you like a soft drink?' he asked when he returned.

Leonora shook her head. 'I'll take a glass of water to bed later, but that's all.'

'An early night would do no harm. Not,' he added

swiftly at her frown, 'that I'm anxious for my own company, I assure you.'

'I only wish I had some anecdotes of my own to compete with yours.'

'I've probably bored you rigid!'

'Far from it—I could listen all night!' She hesitated. 'I'd like to stay down a little while—hear more about your family, too. At the moment it helps to console me for my lack in that direction.'

'All right—but not for long.' He slid down in the chair comfortably, his long legs stretched out in front of him. 'I saw my mother only last week. She stayed with me for a couple of days before going on to Spain to my sister. Charity runs a couple of hotels there with her husband Luiz Santana. Mother generally visits them in March before the season hots up so she can see something of Charity and spoil her grandchildren unmercifully.'

'Lovely,' said Leonora wistfully.

Penry's eyes softened as he went on to describe the rest of his family; Katharine, married to a merchant banker and mother of two teenage sons, and Clemency, Charity's twin, married to a writer and broadcaster and mother of twin girls and a son.

'Are your sisters identical twins?' asked Leonora.

'Unfortunately, yes.'

'Unfortunately?'

'You try walking down the street with two identical, sexy-looking blondes!' He pulled a face. 'Don't get me wrong—I'm very fond of them both, but I prefer them one at a time.'

'What about your other sister? Is she blonde too?'

Penry smiled warmly. 'No. Kit's the same colouring

as me. Not as tall as the other two, and a different personality altogether from the heavenly twins.'

'She's your favourite!'

'I suppose she is. The other two are a set, so to speak—a unit—so I suppose it's only natural I've always gravitated towards Kit.' He paused, eyeing her in the clinical way she'd come to recognise. 'You look very tired, Leonora. Enough chat for tonight. If it's fine tomorrow I'd like to be up to catch the tide. When you're in bed I'll bring up a hot drink.'

Leonora felt a deep reluctance to go upstairs, to face the night alone. She longed to stay where she was, listening to Penry talk in the resonant voice with the attractive trace of Welsh lilt, but she got up promptly, conscious that he probably wanted to get off to bed himself.

'Thank you. You're very kind.' She put the knitting away carefully. 'I feel I should say that if I had to get washed up on a beach minus my memory I was lucky the beach was yours, Dr Vaughan.'

His mouth tightened. 'Your luck was in surviving at all, Leonora. You escaped death by a hair's breadth.'

A shiver ran through her. 'Don't I know it! Instead of whining about my memory I should be thanking my lucky stars I'm alive at all.'

'And since you are, you'll feel a lot better if you get a good night's rest,' he said briskly. 'Don't hang about in the bathroom; it's cold up there.'

Leonora did as she was bidden, shivering as she brushed her teeth. A look in the mirror confirmed that the bruise round her eye was fading rapidly. If she could buy some make-up after the X-ray expedition the discolouration would be hardly noticeable—only she'd have to borrow some money from Penry, she realised, frowning. Which seemed like colossal cheek on top of everything else.

When Penry arrived with the promised drink he also brought a hot-water bottle.

Leonora received it with rapture. 'Wonderful,' she said, snuggling her feet against the warmth. 'It seems colder than last night.'

'It is. But it's not freezing. We rarely get frost here.' Penry stood over her while she drank the milk, then put a hand to the lamp, but she smiled at him coaxingly.

'Will the generator object if I keep it on? Sorry to be a coward, but I don't want to be left in the dark.'

'Not surprising, under the circumstances. And if the generator gives up the ghost in the night you've got a torch on the table, and a candle. Or you can holler for me. I won't mind.' Penry Vaughan smiled down at her, then yawned hugely. 'Sorry! Goodnight, Leonora. Sleep well.'

'Goodnight.' Her answering smile was thoughtful as she watched him duck gracefully through the doorway. With a sigh she slid down further into the blissfully warm bed, realising she was no longer in the least uneasy at the thought of Penry only feet away beyond the bedroom wall. Disturbingly attractive male though he might be, Dr Penry Vaughan was nevertheless a match for any peril which might threaten in the small hours.

The dream came again in the night. Once again Leonora found herself fighting with the tiller in a dinghy threatening to stand on its head in a mountainous sea, but this time when the engine cut out she was plucked from the boat before she could hit the water.

'All right, all right, Leonora,' said Penry, holding her close. 'It was only a dream. You're safe now.'

She clung to him convulsively, gasping as the wound on her temple struck his collar-bone. She pulled away a little, opening her eyes to find herself cradled on Penry's lap like a child.

'It was the same dream,' she said hoarsely. 'I'm sorry I woke you. What time is it?'

'Just after three.' He set her on her feet, then tidied the bed. 'In you get.'

She climbed into bed, leaning back against the pillows he'd stacked so expertly. 'Three in the morning,' she said sombrely, 'when life's at its lowest ebb.'

'Yours isn't,' he said sternly. 'Enough of the self-pity.'

She sniffed hard. 'Right. Sorry.' She tried to smile. 'Thank you.'

'Nothing to thank me for,' he said on his way to the door. 'I merely shut you up so I could get some sleep!'

She lay rigid and wide-eyed once he'd gone, afraid to sleep in case the nightmare returned, then to her relief Penry came back into the room.

'I thought you'd gone to bed!' Feeling unutterably guilty, she saw he'd brought her another drink and a fresh hot-water bottle. 'Coals of fire,' she said ruefully, as he slid the bottle in the bed.

'No, just a glass of hot milk—half a glass, actually, so we can have some breakfast.' He smiled. 'I wasn't expecting visitors. We'll buy more tomorrow.'

Leonora sipped the milk, frowning, then looked up at him. 'When I thanked you just now, by the way, it was because you got me out of the boat before I hit the water this time.' Her eyes held his. 'And I know the name of it, I think—or part of it. Do the letters SEREN mean anything? Part of *serenade*, perhaps?'

He shrugged, then sat down on the edge of the bed

and took her hand. 'I'll ask the coastguard and the police tomorrow before we set out. It's certainly a lead. Take heart, Leonora. It's another piece of the puzzle. Soon you'll have the complete picture.'

She nodded despondently. 'I suppose so.'

'In the meantime stop fretting yourself to fiddle-strings!' He leaned closer, his smile teasing, but as their eyes met the smile faded slowly.

Leonora lay hypnotised, unable to look away. She forgot her dream as she saw the blue eyes darken almost to black. She ran the tip of her tongue over her lips, heard the sharp hiss of Penry's intake of breath, then his head blotted out the light as his mouth met hers in a kiss which shot a jolt of electricity through every vein in her body.

She tore her mouth away, averting her burning face as Penry got unhurriedly to his feet.

'A mere kiss goodnight,' he said softly. 'It can't have been your first.'

Leonora forced herself to look at him. 'I—I don't know. I don't remember.' She blinked back tears fiercely. 'You may not believe me, but I honestly *don't* remember. Anything. Lord knows I wish I did. This blankness terrifies me!'

Penry sat down again on the edge of the bed. He put a hand under her chin to raise her face to his, so much the physician again that Leonora wondered if she'd dreamed the kiss. 'You will remember,' he said with emphasis. 'Sooner or later something will trigger off your memory and everything will come flooding back.'

CHAPTER FIVE

BUT when morning came, bright and clear with only a slight breeze, it arrived alone. Leonora woke up to find her mind as stubbornly blank as before.

'I feel much better otherwise,' she told Penry, trying hard to be cheerful. She held up her face. 'Look, my bruise is fading.'

'You'll soon be good as new,' he agreed. 'I've phoned in the news about the boat, by the way. There's no report of a missing dinghy, but I mentioned the name you saw in your dream and both police and coastguard promise to look into it.'

'They must think you've got a right lunatic on your hands,' she said, grimacing, then brightened. 'But at least I can go outside today. Can we explore the island when we get back? If you're not too busy, of course,' she added guiltily as she put on her jacket.

'We'll see how you feel.' Penry took the paper from her shoes, which felt stiff and hard as she slid her feet into them. He pulled on a bright yellow weatherproof jacket over his thick jersey and moleskin trousers, slid his long feet into rubber boots and collected some keys from the study. 'Right, then. Ready to face the great outdoors?'

Leonora emerged from the house into a bright spring day which belonged to a different world from the gales and rain of before. She held up her face to the pale sunshine, sniffing ecstatically at the salt air. As she followed Penry as quickly as she could she looked about her at the island with interest, curious to see what had lain behind a veil of sea mist and rain since her dramatic arrival. The house itself, she found, had been erected in a shallow depression in the mound surmounting the central part of the island.

'Old Joshua decided to use the site of an Iron-Age settlement when he built his new home,' said Penry, and pointed out an unhewn standing stone at the edge of the cliff. 'That was probably some cult object for the prehistoric island dwellers.'

'Creepy! Do you make offerings in front of it on Midsummer's Eve?' asked Leonora, impressed.

'Absolutely. We tie a maiden to the stone and dance round it by firelight!' He laughed, taking her hand to hurry her along. 'The maiden arrived a bit early, this year.'

'How do you know I qualify?' she said without thinking, then flushed as he halted in front of her, his eyes mocking and very definitely blue in the bright morning light.

'Informed guess. Now watch your step; the path gets a bit steep further down.'

She had no time to spare for embarrassment, due to shoes totally unsuitable for climbing down a cliff path. With Penry in front of her to see she didn't slip, their progress was slow down the steep path towards the strip of land which formed the waist of the figure-of-eight. She tugged on Penry's hand as the path levelled out.

'This must be the Neck. Show me where you found me, please.'

He looked at her searchingly, then stopped and led the way across the rabbit-nibbled turf to a point where she could look down on the inlet he called Seal Haven.

She stared down at water foaming round a row of rocks which looked horribly like jagged teeth in some monster's half-open mouth.

Penry pointed. 'See that small, needle-like rock at the mouth of the inlet? You were very lucky. You got caught on that. If you'd been tossed around in the eddies down there I wouldn't have given much for your chances.' He looked at her colourless face. 'Come on—we'll be late.'

Leonora felt very subdued as she followed him down to the relatively peaceful little beach of Lee Haven, where years before Joshua Probert had built a safe anchorage for his boats. The *Angharad*, a sturdy fishing-boat with a fair-sized cabin, had weathered the storm safely, well out of harm's way. Penry lifted her aboard, then untied the moorings and leapt on deck after her.

She eyed the distant shoreline with misgiving. 'Is it far?'

'You'll be there before you know it.' He smiled reassuringly as he started up the engine, which obliged first time. 'Good girl!' He patted the bulkhead affectionately, then gave all his attention to manoeuvring the *Angharad* out of Lee Haven and into the fast-flowing sound which separated Gullholm from the Welsh coast.

Leonora gripped a rail with white-knuckled hands when the boat bucked as it met the wilder waters of the sound. Teeth clenched, she held on like grim death, determined not to embarrass Penry Vaughan with a fit of hysterics just because she was in a boat again. Besides, she told herself firmly, this time the sea was merely a bit choppy. The wind was brisk, but it was only a wind, not a gale. And the sun was shining.

Bracing her feet against the *Angharad*'s deck, she fixed her eyes on the grey smudge of land in the distance, willing it to come nearer.

'Are you OK?' shouted Penry above the cabin noise.

'Fine,' she assured him loudly. She'd be even better, too, she thought prayerfully, once she was on dry land. But Penry was right. The trip was mercifully short. All at once the shore was suddenly very close indeed, the grey smudge resolving into green fields and a sandy beach with houses in a grey and white arc behind it. And then they were over the bar into a small, natural harbour and the deck steadied beneath her feet as Penry piloted the boat skilfully into a mooring where the *Angharad* would wait for their return. As a boy raced to take the ropes Penry flung out, Leonora began to breathe more easily again, her pulse-rate calming as she felt the usual shamed reaction to terror once safety was assured.

'You can let go now,' said Penry quietly.

Leonora flushed as he prised her stiff hands from the rail. 'Sorry. I was a bit tense.'

'You were very brave, my lovely.' He smiled down at her with warm approval. 'After your nightmares a boat trip must have been an ordeal.'

Her knees rattled together like castanets as he helped her down on to the jetty. 'I suppose it was like getting straight back on a horse after being thrown.' She breathed in deeply and smiled. 'I'll be fine on the trip back, I promise.'

'Good girl. Come on, then. We've a lot to do before then.'

Penry hurried her off to a row of garages on one side of the road leading from the beach into the village. As they walked along there were smiles on all sides as they passed. Dr Penry Vaughan, Leonora noted, was popular with everyone in Brides Haven.

Halfway along he unlocked a garage and let the door slide up to reveal a newish Range Rover. He lifted Leonora into the passenger-seat then leapt up to back the vehicle out into the narrow street, waving his thanks as a weather-beaten old man slammed the garage door shut with a wide smile before waving them on their way.

Brides Haven was small. The Range Rover left it behind quickly on a steep road which wound up in hairpin bends for a mile before levelling out on the road to Haverfordwest.

'I know how you felt in my boat,' said Penry, glancing sideways at her. 'How are you in a car?'

'Great,' said Leonora, relaxing. 'How far is it to St Mary's?'

'Sixty miles or so.'

'Goodness—that far!' She bit her lip. 'You'll be glad to see the back of me, Dr Vaughan.'

'Nonsense. If it's any consolation to you I needed to check up on a patient anyway. I'll kill two birds with one stone.'

'Not the happiest of metaphors for a man of healing!'

He laughed, then gestured at the surrounding farmland, which stretched away to the purple rise of the Preseli hills in the distance. 'Any of this ring a bell?'

'No.' She sighed. 'I was hoping Brides Haven would, I must confess, but it didn't. None of this looks remotely familiar. Have you got a comb, by the way?' she added. 'I feel a bit wind-blown—among other things.'

'If you reach over in the back you'll see a suede jacket. There might be a comb in the pocket.'

To Leonora's relief there was. She untied the shoe-lace and did what she could to tame the unruly curls, then took off her red scarf and used it to tie her hair back firmly at the nape of her neck. 'I don't want to disgrace you in front of the nuns.'

'I've already had a word with Sister Concepta. I gave her the bare outline of your problem, Leonora—it was necessary to explain why I wanted an X-ray in a hurry. There'll be a radiologist waiting for us.'

'Won't that cost a lot?'

'Don't worry about that,' he said dismissively, and focused his attention on the traffic of Haverfordwest as he skirted the town to make for the road to Carmarthen.

St Mary's was a modern, purpose-built nursing home erected in the grounds of an older house, once the property of a Member of Parliament in Gladstone's government. The nuns were kindness itself to Leonora. They fussed over her as though she were a sick child, then, once the X-rays were completed, returned her to Penry, who was chatting over coffee with Sister Concepta in her office.

'Take Leonora into the gardens for a stroll round in the sunshine while you wait for the results, Doctor,' advised the serene, smiling nun. 'She's a bit pale, poor child; she could do with some fresh air.'

Penry, who had changed his rubber boots and yellow waterproof for heavy shoes and suede jacket before entering the hospital, ushered Leonora outside, agree-ing with Sister Concepta that his charge looked a bit peaky.

'Are you all right, Leonora?' he asked as they strolled along the gravelled paths.

'Yes. I don't think I'm ever the rosy-cheeked type.'

She smiled cheerfully as they passed beds massed with daffodils. 'I can tell we're in Wales. Is there a kitchen garden full of leeks, too?'

He chuckled. 'Probably.'

'How was your patient?'

'I've sent her home. Her tests confirmed my diagnosis, so I prescribed some mild medication, a strict diet and bullied her into taking more exercise.'

'Will she do as you say?'

Penry smiled with supreme confidence. 'Of course. People always do as I say—in the end.'

The X-rays confirmed that Leonora's skull had come off surprisingly scot-free from her adventure.

'Not that I had any doubts on the score,' Penry assured her as they set off towards Haverfordwest. 'But I wanted confirmation.'

Leonora was silent, frowning at the passing countryside in deep preoccupation.

'What's bothering you now?' he asked.

'I'm trying to screw up enough courage to ask you a favour,' she muttered, flushing.

'Ask away.'

'Could I possibly borrow some money?' she asked, turing in her seat to look at him. 'I hate to ask, after all you've done, but there are one or two things I need.'

'How much do you want?'

'A few pounds?' she asked hopefully. 'Once I—I get back to normal I'll repay it immediately, I promise. And I won't spend more than I can help. I just want some shampoo and so on.'

'Of course, child. Buy what you want. We'll get some food, too.' He shook his finger at her. 'Was that so very hard to ask, Leonora? Am I such an ogre?'

'Today no,' she said bluntly. 'Yesterday very much so.'

'Let's draw a veil over yesterday,' he suggested. 'It won't happen again. And to make up for it I'll treat you to a slap-up lunch in Haverfordwest.'

Leonora stared at him in dismay. 'Not the way I look at the moment! I'd much rather go home, please.'

Penry made no answer for a moment as he edged past a cattle-truck on a straight stretch of road. After a while he gave her a sidelong glance under his enviable black lashes. 'Was that a slip of the tongue, Leonora? Do you really think of my island as home?'

She bit hard into her lower lip. 'For the moment I don't have much choice. It's the only home I know.' Tears trickled from the corners of her eyes, and she knuckled them away fiercely. 'Sorry to be so feeble.'

'Don't be. It's bound to get you down.' He put a large hand on her knee, then withdrew it swiftly as she cringed away. 'Hey!' He eyed her askance. 'I was trying to comfort you, not grope you, girl.'

Leonora flushed bright red. 'Sorry,' she muttered.

'You need food,' he said decisively, and began to slow down. 'There's a nice little pub along here. Very quiet; no one will stare at your black eye. Which isn't black now, anyway,' he added. 'It's barely noticeable.'

'I'm not hungry,' she said mutinously.

'Too bad—I am!'

Minutes later they were installed in the bar of the White Lion, where the dish of the day, to Leonora's astonishment, proved to be roast beef and Yorkshire pudding with vegetables from mine host's own garden.

'I thought it would be chips with everything,' she whispered.

'Oh ye of little faith! People come from miles around

for Myra's Yorkshire pudding—not to mention the gravy!'

The substantial lunch sent Leonora to sleep in the car on the next stage of the journey. When she came to with a start she found they were in the car park below the ruins of the castle in Haverfordwest.

'Come on, sleepyhead. Time to get out.' Penry took out his wallet and handed her some notes. 'There's your pocket-money. Where do you want to spend it?'

She rubbed her eyes, frowning when she saw how much he'd given her. 'I don't need all this.'

'You might. You can always give me change!'

Penry was tactful enough to leave her to her own devices once he'd directed her to a chemist. 'I'll be outside in twenty minutes. Will that do?'

Leonora darted into the shop, eager to utilise her time to the full. Determined not to hold Penry up, she made her purchases at such speed that she was outside, waiting, when he came striding down the narrow street to collect her. He walked head and shoulders above the crowd in every way, she thought, with such a sudden, overwhelming rush of pleasure at the sight of him that she was tongue-tied.

'We'll call at the supermarket en route,' he announced on the way back to the car. 'Did you bring a list?'

'Just basics—I wasn't sure what else you'd want.'

The Range Rover was crammed with so much food as they finally set off for Brides Haven that Leonora expressed doubt that the boat would carry it all.

'Nonsense. The *Angharad* can cope with a lot more than this! How do you think I get my oil to the island for the generator and the Aga?'

Leonora confessed she hadn't really given it much

thought, all her attention on the weather as Penry loaded the boat. The sun had disappeared behind swollen grey clouds which threatened a rougher crossing back to the island than the trip earlier on. She was right. But when they cast off Penry seemed reassuringly unconcerned, and sang under his breath as the *Angharad* headed for the turbulent stretch of sea separating Gullholm from the coast.

'OK?' he asked, as the *Angharad* bucked over the harbour bar into the open sea.

Her stiff lips tried to smile. 'Fine,' she gasped.

'Come here.' Penry reached out a long arm and drew her in front of him so that she stood in the shelter of his arms as he held the wheel. 'You're quite safe. The wind won't strengthen until after dark.'

Leonora, aware of Penry's warmth in every fibre, found the security of his arms an effective antidote for her fear as the *Angharad* butted her way across the choppy waters of the sound. By the time Gullholm was in full view she was sorry the crossing was over.

'There,' said Penry, putting her aside gently as he prepared to pilot the *Angharad* into her anchorage. 'That was pretty painless after all, wasn't it?' He killed the engine, then leapt out to secure the boat. He held up his arms to swing Leonora to the jetty. 'Can you manage to get up to the house under your own steam while I bring up the food?'

'Of course.' She became very busy with the packages he was stacking on the jetty. 'I can carry some myself as well. You don't know how grateful I am! Thank you for being so kind. I won't be frightened again.'

His lips twitched as he patted her cheek carelessly. 'My dear girl, it was no hardship to hold you in my arms for a while, I assure you!'

She flushed scarlet, hastily collected as much as she could carry and started off up the cliff path. 'Will I hold you up?' she called over her shoulder as Penry came behind her.

'A bit, but I'd rather you went first. I can catch you if you fall. Stop immediately if you feel giddy.'

'I won't!'

She toiled up the path with her packages, sheer will-power keeping her going until the four-square shape of the house came into view.

'I'm out of condition,' she panted, as Penry opened the door and pushed her inside the kitchen. 'You're not even breathing fast!'

'I'm used to it. Go and collapse on the sofa in there. I'll light the stove as soon as I've stowed everything away.'

Leonora nodded obediently, but the moment he'd gone she drew the kettle over the heat on the Aga before going upstairs with her little hoard of shopping. She hurried back down to put away the food already in the kitchen, and by the time Penry returned with the last couple of boxes she had a tea-tray waiting, complete with a plate of tempting cakes from the small bakery in Brides Haven.

'I thought I told you to rest,' he accused, dumping the boxes on the kitchen counter.

'I fancied some tea.'

'Right.' He stripped off his yellow waterproof. 'I'll take it in there, and you can drink it while you watch me light the stove. I cleared it out and relaid it this morning, fortunately. I thought you might be cold when we got back.'

'After that scramble up the cliff? You're joking!' She followed him into the other room and sat down on the sofa to pour out while Penry put a match to the kindling in the stove. One cup of tea and half a custard tart later it dawned on her that she felt a remarkable glow of well-being, for someone in her particular dilemma. She looked down on Penry's wind-blown dark head as he knelt in front of the stove to make sure the fire was established. 'Shall I pour a cup for you now?'

'Yes, please.' He got to his feet in one sinuous movement, stretching hugely, his arms above his head, before he sank down in the chair opposite. 'I hope you haven't eaten both those tarts.'

'No. I forced myself to leave one for you.'

He surveyed her at length as he demolished the cake. 'All in all you don't look too bad at all, Leonora, considering the exertions of the day. How's the head?'

'The stitches tweak now and then, but otherwise it's not aching much.' She smiled cheerfully. 'Basically I fancy I'm fairly tough.'

'You've got guts, I grant you that. You faced your ordeal pretty well today, young lady.'

She frowned thoughtfully as she refilled her cup. 'I was frightened, I admit. But only because of the dream. Somehow I don't think I'm nervous of boats and water normally. Otherwise,' she added, looking across at him, 'I would never have been in a boat alone, would I? Unless all that *was* just a dream, after all, and nothing to do with what really happened.'

'I think it happened, right enough.' His blue eyes held a hint of warning. 'It's quite possible you'll dream again tonight, Leonora.'

She shrugged. 'I know. But if that's what it takes to find out what happened—and who I am—I'll just have to put up with it every night until the last piece of the puzzle falls in place. I'm only sorry you have to put up with it too.' She smiled ruefully. 'You'll be thankful to see the back of me, one way and another.'

'Not at all—I'll lose my cook!'

'Ah, but you've only sampled my pasta. I can't make Yorkshire pudding like Myra's, you know.'

'We all have our crosses to bear,' he said piously. 'And because you were so brave today, Leonora, I bought you a present in Haverfordwest.'

She jumped up, frowning in dismay. 'But you can't give me presents as well. I'll never be out of your debt at this rate.'

'Hey—steady on.' He took her by the elbows, his frown mock-severe. 'I shall not only be deeply wounded if you spurn my offerings, I shan't know what to do with the things. All my womenfolk are at least six inches taller and a few sizes bigger than you.' He went off to the kitchen and returned with a carrier-bag. 'Nothing exciting—just a couple of things to make life easier, since you can't fly away home just yet, ladybird.'

The 'things' were a pair of rubber-soled navy canvas deck-shoes, a miniature version of Penry's rubber boots, and a strawberry-pink lambswool sweater. Leonora looked at the haul, wide-eyed, a lump in her throat.

'Well?' demanded Penry. 'Will they do?'

She cleared her throat noisily. 'Of course they will. Exactly what I need—except for the sweater, which was sheer extravagance!' She blinked hard. 'How will I ever repay you for all you've done for me?' On impulse she stood on tiptoe and kissed his cheek. 'Thank you very much indeed.'

Without warning Penry's arms shot out to pull her on tiptoe against his broad chest, returning the brief little caress with a kiss which left them both shaken when he finally set her square on her feet again.

'Do you require an apology?' he demanded roughly. 'I warned you this type of thing might arise from our particular situation, Miss Castaway.'

Leonora's chin went up. 'Please don't apologise. I'm to blame. I was stupid to kiss you first. I'll take care never to do it again. Now,' she added, deliberately matter-of-fact, 'what time do you want supper?'

'Later!' he snapped, his face like thunder. 'I've wasted too much bloody time today as it is. I need to put in a couple of hours' work before I can think of eating.' He flung away to his study, slamming the door behind him.

CHAPTER SIX

IT WAS almost eight that evening before Penry emerged from the study. Leonora eyed him warily as she switched off the transistor.

'Are you ready to eat now?'

He stared at her, sudden heat in his eyes for an instant before the shuttering lashes came down to hide it. 'What the blazes have you done to yourself?' he demanded.

Leonora glared back, incensed. Her motives unclear, even to herself, she'd taken enormous trouble with her face after her bath, disguising the bruise with a cover-up stick, accenting her eyes with a hint of shadow. She'd lavished the new moisturiser on her face, outlined her mouth with a muted pink lipstick, and for the finishing touch gathered her hair into a loose knot on top of her head with a length of black velvet purchased along with the cosmetics. And until now she'd been naïvely pleased with the result. Penry's derision acted like a red-hot needle, pricking the fragile balloon of her vanity.

'I thought it was time I began looking like a human being,' she snapped.

'Exactly like every other female, you mean!'

Leonora gave him a look of active dislike. 'Ah! Return of Heathcliff, I see.'

'You've got your casting wrong. Not Heathcliff. Pygmalion, perhaps, or Dr Frankenstein.'

Her eyes flashed angrily. 'And I'm the monster, I suppose!'

'Don't be childish.' He looked mortifyingly bored. 'Since you've gone to so much trouble I suppose I'd better change into something more in keeping with your splendour.'

'Don't be so damn patronising! I'm wearing jeans and a jumper and a spot of make-up—big deal!' She turned back to the salad, chopping herbs for the dressing as if she had Penry Vaughan's neck under the blade.

'You're angry. I'm sorry, Leonora.' He reached out to touch a hand to the elaborate topknot, but she dodged away, retreating in haste along the counter, her face flaming at the scathing glitter in his eyes.

'My dear young woman,' he drawled, 'must you shy away like a startled horse every time I get within yards of you? It's bad for my nerves—*and* unnecessary. I'm sorry I kissed you earlier, but I swear on the Bible I've no intention of ravishing you on the kitchen floor before supper—or any other time.'

She hugged her arms across her chest, hot all over. 'I know that! It's just that I—well, I don't seem to like being touched.'

'I'll remember that next time you start screaming in the night!'

Her chin lifted. 'That's different. Then you're just a doctor, not a man.'

'The two are not incompatible!' Penry eyed her flushed face with rancour for a moment, then shrugged. 'Come on—pax! Put the knife away, you're making me nervous.'

The rest of the evening passed without further reference to Leonora's attempt to gild the lily. After the meal she went on knitting the complicated sweater while Penry immersed himself in the newspapers he'd bought earlier in the day. At first there was an uneasy silence, but after a while he thawed enough to read odd items of news aloud to her. When he put down the papers at last he looked abstracted.

'I didn't expect anything in the nationals, of course,' he said, frowning, 'but I thought one of the local rags might have had something about a missing boat.'

'Or even a missing person. Would you stand up, please?' she added.

'Are you sure that's meant for me?' he asked, as she went on tiptoe to measure her knitting against his back.

'Don't you like it?'

'Yes. It's very striking, but not my usual sort of thing. I'm not convinced Mother intended it for me.'

'From the measurements she must have,' she assured him, as her needles resumed their swift, effortless rhythm. 'Surely no one else in your family is built to the same scale?'

'No,' he admitted. 'Something for which, I imagine, the girls are profoundly grateful. I'm a throw-back to old Josh Probert, according to my lady mother. Only *he* was six and a half feet in his socks, apparently, which tops me by an inch or two.'

'I pity his wife if she knitted much for him!'

Penry laughed as he went over to the stereo to put on a compact disc. 'They ran sheep here in those days, so I imagine she did, if only to keep him in socks.'

As the ethereal strains of Ravel stole through the room, Penry let himself down on the sofa, eyes closed. Leonora looked at him, unobserved, as she worked. His mood seemed to have lightened now, she noted with some relief, and pondered, frowning, over his unexpected reaction to what must certainly be her normal other-life guise.

Unaware of her scrutiny, Penry lay full length, guernsey and shoes discarded, his long, bare feet crossed at the ankles as they hung over the arm of the sofa. He was, thought Leonora with detachment, well worth looking at. His face, less hollowed and drawn already than her first impression of it, possessed a quality in repose she could only describe as beauty, of a very virile, masculine variety. Where the skin stretched taut along his cheekbones it held a faint flush of colour after the day out, the disfiguring bitterness in the blue eyes hidden for the moment behind closed, black-fringed lids. Leonora counted stitches for a moment, then let her eyes stray over Penry Vaughan's magnificent physique. He was all muscle and sinew, with no spare flesh as far as she could tell, the aura of strength very marked even in repose as he lay relaxed, his hands clasped behind his head, his face shuttered and dreaming as he listened to the music.

'You like Ravel?' he asked without opening his eyes.

Leonora applied herself to her knitting hastily. 'Not the piano music, nor the hackneyed old *Bolero*, but Ravel in this mood I find irresistible.'

'Know the piece?' he asked idly.

'*Daphnis and Chloe. . .*' She turned to find him watching her. 'Ah! There I go again.'

He smiled. 'So you do.'

'But why is my memory so selective?' she demanded, and thrust the knitting in its bag, suddenly tired of it.

'For the moment it's simply refusing to remember anything other than the pleasant things, Leonora.' He sat up, thrusting his feet into his shoes. 'Mind you, I'm a mere physician, not a psychiatrist——'

'You could never be a "mere" anything!'

'Ah, but you don't know me very well, Leonora.' His face set in harsh, familiar lines. 'I'm as subject to the frailties of human nature as the next man—or woman.'

She looked at him consideringly. 'It's hard to be believe. You seem like a man who gives frailties of any kind short shrift.'

'I said I was subject to them, not that I let them rule me!' He stood up, holding out his hand. 'Come on, young lady. Time for bed.'

Leonora contemplated argument, abandoned it, and, without taking the hand, got up and started for the stairs on leaden feet, full of foreboding about the night ahead.

'Don't worry, child,' he said kindly. 'If you dream, I'll come running, I promise.'

She gave him a melancholy little smile. 'At the risk of sounding ungrateful, I sincerely hope you won't have to.'

Penry stood at the foot of the stairs, looking up at her. 'Get some sleep. You look exhausted.'

'The constant battle to remember's a bit draining.'

'Then stop it. Make your mind a complete blank.'

'You mean more of a blank that it is!'

He frowned impatiently. 'Look, Leonora, trying to force yourself to remember will do a lot more harm than good. Things could be a hell of a sight worse for you, remember. You've got shelter, food, and although I'm not the easiest of companions at least you're not facing your problem alone.'

Leonora felt a sharp pang of remorse. 'I know, and I'm sorry to sound ungrateful. Goodnight.'

She prepared for bed in haste, then got into bed

without turning off the bedside lamp, willing the friendly glow to hold off the dreams which came with the night. It was something of an anticlimax to wake next morning to pale dawn light after a night of sleep unbroken by nightmares or dreams of any kind. Leonora sat up, rubbing her eyes as she switched off the lamp, so exhilarated to find she'd slept the night through that she was less cast down than expected to find her identity was still a mystery. Today, she decided, she would forget that she couldn't remember. Her body was healing rapidly. No doubt her mind would do the same if she stopped chivvying it. She snuggled back down under the covers, deciding it was too early to get up yet. If she kept quiet Penry might sleep longer, and wake in a better mood.

When Leonora surfaced next she found Penry, fully dressed, standing at the edge of the bed. She sat bolt upright, pushing her hair back from her face guiltily. 'Goodness, what time is it?'

'Only a little after eight.' He smiled. 'How did you sleep, Leonora? If you had any nightmares there was no soundtrack last night.'

She smiled radiantly. 'There weren't any! Just wonderful, wonderful sleep—twice, too! I woke earlier on, but I thought I'd disturb you if I got up so I had another nap.'

'You look very much better.' He took her wrist between impersonal fingers and consulted his watch. 'Good. Pulse normal.' He bent slightly to examine her face. 'The swelling's down, and the bruise almost gone, but I'd better change the dressing on your wound after you come downstairs.'

'Right. I'll only be a few minutes, then I'll cook you some breakfast,' she said briskly.

Penry smiled faintly as he made for the door. 'When you finally go back to wherever you belong, Leonora, what shall I do without you?'

She looked sceptical. 'Enjoy the solitude you came here for, I imagine. And in any case,' she added, 'if you are lonely I'm sure there must be any number of—of people you can ask here to keep you company.'

'You mean women,' he said swiftly, his eyes icing over. 'For the past three years I've been a respectable married man, young lady. I never had enough time to spare for my wife, let alone other women—even if I'd been so inclined, which I was not.'

'Oh, come on! In your position you must know a gorgeous nurse or two, or a pretty lady medico, Dr Vaughan.'

His black brows flew together forbiddingly. 'If I do,' he said cuttingly, 'that's my business.'

As he ducked through the door Leonora stared at him in astonishment, then stuck out her tongue irreverently as she slid out of bed, refusing to let Penry's snub spoil her new well-being. She washed hurriedly, then pulled on her old jeans and jersey and tied her hair back with the shoelace. If Dr Penry Vaughan preferred scruffy, she thought resentfully, scruffy was what he'd get. When she went downstairs Penry was feeding wood into the stove in the living-room. She went past him without speaking on her way to the kitchen, and soon had breakfast under way. She began frying bacon and eggs, then filled the kettle and sliced bread for toast. She put cutlery and napkins on two trays, then went to the door.

'It's nearly ready.'

He got up, dusting off his hands. 'Thank you. It smells marvellous. Have I time to wash?'

Leonora nodded silently then returned to her labours. While Penry went upstairs she took his tray into the study, then went into the other room with her own. When he reappeared she gestured through the open door. 'Yours is on your desk.'

Penry stood at the foot of the stairs, frowning as she plugged in the transistor to listen to Radio Four while she ate. 'Are diplomatic relations severed?' he enquired drily.

Leonora buttered toast with a steady hand. 'I don't know how much longer you'll be forced to put up with me, but until the happy day I can bid you farewell I'll try to keep out of your hair as much as I can. To be honest,' she added, 'I find your swings of mood rather a pain. Just when I think you're the kindest man in the world you suddenly get the glooms again. Since I'm obviously the cause of them I'll do my best to keep out of your way.'

Penry looked as though he was about to burst into speech for a moment, then his face set in the familiar harsh lines, and without another word he turned on his heel and made for his sanctum, slamming the door behind him.

Leonora lost interest in her breakfast. Penry's displeasure gave her a sudden, desperate longing to get back to wherever—and more importantly whoever—she belonged. Swallowing her tears, she went back to the kitchen to clear up. She knocked on the study door and put her head round it.

'May I take the tray?'

Penry looked up. 'I'll look at your forehead first.'

Leonora sat in the kitchen chair alongside the desk while Penry removed the old dressing. She sat very still, eyes closed, as he examined the wound, willing herself to remain immune to his nearness, to think of him only as a doctor.

'There,' he said at last, standing back. 'That should do now until I take out the stitches.'

Leonora got up. 'Thank you. How long will that be?'

'A day or two.' He picked up the tray and followed her from the room. 'I'm sorry, Leonora. You happened to hit on a sore subject.'

'As you said, it's none of my business,' she said flatly, and began washing up, her back to him.

'Unlike you I couldn't sleep. Which is an explanation for my bloody-mindedness, I know, but no excuse.' He leaned against the counter, eyeing her withdrawn face. 'Being a Celt, I'm prone to moods. A broken marriage hasn't done much to lighten them, either.'

She maintained a stony silence until she'd finished, then turned briskly. 'Right. Since it's such a lovely day I think I'll go exploring.'

'Not on your own!' he said quickly.

Leonora thrust out a foot clad in one of the new rubber-soled shoes he'd bought her. 'I'll be fine in these. I'll keep to the paths, I promise. I shan't climb down cliffs, or do anything stupid.' Her eyes flashed. 'I may be missing in the memory department, but I do have a brain. Of sorts.'

He eyed the small foot, unimpressed. 'Brain or no brain, I'd rather you didn't go out alone, at least not the first time, please.'

Their eyes clashed for a moment, then Leonora shrugged. 'Oh, very well. Will the generator expire if I use the vacuum cleaner, then?'

'There's no need——'

'I must do something, or I'll go mad!'

Grudgingly Penry agreed to a little housework, after

which, he said firmly, she must rest. Leonora set to with a will. An hour later every room was spick and span except for the bedroom Penry was using. A large suitcase lay on the bed, still full of the clothes he'd taken from the other room. Leonora took out sweaters and shirts and underwear, putting them away with a vague feeling of trespass which failed to keep her from peeping into a folding leather picture frame lying at the bottom of the suitcase.

One half was crammed with snapshots of various adults and children, presumably all members of the Vaughan clan. But it was the single large photograph in the other half of the frame that caught Leonora's attention. Melanie was dark and very lovely, with an aura of warmth and tenderness which filled Leonora with unexpected dismay. But then, Leonora reminded herself sternly, what little she knew was Penry Vaughan's side of the story. Melanie might have a different tale to tell.

Suddenly Leonora felt restless, penned in. She leaned on the wide sill, looking out with longing at the part of Gullholm visible from the window. A path wound away from the house, leading through the ridges and furrows of fields long left to nature. There wasn't a tree in sight, but nearer the cliff edge she could make out carpets of thrift and sea-campion, and yearned to explore.

She turned away, frustrated, and went downstairs to make lunch. After handing over a tray to the absorbed, absent man behind the desk, Leonora ate her own sandwich at the kitchen counter, staring mutinously at the sunshine pouring through the window. The booming surf far below called to her like the beat of a jungle drum. With sudden resolve she began to prepare a beef goulash for dinner. When it was simmering slowly in the Aga she went into Penry, who was searching distractedly through piles of medical tomes.

'If you don't need anything else,' she said distinctly, 'I thought I might take the transistor up to my room for company and have a rest on my bed.'

'Sensible girl. I'm fine—run along.' He plunged back into his work, forgetting about her before she was through the door.

Leonora hurried upstairs gleefully, inserted a new set of batteries in the transistor, turned up the volume and left her bedroom door open a crack. She collected her jacket then crept downstairs on noiseless, rubber-soled feet, taking extra care as she skirted the study on her way out. Exulting in her escape, she closed the outer door behind her and made for the great outdoors like a child let out of school.

Leonora restricted herself to the main tableland of the island, knowing perfectly well that Penry had her safety in mind in his veto of exploration on her own. She kept well away from the edge of the cliffs, perfectly happy to stay in the fields which displayed such fascinating evidence of Iron Age occupation. Excited to find she could just make out traces of narrow fields with dividing banks and walls, she ventured further towards a rounded mound which could well have been an Iron Age barrow, and just beyond it she found the standing stone, where she shivered pleasurably, her imagination running riot about the monolith's precise function in the days when the settlement had been a live, thriving community.

Leonora turned her back on the past, bracing herself against the wind as she walked briskly towards the spot where the cliff path began its decent to Seal Haven.

Shading her eyes with a hand against the bright sunlight, she paused to watch the acrobatics of a troupe of black-backed screaming gulls, but the wind blew suddenly colder, tearing at her hair. Reluctantly she made her way back to the house, then gave a gasp of dismay as Penry erupted from it like a rocket. He tore towards her, menace in every line of him as he caught up with her and grabbed her by the shoulders, his eyes blazing.

'What the hell do you think you're doing?' he shouted.

'I came out for a walk,' she said, shrugging off his hands. 'I'm coming back now.'

'You bet your life you are!' He glared at her as he dragged her along by the hand at top speed. 'When I went up to your room I found Goldilocks wasn't sleeping in my bed after all. The transistor was a nice touch! Planned your escape well, didn't you?'

'Let me go,' she said breathlessly, trying to break free. 'I can't—run as—fast as—you.'

Penry slowed down, his eyes on her face. 'Are you giddy?' he demanded.

'No. Not that it's any thanks to you!'

'Sorry.' Penry ushered her into the kitchen, unzipping her jacket as though she were a child. He lifted her up and perched her on one of the kitchen stools, then filled the kettle. 'Stay there,' he ordered. 'I'll make you some tea.'

Leonora kept her temper with difficulty, feeling ridiculous with her legs dangling from the high stool. 'Dr Vaughan, I crept from the house like a thief to avoid the very fuss you're making right now. I am perfectly all *right*! A gentle stroll in the spring sunshine is hardly a capital offence.' As a blast of hail hit the window she shrugged. 'It was sunny when I went out.'

Penry handed her a mug of tea. 'I know.' He thrust a hand through his hair. 'Sorry I blew my top, but I had visions of finding you down there on the rocks like the first time.'

'I wasn't anywhere near the edge!'

'How was I to know that? I imagined you getting vertigo, even falling!'

'I never dreamed you'd look in my room,' she muttered.

'My sole reason for invading your maiden privacy,' he said with sarcasm, 'was because I'd heard from the police. I assumed you'd want to know that wreckage of a dinghy was washed up a few miles north of here on the Welsh coast last night. There was enough of it to identify her as the *Seren*—or "star" to you barbarians across Offa's Dyke.'

CHAPTER SEVEN

THE police had traced the dinghy to Londoners who owned a weekend cottage a few miles away up the Welsh coast. Because several locals had permission to borrow the boat for a spot of fishing, its absence had gone unremarked.

Penry took Leonora by the shoulders. 'Does any of it ring a bell? Could you be one of the owners of this cottage they're talking about?'

She shook her head wildly. 'I don't know, I don't know.' Tears of frustration and disappointment welled up in her eyes. 'I wish I did. I just want to go home, wherever it is.'

Penry put his arms around her very carefully. When she leaned against him without flinching away he stroked her hair as she buried her face against his chest, and at the delicate caress she sobbed into the thick navy wool without inhibition. It was a long time before she drew away, knuckling the tears away from her reddened eyes.

'Hey—come on,' he said softly, and smiled at her as he reached over to tear off a sheet of kitchen-towel.

Leonora mopped herself up drearily. 'Sorry. Only I was happy out there for a while. For a few minutes I was free of this terrible worry about who I am, about my family. I can't stop thinking about them. They must be going out of their minds with worry.' She blew her nose forcibly. 'Not only that, you could be sheltering a criminal of some kind. What was I doing with someone else's boat, for a start?'

'Stop worrying—that's an order!' He patted her good cheek lightly. 'Now, off you go. Have your bath. By the wonderful smell I assume dinner is already under way, so just tell me what else you intend us to eat and I'll see to it.'

'No, I'll do it,' she insisted, and slithered down off the stool. She bent to transfer the casserole from the oven to the top of the Aga, too depressed to note the lack of protest from her head.

Penry sniffed appreciatively. 'Frankly, if you can cook like this I don't care if you're the greatest lady criminal of all time.'

She gave him a wry smile as she added seasoning to the pot. 'It obviously takes food to keep you in a good mood, Dr Vaughan.'

'I'm sorry if I was a bear this morning. I haven't had much chance to run in the mornings since you arrived. Makes me introspective about certain things missing from my life these days.'

Leonora frowned. 'You mean women, and—and so on? I find it hard to believe that an attractive man like you lacks feminine company.'

'Why, thank you, Madame X.' He gave her a mocking bow. 'And of course your former remarks about lady doctors were quite right. I know several. The trouble was that Melanie believed I was in bed with one of them every time I was half an hour late.'

'Were you?'

'No, I damn well wasn't! I'm a consultant,' he added. 'Part of my function is to supervise and instruct those junior to me, male *or* female. After a hard day it wasn't unusual to gather for coffee with a bunch of registrars of both sexes, and sometimes I was late home.' His mouth tightened. 'Melanie refused to believe the truth. I wish now her suspicions had been correct. I might as well have had the game as well as the name.'

Leonora restored the pot to the oven and straightened. 'There. I'll leave the rest until after my bath.' She eyed him diffidently. 'I tidied the bedrooms today. When I did yours I couldn't help looking at the photographs in the leather frame.'

'My rogues' gallery! Handsome lot on the whole, we Vaughans, don't you think?' he said smugly.

'Very.' Leonora felt a sudden pang to learn he still thought of the fair Melanie as a Vaughan. 'Your wife—your ex-wife, I mean, is very lovely.'

Penry frowned. 'How do you know?'

'Isn't she the dark lady in the studio portrait?'

His face cleared. 'No, that's Kit, my sister—taken years ago when she got engaged. She's been Mrs Reid Livesey for a fair time now. The demon sailing duo opposite her are Rick and Harry, her sons.'

Leonora went off for her bath, feeling oddly pleased by this information, but otherwise very depressed. The news of the *Seren* had ignited a bright flame of hope which left her cold and utterly despondent when it shed no light at all on the mystery of her identity. To warm herself up she lay in hot water up to her chin, her hair tied up on top of her head, consoling herself with the fact that physically she was almost back to normal. She could, she told herself stringently, be a lot worse off.

After dinner Leonora returned to her knitting, glad of its soothing monotony, when Penry began musing about her background.

'I wonder what you do for a living?' he asked

thoughtfully. 'Maybe you haven't started working yet—you could be a student.'

She shook her head. 'I'm sure I'm not, somehow.'

'Well, don't fret about it.'

Leonora, doing her best to obey, changed the subject firmly. 'What do *you* do?' she asked. 'Apart from treating patients, I mean. Do you play golf?'

He sat back in his chair, staring into his glass. 'No. When I was young rugby was the love of my life, but these days I just manage a game of squash now and then. Lately these blasted articles have taken up all my spare time. I've just got to get them out of the way before I get back to work.'

'Where are you based?'

'In a hospital which serves a large area of Wales. I also have a fairly flourishing private practice.' He raised his eyebrows. 'You look surprised.'

She nodded. 'Only about the location. Somehow I just took it for granted you worked in London.'

'I did until last year. I'd spent all my post-Oxford life in London hospitals. I decided it was time for a change.'

'To get away from painful memories?'

He smiled mirthlessly. 'What a romantic you are! Actually it was the change of job which finally decided Melanie to divorce me. She was appalled at the idea of living in the "wilds", as she put it. To expect her to bury herself in the back of beyond, away from all her friends with just Penry Vaughan for company, constituted adequate grounds for divorce in her view.'

'How on earth did you come to marry her?' asked Leonora before she could stop herself, then pulled a face. 'Sorry!'

'Don't be. Lord knows it's a question I've asked

myself often enough. Melanie's beautiful, wilful, and she's been spoiled rotten all her life.' He smiled wryly. 'I was a challenge to her. When I was a young houseman I—well, enjoyed a hectic love-life. Lord knows how I managed it. A working week of over a hundred hours should have been ruinous for the libido, looking back. But I was young, then. And I came in contact with a lot of pretty nurscs. Mclanie already knew I was popular with the fair sex, but when she discovered I was tipped for the top in my career as well she decided it might be a good idea to marry me.'

'Yet after all that she wanted a divorce. Did you agree to it?'

'Gladly. By that stage I was as keen on it as she was. What I wasn't prepared for was my reaction to her rejection. My ego suffered. To be honest I'm still smarting from the various wounds she inflicted. But there'd been precious little joy in our marriage for some time. Besides,' he added grimly, 'by then Melanie had found husband number two. Pots of money and willing at first to squire her to the latest "in" restaurants and nightspots, charity balls, Henley, Ascot, the whole shebang.' He jumped up, looking restless. 'Right. Enough soul-baring for tonight, Leonora. Time you went to bed.'

To Leonora's relief there was no nightmare that night, nor in the nights that followed. Life on Gullholm settled into an uneasy, hard-won routine. After Leonora's stitches were removed, painlessly, to her relief, Penry pronounced her well enough to help with his articles, since typing proved to be another of her accomplishments. Her help proved less of a boon than expected. Once the work was finished, much sooner than he'd ever dared hope, Penry was left without occupation. While the weather was fine he worked off his surplus energies by a twice-daily run, sandwiching an outing of exploration with Leonora in between. But when the gales returned and rain swept the island, penning them both indoors, Penry's mood worsened, darkening, it seemed to Leonora, like the weather. His restlessness permeated the entire house, and she felt guilty, certain that her presence was tying him to Gullholm, that if it weren't for her he would go home, or visit one or other of his sisters or his mother, all of whom made regular telephone calls.

'Do they know about me?' asked Leonora, after a day of sheeting rain.

'No,' said Penry shortly.

'Why not?'

'If they knew they'd never leave me in peace. One or the other of them would insist on having you to stay. But in my opinion the best way to recover your memory is to stay close to the place where you lost it.'

She stared at him, resentment flaring suddenly. 'And you, of course, Dr Vaughan, are never wrong!'

Suddenly the atmosphere in the comfortable room thickened with hostility.

'Of course I can be wrong,' said Penry, a pulse throbbing at the corner of his mouth. 'And the moment I feel you need proper psychiatric help I shall enlist it for you, believe me. But for the time being I happen to think it best to wait a little, in the hope that something triggers your memory into returning of its own accord.' He looked at his watch. 'It's time you went to bed.'

'I suppose I might as well,' she said bitterly. 'Goodness knows you're not much company. In fact you've been downright unbearable ever since we finished your articles for the journal.' She stabbed her needles through her knitting, and stuffed it into its bag. 'May I have some more batteries for the transistor, please?'

'I'd rather you tried to get to sleep,' he said dismissively.

She jumped to her feet and stood over him, her eyes flashing. 'And of course I must obey your slightest wish as if you were God. I'd heard that consultants suffered from delusions about their own deity—you're the living proof of it.'

Penry got to his feet very slowly, standing over her in a way which made Leonora long to back away, but she stood her ground, refusing to let him intimidate her.

'What's the matter with you these days?' she damanded. 'Is it me? Are you regretting that you ever brought me back to life, Pygmalion? Would you rather Galatea had remained a cold block of marble after all?'

'What a lot of questions,' he said coldly, and put her out of his path rather less gently than he intended.

Leonora jumped away, rubbing her forearms resentfully. 'All right, I'm going—no need to use force.'

Penry closed his eyes tightly as though praying for patience. When he opened them again they fastened on hers, blue and cold as tempered steel. 'If you must know, Leonora, I am irritable these days for a very simple reason.'

'You mean you're itching to be rid of me so you can get off this island!'

'Not quite. Something more basic than that.'

She frowned. 'What do you mean?'

'To put it in words of one syllable,' he said, each word encased in ice, 'we are a man and a woman shut up together alone in a house, separated from all other humans by a stretch of Atlantic. Ah,' he added as she backed away. 'Comprehension at last.'

'I'd better go to bed,' said Leonora hastily, moving further away, but he held up his hand.

'Not yet. You started this. You can stay to hear me out.'

She stayed where she was. Penry Vaughan in this mood looked too dangerous to cross.

'Sensible girl,' he said silkily. 'To proceed with the lecture, I'm aware that my somewhat variable moods disturb you. But surely you're not so naïve that you can't understand that for any normal man to be in close contact with a girl for days on end without wanting her is damned impossible?' His eyes lit with a gleam which frightened her badly. 'And this man, Leonora, has been celibate for a long time. Not from choice, you understand, but because Melanie withdrew her favours as a punishment when I wouldn't relent about the move to Wales. Bloody fool that I am, my pride wouldn't let me accept other consolation, even when offered, neither before the divorce, nor since.'

Leonora gazed at him in silence, her heart beating against the blue chambray shirt like a tom-tom.

'Don't be nervous,' he said lightly. 'I've no taste for rape. And I assume that's what it would amount to, since you flinch at the slightest touch of my hand.' Abruptly his face set in bitter, angry lines. 'Oh, go to bed, child. You're in no danger. If it makes you feel better I'll sleep down here tonight.'

It was an effort for Leonora to wish him goodnight, an even greater effort to walk upstairs slowly, instead of running headlong to her room, where she lay sleepless for hours, unable to get Penry Vaughan's handsome, cynical face out of her mind.

She slept at last, but in the small hours the nightmare returned. This time it spared her nothing. She relived the agony of trying to control the boat, the moment of horror when the engine cut out, the desperate struggle to keep the dinghy from capsizing, and the ultimate horror as a giant wave swept her into the sea. For a while she managed to swim, but eventually she grew tired and her mouth filled with water, and she sank choking beneath the waves. . .

CHAPTER EIGHT

'ALL right, all *right*, Leonora, I've got you.'

She opened desperate eyes on Penry's face and collapsed against his bare chest in relief, shuddering. 'I was drowning,' she gasped. 'I was drowning.'

He held her tightly as violent tremors ran through her slender body. 'It was only a dream, child. It's all over. You're safe.'

Leonora clutched at him, terrified he'd leave her. As she quietened Penry heaved himself upright against the head of the bed, taking her with him as he pulled the bright quilt up over her shoulders. She clung to him as he smoothed her hair in wordless comfort, reassured by the sheer size and solidity of him, but at last Penry stirred, and she panicked.

'Don't go!'

'I'm going to tuck you in, then go downstairs and make you a hot drink.'

Leonora scrambled inelegantly to the floor, barring his way. 'I'll come with you. I don't want to be alone.'

Penry slid to his feet, the hollows and planes of his face in sharp relief in the shadows above the lamplight. 'You'll get cold.'

'Then stay with me. I don't want a drink.'

He frowned, then swiftly remade the bed, shaking up the pillows. 'In you get.'

'Bathroom first,' she muttered.

'Right. While you're in the bathroom I insist on making that drink. Two drinks. Then I'll come back with them and stay with you until you fall asleep. Agreed?'

Leonora nodded, eyeing the dark hall nervously. 'Will you put the light on for me, please?'

'Afraid of the dark?' he said gently, as he shepherded her to the door.

'Right now I'm afraid of everything.'

'Not me included, I hope!'

Leonora gave him a wavering smile as he switched on the hall light. 'No, not you. There's a black, uncharted place at the back of my mind labelled "here be dragons". You're my only defence against them, Dr Vaughan!'

'Fanciful child!' His smile was wry as he turned away. 'Go on, get a move on. I want you tucked up in bed, stat.'

Leonora flew to do his bidding, feeling better once she was back in bed, her face sponged and the tangles brushed from her hair. When Penry returned he smiled in approval to find her propped tidily against the pillows, covers drawn up to her chin.

'Good girl.' He smiled as he poured hot chocolate from a vacuum flask for her, then drew a chair up near the bed. 'Now then, Leonora. I know it's harrowing for you, but think hard. Was there anything different in the dream this time? Some other clue we can go on?'

Leonora forced herself to go back over the dream sequence in every terrifying detail. 'It went on longer, that's all. This time I—I began to drown.'

'Since we know perfectly well you didn't, let's forget that bit,' he said crisply. 'Now think. Did you see the name of the dinghy again?'

Leonora nodded. 'Yes. I did. And I had to struggle to start the engine. It took several pulls of the cord before it caught. There was a strong smell of fuel, and the water was like ice round my feet as I pushed the boat out before jumping in. . .' She stared at him, breathing faster. 'Penry! That part wasn't in the dream.'

He leapt up to take the mug from her shaking hand. 'All right, my lovely. Gently now.' He sat on the bed and slid his arm round her shoulders.

She twisted round to look up at him. 'I was actually *remembering* the first part! Clearly, too. But from then on it's all mixed up. I can't tell where the real bits and the dream overlap.'

Penry's arms tightened. 'Don't worry about it. It's probably an indication that your memory's about to return.'

Leonora tried to smile back, shocked to find herself suddenly unsure about wanting her memory to return. Gullholm had been her entire world for almost a fortnight, except for the trip to the nursing home. Suddenly she was deeply afraid of what awaited her in the other world beyond it.

Penry put a finger under her chin to raise her face to his. 'What is it?' he asked softly. 'Got cold feet about meeting yourself face to face?'

She nodded dumbly. As their eyes held Penry's changed, narrowing to a sudden glitter between his lashes.

'I'd better go,' he said huskily, and removed his arm, but Leonora shook her head violently, catching his hand.

'Don't leave me. Please!'

'Leonora, stop that! You know I can't stay.'

She took her hand away, turning her back to him. 'Go, then.' She buried her face against the pillows, biting hard into her lower lip to keep from begging. At the touch of his hand on her hair she twisted round, her eyes alight with hope, and Penry breathed in deeply, his face set.

'All right,' he said grimly. 'You win!' He threw himself down in the chair, like a man beset by demons. 'Now for pity's sake go to sleep.'

Leonora turned to face him. 'I'm afraid to go to sleep. Couldn't we just talk?'

'No, we could not,' he snapped, and drew his chair nearer the lamp. Ignoring her, he looked through a small pile of paperbacks on the bedside table then settled down with the latest Ken Follett.

'You'll get cold sitting there,' ventured Leonora.

'That's the least of my problems!'

Afraid to be alone, Leonora nevertheless found it impossible to sleep with the large figure of Penry Vaughan beside her bed. She lay watching his face as he tried to concentrate on the complexities of the novel. It was no hardship to look at him, she thought dreamily. This Melanie of his had to be a complete idiot to prefer someone else.

'If you keep looking at me,' said Penry, without raising his eyes from the page, 'I shall go back to my room.'

'Sorry.' Leonora turned on her back and stared at the ceiling. The wind was rising again, mocking the arrival of spring as it lashed rain against the windows. 'You must be tired. I'll be fine on my own now.'

Penry shot to his feet with unflattering alacrity. He stood at the edge of the bed, looking down at her. 'Are you sure, Leonora?'

'Quite sure.' She smiled up at him valiantly, the smile fading as his eyes began to darken in a way she recognised. Afraid to move, even to breathe, she stared, mesmerised, as Pentry leaned down slowly until his lips met her cheek. Leonora tensed, colour rushing to the spot he kissed. Her mouth turned blindly to meet his, and Penry's breath caught in his throat, his arms closing round her like steel bands. She reached up to lock her hands behind his neck, her mouth parting beneath his. As Penry's breathing quickened she pushed herself closer without shame, desperate to keep him with her, fired with triumph at getting her own way rather than with sexual response when he laid her flat on the bed. He let himself down beside her and took her in his arms, and Leonora yielded to him without a qualm. If letting him make love to her was the price for keeping him with her all night she would pay it gladly. Not that Penry Vaughan's lovemaking was a hardship. For a while she even forgot why she was letting him make love to her in her surprise at the pleasure of it.

But inevitably the quality of kisses changed, his hands became urgent, and she tensed as with sudden impatience he pulled her nightshirt over her head. The moment his body covered hers she felt a great tide of revulsion and panic surge upwards until it threatened to choke her, and she threshed her head from side to side in blind, unreasoning panic, thrusting him away with frantic hands. Penry shot upright and Leonora slid from beneath him, scrambling from the bed towards the door. Hands at her mouth, she bolted to the bathroom, slamming the door behind her to shut out the sounds of her vomiting as her stomach relieved itself of its contents with such violence that she was left retching drily long afterwards until the spasms died away.

She dragged herself to her feet as Penry came into the room, wearing a dressing-gown. His face set grimly, he wrapped her in a warm, dry bathsheet, then sat her on a stool and sponged her face, smoothing the tangled curls from her pallid face.

'Did my lovemaking revolt you so much, then?' he demanded roughly at last.

She shook her head, her teeth chattering. 'No. I'm sorry. It wasn't my intention to—to tease.' She shut her eyes tightly, a dry sob catching in her throat.

Penry bent to hold her wrist between his fingers, his mouth tightening as he took her pulse. 'Don't say any more for a moment. Back to bed for you, young lady.' He swung her up in his arms, tense for a moment before she burrowed her face into his neck like a tired child.

Back in the bedroom, he handed her the discarded nightshirt, his face carefully blank as Leonora scrambled into it, so unsteady on her feet that it was a relief to get back beneath the covers.

Penry's face wore a forbidding look as he propped the pillows behind her. 'Will you be all right now?'

'No! Don't leave me alone,' she said hoarsely.

He raised an eyebrow. 'I thought you'd want me to get out of your sight—and stay out.'

She shook her head violently. 'No, no! That's the last thing I want.'

His eyes searched her face, impersonal and assessing now, the man replaced by the physician. 'You've regained your memory, I assume.'

She shuddered. 'Yes. Totally.'

His mouth took on a sardonic twist. 'I've had varying success with the women I've made love to in the past, but I've never made one throw up before!'

'*You* didn't make me sick, Penry! You see, when you——' She halted, swallowing hard, then started again. 'When we came together like that, at the last, it all came back, complete in every nauseating detail.' She tried to smile. 'Perhaps you could write an article on it—new shock treatment for amnesia.'

Penry took her hand in his and squeezed it. 'A fascinating thought! But before you tell me about it, frankly I'm in need of a stiff drink. How about you?'

'Just a glass of mineral water, please.' She eyed him remorsefully. 'I'm desperately sorry, Penry.'

'I'll survive. Shan't be long.'

Left alone, Leonora found her newly restored memory an unwelcome bedfellow. Clenching her teeth in disgust, she burrowed her face into the pillow to shut it out until Penry returned.

'Right,' he said as he settled himself in the chair. 'Get it off your chest. I'm sitting comfortably, so begin.'

Leonora sipped some water to easy her dry throat, at a loss to know how to start.

Penry leaned forward. 'Look, if you don't want to tell me who you are, or what gave you the horrors, then don't. My role in life is to alleviate pain, not cause it.'

'I *want* to tell you. It's just that I wish I'd got my wretched memory back some other way.' She flushed painfully.

'Frankly, so do I!' Penry shrugged, then swallowed some of his whisky. 'But this is the point where you stop thinking of me as a frustrated lover, or even as just a man. For the moment I'm a doctor, one you can talk to in complete confidence. So relax, Leonora. By the way, before you get to the bad part, was I right about your name?'

'Yes. I'm Leonora right enough, just as you worked out,' she said, feeling rather better. 'The brooch gave us the right clue—in fact it gave us two. My other name is Fox. I live in a town called Chastlecombe, where I create expensive hand-knitted sweaters to sell to tourists. No wonder I can cope with the pattern which beat your mother. It's the way I earn my bread and butter.'

'And is Leonora Miss or Mrs Fox?' asked Penry quietly.

She smiled shyly. 'Miss Fox, Dr Vaughan.'

'And are you attached in any way?'

Leonora turned away, a shadow crossing her face. 'I thought I was. Which turned out to be a rather spectacular mistake. It's a silly story, really.'

Leonora Fox was the youngest of three children born rather late to parents who had died when their last-born was still a child. Left in the care of Jonathan and Elise——

'Your father *was* a Beethoven fan!' interrupted Penry.

'Not my father, my mother. First-born Fox sons are always named Jonathan, but my mother, who was quite a gifted pianist, insisted on her own choice for Elise and me.'

Jonathan Fox, the eldest, was a highly successful systems analyst in the City, and, though newly married, exerted himself constantly with professional advice for his sisters, who ran a shop in an arcade recently built to blend with the architecture of the Cotswold town of their birth.

'We sell my hand-knitted sweaters—at a very steep

price—some very high-class clothes of the classic, tailored type, and pieces of silver and jewellery and wood carvings made by local craftsmen,' said Leonora.

'Hence the brooch,' remarked Penry.

'Right. Want to guess the name of our shop?'

'Surprise me.'

'Elise insisted we call it "Fox's Lair". Eye-catching, she said, and Jon agreed. I loathe it.'

Penry eyed her speculatively. 'If you live *and* work with your sister, why on earth hasn't she missed you?'

'I'm coming to that.'

Elise, ten years older than her sister, was the brains of the business. It was Elise who saw to the accounts and the buying, who had a flair for salesmanship. Leonora, the creative one, was perfectly happy to get on with her knitting in her little nook in the shop, help with the customers when trade was brisk, type what correspondence was necessary and otherwise leave Elise to the hard sell. Leonora also did the cooking when the two of them were at home, but Elise was often out dining with someone, or in Stratford at the theatre with someone else. Elise Fox, happily unmarried at thirty-two, was rarely without an escort, but never showed the least sign of tying herself to one man for good.

The love of Leonora's life was sailing, and during the summer months she spent her Sundays on the water at the local reservoir, weeknights at the tennis club or the cinema, and in the winter she took part in as many activities as possible in the small town where she'd lived all her life.

'Sounds horribly humdrum, doesn't it?' She smiled ruefully. 'My parents left enough money to make sure I went to the same school as Elise, but I was never the academic type—too fond of games. My career was shaped, I suppose, when I sold my first sweater to a smart shop in Stratford at the tender age of sixteen. When I left school I automatically went into the shop with Elise, and began to knit full time.'

Penry eyed her searchingly. 'Have you never wanted wider horizons than that?'

Leonora shrugged. 'Of course, now and then. But never enough to desert Elise. She was only twenty when she was saddled with me, yet she never made me feel I was a drag, and heaven knows a kid sister must have been at times.'

Penry waited patiently as Leonora paused. When she resumed her story her voice was different, flat and uninflected, as she told him that one day a journalist and a photographer had come to Chastlecombe to do a feature on the shopping arcade for the colour magazine of one of the Sunday papers. Much was made of the sympathetic architecture, and the fact that the arcade brought trade to both new and old shops from the tourists who thronged the town summer and winter.

The Fox sisters attracted a lot of attention. Despite competition from shops offering antiques and locally crafted furniture, Fox's Lair came in for the bulk of the publicity. Elise, tall, red-haired and elegant, occupied pole position on the centre-page shot, wearing one of Leonora's sweaters, a silver fox-head brooch pinned to the scarf thrown carelessly over one shoulder, the interior of the shop in the background.

'Where were you?' asked Penry.

'Hiding. I'm hideously unphotogenic. My hair comes out like a bird's nest and my eyes look slitty. Guy. . .' She faltered for a moment. 'Guy Ferris, the photographer, gave up trying to get a good shot of me in the end. Whereas you can't take a bad picture of my sister. Her bones are so good.'

Penry's eyes lit with a deliberate gleam. 'So are yours—you could do with a trifle more meat on them, but otherwise they compare very favourably with other bone-structures I've met.'

Leonora chuckled. 'Why, thank you, Doctor.'

'So what happened next?'

'I fell in love.'

'With Guy?'

'With Guy.'

Guy Ferris, already making a name for himself in the right circles, made a surprisingly determined play for the younger Miss Fox. Elise, oddly unenamoured of him, became worried when he took to coming down from London quite often at weekends. But Leonora was in seventh heaven. And to crown her joy Guy Ferris was an expert sailor. He would collect her in his Morgan two-seater with the original strap round the bonnet, then take her off to the sailing club to commandeer the helm of her Enterprise dinghy, dressed in the latest sailing gear. Leonora, bedazzled, crewing for him with devotion, was the envy of her friends.

'What a dope,' said Leonora bitterly.

Penry frowned. 'Didn't he want more than just sailing?'

'What do you mean?'

'Don't play the innocent, my child. You know perfectly well our enforced intimacy was a great strain on *me* after only a day or so.'

Leonora looked sceptical. 'Even though I looked as though I'd gone ten rounds with Mike Tyson?'

'You improved at a very disturbing rate, *cariad*!' He

smiled encouragingly. 'Go on with the story. I want to know what caused the amnesia.'

Leonora took a deep breath and informed Penry that Guy had, indeed, made love to her to a certain extent. Lots of kissing and stroking, but nothing more. She'd been convinced he respected her so much that he had intentions of a more permanent nature.

'I read too many fairy-tales when I was young,' she said bitterly.

The romance continued through the autumn and over Christmas, with intimate dinners and spins in the glamorous car in place of sailing once the season was over.

Then Guy told Leonora he was going away for three weeks to Wales, to take photographs for a travel book, and suggested she went with him. It would do her good, he said persuasively. Elise, however, opposed the idea with surprising violence. And, because Elise hardly ever came the heavy older sister, Leonora, with infinite regret, told Guy she couldn't go. He made quite a fuss about it, saying it was time she left the nest, stood up to the forceful Elise and lived her own life. One day, he hinted, he would insist she did, and for more than just a holiday.

'I was so sure he meant marriage,' said Leonora quietly. 'I pined after he'd gone. I was such a misery that by the end of the first week Elise asked a friend to help out in the shop, and packed me off to join him.'

There'd been no word from Guy after he went away, but, knowing his friend's house was isolated, with no telephone, Leonora was unconcerned. Full of excited anticipation, she caught an overnight train, managed to get a taxi to turn out at the crack of dawn to take her to Morfa, then set out along the causeway to Brynteg.

'Brynteg!' Penry turned her face up to his. 'Was Ferris staying in the house of that artist chap there?'

She nodded. 'You know him?'

'Of him—and the company he keeps. Go on.'

It had been a wonderful, exciting adventure to Leonora that morning. Undaunted by the rain, she set out along the causeway, feeling like a princess in a fairy-tale about to join her prince. Not even the rising wind had any power to damp her ardour as she flew along the causeway. The house stood at the summit of a rocky mound at the end of it, like a miniature St Michael's Mount, but to Leonora it was Mecca to a believer as she began the steep climb from the beach towards journey's end, and Guy.

'The house is a bungalow, with a studio built on the back of it, facing out to sea. I knocked on the front door, but there was no answer.' Leonora paused for a moment, then steeled herself to go on. 'I was cold and wet by this time, but after a tour of inspection I found the house was deserted. So I went round the back to the studio and looked through one of the windows. There was a raised dais at one end underneath a skylight, with a sort of bed on it. Guy was in the bed——' Her voice cracked, and Penry got up to take her in his arms.

'With a woman?' he said harshly.

'No. With another man.'

CHAPTER NINE

PENRY held her in a loose, impersonal embrace as her tears fell thick and fast, bitter and scalding enough to cauterise the wound in her memory. At first Leonora's body convulsed with shudders as she wept, but little by little she grew quieter. In the warmth of Penry's arms she came face to face with the truth, survived it, and after a while she detached herself from the comforting embrace, accepting the box of tissues Penry passed to her before resuming his chair. She mopped herself up, then eyed him uncertainly as she saw the set, cold expression on his face.

'You're disgusted,' she said.

His eyes glittered like steel. 'I wish I had this Guy of yours here in my hands. I'd like to wring his bloody neck.'

'Thank you. Oddly enough that's rather comforting.' She blinked her swollen eyes, and tried to smile. 'Not, of course, that Guy can help being—being what he is. And he wasn't expecting me. He didn't know I'd changed my mind about joining him.'

'Making excuses for him?'

'No,' she said wearily. 'Just facing the truth.'

Penry looked grim. 'Did he see you?'

Leonora shuddered. 'No!'

With every nerve straining to turn tail and run, she'd backed away as quietly as possible and once she was out of earshot raced back down to the beach to find the tide had turned.

'Picture my feelings when I found the causeway was under water! I tore along the beach like a maniac, looking for some kind of boat I could borrow to get away. I was lucky. There was an old Heron dinghy drawn up on the beach, with an outboard motor ready attached. I commandeered it without a second thought.'

'Ah. Enter the *Seren.*'

'Yes. I dragged it down to the water on the launching trailer, and pushed off. For a few horrible moments I thought the motor wouldn't fire, but after several pulls it caught, then I just hooked my overnight bag over one shoulder, took the tiller and made for the shore, which looked so close that I felt I could have swum across.'

'At which point, I assume, the engine cut out and the notorious cross-currents of the sound hurled you all over the place until you were swept overboard.' Penry shook his head. 'Miraculously they swept you round to Gullholm, where I must have found you minutes after you got caught in that inlet.' His eyes met hers. 'Have you any *idea* how lucky you were?'

She nodded dumbly, the reality of her escape hitting her suddenly like a body-blow.

Penry frowned. 'When are you expected back, by the way?'

Leonora's eyes opened wide in horror. 'Oh, good heavens, what date is it?'

'The fourteenth.'

She sagged with relief. 'I'm due back tomorrow, then. And I've got to get there on time, too, or Elise will go up the wall.'

He nodded briskly as he jumped up. 'I'll drive you.'

'But I'll be spoiling your holiday. And it's miles out

of your way. If you could just get me to the nearest station——'

'Don't be silly. Like you, it's high time I returned to the real world.' He paused on his way to the door, smiling. 'Besides, without my castaway life on Gullholm will lose its charm.'

Leonora barely heard him, suddenly stricken with dread at the thought of long night hours ahead alone. After a pause she said in a stifled voice, 'Must you go back to your room? Couldn't you stay with me tonight? Please?'

Penry's face darkened. 'No, Leonora. We've been through this once. You know perfectly well I can't. You'll be fine now. You've slain the dragons. They can't hurt you any more.'

He turned, their eyes met and held for a long, tense moment, then suddenly Penry flung away, so precipitate in his hurry to leave that he forgot to duck. Leonora flinched as his head cracked painfully against the lintel. She leapt out of bed as he rubbed his head, cursing.

She caught him by the hand. 'Does it hurt?'

'Of course it bloody well hurts!' Penry glared down at her, trying to yank his hand away, but Leonora hung on to it in desperation.

'Please stay. *Please*. Penry, listen to me. I want you to make love to me. I need you to!' Colour flared in her cheeks as she met his blazing eyes head on.

'You don't know what you're saying,' he said through clenched teeth.

'On the contrary. I know exactly what I'm saying. Look on it from a medical angle if you like, as a cure for an ailment.' She moved closer. 'Penry, don't you understand? What I saw that morning could spoil me for a sexual relationship forever. I need another picture in place of it. If you make love to me I'll have something to look back on with pleasure and gratitude for the rest of my life.'

'That's blackmail!' he said harshly.

'No—just a cry for help.' Leonora flushed painfully. 'Unless the last time put you off completely, of course.'

He stood very still. 'In as much as I cringe at the thought of making you sick a second time, yes. It does. I may be a doctor, but I'm also a man with the usual vanity. I won't deny I find you damn near irresistible when you plead like that, but I don't think my ego could take a repeat of last time.'

Her dark eyes lit with sudden hope. 'There's no danger of that. I just want you to blot out everything about that morning. Just by making love to me. Is it so much to ask?' Suddenly she dropped his hand and slid her arms about his waist, knowing she'd won when she felt the thunder of his heart against her cheek as she burrowed her face against his chest. She wriggled closer, and suddenly Penry's arms crushed her cruelly tight against him.

'Leonora,' he said harshly, his voice muffled against her hair, 'have you any idea what you're doing to me?'

She tipped back her head, exulting as she met the blaze in his eyes. 'No. Not really. I was hoping you'd show me.' She stood back and peeled off the shirt with a nonchalance only a trifle marred when a button caught in her hair.

The air left Penry's lungs with an audible hiss as he helped disentangle her, his square white teeth biting into his lower lip when she stood naked in front of him, hands behind her back as she eyed him diffidently. 'I suppose bodies are pretty everyday things to a doctor——'

He caught her in his arms, swinging her high against his chest, his mouth seeking hers. 'But this isn't every day,' he muttered against her parted lips. 'It's night. And you've won. I know I'll regret this in the morning, but I want you so badly it's a risk I'll just have to take. Are you sure about this?' He set her on her feet suddenly, his eyes like blue flames in his taut face. 'Because this time, *cariad*, I warn you, I shan't let you go.'

'Of course I'm sure,' she said crossly. 'Do you want me or not?'

For answer Penry picked her up and tossed her into the bed, stripped off his dressing-gown and turned out the light. Then his warm, naked body was against hers beneath the covers and this time everything was magically different. Leonora forgot Guy and everything else in her rediscovered world as Penry's presence transformed the darkness into an exciting, intimate microcosm inhabited by two people oblivious of everything but the sheer physical pleasure of being together.

Leonora, expecting to be taken by storm after she'd flung down the gauntlet, found Penry in no hurry at all. She felt a warm rush of gratitude for his sensitivity as he kissed and played with her in a teasing, light-hearted way which both excited and disarmed her at first.

But gradually the tempo of Penry's caresses changed, became more urgent. Skilfully he tuned every nerve in her narrow body to such a concert pitch of response that she began to initiate caresses of her own, delighting in her power as rippling muscles tightened beneath her questing hands. His mouth crushed and coaxed in turns, his tongue subtle and importunate, before he moved lower, sliding his mouth down her throat until it reached her breasts. Leonora quivered, her teeth caught in her lower lip as he kissed each breast in turn, his lips lingering over their slight curves. Then abruptly he took one pointing nipple between his lips, pulling on it, and she gasped as a streak of fire ran through her, and his hands grew urgent, the thrusting caresses of his long fingers so expert that fulfilment soon came flooding in shock-waves which surged through her entire body.

Leonora lay gasping, arms outflung, eyes closed, her hair a tangled mass of damp curls against the pillow. Penry reached over her to turn on the lamp, and she opened her eyes to find him looking down into her face, a triumphant, indulgent smile curving his mouth as he slid his arms around her, throwing one long leg over hers in careless intimacy.

Colour rushed into her face and she moved restlessly, her eyes sliding away from the gleam in his. 'What—what happens now?'

'What would you like to happen?'

'I don't know. But surely what—what just happened to me couldn't have done much for you, could it?'

He laughed softly. 'On the contrary, my lovely, it did a great deal for me. Would you care to find out just how much?' He slid her hand lower until it rested on the irrefutable proof of his desire for her.

Leonora blinked, her hand closing over him involuntarily, and she smiled in triumph as he groaned, his eyes dilating as they stared down into hers.

'How do you feel?' he asked raggedly, astonishing her.

'You know exactly how I feel!'

Penry bent his head and kissed her deeply, and Leonora slid her arms round his neck, responding with a fervour which answered his question without words. A long time later he raised his head and said huskily, 'Are you sure?'

'Yes. Oh, yes—now. *Please*!'

Yet even now he took his time to stroke and caress her until she was drugged and dazed with longing. He parted her knees, bending his dark head to kiss both in turn, sliding his mouth in a series of kisses along each smooth inner thigh until Leonora began to plead hoarsely. At last, slowly, victoriously, his eyes never leaving hers, he granted her wish. Leonora clenched her teeth for an instant as her body yielded to his with a fleeting moment of pain, then she relaxed as they lay still for an instant in the very eye of the storm.

'Did I hurt you much?' he said against her lips.

'Not much. And not now, which is strange. Why aren't you crushing the life out of me?'

'Because I'm very, very clever.'

'And practised!'

'Not lately.'

'I'd never have known.'

'It's like riding a bike—you never forget.'

'I can ride a bike. But I've never done this before.'

'Ah, *cariad*, I know, I know! Let me teach you how it's done.' And he began to move, slowly at first, his forbearance rewarded by the wonder in her eyes as they stared, delighted, into his. With every move she gave a little gasp, as her body, previous experience or not, proved an apt pupil. Without consulting her it began to move faster, inciting her lover to a rhythm which he responded to triumphantly, accelerating in time with their heartbeats, taking her with him towards the culmination she'd been given a foretaste of, which paled in comparison to the flooding rapture which overtook her seconds before Penry gasped, stiffened, then crushed her in his arms as their breathing slowed in the shared diminuendo of the aftermath.

When Leonora opened her eyes again it was morning and she was alone. She stretched experimentally, wincing as various parts of her ached in a way which brought the experiences of the night flooding back in full force. Heat swept over her as she remembered every little detail of Penry's lovemaking, and she closed her eyes, breathless at the memory. But at last, as a tongue probed an aching tooth, she forced herself to think back to the scene at Brynteg, and found the exercise distasteful and painful, but reassuring. It was possible to think of the episode in a detached sort of way, she found with relief, as though it had happened in another time and place to someone else.

From now on, she realised, her life would be forever divided into two separate halves—the time before her loss of memory and whatever was to come after recovering it. This interlude with Penry Vaughan on Gullholm would be something to remember with gratitude as a sort of enchanted no man's land in between. At the thought of Penry she stretched, cat-like, her mouth curving in a dreamy smile. As an experience to blot out the horror of her discovery on Brynteg it had been blissfully successful. Penry's wonderful, gratifying desire for her had been a healing fire which had cured her forever of the wounds dealt by Guy. Then she shivered, as though someone had walked over her grave.

Ah, but who, she asked herself with sudden foreboding, is going to cure you of Penry Meredith Vaughan?

Leonora got up quickly, and took a speedy bath, then dressed at top speed in jeans and jersey, securing the red scarf at her throat with the silver brooch. As she brushed her hair she examined her face in the mirror, amazed when no trace of the experience of the night showed on it. She turned away to strip the rumpled bed, then straightened the room and packed her few belongings in her bag, feeling more reluctant by the minute to face Penry in the cold light of day. At last, unable to delay confrontation any longer, she went downstairs to find Penry emerging from the study as she reached the kitchen.

'Good morning,' he said, no trace of a smile on his face. 'I've informed the police about your recovery.'

'Thank you.' Leonora filled the kettle, utterly shattered to find no trace of last night's lover in the Penry Vaughan of this morning. 'I'd forgotten that. Shouldn't I be compensating someone for the loss of the *Seren*?'

'If you want the episode kept quiet I don't advise it. The owners will claim on the insurance.'

Leonora began frying bacon and eggs, slicing bread for toast, spooning coffee in the pot to cover her secret dismay. 'What will you do with the food in the fridge?' she asked, not looking at him.

'Bryn Pritchard can collect it after I leave the keys with him.' Penry leaned against the counter, his eyes on her face. 'How are you this morning, Leonora?'

'Fine,' she said brightly, flipping the eggs over. 'It feels rather strange now I've got my other world back again, I admit. But it's good to be all in one piece again.'

'Not quite,' he said deliberately, and caught her chin in his hand so she was forced to look at him. 'Memory or no memory, I wouldn't describe you as all in one piece, exactly, after last night.'

Leonora flushed scarlet as she jerked her head away. 'If I'm not it was entirely my own idea, so I can hardly complain.' She handed him a plate. 'Where do you want to eat this? Here or in the other room?'

Penry looked at the food without enthusiasm. 'I don't know that I want it anywhere.'

'Then throw it in the bin,' said Leonora, incensed.

'All right, all right, I'll eat it.' He put the plate down on the counter in front of him then lifted her on to a stool. 'How about eating something yourself while we talk?'

'Talk?' She eyed him askance as she buttered a slice of toast.

Penry ate some of the meal in thoughtful silence, then laid down his fork. 'We need to talk, Leonora. After last night——'

'Let's forget last night.'

'How can we?' His eyebrows shot together in a black bar. 'It may be something you can dismiss easily. I can't.'

Leonora abandoned any pretence of eating. 'Look, Penry. Last night I asked—begged—you to make love to me. You supplied a deep-seated need in me to blot out what I'd seen. You showed me how beautiful love between a man and woman can be, and afterwards I felt healed and whole and normal again.'

Penry refilled their cups with a steady hand. 'Which puts me on a par with a dose of medicine. Thank you.'

'You know that's not what I meant,' she said impatiently. 'What I'm trying to say is how grateful I am, and how miraculous it was, but that's it. I'm off your hands. You needn't feel responsible for me from now on in the slightest.'

'How extraordinarily civil of you,' he said cuttingly, 'but aren't you missing a rather important point?'

She frowned. 'What point?'

'Think, Leonora! Surely you don't need a lecture on the birds and bees?'

She stared at him for a moment, then flushed. 'Oh. I never thought——'

'*I* did—fleetingly.' His jaw set. 'But by then it was too late. The basic urge for gratification blotted everything else from my mind.'

'Gratification!' Leonora eyed him with dislike as she slid from the stool and began clearing away. 'What a ghastly word.'

'What else would you call it?' he demanded.

'A service? You provided it. I'm grateful. Now forget about it. It's entirely my own fault if there are consequences.'

Penry grabbed her by the shoulders and turned her to face him. 'Forget about it? What kind of monster do you think I am?'

'I don't think you're a monster at all.' She looked up at him defiantly. 'But one way and another I've been quite enough trouble to you already. If there should be a—a problem, I'll deal with it myself.'

Penry's fingers bit into her flesh cruelly for a moment, then his face drained of expression as he released her. 'As you wish.'

Leonora stared after him, stricken, as he went upstairs to pack his belongings. Her fine words had been so much whistling in the dark. She had fully expected Penry to dismiss them as nonsense, and felt so shattered that he hadn't that it took her longer than usual to clear away and leave the kitchen immaculate. While Penry was outside seeing to the generator she fetched her belongings, then collected the knitting, stuffing it inside her bag guiltily.

'Are you ready?' asked Penry a little later.

'Yes.' She took a last look round the room which had been her world, then hurried quickly out of the house.

Their progress down to the *Angharad* was slow. There was a fair wind spattering them with rain as they made their descent to the beach. As they reached the little anchorage she looked at the sea with resignation. It would be a rough crossing. Once the luggage was stowed away on board Penry lifted her on the deck of the *Angharad* and cast off. At once the crabber began to bounce about on the waves, as though the *Angharad* was dancing a jig over the water in her pleasure at taking a trip.

Leonora watched the grey smudge of shoreline growing closer, knowing that once she was there this part of her life would be over, and she might never see Penry Vaughan again. Her eyes flew to him, trying to imprint his tall, commanding figure on her memory as he stood with legs braced, his hands on the wheel.

'Are you frightened?' he asked. 'No need to be—it's just a stiffish breeze.' He extended an arm. 'Come here.'

Leonora, depressed rather than frightened, moved to the shelter of his arms for the remainder of the journey. It was a bitter-sweet experience. Through the layers of their clothing she could feel Penry's heart beating steadily against her back, and dreaded the moment of parting which would come all too soon when they reached journey's end in Chastlecombe.

'You're very quiet,' he said into the back of her neck.

She kept her eyes on the heaving sea. 'I was busy composing a graceful speech of thanks for all you've done for me.'

'Unnecessary. You typed the articles, relieved me of the household chores and fed me royally. The debt is on my side.'

She felt glad her face was hidden from him. 'Ah, but you saved my life, remember!'

He moved closer as Brides Haven came into focus in the distance. 'In some cultures that has great significance. Is it the Chinese who would now consider you my responsibility?'

'It's a good thing we're British, then,' she said lightly, and ducked from under his arm. 'We're nearly there.'

The process of visiting Bryn Pritchard to leave keys and instructions took longer than anticipated, since Mrs Pritchard insisted on making coffee and feeding them newly baked scones before they went on their way.

'Is your sister expecting you at a specific time?' asked Penry when they were on the way to Haverfordwest at last.

'I think I said I'd be back this evening some time. Could I ring her en route to say I'm on my way?'

'Of course. We'll stop off somewhere for lunch.'

Leonora thanked him quietly, not quite sure how she felt about this idea. Half of her wanted to get the journey and the parting over, to make a quick, clean break. But the other half wanted the day to go on forever, for Penry to drive at a snail's pace on the way back to prolong their time together to the last possible minute.

As if he'd read her mind Penry took a cross-country route instead of the motorway, driving her through Carmarthen and Llandeilo, then on past Brecon to head for Leominster. When he turned into the car park of an attractive roadside pub Leonora went off to ring her sister while Penry gave their orders.

'Is all well?' he asked when she joined him at a small table in a corner of the crowded bar.

Leonora pulled a face. 'Elise was delighted I rang, but gave me a terrible dressing down for not ringing before or sending a postcard. I told her there were extenuating circumstances and would tell all when I got home.' She gulped down some orange juice hastily.

'What's the matter, Leonora?' asked Penry, his voice so unusually gentle that it brought a sheen of tears to her eyes.

'It suddenly struck me how difficult it's going to be to explain everything to Elise.'

'Surely she'll understand?'

'Of course she will. I just loathe the thought of telling my nasty little tale a second time.'

'It probably won't be as bad as you think,' said Penry briskly, and launched into a description of the house he'd bought on the banks of the River Wye near Builth Wells. Leonora listened wistfully as she toyed with her sandwich, thinking it sounded idyllic, and a great waste for one man on his own. She said appropriate things in the right places, and hardly knew whether she was glad or sorry when it was time to go.

After a leisurely drive through the spring sunshine they arrived in the broad main street of Chastlecombe just after four. Penry parked the Range Rover in the open space behind the arches of the ancient market hall, then reached over into the back for Leonora's bag.

She smiled at him brightly. 'Thank you for the lift. I'll be fine now. Don't get out.'

Penry's brows drew together. 'Don't be silly. I'll see you home,' he said shortly and got out of the car, striding round to lift her down.

Leonora's heart sank, but she knew better by this time than to argue with Penry Vaughan. She led the way along the pavement of the wide main street typical of most Cotswold towns, smiling at familiar faces as they passed. The new arcade looked very attractive in the spring sunshine. Tubs of daffodils stood outside every shop, except for Fox's Lair, where a pair of bay trees flourished in ceramic pots.

'We live in a flat over the shop,' said Leonora, her feet dragging now they were nearly there.

'Come on,' said Penry firmly. 'Let's get it over with.'

And right on cue there was Elise at the door of the shop, elegant as always in slim skirt and silk shirt, her face alight with welcome which changed quickly to surprise as she realised the man with her sister was a stranger.

'Hello, love,' said Leonora, hugging her. 'This is Dr Penry Vaughan. He was kind enough to give me a lift home.'

Penry held out his hand, smiling courteously. 'How do you do, Miss Fox? Could you possibly spare me a few moments in private? Leonora's had rather a disturbing adventure. Don't be alarmed. I just want to make certain she tells you exactly what happened.'

CHAPTER TEN

ELISE FOX was a woman who prided herself on her ability to deal with crisis, but at eleven o'clock that Saturday night she still lay limp on the sofa in the flat, looking utterly shattered when her young sister came in from the kitchen with yet another pot of strong black coffee.

'I'm sorry, Elise,' said Leonora for the hundredth time. 'None of it would have happened if I hadn't gone chasing after Guy.'

'You mean if Guy hadn't come chasing after you!' said Elise hotly. 'I was against it from the first. I couldn't put my finger on what it was I disliked about him, yet now it seems plain as the nose on your face. What a ghastly thing to happen to you. I could kill him!'

'Penry felt like that, too.'

Elise looked across at her searchingly. 'Ah, yes. The impressive Dr Vaughan. Full marks to him, anyway.' Her eyes narrowed. 'Was I imagining things, or was there a definite hint of electricity in the air between you and the dashing doctor?'

'Certainly not.'

'Liar!'

Leonora shook back her hair, looking fierce. 'If you don't mind I'd like to drop the subject now. As far as I'm concerned I'd like to forget that the last couple of weeks ever happened.'

Elise jumped up, looking contrite. 'Poor darling,

you've had such a time and I keep rabbiting on and on about it. I'm sorry. I should be the one dispensing coffee and condolences, not you.'

Glad to be alone in her familiar little room later, Leonora forced herself to face the indigestible truth. Forgetting Guy Ferris would be child's play compared to her other problem. Two weeks ago she had never heard of Penry Meredith Vaughan. Now she couldn't imagine life without him. The conclusion kept her tossing and turning in despair for hours, the sound of traffic in the High Street a poor substitute for the lulling boom of the sea round Gullholm. She had never imagined she would miss Penry so much. The memory of their night together haunted her so relentlessly that it was daylight before she fell into an uneasy, exhausted sleep.

Leonora found the next day very long. Normally she loved Sundays. In the summer it was her sailing day, but in the winter she spent it at home, cooking lunch, reading the papers, and generally lazing around. Sometimes Elise was at home all day, sometimes not. This particular Sunday she had an invitation to a dinner party, and was all for cancelling, but Leonora wouldn't hear of it.

'I ruined your Saturday night, so please go off and enjoy yourself. I'll be fine. Besides, Priscilla's probably got some man lined up for you as dinner partner.' Leonora summoned up a grin. 'Think of her anguish if you upset her seating plan!'

Secretly Leonora was relieved to be on her own. Overnight the full force of what might have happened had finally come home to Elise, and she'd spent most of the day clucking round her young sister like a hen with one chick. Leonora was heartily glad to wave her off to her party. But once she was alone with her knitting depression crept up on Leonora like an incoming tide. Only a short time before she'd had Penry for company while she knitted. Now her sole companion was the television, which was intrusive after two weeks without it.

When the telephone rang Leonora got up listlessly, so certain it would be one of Elise's friends that she slid down on the floor in a heap, heart thumping, at the sound of Penry's voice.

'Leonora? Are you there?'

'Yes. I'm here.' She breathed in deeply. 'Did you get home safely?'

'I did. How are you today?'

'I'm fine.'

'Are you? Honestly?' There was silence for a moment, then he said huskily, 'Leonora—look, there's no easy way to say this, but I hope you're not full of some quixotic notion about keeping it from me if you find out you're pregnant.'

Leonora's hackles rose. 'Why? So you can arrange for an abortion as soon as possible?' she blurted. 'It must be easy enough for someone like you.'

She heard a sharp intake of breath, then an ear-splitting crack as Penry Vaughan slammed down his receiver without another word.

Leonora had a good cry, made herself some tea, then settled down to knit furiously. Before long the sweater was finished and the various parts stitched together with her usual professional finish, ready to post off to Penry next day to make certain he had a keepsake to remind him of his castaway.

The following evening Penry rang again, but this

time he spoke to Elise, who was rather mystified when he politely declined to speak to Leonora.

'He just asked how you were, made me promise to keep an eye on you, then rang off,' she said, frowning.

'He rang last night. I was a teensy bit rude,' said Leonora, trying to look unconcerned.

'Oh, I see.' Elise eyed her thoughtfully. 'Never mind. Perhaps he'll look on that amazing jersey you sent off as an olive branch.'

Instead of ringing again Penry sent Leonora a very formal letter of thanks for the sweater. The sight of his indecipherable scrawl gave her a sharp pang of nostalgia for the strange, lost time spent on his island, underlining her dissatisfaction with life in Chastlecombe very heavily now her adventure was over.

When Leonora learned there would be no sequel to her adventure after all, she was totally unprepared for the desolation which swamped her. She hid it away behind a bright, brittle insouciance which plainly worried Elise to death, but for several nights wept silently into her pillow, utterly shattered to find she'd wanted Penry's child quite desperately without even realising it. Now there would be no reason for further contact between them of any kind, a prospect which painted dark shadows beneath Leonora's eyes, and bleached the colour from her face to the point where Elise began muttering darkly about anaemia.

Leonora pooh-poohed this. Her problem had been amnesia, not anaemia, she told Elise flippantly. Nevertheless she agreed to the luxury of a lie-in the following Sunday morning, even allowing her sister to fuss over her a little.

'I should stay there for a while,' said Elise, when she

brought in a breakfast tray. 'You look like something the cat's dragged in.'

But after an hour Leonora grew bored and irritable with herself and went off to have a bath. Afterwards she spent more time than usual on her appearance, determined that from now on she would stop behaving like some Victorian miss with the vapours. She even put on sheer stockings and a brief pleated skirt instead of her usual jeans, then, as final proof of her new outlook on life, she put on the new pink sweater and danced out into the sitting-room, calling. 'How do I look——' She stopped dead, her heart flipping over under the sweater as Penry Vaughan leapt to his feet at the sight of her, the height and breadth of him overpowering the entire room.

'Good enough to eat, *cariad*!' He held out his hand, and Leonora took it, dumbfounded.

'Well?' he demanded, 'aren't you even going to say hello?'

She pulled herself together. 'Hello, indeed. What a surprise. Where's Elise?'

'She had to go out for a moment.'

Storing up a ticking-off for her sister, Leonora managed a rather stiff smile to hide the joy bubbling inside her. 'Do sit down.'

Incensed at being taken by surprise despite her pleasure at seeing him, Leonora was somewhat mollified to see that Penry was wearing the sweater she'd knitted. The complex, serpentine weaving of colours emphasised his impressive shoulders, and in faded old Levis and scuffed desert boots he looked so wonderful as he lounged on the sofa that she could have thrown herself in his arms there and then. Instead she blurted the first thing that came into her head.

'You've had a wasted journey. I'm not pregnant after all.'

He nodded. 'I see. I wondered.'

'About what?'

'Elise rang me to say you were crying your eyes out every night.'

Leonora eyed him in horror. 'She heard me?'

'Yes.' Penry leaned forward peremptorily. 'And I want to know why you cried, please.'

Her eyes flickered. 'You're a doctor. You know perfectly well that women get depressed at—at certain times. I'm no exception.'

'Is that the real reason?' His eyes held hers inexorably. 'Or is it just possible you wanted to be pregnant?'

But Leonora had herself well in hand by this time. She gave him a scornful little smile. 'Oh, come *on*—I'm not a complete idiot!'

He looked unconvinced. 'No, just unhappy. Elise can't have been mistaken about the tears.'

'I can't say I care for the idea of you two discussing me behind my back, but if you must know I was suffering from reaction,' said Leonora with dignity. 'After my recent adventures it's not really surprising, is it?'

Penry's eyes held a sceptical gleam. 'All right, Leonora, if that's the way you want it. Let's talk about why I'm here instead.' He paused deliberately. 'To come straight to the point, I drove down here to make a suggestion. Are you prepared to listen?'

'Since you came so far I can hardly say no.'

'Very well, then. I propose we carry on where we left off, unless you never want to lay eyes on me again, of course.'

Leonora sat very still, her eyes locked with his. 'I'm—sorry—*what* did you say?'

'You know exactly what I said. Now that the spectre of pregnancy is out of the way, is there any reason why we can't just continue with the relationship begun on Gullholm?'

She stared at him uncertainly. 'Are you serious?'

'Why not?' Penry leaned forward to take her hands. 'I'm not asking to be your lover, Leonora. Yet. Ravishing experience though that was, we came to it too precipitately, and for all the wrong reasons. But is there any reason why we can't be friends?' He smiled, a gleam in his eyes she recognised with a sharp pang. 'I've missed my castaway rather a lot, you know.'

She frowned. 'You were pretty fed up with me the other night—on the phone.'

'Are you surprised? It was a bloody awful thing to say. I thought you knew me better than that.'

She shrugged. 'My recent brush with the seamier side of life has made me cynical. Tell me,' she added, determined to put things straight between them, 'purely as a matter of interest, what would you have done if I had been pregnant?'

'I'd have asked you to marry me.' He raised an eyebrow. 'Old-fashioned, I suppose, but none of the other options seemed remotely possible for you—or for me.'

Leonora withdrew her hands and got up. 'I see.' She looked down at him consideringly for some time. At last she nodded. 'All right. In that case I don't see why not.'

Penry rose slowly, his eyes narrowed. 'Why do I have the feeling I've passed some kind of test?'

'Because you have.' She smiled at him, feeling very much better. 'I wonder what's happened to Elise.'

'She said something about tidying the shop.'

'Poor darling, I'd better go and put her out of her misery.'

Penry reached for her, barring her way to the door. 'Wait a moment. Convince me that all's well between us now—one friendly little kiss would do.'

Leonora hesitated, then held up her mouth. At the first touch of his lips she trembled, and Penry took her in his arms, his kiss suddenly fierce until a tactful little cough from the doorway brought an untimely end to the embrace.

'Can I come in now?' asked Elise apologetically. 'I can't think of another thing to do down there.'

Penry relinquished Leonora without embarrassment, smiling at the relief on Elise's face.

'I gather diplomatic relations have now been resumed,' she remarked with satisfaction.

'I suppose they have.' Leonora smiled happily at Penry. 'Are you in a hurry to be off, or would you like some lunch?'

That Sunday marked the beginning of a new phase in Leonora's life. The mere fact that Penry Vaughan wished to go on seeing her, however few and far between their meetings, did wonders for her self-esteem. It also compensated very thoroughly for the disaster of her relationship with Guy, who received short shrift when he telephoned on his return to London from Wales. She made no mention of her disastrous trip to Brynteg, told him she'd met someone else, and wished him good luck with deliberate finality when she said goodbye.

At first Leonora wasn't sure precisely what Penry had in mind regarding their relationship, and lived in a state of tension between his phone calls. But after a while he augmented the phone calls with occasional visits, and as the summer wore on came to see her with increasing regularity, eventually as often as his professional commitments allowed. On free weekends he drove to Chastlecombe on a Saturday afternoon, took Leonora out for a meal somewhere, stayed the night at the Kings Arms in the town, and spent most of Sunday with Leonora before driving home to face his Monday morning clinic next day. To her delight he even took to discussing his work with her, and Leonora listened, rapt, utterly fascinated by glimpses of the other, professional Penry Vaughan she secretly found so impressive.

Their relationship was an oddly comfortable one, with nothing more demonstrative about it than a swift goodnight kiss, or hands joined on a walk in the beautiful countryside around Chastlecombe. At first Leonora felt strangely happy. It was enough for a while just to have this clever, charming man as a friend, flattering to have him travel so far when he could just for the pleasure of her company. As the weeks passed she finally began to believe that Penry Vaughan meant what he said, that their relationship was important enough to him to nurture with delicacy and care.

But after a while the chaste quality of their relationship grew irksome. Leonora dreamed of the fierce rapture they'd shared on the island and began to long for Penry to want her violently, to stop treating her like a younger sister, and sometimes after he'd gone she'd stare in the mirror in discontent, wishing she were tall, or voluptuous, or blonde. Anything other than dark-eyed and boyishly slender.

'What's up?' asked Elise one night, as Leonora was trying to find some new, madly attractive way to arrange her hair. 'Mirror, mirror, on the wall, who's the fairest one of all, and so on?'

Leonora turned away, sighing, to slump down on the side of her bed. 'No need to ask that,' she said despondently. 'You are, Elise Fox.'

Elise gave her a hug. 'Darling, what nonsense!' She grinned mischievously. 'It's not me Penry Vaughan drives all this way to see, remember.'

Leonora refused to be consoled. 'Possibly not. Which doesn't stop me wishing I were less unspectacular.'

'The ex-Mrs Vaughan being very spectacular, I take it.'

'Very, from what little he's said about her. So are his sisters. I saw photographs of them.'

'Perhaps it's the contrast Penry finds so appealing——'

'Thank you very much!'

'You know what I mean!' said Elise impatiently. 'Perhaps Dr Penry Vaughan is surfeited with so much glamour and finds your subtler style more to his taste.'

Leonora gave her sister a scornful look. 'Then why doesn't he——' She stopped dead, blushing to the roots of her hair.

'Ah!' Elise nodded sagaciously. 'I see. Dr Vaughan is a shade too platonic for your taste, little sister!'

Leonora shied a pillow at her sister, her face scarlet as she remembered how she'd once pleaded with Penry to make love to her. Next time, she vowed secretly,

Penry Vaughan would do the begging. If there was a next time.

Penry did use persuasion on Leonora next time they met, but it had nothing to do with becoming her lover.

They had just returned to the flat after a long, lazy picnic in the September sunshine, to find Elise out. A note left taped to the fridge informed Leonora that her sister would be back in time for supper.

'Elise goes out a lot on Sundays,' remarked Penry. 'I hope we're not driving her out.'

'No, of course not. It's the only regular free day she has to visit friends. When you're not here I go sailing on Sundays, remember.'

He settled himself on the sofa as he always did, looking fit and rested as he eyed her speculatively. The dark, brooding look about him, so daunting at their first meeting, was missing these days, replaced by a zest and animation she knew must have been the norm for Penry Vaughan before his marriage—or before his divorce, she corrected herself. It was the parting from his wife, unquestionably, which had etched the lines of disillusion on his handsome face.

'Why are you looking at me like that?' asked Leonora.

Penry patted the cushion beside him. 'Come and sit beside me, *cariad*, and I'll tell you.'

Leonora needed no second bidding. These days she was glad of any invitation to proximity, and curled up beside him so promptly that he gave her an amused sidelong glance as he took her hand in his.

'I was just thinking what guts you had to start sailing again after what happened on Brynteg,' he said, surprising her. Brynteg was a subject they never discussed.

She nodded soberly. 'The first time afterwards was

terrifying. When the wind got up, Julian Parker had to get the Enterprise back almost single-handed I was so rigid with fear.'

Penry's eyes narrowed. 'Who the devil's Julian Parker?'

Leonora, deeply pleased at his tone, shrugged airily. 'Just a friend. He crews for me—or I crew for him. But wc haven't raced competitively this season because I'm not there regularly enough.'

'Is this where I make the noble suggestion of keeping away at weekends to leave you free to sail as much as you want?' he demanded.

'If you like,' she said cheerfully. 'Are you going to?'

'No, Leonora. I am not.' He paused, then slid his free arm round her shoulders. 'Unless,' he said silkily, 'you specifically request me to do so, of course.'

'The season's almost over now,' she said obliquely, not looking at him, and suddenly the arm descended to pull her against him. Penry released her hand to turn her face up to his.

'I take it that means you're still agreeable to my company when I can make it?'

Leonora longed for his company in much larger doses than he was able to spare, but had no intention of telling him so. She nodded slightly, and he bent his head to give her a kiss which was meant to be fleeting, but which went on and on until they were breathless and shaken when he put her away from him at last.

'Why did you stop?' she whispered.

Penry breathed in deeply. 'You know why!' He smiled at her crookedly, changing the subject with determination. 'Leonora, am I allowed to ask how you feel these days about the ambivalent Mr Ferris? Any hang-ups, or regrets?'

Leonora swung her feet to the ground, disinclined to discuss Guy Ferris. 'No, none.'

He put out a hand to smooth her untidy hair. 'Has he been in touch?'

'Yes.' Leonora sat very still, every nerve-end alight at his touch.

'Did you tell him about me?' demanded Penry.

'No,' lied Leonora shamelessly. 'Should I have?'

Penry frowned, then kissed her again, hard, but Leonora dodged away, scowling.

'What's the matter?' he demanded. 'I've been so unnaturally virtuous lately that you can surely grant me two kisses in one day!'

'I would appreciate it more if this one hadn't been prompted by resentment of another man.'

'If you can call Ferris a man!'

Leonora got to her feet, suddenly and unreasonably furious. She folded her arms across her chest, careless of her untidy hair and sunburned, shiny face. 'I suppose that what you're really saying is that Guy was attracted to me because he could pretend I was a boy!'

'I'm saying nothing of the kind,' snapped Penry, leaping to his feet.

Refusing to be intimidated by the sheer size of him, Leonora glared up into his face. 'Except for that one, never-referred-to night on your island, Dr Vaughan, you're no different. I might just as well be a boy for all the interest you take in me as—as a woman!'

Penry glared at her in sudden fury. 'What the hell do you mean? Are you inferring that my sexual preferences have any remote resemblance to your fancy photographer's?'

'I could be forgiven for thinking so lately,' Leonora

muttered unwisely, then backed away in a hurry from the blaze in his eyes.

'Don't be nervous,' said Penry with dangerous calm. 'I shan't hit you.' He seized her by the shoulders, his fingers biting into her flesh. 'But I'd like to put you over my knee and paddle your behind, young lady. Dammit, Leonora, I thought you understood I was bending over backwards not to rush you.'

Leonora shrugged off his hands with sudden violence. 'Did you have to take a whole summer?' she demanded angrily. 'All you've done, Dr Vaughan, should you be interested, is wreck my self-confidence and give me an inferiority complex about my looks.'

Penry stared at her in silence, visibly pulling himself together. 'How did I manage that?' he asked at last, in a flat, uninflected tone very different from the passionate outburst of a moment earlier.

Leonora let out an unsteady, shuddering sigh. 'It doesn't matter,' she muttered, and turned away, but Penry seized her by the waist and turned her to face him.

'Of course it matters!' He shook her slightly. 'Are you saying that all my bloody unnatural restraint has achieved is to convince you I don't find you attractive?'

She nodded. 'All the women you know are so good-looking. I assumed I was just too ordinary to interest you—in that way.'

'Then why the hell do you think I keep coming to see you?' Penry pulled her down on the sofa forcibly. 'Now sit still, shut up, and listen! Before I got married I led a pretty lively existence where women were concerned, and enjoyed it to the full. I married Melanie, if I'm honest, because she was the only one who'd held out for a wedding-ring.'

'Why are you telling me all this?' asked Leonora, trying to move away.

'Because we need to clear the air, I think, if we're to go on seeing each other.' His eyes narrowed with sudden hostility. 'Unless, of course, you don't want that.'

Leonora shook her head, flushing. 'You know very well that I do. Very much.'

'I'm relieved to hear it. And I took you in my confidence—something, incidentally, I don't do lightly—because I couldn't face another relationship based on misunderstanding. Melanie was like an empty chocolate-box, tempting on the outside, nothing inside—to be blunt, frigid. Yet she was determined to marry me. Beats me why!'

'It's perfectly obvious why!' said Leonora, astonished.

Penry smiled slowly, his eyes lighting up with the gleam she found so irresistible. 'Thank you, *cariad*. You're very good for my ego.'

But Leonora was still thinking over what he'd said. 'Penry,' she said, frowning, 'are you saying you—well, that you wouldn't want a relationship with me if I were frigid, like Melanie?'

Penry shook his head. 'No. I'm not saying that at all. I married Melanie in a rush, for reasons which embarrass me to remember. With you I just wanted to savour the initial stages, step by step, to enjoy just being with you, whatever we were doing Besides,' he added very softly, his fingers stroking the back of her hand, 'you're not frigid, my lovely. I know that beyond all doubt.'

'So you're not sorry you made love to me that night?'

'How could I be? It was a uniquely beautiful experience—for me at least, if not you.'

A weight rolled off Leonora's shoulders. 'It was for me, too. I'll always be grateful to you for that night.'

He picked up her hand and kissed it, then replaced it on her bare brown knee. 'I don't need gratitude for something which gave me such infinite pleasure. On the other hand, if you really feel indebted, Miss Fox, there is a small favour you could do for me in return.'

'Oh, yes?' Leonora eyed him warily. 'What kind of favour?'

'I've been invited to a party next weekend. Will you go with me?'

'Where?'

'That's the snag.' Penry smiled wryly. 'The party's in London. It's to celebrate my sister Clem's tenth wedding anniversary—and my family will be there *en masse*, including my mother, who commands my presence.'

Leonora eyed him in alarm. 'And you want me to go with you? No way!'

He smiled coaxingly. 'Please don't say no, *cariad*. I told my mother I was bringing you. Otherwise one of my sisters will have some unattached female ready to pounce on me. I need you for protection!'

She thought it over uneasily. 'Won't they mind if you bring a stranger to a family party?'

'Not in the least. Nick and Clem will have invited half the world and his wife, anyway. Besides,' added Penry with cunning strategy, 'if you turn me down we shan't see each other for quite a while. I'm tied up at the hospital the weekend after.'

Leonora's heart sank at the prospect of a whole fortnight without him, and as if scenting victory Penry moved closer, his long forefinger caressing her drooping lower lip.

'Is there no way I can persuade you?' he whispered.

Leonora nodded, her eyes bright with mischief. Very deliberately she closed her teeth gently on his fingertip, her eyes holding his, and with a smothered sound Penry jerked his hand away and seized her in his arms, his kiss igniting a response which set them both alight.

Leonora shivered with pleasure as Penry's long fingers caressed the length of brown thigh below her brief denim shorts. Her mouth parting ardently beneath his, she began to unbutton his shirt with unsteady fingers, then slithered lower to kiss his bare brown chest, exulting in the thunder of his heart for a moment before she found herself flat on the sofa as Penry slid her jersey over her head, then dispensed with the scrap of satin beneath. His dark hair brushing her skin, he bent his mouth to each breast in turn, paying such delicately agonising attention to each one that Leonora gasped and thrust her hips hard against him. With a groan Pentry thrust her away then crushed her against his chest, his cheek on her hair.

'This is torture!' he said hoarsely.

She nodded violently, and turned up her face, her eyes sloe-black in her flushed brown face. 'But you're not going to make love to me.'

He let out an unsteady breath, his blue eyes almost as dark as hers. 'No. You must know how much I *want* to make love to you, Leonora, but not here, not like this. I want much, much more than a few snatched moments. Next time we make love I want it perfect, with all the time in the world for each other. Can you understand that, *cariad*?'

Leonora drew in a deep, unsteady breath and nodded. 'Yes.' She glanced at the clock and leapt to her feet, her colour deepening at the look in Penry's eyes as she pulled her jersey over her head. 'Just as well your particular brand of persuasion came to a halt when it did Dr Vaughan. Elise will be home soon.'

He smiled wryly as he fastened his shirt. 'I know. Otherwise. . .' He sighed with wry regret as he took her into his arms, tipping her face up to his. 'Tell me, Miss Fox, was my persuasion powerful enough? Will you come to Clem's party with me?'

'Yes.' She stood on tiptoe to kiss him. 'Otherwise I'd spend the evening wondering if you were using that particular form of persuasion on someone else.'

'Would you mind?'

'You bet I would!'

CHAPTER ELEVEN

LEONORA was suffering serious doubts about her sanity by the time the train drew in to Paddington Station the following Saturday evening. She sighed as she folded Elise's cream linen jacket over her arm before making her way along the compartment. An evening spent in the bosom of Penry Vaughan's relatives had all the appeal of Daniel's soirée in the lion's den. Not even the sight of Penry's dark head, clearly visible above the crowds on the platform, had the power to raise her spirits as he forged his way towards her, looking spectacularly attractive in a lightweight grey suit with a white silk shirt striped in Cambridge blue, open at the throat.

'Hello, *cariad*!' He lifted her down from the train, kissed her swiftly, then began to lead her towards the taxi rank. 'I left the car in Parson's Green and came in by Underground so I could hold your hand all the way back.'

Leonora hung back. 'Hello, Penry—hold on. I need to change my clothes first.'

Penry looked at her violet cotton shirt and cream denims in surprise. 'Aren't you wearing that to the party?'

'Of course I'm not,' she snapped.

He eyed her searchingly, then stood still, holding her by the shoulders, oblivious of the crowds which parted to avoid them. 'What's the matter? Sorry you came?'

She nodded vigorously, and he grinned.

'Don't worry, my lovely. I'll protect you. Not that you'll need it. My family are a nice lot by and large.'

'I'm sure they are. How much do they know about me?'

'No details. Your presence tonight won't cause comment, I promise.' He kissed the tip of her nose. 'At one time they'd have thought it odd if I didn't have a girl in tow. It was different when I was married, of course, but I'm not married any more.'

'True. Otherwise my presence wouldn't be necessary!'

'But, since it's not only necessary, but vital, get a move on, *cariad*. If I'm to drive you home afterwards we'll have to leave as soon as we arrive at this rate.'

A few moments later Leonora rejoined Penry, who was prowling around the central bookstall impatiently, looking at his watch. When she tapped him on the arm he turned swiftly, his eyes suddenly narrowed at the sight of her.

'Is this all right?' asked Leonora anxiously. 'Elise said I couldn't go wrong with a little black dress.'

'Little's the word,' he said gruffly, looking her up and down. 'I don't know that I approve of quite so much black silk leg on view, but otherwise you look wonderful.'

She smiled happily. 'Why, thank you, Doctor, you say the nicest things. I wanted to wear my hair up in a knot but Elise said you'd prefer it loose like this.'

'She's right!' Penry put his arm round her to shepherd her towards the moving row of taxis. 'Now get a move on, there's a good girl.'

Leonora felt better once she was in the taxi, particularly since Penry not only held her hand, but kept his arm round her for the entire journey, taking her mind very successfully off the evening ahead by the sheer joy of just being with him after a week apart. She gazed into his face raptly as he described his clinic the day before at St Mary's and passed on good wishes from Sister Concepta.

'What's the matter?' he said at last, as he realised she wasn't paying quite the attention he would have wished.

'I was just thinking how glad I am to see you,' she said candidly.

His arm tightened as he bent to kiss her cheek. 'Why, thank you, Miss Fox. I'm very happy to hear it.'

The moment they arrived in Parson's Green Penry rushed Leonora to the Range Rover, gave her a moment to fish out a gift-wrapped package from the bag containing her change of clothes, then stowed the latter in the car. He fairly hauled her along the street afterwards, giving her no time for nerves as they reached a white-painted door with a large brass dragon for a knocker. Almost at once it swung open to let out a surge of laughter and music as a tall dark man with a scar on one cheek clapped Penry on the back and introduced himself to Leonora as Nick Wood, then beckoned to a tall, beautiful woman with a mane of ash-blonde hair, who excused herself from a group of people to come running to throw her arms round Penry's neck.

'Hello, you finally made it.' She turned to Leonora with a radiant smile. 'Welcome to the Wood ménage, I'm so glad you could come.'

Leonora wished her hosts happy anniversary as she presented her gift rather shyly. 'I looked up the tenth anniversary and it said tin, which was a bit limiting. It's not very original, I'm afraid.'

Her gift was an oblong tin containing a bottle of venerable malt whisky, received with much pleasure by both recipients before Clem swept Leonora away on a round of introductions. At last a man with silvery smiling eyes in a brown face introduced himself as Luiz Santana, husband of Clem's twin, Charity, and took Leonora into the dining-room when Clem was called away to great more arrivals.

'*Queridas*,' he announced, 'this is Penry's guest, Señorita Leonora Fox.' The two women putting finishing touches to the buffet supper turned as one, surprise in the smiles they gave the slender figure standing alone in the doorway. Luiz introduced his mother-in-law and his wife, then excused himself to go off to help distribute drinks.

Leonora smiled diffidently, blinking with surprise at the sight of Charity, who was such a mirror image of her twin that the effect was electrifying. But her real interest lay with the older woman, whose smoke-blue eyes and distinctive bone-structure proclaimed her Penry's mother in a way which made an introduction unnecessary.

'How do you do?' she said shyly, since both women seemed momentarily at a loss for words. 'It was kind of Mrs Wood to invite me.'

'My dear child,' said Mrs Vaughan, a look on her face Leonora could have sworn was relief. She stretched out her hands in welcome. 'How very nice to meet you.'

'Why didn't Pen bring you straight to us?' demanded Charity, adding her own dazzling smile to the warmth of her mother's greeting. 'Honestly, he is the end.'

'Oh, it wasn't his fault!' said Leonora instantly, flying

to Penry's defence. 'Your sister took me off to introduce me to everyone.' She smiled ruefully. 'Not that it was much use, I'm afraid; I met so many people the faces were just a blur.'

Charity exchanged a few pleasantries, then, at a look from her mother, excused herself to go off to the kitchen, leaving Leonora alone with Mrs Vaughan.

'Penry was rather mysterious about you, my dear,' said the latter, and patted one of the dining chairs ranged along the wall. 'Come and sit here and tell me about yourself. Penry has already given me, and *only* me I would stress, a brief account of your adventure on Gullholm. Dear heaven, child, you were so lucky to survive!'

'I know, Mrs Vaughan,' agreed Leonora soberly. 'Your son saved my life.'

'Thank God he was on hand. The island's usually left to the gulls at that time of year.' Mrs Vaughan shuddered slightly, and touched Leonora's hand. 'Fate was kind to arrange for Penry to be there just when he was needed most.'

'Someone taking my name in vain?' asked Penry, coming into the room. 'There you are, Leonora. I see you've met my mother.'

'No thanks to you,' said Mrs Vaughan in dry reproof.

'Clem spirited her off before I could even get her a drink.' He handed a glass of wine to Leonora. 'Would you care for something, Mother?'

'No, thank you, darling,' said Mrs Vaughan, then met her son's eyes, stiffening, as feminine laughter rose above the general hubbub in the hall. Penry turned, his face set, as the door flew open and a tall woman in a clinging white dress paused theatrically on the threshold. She moved across the room with an indolent, hip-swaying saunter, tossing back her shining black hair as she smiled at Penry.

'Hello, Pen. Long time no see.' She turned to Mrs Vaughan. 'Hello, Mrs V, don't look so stern. I couldn't keep away from my darling brother's anniversary party, now, could I? How *are* you—and who's this?'

'Good evening, Melanie,' said Mrs Vaughan shortly. 'What a surprise. Where is—what's his name?'

'Oh, Nigel—on some beastly business trip on the Continent.' She looked at Penry challengingly. 'Haven't you got a friendly little greeting for me, Pen, darling?'

'Good evening,' he said expressionlessly, pulling Leonora to her feet. 'Allow me to introduce you. Leonora, this is Melanie, my ex-wife. Melanie this is Leonora Fox—my fiancée.'

The cruel grip of Penry's fingers conveyed an appeal which Leonora responded to without batting an eyelid at the word 'fiancée'. She smiled serenely. 'How do you do?'

The other woman swept hostile green eyes from the crown of Leonora's curly head down the brief black silk dress and long, slender legs. '*Hello*! Well, well, this is a surprise. I'd no idea you were contemplating matrimony again, Penry.'

'He thought Clem's wedding anniversary an appropriate time to announce the glad news,' said Mrs Vaughan smoothly, and rose to her feet rather stiffly to take Leonora's free arm. 'Come on, Penry. I think Katharine's arrived. She's eager to meet Leonora.' And with a cool, excluding smile for her former daughter-in-law she accompanied her large son and his slender young companion from the room, leaving Melanie staring after them in umbrage.

Leonora was never alone with Penry for a moment. She met Penry's favourite sister Kit and her husband, Reid Livesey, ate some supper, laughed and chatted with more of Penry's friends, and all the time she burned with the need to ask Penry what he was playing at, why he'd thrown down his unexpected announcement like a gauntlet in front of his voluptuous ex-wife.

As the evening wore on, with plenty of opportunity to study Melanie as the latter flitted from group to group, Leonora grew more and more furious with Penry. If his real reason for inviting her was a kind of face-saving operation in front of his former ex-wife, he might at least have had the honesty to say so. He, after all, was the one so determined to do away with sham and misunderstanding. After a couple of hours she was seized with a longing to go home, but Penry, she realised with misgiving, was suddenly nowhere to be seen.

Pressed by Clem and Mrs Vaughan to stay the night, Leonora declined with grateful thanks, hoping her longing to escape wasn't visible to Penry's family, all of whom she would have liked to know better under other circumstances. She went off on a determined search for Penry, but he was still nowhere to be seen. Leonora found a bathroom instead, and spent a few quiet minutes tidying herself up in peace. As she went back along the landing she paused, frowning.

The sound of Penry's unmistakable resonance removed any scruples Leonora might have had about eavesdropping. Through a half-open door she saw a glimmer of white and stiffened, nauseated, as she saw Melanie over Penry's shoulder, her face held up to his in impassioned invitation.

'Please, Pen,' Melanie pleaded, her husky whisper

carrying all too clearly to the girl outside in the hall. 'Just this once. For old times' sake.'

'It's out of the question,' he responded harshly, but Melanie threw herself against him. Red-tipped fingers slid up to encircle Penry's neck and Leonora turned away in blind haste, running downstairs to plunge into the crowd below.

Whcn Penry rejoined her some time later Leonora was the centre of a group discussing the rival merits of various sailing craft. Reid Livesey turned to him with a smile.

'Your lady's a sailor, then, Pen. You must take her over to Rico's place in Portugal.'

'Good idea,' said Penry absently, eyeing Leonora's brittle gaiety with a frown. 'But now I'm afraid it's time we were off. Leonora's determined to make me drive her all the way home tonight.'

There was a flurry of farewells, repeated invitations to Leonora to come again soon, then at last they were in the car and heading out of London.

'What's the matter?' asked Penry at last, breaking a silence which threatened to last all the way to Chastlecombe. 'Didn't you enjoy the party?'

'Not as much as I might have.'

'Didn't you like my family? They certainly took to you!'

'I liked your family very much, but you deliberately gave them the wrong impression about me,' she said angrily. 'Particularly your ex-wife!'

There was a pause. 'Is that what this is all about? Because I embroidered a little and introduced you as my fiancée, or because Melanie was there?'

'I assume the two are interconnected,' said Lenora stonily. 'You conveniently forgot to tell me she was

Nick Wood's sister. You knew she'd be there tonight, which is why you needed me as protective cover. Not that it worked very well, ultimately!'

'What are you getting at?'

'When you were missing I went to look for you. I didn't find you at first, so I went to the bathroom. On my way back downstairs I saw you in one of the bedrooms with Melanie.' Her voice was bitter. 'So absorbed you even forgot to close the door!'

Penry swore under his breath. 'Damn it, Leonora, it wasn't what you thought——'

'I didn't hang about long, but I saw enough to convince me that all that rubbish about Melanie's frigidity was pure invention on your part.'

'Leonora,' began Penry, sounding weary, 'Melanie didn't want me to make *love* to her. She needed a favour from me, which is why she came tonight.'

'Straight into your ever-open arms.' Leonora stared angrily through the windscreen. 'I'm sure she wasn't taken in for a moment about—about me.'

'You're wrong, as it happens. One look at you convinced Melanie of my intentions beyond all doubt.'

'Oh, really. Why?'

Penry hesitated. 'To be blunt, you're the exact opposite of all the other women in my life. Like Melanie they invariably ran to small IQ's and big bust measurements.'

'And one look at my flat chest convinced her I was the love of your life, I suppose!'

'Don't be so childish!' he snapped unforgivably.

As an end to the argument this remark was a great success. To avoid further childishness Leonora took refuge in stony, obdurate silence. Penry made several attempts to break it, but gave up at last, his face like thunder as he drove at a speed which frightened Leonora to death. By the time they finally arrived in the deserted car park behind the arcade she was trembling from head to foot, racked by every emotion from fear to rage. She yanked her seatbelt free then gave a squeak of protest as Penry pulled her into his arms to kiss her with a ferocity she fought against at first. But the upheaval of the night proved too much for emotions which see-sawed from anger to white-hot response with mortifying speed.

She could hear Penry's heart pounding against hers, as her kisses matched his in utter frenzy. He tore his mouth away at last to rub his cheek against her untidy hair as he crushed her against his chest.

'You're hurting me,' gasped Leonora at last.

Penry held her away a little, his eyes glittering into hers. 'You deserve it,' he said, breathing hard, 'for harbouring such bloody awful suspicions about me. Listen, Miss Doubting Thomas—and listen well. I can't tell you what Melanie was asking me because I don't betray other people's confidences. But one thing I want to make clear once and for all. Even if she had been asking me to make love to her—which she wasn't—the answer would very definitely have been no. For one thing she happens to be another man's wife these days. But there's a *much* better reason than that,' he added, and paused tantalisingly.

'What is it?' asked Leonora hoarsely.

'These days,' he said, looking at her in a way which took away what little breath she had left, 'I have this picture etched in my brain. Of a certain unforgettable night on my island. The experience seems to have rendered all women's attractions null and void. Except yours, Leonora Fox. Do I make myself clear?'

She nodded rapturously, and suddenly the night was beautiful and the moon shone brighter than it ever had before. 'I'm sorry,' she said, hiding her face against him. 'But Melanie's so gorgeous to look at. I was jealous. Horribly.'

Penry crowed softly in triumph then began kissing her again, and she responded ardently, all her anger and hurt melting away in the warmth of his embrace. At last he drew away, his smile rueful. 'I can think of better places to make love, *cariad*.'

'So can I,' she agreed fervently, rubbing her elbow. 'Bits of me keep coming into contact with bits of your car.'

'I'd better let you go in.'

She sighed. 'I don't want to go.'

'Nevertheless, if you have any respect for my blood-pressure, lady, I think you'd better retire to your lonely bed, while I continue my journey to Wales.' Penry kissed her again, lingeringly. 'I wish you were coming with me.'

'So do I.'

They gazed at each other in silence, then Penry touched a finger to her lower lip. 'Leonora, will you come to Wales next weekend? See my house—try it on for size, as it were? I'm tied up at the hospital for a while each day, but we could be together most of the time. Will you come?'

She nodded, her eyes like stars, her pulse racing at the implication in his words. 'I'd love to.'

'Bring Elise, too, if you like.'

'Do you want me to?'

'In a word, no.' He smiled, stroking her cheek. 'But if you're afraid I'll lose my head once we're alone together, by all means bring a chaperon.'

'I'll think about it,' she said demurely.

Leonora went round in a dream the following week. Fortunately she had an order for a full-length wool coat and dress, and worked in happy isolation in the small room at the back of the shop, her mind lingering on the implication of Penry's invitation as her fingers flew independently to finish the order for a customer due to return to the States a few days later. Penry rang each night, to remind her about the weekend, he said, in case she'd forgotten. Fat chance, thought Leonora, unable to resist keeping him in the dark about whether Elise was going with her.

'As if I would,' said Elise, laughing. 'I've no taste for playing gooseberry to a couple of lovebirds, I assure you. Off you go alone, with my blessing, love, since it seems pretty obvious Penry intends to pop the question.'

'Nonsense,' said Leonora, who had given her sister a very much edited version of Saturday night. 'He's just keen to show me his house.'

'In that case, why not surprise him? Drive to Wales on Friday evening instead of waiting for Saturday. Sue Parker will help in the shop.'

Leonora assented rapturously, keeping her change of plan gleefully secret from Penry. She started out on the Friday evening with suppressed excitement, timing her arrival long before he was likely to make the now nightly telephone call. She sang along with the radio as she drove up through Gloucestershire and crossed into Wales by way of Abergavenny and Brecon, then took the road north towards Builth Wells, to the wooded hills south of the town where Penry's house occupied a vantage point above the River Wye. His instructions had been so clear, and so often repeated, that Leonora felt she could have found her way blindfolded in the dark. She had no problem in finding the turning which led her along an unadopted road for half a mile before she drove through open gates up a steeply ascending drive past lawns on several different levels until she finally reached a gravelled circle in front of Penry's house. She gazed up at it with a deep sigh of pleasure. Built, as Penry had told her, almost a century before, its mellow brick and gleaming windows blended into the picturesque hillside, welcome in every line of it to the girl who gazed at it in bliss as she turned off the engine.

Leonora jumped out, stood looking up at the house for a few moments more, then ran up the steps to ring the doorbell, laughter bubbling up inside as she anticipated Penry's surprise at the sight of her. She waited a few moments then rang the bell again, and this time the door opened with maddening slowness. All her joy drained away like water spilled on sand as instead of Penry Vaughan's tall, broad-shouldered figure she came face to face with the woman who'd once been his wife. Melanie smiled lazily, smoothing back her hair, the opulent curves of her body outlined by the satin dressing-gown which was very blatantly the only garment she had on.

'Well, well, fancy meeting you. Leonie, isn't it? Surprise, surprise.'

'My name is Leonora.' Sick and numb with shock, Leonora felt vaguely surprised to hear her voice functioning normally.

Melanie took her by the hand and drew her inside.

'Do come in. Pen won't be long. I've been paying him a little visit.'

Leonora snatched her hand away, her eyes hunted as they scanned the large, square hall. 'Is Penry here? He's due back today, from a medical conference.'

Melanie's eyes gleamed. 'Is that what he told you? Naughty Pen. In actual fact we spent last night together, here. We've not long got up. He's just popped out for supplies. Sex does make one so hungry, doesn't it? Or perhaps you don't know about that—goodness, dear, you've gone a very funny colour!'

Leonora gulped, a hand to her mouth, and with an exclamation Melanie hauled her upstairs and through a large bedroom into a bathroom, then left her alone to part with her lunch. It was a pity, Leonora thought with bleak detachment afterwards, that shock always had such an inconvenient effect on her digestive system. After a moment or two to pull herself together and wash her face, she went back through the bedroom, her stomach heaving again when she saw the crumpled disorder of the bed. She shuddered, and ran like the wind down the stairs to escape, but as she reached the hall the door flew open and Penry burst into the house, his face alight at the sight of her.

'Leonora! You came tonight!' he said, pulling her into his arms.

She leapt away. 'Don't dare touch me!' Her eyes flashed coldly as they met the blank astonishment in his. 'I never learn do I? Like a fool I came to surprise you, just like I did once before on Brynteg. Needless to say, the surprise backfired on me. Again.'

Penry stood rigid, his eyes incredulous. 'Can you please tell me what you're talking about?'

'She's talking about me,' said Melanie, emerging

from one of the rooms off the hall, fully dressed now, every shining hair in place.

'*Melanie*? Why the hell are you still here?' demanded Penry wrathfully.

Still? Leonora could take no more. She brushed past Penry, eluding the hand he put out to detain her as she ran outside to the car, deaf to his entreaties as she jumped in the car and started it up with a violent rev of the engine. She reversed in a reckless sweep, scraping the Range Rover with a hideous scream of metal, then tore off down the hairpin bends of the drive, blinking away tears furiously to see where she was going. After a mile or two of expecting the Range Rover in pursuit it finally came home to her that Penry had no intention of following her. The discovery started her crying in earnest, which meant a stop in a lay-by for a while before she was in a fit condition to resume her journey home.

When Leonora finally arrived home, red-eyed and white-faced after a nightmare journey, she found Elise in a terrible state.

'Leonora, what on earth's going on? I've been worried to death! Penry's been on the phone every few minutes to see if you've arrived. He's out of his mind in case you've had an accident or something, but he couldn't come after you because he was due back at the hospital for a clinic.'

Leonora huddled in a little heap on the sofa, pleading for coffee before she'd say a word. Once she'd downed some of the extra-strong brew she gave her sister the bare bones of the story, then turned dull eyes on Elise's horrified face. 'Did Penry say anything about Melanie?'

'No. He just said there'd been a terrible misunderstanding, and you wouldn't listen when he tried to explain.' Elise hugged her sister close.

'What explanation could there be?' Leonora gave a dreary little laugh. 'I saw the evidence with my own eyes, Melanie wearing only a dressing-gown, her hair all over the place. I even saw the bed——' She swallowed hard. 'No, I am *not* going to be sick again,' she added fiercely as Elise eyed her in alarm.

When the telephone rang, right on cue, Leonora started up, wild-eyed. 'If that's Penry tell him I don't want to speak to him or see him again. Ever.'

The following Monday afternoon, shortly after lunch, two customers poring over the jewellery in Fox's Lair looked up in surprise as a tall man came into the shop like a whirlwind and gave Elise a brief, unsmiling greeting.

'Where is she?' he demanded.

'In the office, working. Do go through,' said Elise, unnecessarily, since Penry was already on his way.

He wrenched open the office door then slammed it behind him and stood against it, glaring into Leonora's frozen face.

'What are you doing here?' she said icily.

'I want a word with you. I've come straight from the hospital, and now I'm on my way to St Mary's, where I'm due at five. It was not part of my plan to make a detour via Chastlecombe, but since you won't talk to me on the phone I didn't have much choice. You knew perfectly well I had to stay within reach of the hospital over the weekend. I couldn't get here until now.'

Penry, hostile and intimidating, was too large a presence for the small office. Leonora felt claustrophobic as he loomed over her. She folded her work carefully and stood up, backing away.

'Elise passed on my message, I know,' she said crisply. 'Perhaps it lost something in translation. I don't want to talk to you. Ever again.'

Penry grabbed her hands. 'Just give me the chance to explain, you obstinate little fool——'

Leonora snatched her hand away, eyes blazing. 'I saw with my own eyes. You don't need to explain. You lied to me about Melanie——'

'I have never lied to you,' he broke in, white about the mouth. 'She was bent on making mischief because I wouldn't do her the favour she wanted, and she bloody well succeeded, didn't she?'

Leonora clenched her teeth. 'Ah, yes, the celebrated favour again. Tell me what it is and just possibly I might believe you.'

The dark blue eyes iced over. 'How extraordinarily good of you, Leonora. Nevertheless I can't do that. Melanie or not, it was still in confidence. All I can say is that I didn't even know Melanie was still there that night. I thought she'd gone. She'd come to persuade me——'

'And succeeded, by the look of the bed!' Leonora turned away blindly, and Penry caught her by the shoulders, forcing her round to face him.

'I did *not* make love to her, Leonora,' he said forcibly. 'Can't you believe me?'

She stared up at him despairingly. 'I want to believe you—but she's so beautiful——'

With a smothered curse he pulled her into his arms and began to kiss her, using a more powerful argument than words as the first touch of his mouth on hers sent everything out of Leonora's head other than the fact that she loved and wanted this man to the point where she was almost ready to believe that she'd been mistaken. Somehow she found the strength to pull away.

'Tell me why Melanie was there at your house?' she pleaded.

Penry stood back, looking grim and formidable. 'I can't, Leonora. All I can say is that there was an innocent explanation for what you saw. If you can't accept that, and trust me, then there's nothing more I can say.'

Leonora straightened her shoulders, pale and vulnerable in the plain black sweater and skirt she wore in the shop. She saw Penry's eyes on the silver brooch on her shoulder, knew he was remembering their time together on the island, and for a moment she was tempted to throw herself into his arms, to assure him that nothing mattered as long as he loved her, Leonora Fox, not Melanie. Then her resolve hardened. 'I saw what I saw, Penry, and I don't blame you. It's crystal-clear that whatever defects your former wife possesses you're still attracted to her. Who can blame you? When I gatecrashed your life I suppose you thought I might come in useful as some kind of antidote—but it didn't work.' She smiled frostily. 'It was a case of "physician, help thyself". It's not your fault you couldn't, Dr Vaughan.'

Penry heard her out in silence. 'I've had a wasted journey,' he said at last. 'You weren't prepared to listen to a word I had to say, were you?'

Leonora shrugged. 'What was the point?'

'What, indeed?' He gave her a chilling little bow. 'Then I'll say goodbye, Leonora. I hope I didn't shock your customers by barging in so unceremoniously.

'I imagine it made their day.' She felt quite proud of

her composure as she escorted him through the shop, relieved, for once, to see it empty. 'Goodbye,' she said as they reached the door. 'Give my love to Sister Concepta.'

Penry put out a hand, then dropped it, and with a strangled curse turned away to stride off over the cobbles of the arcade, an arresting figure in the autumn sunlight as he went out into the street without a backward glance for the girl watching him go.

CHAPTER TWELVE

THE winds of late October were lashing Haverfordwest as Leonora left the train. She smiled wearily as Bryn Pritchard came to take her case, blessing his tact when he made no comment on the reason for her visit. He installed her in his battered van, chatting volubly on every subject under the sun other than Dr Penry Vaughan on the journey, but Leonora was hard pressed to make suitable rejoinders, every nerve in her body stretched to breaking-point at the thought of what lay ahead.

When they arrived in Brides Haven Rachel Pritchard welcomed Leonora with a cup of hot, strong tea, but Bryn soon cut across his wife's chatter, pointing out that they must set out at once if he was to make the return trip before dark. His wife packed a box with various goodies for Leonora to take to Penry, then walked with them to the jetty, and waved them off on the *Sea-Fret*, a sturdy fishing-boat a lot newer than Penry's. As the boat crossed the bar into the open sea with a stomach-clenching lurch, Bryn gave his passenger an encouraging smile.

'A bit rough, but nothing to worry about, Miss Fox.'

Leonora, too wrapped up in her thoughts to be afraid, smiled back, unconcerned. 'I'm only sorry I had to bring you out in it.'

Bryn shook his head good-naturedly. 'No trouble at all. The wind's increasing to gale force later, according to the shipping forecast, but I'll be home safe and sound long before then.'

'You didn't phone Dr Vaughan to say I was coming?' asked Leonora anxiously, as Gullholm loomed nearer on the horizon.

'No. Not a word. He said he wanted peace and quiet, mind,' Bryn warned.

Leonora scanned the turbulent stretch of sea anxiously. 'I only intend to stay a few minutes. I hope Dr Vaughan will run me back in the *Angharad*.'

Bryn looked doubtful. 'You'd better not hang about, then.'

Soon the *Sea-Fret* was alongside the jetty at Gullholm and Leonora leapt out nimbly. She received her overnight bag and Rachel's box from Bryn and thanked him warmly. As he headed back across the sound she began to toil up the cliff path, pausing for breath now and then as the wind battered her and tore at her hair, which soon broke free of its restraining scarf and whipped into her eyes, slowing her progress up the wet, slippery path towards the house. Halfway up she paused, fighting for breath, suddenly struck by the enormity of what she was doing. What if Penry took one look at her and threw her out, bag and baggage? She resumed her climb doggedly. He could hardly throw her off the island. The worst he could do was take her back to Brides Haven. Then a fiercer gust of wind almost blew her from the path and she hung on to bag and box like grim death. Bryn was right. The wind was increasing to gale force, and fast. She turned to look towards the shore, relieved when she saw the *Sea-Fret* making good headway back to Brides Haven, then a flock of screaming gulls startled her into resuming her climb, and soon she was on the Neck and starting the last, steep push towards the plateau.

As the path flattened out to lead across the close turf

to the house Leonora's feet slowed. At the sight of windows lit against the gathering gloom she had a sudden desire to turn tail and run, to take refuge below in the *Angharad*. Which, she told herself trenchantly, was nonsense. She'd come this far to say her piece and say it she would, come hell or high water. She smiled at this last. If the weather went on deteriorating at this rate there'd be plenty of the latter around Gullholm.

Sodden by the now driving rain, breathing hard from the climb, Leonora crept round the house to the cluster of outbuildings at the back, where the familiar throb of the generator welcomed her like a friend. Which, she thought drily, was probably the only welcome she'd get. Penry was unlikely to look kindly on someone who landed on his island uninvited twice in a row.

Uncertain whether to knock politely on the kitchen door, or just thrust it open and make a dramatic entry, Leonora dumped her bag on the flagstones and pushed wet rat's-tails of hair back from her face. Somehow it seemed silly to knock. Taking her courage in both hands, she left her bag where it was and turned the knob, pushing open the door into the kitchen which smelled so warm and inviting and blessedly familiar that a lump rose in her throat. She closed the door softly, then advanced cautiously across the room to deposit the box on the counter. The door to the study was half open but the room itself was in darkness. No Penry there. Slipping off her muddy shoes, Leonora went on into the big living-room, every nerve on edge as she crept silently across the familiar worn carpet towards the seductive warmth from the stove, but there was still no sign of Penry. In deference to the generator, presumably, only one of the table lamps was lit, giving the room a shadowy, ghostly look. Steam rose from her clothes as she hesitated, wondering what to do next. Somehow she'd imagined Penry leaping up from the sofa at the sight of her, angry at her intrusion. Or even smiling in welcome, in some of her wilder dreams. The silence of the deserted room was eerie. There was an open book on the sofa, a basket of ready-chopped wood near the stove, even a half-full glass on a table. Leonora shivered and held out her hands to the stove, then stood motionless as she realised she was being watched. She turned slowly to face the forbidding figure standing in semi-darkness halfway up the stairs.

'They say an Englishman's home is his castle,' said Penry tonelessly, his face invisible in the shadows. 'I'm Welsh, but the principle's the same. I should have fortified myself better against invaders.'

Leonora, wishing with all her heart she'd listened to Elise and telephoned, instead of rushing to the island uninvited, squared her shoulders. 'I've come to say I'm sorry,' she blurted. 'It seemed like the only thing to do before I set out. Now I'm actually here I realise I'm intruding. I'm sorry. It was stupid to barge in here like this.'

Penry walked slowly down the remaining stairs and crossed the room towards her, stumbling over a rug en route. He wore a navy guernsey and salt-stained Levis, and he needed a shave. He needed a haircut, too, noted Leonora with misgiving, and from the look in his eyes he was in a foul mood.

'Are you ill?' she asked sharply.

'I was; but no longer. I've had a drink or two. And if this were any other place I'd tell you to get the hell out of here and out of my life.' He reached over for the glass and swallowed down the rest of its contents, eyeing her malevolently. 'As it is we're on an island

and the bloody weather's deteriorating fast. If I were completely sober I might just manage to get you back to Brides Haven, but I doubt it. In any case, as you can see, I am not sober. So I'm stuck with you, Miss Castaway, yet again. How the hell did you get here?'

'Mr Pritchard brought me.'

'Why the devil didn't he ring me to say you were coming?'

'I asked him not to.' Leonora stuck her chin out. 'I thought you wouldn't let me come.'

'You thought right!'

'I'm sorry. I shouldn't have come.' She looked away. 'I'll ring Mr Pritchard to fetch me in the morning if you'll just let me stay the night.'

'What choice do I have?' he demanded irritably. 'I'm hardly likely to throw you out in this weather.'

'Thank you.' She eyed him cautiously. 'Perhaps you'll let me cook dinner in return for your hospitality.'

'My hospitality!' He eyed her with derision. 'All right, Leonora, let's keep it civilised, by all means. I'd planned a liquid dinner for myself——'

'A square meal would do no harm, by the look of you,' she retorted. 'May I take my jacket off, please?'

'Do what you like,' he said without interest, and stretched out on the sofa. 'I think I'll have a nap.'

In sudden fury Leonora caught hold of his legs and swung them to the floor. 'No, you won't. You'll go upstairs and have a hot bath and a shave. I'll have some black coffee waiting when you get down. It's a good thing your patients can't see you now, Dr Vaughan!'

He staggered to his feet, swaying a little, his eyes like chips of blue ice. 'I happen to be here on holiday, Goody Two-Shoes. A few hard-earned days of R and

R, as the Americans put it, away from everything and everyone—or so I thought. I had a bad dose of influenza, if you must know. My mother wanted to fuss over me in Lanhowell, but somehow I couldn't take that. I needed solitude—so where better to find it than my island? Or so I thought,' he added morosely.

'I see,' she said, unzipping her jacket. 'You obviously haven't been eating properly——'

'And I've had a couple of glasses of Scotch to celebrate finishing a course of antibiotics for a chest infection,' he finished wearily. 'Not exactly a punishable offence. But then, I forgot. Your opinion of my integrity is not exactly high, is it, Miss Fox?'

'I came a long way to say I'm sorry,' Leonora reminded him. 'Go on. Go up and have a bath—even a nap, if you like.'

Penry eyed her broodingly, then shrugged. 'Why not?' he said carelessly, and made for the stairs with the care of someone not absolutely steady on his feet.

Leonora watched him go, frowning, then went to fetch her bag. Alone in the kitchen, she towelled her hair dry and stripped off her wet jeans and socks, draping them on the rack of the Aga with her jacket. In dry denims with a heavy black jersey over her scarlet wool shirt, she looked through the refrigerator and cupboards and began to concoct a dinner likely to appeal to a newly recovered—and fractious—invalid.

Once a pan of vegetable soup was simmering fragrantly on the stove she put potatoes to bake in the oven then sprinkled rosemary and garlic slivers over some lamb chops, ready to grill when her dinner companion chose to put in an appearance. Refusing to let herself think beyond the tasks she was performing, Leonora listened to the radio as she worked, and when the meal was well advanced she went quietly upstairs to find the bathroom empty, and Penry, fully dressed in fresh clothes, fast asleep on his bed.

She washed swiftly, brushed her drying hair into softer curls, then flicked on some mascara and gave her lips a touch of colour before bearding the lion in his den.

Standing at the foot of the bed, Leonora touched one of Penry's bare brown feet. 'Dinner's almost ready. Shall I bring you up a tray, or will you come down?'

Penry shot upright, yawning mightily as he rubbed eyes which focused on her with a noticeable lack of warmth. 'So you weren't a dream.'

'No.' She smiled cheerfully. 'Do you feel well enough to come down?'

He slid to his feet, stretching. 'Of course I do.' He frowned, surprised. 'In fact I feel very much better.'

'Good. Put something on your feet before you come downstairs,' she ordered as she went out.

'You sound like my mother,' he called after her.

'Thank you,' she shouted as she went downstairs. 'Having met your charming mother I'll take that as a compliment.'

Without anything said a truce seemed to have been tacitly agreed. Penry, obviously very much better after his sleep, admitted that the meal was a great improvement on the one he'd planned.

'I haven't felt much like cooking.'

'I can tell,' said Leonora, removing their soup bowls. 'The fridge is full—so are the cupboards.'

When she returned with the main meal, Penry sniffed ecstatically. 'If this is an apology, Leonora, I accept whole-heartedly.'

'Good. There's some apple tart afterwards, if you like.'

He regarded her with awe. 'Don't tell me you made that, too, while I was sleeping off my drunken stupor?'

'It wasn't a drunken stupor, nor did I make the tart.' She grinned. 'Mrs Pritchard sent it over, along with a pile of Welsh cakes and something she called *bara brith*.'

He nodded, mouth full. 'A sort of tea-bread with currants and so on. She's a great cook. So are you,' he added, then smiled wryly as the wind howled in the chimney like a lost soul. 'This is where we came in first time round, Leonora. Just you and me and a force-ten gale.'

There was a sudden, charged silence which Leonora broke hastily, pressing him to apple tart, but Penry shook his head.

'I'll leave the tart for tomorrow—sinful to cancel the flavour of that lamb.' He stretched luxuriously. 'Coffee would be nice.'

Leonora gave a little bob. 'Certainly sir. Coming up.'

When the meal was cleared away and they were settled before the fire, Penry looked across at Leonora thoughtfully.

'Strange, really. It seems like only yesterday we were here like this before, as if the months in between had never been.' His mouth twisted. 'Which would be a good thing in some ways.'

'Penry,' said Leonora, bracing herself. 'I think that's my cue to explain why I'm here.'

Penry shrugged. 'It isn't necessary.'

'I think it is.'

'You mean you came because you're ready to listen to me now?' He said with sarcasm.

Leonora flushed. 'I wish I could say yes. But I can't.'

'Then what in hell's name made you come all this way in weather like this?'

'Your sister wrote to me.'

Penry stretched out his long legs to glower at his battered espadrilles. 'Which one?'

'Clemency.'

'Ah!'

'She told me Melanie was expecting a baby soon after Christmas.'

He shot a hostile look at her. 'And you assumed I was the father, no doubt!'

Leonora met the look squarely. 'At first reading I did. The word "baby" came off the page like a fist. But as I went on reading I found that wasn't what Clem was telling me at all.' She cleared her throat. 'The favour Melanie wanted was an abortion, wasn't it? And as a doctor it was against your ethics to tell me.'

'Something like that,' said Penry bitterly. 'Melanie always had hysterics at the mere mention of motherhood. Nigel wasn't as forbearing as me. He made very sure she got pregnant. Melanie was furious, and desperate enough to go to any lengths to terminate the pregnancy. She couldn't pay for an abortion herself because Nigel won't let her have a cheque book or a credit card, let alone any cash. She's forced to ask him for everything, loaded as he is. Nigel is by no means the fool she took him for. So Melanie actually had the gall to ask her brother Nick for the money for an abortion that night. At a party to celebrate ten years of marriage to Clem, would you believe? He wiped the floor with her. Nick's a straight arrow. He wouldn't have anything to do with it.'

'Was she asking you for money?'

Penry's lips curled with distaste. 'No. What you witnessed that night was Melanie trying to persuade me to perform the operation for her—or, failing that, to get someone else to do it as a favour.' He looked Leonora in the eye. 'I gave her short shrift. As you know, I'm sensitive on that particular subject.'

She flushed, her eyes falling. 'Yes. I do. But to continue with Clem's letter—she told me Melanie went to Wales after you to try more persuasion.'

'She did. Melanie was determined to get her own way. She rang up to make an appointment with my receptionist, using a false name. When I found her the other side of my desk I told her in no uncertain terms I wasn't having anything to do with it. I spiked her guns by the simple expedient of ringing Nigel right away, told him the truth, and instructed him to fetch her home and keep her there. I was called away to the hospital so I left her at the house waiting for Nigel to turn up to collect her.' Penry smiled morosely. 'Unfortunately fate delivered you into Melanie's hands before Nigel arrived. She saw you coming up the drive, and hit on the ideal way to take her revenge. She tore off her clothes, made a mess of the bed and—you know the rest.'

Leonora stared at him in horror. 'Why would she do something so horrible? Does she hate you, Penry?'

'No.' Penry shrugged. 'She's terminally immature, that's all. She was furious because I wouldn't do what she wanted and paid me back as spitefully as she knew how. Her punishment is having to bow to the inevitable. Motherhood has overtaken her whether she wants it or not.' Penry got up to put more logs on the stove. When he sat down again there was a long, tense silence.

Leonora knew perfectly well it was time for her to grovel, but found it difficult to make a start. 'I'm so sorry I wouldn't listen to you,' she said at last.

'I'm sorry, too.' He looked at her curiously. 'Why did Clem take it into her head to write to you?'

Leonora looked down at her hands. 'Your family was worried about your—your frame of mind. Clem seemed to think it was something to do with me.'

'She knew damn well it was something to do with you. I told her that her precious sister-in-law had made a mess of my life yet again, so I suppose she felt obliged to make amends.'

'It wasn't like that at all!' flared Leonora. 'Clem was deeply concerned because you were unhappy, and because she loves you she decided to interfere. Her word, not mine, by the way. I'm glad she did.'

'But if she hadn't you'd never have got in touch.'

'I wanted to, but after the way we parted last time I didn't dare.' She looked at him squarely. 'Do you accept my apology, Penry?'

'Yes. Of course I do.' He held out his hand to help her up. 'But that's enough emoting for tonight. Right now I think it's time you went to bed. You look tired. I've put hot-water bottles in the room next to the bathroom.'

'Thank you.' Leonora eyed him uncertainly. 'Goodnight, then.'

'Goodnight.' Penry's eyes were inscrutable as she turned away.

'I'll just collect my bag from the kitchen,' she murmured.

'Shall I carry it up for you?'

'Oh, no. There's not much in it. Just enough for one night.'

'So you definitely expected to stay, then!'

Leonora looked at him levelly. 'Yes, but not here. Mrs Pritchard was going to put me up.'

Leonora felt horribly depressed as she prepared for bed. On the way in the train earlier she had pictured her meeting with Penry over and over again, but none of her imaginings had been remotely like the reality. She'd been a fool to think one polite little apology would be enough to put everything right between them. Penry was a mature, proud man who obviously no longer thought it worth the trouble to cultivate a relationship with someone as jealous and unreasonable as Leonora Fox, spinster of the parish of Chastlecombe.

Perhaps, thought Leonora, turning out the light, she would never have learned the truth if Clem hadn't written. Penry's ethics would never have allowed him to reveal the reason for Melanie's visit to his home. A home, she thought in sudden pain, which I'll never share with him now. Penry had quite plainly lost interest in her. And who could blame him?

Leonora lay hugging a hot-water bottle in the noisy darkness, grateful for the warmth as she listened to the wind howling in counterpoint to the boom of the sea on the rocks below. Her mouth twisted at the thought that this time, at least, there was no danger of a nightmare. Those had vanished since the return of her memory.

She tensed, struck by a sudden brainwave. She lay thinking about it for some time, then decided she had nothing to lose. Not daring to put on the light, she sat up and felt for the glass of water on the bedside table. For a moment she hesitated, then, her mouth set in a determined line Elise would have recognised with misgiving, set about dampening her cotton nightshirt and then her hair and face to simulate perspiration. Replacing the glass with care, she slid back down in the bed and deliberately conjured up the scene in the *Seren* at the moment the engine cut out and she was about to capsize. The horror of the memory made it all too easy to choke and scream, but to her relief her performance was cut short in seconds as the door burst open, the light snapped on and she was in Penry's arms, held close to his chest, and so glad to be there that not even her guilt could mar the joy of the moment.

'It's all right, it's all right,' said Penry hoarsely, as her tears, hot and flooding in relief, streamed down his bare chest. 'I've got you, my darling, I've got you.'

Leonora held up her face blindly and he crushed her even closer, kissing her until neither could breathe.

'You're wet,' he said at last, and picked her up and carried her into his bedroom. 'I'll find you something dry.'

But when they reached his room Leonora wriggled out of his arms and stood on the bedside rug, hands behind her back, guilt flooding her now in full force at the look in his eyes. 'I didn't have a nightmare,' she blurted, her small breasts rising and falling convulsively under the clinging, damp cotton. 'I doused myself with my glass of water and then I screamed, hoping to bring you running.'

Penry stared at her incredulously, then to her relief the tension drained from his face before her eyes as his muscular, beautiful torso began to vibrate with laughter. 'You little witch! I *came* running, too, didn't I?'

'Are you angry with me?' she muttered, blushing furiously.

'Only for courting pneumonia,' he said softly and closed the gap between them to lift her face to his. 'Since this nightshirt's damp the sensible course, Miss Fox, would be to remove it, don't you agree?' And slowly and carefully he peeled the garment over her head, his hands unsteady as he completed the task. 'You should dry your hair——' he began, but Leonora shook her head violently and brushed past him to leap into his bed. She held up her arms in entreaty, her eyes glittering darkly in her flushed face.

'Just make love to me, Penry, *please*. If you don't I think I'll die——'

The rest of her sentence died on her lips as Penry took her in his arms with a sound somewhere between a sigh and a groan as their lips met and their bodies flowed together in a deep, primeval need which united them almost at once in a storm of love and need as fierce as the one which raged, unheard, outside.

'Damn,' said Leonora a long time afterwards.

Penry raised his handsome head in enquiry. 'You spoke?'

She gave him a rueful, slumbrous look. 'I made a sort of vow.'

He turned over on his back and drew her up so that her head lay on his shoulder. 'Of chastity? If so, it wasn't much of a success.'

He yelped as she bit him, but Leonora grinned up at him, unrepentant. 'You may remember that I begged you to make love to me the first time, Penry Vaughan! So I made a vow that the next time you'd beg me.'

'And I will. Promise.' He detached a hand to look at his watch. 'But not for half an hour or so—what's the matter?' as Leonora stared at him, wide-eyed.

'I didn't mean tonight,' she muttered, burying her face against his shoulder.

Penry stretched luxuriously, moulding her closely against him. 'Ah, but I did. Unless you object?'

She shook her head emphatically.

He laughed softly. 'I love you so much, you know, my little vixen. You were blazingly angry with me that day at the house.'

'I was jealous. Horribly, mortifyingly jealous of your beautiful wife.'

'Ex.' Penry rubbed his cheek over her hair. 'Leonora, does the fact that I've been married before put you off the thought of becoming my wife?'

'No,' she said decisively, raising her head so that he could see her eyes. 'Nothing could. Are you proposing, Dr Vaughan?'

'Oh, my darling, I am, I am!'

'Then I accept. With great pleasure.'

'I was going to propose to you properly that week-end,' he went on after a long, blissful interval. 'I had champagne chilling ready for a romantic dinner *à deux*. And when you were in suitably softened mood I was going to tell you how this time I'd found what I'd really been looking for all my life.'

'And only an hour or so ago,' said Leonora wonderingly, 'I was thinking you'd lost interest in me completely.'

'Then I must be a bloody good actor!' He turned her face up to his. 'What's going to happen about Elise and Fox's Lair once we're married?'

'Elise has it all cut and dried already. Sue Parker—

mother of Julian, who's only eighteen, by the way,' added Leonora with a wicked little grin, 'is keen to go into partnership with her, and I can do what I do just as easily after I'm married as before.'

Penry gave her a smile which brought the blood to her cheeks. 'Yes, definitely,' he said softly, brushing her hair back from her forehead.

'I meant knitting!' Leonora giggled, then bit her lip, eyeing him anxiously. 'You must think I was taking a lot for granted, sorting all this out before—well, before I even knew you'd let me on the island, let alone still want me.'

'You knew damn well I wanted you!'

'I didn't! But Elise was absolutely sure you did. She said that if I came here to the island and said I was sorry you'd welcome me with open arms.' She eyed him accusingly. 'You didn't, though. You weren't very welcoming at all.'

Penry opened his arms wide, then closed them about her. 'I couldn't believe my eyes, Leonora, when I saw you standing in the middle of the room down there. I'd been lying on my bed, thinking of you, and suddenly I couldn't bear it a moment longer and jumped off the bed intending to phone you—and there you were, looking half drowned and so nervous I was afraid to put a foot wrong.'

'All you had to do was kiss me, Dr Vaughan!'

'With a day's growth of beard and reeking of Scotch? I could have smacked your bottom for taking me by surprise. If you'd just rung from Bryn's place I could have at least made myself presentable, *cariad*!'

'You looked quite wonderful to me,' she said matter-of-factly, and resisted when he'd have hugged the life out of her. 'Besides, I was afraid you wouldn't let me come if I phoned.'

'Are you joking? I'd have cast off in the *Angharad* to fetch you the minute I knew you were there!'

'Would you? Really?' Reading the confirmation in his eye, she sighed happily, then detached herself. 'I'm going to tidy myself up. I must look a wreck.'

'Don't go!' Penry drew her back into his arms slowly. 'You look utterly ravishing to me. So much so that I want very much to make love to you again. Are you going to make me beg?'

Leonora shook her head in revulsion. 'No. Not now. Not ever! I love you too much——'

'At last!' said Penry gruffly.

'At last what?'

'You've told me you love me.'

She frowned. 'Of course I love you. I have right from the first. Didn't you know that?'

He shook his head, his eyes blazing with a light which sent everything out of her head. 'Go on,' he prompted after an interval spent in convincing her that her sentiments were returned in full.

'What do you mean?' she asked breathlessly.

'You said you loved me too much—and then stopped.'

Her face cleared. 'Oh. I merely meant that I love you too much to refuse you anything—only I'm probably an idiot to admit it!'

Much later that night, when the storm had died down and they lay at rest in each other's arms, on the verge of sleep at last, Leonora said very quietly, 'Penry.'

'Mm.'

'Will you be offended if I ask you a question?'

He chuckled. 'I won't know until you ask it. Besides, the way I feel now nothing could offend me.'

'Don't count on it. I want to know whether you and Melanie slept in this bed together.'

Penry laughed, cuddling her close. 'No, we didn't. In fact, my little castaway, she never set foot on the island at all—wouldn't come near the place.'

'Great!' said Leonora with satisfaction. 'I'm glad. This is something of yours that belongs just to me, then.'

Penry shook her slightly. 'Correction. Everything I have and am and ever will be belongs to you, Leonora. All of me. Satisfactory?'

'Very.' She gave an ecstatic little wriggle. 'Are you sorry now that I invaded your castle?'

'Haven't I shown you how delighted I am that you did? If you're not sure I'm perfectly happy to convince you again,' he whispered, kissing her. 'It was a lucky day for me when the storm washed you up on my island, my darling.'

'Neither of us had a clue who I was, then!'

'*I* knew who you were, *cariad*. I'm a Celt, remember. I knew I'd met my fate right from the start!'

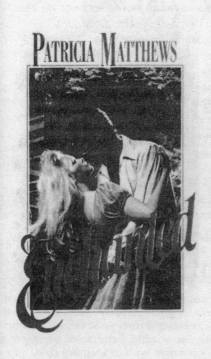

'You're so lovely,' Kyle whispered raggedly. 'So slender and graceful, so cool and elusive...' His hand was caressing her hip, the satiny skin of her thigh. 'From the moment I saw you, I've been burning for you. And I know you feel the same way, too.'

'You don't know anything of the kind,' Sophie retorted. But she had to speak between his kisses, and the blood was rushing in her veins, like molten gold being poured into a new mould, a new shape.

Then she remembered Maisie. Before he could stop her, she slid away from him, rose to her slender, shaky legs, and ran down the moist sand to the sea.

The warm water enveloped her, too warm and too salt to do much in the way of rinsing away her emotions, but at least she had escaped from the drowning maelstrom of Kyle's lovemaking.

For the time being.

Books you will enjoy
by MADELEINE KER

A SPECIAL ARRANGEMENT

It might be the twentieth century, but arranged marriages still existed, as Romy found out when Xavier de Luca blackmailed her into marrying him. He wanted heirs for his Sicilian estate, and in return he would save Romy's father from bankruptcy. But could she cope with such an arrangement when her feelings for him were so extreme?

PASSION'S FAR SHORE

Dorothy had accepted the job as governess to Pearl, not because she wanted to go to Japan, but because the little girl needed her. But it seemed Pearl's father, Calum Hescott, thought differently...

TIGER'S EYE

Working so closely with Blaize Oliver in Spain, Leila couldn't help but acknowledge his powerful charm. But Blaize's hostile teenage daughter had warned Leila off her father—and it was a warning Leila, with her inbred instinct for self-preservation, was determined to heed...

DUEL OF PASSION

BY

MADELEINE KER

MILLS & BOON LIMITED
ETON HOUSE 18-24 PARADISE ROAD
RICHMOND SURREY TW9 1SR

First published in Great Britain 1990
by Mills & Boon Limited

This edition 1990

ISBN 0 263 76657 8

Set in Times Roman 10 on 10½ pt.
01-9004-60366 C

Made and printed in Great Britain

CHAPTER ONE

THE rhythm of the Caribbean surf was the most soothing sound Sophie had ever known. It was so different from the pounding of the North Sea, that gravelly hammering she had listened to all her childhood on the North Yorkshire coast; and different, too, from the peaceful lap-lapping of the Mediterranean, the only other sea she'd known.

Lying on her back in the baking sun, her eyes shut behind the opaque sunglasses, she had been listening to the alternate rush and hiss of the ocean waves all morning, wrapped in a world of peace and warmth.

Now and then there had been the distant voices of other people sharing this Jamaican morning; but the exclusive San Antonio Hotel owned the whole white sweep of beach, and since Sophie had walked almost half a mile from the hotel to find the most sheltered spot in it, encircled by rocks and sheltered from the breezes, she'd had the surf and the sun and the sand all to herself all morning.

She hoped it was going to be like this every day for the next three weeks.

For a single girl in her early twenties to have chosen to spend a three-week holiday by herself in Ocho Rios, on the beautiful north coast of Jamaica, was slightly unusual. But then, Sophie Aspen was a slightly unusual person. And she'd had strong reasons for choosing this kind of break.

After less than four days of her holiday, Sophie was already starting to tan a rich golden-brown. Her slim body, as she lay completely relaxed in her black bikini, might have served as a mouth-watering image for some lavish advertisement.

She was tall for a woman, and her figure was delectable, with slender and graceful limbs. The outsize sunglasses covered a lot of her face, but what showed was distinctly interesting: a short, straight nose and a neat chin, framing a full, rather passionate mouth, and an abundance of mahogany-rich hair, now taking on golden highlights under the influence of the sun.

It was the mouth to which one's attention returned. Warm and sexy, it was also determined. There was courage in its curves, evidence that the owner possessed strong and definite feelings. Whatever the eyes were like behind those sunglasses, the casual observer might have guessed that they would be both beautiful and marked by a strong character.

The casual observer, if asked to guess her occupation, might have suggested modelling, the theatre, or television. In fact, all three would have been accurate guesses, because Sophie Aspen had worked intermittently in all three of those fields.

But since leaving drama school she had thought of herself primarily as an actress. That was the goal she had always had throughout her adolescence. During the past two years, however, she had struggled through one of the worst periods for the theatre in recent years, counting herself lucky to have got walk-on parts in minor productions, with the odd bonanza of an appearance in a television commercial. Until last autumn, that was.

Last autumn—in October, to be precise—she had been given her first real, meaty role. And not just in some small company, either; she had landed the part of Maisie Wilkin in *The Elmtree Road Murders*, a glamorous period murder mystery being made by BBC 2's drama department.

The play was scheduled for a peak-viewing two-hour slot this summer, on Thursday the fifteenth of August. Only a few weeks away, in fact.

It had been her biggest break ever, and it had called forth her finest performance so far.

Yet, now, she could not think of *The Elmtree Road Murders* without a touch of sadness. What had started out as such an exciting challenge for her had ended on a note of bitterness and hurt.

It had taken all the eight months since then to get over that hurt.

The past days of swimming and long walks along the beach had already seen a few ounces of excess weight disappear from her hips and thighs, and, in fact, she was slimmer now than she'd ever been since leaving drama school. Her body was honing down to exquisite lines, and her skin was recovering from the awful period of greasy lifelessness it had gone through.

She felt optimistic and healthy...

All that remained to fix now was the old-fashioned hairstyle that she'd worn for the three modern dramas. The hairdressers had advised her to let it grow out before she had it cut.

As soon as she got back to London, she would have to start preparing for her next job: a television commercial for bath oil, scheduled to be filmed in six weeks' time. The fifty-second sequence of her soaping herself languidly in a bathtub would hardly be great theatrical art, but it would certainly pay a few bills!

She would have to contact the art director of the advertising company about her hair. She wanted it cut into something glamorous and short, but she would have to go by what they decided.

There were voices nearby again: the soft laughter of a child, and the husky bass of a man. Too soft to contend with the musical suck and rush of the surf, they scarcely intruded into Sophie's thoughts.

'Give me your hand. Come on, don't be frightened.'

Lazily, Sophie turned her head to half open her eyes. A man, the owner of the bass voice, was hoisting a little girl up to stand on the rocks beside which Sophie was lying. They were against the sun, and through her sunglasses they were just two silhouettes.

'Oh, look at that beautiful boat!'

'Which one?'

'The one with the red sail. There!'

'Ah, yes. That's rather nice. Want one like that for your birthday?'

Something about that husky voice was starting to make Sophie's nerves prickle with tension.

'Uncle Kyle! Look at this.'

Kyle? It couldn't be. Not here! It had to be a figment of her imagination.

Her peaceful reverie had turned into a waking nightmare. She listened tautly as the man answered the child's chattering questions, trying to establish whether that husky voice was the one that had once cut into her with the force of a rhino-hide whip.

The last time she'd heard *that* voice had also been on a beach, almost nine months ago. On that occasion, his words had carried, clear and deep, across the beach. But today the sea and the wind made voices sound different, softer...

'Let's go down there. It looks interesting.'

They were clambering down the rocks towards the little enclave where Sophie lay. Let them not come down here, she prayed hastily. Escape was impossible—there was no way out of her little inlet. But it was too late for prayers. They were down now, and walking towards her.

'Uncle Kyle,' she heard the child exclaim, 'someone's already here!' Then, in a confidential voice, she added, 'Gosh. She's *lovely*.'

Sophie sat up quickly, and lifted her sunglasses to stare at the pair.

'I'm so sorry,' the man said, speaking directly to Sophie. 'We didn't mean to wake you.'

Recognition of that husky voice was superfluous. As soon as she'd looked into the dark-fringed, deep green eyes, she'd felt a giant fist close around her heart and start squeezing.

It was Kyle Hart.

Unbelievably, it *was*. Wearing only a dark blue Speedo that emphasised, rather than concealed, his manifest masculinity, he stood between her and the sea, considering Sophie with that assessing, smouldering gaze she knew so well.

A formidably male face, etched with lines that said he'd lived through plenty of experience, in more departments of life than one. The mouth looked as though it had kissed a thousand women, and had left them all crying for more.

The silvery streaks among the dark, almost black hair said that he was no boy. Yet his potency and vigour were unquestioned. His lithe body was tanned darker than her own, a symphony of lean muscle, emphasised by the dark hair that curled lazily down his flat belly to his loins. His legs were long and muscular, and he had the powerful shoulders and taut waist of a man who took his exercise seriously.

The child beside him was dark-haired and pretty, and was carrying a red plastic bucket full of pebbles and sea shells.

Sophie's throat had been too choked with shock to answer him. She was waiting for him to recognise her, to remember, to say something. She found words with an effort.

'I—I wasn't asleep.'

His gaze was moving down the satiny skin of her body appreciatively, with no sign that he had ever set eyes on her before now. He swung his wide shoulders to glance round her little cove. 'Nice place you have here.' he smiled. '"A fine and private place."'

...But none I think do there embrace. Her memory finished the couplet for her, but her voice was still frozen.

'You *are* English?' he asked, turning the dark green eyes back to her with a quizzical look.

The direct question forced an answer out of her.

'Yes. I'm English.'

He laughed, a pleasant, husky sound. 'For a moment I thought you might be French or Italian. You could be, with that tan, although the grey eyes are a give-away. You're staying at the San Antonio?'

'Yes,' she said again, dry-mouthed.

He considered her blank expression, her hand still holding the sunglasses up against her forehead. 'Are we bothering you?'

'N-not at all.'

He nodded, evidently deciding not to attempt any more conversational gambits, and squatted next to the little girl, hard muscles tightening along his thighs. 'Look at all these lovely shells, Emma. Isn't that a cowrie?'

Together, they wandered away from Sophie, the man holding the child's hand. He didn't look back.

He had stared her straight in the eyes, and hadn't known.

Don't you recognise me? The disbelieving cry was still echoing in Sophie's head as she lowered the sunglasses again, and wrapped her slim arms around her knees.

Her heart was pounding behind her breast-bone, making her breathing quicken involuntarily. What was he doing here?

What perverse fate could have brought him all this way, to land in the very little cove where she had been lying? It just didn't seem possible that his presence here could be a coincidence. Was it possible that there was a connection, that he had followed her here——?

She rejected the idea before it was even half formed, with a flicker of scorn. Of course he hadn't. That was absurd. If he'd wanted to contact her after Brighton, he'd had eight long months to do it in.

And she'd told no one except Joey that she was coming to Jamaica. Hélène didn't know: she was filming in Scotland. No, it had to be coincidence.

Sophie sat in a kind of trance, watching him stroll along the beach with the child, as if the slightest movement would break the spell and make him vanish.

But he didn't vanish. It was Kyle Hart, here in Ocho Rios. She was still getting to grips with the idea. The little girl had called him 'Uncle'. His real niece? The daughter of his current lover? There was no way of telling.

The situation would be almost funny if it weren't so weird. A mad desire to laugh rose up in her. They hadn't seen each other since last October. Had she really changed that much in the eight months since then?

Yes, of course she had changed. Though why should he remember her, whether she'd changed or not? It was as inevitable that he would forget her as that she would remember him with needle-sharp clarity. Their meetings had been brief, forgettable, and he would probably never know how much he had offended her.

A slow, ironic smile tugged at her lips. Well, *he* hadn't changed much, anyway. Kyle Hart was still the most beautiful male animal she had ever set eyes on.

The last time she'd seen him, on Brighton beach at the end of last year, he'd worn an elegant cream linen suit. He was even more magnificent now, more complete, as he wandered semi-naked along a very different beach.

The child laughed happily as she and Kyle moved along the waterline, searching the white sand for treasures. Sophie followed them with grey eyes that were starting to mist behind the sunglasses, as she remembered the way it had all started, in the summer of last year...

'You'll have to put on three stones, of course.'

'What?'

'There's a limit to what padding can achieve. It's the arms and legs, you know. And the face, of course.'

Sophie's agent, Joey Gilmour, had been excited about the role from the very start. He'd felt that it was the right opening for Sophie, and he'd been proved right. Though the big roles had already been earmarked for popular and established actors like Hélène le Bon, there was going to be a sprinkling of new faces in the cast.

And the part of Maisie Wilkin had been one of those scheduled to go to an unknown.

The blackmailing housemaid, Maisie Wilkin, was a grotesque character in every respect. Not only was she a leech who had battened on her erring but beautiful mistress for two years, but she was physically far from inspiring. The scriptwriters had been very firm about that.

Her being plain, overweight and ungainly was an essential part of the story, as Sophie's agent had impressed upon her while he'd been grooming her for the auditions. It explained her bitter jealousy and resentment of her elegant employer's many affairs with men.

Maisie Wilkin was certainly a challenge, a role for a character actress to get her teeth into. If she landed the job of playing Maisie, it would be Sophie's most important part since leaving drama academy. And, considering that a large proportion of that period had been spent sitting in her agent's waiting-room, or casting for parts she'd never got, Sophie had launched into the task of landing Maisie with every ounce of enthusiasm at her disposal.

She had embarked on the task of putting on thirty more pounds of adiposity. Before the audition, Joey had also made her have her hair cut in a hideously unflattering 1920s style, with a parting down the middle, and short, ungainly bangs like spaniel's ears. She'd completed the outfit with low-heeled shoes that reduced her height, old-fashioned horn-rimmed glasses that were alternately like Billy Bunter and a particularly hung-over barn-owl, and a thick coating of sallow make-up.

Similarly, she'd had to overlay her hint of a northern accent with a southern counties intonation. She'd had to unlearn the elegant model's walk that had taken so long to perfect, and had developed a shuffling, flat-footed gait.

It had all been a challenge. But she'd risen to it with the will of one who hadn't worked in a long while, and the results had bowled the casting director over.

'That's it,' she'd all but shouted, as Sophie had finished the speech they'd given her to read. 'That's Maisie Wilkin!'

All she needed, she had been told, was to dye her hair black, and put on just fifteen more pounds.

'It'll come off again in a flash,' she'd been assured, 'and it really is essential for the part. Don't you like cream cakes?'

'Well, yes——'

'Just let yourself go, darling. Fifteen pounds'll go on in no time. Frankly, an order like that is my idea of heaven!'

That was the way it had begun.

The first time she had met Kyle Hart had been several weeks after that.

It had been in Brighton, during the final stages of filming *The Elmtree Road Murders*, before they'd gone back to London to do the courtroom scenes. She remembered it all so well. It had been at a stage when she'd been most preoccupied with her characterisation, and most concerned to give a good performance in her first major role.

She and Hélène had eaten in the mobile canteen, in the courtyard of the rambling old boarding-house where they'd been filming. the two of them had been alone at a table, under an umbrella to shade them from the morning sun.

Hélène had had the chicken salad, and Sophie had had a pie and chips. She'd been asking Hélène for some precious advice about her role, and Hélène had said something about Maisie being a crow...

'Of course it's a challenge for you, darling,' Hélène had said. 'Maisie Wilkin is a crow, and you're a swan.'

'I don't feel very swanlike at this moment.'

'You're not *meant* to, darling. You're meant to be a very plain, overweight, dim-witted, nasty-minded housemaid. It's a part I would have given my eye-teeth for at your age.'

Sophie smiled. Slim, elegant, and looking ravishing in the 1920s suit she'd worn for that morning's filming, Hélène le Bon was luminously beautiful as she studied the menu.

The mobile canteen wasn't renowed for its cuisine, which was why some of the cast chose to eat in restaurants in Brighton. Sophie and Hélène, however, always ate in the canteen—Hélène because she was utterly indifferent to food, and Sophie because she was too shy about her appearance to venture far from the set these days.

Like Hélène, she was still in costume. If you could call a shabby pinafore, wrinkled stockings and a lumpy grey cardigan a costume.

Unlike Hélène, she hadn't been dressed that way by choice. The trouble with having put on thirty pounds was that almost nothing of her own fitted her any more, which meant that she was forced to wear Maisie Wilkin's clothes around the set.

She certainly wasn't going to equip herself with a whole new size eighteen wardrobe just for the duration of *The Elmtree Road Murders*, because the first thing she was going to do once the last foot of film was in the can was go on a crash diet.

A diet which didn't include a single ounce of any fat, oil or carbohydrate.

'I'm going to have the chicken salad,' Hélène decided. She glanced at Sophie with a glint of amusement. 'You'd better have the pie and chips, Maisie. Don't want you losing your figure.'

'Do I have to?'

'You're starting to melt away, unless I'm much mistaken.'

Sophie wriggled in her grimy beige pinafore. It was certainly looser on her these days. If she lost any more weight, Percy Schumaker, the director, would start complaining again.

'You're right. I definitely have trouble identifying with Maisie's diet,' she smiled, sitting back in the chair.

'What exactly is worrying you about your performance?'

'I don't really know, Hélène.' She fidgeted with her ring. Even that was tight, these days. 'I just feel I'm not getting to the depths of my part. Maybe I'm simply not experienced enough an actress to cope with a role like Maisie.'

'Oh, nonsense. You're doing a marvellous job, darling. But if you feel you're not getting deep enough down into Maisie, perhaps the answer is that you're not . . .' Hélène le Bon frowned as she searched for the word, her slim eyebrows drawing down in a V over luminous brown eyes. '. . . perhaps not *compassionate* enough towards her.'

The waitress brought their food, and Sophie contemplated her pie, which was swimming in gravy and surrounded by glistening chips, with distaste. Feeling eyes on her, she'd looked up, and met the gaze of a handsome blond man a few tables away. He was one of the extras, and she'd noticed him several times. He had the kind of rugged looks that appealed to her, and a fine, athletic figure.

But as her eyes met his he looked away hastily, and started talking animatedly to the woman next to him.

Sophie, flushing, tackled her pie and chips with the true Maisie Wilkin spirit of grim doggedness.

Men never used to look away from her. In fact, the looks she used to get were downright appreciative. And now . . .

She brought her mind back to acting. 'Not compassionate enough?' she echoed.

'Yes,' Hélène nodded. 'I don't mean pity. That's something else. I mean understanding. During the scenes we're shooting here, it isn't that important. But once we're back in London you'll certainly have to dig a little deeper into Maisie.'

Within a fortnight they were due to conclude the location filming here in Brighton, and take the circus back to London. The climax of *The Elmtree Road Murders*, the trial and the emotional courtroom scenes, would be done in the studios after the boarding-house scenes were over.

'The trial is the real heart of the film, you see. It's where we get to see what Patricia and Maisie are really like inside, and the deep-down reasons why they acted as they did. The focus is very much on character and motive. This is your time to shine, Sophie. Those final speeches of yours—well, I think you can see how effective they could be if you treated them right.'

Sophie concentrated. Advice from Hélène le Bon was worth rubies. 'How do you mean, treated them right?'

'Well, up until now your part has been all motiveless malignity,' Hélène had said. 'After all, Maisie has been really rather vicious. Blackmail, betrayal, hypocrisy. The audience isn't exactly captivated with her morals.' She leaned forward. 'But in those courtroom speeches, you can give a real *cri de coeur*. You can make the audience feel what it's really like to be someone like Maisie Wilkin—ugly, slighted, disadvantaged, the kind of person nobody really bothers to understand until it's too late. You can leave them with a feeling of compassion, almost of wonder...'

Hélène was, by her own admission, pushing forty-five. A deeply experienced and much-loved actress, she could have been a very intimidating person for Sophie, twenty-three and in her first significant role, to play against. But Hélène had taken her under her wing from the start, and Percy Schumaker was a good enough director to let Hélène guide Sophie through the part without contradicting her judgements too much.

Sophie listened in attentive silence as Hélène outlined the emotional peaks and valleys of the scenes that lay ahead. Though she knew the script backwards, it always astounded Sophie how much light Hélène could shed on characters other than the one she herself was playing. She had the true actress's ability to empathise with all the roles in a script, and she made Sophie feel hopelessly amateurish at times.

She'd been listening so intently to Hélène that she hadn't noticed the tall figure that had approached their table, and was now looming over them.

That was when Kyle Hart had first appeared in her life.

Despite the Caribbean warmth, a shiver of goose-flesh now swept across Sophie's tanned skin as the memory flooded back.

Her eyes, which had lost their focus while she'd thought back, now flicked to the tall figure of Kyle Hart, stooping twenty yards away from her with the child.

That moment would stay with her for a long time. The recognition that she was looking into the eyes of one of the most beautiful men she would ever meet.

Not that she'd been conscious of the rest of his face at first. It had been Kyle's eyes that had electrified her.

Though he hadn't been as dark in Brighton as he was now, his skin had been tanned enough to make those tawny-green eyes as cool and startling as lake-water in some sandstone desert. They had held a directness that was animal, shocking. Utterly sure of his own strength.

For a split second, Sophie had met that heart-stopping gaze with unthinking, wide-eyed shock. Then she'd remembered what she looked like, and how he must see her, and embarrassment had washed over her in a tide that had flushed her plump cheeks crimson.

'Kyle!' Hélène had risen to give him a hug and a kiss, then had introduced him to Sophie as Kyle Hart, a financier in the City, and one of her oldest friends.

The fact that he was smiling at them both had softened the lines of what she'd instinctively known would be a merciless face in repose, darkly virile. His self-assurance went with not having to question his own sexuality, mastery or wealth.

Sophie had felt a keen sense of frustration. If only this magnificent male had chosen to arrive in her life a few weeks earlier, he would have met a reasonably pretty woman, reasonably poised, and reasonably attractive.

As it was, those green eyes had glittered with inner amusement at a frightful, overweight frump with greasy black hair and owlish glasses, wearing the most unflattering garments ever devised by a satanic wardrobe-mistress, and quailing into her seat with embarrassment and shame.

Not that Kyle Hart had betrayed his contempt in any way then, or during the days that had followed.

Kyle's relationship with Hélène was warm and intimate; though she was older than he was, they were evidently good friends, sharing a lot in common. He had been in Brighton on business to do with the merchant bank for which he worked, and had dropped into the set regularly, watching the filming from the sidelines. Obviously a connoisseur of acting, he had complimented them both on their performances.

He'd also been very kind in other ways. He'd taken them both out, twice to lunch, three times to dinner, invariably at the best restaurants in town.

Sophie had done the best she possibly could to eradicate Maisie on those occasions, but no amount of make-up could have hidden the extra pounds, the lank black hair, and the awful clothes she'd been forced to wear. Even the heavy black glasses had had to go with her: she needed them for reading, and she'd got into the habit of twitching them on and off nervously.

In any case, they had been finishing off the Brighton episodes, and there was no way she could have got too far out of Maisie's character and still kept the integrity of her performance in front of the cameras.

And, despite all that, she'd let herself nurture those crazy delusions. Delusions that it was herself, and not Hélène, that Kyle was really interested in. That it was by his wish that she went everywhere with them, rather than through Hélène's kindness. That he could look under the surface of her less-than-beautiful image, and see the woman beneath.

Not exactly experienced with men, she had found her contact with this devastatingly handsome, sophisticated, witty tiger dazzling. He had had an impact on her emotions that had bowled her over.

What was so exciting was that it went beyond a physical attraction. They shared so much in common, it seemed. They both loved the theatre, the same kind of music, had the same views about so many things. Kyle was amused by the same odd moments that made her laugh, and they shared an off-beat sense of humour, so that they two had sometimes been helpless with laughter at things that had made Hélène only smile in puzzlement.

Kyle, in fact, had been flatteringly attentive towards Sophie, and so apparently interested in her, her views and her work that her stupid head had been utterly turned.

Oh, the fluttering heart, the shallow breathing, the hot, mad dreams!

Sophie's fingers clenched into tight fists, her nails digging into her palms as if to punish herself for her incredible stupidity. Had she really imagined that a man like Kyle could have been seriously interested in someone like Maisie Wilkin?

Yes, she had. She forced herself to conjure up the misery all over again.

She'd fallen into an infatuation swifter and deeper than anything she'd known before. Dreaming of the day when she could cast off Maisie, and present herself to Kyle as she really was, she had been drawn into something she'd never had as a schoolgirl—a schoolgirl crush. And the fact that her emotions had been as yet largely untried had made the crush all the more fierce, all the more hopeless.

She'd been like a convert exposed to a new religion, embracing her passion without thought or logic. Like a teenager in the front row of a matinée, dreaming an impossible dream.

Until the memorable afternoon of her disillusionment.

Then, as now, they had been on the beach. Taking a break during the late afternoon filming, she and Hélène and Kyle had walked from the set down to the beach with a party of the crew and the cast.

It had been a mild, warm autumn day, with no hint of the winter that was to come. Hélène and Kyle had gone off for a walk on their own. After twenty minutes, Sophie had followed, hands thrust into the pockets of her housecoat as she trudged barefoot across the warm pebbly beach, her thoughts happy and free.

She'd come upon them sitting on a pair of deck-chairs, facing the sea.

The stiff breeze had been flowing inland, from them towards Sophie. Which was how they hadn't heard her approach.

And why she'd caught every word of their conversation.

'Oh, come on, Hélène,' Kyle had been saying, his voice somewhere between frustration and amusement. 'Why don't you speak to the girl about her appearance? She's like an overweight owl!'

Sophie had frozen where she'd stood, the blood draining away from her heart.

'Sophie isn't that overweight,' Hélène had rebuked.

'Well, she's not exactly sylph-like.'

'She's a splendid young actress, and she's doing an excellent job with a difficult role.'

'Maybe so, but her appearance is absurd. She wears such terrible clothes, not to mention her hair—how could any young girl let herself go like that? She must have no pride in herself whatsoever.'

'You don't understand, Kyle.' Hélène's voice had been patient. 'Sophie isn't normally like that. She hasn't "let herself go", as you so crudely put it. She's supposed to be unattractive, for the part. You'll understand why when you see the film.'

'Well, if she's supposed to be unattractive, she certainly fits the bill.'

'Is she getting on your nerves?'

'She does rather irritate me, snatching those glasses off and on like a railway signal the whole time.'

'Well, she's embarrassed about them.' Hélène had lit a cigarette, and Sophie had numbly watched the smoke drifting towards her. 'Sophie's had to put on nearly three stones to play Maisie,' she had explained. 'So, naturally, her own wardrobe doesn't fit her any more. She has to wear Maisie's clothes. The hair's dyed, of course. And she's even gone to the length of having her own lenses fitted into those heavy black frames. That's why she looks like an owl to you. You're really looking at someone in heavy disguise. If you can't see that underneath it all she's a very intelligent, pretty girl——'

'I'll grant you the intelligence. She's good company, poor thing. But *pretty*?'

'Yes. She has a beautiful face.'

'If you think suet pudding is beautiful.' Kyle's laughter had been soft, mocking.

'You're cruel,' Hélène had said. 'I've rather taken her under my wing, you see.'

'Yes, I've noticed. Another of your lame ducks. She doesn't benefit from the comparison, I assure you. Do you know what she looks like, next to you?'

'Kyle, don't. Sophie Aspen is very far from being a lame duck. She's just young, and rather inexperienced. It's good for her to be around a sophisticated man like you. That's why I like to have her along with us. And you've been very sweet to her so far. Think of it as a charity.'

'Yes, well, I've been a little too charitable, I think.'

'Hmm?'

'You can't mean you haven't noticed?' Kyle had demanded, the husky laugh drifting back to where Sophie had stood like stone on the twilight beach. 'The poor girl is falling in love with me.'

'Oh, dear,' Hélène had sighed. 'I think you're right. I have noticed her being rather moony in your presence.'

'There's no doubt about it. I know the signs. It would be amusing if it weren't so pathetic.'

'Well, you're used to that, at least,' Hélène had smiled. 'And I can assure you that you've had less worthy women than Sophie Aspen in love with you.'

'Have I? I've certainly had slimmer.'

'I just hope that you're not going to——'

'Laugh in her face?' Kyle had concluded for her. 'No, Hélène, I'll restrain myself from that. Though it won't be easy. She looks like...'

Kyle had gone on to describe exactly what she'd looked like. He had a talent with words. He could make them glitter like surgeons' knives, could make them stab and slash and puncture the flimsy bubble of vanity and illusion.

But Sophie hadn't stayed to hear the end of it.

She'd willed her paralysed legs to start moving, to turn around and carry her bleeding soul back towards the others, where she'd come from.

There wasn't any way she could describe how she'd been feeling. The pain and humiliation had been glowing in her, like coals in a stove. It had been something she'd known she would never forget.

To see ourselves as others saw us—a gift that could be terrible. But he hadn't needed to be so cruel! The frivolous, superficial, callous pig——

If she could have confronted him there and then, and thrown it all back in his face, she would have done. But the awful thing was that everything he'd said about her had been true.

She *had* been infatuated with him. And she *had* been an absurd sight. It was just that she'd forgotten. And had forgotten how much value the world placed on images. She'd known that she'd looked less than ravishing, but she hadn't known just how important appearances were to people.

Kyle hadn't known her at all. That was what had really hurt her. He'd never looked beneath the surface. He'd never bothered to see beneath the exterior, to the real person she was under the dyed hair and thick make-up, the ugly glasses, the extra weight, the shabby clothes.

He'd never bothered to find out that she wasn't absurd inside, that she wasn't some kind of freak. To him, she'd never been Sophie Aspen at all. She'd only been Maisie, a physically unattractive woman whose so-obvious infatuation with him had been laughable, a thing to hold in contempt...

Well, pain was valuable to an actress. It was like raw stone to a sculptor. And this pain was Kyle Hart's own special contribution to her development as an actress. He had changed her, had shown her a great deal about the world, and the way the world was obsessed with appearances. And for that, she felt a kind of bitter gratitude.

But, for the rest, he was a man she would loathe for the rest of her life.

That night she'd excused herself from the dinner that Kyle had offered, pleading an upset tummy. He had been exceptionally kind to her that night, and over the next few days until he had left Brighton to go back to the City. Kind! That had been the final straw. His scorn she could live with. His kindness could go to the devil! She had not gone out with him again, despite pressing invitations. And she'd never spoken to him again.

Not until ten minutes ago, at least.

Though her hurt and anger had lain too deep for words, it had been within her powers to act out her feelings on the set.

And the understanding of her role that had eluded her until then had suddenly been there, shimmering in her performance the next morning.

During the last days at Brighton, and the final episodes in the studio, she'd brought a quality of fury against the world to Maisie Wilkin that had made Percy Schumaker kiss her on both cheeks, and the studio crew give her standing ovations on several occasions.

It was as if, for the first time, she had really known what it was like to be someone like Maisie Wilkin—ugly, slighted, disadvantaged, the kind of person nobody really bothered to understand until it was too late.

Sophie had never spoken to Hélène about what she'd heard that afternoon on the beach.

Once or twice, she'd caught Hélène staring at her as though she'd half suspected the truth, but neither of them had ever brought it up. Nor had Sophie ever laid the slightest blame at Hélène's door. To her, Hélène le Bon would always be someone who had helped her profoundly in her career, and since *The Elmtree Road Murders* they had remained friends.

'You're a very talented actress,' Hélène had said gently, on the last day of filming. 'You have a bright future ahead of you, Sophie.'

But she'd been drained and exhausted by the time filming had ended.

Her first concern, once filming had ended last November, had been to slough off Maisie Wilkin, the way a snake shed its unwanted skin. She had gone back to her St John's Wood flat, and had retreated deep into her shell, had embarked on a crash diet, had seen no one, gone nowhere. She had superintended the eradication of Maisie without sorrow or remorse. Diet and exercise had taken care of the extra weight. The black hair-dye had washed out, and the rest had been mainly cosmetic.

Getting back to work, she had spent the first five months of this year touring with a repertory company, staging a trio of very modern dramas called *Here*, *There*, and *Nowhere*, which had never played to more than half-full houses. It had been her second substantial job in acting, but it had been far from a success. Most of the cast had been young hopefuls, like herself. She, in fact, with her experience of television, had been better off than most of them.

The pay had been minimal, the conditions had been exhausting, and everyone had let out a silent sigh of relief when the director had finally announced, at the beginning of June, that the tour was folding. None of them had been paid for more than three months out of the five. Without her fee from *The Elmtree Road Murders*, which she'd been hoarding in her building-society account, she would have had a thin time of it.

When the tour had folded, Sophie had found herself at a loose end. And she'd been very run down. After the pain of what had happened in Brighton, the débâcle of *Here*, *There*, and *Nowhere* had taken a lot out of her. She'd felt that she desperately needed a break, some kind of sun-drenched holiday to restore her calm and help bring back her dented self-respect.

She'd seen the cancellation in the travel agent's window. Though the price of the holiday had been halved, it was still expensive. And three weeks was longer than she'd wanted to go for. But she'd felt somehow drawn to the idea, and the lure of Jamaica had been irresistible in the end. She'd dipped into her little hoard from *The Elmtree Road Murders*, and had bought the ticket, hoping she was doing the right thing.

She was now feeling that three weeks of sun, sea, and salads were definitely going to be the right thing. She hadn't needed to come all this way just to get a tan and relax. But she'd needed the psychological break, and the glamour of Jamaica was proving marvellously beneficial to her weary psyche, as it was to her physical well-being.

She'd tried so hard to forget Kyle over the disastrous five months of the tour. But, at the end of it all, she knew she had only half conquered the hurt. It was still there, inside her, overlaid with a veil that any casual word could whisk away.

That was really why she had come to Jamaica. Because of Kyle Hart. To get over him once and for all.

And now he was walking towards her, on a sun-drenched beach in Ocho Rios, and he didn't even know who she was.

CHAPTER TWO

IT WAS the child who reached her first.

'I've found somc beautiful shells,' she said, sitting down next to Sophie and overturning her bucket of treasures to sort through them. 'Aren't they lovely?'

'Lovely.'

''Course, most of them are broken,' the child sighed. 'You have to go diving to get the ones that aren't broken. My uncle's going to dive for me soon. Look—mother o'pearl!'

'That's very pretty,' Sophie said, taking the shell from the child. Her pulse-rate was just settling down to normal as Kyle approached.

He looked down at her speculatively. 'This is going to sound rather weak—but we've met somewhere before, haven't we?'

'No.' The lie came to her mouth at once, unbidden. 'No, I don't think we have.'

'Well, then you remind me very strongly of someone I've met once before, though I can't think who.' Suddenly he smiled. 'That sounds like the crudest kind of come-on line, doesn't it? Worse than "do you come here often?"'

Sophie smiled blankly. She didn't want him to recognise her, not any more.

Kyle was taller than she had remembered, a big, leanly built man who wore his rangy body with the assurance of complete authority. In Brighton, the naked power of his body had been cloaked in linen and silk. Out here, practically naked but for the black triangle of his swimming-trunks, he made Sophie aware of the aggressive mastery that burned in his every movement. It was as though she could physically see the calm, potent maturity that set Kyle apart from every man she'd ever met before.

'Can I ask you your name?'

'Sophie Webb.' Again, she hadn't meant to lie. The words had just been there in her mouth. Actually, it was almost the truth—Sophie Webb Aspen was her full name. Would 'Sophie' ring any bells?

Apparently not.

'My name's Kyle Hart. And this is Emma, my niece.'

'Pleased to meet you,' Emma smiled, and wandered off down to the water's edge to look for more shells.

Kyle sat down in the space his niece had vacated, the warm skin of his shoulder brushing hers for a moment, making her flinch as though she'd been touched with a hot branding-iron. 'We're also staying in the San Antonio. We arrived yesterday.'

'Are you with Emma's parents?'

'No.' He glanced at the figure of the little girl. 'My brother and his wife are going through a rough patch with their marriage. In fact, they're on the brink of a separation. I volunteered to take Emma on holiday, partly to get her away from the atmosphere at home, and partly to give her parents a breathing-space. A chance to save their marriage before the ultimate break-up.'

'I see.'

That was why he was here. At least she now knew who Emma was, and why Kyle was in Jamaica. Her idea that he'd come to find her had been just as absurd as she'd known it would be.

'And you?' He glanced at her briefly. 'Are you here with friends?'

'I'm on my own,' she replied.

He didn't look surprised, but she sensed that he was. 'Your first visit to Jamaica?'

'Yes.'

'England to the Caribbean is a long way to come on your own.' His expression told her he was still puzzled by her, still trying to place her. 'May I ask what you do for a living?'

'I'm . . . a model.'

'That figures,' he smiled, his eyes drifting over her figure. 'I'm afraid my own occupation is nothing so glamorous. I work in a bank.'

'Really?' The tension was too much for her. Making small talk with Kyle was just too much. She knew that if she didn't get away now she would say or do something really stupid.

With nervous movements, Sophie gathered up her towel and straw bag, and rose fluidly to her feet. 'I'm awfully sorry,' she said, 'but it's time for me to get out of the sun.'

He glanced up at her, dark lashes veiling a slow smile. His eyes took in the honey-tanned length of her body, slow and sultry as a caress, before he spoke. 'You should have said at once if my presence disturbed you.'

'No,' she replied, slightly breathless, 'I really am too hot. I'm going to have a shower before lunch.'

'Then I might see you at lunch?' He couldn't see her eyes behind the dark glasses, but his glance was disturbingly penetrating all the same.

'Of course,' Sophie replied, turning away. 'You might.'

She walked quickly up the beach away from him. She felt his eyes dwelling on her back, and knew in her bones that he was watching the swing of her long legs.

By the time she got back to the hotel her skin was damp with nerves. She took the lift up to her room, wriggled out of her bikini, and stepped under a cool shower.

Whew! What a weirdly tense little experience that had been!

Well, if nothing else, that chance meeting with Kyle Hart had just boosted her ego by several degrees. She'd come here to unwind, to relax, and to restore her self-image. If he didn't even recognise her any more, then her self-image was well and truly restored!

She evidently presented a very different picture from the one she'd presented last autumn.

She felt a smile creep across her lips. What had possessed her to tell him she was a model called Sophie Webb? Mischievously, she was now pleased she had done so. Let him find out who she really was, if he could. She was going to enjoy seeing the look on his face when he did!

She stepped out of the shower, brown and dripping, and dried herself.

Saying that he worked in a bank was almost more of an untruth than her own claim to be a model. She knew that he was, in fact, a partner in a very prestigious firm of merchant bankers, and that 'Hart' was one of the names carved over the lintel of the neo-classical building in the City.

But what she'd said was also at least partly true. She'd done a fair bit of modelling for fashion magazines, especially during her time at drama school, and if her acting career didn't work out she might be doing a lot more in the future. She had never commanded anything like good pay, of course, but it had helped to pay the rent and tuition fees.

So she hadn't really lied to him.

There was, in fact, no immediate prospect of further work for Sophie. Joey Gilmour, her American-born agent, had assured her that in the wake of *The Elmtree Road Murders* there would be further offers, which was always a possibility. She was hoping that her substantial fee from the film, plus what she made from the bath-oil ad, would tide her over until something else came in.

In any case, she wasn't here to worry.

Sophie dressed in a light and airy blue and green dress that brought out the naturally rich colouring of her hair and skin. She looped a string of rose-quartz beads round her neck. The jewellery wasn't expensive, but against her throat the colours glowed prettily.

Come to think of it, this situation might be fun, after all. And perhaps, for once, she would have a more interesting companion over lunch than the thick paperback she was still only a third of the way through.

Would he join her at her table? Would he have remembered who she was since this morning?

She touched her lips with a pink lip-gloss, and went down to lunch feeling as though she were going on stage.

He hadn't recalled her yet. He and Emma joined her table, and all ordered the same thing: a light salad with cold meats. Sophie was now feeling a lot more poised in his company, and was drily awaiting the moment when it suddenly dawned on him who she was.

'Do you always wear those sunglasses?' Kyle enquired, leaning back in his chair to survey her.

'My eyes aren't used to this bright sunlight.' Actually, the sunglasses had prescription lenses, and she could see much more clearly with them. Not that he would know that—the Dior frames looked anything but practical.

'Or is it that you don't want to be recognised?' he asked lazily. Sophie couldn't stop herself from jumping, but he went on, 'After all, you must be a fairly famous model.'

'Why should I be so famous?'

'This place doesn't come cheap,' he shrugged, glancing round the glamorous palm-lined dining-room. 'Money means success. And, in your line of work, success means fame.'

She ate a mouthful of salad before answering. 'I'm not famous, and I probably never will be. I certainly don't want to be.'

'That's a very unfeminine sentiment.' The wicked smile made him suddenly dazzlingly handsome. It was the smile and the eyebrows that gave his face such a cruel cast, she realised suddenly. The dark brows curved down over those tawny eyes in a way that conveyed passion, and the level grin, inlaid with beautiful white teeth, held a predatory quality, the smile on the face of a tiger. 'I assume that's why you look so familiar,' he said, pouring the fresh orange juice that the waiter had brought. 'You must have been on the cover of a magazine at some time, and I'll have seen your face on the news-stands. Something like *Vogue*, I'd guess.'

Sophie shook her head, trying not to laugh. 'Not *Vogue*. But you've probably seen my face here and there.'

'Where would I have been likely to see it?'

'Here and there,' she repeated, shrugging her slender shoulders.

Kyle smiled again at her evasive reply. 'Mystery lady,' he said softly. 'You don't like answering questions, do you?'

'I just don't like talking about myself.'

'Another unfeminine quality,' he observed. Sophie watched his hands as he cut his food. Strong, capable hands, the knuckles etched with glinting hair. On his wrist he wore a black diver's watch, evidently expensive, but not flashy. She knew he was a wealthy man, but he adopted few of the accoutrements of wealth. He didn't adorn himself with gold jewellery or conspicuous clothes, as if he didn't need to prove anything.

'As for the cost of this holiday,' she said, sipping the orange juice, 'I assure you it's an unwonted extravagance, and not the sort of thing I do every six months.'

'You must be rewarding yourself for something, then.'

'Exactly,' Sophie said. He couldn't see the glint in her grey eyes behind the sunglasses, but he caught the tone in her voice.

'Intriguing,' he purred. 'May I ask what?'

'Oh . . . having come through something.'

'What?'

'Something private.'

He grimaced. 'And the curtain comes down again, leaving the mystery intact.'

She put down her knife and fork, and propped her neat chin on her clasped hands. 'I just felt I needed a break from work. I finished a tough assignment a while ago, and I was a bit run down, so I decided to get away from it all. There's nothing mysterious about that at all.'

'It's a mystery to me that you should have decided to come to a place like Jamaica all on your own,' Kyle replied calmly, finishing his grapefruit, and breaking a roll. 'A woman with your beauty and personality shouldn't have to endure solitude.'

The irony of it all kept laughter bubbling just beneath the surface of her deliberately cool poise. The man who'd once described her as an overweight owl with a face like suet pudding, among other things, was sitting here complimenting her on her beauty and charm. Such was the power of a slight change in appearance.

'To me, solitude is a gift, rather than a penance,' she told him. She was rather enjoying her Mystery Lady role. She could see that it piqued and intrigued him, and there was no harm in hamming it up a little. 'I like to get away from the madding crowd from time to time.'

'Can I go and play now?' Emma demanded, plainly bored with the adult conversation.

'Go on,' Kyle nodded. 'But stay out of the sun, or you'll roast.' He watched the little girl scamper off, then turned to her with a smile. 'This is the first time she's been abroad. She's a real London child. Do you live in London?'

'Yes, nowadays. But I grew up in Scarborough.'

'Where the Fair is? Parsley, sage, rosemary and thyme?'

'The same,' she smiled.

He considered her thoughtfully. 'Well, well. A country girl. I wouldn't have thought it. You have the poise of someone whose ancestors danced the gavotte.'

'My ancestors were Yorkshire farming folk. My father has a small sheep-farm—just twenty acres of moorland, really, overlooking the sea.'

'Is it pretty?'

'I think it's lovely.'

He studied the elegant, sophisticated woman in front of him. 'And may I ask how you got the Yorkshire out of your voice?'

'It's still there, if you listen. Or would you rather I prefaced every sentence with ee ba gum?'

He grinned. 'Any more at home like you?'

'I haven't any brothers or sisters, if that's what you mean.'

'Ah. So that explains why you're always so collected. You never had any competition as a child.'

'Oh, I wouldn't say that,' Sophie said wryly. 'My cousin Jenny gave me as much competition as half a dozen sisters!'

'She sounds like quite a girl,' Kyle smiled.

'She's two years younger than me, but she's a real beauty. Much prettier than I'll ever be.'

'Really?' he said, his disbelief flattering.

'She's the one who ought to be the model, but she's got more brains as well as more looks. She's studying maths at the University of York now.'

'What a paragon she must be,' Kyle said gently.

'If I were the jealous type,' she assured him, 'I could get quite worked up about Jenny.'

He studied her. 'Has she the same rich chestnut hair and cool grey eyes?'

'Oh, she puts me in the shade. She has the most beautiful hair, long and golden-red, and bright blue eyes. We grew up together. Her mother and mine are very close. As a child, I was always being asked why I wasn't more like my cousin Jennifer.' Sophie couldn't help her lips tightening slightly. 'When we got older, she used to steal all my boyfriends.'

His eyes were warm. 'But not any more?'

'Well, she meets enough men of her own at university nowadays. But it's a good job I've moved to London. I never particularly like losing my favourite men to my younger cousin.'

Kyle looked amused. But it was the truth. She knew for a fact that Jenny was sexually far more experienced than she herself was. They had always been a paradoxical pair—Jenny, the scientist, supposed to be so cool and precise, yet in her teens an expert on men; Sophie, the actress, who had still, at twenty-three, never been made love to by a man...

She had finished eating. And he still didn't know who she was. 'Well,' she said lightly, rising, 'please excuse me. I'm going to have a little lie-down until it's cool enough to swim.'

He rose with automatic courtesy. 'See you on the beach, then,' he said.

She felt his eyes boring into her back as she walked away.

'There's something very familiar about you, Sophie Webb.'

Sophie's poise didn't falter in the slightest as she looked up from the breakfast table a few mornings later.

He'd said that twice over the past few days. Whenever they had met, in fact. But if he hadn't recognised her by now, after all the hours he'd spent in her company, he wasn't going to recognise her this morning, with her wearing her sunglasses and a wide-brimmed straw hat as she breakfasted on the hotel terrace, against a backdrop of palms and blue sea.

She was wearing a pale gold sun-dress over her metallic scarlet one-piece costume, and the colour made her toffee-tanned skin look lusciously smooth.

'It's a little late for that line, isn't it?' she said with light irony. 'Maybe you should ask me if I come here often.'

'I'm being serious,' he smiled, standing in front of her. 'As I came on to the terrace, it struck me again. You're very like somebody I've met once before, but I just can't place who or when. Can I join you for breakfast?'

'If you insist on sharing your every meal with me,' she said gently, 'people are going to talk.'

They'd got into the habit of lunching together, and had had dinner together the night before, too. He sat down anyway, looking amused. 'I'll take the chance on my reputation. And, considering that we're both here on our own...'

She scooped the seeds out of her papaw, and gave him a glance. He was wearing trousers and a loose cotton shirt, open to show the tanned column of his throat. He looked stunning. She forced herself to keep up the light, cool tone she'd adopted from their very first exchanges. 'Considering we're both here on our own?' she prompted.

'Well, eating at the same table is hardly cohabitation.' He picked up the menu. 'Sleep well last night?'

'Fine,' she lied. 'Where's Emma?'

'Coming in a minute. I'm starting to realise that I'm not very good at dealing with grooming an eight-year-old girl.' He turned to the waiter who had materialised beside them, and ordered grapefruit, rolls and coffee. Sophie took advantage of the waiter's presence to ask for a fresh pot of Earl Grey tea.

They'd spent most of yesterday afternoon on the beach, talking and swimming, and he hadn't suspected for a moment that he knew her.

Last night, over their dinner of lobster, oysters and a variety of seafoods, she'd wondered if memory would return. After all, it wasn't exactly the first time that Kyle Hart had faced her across a restaurant table.

But though he'd frowned, and kept probing her for information about herself, recognition had not dawned. Nor, on the other hand, had he made any secret of his attraction towards the woman he still thought of as a stranger met by chance on holiday. He'd made no effort to hide the fact that he was interested in her. Very interested.

She'd looked into those tawny-green eyes last night, and had seen the speculation in them. She knew he was intrigued by her. And she'd remembered that this man had once had to restrain himself from laughing in her face.

Well, now the boot was on the other foot. Now it was she who had to bite back her amusement, to stop herself from telling him what a complete fool he was making of himself.

Would he ever see Sophie Aspen as she really was?

History was repeating itself. Once again, Kyle Hart's eyes hadn't looked beneath the surface. Once again, he was focusing on the external image. Once again, her appearance was all that mattered to him, as though what she was inside was irrelevant. The only difference was that last time he had seen only Maisie Wilkin, the overweight owl. This time he was seeing only Sophie Webb, mysterious and attractive model.

It had been on the tip of her tongue several times over the past few days to tell him who she was, and see the look on his face as realisation set in. But, as it had grown clearer that he still didn't have the remotest idea who she was, she'd decided not to tell him. Not yet, anyway. She was waiting to see how things would turn out.

And things were turning out in a rather amusing way.

He had even kissed her goodnight after dinner last night. She'd just let his lips touch her cheek before she'd drawn quickly away, and with a faint smile had locked herself into her room.

Once, she'd have given her right arm for a kiss from Kyle Hart.

Now, knowing what she did about his shallowness, his cruelty, his superficiality, she was left cold by him.

Almost.

Emma arrived to join them. The eight-year-old had taken a strong fancy to Sophie over the past few days, and she was chattering brightly as she clambered up on to the chair next to her.

'Are you coming to the beach this morning?' she asked hopefully.

'Yep.' Sophie pulled down the shoulder of her sun-dress to show the red strap of her costume against her brown skin. 'I'm all ready.'

'Great! Can we come?'

'I'll think about it,' Sophie smiled. 'What do you fancy for breakfast?'

'Kippers and scrambled egg,' came the unhesitating reply. 'It's my favourite.'

'No kippers,' Sophie said regretfully, consulting the menu.

'Kingfish and ackee come pretty close,' Kyle suggested. 'Kingfish isn't kippers, and ackee isn't egg, but I think you'll enjoy it.'

'OK,' the child conceded. 'I'm going to build a huge sand-castle this morning, bigger than yesterday.'

'Her father,' Kyle smiled, 'is an architect.'

'What *is* ackee?' Sophie wanted to know, after they'd given the order to the waiter. 'I've seen it on the menu every morning, but I've never risked it.'

Kyle was trying to put Emma's dark curls into order. Competent as his long fingers were, they weren't doing much of a job. 'It's very tasty,' he said. 'Actually, it's a fruit, but it ends up a vegetable equivalent of scrambled egg. It was introduced by Captain Bligh.'

'The *Mutiny on the Bounty* man?'

'Yes,' he nodded. 'Another odd thing about it—it's poisonous until it's ripe, and then it sort of pops open, ready to cook.'

'Here.' She took pity on his amateurish efforts with Emma's hair. 'Let me do that. What do you want, Emma, a plait or pigtails?'

'Pigtails,' Emma decided. Sophie found rubber bands and a comb in her beachbag, and started neatening the child's hair, watched by Kyle. 'How do you know so much about Jamaica?' she asked him. 'Have you been here before?'

'I've worked all over the Caribbean,' Kyle smiled. 'In my younger, wilder days.'

'Worked? As a banker?'

'Mainly on yachts,' he answered.

Sophie's eyebrows rose. She glanced at him over Emma's head. 'Do tell.'

'Not likely,' he said easily. 'My disreputable past isn't a fit topic for the breakfast table. Besides,' he added with a glint, 'everyone needs a little mystery.'

'Touché,' she nodded, amused.

When Emma's ackee arrived Sophie sampled it, and found it every bit as delicious as Kyle had promised. After breakfast, the three of them went down to the beach.

It was another glorious morning, the sun blazing down from a cloudless sky. Sophie watched while Kyle swam, his muscular shoulders cutting an easy swathe through the surf. The child's presence had curtailed the rather dangerous flirtation that had been developing between them, which had been something of a relief. She was finding flirting with Kyle Hart to be a definite strain.

After a while Kyle emerged, dripping, and dried himself vigorously. Sophie couldn't take her eyes off him, fascinated by the way his body moved, the powerful muscles pulsing and relaxing in such perfect harmony. He was a man who would do everything to perfection, from dancing to making love...

He flopped down beside her on his back, closing his eyes with a sigh.

'This is the life. God, to think I have to go back to work some day!'

'It *is* rather hard to see you in a bank,' she admitted.

She pretended to be absorbed in her book, but she was really thinking about herself, about Maisie Wilkin, and about Kyle Hart.

Especially about Kyle.

He was magnificent, really. No wonder he had an oversized ego. And no wonder he'd been so contemptuous about Maisie. Beautiful people tended to be very unkind about those not so favoured as themselves.

But such shallowness deserved punishment. He shouldn't be allowed to get away with such a callous attitude. Somehow, she knew she could turn the present situation round to get her own back.

Somehow...

Last night, after showering, she'd gone to stand on the balcony to look at the midnight sea, and she'd realised that if she wanted to she was in a position to deal a blow to Kyle's pride that would make up in some way, at least, for the blow he had dealt to hers.

The only question was how to deal it in the fortnight she had left on Jamaica.

Sophie turned her head slightly to study Kyle. In repose, his face was cruelly beautiful. No man had any right to be so damned beautiful. No man had any right to possess a figure like that.

His broad chest moved in a slow, tranquil rhythm as he dozed off in the sun. Beads of water glistened like pearls against the bronzed skin that was so fine for a man's. What would it feel like to reach out and caress that muscular throat, trace the way it met the bending curve of his collarbone, continue across those broad pectoral muscles to the dark, hard points of his man's nipples?

The idea was both exciting and frightening. Any woman would be half afraid to awake the animal in this man. His masculinity was so very formidable; it was evident in every movement, in his speech, in the crisp hair that started just below the arching wings of his ribcage, making its way across the tightly defined muscles of his stomach to the dark triangle of his Speedo.

She looked away, weird feelings turning her blood into ice, then into flame. Well, she'd once had a monumental crush on this man, and it was too soon to pretend that she felt indifference. In any case, very few female hearts would ever feel totally indifferent to Kyle.

Then what did she feel?

Avoiding the question, she moved her gaze to little Emma, who was adding another turret to the sand-castle she was building, far too close to the threatening waves. Poor kid. Sophie really hoped that she would still have a home to go back to once this holiday was over.

A larger wave than the rest suddenly came rippling up the beach, flooding Emma's sand-castle. With a squeak of dismay, she tried to protect her creation, but it was too late. The retreating water left only a shapeless lump where the castle had stood.

'Oh, *no*!'

Smiling, Sophie got to her feet, and went over to help Emma rebuild her palace. 'You'll have to make it further back from the sea,' she told the woebegone little girl. 'I know all the lovely moist sand is down here, but we'll carry it up in the bucket.'

In a few minutes, Emma was intently decorating the walls of a new, even bigger castle with sea shells. Sophie sat beside her, watching and giving advice.

As the topmost turret went into place, she nodded approval. 'What you need now is a Union Jack to fly from the top.'

Emma's eyes shone. 'Oh, that would be perfect! But I haven't got one.'

'I have.' Smiling, Sophie produced the little paper flag on its toothpick. 'It was on the breakfast table. When you said you were going to build a sandcastle, I knew you'd need it.'

Delighted, the child planted the flag on her battlements, and Sophie left her playing imaginary kings and queens in her palace and went back to her book.

As she settled down beside Kyle he turned his head lazily towards her, opening his eyes to smoky green slits.

'You're being very kind to the kid,' he said softly.

She shook the sand off her book. 'I like children. And Emma's a lovely little girl.'

'I was thinking of taking her to Dunn's River Falls this afternoon, in the car. It's a spectacularly beautiful place. You can climb up the waterfall from the sea, along a sort of a ladder of pools and shelves. You have to go in a bathing costume, of course, but it's quite an experience.'

'It sounds it.'

'Care to come?'

There was a silence after the casual invitation. Sophie found herself staring blankly at the surf, wondering just what the hell she was getting into. Why hadn't she told him, right away, who she was?

Then she shook away the feeling of doubt. Let him stay fooled. It would make the truth, when it came, all the more of a shock to his arrogant system!

'I might,' she said coolly. 'Can I tell you how I feel after lunch?'

Kyle's eyes were closed again, absurdly long lashes fanning his tanned cheeks. 'As you please. It isn't just your face that's familiar, you know,' he said in the same relaxed tone. 'It's your voice, too. Your voice reminds me of some other woman even more than your face does. I just can't think who.'

She sat very still. 'Have you known so many women, then?' she asked lightly.

'A few.' He rolled on to his stomach, catlike, and suddenly the tawny eyes were open, and staring into hers. She'd taken her dark glasses off, and the glowing stare seemed to reach deep into her soul, searching after the truth.

For a shuddering moment she felt totally certain that he knew exactly who she was. How could any woman hide anything from a man with eyes like that? Frozen, she waited for the recognition.

Then the passionate curve of his mouth moved in a wry smile, and he shook his head. 'Whoever you are,' he said huskily, 'I'm glad you're here. You make the morning beautiful.'

Sophie's fingers were shaking slightly as she reached for her sunglasses and started to put them on.

His long fingers stopped her, trapping her hand in his own.

'Don't put them back on,' he requested quietly.

'Why not?'

'Because your eyes are remarkable. Cool and grey and calm. Put up with the sun for a while. For my sake.'

She felt her cheeks flush as she withdrew her hand from his, and defiantly put the sunglasses back on. 'If I didn't know you were a respectable banker,' she said drily, 'I'd suspect you of trying to flirt with me, Mr Hart.'

'I'm too sensible to try anything like that, Miss Webb.' Denied the enjoyment of her eyes, he was watching her satin-smooth mouth, his lids hooded. 'You're not the flirtatious type.'

'No?'

'Definitely not. Flirtations are for shallow people. You are as deep as well-water. With you, only a profoundly passionate love-affair would be possible.'

She opened the book, a thick best-seller, and stared at the pages.

'And you?' she heard her own voice asking. 'Are you deep or shallow, Mr Hart?'

'Well,' he grinned, 'let's say I'm getting a little deeper with each year that passes.'

'But you're still shallow?'

'Better than I was. At your age, I certainly wasn't as grave and solemn as you are.'

She still didn't look up from her book. 'I'm not exactly a child.'

'How old are you? Twenty-two? Twenty-three?'

'Twenty-three.'

'I'm almost fifteen years older than that,' Kyle said gently. 'Yet you make me feel... daunted.'

'That's an odd word.'

'I'm always daunted by the inaccessible. You remind me of a teacher I had at infant school. Miss Willoughby, her name was. We called her Miss Willowy, because she was so slender and unapproachable. She had the same iceberg poise that you have.'

Sophie looked up at last. He was studying her figure with that provocative gaze, as though wishing that the one-piece costume wasn't there. His eyes dwelled on the scarlet V between her thighs, caressed her slim midriff, and took in the slight but definite curve of her breasts against the clingy metallic fabric. If he'd looked at his kindergarten teacher with those eyes, she thought wryly, turning slightly away from him, he had definitely been a precocious child!

'I'm sorry to hear that I daunt you,' she said, returning to her book, though she hadn't read a word of the last ten pages. 'But I wouldn't like to be thought of as too accessible.'

'You aren't,' he assured her, sunlight making her eyes smile like emeralds beneath their fringe of black eyelashes. 'The way you talk intrigues me, Sophie. You have the immaculate enunciation of a newscaster. No, not a newscaster... an actress.'

'How odd,' she said, trying to stop her expression from changing. 'I've never done any acting.'

'"I've never done any acting,"' he echoed her, his husky voice parodying her accent. 'You close your mouth so primly after every sentence, as though determined not to let any secrets out.'

'As you said earlier on, everyone needs a little mystery.'

Kyle laughed softly. 'Are you really reading that book?'

'It's extremely fascinating, as it happens.'

'It must be. You've just flipped two pages over at once, and you don't seem to have noticed.' He reached out and unstuck the two leaves that had clung together. 'There,' he said with a glint in his eye. 'Perhaps the story will make more sense now. If you've never tried acting, then you should do so. You certainly have the sex appeal and the beauty.'

'You think beauty is very important in a woman, don't you?' she asked drily.

'Well, isn't it?' Kyle smiled.

'It's a gift which very few women have.' She made no pretence of reading any more. 'Does that mean that you're only interested in those few women who *are* beautiful? Irrespective of what they're like as people?'

'You make it sound like a crime to admire a pretty face,' he laughed. 'As a matter of fact, I've always found that people who are lovable inside also possess a lovable exterior.'

'Now, that *is* shallow,' she retorted hotly. 'Beauty is an accident of birth. Possessing a good mind, or an upright nature, or kindness of heart—that isn't. By your lights, you would laugh at an ugly saint and admire a beautiful fraud!'

'I haven't ever seen a saint, ugly or otherwise,' he said, amused at her heat. 'But I would argue that intelligence, honesty or kindness of nature are just as much accidents of birth as beauty.'

'You're splitting hairs.'

'I don't think so. In any case, you're taking me far too simply. My views aren't as crude as you're trying to make out. Otherwise I would fall in love with a statue, like Pygmalion. A woman can have all the trappings of conventional good looks, but without the inner light to illuminate that mask she is not truly beautiful. She's pretty, but she's vapid and uninteresting.' His eyes met hers. 'That is what I meant. By the same token, a plain face can be made beautiful by the fire in the eyes, or the expression on the mouth.'

'You're confusing image with reality!'

'But how can you separate the two?' he challenged. 'My dear Sophie, I'm sorry if my compliments just now sounded patronising. When I said that you had the beauty to succeed as an actress, I meant that you had beauty in addition to a natural talent.'

'Now, how would you know whether I have any natural talent?' she asked him, her lips curling into a mocking smile.

'It's obvious. You're acting all the time.'

Her smile faded. 'I don't know what you mean.'

'Of course you know what I mean,' Kyle contradicted her calmly. 'Whoever or whatever you are, Sophie Webb, you're as well hidden behind your beautiful façade as a she-leopard sitting in the long grass. Or as any actress behind a role.' His eyes were as hard as diamonds, and, though he was smiling slightly, that cruel intentness was suddenly very disconcerting again. 'You accuse me of being shallow, of only being interested in your beauty. And yet, for some reason, you don't want me to get through to the real you, and you're devoting a lot of care to keeping me well away from whatever it is you hide behind those dark glasses.'

'You're lying right next to me,' Sophie pointed out, but her mouth was dry.

'In terms of getting near you, I might as well be lying somewhere on the other side of the world.' He shifted, sleek muscles coming into relief beneath his smooth skin, but he did not take his eyes from her face. 'No, you're an actress, all right. The best kind. The most elusive kind. You have that quality, that very special calibre, that either comes with years of experience or as a godsent gift.'

Sophie stretched her long legs, trying to maintain her casual pose. 'You sound as though you're something of an expert.'

'I enjoy the theatre. And I know several actresses. In fact,' he added, his eyes narrowing, 'you have a certain quality of one very fine actress, I know, Hélène le Bon...'

To her horror, his voice trailed off as he said the name, his stare fixed on her face with a concentration that made her heart suddenly leap into her throat. His mouth was half open, as though recognition was on the tip of his tongue.

For the second time in twenty minutes, she felt totally certain that the game was up. Then, out of her paralysis, she dredged up a languid tilt of the head.

'Hélène who?' she asked casually.

'Hélène le Bon,' he said slowly, a frown drawing his brows deep over his eyes.

'Oh, yes.' She made it sound utterly unconcerned. She sat up, turning her face away from him, and reached for the sun cream. As she smoothed the cool, sweetly scented stuff over her arms and shoulders, she said lightly, 'I've seen her in one or two things. She's very good. I'm flattered by the comparison, but I know you're really mocking me outrageously.'

She could sense his puzzled, fixed stare, and her heart was in her throat. She was certain that her skin had paled under her tan.

And then Emma came running over to them. 'Uncle Kyle! Come and see my palace!' She seized her uncle's hand, and started dragging him over to her sand-castle. With a wry smile he acceded, and the moment was broken.

Sophie started breathing again as he walked off with the child. Hell! There had been a damned sight too many close shaves so far! How long could she keep this little charade up?

She stared thoughtfully at Kyle's splendid figure as he examined Emma's castle. He was a hell of a lot more perceptive than she'd given him credit for. Though it was true he hadn't recognised her yet, despite a few close calls, he had very swiftly picked up the fact that she was concealing something from him. Given no more than the tiniest hint, she felt in her heart that he would see through her, once and for all.

She would have to be very, very careful. Kyle would have made an excellent interrogator, she thought, enjoying the jasmine scent of her sun cream. He observed with the keenness of a predator, and he let no slip pass unnoticed. There was a formidable intelligence behind that devastatingly male visage.

The closer he got to discovering her identity, the more determined she became to keep up the defence. She was enjoying this game intensely. Those moments when she'd thought he'd recognised her had been terrifying, yet had thrilled her to the core. Keeping him from recognising her had turned into a challenge every bit as stimulating as becoming Maisie Wilkin had been.

If he was really the connoisseur of acting that he'd said he was, she felt sure that he would appreciate the quality of the performance that she had put on, just for his benefit, over three Jamaican weeks.

But that was not to be until she willed it. She was determined that he should not discover her secret before she left the island, and determined that realisation should come in a way of her own choosing. Maybe she would suddenly be gone one morning, leaving him a mocking note, telling him who she really was and reminding him of how he had once found her so absurd.

Hmm, that was good.

She wanted to leave him with just a touch of the humiliation and anger he had once awoken in her.

She wanted to leave Kyle Hart grinding his beautiful white teeth!

CHAPTER THREE

NAKED in her bathroom after her shower that evening, Sophie smoothed an after-sun gel all over her body. Ever since coming here, she had been determined to take extra-special care of herself, and the cooling, moisturising lotion would give her skin an added lustre, replacing the oils that exposure to the Caribbean sun would have destroyed.

Sophie turned to the full-length mirror and studied her reflection dispassionately. This holiday in Ocho Rios was putting a fine gloss on her physique. She was a very different woman from the one Kyle had known eight months ago.

Not a trace of excess fat was left on her tall, slim frame. Her face, which had tended to become moonlike under the influence of three extra stones, was now a delicate oval, framed by tawny-brown hair, curling after a day of being constantly wet. Her breasts, too, which had been puppyishly rounded in Brighton, were back to their usual high curves. She'd always thought them far too small, so slight that they hardly cast a shadow on her ribcage, the rose-petal discs in their centres the only sensual thing about them; but she'd been glad to shed the unwonted heaviness, and to dispense with her B-cup bras.

She turned, and studied her back view over her shoulder. Trim bottom, long, elegant legs, a smoothly lovely back that gleamed with the coating of lotion. Already, she was tanned to the colour of burned honey, and would have to be careful not to let her skin get too dry.

Kyle was interested in her; she could say that without vanity, and know it was true.

The afternoon had been marvellous fun. There had been no more nerve-jittering moments of recognition—the three of them had been having far too much amusement for that.

Ostensibly organised for little Emma's benefit, the trip to Dunn's River Falls had been a huge success. The place had been just as exquisite as Kyle had said it would be, a primevally lovely spot from the first dawn of creation. They'd all got soaked clambering up the cascades, wallowing in fresh-water pools, and discovering caves and grottoes where luxuriant ferns grew in abundance.

From there they'd driven up to Runaway Bay, where there were more caves to explore, romantic enough to have Emma squealing with excitement. By the time they'd got back the little girl was happily exhausted, declaring it to be the best day of her life.

It had certainly been one of Sophie's better days.

She'd felt Kyle's eyes on her all day. And once or twice, when he'd helped her up some particularly awkward spot, his strong hands had touched her body with a possessive appreciation that had set her blood racing.

He was certainly all man. If she was toying with him, then it was a dangerous game. And, like all dangerous games, it had both its perils and its rewards. Revenge in this case was going to be very sweet. She just had to be careful that she didn't burn her own fingers in the bright flame of her sport!

On the way back, he had casually invited her to spend the next day with them, describing an alluring trip round the island as bait. After an initial hesitation, she'd accepted. It was easy to tell herself that it was all part of her plan for revenge.

Well, not quite revenge, maybe. But retribution of a kind was certainly within her grasp.

Really, he had already walked into the trap so neatly that she didn't have to do a thing. The irony of it was so perfect that she was aching for someone to share it with. All she needed was the right moment to tell him who she was, and to tell him that she'd overheard him that afternoon on Brighton beach.

And then she could walk away from Kyle Hart, and never think of him in her life again.

In the meantime, why should she feel any guilt about abusing his trust or his hospitality? If he wanted to appoint himself as her personal guide to Jamaica, then let him. By her calculations, he owed her a little atonement!

She dressed for dinner in a cool chiffon blouse with a narrow grey skirt. One of the nice things about the San Antonio was that its guests treated dinner as a dress-up occasion, and, considering the excellent restaurant, and the beautiful dining-room with its view of the bay, there was no artificiality about that.

Kyle and Emma weren't in the dining-room; Kyle had told Sophie that he would be dining with friends in Kingston, and had taken Emma with him. He evidently knew Jamaica well, and had many acquaintances on the island. All to do with that shady past, no doubt.

So she ate alone, thinking about the afternoon, and what it had felt like to be with Kyle Hart again.

It had felt very strange. There was a sense of *déjà vu*, inevitably. Yet the fact that she knew who he was, but he didn't know who she was, threw a strange spice into the mixture. There was something oddly erotic about it all. Why that should be, Sophie could not tell. But somehow the situation was one she found exciting, amusing, even sexy. Having got over the shock of seeing him again, she was enjoying the strange feeling of being half in control of events, half at the mercy of whatever would happen.

She must be one of the few women, she thought with a smile, to have ever stayed one step ahead of Kyle Hart!

'What would you like tonight, Miss Aspen?' Franklyn, her favourite waiter, was beaming down at her, and she smiled back at him. He was middle-aged and fatherly, and had pampered her right from the start, always making sure no one served her except himself.

'What do you recommend?' she asked.

'The seafood platter is extra good tonight,' he assured her. 'Good crayfish, fresh from Port Maria this afternoon. And lots of those prawns you like so much.'

'That sounds lovely, then.'

'Shall I call the wine steward?'

'No,' she decided, 'I'll stick with mineral water, thanks.'

He brought the splendidly presented platter a few minutes later. As she was becoming something of a pet of the Jamaican staff, the dishes she got tended to be a little special, and tonight was no exception.

'Wow!' she gasped at the array of shellfish. 'I'll never get through all that!'

Franklyn took the silver lobster-crackers and dealt with the crab's claws for her. 'I see you been makin' friends with Mr Hart and his little girl.'

'Well, we got talking,' Sophie said, not rising to the bait.

'Mighty fine-lookin' man,' Franklyn said, dealing efficiently with the hard shells. 'Knows Jamaica pretty well, so they say. Used to live here.'

'Do they? What else do they say?'

'They say Jamaica knows *him* pretty well,' Franklyn grinned.

'What does that mean?'

'Means he's a popular man with the ladies.' Franklyn straightened and started serving up the food. 'Got an eye for a pretty face. Which I guess is why he so interested in you, Miss Aspen.'

Sophie looked up quickly. 'He's been asking you about me?'

'This morning,' Franklyn confirmed, dark eyes twinkling. 'Seen me talkin' to you last night, and I guess he thought I could fill in a few details for him. Seemed to think your name was Miss Webb.'

Sophie bit her lip. 'Did you...?'

'I didn't tell him no different,' Franklyn said with a chuckle. 'In fact, I didn't tell him a thing about you. Just that he was the tenth feller to have asked about you in a week!'

'Thank you for not giving the game away, Franklyn.' Sophie sighed. She struggled to find an adequate explanation for her deception of Kyle. 'You see, I'm playing a sort of joke on Kyle Hart——'

'You don't need to explain a thing, Miss Aspen.' He put the immaculate napkin over his arm, and beamed down at her. 'But I tell you one thing—you got that gentleman bamboozled.'

'What does that mean?'

'Reckon he's heading into the lobster-pot as sure as that old crayfish there on your plate.'

Seismically amused by his own wit, Franklyn glided away from her table.

Sophie was awakened the next morning by a persistent tapping on her door. Wrapping herself in her lightweight gown, she went yawningly to open it.

Emma's eager face looked up at her shyly. 'You haven't forgotten? You promised you'd come!'

'I hadn't forgotten,' Sophie smiled, shaking her tousled head. 'Where's your uncle?'

'Getting dressed,' Emma replied. It was just eight. She was all ready for the day's excursion, a wide-brimmed straw hat perched on her dark hair, and her pretty little face alight with excitement.

'OK,' Sophie said, stifling another yawn. 'I won't be long. Want to come in while I get ready?'

The child nodded, and Sophie let her in. She hopped on to Sophie's tumbled bed, chattering joyously as Sophie went into the bathroom and stepped into the shower.

'We're going to dig for treasure,' she announced. 'And then we're going to dive for pearls. And then we're going to eat crayfish...'

Sophie smiled to herself as she listened to the recital through the spray of her shower. She was looking forward to the day, though her expectations weren't as sanguine as Emma's.

She washed her slim body, dried herself, and got straight into her costume. Like yesterday's, it was a one-piece, but this time in stretchy mauve Spandex, clinging to her form with flattering sexiness. It was really a little too revealing, but it gave her a kind of wicked pleasure to parade in front of Kyle the wares he'd once held in such contempt!

She went back into the bedroom to finish dressing.

'You've got such lovely clothes,' Emma sighed. At eight, she was already alert to fashion, and loved bright colours. 'My mum wears pretty things, too.'

'Does she?' Sophie asked, stepping into a deep blue sun-dress and zipping it up.

'Yes. Mum and Dad are talking about getting divorced, you know.'

Sophie tried not to wince at the blunt announcement. 'Oh. I'm sorry to hear that.'

'That's why Uncle Kyle's taking me on this holiday. I'm not supposed to know. But I do.'

Sophie put some underwear, a sun-dress and an extra towel in her basket, along with an assortment of toiletries, sunglasses, hairbrushes and general feminine accoutrements. 'I suppose you couldn't help knowing about something like that,' she said slowly.

'They might be divorced by the time I get back.' Emma obviously had a rather vague idea of what was involved, which was just as well. She looked relatively unconcerned. 'My best friend's mum and dad got divorced last year. Lots of the girls at school have got divorced mums and dads, too.'

'Well, let's hope it doesn't happen to you,' Sophie smiled. 'Think you can wait while I do my hair in a plait?'

'I'll help,' Emma offered. 'I always help Mummy do hers.'

'OK.' Sophie got on the bed next to her, and sat cross-legged while the girl busied herself with the thick chestnut hair at the back of her head.

'Do you like your Uncle Kyle?' she asked.

'Oh, he's *fabulous*!' Emma enthused. 'He's the handsomest man in London.'

'Is he?' she replied, amused.

'Don't you think so?'

'I've seen worse, I guess. He seems very fond of you, for some unknown reason, too.'

Emma giggled. 'Daddy says he used to be the black sheep of the family, but not any more. What *is* the black sheep of the family?'

'You'll have to ask your Uncle Kyle that,' Sophie hedged discreetly.

'And Mummy says he should get married and settle down. Except,' she added, 'he hasn't found the right woman yet.'

Sophie tried to hide her smile. It was odd to hear these scraps of grown-up conversation coming out of Emma's mouth. 'And did you have a nice time last night?'

'Oh, *yes*!' Emma enthused. 'We went to some friends of Uncle Kyle's. There was music and dancing, and a feast——'

'A feast?'

'That's what they call it in Kingston. Where the food's all laid out, and you sort of help yourself.'

'A buffet?'

'I think so. It was scrummy, anyway.'

'Lots of pretty ladies wearing lovely clothes?' Sophie probed.

'Mmm! There was a *super* Jamaican lady dancing with Uncle Kyle. She looked like a model. Not like you, though. Different.'

'Prettier?' Sophie asked casually.

'Well...' Diplomacy struggled with accuracy as Emma concentrated on the plait she was making. 'Maybe just a tiny bit. She was ever so tall and smart, with a lovely figure. She had beautiful hair, too, done in sort of an Afro style. Like in the films.'

'I see.'

'Her name was Francie. She and Uncle Kyle go way back.'

'Oh, they do, do they?' Sophie commented, feeling the flame of jealousy flutter into life. 'Did he dance with this beautiful Francie all night?'

'I don't know,' Emma answered with devastating honesty. 'I got put to bed at ten. But he seemed very fond of her. Is that all right?'

Tying the plait, Sophie checked in the mirror. It was surprisingly proficient, and gleamed glossily at her nape. 'That's lovely,' she smiled. 'Let's go!'

They went downstairs to the car, where Kyle was already waiting, wearing figure-hugging denims and a loose tank-top. He greeted her with a grin, and Sophie found herself wondering rather bitterly whether Francie with the lovely figure and Afro hair was responsible for a certain cat-that-got-the-cream air about Kyle this morning.

'Did you sleep well?' he asked.

'Very well,' she nodded. The impact of Kyle's beauty was hitting her all over again. His tan was deepening visibly after days in the sun, and in the denims that hugged his hips and the crisp cotton shirt he looked anything but a banker from London. More like a Hollywood sex symbol doing a bit of beach-combing.

He took her hand and lifted it to his lips. The light kiss gave her a shivery sensation of goose-flesh.

'Blue suits you well,' he said, studying her calmly. 'You look stunning. You could pose for Aphrodite rising from the foam.'

'Thank you, kind sir,' she said, and cursed herself for the blush that rose to her face.

Kyle opened the door for her, amusement registering on his bronzed features.

'You're not very poised for a top model,' he said. 'Aren't you used to compliments?'

'You say things that are just outrageous. They aren't compliments.'

Getting into the convertible, Sophie was having the weirdest feeling. It was exactly like being a young family, going on a glamorous outing together. Except that she wasn't married to the man, and the child wasn't theirs.

They set off inland, and drove across the centre of the island towards Mandeville, a hilltop town of cool English elegance. Its white houses were dazzling in the morning sun. Pausing there to wander along the Georgian avenues, and to buy Emma a glass of iced coconut-milk, they headed on towards the coast and Treasure Beach.

The vast sweep of golden sand, fringed on one side by a sea of impossible blue, and thick tropical vegetation on the other, was an incredibly beautiful sight. Sophie was enchanted, but Emma, clutching her spade and bucket, looked dismayed.

'But where's the treasure *buried*?' she wailed.

'That's for you to find out,' Kyle smiled. 'I didn't say it was going to be easy, did I?'

'It could be anywhere!'

'You never know your luck,' Kyle said solemnly. 'And I've got a clue. The treasure is buried under the biggest palm tree on the beach.'

'It must be that one! Or that one!'

'Well, let's cool off with a swim before you start digging,' he suggested.

The sand was already burning hot as they walked down to the sea across the dunes, and Sophie couldn't resist the delicious turquoise water. As soon as they'd found a satisfactory place to settle, she pulled off her shorts and shirt and ran into the sea.

The water was ravishingly cool as it flooded round her body. She struck out towards the horizon, splashing blissfully. It was a perfect day. The sky overhead was a vault of sapphire-blue, the sunlight pouring down like gold. Kyle and Emma followed her. He was completely at home in the water, moving with the easy grace of a big fish. He smiled at Sophie, the deep blue of the sky reflected in those green eyes, turning them the colour of the sea.

'You look as though you're enjoying yourself.'

'I love Jamaica,' Sophie sighed rapturously. 'I just know I'll come back some day.' They swam for almost an hour, just revelling in the sea and the natural beauty all around them.

When at last they were lying in the baking sun, with Emma digging hopefully for treasure under the biggest palm tree she could find, Kyle turned to her.

'When are you thinking of leaving Jamaica?'

'I don't know,' she answered idly.

'Don't you have a job to go back to?' Kyle probed. 'No assignment waiting for you back home?'

'Not for the moment,' she replied.

'Does that mean I have you to myself on an indefinite basis?' he asked, the smile warm in his voice.

'You don't have me to yourself on any basis,' she replied tartly. She looked up. He was watching her. Once wet, the mauve Spandex costume clung to her in a very revealing fashion, and he wasn't bothering to disguise his interest in her anatomy. She fought down her prudish instinct to cover up. After all, she enjoyed looking at his body. Why should she feel so awkward? Stop being Maisie, she warned herself, and remember that you're Sophie again!

A beaming Jamaican beach vendor had arrived, with a vast basket of fruit balanced on her head. Kyle bought them bananas, pineapples and some strange, knobbly looking things that were called sweet-sop. He washed the pineapple in the sea, and started peeling it with a knife.

'What about you?' she asked, watching him carve the dripping fruit. 'How long are you planning on staying here?'

'I'm in no hurry to leave,' he said, his eyes holding hers. 'But if my brother and his wife take a long time sorting out their marriage, I'm thinking of chartering a yacht, and taking Emma across to Haiti and the Dominican Republic. To the Cayman Islands as well, if we have the time. Maybe even to Cuba.'

'Not exactly the well-beaten tourist track,' Sophie remarked, glancing at him.

'No,' Kyle agreed. 'But it's worth it, just for the Creole cooking.' His smile glinted in the sunlight as he sliced the golden pineapple into juicy rounds. 'Besides, I know those islands well enough to be able to take care of myself—and Emma.'

'Knowledge gleaned during your misspent youth?'

'Mmm.'

She assessed the powerful muscles of his chest and shoulders from under her thick lashes. 'You're very discreet about that misspent youth of yours. Was it so very wicked?'

'Well, I wasn't always a dull pen-pusher, slaving away in a City bank,' he said in amusement.

'So what took you to the Caribbean?'

'It's a long story.'

'We've got all morning,' she hinted. He passed her some pineapple, and she bit into the fruit. It was nectar, with none of the acidity she associated with pineapples in England.

'Nice?' he asked, watching her.

'Heavenly.' She was getting the juice everywhere, but with the sea two steps away who cared? She brushed her chin with the back of her wrist. 'But I want to hear about why you came to Jamaica.'

'Well, the essence of it is that my father is one of the directors of a merchant bank in London. It isn't a very big one,' he smiled, catching her expression, 'but it's very well established, and it has a good name in the City. It's been going for a hundred and thirty years.' He consumed a chunk of pineapple, making a neater job of it than she had done. 'The tradition in our family is that the eldest son always goes into the bank. I happen to be the eldest of the three of us, but when I came out of university I just wasn't ready to go into servitude.'

'Poor thing,' she condoled in a voice like lemon drops, 'born to such a dreadful fate. Fancy having wealth and a distinguished career thrust upon you so cruelly.'

He laughed huskily. 'I didn't see it quite like that at the time.' He passed her another piece of fruit. 'All I knew was that people who worked in banks were dull and staid and grey. I had the idea that bankers just sat around counting money all day. Well, I was crazy about yachts and yachting, and all I wanted to do was see the world. I told my father that I needed two years to settle down, and he reluctantly agreed. So I took off.'

'How, exactly, took off?'

'I got a job, crewing on a yacht bound for Montego Bay. When I arrived, I just fell in love with the place.'

Sophie smiled, and hummed from 'Jamaica Farewell'. 'I took a trip on a sailing ship, and when I reached Jamaica, I made a stop.'

'Exactly,' he laughed. 'I spent the next twenty-six months in the Caribbean, mainly working on yachts between the islands. Sailing and . . . seeing life.'

'Was she dark-skinned or light-skinned?' Sophie enquired, deadpan.

Kyle laughed softly. 'There were two, actually, and both had skins the colour of *cortado*—what the French call *café au lait*. They taught me a great deal about life...and love. But they weren't the only reason I stayed. I really did come to love the Caribbean. The work was hard, but I was fit and ready for most things.'

He didn't need to elaborate. Wisely, Sophie resisted the impulse to ask whether one of the ladies had been called Francie. 'It sounds like fun.'

'Life was good,' he agreed. 'There was a lot of hard physical work, but I didn't have many responsibilities or worries. I was just living from day to day, doing what I loved. I had a lot of good times. Then, one time, we went up to Florida on a fishing trip, and I found a rusty old steel-hulled yacht for sale in a mooring in Miami. I had just enough money to buy her. I sailed her back to Kingston, and cleaned her up, begging and stealing the paint and varnish where I could. A month later, I went into the charter business.'

Sophie couldn't stop herself from smiling. 'Trust you. The mercantile genes were coming out, despite the attempt to break free.'

'There's more truth in that than you know,' he agreed. 'It must have been my destiny.'

'What astrological sign are you?' she asked.

Kyle snorted. 'You don't believe in all that silliness, do you?'

'I don't knock it,' she replied. 'You talked about destiny just now, didn't you? So tell me, what sign are you?'

'Scorpio.' He gave her a dry look. 'Now you're going to tell me I'm ambitious, vindictive and deeply passionate, right?'

'I wouldn't know,' she smiled, 'but those are typical Scorpio characteristics. Especially the vindictive bit. Most Scorpios I've known have been great ones for getting their own back. Their motto seems to be "don't get mad, get even"!'

'Could be true,' he shrugged. 'I hate anyone to get one over me.'

'There you are, then. Do you always get your own back?'

'Always,' he said with a glint. 'Preferably in spades.'

Sophie felt a slight chill touch her skin, despite the tropical sun. But Kyle was smiling easily. 'And you?' he asked. 'Where do you come in the zodiac?'

'I'm a Virgo.' Somehow, that made her blush stupidly, and his keen eyes didn't miss that fact.

'That suits you rather well,' he smiled. 'Didn't I say you had a cool, touch-me-not quality? So—what happens when a passionate, ambitious Scorpio male meets a cool, vestal Virgo female?'

That was not a question she cared to go into! 'We were talking about your misspent youth,' she reminded him firmly. 'What happened after you got into the charter business?'

He sighed. 'Well, it was the beginning of the end, of course. I went at it with all my enthusiasm. In six months, I was buying two more yachts and starting to hire my own crews, and six more months later my bank manager was starting to talk about the benefits of floating a company.'

'Sounds like everybody's dream,' Sophie commented.

'It wasn't *my* dream.'

'The magic had worn off?'

'Unfortunately,' he nodded. 'While I was just lazing around, making love and having fun, it was paradise. Once money came into it, everything changed. I found I was thinking about the business all day long. Where I used to be content lying on the beach with a bottle of rum and a girl in my spare time, now I was making plans, working on boats, adding up figures.' He smiled at Sophie gently. 'One morning, I woke up, and I realised I was out of my place. I could be doing the same work in the bank, and that was where I belonged.'

'Just like that?'

'I discovered that I wasn't doing what I wanted any more. I was twenty-three, just your age, and I was playing truant from my real life.'

'Did you sell up?'

'Lock, stock and barrel. I was a little late on my promise to my father, but by the time I was twenty-five I was working in the bank, and heading for a seat on the board.'

She watched his face. 'And did you miss Jamaica?'

'On grey, drizzly days, yes. But I'd realised by then that I had sown my wild oats, and that responsibility couldn't be avoided for ever. But I've always been able to come back for holidays—though if I didn't have Emma,' he added with a glitter, 'I'd be staying somewhere very different from the San Antonio.'

'With one of your *café au lait* charmers?' she suggested, tilting a dry look at him.

'Somewhere like that,' he agreed easily. He evidently took no trouble to disguise the fact that he was footloose and fancy-free as far as women were concerned. 'As a matter of fact,' he went on, 'I learned a lot in the Caribbean, about myself, and about business. And one of the things I'd picked up was that work doesn't have to be dull.'

'I assume you've added your own particular style to merchant banking?' Sophie asked.

He smiled faintly. 'In a way. My speciality is financing projects which other banks have rejected as too avant-garde, or too risky, but which I think are basically sound. Ninety-eight per cent of the time it pays off handsomely.'

'And the other two per cent?'

'The other two per cent has to be explained away to the board...very convincingly.' He smiled into her eyes. 'But I can be very persuasive.'

'I'm sure you can.' Her eyes dropped to the curve of his mouth, so temptingly male. 'So how do you judge the sound projects from the cranky ones?'

'Instinct.'

'Did you also learn how to judge the worth of people while you were sowing your wild oats in the Caribbean?'

'That,' he said gently, 'is the most difficult art of all. But I think I'm good at it.'

She raised an ironical eyebrow. 'Really? And you never go wrong, say...make a snap judgement on the face value of things?'

'We all do that, from time to time. But I try not to.'

'That must be a great talent,' she said with well-veiled sarcasm.

'Why do I have this idea that you're laughing at me all the time?'

'Why should I laugh? Your life has evidently been a mixture of Errol Flynn and Pierpont Morgan.'

He laughed out loud at that, throwing his head back. He was so handsome that he made her heart ache. 'You're an ironical creature,' he observed, meeting her eyes in amusement. Laughter was still rumbling in him as he rose to his feet. 'I'd better go and make sure Emma finds some treasure.'

'Have you brought something?'

He showed her a little silver ring, set with a 'ruby'. It was clearly inexpensive, but quite authentically antique-looking all the same. 'I bought that from one of those Rastafarian stalls. Think she'll like it?'

'She'll adore it,' Sophie nodded.

'I think the kid needs a little spoiling.' He looked down at her, tall and tanned. 'I'm not much good at entertaining little girls, but I'm learning from you. I don't know how I would have managed if you hadn't been here.'

'She's not entirely unaware of what's going on at home,' Sophie said, wiping her sticky hands. 'She told me this morning that her mum and dad were talking about a divorce.'

Kyle's face changed. 'Damn. How do you stop a child from picking up these things?'

'You can't.' They looked at each other for a moment in silence. 'Have you heard from her parents yet?'

'My sister-in-law rang last night,' Kyle nodded. 'Things aren't going too well.'

'I'm sorry to hear that,' Sophie said.

'Yes. Well, it's just one of the things that happen, isn't it?' The bitterness on his face told her how much he cared, really. He walked across the beach to plant the ring in Emma's excavation.

Sophie went down to the sea to wash her hands. He was a strange man. So caring in some ways, so hard and ruthless in others. She basked in the sun for an hour, almost dropping off to sleep while Kyle entertained his niece. At noon they went back to the car, heading on down the coast towards Black River.

It was now fiercely hot. At a roadside stall they bought crabs and crayfish roasted over the coals, together with 'bammies', manioc bread, and stopped in a particularly scenic spot to eat their feast. The food was delicious and fresh, given added zest by being eaten in the open, in such glorious weather. Emma was bubbling with delight over her ring, apparently completely unsuspecting that it hadn't been lying in the sand since Captain Morgan's time.

At Frenchman's Reef, they swam again, this time wearing face masks, and using snorkels. The water was clear and calm, and though they didn't find any pearls the underwater scenery was weirdly beautiful, bright shoals of fish flickering through miniature forests of corals, and waving fields of sea-grass patching a submarine landscape of pure silver sand.

In the late afternoon they drove on to Bloody Bay. All day they had been getting further and further from the well-beaten tourist areas, and now they were in almost completely unspoiled countryside. The wide and empty scenery had exerted a powerful hold on Sophie, and she was realising how much she'd missed by staying around Ocho Rios. Bloody Bay had an even longer beach, and even warmer water, than Treasure Beach.

After a final swim, Emma curled up in the shade of a sand-dune and fell asleep, while Kyle took Sophie on a gentle ramble along the water's edge.

The relationship between them had been growing more warm and intimate all day, and now they just walked in silence, not talking much, just sharing the beauty of the day and the landscape.

'It really is extraordinarily lovely,' Sophie sighed at last, as they stopped and looked back along the shimmering sand. The warm, lapping sea had all but obliterated their footprints. They were the only two solitary figures in all the vast beauty of sea and sand.

'You fit in well,' he said softly, 'because you're an extraordinarily lovely woman. I find it hard to believe that you're not surrounded by a coterie of pursuing men,' he went on. 'You must have left them in England.'

'No, there's no one in England.'

'Not a soul?'

'There are always men in my life,' she said, meeting his eyes briefly. 'But not in the sense you mean.'

'What sense do I mean?'

'Well, I presume you're asking me whether I have a lover,' she smiled.

'And the answer is no?'

'Not at the moment.'

'A true Virgo?' Kyle was looking at her with an expression that made her heart suddenly clench in reaction. He was wearing only faded denims, his powerful torso naked to the sun. She, in her mauve one-piece, with a frayed straw hat shading her eyes, looked captivatingly graceful and feminine.

'You're exquisite in this light,' he said in a quiet voice.

She tried to laugh the comment off, and turned away. Despite her daily swims and exercise, she was feeling pleasantly tired. She couldn't match the power of that hard body of his. 'My legs are aching exquisitely, at any rate.'

'How else could exquisite legs ache?' he smiled. 'I must have worn you out with all that swimming and walking.'

'I'm not as strong as you are,' Sophie pointed out. 'I've loved it—I just feel a bit the way Emma does.'

'I ought to be shot. Let's go and sit on the sand over there.'

They walked over, and settled down in the lee of the breeze that had sprung up. The sand was warm, radiating back the heat of the day. With a sigh of bliss, Sophie lay back against its soft, yielding warmth, and closed her eyes. 'To think that all this has to end,' she said dreamily. 'It doesn't seem fair. Beauty should never have to end.'

She felt his fingers touch her hair, caressing the salt-stiffened tangle gently. She half opened her lids languidly, looking up at him with eyes that had taken on the colour of the evening sky.

'This is what I like about you,' he said.

'My awful hair?' she smiled.

'Your beautiful hair,' he corrected. 'The way you don't fiddle and fuss with it all the time. I like women to be natural. I hate that neurotic, twitchy way some women behave.'

She thought of the way her fiddling with her glasses had irritated him in Brighton. He was leaning over her, smiling down at her, and at that moment she felt very close to him, and that she wanted him very much.

'Is it a cliché to say that you're radiant?' Kyle asked. His fingers trailed down the satin-smooth skin of her cheek to trace the delicate arc of her jawline. 'Your skin is the colour of gold, yet it's got an almost pearly quality, finer than the finest silk that was ever spun.'

'The afternoon has gone to your head,' she said, trying to ignore the long fingers that were caressing her neck.

'Maybe,' he conceded. 'How are your legs?'

'Better.' His caresses were not having a soothing effect on her. His touch was deliberately sensual, yet as light as thistledown. 'We must have walked miles today.'

He did not answer, but bent slightly to touch her lips with his.

A touch, no more. The velvety warmth was there on her mouth, then gone. She felt her lips part, her eyes closing with the reaction that had swept across her skin.

'You've got goose-bumps,' he said softly, his fingers trailing down her arm where the fine golden hairs were erect. The extra-responsive condition of her skin made his touch something between torment and ecstasy. Sophie felt his lips touch her forehead, drifting down her eyelids.

The warm moistness of his tongue told her he was tasting the sea-salt on her temples, and she shuddered involuntarily. She was in the grip of a kind of sweet hypnosis, immobile in the warm sand while Kyle kissed her face, his mouth never touching hers, drawing close, then moving away with maddening deliberation.

When at last her lips touched his, Sophie knew that it had been by her own movement. She lifted her full, sensitised mouth to his, and felt him kiss her there at last, his arm sliding round her to draw her close.

Her lips clung to Kyle's, possessed of a will of their own. His tongue traced the shape of her soft lower lip, touching her white teeth, meeting the sensitive tip of her own tongue. His lips pressed harder as passion took the place of exploration. He was tasting the deep inner secrets of her mouth for a dizzy moment; then he drew away, as though trying to discipline them both.

'I've been dying to do that all day,' he whispered.

He kissed her cheeks, her delicate eyelids, his mouth moving down her throat to find the scented hollow where her pulses fluttered madly.

She couldn't stop the soft moan of desire from escaping her parted lips. She had hungered for Kyle for so long, and this moment was so sweet. It was happening at last, the impossible dream she had ached for long ago...

Her slim arms slid around his neck, pressing his face to her throat, her neck arching as she felt the harsh touch of his teeth.

Who was conquering whom? She felt his palm caress her ribs, drawing closer to the gentle swell of her breast, where the skin was already tightening in reaction. His touch was possessive, yet thrilling. She was melting inside, her adoring heart starting to fail her.

Kyle whispered her name, his hand sliding into the V of her bathing costume to stroke the silky skin of her breasts. The sensation was so much more erotic than she could ever have dreamed. His touch was tender, yet accomplished; he knew how to touch a woman. She moaned aloud as his palm caressed the sultry tips of her nipples, drawing them into concentrated stars of aphrodisiac passion. His very gentleness was tormenting. The sensitive areas of her body were starting to throb with hunger, and Sophie felt her self-control start to slip.

With a supreme effort she drew away from him and unclasped her hands from round his neck.

'We'd better get back to Emma,' she said, in a voice that shook slightly. 'And we'd better stop what we're doing right now.'

'Why?' he wanted to know, smiling down at her with smoky eyes. His fingers eased aside the stretchy mauve top of her costume, revealing the paler curve of her breast, the rosebud tip tight and demanding at the centre.

The dark expansion of his pupils registered the way her nakedness had affected him; then, obeying the tacit demand, he bent his head, his mouth closing over her nipple.

Sophie gasped at the intimate kiss, his tongue feeling as rough as a cat's against her tender skin.

She ran her palms shakily over his powerful shoulders, up his neck. His hair was thick and crisp under her fingers as she drew his head down, wanting him to touch her harder, more fiercely. Kyle's teeth closed around the aroused flesh of her nipple, the caress becoming almost cruel. The pleasure was wickedly intense, drawing a whimper from deep in her throat. His hand was finding her other breast, seeking her other nipple, making forked lightning dart along her nerveways into her loins, turning desire into quivering hunger.

Unable to bear it now, Sophie arched away, and pulled the soft material of her costume back over her naked breasts. Suddenly the Spandex seemed a painfully flimsy protection, her aroused nipples making flagrant peaks against the mauve material.

'Please,' she begged, her eyes misty, 'if you respect me, don't touch me any more.'

He stared at her, his expression unmistakably desirous. 'Are you deliberately trying to drive me crazy?' he asked huskily. 'I want you, Sophie! Don't you know how I feel about you?'

'I know that I don't know you well enough to let you do this to me,' she replied, sitting up. Her mouth was dry with passion. 'Secondly, this isn't the time or place for what you feel, and thirdly, there's a little girl all alone over there——'

'Emma's quite safe.' He tilted his head to kiss her mouth again, and she felt the world spin around her. 'God, I want you,' he murmured, drawing her close.

'Kyle, don't——'

'You're so lovely,' he whispered raggedly. 'So slender and graceful, so cool and elusive...' His hand was caressing her hip, the satiny skin of her thigh. 'From the moment I saw you, I've been burning for you. And I know you feel the same way, too.'

'You don't know anything of the kind,' she retorted. But she had to speak between his kisses, and the blood was rushing in her veins, like molten gold being poured into a new mould, a new shape.

Kyle's hand slid into the smooth coolness between her thighs, caressing the delicate skin, so close to the aching, melting centre of her need that the slightest movement would be fatal.

His mouth claimed hers with hungry intensity, and then she felt his palm cup the mound of her womanhood, only the soft material coming between his possessive touch and her arousal.

Her eyes widened, her whole body tensing like a coiled spring at the feelings he was unleashing in her.

Then she remembered Maisie. Before he could stop her, she slid away from him, rose to her slender, shaky legs, and ran down the moist sand to the sea.

The warm water enveloped her, too warm and too salt to do much in the way of rinsing away her emotions, but at least she had escaped from the drowning maelstrom of Kyle's lovemaking.

For the time being.

Kyle followed her after a few moments, his magnificent face looking partly amused, partly frustrated. She was expecting some acid comment at the way she'd chickened out, but he didn't say anything to her, just swam beside her in silence until she was ready to get out again.

'We'd better set off,' he said, as they walked, both dripping, back to where Emma lay sleeping. 'It's a long drive back to Ocho Rios.'

'Yes,' she said flatly.

'Are you angry about what's just happened?' he asked, sliding a strong arm around her waist and pulling her close.

'No,' Sophie said, rather tensely. 'But I don't want it to happen again.'

'Oh, Sophie,' he said, in mock reproof. 'You don't really think it's going to end there, do you?'

She didn't answer him.

But later, when she was alone, she could no longer pretend that it was all just a mischievous game any more. She'd wanted to let Kyle's misconception about her run. She'd wanted to play some kind of joke on him, to sting him back for the way he had once stung her.

Yet somehow it wasn't working out as simply and as neatly as she'd expected.

Kyle wanted her. There was no doubt about it any more. If her ambition was to be desired by the man who had once spurned her, she knew deep down that her wish was fulfilled.

There ought to have been a delicious enjoyment in that. This was a man who had once ridiculed her infatuation with him. And today he had held her in his arms, and had wanted to make love to her, right there on the beach. If she'd wanted, she could have had him...as her lover.

Enjoyment? Yes, after a fashion.

But there was pain, too. That old, sharp pain, reminding her so keenly of a certain evening in Brighton. The pain of feeling that he was only looking at her exterior. Only looking at her body. As though what lay inside her counted for nothing, as though all the feelings and emotions, the intelligence and the wit, were all irrelevant to looking good and dressing well.

What was worse: being humiliated because of her appearance, or being desired for it?

Damn him, she thought with quick hurt. Damn him for his triviality! If she'd once thought he cared about her, about what she was like inside, today would have been the happiest in her life, instead of a moment of acute, bittersweet irony.

And there were further problems. Mainly her own, that was. She ought to have known herself well enough to foresee just how deeply she would become enslaved by him. Enslaved? Yes. There was no other word.

Sophie knew her own feelings. They ran deep and strong. Though she'd never committed herself to any man in the full physical sense, she'd always known that when she did fall in love with a man it would be forever. She'd always cherished the old-fashioned ambition of having, in the same man, her only lover, husband and partner through life.

Maybe that was just the naïve conservatism of her rural Yorkshire upbringing. But it was a part of her, and she felt with deep pain that she could never survive a casual affair, not with Kyle Hart.

Kyle was by his own admission a roamer as far as women were concerned. He was hardly the forever kind.

How could she be sure that their relationship had any prospects other than those of a pleasurable holiday romance, which would end, on his part, with no possibility of anything deeper or further? She could not. All that lay in front of her, as far as she could now see, was pain.

What on earth was she going to do? She had already played this game for so long that it had gone too far to call the chips in.

If she told him who she really was, could she be sure that he wouldn't reject her completely? The thought that he would react with fury, or with disgust, terrified her. That Scorpio temper was something to fear. She was no slavish adherent of astrology, but somehow Kyle fitted the Scorpio bill very well indeed. If he was true to the type, he would react badly to having been duped, and that sting in the tail could be fatal. She could either have told him who she was right at the very beginning, or——

Or not tell him at all?

The temptation was so strong. On the one side she risked losing Kyle forever. On the other, she had the prospect of two more weeks of certain heaven.

Perhaps there was a way she could have her cake and eat it. If she could avoid a physical affair, if she could just keep it to the kind of happy friendship they'd had until this afternoon, then what harm was there in letting him remain ignorant about her identity?

The decision was made. She wouldn't tell him. Not until the very end. Then, if he really cared about her, it would all work out. And if he didn't—well, she would have had her three weeks of heaven.

CHAPTER FOUR

SOPHIE sat down at the dressing-table to put on her make-up, and stared at her own face in the mirror. The cool grey eyes looked back at her with a misty hint of melancholy, and the full, passionate mouth was touched with sadness.

It was her last night in Jamaica.

Three weeks of heaven had flown by so quickly, the happiest three weeks of her life. She had known love, excitement, had seen her most secret dream come true—that she would meet Kyle Hart again, and that he would be as attracted to her as he had once been repelled.

He still didn't suspect a thing. He didn't even know she was going tomorrow. She hadn't told him.

Lying on her bed, her tan suitcases were almost completely packed, bright summer colours peeping out from under the lids. The cupboards and shelves were empty. The taxi was booked to take her to the airport at seven-thirty tomorrow morning; the hotel bill was paid; she'd rung London to ask Mrs Flanagan, her cleaning lady, to air and clean the flat for her arrival tomorrow night. Tomorrow night she would sleep in London, and all this would be just a dream. Including Kyle Hart.

Everything had come to a focal point tonight.

They'd spent so many beautiful days together, sometimes just lying on the beach, talking and laughing with the intimacy of lovers, sometimes exploring Jamaica together, Kyle's expertise about the island making him a fascinating guide.

But they had never become lovers—not in the physical sense. She'd been so careful to avoid letting him kiss or caress her, knowing full well by now the devastating physical effect he could have on her. Though she knew her reserve had frustrated him intensely, she had deliberately shied away from the sensual relationship she knew he wanted so badly. For that, at least, she was now profoundly grateful.

She was wearing only a cotton wrap, and it had drifted aside to reveal the curves of her neat, high breasts, with their delicate tips.

In the afternoon, on the beach, Kyle had asked her to have dinner with him tonight—not in the hotel, but in a restaurant in Kingston that he claimed was unmatchable—and she'd accepted.

Her plans for tonight weren't definite. It was her last performance, though, and she was determined to play it to the hilt!

She checked her watch. She'd sat here mooning so long that she was already running fifteen minutes late. If Kyle was on time, then he would be cooling his heels in the foyer already. Well, let him! A little waiting wouldn't hurt that massive male ego.

Her face didn't need more than a touch of lip-gloss and a hint of eyeshadow to leap into glamorous definition. She darkened her lashes with mascara, and brushed her chestnut hair as vigorously as she could bear. Her hair was the only incomplete note; not in any definable style, it tended to become a glossy chaos of curls and waves. But it was not an unattractive chaos, and it would have to do.

She touched her wrists and the valley between her naked breasts with a Giorgio Armani perfume, a fragrance she had discovered recently, and which captivated her with its mysterious seduction.

Letting the wrap drift to the floor, she stepped into a pair of lacy silk briefs, pulling them up over her slender hips, then she lifted the dress off the chair where she'd left it.

It was the only garment she had which was really suitable for an occasion like tonight. She'd bought it in Kingston a few days ago, knowing at the time that she would probably never wear it in London, but thinking of it as a souvenir. A plain black sarong dress in silk chiffon, it looked demure, apart from having no straps and leaving her tanned shoulders bare.

Until she took a step forward, when the slit in the front opened from ankle to the top of her thigh, revealing a devastating length of honey-coloured leg.

Half-amused at her own daring. Sophie fastened the dress and stepped into black high heels. Stockings, she guessed, weren't *de rigueur* in Kingston in summer. She didn't have any jewellery except cheap costume stuff, so she did without. A final glance in the mirror confirmed that she was looking just as she wanted to look. The image was right. He would be dazzled.

She picked up her little evening bag, and walked out of the room to meet Kyle.

She was exactly forty minutes late. He was waiting in the foyer, in a white jacket, with his hands thrust into the pockets of his black dress trousers. He looked magnificent enough to make her heart miss a beat, a sensationally male presence, radiating an animal aura of potency.

He also looked very impatient. In fact, his white teeth were biting into his tanned lower lip as he glowered across the palm-filled acres of cream carpeting, the green eyes smouldering under the dark brows.

Sophie stepped out of the lift, and walked towards him, keeping her expression neutral. This was probably the only time in her life she would walk across a room like this, dressed like this, to meet a man like Kyle Hart.

He turned and saw her, and his left wrist instinctively came out of his pocket, turning the diver's watch so he could tell her just how long she'd kept him waiting.

But his eyes did not leave her to consult the time.

Instead, they widened slightly as they took in her face, then drifted down her figure to watch the way her right leg parted the black silk chiffon as she walked.

And one thing her experience as a model had taught her was how to walk across a room.

'Hello,' she said as she reached him, and gave him a cool smile. 'Isn't it a warm evening?'

'Uh—very warm,' he agreed, as though still trying to come to terms with her appearance. 'Sophie, you look...'

She tilted an eyebrow at him. 'Yes?'

'Come on,' he said, shaking his dark head slightly. He didn't mention that she'd kept him waiting for the best part of an hour, though Sophie guessed that he was the kind of man who didn't usually let things like that ride!

As he opened the passenger-side door of the white convertible to let her in, he touched the cool skin of her arm.

'Sophie,' he said quietly, 'you're utterly lovely.'

She settled into the seat, and looked up at him without missing a beat. The slim length of her thigh peeped through the silk. Kyle's almost tense expression told her how completely she had succeeded in her intention. She let a slight smile play across her mouth.

'Are you going to stand there all night, or shall we go and eat?'

He grinned, and leaned down to arrange the skirt so it covered her leg more demurely. 'That's a hazard to safe driving. Keep it covered if you want me to concentrate on the road.'

He closed the door, walked round the car, and got into the driver's seat. The roof was down, letting the balmy night air play around them.

'Top up or top down?' he enquired.

'Top down. It's hot.'

'OK.' He fired up the engine. 'Let's go.'

It was three-thirty in the morning, and the moon was a mother-of-pearl disc, high in the velvety dark blue sky, as they drove down the avenue of ghostly palm trees back to the San Antonio. In a very few hours, she would be on her way back to England.

But she didn't want to think about that.

Only now had the air started to cool down, and, after the evening they'd had, Sophie was glad to just lie back in the passenger seat and feel the crisp breeze caress her throat and shoulders. She raised her arms to lift her tumbled hair and let the cool wind get round the back of her neck, and sighed.

It had been a night of magic and enchantment. The restaurant he'd taken her to had been in the heart of downtown Kingston, the old part of the city. It had been the kind of place she'd never have dreamed of going to on her own, a dockside basement throbbing with reggae music and filled with an assortment of clients which had been, to say the least, picturesque.

But Kyle had been greeted as an old friend by the villainous-looking staff, and the meal they'd had—stuffed crabs, jerk pork cooked over pimento wood, yams, fried green bananas, and an exquisite pudding like a fruit fool, which Kyle had told her was called 'matrimony'—had been like nothing she'd ever eaten before. Washed down with lager, and concluded with rum and coffee, it had left her happily light-headed, a feeling which had persisted for the rest of the evening.

From there they'd moved on uptown to a nightclub with a terrace where they'd danced to the brilliant music of a calypso band. Kyle was being a charming companion, amusing her with the trenchant ease of a man who'd entertained a great many women in a great many different ways.

She hadn't tried to fool herself about her reaction to Kyle; he was sweeping her off her feet, and she loved it. She loved being held in his strong arms, losing herself in the bliss of snuggling up to his big, powerful body. Loved talking to him, listening to his pungently amusing conversation. Loved the fun he seemed to generate around himself.

He'd explained what some of the lyrics to the songs had meant, and they'd been wicked—and witty—enough to have her giggling helplessly.

Later, they'd gone on to a third locale, where they'd watched limbo dancing. The real thing. That had been very different from what had gone before, a pagan hint of voodoo accompanied by throbbing drums that spoke of dark magic and ancient ritual. Sophie had watched in taut fascination as the glistening, lithe brown bodies had performed almost impossible feats of agility, dancing beneath a flaming bar no more than a foot off the ground.

She'd been so sure some of the dancers would burn themselves that she'd found herself holding Kyle's hand tightly in her own. During one of the breaks, he'd kissed her. Nothing serious, just a gentle contact of lips, and yet the underlying message had been plain. A question, an invitation. A message that tonight didn't have to end.

'What are you thinking about?'

The question roused Sophie from her dreamy reverie. She curled in the seat to look at his profile.

'Tonight.'

'Have you enjoyed it?'

'Immensely.'

'We can do the same thing tomorrow night. And the next night, and the next...'

Sophie was silent, thinking of the packed suitcases lying on her bed, and the ordered taxi.

Suddenly, she was wishing that his promises were true—that her time here with Kyle was unlimited.

But that would only have been a consummation to be wished if she really had been an unknown to him, a mystery woman embarking on a holiday love-affair with a beautiful stranger.

As it was...

Earlier, he'd bought her a beautiful white gardenia from a street vendor, and now she touched the flower to her mouth, inhaling the sweet, exotic scent. 'Who is Francie?' she asked.

Kyle glanced at her, then smiled. 'Shame on you, to interrogate a child like that.'

'We girls have no secrets from one another. Was she one of your lovers when you lived in Kingston?'

'She's an old friend,' he hedged, his expression amused. 'You can't ask a gentleman to say more than that.'

They had arrived at the hotel. He parked the car, and they walked into the silent, beautiful foyer together. Apart from the night staff, the place was deserted.

Kyle turned to her, green eyes assessing. 'The bar's closed. So is the restaurant. Would you take it wrongly if I said I had a bottle of cognac in my room, and offered you a nightcap?'

Sophie considered him with a cool smile. 'How does one take an invitation like that rightly?'

'One accepts a gentleman's assurance that he won't try any funny business,' Kyle replied, holding her gaze. 'Despite the very considerable temptations.'

'Won't we disturb Emma?'

'Not unless you gulp your cognac very loudly. She's got the room next door, and there's a hotel baby-sitter with her.'

Sophie hesitated. She didn't want the evening to end, yet she was wary. It might be perfect to let it end here, and to be gone in the morning, leaving a letter for him at reception.

Then he smiled into her eyes, and caution melted into acceptance.

'I'd like a nightcap.' She nodded.

'Good.' He took her arm, and led her to the lift.

Kyle's room was bigger and more luxurious than her own, and the balcony commanded a spectacular view of the beach, and the moonlit sea that stretched out forever towards the horizon. She could hear the breakers rustling far below, and smell the faint scent of some night-blooming creeper.

He poured two brandies and brought them on to the balcony. They toasted one another silently, and Sophie sipped the fiery liquid.

Kyle tugged his tie off, and unbuttoned his collar. Suddenly, with that V of tanned skin and dark, curly hair showing, the pagan, animal quality in him was re-inforced. He moved to stand beside her at the railings, and stared out over the sea.

'It's so beautiful. On a night like this, I want to be out at sea, on a yacht. The dark water beneath my keel, a sail against the moon . . . and you, by my side.'

'What would I be doing there?' she smiled.

'What comes naturally. Don't be so cautious with that cognac.'

'It's showing signs of going to my head.' She gulped the liquid fire down, none the less, and felt its heat spread through her system.

Kyle took the cognac glass out of her fingers, and put it down. 'I know who you are, now,' he said softly.

Sophie's blood turned to ice, the heat of the cognac going out like a quenched flame. 'You—know?' she whispered.

'Mmm,' he nodded. 'You're the White Witch.'

Her breathing resumed. 'The White Witch?'

He smiled slightly. 'It's a local legend, but she really once existed. Her name was Annie Palmer, and she came to Jamaica in the 1820s, to marry the master of one of the great estates, Rose Hall. She was young and beautiful, like you. But they said she was a witch. She certainly had a fatal effect on her three husbands, not to mention her lovers.'

'Wow.'

'They always said she would come back. Maybe I'd better get me a mojo,' he smiled, his eyes warm.

'What's that?'

'A hex to ward off a woman's spell.'

Sophie laughed rather breathlessly. Let that be the last close call she would have to deal with for a long time!

He drew her to him. 'Sophie...'

'A gentleman's promise,' Sophie said, laying a finger against his chest, to stop him getting any closer, 'ought to be inviolate. No funny business, you said.'

He looked down at her with brooding eyes. 'I can't get over that feeling that I know you from somewhere.'

It was time to go. 'You don't know me,' she said with a light smile, 'not from anywhere. It's been a lovely evening, Kyle. I won't forget it.'

'Neither will I.' He touched her cheek. 'One thing more. That trip to Haiti and Dominica I mentioned last week.' His eyes held hers. 'I want you to come with us.'

'Oh, Kyle——'

'I'm serious. It won't cost you anything, and if you haven't any work lined up at home, then you won't be missing anything.'

'Kyle, I can't——'

'We'll charter a yacht,' he cut through her protests. 'Haiti and Dominica are incredibly beautiful. They're fascinating places, with a unique art and culture. I'll take you to see real voodoo dancing—not the tourist stuff you saw tonight, but the authentic thing. We'll go to Sans Souci—I can promise you that you'll never see anything like it in your life again. If there's time, we'll go to the Caymans, where you can do some of the best diving in the world. The water at Spanish Bay Reef is crystal-clear—it's like drifting through the air.'

He had her hands in his now, and he was staring down at her with an almost pleading expression. 'Say you'll come, Sophie, and I'll start organising it tomorrow.'

'I can't say that,' she replied quietly. 'I hardly know you, Kyle. I can't commit myself to setting off with you on a yacht for an indefinite tour of the Caribbean. Not at four o'clock in the morning!'

'Then think about it,' he said forcefully. 'I'll start arranging a boat anyway, and you can give me your answer any time over the next few days. Is that agreed?'

'Nothing is agreed,' Sophie retorted, feeling painfully uncomfortable. She withdrew her hands from his. 'If you insist on making arrangements, then I can't stop you. But don't count on my coming with you. In fact, you might as well know here and now that it's extremely unlikely that I will come with you.' More unlikely than he knew, she added mentally.

'Why not?' he challenged. 'I'm promising you a little slice of heaven, and all you can do is shake your head.'

'My idea of heaven doesn't come in little slices.'

'What does that mean?'

'Oh, I don't know what it means,' she said restlessly, turning away from him. 'You're too sudden, Kyle. People just don't behave the way you want them to.'

'All I know is that you're having a very special effect on me,' he said quietly. She felt his hands take her arms and turn her to face him. He looked down intently into her face. 'There's something about you that tantalises me, eludes me. I don't really know what to do about it, but I want the feeling to stay.'

Sophie looked up at him, her heart starting to thud against her breast-bone. He drew her close, and kissed her parted lips with gentle force.

'Sophie,' he said gently, 'don't turn me away.' His hands were caressing her slim flanks, moving up the bare skin of her back to touch the thick tumble of her hair. 'You're a very special woman, my love.' His voice was rough, but quiet. 'I just know we've met before. But if it wasn't in this lifetime, then it must have been in some other one, because I feel that I'm acquainted with you. The important thing is that we don't lose one another again.'

'Hmm,' Sophie said, keeping her casual smile with an effort, 'the cognac is making you unwise, Mr Hart. That kind of talk is for shallow people—not persons of deep feeling, like you and I.'

'I mean it,' he said, his eyes tightening. 'I know we've barely met each other, but there's something about you that...' He didn't finish the sentence. 'You must feel that, too. I know you do.'

'I feel that it's past my bedtime,' she said, trying to sound relaxed. 'So if you'll let me go——'

'Damn you!' he whispered. 'How can you be so cool when I'm burning?'

Then, with smooth power, he had lifted her off her feet, into his arms. She gasped in shock, clinging to his neck, her long legs dangling.

'Kyle!'

He carried her into the bedroom, and laid her down against the white coverlet, sitting beside her and trapping her by leaning over her on one arm. He smiled down at her as she lay helpless, her breasts rising and falling as she panted slightly. 'Now I've got you where I want you.'

'This is the basest kind of treachery,' she protested. 'Let me up!'

'In a moment.' He bent to kiss her neck, his breath warm against her fine skin. Sophie tried to turn away, but he had put her in a helpless position. His mouth moved across her throat, finding the soft hollow at its base, his lips warm and hungry. She gasped involuntarily as his warm breath brushed the sensitive shell of her ear.

'Kyle, you promised! Please, let me go——'

His kiss stopped her words, his warm mouth dominating her without effort. An electric thrill rolled down her stomach as she felt his tongue, smooth and moist, probe between her lips.

She arched against him, fear and desire struggling in her. He was caressing her body with rough tenderness, brushing the curve of her breasts, the swell of her hips underneath the black silk.

'Let's take your mask off, just for once,' he said huskily. 'Let's see who you really are.'

'Kyle, *no*!' she protested, as he started easing the material away from her breasts.

'I want you so much.' His deep voice was almost a whisper, and she sensed, rather than heard, the tremor that underlay it. He stared down into the wide grey depths of her eyes. His face was half in shadow, all his male desire concentrated in the tawny eyes that devoured her.

He was so strong; she tried to stop him from pulling the strapless top down, but she could not. In the soft light, her skin was the colour of burned honey, her breasts creamy-pale, demarcated by the line of her costume.

'I'm glad you don't suntan topless,' Kyle said quietly. 'You're so demure, so cool and maidenly. It's driven me mad, right from the start...' He leaned forward to kiss the valley between her breasts, inhaling the scent of her flesh. 'And you smell so sweet.' He spoke with his mouth close against her skin. 'That perfume has been haunting me all night. It's like you, it tantalises me. I feel I know it, and yet it's so new and strange to me...'

It was so hard to control her reactions; a kind of electricity was flowing from him into her veins, charging her with his desire, until she felt as though every nerve were stretched tight. His mouth roamed over her breasts, his kisses warm and tender against the soft flesh, the delicate arch of her collarbone, the aching stars of her nipples.

Sophie's body was moving with a will of its own, a primitive hunger that paid no heed to her reason. She was arching to him, her fingers roaming through the crisp hair that clung and twined round them, as though it had an amorous life of its own.

Her mouth was forming his name, her panting breath making the words ragged and uneven. Her mind was screaming commands at her, to get out, get away, run home as fast as her legs would carry her.

But what had she worn this dress for, what had she made herself beautiful for—what did she exist for—if not for this?

Sophie drew him close, as if it were suddenly she who was the demanding one, and he the pursued. His body was so hard and strong, its potency overwhelming her senses. She had longed to touch him for so long that her caress was almost rough in its explosive release.

She gasped out loud as his mouth tasted the tender pink tips of her breasts, the caress of his tongue a passionate adoration. Sophie could feel them tighten with desire in his mouth, hardly aware that she was digging her nails into the hard muscles of his back, as though urging him to unleash the cruelty she had always suspected was in him.

His teeth closed gently around the taut buds, the sensation at first shockingly intense, then changing to a languorous heat that invaded her thighs, her womb, the centre of her need.

At last, he drew away from her, and rolled on to his back, pulling her on top of him. The face that looked up at her was magnificent, passion making it more beautiful than she had ever seen it before. The curving male mouth was imperious.

'Take my shirt off.'

Why could she not disobey the whispered command? Her shaking fingers were fumbling with the buttons, her hair tumbling about her face as she pressed tiny, shy kisses on each inch of velvety bronze skin that was revealed. He smelled so good, warm and male and clean, and she thrilled to the way his breathing grew harsh and fast at her clumsy, timid caresses.

The night was like silk, cool and silent, wrapping them in dark arms. The world outside was ceasing to exist, their bodies becoming the only universe that mattered.

Tender with passionate hunger, Sophie tasted the dark skin of his belly, feeling the curling black hair brush her lips as her tongue drew moistly towards the dark core of his navel. He groaned, his arms reaching for her.

'I want you, Sophie,' he said, almost fiercely. 'I've never wanted anyone the way I want you.'

She sank her cheek against his bare skin, closing her eyes. Her arm touched his loins unwittingly, brushing the hard, swollen arousal there; Kyle's half-stifled gasp of reaction made a wave of dizziness wash through her mind. He lifted himself on one arm, staring into Sophie's dark bewildered eyes with ruthless intensity.

'The moment I set eyes on you, this was already happening in my mind. I've made love to you a dozen, a hundred times already.' He smiled briefly, tawny eyes seeming to speak to her very soul. 'Sometimes it was slow and unbearably drawn-out. Sometimes it was swift and savage. But I never dreamed, not once, that it could be as beautiful as this.'

'Oh, Kyle,' Sophie whispered, helpless in the force of her feelings for him.

'Let's not hurry,' he murmured, his mouth seeking hers. 'We've got all night...'

He cupped her breasts as he kissed her, his thumbs moving with slow appreciation across her sensitised aureoles. She was lost, her mind flooded with patterns of colour, like the bright depths of a kaleidoscope, ever changing, never escaping the brilliant circle of desire.

Her own hand had come to rest at the base of his belly, sensing the heat of his manhood through the thin material. The way he moved begged her to move her hand lower, and her fingertips moved like shy butterflies to obey, tracing the shrouded mystery of his desire so gently that it was almost impossible he could feel it; and yet he moaned, deep in his throat, as though her timorous touch had been the most expert of caresses.

Her heart was pounding, her mind spinning on waves of dizzy heat as she stroked him there, feeling his possessive touch at her breasts.

Had she meant this to happen? Was this part of her so-called plan, that she should wind up making love to Kyle Hart on the eve of her departure?

He was kissing her mouth as he caressed her naked back, her flanks, her hips, the slit in her sarong now proving a fatal breach in her defences as he slid his hand along the inside of her thigh, her position offering no resistance to the questing fingers that moved expertly towards the wisp of lace that was all that protected her virginity.

Sophie had never gone this far with any man before. These were regions where she had never trodden, feelings she had never dreamed of. But then, she had never been with a man like Kyle before. The compelling sexuality of this man had overwhelmed her from the start. But she had never stopped wanting him.

She, too, had done this a hundred times in her imagination already. But she had not possessed the honesty, or the self-knowledge, to admit it.

Her thoughts broke up in a silent explosion of colour as she felt Kyle's fingers reach the moist, silken skin of her loins, touching the melting substance of her womanhood, finding the soaring apex of her desire with a caress that brought both gasping release and a completely new surge of hunger.

The time for reserve was over. Suddenly, their bodies were pressed together, their mouths kissing with a feverish intensity as their hands caressed, tormented, excited one another beyond endurance.

There was no more doubt, no more thought of the consequences of the morrow, or the morality of what she was doing, in Sophie's mind. Her mind was his, both of them focused on the ever more urgent necessity of union, of knowing each other well enough for the act of love.

An eternity later, they both paused, staring at one another in tense wonder as they lay on the white bed-cover. He was naked to the waist, his body dark and formidably male in the soft light. She, with her chestnut hair tumbled round her flushed cheeks, and her black dress rumpled about her slender waist, made a picture of wanton eroticism.

'Kyle,' she said tightly, her voice feeling as though she hadn't used it for months, 'there's something you don't know.'

For a moment, amusement took the place of desire in his eyes. White teeth glinted between tanned lips as he laughed softly. 'Is there, little cool Sophie? And what might that be?'

Her mouth opened, but no words were formed. She could not go on without telling him. And yet, if she told him now—if she told him, and he was angry, or laughed...

Unlike last year in Brighton, Kyle's attraction towards her in Jamaica had been swift and warm. As she'd seen the interest in her awaken in his eyes, so she'd started to dread discovery. It had stopped being a game, long ago. If he once remembered her as Maisie Wilkin, that ugly, drab creature he'd once found so repulsive, would all his interest in her not swiftly evaporate, and vanish forever?

She flinched suddenly, as though a rough blow had landed across her mouth.

At first, all she'd wanted was to have a bit of mischievous fun with him. At least, that was what she'd told herself. She'd had something in mind when her little game with Kyle had started, but the logic of it had somehow got distorted, broken up like a reflection in troubled waters.

And now she was deathly afraid. She had been afraid from the very start. Afraid that, once again, her feelings were going to be trampled on.

She'd faced this moment from the very beginning, when she had first set eyes on him down at the beach. And she had already weighed up the prospects, and had come down on the side of three weeks of certain heaven, rather than risk the chance of nothing at all.

But had she made the right choice?

She'd never known such perfection as these three weeks. And tonight, as he'd held her in his arms, she had felt that Kyle's feelings were real, and that they had been on the brink of an experience that had depth and beauty in full measure.

But it had all been false, it was all tottering on the edge of a horrible disaster, because of what she knew and he didn't.

'What is it?' he asked in concern, seeing the colour drain from her glowing face. 'Sophie?' Kyle drew her close, his mouth seeking hers for the gentlest of caresses. 'What is it, my darling? You look as though you've seen a ghost.'

'I have,' she whispered.

'What is it that I'm supposed to know? Tell me.'

'Oh, Kyle,' she whimpered. 'If you only knew how I've prayed that you wouldn't do this to me...'

'Don't you want me to make love to you?'

'Oh, yes... but you don't understand. And when you do understand, I'm so afraid of what you'll feel...'

He stared at her, eyes dark and puzzled as he tried to fathom what she was saying.

And in the taut silence came the faint, muffled crying of a child from the next room, desolate and afraid.

'Emma,' he said quietly. 'She has nightmares. The baby-sitter will put her back to sleep.'

But the crying only increased in volume and intensity. 'You must go to her,' Sophie said, releasing him with a deathly ache in her heart. 'She needs someone she knows.'

His fingers bit into her wrists like manacles.

'God, I'm suddenly so afraid you won't be here when I get back,' he said tautly.

'I will be,' she promised, feeling a thick lump in her throat.

Kyle stared into her eyes for a tense moment longer. Then he rose fluidly to his feet, and pulled his silk dressing-gown off the chair.

He left without a word, closing the door behind him.

Sophie, too, got unsteadily to her feet. Her breasts and loins were aching with unfulfilled desire. She caught sight of herself in the mirror, the intense eroticism of her own appearance shocking her raw sensibilities.

Clumsily, she hooked the dress back over her naked breasts, trying to restore some order to her dishevelled clothing. It was not going to happen tonight. In a moment she was going to go back to her room, and tomorrow she was going back to England. Her eyes were blurred with unshed tears as she groped for Kyle's hair-brush, and started blindly brushing her hair.

She listened to the distant sound of Emma's crying, hearing it fade away into silence.

She had reached a point in her relationship with Kyle beyond which she could not go.

She couldn't let him make love to her, not without telling him who she really was.

And she couldn't face what his reaction might be to that disclosure. Not now, not tonight.

The door opened, and Kyle came back into the room, his eyes darkening as they saw her dressed.

'Sophie . . . *damn*! I knew that would be the end of it.'

'Tomorrow is another day,' she said, taking a deep breath of the cool night air in an effort to steady the surging in her veins.

'Do I have to take that as a dismissal?' Kyle asked, coming to take her in his arms.

Sophie's mouth drew into an unsteady smile. 'Tomorrow is another day,' she repeated.

'Then what are you crying about?' he replied, kissing her temples gently. 'What did you want to tell me that was so important?'

She looked at him from under thick lashes that were wet with tears. Tomorrow was going to be a very different awakening from the one he expected. 'Nothing. I'm just not . . . not very experienced at all this.'

Kyle looked down at her with an expression in his green eyes that made her heart turn over inside her.

'Are you telling me that you're a virgin?' he asked quietly.

She hesitated, then nodded with a laugh that was midway to a sob. 'Yes. Partly that, yes.'

'And you want more time to think about it?' he said, even more gently.

She nodded, her throat too choked for speech.

Kyle smiled slightly, but not mockingly. 'Don't think about it for too long. I might just get ill with wanting you in the meantime.'

Again, that half-laugh, half-sob rose in her throat. 'Thank you for a lovely evening. All of it. It's been like nothing I've ever known before.'

'If I said the same thing, you probably wouldn't believe me. But it's true.' He kissed her vulnerable, slightly swollen lips softly, cupping her oval face in his hands. 'Do you really want to go?' he whispered huskily.

She nodded, and he walked her to her own room. Outside her door he reached for her again, but Sophie gave him a warning glance.

'I think you've kissed me quite enough for one night,' she pleaded. 'I don't think I could take much more.'

'If I get any sleep,' he promised, 'I'm going to dream of number one hundred and one.'

She smiled up at him, her eyes lingering on one of the most magnificent male faces she would ever see. Then she held out the gardenia he had given her. 'I've loved tonight. All of it. Until tomorrow.'

He took the flower. 'Until tomorrow.'

She let herself into her room, and locked the door.

Her eyes were blurred with tears again, tears that now spilled hotly down her cheeks, unchecked. She fought her emotions down fiercely. There wasn't time for absurd sentimental indulgences. She brushed her wet cheeks, and checked her watch. Almost five. Already, the sky was lightening outside, and she caught the smoky morning smell of a distant fire. In two hours' time, she would have to be ready to leave.

It wasn't worth taking off her make-up, but she stripped off the sarong dress. The tips of her breasts were still painful with eager desire, her loins liquid and throbbing, but she fought that feeling down, too. She packed the dress, and the last of her belongings, and started getting ready for her departure.

The only things she didn't pack were her pyjamas, which she put on, her sponge-bag, and a light dress to wear on the flight.

There was only one way for her to know how seriously Kyle Hart felt about her, and that was to do what she had originally planned to do: go back to England, leaving him a letter telling him who she really was.

She sat at the desk, and pulled a sheet of hotel writing-paper towards her. There were no more tears in her eyes as she started to write.

> Dear Kyle,
>
> Once upon a time there was a girl who went for a walk on Brighton sands, and overhead a man talking about her to her friend. What she heard him say about her was painful. It wounded her vanity, and made her wish, for a while, that she were someone else.
>
> By the time you read this, I'll be on my way home. I'm sorry to have perpetrated a deception on you. You were right all along, of course. You and I have met before, but it was not an occasion which I remember with any pleasure, and so I took care not to remind you of it. Now I wish I had done

so, at the start. But it's too late for wishes.
If your memory needs further prompting, you can see me as I was on BBC 2 at eight p.m. on Thursday the 15th August. I've changed since then, but I was the absurd one, with those awful clothes and glasses.
I can only hope that you'll understand why I deceived you, and how much it has cost me.

Sophie hesitated for a long while, staring at the paper with absent eyes. Should she add something like, 'Please get in touch with me again?' She could just add her London phone number, or even her address. But her pen hesitated over the paper.

If he wanted to find her again, he could locate her easily enough. Hélène, for one, could tell him where she lived. And if he didn't want to find her...

Well, there was nothing she could do about that. She would have to leave it up to him. She had no other choice.

If he really cared about her, he would come to her again, and they could start their relationship on a fresh footing. If he felt only disgust at the revelation, or if his feelings had never been serious to start with, then she would never see him again. It was as simple as that.

There seemed nothing more she could say. After a moment, she signed the note, 'Maisie'. As an afterthought, she took the Giorgio Armani bottle out of her bag and let one small drop fall on the paper.

She read the note. It would sting, and at first it would seem to have hit too hard, and too far below the belt. But what else could she do?

She folded the note, sealed it, and wrote Kyle's name and room number on the envelope. She propped it up on her desk, ready to give to reception later, as she left.

Then she climbed into bed, and curled up under the sheet. She pushed sorrow firmly away from her mind.

There would be time enough later to think about what she had done, and grieve for what might have been.

Now she closed her eyes, and let memories of the brightest night of her life take her down the tunnel of sleep.

CHAPTER FIVE

WHAT had been the point of it all?

As the Jumbo descended through layers of misty cloud towards Heathrow, at twenty minutes to midnight, Sophie was thinking about what had happened over the past three weeks.

She'd once adored Kyle Hart. Meeting him again hadn't exactly quenched the glowing embers of that feeling. In fact, being in his company for three blissful weeks had been more like a gale, fanning the glow into a full-scale forest fire.

Why hadn't she told him who she really was right at the start? Why hadn't she just given their relationship a chance to recover from what had happened in Brighton last year, and let the Caribbean sunshine ease away all pain, all anger, so that they could make a new start?

It was too late for such reproaches. His awakening this morning would have put a cold end to any such dreams.

She thought of him reading her note, thought of his expression, the way his face would have changed. She'd once thought of that moment with relish. Not any more. If that was a triumph, then it was a mean one, and one she hadn't even stayed to witness.

What kind of brainstorm had she been through? Looking back, she must have been insane to have played that kind of trick on a man like Kyle.

Now, approaching a rainy London, she was wondering who had really been punished, and who had really been hurt.

'Ladies and gentlemen, this is your stewardess speaking. Please fasten your seat-belts and extinguish your cigarettes. Passengers are requested to make sure their seats are in the upright position for landing, and to refrain from smoking until they are in the terminal building.'

Sophie reached absently for her seat-belt.

A song was running through her head, the bitter-sweet refrain of 'Jamaica Farewell': 'My heart is down, my head is turnin' around, I had to leave a little girl in Kingston town...'

But she knew that Kyle wasn't the forever kind. Had she let herself be drawn into the maelstrom of an affair with him, blown on the wings of a Caribbean hurricane from Ocho Rios to the Cayman Islands, she would almost certainly have ended up with a broken heart and broken dreams.

So maybe getting away from Kyle, and leaving him with that slap in the face, had been the best thing she could have done.

But no amount of rationalising could take the ache away from her heart, or the depression from her mind. All she knew was that she was a day away, a lifetime away, from the only man who had ever really touched her heart.

The landing was bumpy, and the tarmac was wet with drizzle. The ground staff seemed to look at the incoming passengers with world-weary, cynical eyes. The familiar smells of Heathrow hit Sophie with a wave of melancholy. Fighting through the crowds of people, she decided to take a taxi home rather than battle with her heavy suitcases in the Underground late at night. She didn't want to come down to earth with too much of a bump just yet.

Two and a half hours later, she was falling into bed in her tiny flat in St John's Wood.

It was on a main road, and after the peace of Jamaica the noise of the traffic outside when she woke next morning was intrusive. Despite Mrs Flanagan's languid efforts, the pokiness of the place was something of a blow after the airy room at the San Antonio, and when she remembered the rent she was paying for it distaste for her surroundings settled like a cloud over her head. Would she ever make enough money at her job to afford a better place? London was so hideously expensive these days, yet no one with aspirations to a career in acting could afford not to live here.

The black silk sarong was the first thing she found when she opened her big suitcase. She lifted the dress out, and stared at it, grey eyes sombre. The faint smell of the Giorgio Armani perfume was still on it, reminding her poignantly of her last night in Jamaica.

The night before last? It all seemed to have happened an eternity ago. His kisses, his touch. The way he'd asked her to sail away into the mists of romance with him...

Would he ever get back in touch with her?

She was starting to have a terrible feeling that she would never hear from Kyle Hart again.

Why should he bother to get back in touch with her, anyway? She'd left no invitation for him to do so. In fact, that note might be construed as deliberately final. She thought back, biting her full lower lip, and wished she could remember exactly what she'd said. Five o'clock in the morning, under the influence of Jamaican rum and Kyle's kisses, had not been exactly the best time for balanced literary composition.

Had she made it more harsh than she'd wanted to?

Had she really envisaged her return here as being like this, with no possibility of ever seeing Kyle again?

Suddenly, she dropped the black dress and ran to the telephone. She had the San Antonio's number in her diary, and she hunted frantically through the telephone book to find the STD code for Jamaica.

She dialled the number, and sat tensely by the telephone. It would be eight o'clock in Jamaica right now. She would start off by apologising for that ridiculous note. Or *trying* to apologise. God, he must be feeling so awful by now. She just hoped he would listen to her. Then she would tell him exactly how she felt about him, how much he meant to her. Then she would ask him to——

'San Antonio Hotel, can I help you?'

'Hello! This is Sophie Aspen, calling from England. I've been staying in room 315 for the past three weeks——'

'Yes, Miss Aspen,' the receptionist said brightly. 'Have you left any personal property behind? Anything we can do?'

'No, I haven't left anything. I'd like to speak to Mr Kyle Hart, if I might.'

'Oh, Miss Aspen, you've missed Mr Hart.'

'Has he gone somewhere?'

'He checked out yesterday,' the receptionist replied.

'Checked out?' she gasped. 'Where has he gone to?'

'I have no idea, I'm afraid. He informed Reception he was leaving right after breakfast, and that's what he did. I could take a message, in case he gets back in touch with us, but he didn't say he was going to.'

'If he *does* get in touch,' Sophie said tautly, 'will you ask him to telephone me, please?'

She left her number, and went back to her unpacking with a dark sense of acute frustration. Where had he gone to? What did his suddenly checking out like that mean? She worried miserably for half an hour. Then reaction set in to her mood of loss. Damn it, girl! She made herself a cup of coffee, cursing herself. Forget him, for God's sake. He's a shallow, heartless, careless man, to whom you mean no more than a snap of his fingers. Forget him. You've got him out of your system at last; be content with that. He was never the man for you. Don't let your head be turned a second time!

Forcing herself to face hard practicality, she set about finishing off the cleaning job Mrs Flanagan had started.

There were two telephone calls that evening.

The first, which arrived midway during her dinner of salad and cheese, had her scrambling for the phone, her heart pounding in the expectation that it would be from

Kyle. It wasn't. It was from her mother in Scarborough, to check that she'd arrived safely back.

'You don't sound very cheerful, darling,' she commented, after listening to Sophie's rather lacklustre assurances that the holiday had been enjoyable. 'Maybe you should have had someone to keep you company, after all.'

'To tell the truth,' Sophie admitted, 'I'm just not feeling all that jolly.'

'Disappointed it's all over?'

'In a way. And I think I might be getting one of those summer colds . . .'

'Poor thing! Get an early night. We're all so excited about the film. I just wish you were able to come home to watch it with us.'

'So do I,' Sophie sighed. 'But I just can't. I'm scheduled to be working on the commercial that day, and the next.'

'Our baby, on television,' her mother marvelled. 'I still can't get over it.'

'You'll get a shock when you see me in *The Elmtree Road Murders*,' she warned. Her family hadn't seen her while she'd been playing Maisie, and didn't know what to expect. 'Just remember that I'm not in a very flattering role.'

'We're expecting the worst,' came the laughing reply. 'As long as we can recognise you. Darling, your cousin wants to come down and stay with you.'

'Jenny?'

'Yes. She'll be on holiday from next week, and you know how she loves London.'

'I do,' Sophie said, a shade wryly. That was all she needed right now. She really wasn't in the mood to have her vivacious and rather spoilt younger cousin to stay. Jenny on holiday was, at best, something of a handful, and previous visits had left Sophie exhausted. But blood was thicker than water.

'If you're too busy to have her——' her mother began.

'No, no. I'll be working during the day from the thirteenth to the sixteenth, but apart from that I'll be free. Tell her I'd love to have her.'

'Are you sure?'

'Yes, of course! Tell her to come down as soon as she can.'

'She'll be thrilled. You get yourself into bed now, and take an aspirin. My bet is you'll be right as rain tomorrow. Goodbye, darling.'

''Bye, Mum.'

By the time the second call came at nine, she was less sanguine in her hopes. It wasn't from Kyle, either, but from Joey Gilmour, Sophie's agent.

'Welcome back to civilisation,' he boomed. 'I nearly rang you in Ocho Rios!'

'Why, what's the news?'

'Only two separate and distinct movie directors anxious to secure your services, that's all.'

'Joey!'

'Well, don't get too excited. Neither of them's Steven Spielberg. But apparently word's getting round about the great performance you put in for *The Elmtree Road Murders*. The people who've seen the edited tapes say you're sensational. I knew you would be. Come round to my office tomorrow at ten, and I'll tell you all about it.'

'Oh, please tell me about it *now*,' she begged, sitting down by the phone with bright eyes. 'Who are they? What are the films?'

'The directors are John Payne and Franco Luciani.'

'Never heard of them,' Sophie said, slightly disappointed.

'They're both young and relatively unknown,' Joey replied, 'except in arty circles. However, they've turned in good work recently. I've seen both scripts, and they aren't bad.'

'And the roles?'

'In John Payne's script you'd be playing a psychopath. You go around posing as a nurse, and murdering your patients.'

'Ugh! And in the other?'

'The other role's a young drug addict, called Marjorie. You die tragically just as you discover love. It'll be filmed in Italy, in Pisa. That's where Franco Luciani comes from.'

'What language is the script in?'

'English. The exciting thing is that this is a lead role.'

'Wow,' she laughed. 'I can't believe it. I've never even met this man, and he wants me to play the lead in his next film?'

'He's very keen about you, and apparently his backers agree. He's had access to some of the *Elmtree Road* tapes, and he's very impressed. Quote: "If she can do that, she can do anything," unquote!'

'Gosh! I don't know what to say.'

'There are various problems,' Joey cautioned. 'For one thing, he's working on a very small budget. I've checked out his backers, and they haven't given him much leeway. His last film was praised to the skies by the critics, but it didn't make a penny at the box-office, so this is something of a shoestring operation. That means that he's not in a position to pay anything like the fee you got for *Elmtree Road*. On the other hand, nor is John Payne. Frankly, if we wait around, we'll probably get better offers. But I'll give you the scripts next week, Sophie. I've got them down here in my office. You can have a think about them both.'

'OK.'

'So how was Jamaica?'

'Oh, it was beautiful. I had a lovely time.'

'You can show me your holiday snaps next week. And I'll fill you in on all the gossip since you've been away. You must be worn out. Sleep well, Sarah Bernhardt!'

* * *

Kyle didn't get in touch that night, nor through the week that followed. She rang the San Antonio, just to be sure, but he hadn't been back in touch with the hotel. They had no idea where he might be.

She went to see Joey Gilmour, to pick up the scripts and discuss her prospects.

'There's no rush to accept either part,' Joey counselled. 'If we wait a month or two, you might get an offer of a part you like better. In fact, you might get a whole lot of offers!'

'That seems a little callous——'

'It's a hard world, Sophie! Frankly, I think these two young guys have both had the same idea—to get in before you become hot property, which may just happen after *The Elmtree Road Murders* is screened next month. They're both working on very limited budgets, and they aren't exactly offering top dollar, either of them. They want a talented actress at a cheap fee, and that isn't so easy these days.'

'Am I really a talented actress?'

'You tell me,' Joey smiled. 'I think you're very talented. You'd be making much less than you did for the BBC, and working for a longer period. On the other hand, it wouldn't hurt your reputation to work for either of these two guys. They have something of a cult following in intellectual circles, and they could be the Fellinis or the Viscontis of the future.'

'Can we afford to put them off? Two job offers is two more than I've ever had, even to play a drug addict and a psychopath!'

'Yes,' Joey said, more soberly. 'That's something else. I know you're afraid of being typecast, after Maisie. We don't want you to be playing oddball parts for the rest of your career. So we'll have to think about this situation in role terms, as well.'

'Oh,' she replied. 'I'm delighted about this, Joey, don't get me wrong. But you're right. I do want to pick my next part carefully.'

'Of course you do. And I'm here to help. You go and read those scripts, and have a think. Remember, I can only give advice. The final decision is down to you.'

Sophie started reading the scripts that afternoon, and tried to think logically about the future. But really, she was concerned with little else but Kyle, wondering what he was doing, whether he had taken that tour of the Caribbean with Emma after all, whether he had returned from Jamaica yet, whether he would forgive her for her deception. Wondering whether he would ring.

The only answer to those questions was the silence that deepened, day by day, as the weekend approached.

By the following Sunday, there had still been no phone call, no visit, no letter. Nothing. The days passed, and with each one, a little something died inside Sophie.

Seldom had time passed in such depression for her.

And she had plenty of time to fill in before she started work on the commercial. She had her hair cut and styled, after agreeing with the art director of the advertising agency, into a fairly short modern style that showed off her slender neck, but left plenty of glossy chestnut curls to frame her face.

She also, at the same art director's instigation, paid two visits to beauty clinics for a facial and to get her eyebrows shaped.

She re-read both scripts carefully. John Payne's script, about the psychopathic nurse, was violent and bloody, and didn't ring any bells with her at all. But the other one did.

Franco Luciani, whoever he was, had written his own sensitive and very touching script, based on a recent novel called *The First Day of Autumn*. The film was to have the same title. The more Sophie read the script, the more impressed she was. It was a simple story: a young English girl who can't shake her addiction to heroin goes to Italy, meets and falls in love with a good-looking Italian boy who tries to save her, but dies in the end, leaving him heartbroken. The central role of Marjorie, the young drug-addict, was a good one, anyone with any feel for drama could see that at a glance, and the script as a whole had the feel of a prospect that would succeed. It was a contemporary love story. It was moving, it was glamorous, and it was exciting.

In short, Sophie had the feeling that it was a winner. Discussions with Joey confirmed that he was not so sanguine, believing that she could get far more money if she waited. But he had another bit of news about the film.

'The male lead is going to be Luigi Canotta.'

'Wow,' Sophie said appreciatively. Though Canotta was not all that well known in England, he was very much a rising star in Italy. He was also a strikingly handsome man, and something of a younger generation sex symbol.

'Yeah,' Joey grinned, watching her expression. 'Very good-looking, and quite a man. You'd be in good company, at any rate.'

However, they confirmed their decision to hold off giving any reply, or even meeting the director, until *The Elmtree Road Murders* was screened.

'I'll stall him for another couple of weeks,' Joey said, 'and see what turns up. In the meantime, I've told him you're reading the script and thinking about it.'

The weekend dragged by in an infinity of loneliness and nostalgia. She was haunted by thoughts of Kyle.

Thoughts of his kindness and humour, the fun they'd shared.

Thoughts of his incredible physical appeal for her. That was the hardest thing to forget. Images of his beauty had been stamped into her mind forever, memories of that tanned, muscled body, and the way it had loved her.

She lay in bed, suffocating and restless with the burning heat of the passion he'd awoken in her, remembering the dizzy intimacy of their caresses until she thought she would go mad with frustrated desire.

There was no release, only an increasing imprisonment with her own hunger for Kyle. Where was he? Why didn't he call or write, if only to abuse her with angry names?

Jenny arrived to stay on Monday, looking prettier than ever, announcing that she would stay for four or five weeks.

'Is that too long?' she asked, innocent blue eyes wide.

'Of course not,' Sophie smiled. 'We never see each other these days. How're things at university?'

'Marvellous. I'm having this *wild* affair with one of the lecturers,' she confided gaily to a shocked Sophie. 'Oh, don't look like that! He's practically old enough to be my father.'

'And that makes it better?'

'At least he isn't in the maths department,' she said with a giggle. 'Anyway, I prefer older men—that way it can't ever get very serious, can it?' Jenny said practically, and plunged into the steamy details of her love-life.

Sophie, acutely conscious of her own inexperience, listened in alternating amusement and horror. How had Jenny grown into such an uninhibited womanhood, while she herself, two years older, was still a virgin? How did Jenny always manage to be the one in control of her relationships with men, while Sophie's only real love-affair with a man had just ended in disaster?

From the day of her arrival, the telephone glowed red-hot from Jenny's breathy, interminable phone calls to men, and not just to the love-lorn lecturer in York, either—there seemed to be at least four on the go.

Despite their differences of temperament, they had always been good friends. And the presence of her unashamedly frivolous, flirtatious cousin for company was a distraction, in some measure, from her inner ache about Kyle.

Jenny got her out of the flat, too. They went to all the latest shows, Sophie getting tickets through friends in the profession, met a lot of acquaintances, and went to their fair share of parties—all of which gave Jenny the idea that being an out-of-work actress was a better deal than being employed in any other profession.

On the thirteenth, two days before the screening of *The Elmtree Road Murders*, Sophie stopped being an out-of-work actress, and started filming for the television commercial. It was scarcely demanding work: her part consisted of sitting practically naked in a bathtub of foamy water, lathering various parts of her body, with a dreamy expression on her face.

Jenny, whom she wangled on to the set to watch the performance, was amused.

'You're going to have the cleanest right arm in London,' she announced after the seventeenth retake of Sophie soaping her arm. 'Darling, I'm sure *I* could do that just as well as you!'

Sophie, shivering slightly in her bathrobe, shrugged. 'I'm sure you could.'

'Why do they keep doing the same bit over and over again?'

'Advertising work is so meticulous. They get less than a minute to put their message over—a very expensive minute. So every second has to be perfect. But it can be rather dull.'

'Well, I'm bored stiff!' There was a glint in Jenny's blue eyes. 'There's a rather gorgeous boy over there. Think I'll just go and ask him for a light.'

'What happened to your lighter?' Sophie asked in all innocence.

'It's just stopped working,' Jenny smirked, taking out a Dunhill and slipping off towards the technician in question.

'Sophie!' the director carolled. 'Ready for a retake?'

With a grimace at her cousin's elegant back, Sophie rose to get back into action, this time soaping her throat and shoulders.

'In this sequence we want to emphasise the *tactile* and *fragrant* qualities of the product,' he urged, helping her into the lukewarm tub under the baking spotlights. 'It has to feel slippery, slick, soapy. You absolutely *love* smoothing it over your throat. And then the perfume hits you, and you inhale deeply, *rapturously*...'

Jenny's uninhibited presence distracted Sophie a little from her brooding over Kyle. Her dreams, however, were full of him these days. He came to her almost as soon as her eyes closed, warm and real in memories of Caribbean sunshine, his magnificent body naked and eager for her, his lovemaking overwhelming her like the deep blue sea...

Sophie was thinking of him when she sat curled up on the sofa next to Jenny, with her heart in her throat as the announcer introduced *The Elmtree Road Murders*. She was hugging her stomach, which was aching with nerves.

'What are you so jittery about?' Jenny laughed. 'It's all over and done with now. There's nothing you can do about anything any more.'

'I know. But I'm as tense as though I were going out to do it live at the Palladium!'

'How many people are watching this?'

'They predicted around seven million.'

'Seven million...?' Her cousin shook her head. 'That's a lot of people! I'm going to tell everyone at university that you're my cousin!'

They both stared at the screen as the film began.

It was obvious at once that the production department had done a superb job. *The Elmtree Road Murders* exuded quality right away, from the moody theme music to the 1920s-style graphics of the credits.

The opening scenes, shot in the Brighton boarding-house, had a brooding, atmospheric quality. Hélène le

Bon was on screen with one of the male leads. Coming over very cool and graceful, she radiated professionalism to Sophie's eye.

'Doesn't she look elegant?' Jenny said. Her blue eyes were bright and wide, her golden-red hair glinted in the light. 'She's such a beautiful actress. When do you come on?'

'In the next scene.'

It was all coming back as she watched, the atmosphere of those summery days in Brighton. The happiness, the pain. She would always feel ambivalent about this film; so much had happened to her during it, and after it, to make her emotional. But looking at the finished product now, she felt a thrill of pleasure at having been associated with such a quality production.

She wondered with a sudden stab of pain whether Kyle was one of those seven million, watching the screen now, somewhere in London.

'Sophie!'

Jenny's scream of laughter snapped her out of her reverie. She looked up, and saw herself. There she was, on the screen. Or rather, there was Maisie.

'Is that really you?' Jenny demanded, hands trying to stifle her laughter. 'I can scarcely recognise you! God, I had no *idea* you'd had to put on so much weight. And that awful hair—they've turned you into a fright!'

'Yes, I do look rather depressing, don't I?'

Sophie tried not to wince at Jenny's laughter. Indeed, the black-haired, rotund figure bore hardly any resemblance to Sophie Aspen as she now was. Everything was different, even the movements, the expression on the sallow features, the voice. The glowering housemaid radiated an air of hostility and resentment as a brick wall radiated heat at the end of a summer's day.

'I'm not so sure about telling people we're related any more! No wonder you were embarrassed about yourself,' Jenny gurgled. 'I wouldn't have let anyone make me look as awful as that for a thousand pounds!'

The mixture of feelings inside Sophie was almost too complicated to make sense. She tried to be detached, professional, noting the way the scenes had been cut and edited, trying to pick faults in her own acting.

But inwardly, a dull, throbbing pain in her heart reminded her of Kyle. Of the way he would have seen her during that week in Brighton.

She had been so unattractive. That was her overwhelming thought. No wonder he'd laughed at her. No wonder he'd found her adoration of him absurd!

'Anyway,' Jenny grinned, turning to her cousin, 'you're not a bad actress, despite that hair. In fact, you're rather good!'

Sophie smiled wryly, watching herself playing Maisie Wilkin. The intensity of her own performance was impressive, she had to admit that. The little figures on the screen moved and spoke, strutted and fretted. The story unfolded. But Sophie wasn't involved with the plot any more.

Three weeks. Three weeks without a word from him. If he'd had the slightest intention of seeing her again, he would have been in touch by now.

Damn that letter; *damn* her stupid pride!

If she'd told him who she was, that last night in Jamaica, she might be watching this in his arms now.

What could his mood be towards her? Anger? Indifference?

The latter, most likely. If he'd felt a momentary pique at the one that got away, Kyle Hart was the sort of man who would have no trouble finding himself a consolation prize. In fact, he would probably have done so instantly, just to prove to himself that he could do it . . .

Sophie's eyes blurred with tears, the screen becoming merely a dancing square of light. She turned her head aside so that Jenny wouldn't notice. She was experiencing the horrible feeling that she had lost the only man she had ever really cared about.

* * *

The telephone started ringing before the final credits had finished rolling.

First through were her parents, her mother weepy, even her tough old father husky with emotion. 'You were super, Sophie, just great,' he said. 'You have a real talent, my girl. We're all so proud of you.'

'Weren't you a little shocked to see the part I was in?' she asked.

'Shocked? Of course not. You're an actress. And we know what you look like in real life!'

More professional, but no less enthusiastic praise came from Eleanor Bragg, Sophie's tutor at drama school, who rang immediately afterwards.

'That was a fine performance for someone as young as you,' she told Sophie. 'I can't think of many young actresses who could have held their own so well, playing against a performer of the calibre of Hélène le Bon. As for those courtroom scenes... I'm very proud of you, Sophie.'

Jenny cracked the bottle of supermarket champagne that had been chilling in the fridge all day, but they didn't get much chance to drink it. The telephone kept ringing every few minutes. Several friends and colleagues rang in quick succession, some of them people she hadn't heard from in months, and later on Joey Gilmour got through, characteristically outdoing everyone else.

'You were bloody fantastic,' he boomed down the line.

'Thank you, Joey,' Sophie said. 'I'm glad you enjoyed it.'

'I knew you were perfect for that part. This is your big break, Sophie. From now on, things are going to change for you, believe me! Listen, I think we can forget both John Payne and Franco Luciani.'

'You do?'

'Why should you work for peanuts? If you don't get a really outstanding offer in the next couple of weeks, then I've learned nothing in twenty years in this business!'

It was two hours before the phone calls slowed down, by which time she and Jenny were slightly tipsy, and feeling rather emotionally drained. The last call came at eleven, and was from Hélène le Bon, whom she hadn't seen for some months.

'Hélène!' Sophie exclaimed. 'It's lovely to hear from you! Are you still in Scotland?'

'No, I got back two days ago. I thought I'd wait until the rush was over before ringing you with my congratulations, darling. I presume the phone hasn't stopped ringing all evening?'

'Everyone's been so kind.' Sophie, who was herself starting to feel rather weepy by now, had to clear her throat. 'Anyway, as for congratulations, you're the one who deserves them most. You were brilliant.'

'I've been in this game a long time. For such a young actress, you achieved something remarkable in that film, Sophie. I hear on the grapevine that the job offers are flooding in.'

'Well, not exactly flooding,' Sophie smiled. 'I've had two offers to make films from directors I've never heard of.'

'Oh, I've heard of them both. In fact, I'm a great admirer of Franco Luciani. He's a very gifted young man, you know.'

'Is he?'

'You probably haven't seen *Roman Affair*, his last film? It wasn't exactly a box-office smash, but it was a very beautiful film. I was speaking to him only last week. He saw you in some of the unedited rushes, after Brighton—he has contacts in the drama studios.'

'I was wondering how he'd heard of me.'

'Well, he was very struck by the *Elmtree Road* footage. He seemed to think you had exactly the quality he was looking for in his next picture. He'll be be even more struck now and, frankly, I couldn't think of two people who would go better together. Have you read his script?'

'Yes, I have.'

'What's it like?'

'It's very good. I didn't think it would suit me, but, having read it, I was seriously considering doing it.'

'In my humble opinion, darling, he's just the right man for you. I expect he isn't offering very much?'

'My agent thinks I can get more.'

'Darling, of course you could. But money isn't everything—certainly not in this game. Now, listen. We're having a little party tomorrow night. A lot of the cast from *The Elmtree Road Murders* will be there, and so will Franco Luciani. He's very keen to talk to you. Will you come and meet him?'

'I'd love to come!'

'Good. I'm so looking forward to talking to you. I think Franco Luciani is in for rather a surprise when he meets Maisie in the flesh!' Hélène laughed mischievously. 'He doesn't know that you don't look like Maisie any more.'

'I hope he doesn't want me to go through all that again,' Sophie groaned. 'I don't think I could!'

'He'll be quite happy with you as you are,' Hélène promised. 'The address is seventeen, Cadogan Gardens. Come around eight, and wear something shimmery. I'm dying to see you again. I've missed you.'

'I've missed you, too, Hélène. Oh, by the way—my cousin is staying with me at the moment——'

'Bring her with you, darling, of course. I'd love to meet her. What's her name?'

'Jenny.'

'Tell her I'm looking forward to talking to her. See you both tomorrow?'

Sophie rang off after a few words of goodbye, and told Jenny about the invitation.

'Oh, I'd *love* to meet Hélène le Bon in person! Will there be lots of gorgeous males?'

'I expect so,' Sophie nodded. 'Hélène knows everyone in the profession.'

She was definitely intrigued at the prospect of meeting Franco Luciani, the young Italian director who had taken such a fancy to her.

In the midst of her excitement, it suddenly occurred to her that there was someone else that she and Hélène had in common. Kyle.

Hélène would probably know where Kyle was, and what he was doing. She would be able to ask her tomorrow. If she dared.

If she dared? With a pang of grief, she realised that she couldn't go on like this, not any longer. She thought of nothing except Kyle, day and night, and if he didn't get in touch with her, she must get in touch with him.

She couldn't live in limbo. She had to know how he felt about her, whether he'd been serious in Jamaica, whether there was any chance of their getting together again.

If there wasn't—well, she would somehow have to come to terms with that. But she must know, one way or the other.

Her mind was made up. She would find out where Kyle was from Hélène tomorrow night, and then she would go and see him.

Cadogan Gardens, Sophie reflected the next evening, was exactly the right sort of address for someone like Hélène. Glitzy, expensive, central, it was just a stone's throw away from Sloane Square, located between some of the smartest schools in London and a set of Third World embassies.

Number seventeen had a beautiful neo-classical façade, and the pavement outside it was crowded with Rolls-Royces and Jaguars. All its windows were blazing, and the sound of music drifted through the summer evening. Hélène's 'little party' was obviously going to be a lavish affair.

Sophie paid the cab-driver, and they walked up the stairs together. Jenny was in one of Sophie's dark evening dresses, and looked, Sophie thought, ravishingly pretty in it, while Sophie herself had obeyed Hélène's order to wear 'something shimmery'. The silk blouse and metallic-print red skirt showed off her tan to perfection, and, though she was wearing the minimum of face-paint, as she had on that last night in Jamaica, she felt she looked as glamorous as she ever would.

They were met in the hall by Hélène herself, looking radiant, and obviously delighted to see them.

'Sophie, you look utterly delicious, darling! So brown and slim and lovely! Wait till the rest of them see you. And you never told me you had such a pretty cousin. So pleased to meet you, Jenny. Now come up, and have some champagne...'

The big drawing-room was crowded with people, talking and laughing, and Sophie's entrance caused a sudden uproar among the babble. For a breathless quarter of an hour she was enveloped by friends from the *Elmtree Road* set, congratulating her on her performance, and wide-eyed at the transformation she'd been through.

'I don't believe it,' Lionel Jakobson gasped. He had played one of Hélène's three husbands, and Sophie had got on well with him. His eyes, already rather bulging, were popping out of his florid face. 'We had no idea you looked like that under Maisie!'

'This is the Ugly Duckling turning into a swan, with a vengeance!' One of the other male leads, Julian Pike-Ashmore, made Sophie a mock obeisance. '"You walk in beauty," my dear, "like the night Of cloudless climes and starry skies." May I beg a kiss?'

'Have you seen this?' one of the women asked, holding out a copy of *The Times*, folded open at the television page. The article about *The Elmtree Road Murders* was short, but enthusiastic. After praising the script and the director, Percy Schumaker, it went on to single out some of the performances, starting with Hélène's.

About Sophie, the writer said, 'The performance of newcomer Sophie Aspen, playing the difficult role of Maisie Wilkin, was one of the highlights of the film. She managed to combine the roles of victim and victimiser very convincingly. This young actress has a bright career ahead of her.'

Percy Schumaker himself was present, too, and came over to greet Sophie. He was very flattering about Sophie's contribution to the film's success, and dropped various hints about possible further opportunities to work with him in the coming year.

It was an exhilarating occasion, and Sophie had to leave her cousin to manage as best she could for a while—rather a new experience for Jenny, who was used to being the centre of attention.

After fifteen minutes Hélène approached, with a tall, olive-skinned man in tow. He was very handsome in a refined, rather sensitive way, and had intense, bright brown eyes. He smiled warmly as Hélène introduced him.

'Sophie, I want you to meet Franco Luciani. He wouldn't believe that you were really Sophie Aspen when he first saw you. Franco, you're face to face at last with Maisie Wilkin.'

'No. This is not Maisie Wilkin.' He had a charming accent, but spoke fluent English. 'This is somebody very different from Maisie Wilkin.' He kissed Sophie's hand, and held on to it in both of his as he straightened. 'I do not know which to compliment you on first, Sophie: your performance in *The Elmtree Road Murders*, or your appearance tonight.' His brown eyes gleamed appreciatively as he looked her up and down. 'May I say that both, in their way, are quite unique!'

'You're very kind,' Sophie laughed, colouring.

'I'll leave you to it,' Hélène said, melting away.

Sophie looked up shyly at the good-looking Italian. 'But you didn't think I really looked like Maisie, did you?' she asked.

'Well . . .' His full mouth curved into a smile. 'I knew you were heavily made-up. But I have to confess I didn't think you were so very beautiful, which I now see you are, or so charming, which I now also perceive.' He released her hand at last. 'When I saw the raw tapes of you playing Maisie Wilkin, I felt at once that you were the right actress to play Marjorie in *The First Day of Autumn*. My reaction to seeing those tapes was that an actress of your age who could play so difficult a role as Maisie could do anything. I was looking for someone young, and at the moment there is rather a shortage of gifted young actresses. You had the vulnerability, and yet the strength, that I wanted. But when I saw the full performance last night——' he shook his head '—it was breathtaking. During those final scenes, in the courtroom, I was holding on to my seat. One might almost have thought that you weren't an actress at all, but someone expressing a real hurt, a real anger.'

'Well,' Sophie said, thinking wryly of what had happened to bring out that performance, 'I'm glad I was convincing.'

'The only factor that bothered me was the Marjorie is meant to be very beautiful, while Maisie was . . .'

'Not very beautiful,' Sophie supplied, as he hesitated diplomatically.

Franco Luciani laughed quietly, showing even white teeth. 'Shall we say that Sophie Aspen is closer to my idea of Marjorie than Maisie was. With both talent and beauty on your side, I am more determined than ever that you must play Marjorie.'

'I'm very flattered,' Sophie murmured.

'Do you like the script?'

'Very much indeed,' she nodded. 'It's beautifully written, and I'm thinking about it very hard.'

'But even after three weeks of hard thinking, you are not willing to commit yourself just yet?'

She was rather taken aback by the full-frontal approach. 'Well, I'm still discussing it with my agent, and——'

'And he has advised you to wait and see whether you get a better offer?' He smiled with disarming frankness. 'And you are not sure about committing yourself to this almost-unknown Italian, whose films make no money, and who pays such low fees?'

'I can assure you that I'm not accustomed to high fees,' Sophie smiled. She was taking an instinctive liking to this man, 'And I am very flattered by your interest in me.'

'Have you other offers to consider?'

'Well—yes, I have.'

'Please, listen to me.' He took her hand in warm fingers, and looked intently into her face. 'On the strength of last night's showing, you could command much more money than I am offering. But I cannot raise my fee, much as I would like to. My finances are, as you no doubt know, very limited, and I am having to pay a great deal of money to get Luigi Canotta, the male lead. What I can do, however, is offer you a percentage of my share in the eventual box-office profits of *The First Day of Autumn*.'

'Mr Luciani——'

'That is something I have not offered Canotta. Sophie, I am convinced that this film will make money. It's different from *Roman Affair*, my last film. It's much more commercial, and much more contemporary. Your one or two per cent, whatever we decide on, could be worth a great deal more than the fee I'm offering. It could make money for you for years to come.'

'That's an extraordinarily generous offer, Mr Luciani, and I feel that...'

The words dried in Sophie's throat as her eyes fixed on someone over Franco's shoulder.

It was Kyle.

And Hélène le Bon, talking animatedly, was introducing him to Jenny.

Sophie felt that giant fist squeeze her heart tight as recognition slammed home. Her first thought was, He's been here, in London, and he hasn't contacted me!

Her second was to confirm her gut feeling, as though it needed confirming, that he was the most magnificent man she would ever see.

If anything even more tanned than she remembered from Jamaica, he was smiling lazily down at Jenny's coquettish, pretty face. His eyes were emerald slits between the smoky black lashes. The lithe, muscular body she remembered so well was sheathed in a dark silk suit tonight, the fine material doing no more than hint at the powerful shoulders and taut waist that had once lain naked against her own skin.

She laid her hand against her pounding heart, trying to catch the breath that seemed to have been seared from her lungs all of a sudden. Dimly, as if from far away, she was aware of Franco Luciani asking her something.

'I—I'm sorry.' She tore her hypnotised gaze away from Kyle and Jenny, and looked blindly at the director. 'What did you ask?'

He was frowning slightly. 'I asked whether you found that offer appealing. It's not uncommon these days, and many actors have found it a very profitable arrangement. Of course it's a gamble, but this is a gamble where you cannot actually lose money.'

'No, no, I find it a very interesting proposition,' she stammered, completely off balance. Suddenly, all she wanted to do was get away from Franco and speak to Kyle.

God, why did things work out like this? Just when she needed her concentration most——

'I will be working with a very small film unit,' Franco said. 'Almost impromptu. Costs will be very low. If you agreed to play Marjorie for me, we could bring the first day of shooting forward by two months. Canotta is free at this moment. We could be filming on location in Pisa by mid-September.'

'Mid-September? Next month?'

'Yes. Would that suit you?'

'It's a little short notice... but there's no reason why not.'

'Good,' Franco said, his expression easing. 'This is a film which will be made quickly and cleanly, without too much introspection. You understand me? Your part of it could be finished in less than eight weeks. At the most, ten weeks. The scenes between the hero and his family will be shot in the studios at Cinecittá, in Rome, later in the year. Once you'd finished in Pisa, you would be free to come back to London. Maybe we could even get the Pisa section shot in as little as six weeks. Why not? We have no special effects to contend with, a very small cast, and a relatively simple script. I have deliberately chosen to do it this way, to keep the expenses down. The problem with financing any kind of film in the present economic climate is that...'

Sophie wasn't listening any more. Her eyes had swung back to Kyle, now lifting his head to drain his champagne glass. Why didn't he look at her? He must know she was here! Was he deliberately ignoring her? Oh, look at me, she begged him silently, *please*...

Hélène had moved on to another group, leaving Kyle and Jenny talking. The silvery streaks at Kyle's tanned temples glinted as he turned to get Jenny another glass of champagne from a passing waiter. He smiled at her as he put it into her fingers, that formidably male face wearing its most deliberately charming mask.

And Jenny was moving into top gear, reacting to Kyle like a rose starting to bloom in the summer sunshine. A Venus's fly-trap, more likely, Sophie thought bitterly, catching Jenny's silvery laughter as Kyle murmured something amusing close to her ear.

She felt sick. Faced with Jenny's beauty, Kyle Hart's poised male experience was all too obvious; a slow smile was lurking on his lips, lips that she'd once imagined kissing so many women, leaving them all crying for more.

Something of Franco Luciani's passionate sincerity was making its way through her numbed thoughts. For God's sake, she cursed herself, one thing at a time. This man is making you a marvellous offer!

Once again, she dragged her eyes away from Kyle and tried to fix her mind on what the director was saying to her. 'Artistically, you find no obstaclcs about playing the part of Marjorie?'

'No, on the contrary, I think she's a wonderful character—'

'And you are not, how do you say, put off by the difficulties of playing against an Italian lead? You don't speak any Italian, do you?'

'A—a little. I once did a course...'

'But that's wonderful,' Franco said, his eyes lighting up. He moved slightly, obscuring Kyle and hemming Sophie into a corner. 'When we start filming in Pisa...'

She tried to look interested in what Franco Luciani was saying, but the hollow, dizzy feeling inside wouldn't leave her alone. She tried to see round him, but he had stationed himself so as to monopolise her attention. Like other directors she had known, he was almost obsessive about his work, the project on hand dominating his thoughts to the exclusion of all others.

It washed over her like rain, and it was twenty agonising minutes before the director interrupted his own monologue. 'But this is not the time or place to talk business,' he said. 'I simply wanted to give you some time to think about the idea.'

'Your offer is extremely generous,' she said, trying to smile. 'I'd very much like to discuss it with Joey Gilmour, my agent. I'm no good at business, I'm afraid—he deals with all that side of it for me—'

'Of course. We will arrange a more formal meeting to discuss the details.' He leaned close to her. 'And do not forget, what could be worth even more than that is the chance to star in a film that attracts attention. Believe me, Sophie Aspen, *The First Day of Autumn* will attract a great deal of attention.' He straightened his back proudly. 'I have made commercially unsuccessful films, but I have never made a bad film.'

'I'm ashamed to say I haven't seen *Roman Affair*,' Sophie said, 'but everyone speaks very highly of your work.' She touched his arm. 'I'm terribly sorry,' she said awkwardly, 'this is absolutely fascinating, but I've just remembered something important I must say to my cousin. Could you excuse me for ten minutes?'

'Of course,' he beamed, evidently delighted at finding Sophie in such a receptive mood. He helped himself to a glass of champagne as Sophie started across the room to where Kyle and Jenny were standing.

CHAPTER SIX

KYLE was a head taller than most of the men in the room, his dark presence seeming, in Sophie's eyes at lcast, to dominate everyone else. Her heart was in her mouth, her palms clammy with perspiration, as she approached through the crowd. How was he going to treat her?

'Hello, Kyle,' Sophie said softly. As on a previous meeting, her throat was constricted. She found speech with an effort. 'How are you?'

Kyle's gaze swung her way, but there wasn't a flicker of emotion on his face as their eyes met. 'Fine,' he said with cool politeness. 'And you?'

Sophie felt as though someone had just dashed a bucket of iced water in her face.

'Fine.'

'Do you two know each other?' Jenny said, looking slightly put out.

'We've met,' Kyle said huskily.

'Don't tell me you're another member of the Sophie Aspen fan club,' Jenny groaned. 'All I've heard tonight is how wonderful my theatrical cousin is. Did you watch *The Elmtree Road Murders* last night?'

He shook his head, and Jenny brightened. 'I was tied up with a friend.' He put just enough emphasis on 'friend' to leave no doubt that he meant a lady friend. 'But I understand that Sophie's performance was something special.'

'I've never seen anything like it,' Jenny snickered. 'You really missed something, Kyle.'

'The story of my life,' he said, with a cold smile. 'What was so special about it?'

'Oh, Sophie's make-up was just amazing.' Jenny's eyes were bright with malicious laughter. 'I couldn't stop laughing. She looked like . . . well, like nothing on earth.'

'Really?' Kyle drawled. 'How bizarre.'

'*Grotesque* would be a better word. I couldn't believe it when I saw her,' Jenny gushed. 'I said I wouldn't have let anyone make me look as awful as that for a thousand pounds! You couldn't imagine it, Kyle.'

'Perhaps I could.' Ice-green eyes were holding Sophie's. 'As a matter of fact, I last met your cousin in Brighton, during the filming of *The Elmtree Road Murders*, and she presented a very different picture then.'

'Then you haven't seen Sophie since she was playing Maisie?' Jenny asked, wide-eyed. 'Gosh, you must hardly recognise her.'

'I see her with new eyes,' Kyle agreed, but only Sophie caught the razor's edge that lay beneath the bland words.

'Doesn't it surprise you to find how *beautiful* Sophie really is?' Jenny said, with just enough of a droop of her eyelashes to utterly devalue the statement.

Sophie knew this routine of Jenny's so well, and yet it never ceased to make her wilt. Jenny was an expert at putting her down in the presence of any remotely attractive male. No matter how close they were, as relations and as friends, when a desirable man was involved Jenny suddenly turned into an utterly ruthless bitch, for whom no hold was barred.

Kyle's gaze left Sophie's face at last, and moved down the length of her body with cool assessment. 'You've changed since then,' he said drily. 'I might not have recognised you, Sophie.'

'Yes,' she said numbly, 'I've changed since Brighton——'

'You're another woman,' he said flatly.

By now she knew, with no shadow of a doubt, that Kyle hadn't forgiven her, wasn't going to forgive her. Yet she could not resist probing further, as though there might still be a chance . . .

She found the words with an effort. 'But we've met since Brighton, Kyle.'

'Have we?' he raised a negligent eyebrow. 'I'm afraid I must have forgotten.'

She shook her head at him slightly, fighting down the pain. 'I remember it well.'

'How odd!' Jenny, picking up the tension, had scented something juicy. 'Where was that, Sophie?'

'We bumped into each other once or twice,' Sophie said dully, feeling despair unfold leaden wings inside her.

'Yes,' Jenny persisted, 'but how come Kyle didn't know who you were?'

'Your cousin is such a very talented young actress,' Kyle said ironically, watching Sophie with ice-green eyes. 'Who knows, perhaps I didn't recognise her. Where did we "bump into each other", Sophie?'

'If you don't remember,' Sophie said distantly, 'then it hardly matters.'

'But I'm curious,' Kyle said with a cold smile. 'And you've got your cousin intrigued. Do remind me of the occasion.'

Colour was starting to rise hotly into Sophie's face. 'We met in Jamaica,' she forced herself to say.

'In Jamaica?' Kyle was wearing an expression of cool surprise. 'But, my dear Sophie, I remember nothing about this meeting. I spent quite some time there, and I certainly don't recall meeting any Sophie Aspen.'

Jenny had been following this exchange with bright, inquisitive eyes. Kyle now turned the full force of his smile on her. 'How delicious to see two such beautiful women together,' he drawled. 'You might almost be sisters. Sophie told me about you.'

'Did she?' Jenny preened.

'She told me you had beauty as well as brains, and I now see that she was understating the case.' He gave Jenny a slow, appreciative once-over. 'Yet your cousin gets all the attention.'

'Oh, we have different talents,' Jenny answered with a bright laugh. 'We've never competed.'

'Except for men?' Kyle suggested gently.

'Oh, Kyle,' Jenny said breathily, 'I've *never* had to compete with my cousin for men.'

'I can see why not,' Kyle said meaningfully. 'What a waste for someone as radiant as you to be closeted in the dusty realms of mathematics.'

This was music to Jenny's ears. She glanced triumphantly at a silent Sophie. 'Oh, maths isn't all that dusty. As if happens, I spend most of my time working with a giant computer which positively gleams with cleanliness.'

'In a laboratory where no one sees your beauty. I wonder whether your professors appreciate the loveliness that is under their noses?' His voice was tantamount to a caress, and Sophie watched the coquettish droop of her cousin's eyelashes.

'As it happens,' Jenny said mischievously, 'some are more appreciative than others.'

Kyle arched one eyebrow. 'I thought that sort of thing didn't go on.'

'It goes on,' Jenny said with heavy innuendo, 'believe me.'

'Ah,' Kyle said softly. 'Well, that doesn't surprise me. You must be a devastating temptation.'

They were ignoring Sophie completely. She was standing like a fool, transfixed with the sick hollowness inside. Jenny's eyes were glowing as she basked in Kyle's attention. 'Anyway,' she said, 'as a banker, you must be something of a mathematician yourself, Kyle?'

'Oh, yes. The purity of applied maths has always interested me. Numbers cannot lie. They can't deceive or cheat, or pretend to be something they're not.'

'But that's exactly what I love about mathematics!' Jenny exclaimed. 'I love the way it's all so unambiguous. There's always an answer, or almost always. Life isn't like that.'

'No,' Kyle said. His eyes glittered at Sophie. 'Life isn't like that, and people aren't like that. I detest dishonesty, above all else. It sickens me.'

Sophie's heart was pounding painfully against her breast-bone. It was far worse than she'd dreamed. He wasn't just indifferent to her. She knew Kyle well enough to sense the radiating anger that blazed beneath his impeccable façade. There was no question of his forgiving her for what she'd done in Jamaica. He was, she knew with sudden certainty, intent on making her pay.

'Don't you agree, Sophie?' he challenged meaningfully.

'Perhaps,' she said in a low voice. 'But numbers don't have hearts. A thing without a heart can never lie. On the other hand, it can't love, either, or be loved in return.'

Kyle took Jenny's arm casually. 'Do you agree with that?' he asked.

'Well,' Jenny said, almost purring at the contact, 'I'm no expert on true love. Personally, I reckon it's a lot of irrelevant sentimental idiocy. I prefer straightforward relationships...' she looked at Kyle from under thick lashes '...without emotional strings.'

'My opinions exactly,' Kyle said, looking into Jenny's eyes with a dark smile. 'You and I have much in common, Jenny.'

Sophie couldn't stand it any longer. She turned to Jenny pleadingly. 'Jenny,' she said in a quiet voice, 'would you give me a moment alone with Kyle?'

Jenny looked angrily back at Sophie. 'What?'

'I want a private word with Kyle. Just a few minutes.'

'Well, I really think——'

'Please.'

'But don't go far,' Kyle said, giving Jenny another smoky smile. 'I'm sure your cousin won't detain me for long.'

Jenny flounced off indignantly, and stood sulking by the drinks trolley. Sophie looked up into the tanned, rugged face that had haunted her dreams. 'I tried to ring you, the day I got back to England, but you'd already checked out. Why didn't you get in touch with me?' she asked in a low voice.

'Did you really expect me to?' Kyle asked contemptuously, not bothering to keep up the urbane manner now that Jenny was no longer present.

'I thought that after what happened between us in Jamaica...'

'What happened between us?' He spoke with such concentrated venom that Sophie dropped her gaze. 'You astonish me, Sophie,' he rasped. 'After that despicable little charade in Jamaica, I find it incredible that you have the face to even approach me.'

She gasped slightly at the force of his anger. 'Kyle, please listen to me,' she begged. 'I didn't want it to be a charade. But I found myself in a corner. I didn't know how to get out of it——'

'You two-faced little fake,' he cut through harshly. 'You're the cheapest swindler I've met in a lifetime of dealing with cheap swindlers.'

The colour was draining from Sophie's face. 'That's cruel and unfair——'

'Wasn't what you did to me cruel and unfair?' The skin around his eyes was tight with anger. 'I wonder how all your admiring friends would feel about you if I made a speech about your gifts, right now? Would they still respect you once they knew about the fine performance you gave in Jamaica, for the benefit of your captive audience?'

'It started out as a performance,' Sophie said, struggling to keep her composure. 'But it didn't end up that way.'

He laughed shortly. 'You've had your little game with me,' he said. 'But the game is now over. Don't drag it out any further.'

She was white. 'It isn't a game, not to me!'

'But it's a game to me.' His smile was arctic. 'It's *my* game now.'

'What do you mean?'

'I mean that, as you hurt me, I intend to hurt you.'

'Oh, Kyle,' she said quietly. 'I told you you were a typical Scorpio, didn't I?'

'So you did,' he said silkily. 'Did you think you could just walk all over my pride, and get away with it?'

'You once walked all over my pride,' she shot back. 'If you had any idea how you hurt me in Brighton——'

'You eavesdropped on a conversation you half understood in Brighton.' His passionate mouth curled. 'I don't know what you heard that afternoon, but I would never have said anything unkind about you to your face. I never set out to hurt you. But you set out to hurt *me*. Your vanity was piqued, so you thought you would get your own back. You decided to make a fool of me, the most complete fool you could manage.'

'That's a distortion of the truth!' Her grey eyes were misty with pain. 'You didn't recognise me when we met that day on the beach. I waited to see whether you would remember who I was, but you didn't——'

'And you helped jog my memory, of course, by giving yourself a false name and lying to me about your job.'

'I just wanted to tease you. I never planned it to go so far!' She was begging him to believe what she was saying. 'I had no idea we would get so close——'

'Or that we would wind up in bed?' he finished for her. 'God, I was a fool. A blind fool. There was something about you that haunted me, from the moment we met—but I never suspected the truth.' His eyes burned into hers. 'Three weeks. You had me going for three damned weeks! You must have found it so entertaining, watching me falling for you, watching me get caught in your web!'

'It wasn't like that,' she answered shakily. 'But if it comes to that, didn't *you* once find it amusing that I had fallen for *you*?'

His fingers clamped painfully around Sophie's bare arm, making her gasp with shock. 'I never did what you did,' he grated. 'You let me take you to bed, let me make love to you, let me tell you how wonderful you were, how much I cared about you—and all the time you were laughing yourself sick behind your hand!'

'No! It wasn't like that! If you only knew how much I've regretted the way it all ended. But I didn't know what else to do!'

'The only thing you've regretted is that you weren't there to watch my face as I read your clever little letter,' he retorted. His anger was turning back into cold dislike again. He released her arm at last, and if her skin hadn't been so tanned his fingers would have left livid marks on her flesh. 'You would have had a most amusing spectacle,' he said, with a cold smile. 'I felt as though the earth had caved in under my feet. That's what you wanted, wasn't it?'

She wiped her tear-soaked lashes tremblingly. 'Oh, no, Kyle——'

'You play very dirty, Sophie,' he said bitterly. 'But you'll find I can play dirty, too.'

'Is that why you came here tonight?' she asked unsteadily. 'To tell me all this?'

'I didn't come to see you at all,' he retorted with a tiger's smile. 'I came to see someone else.'

'What do you mean?' she followed his eyes, and found herself staring at Jenny, who was now talking to another man. An icy chill flooded her veins as she looked back into Kyle's hard, unforgiving eyes. 'Jenny? You came to see Jenny?'

'Why not? Your sweet little cousin and I have a lot in common, hadn't you gathered that? We both prefer uncomplicated relationships without falsehood or irrelevant emotions.'

'You don't even know her!'

'That can be rectified,' he said lazily. 'She tells me she's in London for the next three weeks. That is exactly the right period for my purposes. I intend to get to know your cousin very well indeed during the coming three weeks.' His eyes travelled appreciatively down Jenny's slender figure. 'She even looks like you. You were right, of course, she's far prettier than you'll ever be. But the resemblance is there, and that will give me added pleasure.'

'What do you mean, added pleasure?'

'When I taste what was denied me in Jamaica.'

Shock made Sophie numb for a moment as his meaning dawned on her. 'I don't believe you,' she whispered. 'You wouldn't do that!'

'Why wouldn't I?'

'Kyle, no! Having an affair with Jenny isn't a fit pastime for a man like you!'

'You are a very poor judge of what is fit, and what isn't,' he retorted mockingly. 'Since you obviously have no honour or pride to hurt, Sophie, I must hurt you through whatever means I can find.' He tilted his head to look down at her dispassionately. 'When Hélène told me your cousin was staying with you, I remembered what you once told me. About your jealousy and resentment of Jenny. You weren't lying to me about that, were you? After all, Jenny is so much prettier than you. So much sexier, too.'

'Kyle,' she said in horror, 'for God's sake!'

'Yes,' he smiled drily. 'I see I was right. Jealousy is one of the few emotions you're vulnerable to. Like most actresses, your pride is your Achilles' heel.'

Unbearable hurt made her feel physically sick. 'How could you think of something as sadistic as that?' she whispered.

'I call it justice,' he replied softly.

'I'll stop you. I'll tell Jenny. I'll—I'll tell her what happened in Jamaica!'

'Do. Tell her just what a bitch you've been. I'm sure she'll be most edified to hear all about it.'

'Jenny would never do anything to hurt me!'

'Wouldn't she?' His expression was amused. 'I think she would. I think Jenny takes a particular pleasure in stealing men from you. She does steal all your favourite men, doesn't she?'

'God,' she whispered, 'why did I ever tell you that?'

'One look into your cousin's eyes tells me just how different she is from you. That, unlike you, she has the ability to please a man, and be pleased in return.' Sophie stared up into the magnificent, cold face, her blood like ice. 'Tell Jenny all about it,' he invited smoothly. 'Tell her what you did to me in Jamaica, then tell her that I'm going to have an affair with her. See if that puts her off. She'll enjoy it as much as I will. And I'll enjoy it very much.' He reached out tauntingly, and caressed her half-open, velvety mouth. 'Your pride is going to take rather a pounding, my dear Sophie. How will it feel to watch your younger, prettier, sexier cousin get the man you betrayed? Perhaps, when you think of Jenny in my arms, you might regret that little trick you played on me in Ocho Rios!'

'Please,' she whispered, her eyes blurring. 'Please don't do this.'

'It's easy to see why she stole your men. The two of you are like gold and lead. She is the gold, but you, Sophie, are lead. Cold, grey, uninteresting. She's not just more attractive. She's sexually receptive. You are not.' He said it with biting disdain. 'You're clearly incapable of a normal relationship with any man. That's really why you had to go through that incredibly elaborate sham in Jamaica, isn't it? You prefer fiction to reality. What are you so afraid of? That one day a man will find out just how colourless and frigid you really are?'

Sophie was staring at him in horror, silenced. With a last cruel smile into Sophie's eyes, Kyle turned and walked over to Jenny, taking her arm and murmuring something into her ear.

And Franco Luciani, spotting that Sophie was alone, chose that moment to come back over to her. His big, intense eyes searched her face.

'Are you all right, Sophie?' he demanded, looking at her curiously. 'You've gone very pale.'

'I'm fine,' she nodded dizzily, and took an unsteady breath. 'Perhaps the—the champagne went to my head—a little.'

Franco nodded. 'Can we get back to what we were talking about a few minutes ago? I'd be extremely interested to hear your views on the character of Marjorie. How did you read the part?'

Sophie tried to stir her bruised mind into some kind of reply. Dissociated from the empty words that came from her mouth, her thoughts were fraught with pain. *What could she do?*

The answer was nothing. Just brace herself for the crushing blow of seeing the man she loved walk into a shallow, deliberate affair with her cousin.

And Kyle was right. The idea of her, a virgin, being any sort of competition for Jenny was absurd. Despite the two-year age-gap between them, Jenny was infinitely more experienced with men than she would ever be. Infinitely more experienced, and infinitely more attractive.

She felt a wave of acute sickness, as though she'd just been struck in the solar plexus.

Some part of her mind must have been functioning independently of her inner thoughts, because although she had not the faintest idea of what she'd been saying to Franco Luciani, he nodded eagerly.

'That is very profound. You have hit on the essential element in the character of Marjorie. She is a woman in the grip of an addiction stronger than she knows how to deal with. She finds love, but that cannot save her. She embraces the flames that devour her——'

'Sorry to interrupt.' It was Jenny, her blue eyes sapphire-bright as she came over to talk to Sophie. She gave

Franco a pretty smile, and drew her cousin aside. 'Kyle wants me to go to a nightclub with him.'

'Now?' Sophie asked in pain.

'This is your party,' Jenny sneered. 'I don't know a soul here. And Kyle's as bored as I am. Frankly, I'd far rather be dancing with him. Do you mind?'

Sophie fought for control. 'No,' she said, almost inaudibly, 'of course I don't mind.'

Jenny leaned forward, 'God, isn't he fantastic?' she giggled under her breath. 'He's the best-looking man I've ever seen in my *life*, and he's obviously on the loose. I can't believe my luck! Why haven't you told me about him?'

'I—I don't know.'

'What's between you?' Jenny's blue eyes were eager, greedy. 'Have you had an affair with him? I mean, I'm not poaching, am I? I'd hate to be taking yet *another* man from you.'

'There's nothing between us,' Sophie said, feeling as though she were in the grip of some icy paralysis.

'Good,' Jenny sparkled wickedly. 'Because I have very good feelings about tonight. He's got that certain look in his eyes. So don't wait up for me!'

'Jenny,' Sophie pleaded, her eyes as dark as her cousin's were brilliant, 'don't...'

'Don't what?' Her cousin's smile was unmistakably taunting.

'Just—just be careful.'

'Not a chance,' Jenny grinned. 'Kyle Hart isn't the kind of man a woman should be careful with. That was always your trouble, darling. Not knowing when to go for it. Well, good luck with your Italian; he's pretty yummy, too. Bye!'

'What a pretty girl,' Franco said appreciatively, as Jenny hurried off. 'She's younger than you, isn't she?'

'Yes,' Sophie said. The room was blurring around her, only isolated details coming through the haze. Kyle's eyes, meeting hers in cold triumph. His arm sliding round

Jenny's waist as they headed discreetly for the door. The distant laughter of Hélène le Bon. The sound of pulsing music—or was it her own blood, pounding in her ears?

'Sophie, you look ill,' Franco said, peering at her. 'Sophie?'

'I'm sorry,' she tried to say, 'I'd better sit down...'

Franco was just in time to take her in his arms as she sagged against him, darkness flooding her mind.

She awoke late the next morning, feeling panicky and depressed.

Memories of last night flooded in. Where was Jenny? She got up quickly, and pulled on her dressing-gown, then padded out into the corridor in her bare feet.

She pushed the door of her tiny guest bedroom quietly open, and peeped in.

The immaculate bed hadn't been slept in. Sophie fought down the tears as she sagged against the doorway. Jenny had not come home last night. Where she was now was anybody's guess. Especially Kyle's.

Gathering her strength, she went into the bathroom and showered. Last night drifted through her thoughts as she stood under the spray. What a débâcle. Coming out of her faint with a crowd of anxious faces round her. Hélène's concerned eyes and kind words. People blaming the heat, or the champagne, or the excitement. People offering to take her home. Nobody understanding a thing...

Stupidly, she'd kept on announcing that she was fine, and that she wanted to stay on, when all the time she'd just wanted to run a hundred miles away, and bury her pain and humiliation somewhere out of sight. The rest of the evening had been stretched and hazy, like someone on the rack, until Franco Luciani had eventually taken pity on her glazed eyes and white face, and had insisted on driving her home.

She'd never taken a sleeping-pill in her life, but last night she'd wanted one badly.

Come to think of it, she could have crawled back into bed right now, and buried her head in misery...

She had to keep reminding herself that although Jenny was enjoying her latest triumph, she was completely innocent of Kyle's darker purpose, completely ignorant of the relationship Kyle had once had with her.

Jenny could cope with most situations. Sophie couldn't. Maybe Kyle had been right about her. Maybe she wasn't able to have a normal relationship with a man. Maybe that *was* why she'd invented that elaborate charade in Jamaica.

Whatever the truth of it, Kyle was going to make her pay, all right. He'd worked out a torment of hell for her.

How could a man who'd once felt so much for her now be so cruel and vindictive? She'd once thought him shallow. God! Could she ever have been more mistaken? She'd never guessed at the depth of his feelings, had never known a tenth of how deeply he'd really felt about her...

She was making a cup of coffee half an hour later when Hélène rang.

'How are you feeling? Any better?'

'Much better,' Sophie lied, trying to sound sincere. 'I slept like a log.'

'Did something upset you last night?'

'Oh, no.' She fell back on the well-worn excuse. 'It's just not a very good time of the month for me.'

'I see! Well, I'm glad that's what it was, darling. I was worried. I saw you talking to Kyle, and I wondered whether you might have been distressed by something he said or did. I couldn't help noticing... well, that he left the party early with your cousin, Jenny.'

'Yes,' Sophie said with an effort. 'They went to a nightclub together.'

'Did they have a good time?'

'Jenny didn't—didn't come home last night. She's not back yet.'

'I see,' Hélène said quietly. 'I think I can imagine how you feel.' Sophie was silent, and Hélène went on quickly, 'It seemed to me, last year in Brighton, that you grew rather fond of Kyle. I don't want to seem as though I'm prying, but you were obviously very taken with him. It's just that I didn't think your feelings would still be so strong, all this time later—otherwise I would never have asked him to the party. It must be nine months since you last met him.'

'No,' Sophie said wearily. 'We've met since then.'

'I didn't know that.'

'It was in Jamaica...' Sophie struggled to find words to describe what had happened between her and Kyle. But it now seemed so unreal, so impossible to explain.

'While you were on holiday?' Hélène prompted.

'Yes. Oh, Hélène, I've been such a fool. I did something so stupid to him, really hurt his pride, and now...now he hates me.'

'I don't believe that!' Hélène exclaimed. 'Kyle always had a very soft spot for you. And when I say that, I'm talking about a man who has very few soft spots—especially for women.'

'He found me ridiculous in Brighton. And I *was* ridiculous.' Her voice trembled slightly. 'And now that I'm presentable, I've gone and wrecked everything in another way.'

'Kyle didn't find you altogether ridiculous.' Hélène was silent for a moment. Then she asked quietly, 'You overheard us that day, on the beach, didn't you?'

'Yes,' Sophie said dully. 'I didn't mean to, but it just happened that way.'

'I thought you must have heard something. You were so cold to him over those last few days. You treated him as though he'd suddenly stopped existing. As a matter of interest, what *did* you hear?'

'I heard Kyle telling you how...how amusing he found it that I was so obviously infatuated with him. He said a lot of other things, about the way I looked and dressed.

About what a spectacle I was. He was asking you to speak to me about my appearance.'

'Oh, dear. Is that all you heard?'

'Well . . . I didn't stay very long.'

Hélène sighed. 'You didn't hear him say how charming he found you as a person? Or how he admired your acting ability? Or what good company you were?'

'He seemed to think the way I looked was more important.'

'Kyle knew very little about you, then. He didn't know that you had changed your appearance radically to play the part of Maisie. No one had told him that. The afternoon you overheard us, he was asking me about you, and I was explaining how Percy had insisted on the slatternly image for Maisie, and that it wasn't really you.'

'What did he say?'

Hélène laughed softly. 'He said that he couldn't wait to see you once you'd gone back to normal. How did he react when he met you in Jamaica?'

'He . . . he didn't recognise me.'

'I'm not surprised,' Hélène smiled.

'No, you don't understand,' Sophie said tautly. 'He *never* recognised me. You see, he wanted me. I thought he was just making a pass at first, and I thought I'd tease him a little. I lied to him about my name, and just let him go on thinking that he'd never met me before.'

'Oh, Sophie! But *why*?'

'I suppose I must have wanted to get back at him in some way. Prove a point, maybe. But . . . things changed so quickly. I think he was really serious at the end, and I just didn't know how to handle it any more. I behaved so badly. The day I left Jamaica, I wrote him a note explaining who I was. A really stupid, childish note. But by then I was so involved with him. I don't know what made me behave in that way, but I regret it so much now! That's why he's so disgusted with me, Hélène.

'Oh, Sophie!' Hélène mourned. 'How could you have been so silly?'

'I've been sitting here for three weeks asking myself just that, and praying he would get back in touch with me. I didn't realise how angry he was. Last night he...he said such cutting things to me. And he only went out with Jenny to hit back at me. He seems determined to punish me for what I did.' Sophie's voice broke. 'What can I do?'

Hélène paused for a long while, as though thinking. 'I don't know what you can do,' she said slowly at last. 'But I want to tell you something about Kyle Hart. I've known him a long time, and I consider him a good friend. He's an achiever, Sophie. He was a little wild in his early twenties, but he settled down after a year or two in the Caribbean. Did he tell you about that?'

'A little bit,' Sophie nodded.

'Well, he's done absolutely brilliantly since then. He's made a fortune for his bank, and he's now one of the most powerful men, for his age, in the City. He's been responsible for countless projects, and he's very highly thought of. Kyle works incredibly hard at his job, and he plays hard, too. With women... well, I don't need to tell you that he just has to whistle. He's had a succession of the most stunning girlfriends, and none of them ever seem to have meant much to him. Do I sound as though I'm rubbing it in?'

'A little,' Sophie said wryly.

'Well, I'm trying to make a point. The point is that, for all his success with our sex, Kyle is very wary. Whether he's had some bad experiences, or whether it's just constitutional, I don't know. But he's erected some formidable defences, and he tends to be very distrustful of any woman who looks like breaching them. Any time one of his girlfriends seems to be getting close to him, the barrier suddenly comes down, and they're excluded. I've seen it happen half a dozen times. Sometimes they come to me in tears and ask me what they did wrong, and I have to say I simply don't know. I've always guessed that Kyle simply wants happy, mainly sexual relationships with his women, without involvement or commitment on either side. The unfortunate thing,' she added with a little sigh, 'is that he's the kind of man very few women can treat like that. They tend to fall in love with him. Hard.'

'It isn't difficult to do,' Sophie said drily.

'No, I suppose not. What I'm getting around to, darling, is that you seem to be the one exception that proves the rule. It sounds to me as though you actually did get through his defences. You've probably seen a side of Kyle that he's shown to very, very few women. As I said,' Hélène commented gently, 'he always did have a very soft spot for you. But as it's turned out... well, you've probably hurt him far more deeply than you guessed at the time.'

'Oh, no,' Sophie said in dawning horror.

'He's also probably very angry. And when he's angry, he's capable of hitting out with a great deal of force. I can't tell you how to run your life, but I really don't think you have much to gain by trying to face up to him. You'll only collect a lot of unnecessary bruises. Do you want me to talk to him?'

'No, please don't. It wouldn't make things any better.'

'No, I don't think it would. I'll do what I can, without actually interfering. Sophie, I know this is going to hurt, but I've never known Kyle go back to anyone whom he's once cut out of his life. He's a very decisive man. If he's striking up a relationship with your cousin, then it's going to be murder for you to stand by and watch, but there really isn't anything you can do. Except try and get over it, and remember that Jenny is probably far less vulnerable to Kyle than you are.'

Hélène spoke a great deal more, but after that Sophie's mind was numb. How was she ever going to adjust to the truths she had learned this morning?

The things Kyle had said to her in Ocho Rios, things she'd thought he said to every woman he wanted... he'd really meant them. He wasn't the kind of man to talk to a woman like that, not casually.

'You're a very special woman, my love. I just know we've met before. But if it wasn't in this lifetime, then it must have been in some other one, because I feel that I'm acquainted with you. The important thing is that we don't lose one another again.'

And she'd been so blasé, so cool with him.

'That kind of talk is for shallow people—not persons of deep feeling, like you and I.'

He'd felt something special for her, and she had thrown it back in his face. Had insanely thrown away the rarest gift that Kyle could give a woman—his trust. And she would never get it back again.

It was almost ten-thirty that morning by the time she heard Jenny's key in the door. And Kyle was with her.

They were both still in last night's evening clothes, and Kyle's arm was possessively round Jenny's waist as they came into the little flat, laughing. They brought with them a scent of perfume, whisky and cigars.

'God, we've had such a fabulous time,' Jenny said with a giggle, collapsing into an armchair beside Sophie and throwing her red-gold hair back. She looked like a cat who'd just had a bowl of double cream all to itself.

'Have you?' Sophie asked brightly, avoiding meeting Kyle's mocking green eyes. 'Where did you go?'

'Oh, I can hardly remember.' Jenny yawned lazily, showing a pink inner mouth. 'To a disco, first. What was that place called, darling?'

'La Valbonne,' Kyle said, leaning negligently against the mantelpiece. His presence seemed to overpower the tiny flat, making Sophie feel as though she were being crushed into a corner. 'Not exactly your scene, Sophie.'

'I'll say not,' Jenny agreed maliciously. 'Bit too wild for you. But it was *fabulous*,' she sighed. 'We even had a swim in the pool. Then we had dinner at the Café Royal. I've never seen so many celebrities! The place was wall-to-wall film stars and pop stars. Then we went to La Capanina, and danced practically till dawn... We've just had breakfast at the Dorchester!'

Sophie forced a smile. 'And where did you go between dawn and the Dorchester?'

'You wouldn't believe us if we told you,' Jenny gurgled, her blue eyes sparkling.

An agonising flash of memory seared Sophie's mind, as she recalled what she herself had once got up to with Kyle in the early hours of the morning. 'No,' she agreed drily, hiding her pain under a composed face, 'I probably wouldn't.' She grasped after normality with a supreme effort. 'Would either of you like a cup of coffee?'

'Love one,' Jenny nodded. 'And you, darling?'

Kyle glanced at his watch, the black diver's watch she remembered so well. 'Why not?' he agreed easily. 'I don't have any appointments until noon.'

Jenny jumped to her feet. 'I'm going to have a lightning shower while you put the percolator on, Sophie.' She stroked Kyle's cheek. 'You don't mind, darling?'

That made three darlings so far, Sophie noted savagely. She walked stiffly to the kitchen, praying that Kyle wouldn't end up making her hate her own cousin.

She started making coffee in a state of blind tension, her fingers clumsy and disobedient. From the bathroom came the sound of Jenny showering.

'So this is where you live.' She turned. Kyle was watching her from the doorway, his dark face amused. He glanced around without bothering to disguise his disdain. 'Rather a poky little place.'

'It's all I can afford!' Sophie snapped, scattering coffee as she filled the percolator. 'Unlike you, I don't own my own bank.'

'How did you sleep last night?'

'Fine—*darling*.'

'Really?' he drawled. 'You seem kind of ragged this morning.'

'I obviously don't have your stamina for night-life,' she replied bitterly.

'A little birdie tells me,' he said gently, 'that you threw a fainting fit at Hélène's last night. Right after I left the party with your cousin.'

'I was tired,' she said stiffly. 'I got a little giddy.'

'Nothing to do with me and Jenny?' Silent laughter sparkled in his eyes as he watched her. 'My, my. That really must have hit you hard. I hear that Luciani was most impressed.' He mimicked the Italian's accent with wicked accuracy. '"Thees ees exactly what I want for my wonderful new film."'

'Very amusing,' Sophie bit out.

'You're good at doing emotional scenes, aren't you?' he mocked. 'Everyone keeps telling me what a brilliant performance you put in at the end of *The Elmtree Road Murders*. They say the final scenes were quite stunning. I'm starting to be sorry I didn't catch it, but I was very much occupied that night. With a ladyfriend.'

That soft postscript hurt like a barb in her flesh. 'So you've already said. I'm sure you were much better occupied,' she said, pretending indifference. 'But if I did act competently, then part of the credit must go to you.'

He arched one dark eyebrow. 'Indeed?'

'If I hadn't been brought down to earth with a bump one afternoon, I might not have put in such a realistic performance,' she informed him lightly.

'Well, well.' He subjected her to a slow, deliberate scrutiny. 'What happened in Brighton really seems to bother you. You had quite a crush on me then, didn't you?'

The sudden, hectic flush on her cheeks emphasised her paleness. 'I really don't remember.'

'I do. It was painfully obvious.'

'Yes, I should have been much more discreet about my juvenile feelings, shouldn't I?' She gave him a tight smile. 'But unfortunately, I didn't know just how...absurd you found me.'

Kyle smiled drily. 'Want to hear something funny?'

'I could do with a laugh.'

'I liked you in Brighton, Sophie. I liked you a lot. You amused me, really you did. I had the idea that we might become good friends.'

She looked down. 'Is that . . . all?'

'A good friend is a much rarer and more precious commodity than a good lover,' he assured her ironically. 'But it seemed it was not to be.'

'You said awful things about me,' she told him in a low voice. 'Things that hurt me for months afterwards.'

'You weren't meant to hear them,' he retorted. 'And not many people can afford to eavesdrop on what others say about them, and not be hurt. I didn't understand the role you were playing, until Hélène explained about it. I thought you were just being sloppy. I didn't know then how much you were throwing yourself into your part.' He paused. 'As I remember it, that afternoon I was being rather clever about your evident infatuation with me.'

'Yes,' she said dully.

'I never understood why you changed towards me so abruptly. I didn't guess what had happened. I just got the message that my company was suddenly not welcome any longer. But of course, you were already plotting your little revenge, weren't you?'

She lit the gas, and put the percolator on. In the silence, they heard the shower stop. Jenny was humming gaily as she dried herself.

'As a matter of interest,' Sophie asked, 'what *did* you do between dawn and breakfast?'

'I took your sweet little cousin to bed.'

The teaspoons clattered out of Sophie's paralysed fingers into the sink. The world swayed dizzily around her as her eyes flooded with tears.

'Oh, Kyle,' she whispered numbly, staring at his blurred figure. 'You didn't!'

He looked at her grief-stricken face for a moment, then laughed huskily. 'Oh, but I did—*darling*.' Sophie felt so sick that she thought she might throw up. Then Kyle went on, 'However, I didn't get in with her.' He arched a derisive eyebrow at her expression. 'You have a remarkably sordid imagination. We stopped off at home, and Jenny was practically falling asleep. So I let her catch forty winks in my spare bedroom, while I caught up on some paperwork. In my study,' hc added. His eyes showed how much he was relishing her pain. 'Then we had breakfast at the Dorchester, and I brought her here. *C'est tout*.'

Reaction was making Sophie's fingers tremble as she groped for the spoons, and started putting cups out. 'You bastard,' she said in a whisper.

'Poor little Sophie,' Kyle smiled darkly. 'What an innocent you are.' He came over to her, and slid his arms round her in a heart-breaking mockery of tenderness. 'Did you think I was going to make love to her on our first date? That would have spoiled all the fun.'

His touch made her senses swim. 'Do you call this *fun*?' she asked bitterly.

'Of course.'

'I think it's sick. You know I care about you, and you're hurting me in the cruellest way you can think of!'

'*Care?*' he repeated silkily. 'What an interesting choice of words. Are you being extraordinarily naïve, girl? Or are you offering to pay me back in some other way?'

'I don't know what you mean,' Sophie said tiredly.

'Don't you?' He smiled, and touched her chin, tilting her downcast face upward. 'I sometimes could almost believe that you really are a virgin. Now, how could a man find out the truth of that? There's only one reliable way, isn't there?'

'You could just believe me.'

'But I don't believe you.' He was staring at her mouth with intent eyes. 'I don't believe one single syllable that comes out of those soft, sweet, lying lips of yours. I've believed once too often.' He looked into her eyes, and growled softly. 'Why are you looking at me like that?'

'Like what?'

His arms moved to hold her more tightly. 'Damn you, Sophie,' he said softly. 'Those soft grey eyes of yours beg me to make love to you. You know that, don't you?'

'No!' She tried to tear her gaze away, but he held her, as though hypnotised.

'Yes. That would be the only way we could get at the truth of your fabled virginity, wouldn't it?'

'After which,' she said, dry-mouthed, 'the question of virginity becomes irrelevant.'

'It's irrelevant, anyway,' Kyle replied, his gaze hardening. 'You are not the one I'm going to make love to.'

She winced painfully, and caught the flare of satisfaction in his eyes as he saw that his words had struck home.

'But in lieu of that satisfaction,' he said huskily, 'perhaps we could settle for a good-morning kiss?'

She tried to twist her face away from his seeking lips, but he was so strong. His mouth met hers, deliberately erotic as his lips moulded themselves to hers, caressing, pressing warmly and possessively. His hand slid silkily down her back, caressing with calculated sensuality.

'What makes you tremble so much?' he laughed softly. 'The thought of my possessing your delectable little cousin? She's just my type. And she doesn't feel like a marble statue when I kiss her, either. But you'll have to wait, Sophie. I'll tell you when I make love to her, don't worry. But it might not be for a while. Maybe another day or two. Maybe much longer. Who can tell with these things?'

'How can you be so deliberately cruel?' she asked unsteadily, trying to push her way out of his embrace.

'Weren't you cruel to me?' he retorted, his smile tightening. 'Didn't you play exactly this kind of game with me?'

'No, never!'

'Oh, but you did.' His arms tightened, crushing her almost painfully. 'It was a sensational performance. Your professional virgin routine was quite brilliant,' he said, with vitriolic tones in his deep voice. 'You actually fooled me, do you know that? You really are a talented actress, Sophie. For someone like you to convince me that you were a sexual innocent was quite an achievement.'

'It was no achievement.' Sophie's long, dark lashes were wet with unshed tears. 'It was the simple truth.'

'It was a heartless charade.' He kissed her mouth again, but this time cruelly, making her wince as he crushed her lips. 'You had it all at your fingertips—the shy eagerness, the timid touches, the breathy little voice...' He gritted his teeth, as though he wanted to sink them into her throat. 'And then, when you knew that I wanted you, really wanted you, you slipped away, leaving me to read that—that contemptible, insolent little note. Well, I'm going to make you pay for that, Sophie.'

'Perhaps it was contemptible. But what you're doing now is even more contemptible.' A tear slid down her cheek, and Kyle watched it with hard green eyes.

'Tears are a very cheap currency in the theatrical world,' he observed coldly. 'They don't count for much.' His hands slid down to cup her slim waist, drawing her forward. 'However,' he said in a husky rumble, 'they are the first of many, and I must savour my reparation as it comes.'

Sophie's wet lashes fluttered closed as Kyle gathered the tear from her cheek with his lips, tasting the salt of her grief.

The gentle touch of his mouth made yearning flood her aching heart. Her knees buckled, and she sagged against him helplessly, her arms reaching for the hard strength of his man's body.

'Kyle,' she whispered brokenly, 'I need you so much...'

For a taut moment he held her, his mouth pressed against her hair. Then he thrust her away, his eyes glittering.

'It's called frustration,' he said tauntingly. 'Plain, painful, sexual frustration.' It seems we've both got a bad dose of it, my dear Sophie. Except that I have someone who'll relieve it for me. You haven't.' His eyes narrowed. 'Unless you're asking me to do it for you?'

She hated him at that moment. 'I'm not asking you for anything!' The percolator began to bubble, and Sophie turned dully to switch off the gas.

'Isn't that coffee ready yet?' Jenny asked, dancing into the kitchen with a big smile. She looked as fresh and pretty as a daisy, wearing a light cotton dress that made the most of her rather full bust. She nestled up to Kyle with all the possessiveness of a woman confident in her own attractiveness. 'Gosh, I feel better for that shower,' she said, looking up at him.

'You smell delicious,' Kyle said appreciatively, allowing her to mould her lithe body against his. 'I seem to recognise that soap.'

'It's Sophie's.' Jenny lifted her wrist for Kyle to smell her skin. 'Jasmine.'

'It smells different on you,' he smiled, his eyes sultry as they assessed the pretty young girl in his arms.

'I'll bet it does.' Jenny smirked at Sophie. 'Have you been telling Sophie what we did before breakfast?'

'She was intensely curious to know.'

'It was all quite innocent,' Jenny preened. 'But you should *see* Kyle's house, Sophie. It's practically a mansion! Late Elizabethan, you know, all oak panelling and marble floors—and the *biggest* garden I've ever seen in London, going right down to the riverbank.' She turned to look up at Kyle. 'You must be absolutely, impossibly rich, darling!'

'I struggle along. More to the point, where are we going tonight?'

'Somewhere special, darling.' Jenny was obviously delighting in showing off her new intimacy in front of Sophie. 'Somewhere really special!'

'I think I know just the place,' Kyle purred.

'And then,' Jenny giggled, leading Kyle into the sitting-room, 'maybe we can go back to your house again...?'

Sophie clenched her mind against the pain. She leaned against the kitchen wall, trying to find a way out. Her instinctive thought was flight. Get out of London, away from Kyle and Jenny.

Yet how could she just leave? She didn't even have her next job lined up, and for the time being she was tied to Joey.

Just how was she going to survive the ordeal that Kyle had planned for her?

CHAPTER SEVEN

'LUCIANI'S offering two and a half per cent of his cut,' Joey Gilmour said, booming down the telephone as usual. 'Since he's entitled to thirty-three per cent net under his contract with the backers, that means you'd be getting less than one per cent of the pre-tax profits. About point eight-three per cent, in fact.'

'That sounds quite respectable,' Sophie suggested.

'Depends what the profit is,' Joey grunted. 'If you'd had point eight-three per cent of his last film, you'd have had point eight-three per cent of blow-all. Look at it this way—*The First Day of Autumn* has to make a hundred thousand profit before you even get eight hundred back. Out of which you have to pay *my* ten per cent. And I don't think all of Luciani's films put together have made that much. We're not talking Hollywood here.' He made a 'tchah' noise. 'Let's not bother with it, Sophie. The man is offering peanuts.'

'I really want to do it, Joey.'

'My advice is to forget it.' Joey had been negotiating with Franco Luciani over the past couple of days, and had rung Sophie at home to give her the benefit of his opinions. 'Listen, the amount of enquiries I'm starting to get about you, you could have your pick of the plums in a month or two. Just sit tight for as long as it takes, and wait for them to drop into your lap.'

'I can't help feeling you're being far too confident about it, and that isn't false modesty. Besides, I want to be working. I can't just sit around here!'

'Listen, this guy is talking about starting filming in mid-September.'

'Yes. He says the light in Tuscany is remarkable at this time of the year...'

'The light in Tuscany?' Joey snorted. 'That isn't why he wants to bring the date of filming forward by six weeks. He's hustling you off to Italy quick-sticks, before you get a better offer. All kinds of people are asking after you, Sophie. It would be far better if you stayed around in London to be on hand for the right opening. If you disappear to Italy to do an art film with Luciani, you might miss something far more important.'

'But this film is important to me.'

'Why?'

'The script is very special. And I've got a feeling about it. I like Franco.'

'Will you do me a favour? Just give me another week to look around before you give Luciani an answer. If I don't come up with anything better, you can think about doing *The First Day of Autumn*. Is that a deal?'

Sophie agreed reluctantly, but as she put the receiver down, she was regretting having let Joey talk her out of an immediate decision. As far as she was concerned, there really wasn't a choice. She needed to take this film.

Even if the script hadn't had a special appeal for her, which it had, she would have jumped at it just to get out of England, and away from her misery. She couldn't face the prospect of sitting around waiting for a better proposal to come along. Not the way she felt right now.

By accepting Franco Luciani's offer, she would be flying to Italy in three weeks' time, and leaving Kyle behind her. Burying herself in work a long way from London was something that appealed very strongly right now.

She glanced at the clock.

'Damn!'

She was due to meet Hélène for lunch in an hour, at the Gay Hussar in Greek Street, a Hungarian restaurant much frequented by journalists, and one of Hélène's favourites. She had a lightning shower in between changing out of her dungarees into a smart dress.

Her own face in the mirror looked tired. There were shadows under the level grey eyes, signs of tension around the full mouth. The past three days had been almost more than she could bear. Pain and anger built up in her to explosion-point sometimes. It was hard to say which was worse—sitting alone in the flat every night while Kyle and Jenny were out, wondering what they were doing; or having to listen while Jenny enthused about last night's entertainments the next day, letting the bitchy side of her nature have full rein as she savoured yet another victory over her cousin.

Right now, thank God, Jenny was still asleep, after dancing till dawn at discos with Kyle.

As far as she knew, they hadn't yet made love. But Kyle was giving Jenny a tour of the most glittering night-spots and the most expensive restaurants, and Sophie knew it couldn't be long before he offered Jenny more. And Jenny, with her casual, open attitude towards sex, would take whatever Kyle offered.

While Sophie watched, helpless.

That Scorpio thirst for revenge: it was so strong. He hardly took his eyes off Sophie when he was at the flat; he was so intent on observing her reactions that he almost ignored Jenny. It was so obvious that his pleasure lay in wounding Sophie, rather than in Jenny's company, that Sophie sometimes wondered how Jenny could fail to notice.

Maybe Jenny *did* notice. She'd always taken intense pleasure in proving herself more attractive to men than her older cousin. Maybe the sense of personal, female triumph made it irrelevant that Kyle didn't really give a damn about her. Maybe it made the pleasure all the more intense. Kyle Hart, after all, was a prize like no other man they'd fought over.

Fought? That was a laugh. There was no competition here. There was no contest at all.

Sophie sighed shakily. Maybe she was being unjust. Maybe Jenny really didn't know how much she was being hurt. But how could she tell her, without spilling out the whole humiliating story of what had happened between herself and Kyle? And how could she trust Jenny not to take even more advantage of the situation, and make her pain all the worse?

She arrived at the Gay Hussar a little late, because the underground trains were running slow, and pushed her way through the crowded entrance. Hélène le Bon was already sitting at a discreet table at the back of the restaurant, but Sophie paused in shock as she registered that Kyle was sitting beside her, laughing quietly over some joke.

A cold wave of reaction gave her goose-flesh, but she forced herself to go on, and even managed a breezy smile as she arrived at the table.

'Sorry I'm late. Have you ordered?'

'Not yet.' Hélène gave Sophie a kiss on the cheek as she sat down. 'Kyle isn't staying for lunch,' she said brightly. 'Too busy making money. But I talked him into stopping for a glass of wine.'

'I'm not crazy about goulash,' Kyle commented. 'And I have clients to see.' His lazy green eyes drifted over Sophie's dress. 'Well, my dear Sophie, you look as fresh as a spring morning.'

'How kind. You look reasonably fit yourself—considering the marvellous time you evidently had last night.'

'"Pleasure and action make the hours seem short,"' Kyle commented calmly.

'Othello,' Hélène smiled, 'Act two, scene three. Where did you go last night, Kyle?'

'Dancing with a pretty girl.'

Sophie lifted the menu, her face reddening, and wondered what he and Hélène had been talking about before she'd arrived. Hélène, who had been watching them both with her luminous brown eyes, got to her feet.

'Would you two excuse me a moment? I have a couple of telephone calls to make!'

Kyle's expression was pure irony as he rose and watched Hélène head for the telephones.

'That's called bringing two people discreetly together,' he observed laconically, sitting down again.

Sophie looked at him briefly. He was wearing a dark suit with some kind of old school tie, obviously what he normally wore for work. But the exquisite clothes didn't hide the raw masculinity of the man beneath. In fact, he looked stunning, and that only made her feel all the more tense and ill at ease.

'Is it?' she said coolly.

'Hélène has only one flaw. She thinks that everyone has a right to happiness.'

'And you don't agree?' Sophie said, her long lashes hiding her eyes from him as she scanned the menu.

'I'm a realist. I believe in crime and punishment.'

'I've already gathered that. It's in your stars.'

'The fault, dear Sophie, is not in our stars, but in ourselves.'

'Is it my turn to guess the Shakespearean allusion? *Julius Caesar*, but I don't know the act or scene number.'

'Very good. Hélène thinks that a little honest, civilised talk would iron out all the problems between you and me,' Kyle said drily. He poured her a glass of the dark red wine he'd been drinking. Sophie thanked him, and took a sip. It was strong, almost metallic, but not unpleasant. 'Unfortunately,' he went on, 'she doesn't know that you're not honest, and that I'm not civilised.'

'What nice things you say, Scorpio,' Sophie shot at him angrily.

'My pleasure, Virgo.'

Sophie glanced at Hélène, standing at the telephone with her back studiously to their table, and grimaced. 'Hélène is not going to be back for at least a quarter of an hour,' she said wryly. 'So it looks like we have to talk, if only just to fill in fifteen minutes.'

'Even if the subject matter turns out to be uncivilised and dishonest?'

'I'll risk it,' she replied with a lightness she was very far from feeling. 'You've never even told me what happened with Emma's parents,' she reminded him. 'Have they decided on a divorce?'

'No, poor fools,' he growled. 'They've kissed and made up, and are giving the hoary old myth of happy wedlock another spin.'

'I'm so pleased for Emma's sake,' she said, wincing at his cynicism. 'She must be very happy about it.'

'She's delighted. But then, she's too young to understand the falsity of most human relationships.'

Sophie let that one ride, too. 'Did you go on that cruise with her?'

Kyle picked up his glass and drank briefly. 'After your little disappearing trick, we were both rather dazed,' he said drily. 'It wasn't exactly easy to explain what had happened to an eight-year-old child.'

'Kyle, I'm so sorry——'

'Don't prattle apologies,' he rasped, silencing her. 'As it happened, we left the hotel the same day. Somehow, I just couldn't face staying there another night. Not after you'd——' He bit off what he was going to say. 'We stayed with a friend in Kingston for a few days, then chartered a twenty-eight-foot sloop and spent a week sailing round Haiti. By the time we got back to Kingston, Emma's parents wanted her back, so we flew home to the happy family.'

'Did—did Emma enjoy it?'

'I suppose so,' he shrugged. 'It was a bit of an adventure for her. It did me good, too. Put things back in perspective.'

'Kyle, why can't you believe that I didn't set out to hurt you in Jamaica?' Her voice was low, urgent. 'You think it was some kind of deliberate plan, but it really wasn't like that! It was all so confused. When you didn't recognise me, I—I had this crazy idea to play a joke on you.'

'You consider it a joke,' he said bitingly, 'to go to bed with a man, knowing he thinks you're someone else?'

'I had no idea how we were going to turn out. I thought—I thought you just wanted a holiday romance with me. Something shallow and temporary——'

'That's all I ever did want,' he cut in brusquely. 'Don't kid yourself, Sophie. I never wanted anything more than that from you.'

Silenced, she fought back the tears.

He turned the wine glass absently, watching the scintillating ruby lights on the tablecloth, and went on, indifferent to her unhappiness. 'There was something about you that intrigued me, even in Brighton. You were good company in Jamaica, and you were kind to little Emma. But otherwise...' He shrugged his broad shoulders. 'All I really wanted was a painless affair with a pretty girl. So don't kid yourself that there was ever any chance of anything deeper.'

She fought for self-control in a sea of dizzy nausea. 'Then I'm glad we parted,' she said with an effort, 'before I was discarded for the next pretty face.'

'You haven't been discarded yet,' he said, with a return to that panther smoothness of tone. He smiled into her eyes. 'I haven't finished with you yet. You just watch this space, darling.'

Hélène was heading back to their table, and Kyle rose with an air of finality. 'If I don't leave now,' he said, threat turning to a purr, 'I'm going to offend a very important man in electronic components.' He kissed Hélène's hand, then bent to brush his lips against Sophie's cheek. 'I'm sure we'll see each other again soon,' he said with syrupy politeness, and was pushing his way through the crowds towards the bright street outside.

Hélène met Sophie's eyes guiltily. 'Oh, dear. It seemed a good idea at the time,' she said, covering Sophie's hand with her own. 'Judging by your expression, it wasn't?'

'Not really,' Sophie said, struggling to stitch a smile across lips that were quivering downwards in grief.

'Want to talk about it?'

'Not really.' She got a hanky out of her bag, and stopped any tears before they had time to show. 'Let's just have a lovely lunch, and talk about the theatre, shall we?'

Sophie went in to see Joey Gilmour two days later, and announced that she wanted to do the Luciani film.

He sighed patiently. 'OK, it's a very romantic script, and maybe the finished product will get rave reviews in little arty magazines and student newspapers. But it won't make a penny, I guarantee that. You'll come out with a few hundred pounds in direct fee, and you'll be lucky if you ever get a penny on top of that. I can get you ten times that just doing commercials here in London!'

Sophie was staring at a framed picture on the wall, showing Joey shaking hands with a famous stage actor who had died a year or two ago. 'I've never been to Pisa,' she said absently.

'She's never been to Pisa,' Joey repeated, throwing down his pencil. 'Let me get you a real contract to do a real film. Make a lot of money, then go to Pisa on holiday.'

She smiled at him tiredly. 'I think my mind's made up,' she said, and it sounded almost apologetic. 'I want to do Franco's film. I don't care about the money.'

'OK, so you don't care about the money,' Joey growled, slapping the desk. 'But this is a very important time for you, careerwise——'

'Oh, damn my career!' she said with sudden brittleness.

'I'm not sure I understand you,' Joey sighed, running his hand through his hair. 'You don't look happy lately, Sophie. You're pale, you're withdrawn, you sit there with misty eyes and tell me you don't care about your career—what's up with you?'

'Nothing,' Sophie assured him gently. 'I've just got a feeling about *The First Day of Autumn*. Whether it makes nothing, or makes a million, I know it's the right choice for me.'

Joey stared at her hard, then shrugged. 'OK. I'm not going to argue with you if that's the way you really feel. Do you want me to go ahead with the contract?'

'Yes, please.'

'And you're happy to start in mid-September?'

'Yes. I'll probably only be gone for two months, Joey. Franco wants to get the filming done before the early nights set in, so I'll be back well in time to take up anything else that might come in.'

'It's your life, sweetie. You're going to make one Italian movie director very happy, I can tell you that. The guy has hardly been out of my office this past week. Right, I'll get on to it right away.' He got up to usher Sophie out of his office. 'Just don't do a disappearing trick on me,' he warned, patting her shoulder. 'I'll need a contact number where I can reach you in Pisa, any time of the day or night. Your career is just opening up, kiddo, and you need to stay available.'

On the Tube, she sat thinking about her career, and facing up to the feeling that had been growing in her heart for some time, now. The feeling that she no longer wanted to be an actress.

Oh, yes, she had a certain amount of talent, and once she got established she would presumably always have work. A career lay in front of her, a vocation which might even aspire to success. But she doubted whether she would ever achieve true brilliance. She was no Hélène le Bon. And something had happened to her, something which had given her a deep distaste for her profession.

A life based on illusion, on dreams, a career made out of counterfeiting emotions she did not feel, earning the plaudits of people who did not know her, living lives and saying words that were never her own... Was that what she wanted?

It had all seemed so glamorous to her at eighteen, when she'd signed up for drama school. She'd always had a talent for theatricals, had always aspired to be an actress, but in the five years since then she had changed so much. Especially in the last year; especially since Kyle Hart had entered her life.

Like so many things in life, it wasn't nearly as simple as it had at first seemed. Drama as a pleasant hobby was one thing. Drama as a way of life had to satisfy something deep inside you, or it would only lead to disillusionment and failure. Doing *The Elmtree Road Murders* had been a very mixed experience. Touring with *Here*, *There*, and *Nowhere* had been frankly horrible. Unless you loved the stage, be it theatrical or cinematographic, it was a very hard life. So much depended on illusion, on pretence and imitation. And she was deeply wearied of pretence...

But what else could she do? She wasn't trained for any other kind of work. She couldn't even type or take shorthand. There was no escape from acting, not in the immediate future. She thought about Pisa, and *The First Day of Autumn*. Whatever changes were going on inside her, they would have to wait. The prospect of getting out of London was all that mattered to her right now.

She got off at St John's Wood, and walked slowly back to the flat. It was noon as she rounded the corner of her street, and stopped dead.

Kyle's sleek black Jaguar XJS was parked outside the flat, and Sophie's heart lurched, then sank like a stone into her stomach. Jenny wasn't in; she had gone shopping that morning, and wouldn't be back till later in the afternoon.

Kyle himself was reclining in the driver's seat. His eyes were closed, and Sophie thought for a moment of hope that he was asleep. But as she tried to steal silently past the sports car, his deep voice reached out to her.

'In a hurry?'

'I didn't want to wake you,' she sighed, turning slowly to face him.

'I wasn't sleeping.' Kyle stepped lithely out of the car, more pantherine than ever in a black denim shirt and jeans that moulded the hard, muscled length of his thighs. A thick leather belt circled his taut waist, the heavy brass buckle glinting. He was smiling, the green eyes chips of emerald between thick black lashes.

'Where's your delectable cousin?'

'Shopping,' Sophie said shortly. 'Probably buying smart clothes so you can take her out to smart places, and turn her smart little head.'

'Good. That's what I like to hear.' The smile glinted into a grin, making Sophie's pulses race into turmoil. God, she thought, as she faced him with outward defiance, of all the idiotically emotional women in the world, she must be the most illogical. Why did his mere presence reduce her to trembling shock, when she knew what a bastard he really was? 'Are you going to keep me out here all day?' he enquired, tilting one eyebrow. 'You might offer me a glass of wine.'

In silence, Sophie led him into the flat.

'And what,' he asked, as she busied herself in the kitchen, 'have you been doing all morning, little actress?'

'I went to see my agent,' she said shortly.

'Has he got a job for you?'

'As a matter of fact, yes.' She twisted the cork out of the wine bottle with something like satisfaction. 'I'm going to do the Luciani film.'

His eyes narrowed. 'I heard that the man was hardly offering enough to keep body and soul together.'

She flashed him a dry glance from cool grey eyes. 'You seem to know a lot about my affairs.'

'I hear things,' he said. 'When do you start filming?'

'Next month.' Like him, she was wearing denims, together with a suede jacket over a cotton top. She gave Kyle his glass of red wine, pulled the jacket off, and pushed past him into the sitting-room to hang it on the antique bentwood coat-rack. Kyle watched her movements with unsmiling attention.

'What do you mean, next month?'

'Next month. The month after this one. The middle of September, to be even more precise. I'll be flying to Pisa in a couple of weeks.' She caught the angry glitter that moved like summer lightning behind his eyes. 'What's the matter?' she asked softly. 'Are you annoyed that your prey might be getting away? You've got a fortnight left to torment me in, don't worry.'

'I don't want you escaping too soon.' He came towards her, his expression grim. 'How long will you be gone for?' he demanded roughly.

'Luciani's budgeting on being in Pisa around two months.'

He studied her face with grim attention. 'I'll be waiting for you when you get back,' he said in a threatening growl.

Sophie arched mocking eyebrows, instinctively knowing that she had suddenly gained the upper hand in this vindictive struggle for supremacy. 'Will you? But I may not come back. They say the male lead is quite a man.'

'Luigi Canotta?'

'Hmm.' She folded her arms over her neat breasts and tilted her chin up truculently. 'He's beautiful,' she said lightly. 'I'm looking forward to it very much.'

'Bully for you,' Kyle said, a note of harshness in his voice.

She sensed her advantage, and followed it home. 'Since you know so much about the film, you must know something about the script.' She smiled slightly as he shook his head. 'You don't? Oh, it's a very moving love-story. Very passionate in parts. It opens with me naked in bed with my lover. We've just made love, you see, and he's kissing my breasts... But let me get you the script, and I'll read you the relevant sections.'

She was walking over to get Franco's script when Kyle put his wine glass down and grasped her wrist, swinging her round to face him. 'You little Jezebel,' he rasped, eyes smoking at her like gun muzzles. 'I don't want to see the damned script.'

'Then you'll have to take my word about the passion,' she said, masking her intense triumph with a cool smile. 'Luigi Canotta is exactly the right man to do scenes like that with. Why, I'll hardly have to act at all. I'll just let myself go.'

'You've never let yourself go in your life,' he grated. 'And what would a man like Canotta want with a repressed virgin like you?'

She pulled her hand free. 'I thought I was a Jezebel?' she enquired with maddening poise. 'You're getting your metaphors mixed, Kyle.'

'No, I'm not. Because you're an unlikely mixture of both. Your cousin confirmed the truth for me.' Kyle's eyes gleamed. 'She told me you've never had a man in your life. You *are* a virgin, after all!'

'Well, perhaps that'll change in Italy,' Sophie shot back, her cheeks paling.

'Oh, I see,' he taunted. 'You plan to sacrifice your virginity to Luigi Canotta, on the altar of cinematographic art? Well, Franco Luciani likes the *outré* effects. Perhaps you can persuade him to immortalise the magic moment on film?'

Her free hand flew upwards of its own accord, cracking against his cheek. She'd finally been unable to just take it any more, and the slap must have stung. Kyle caught her wrist swiftly, and pulled her hand to his mouth, twisting it so that he could kiss her open palm.

'That way,' he went on, his eyes as bright as a cat's with amusement, 'we can all share the immortal experience that turns you from a spoilt-rotten little girl into a spoilt-rotten little woman.'

'Stop it!' She tried furiously to slap him again, and almost succeeded. He had to pinion both her hands behind her back to stop her.

'You're quite dangerous,' he said softly, looking down into her face with glinting eyes. 'Do you know something? You may not be as pretty as your sexy cousin, but you're a damned sight more entertaining.'

'Let me go,' she panted.

'In fact,' he drawled, drawing her against his hard body, 'Jenny bores me stiff. But you're something else.'

'Yes! I'm fool enough to be hurt by you, and you enjoy that!' Sophie's eyes flared grey fire at him. 'You accuse *me* of vanity. You've got a nerve, Kyle. Only a man whose vanity was colossal could dream up the sort of sick game you're playing. Why should it matter a damn to me whether you make love to my cousin or not?'

'Why indeed?' he purred. 'Why should I bother with Jenny, when it's *you* I really want to chastise?' He was holding her as close as a lover now, but the muscles of his arms were iron-hard as they immobilised her hands behind her back. 'So you really are a maiden,' he said with a husky laugh, studying her face with dark eyes. 'That changes my outlook about you, my dear Sophie. I now know a far better way of getting back at you.'

'What do you mean?' Sophie demanded angrily.

'You do realise that at your age virginity is tantamount to an aberration?' he asked softly. He was pushing her inexorably backwards as he spoke, forcing her towards her bedroom. 'You're twenty-three, and beautiful enough to make any man desire you. You obviously prize that maidenhead of yours very highly, to have clung to it for so long. What are you planning to trade it for? A wedding-ring?'

'Let me go!' she gasped, struggling vainly against Kyle's superior strength. 'You're hurting me, you brute——'

'But people in glass houses should never throw stones,' he went on, ignoring her protests. 'You obviously don't play poker, my love. Nobody puts their prize asset on the table. Not ever.'

He pushed her into her bedroom, and kicked the door shut behind him, then released her stinging wrists to twist the key in the lock and push it into his pocket.

'Kyle, for God's sake,' she whispered, starting to be really afraid. 'What are you doing?'

'What I ought to have done a long time ago,' he replied. 'What you really want me to do, deep down inside.' He smiled mercilessly. 'I'm going to have that precious prize of yours, my dear Sophie. I'm going to make you a woman.'

'No!'

'I think you mean yes.' His voice was a gentle purr to her sharp denial. 'Don't you want to know what all the fuss is about? Don't you sometimes wonder what it feels like, to be made love to by a man?' He walked over to her, his hands reaching to capture her slim waist. 'A man who knows exactly how to give a woman pleasure in bed?'

'Kyle, you've gone mad!' But she knew those flames that were now beginning to lick in his eyes, and she felt the response shudder through her own body.

'Have I? Then why can I feel you trembling with desire?'

'I'm trembling because you frighten me,' she managed. 'Please let me go, and get out of my bedroom——'

'Not until I've made love to you.'

'You can't force me to submit!'

'I won't have to,' he said with a smoky smile. 'By the time I've finished with you, you're going to be begging me to make love to you. Know that feeling? Like someone burning up with thirst, begging for water. That's the way I'm going to make you feel.'

He bent to kiss her mouth, his lips warm and possessive, the red wine on his breath.

She turned her face wildly away from him, struggling in fierce silence. But it was as though some veil in her mind were being torn open, forcing her to face the truth, that she wanted him, that his mood of raw sexuality was exciting her, sending the hot blood coursing through her veins.

'Do you remember that last time, in Jamaica?'

'I don't want to remember!'

'But I do. I want to remember, because that's where we left off...' Kyle's mouth was roaming across her throat, his lips almost devouring the scented skin. 'That's where we left off,' he growled breathily into her ear, 'and that's where my mind's been stuck for the past month, playing the same track over and over again, driving me crazy!'

She heard stitches rip as he pulled her cotton blouse open with contemptuous power, baring the feminine curves of her bra-less breasts, the dark nipples already thrusting eagerly outwards.

'Kyle, please,' she whispered, feeling sanity start to slip away. 'Don't do this to me!'

'Would you rather I were doing this to your cousin?' He slid his hand into her ruined blouse, and cupped one silky-firm breast in his hungry palm. His thumb slid across the aroused peak, making her whimper with response. 'Would you rather Jenny were in your place right now?'

Sophie pulled the torn corners of her blouse defensively over herself, tormented by his caress. 'No,' she whimpered, her mind reeling.

'Nor would I,' he laughed unsteadily. 'To make love to Jenny would mean nothing to me. But to touch you like this makes me burn inside—just as it makes you burn. Isn't that true?'

'No! You disgust me, you always have done!'

'Is that why you shudder when I touch you here?' He pushed her flimsy defence aside, and had only to caress her breasts to make her body arch with desire against him. 'Is that why your heart is trembling, like a trapped bird? Because you feel disgust?'

She tried frantically to fight away from him, but he merely laughed, deep in his throat, and pushed her back on to the bed.

'You won't face reality, will you?' With smooth movements, he stripped off the black denim shirt, revealing the muscled, tanned body that had haunted her memory for so long. 'You're infatuated with me, Sophie. You always have been.' Kyle sat beside her on the bed, his palms smoothing sensuously across the mounds of her breasts. He smiled down at her, handsome as Lucifer. 'You didn't object the last time I held you in my arms. In fact, you were melting like ice-cream in the sun. Or was that all part of the charade, too?'

'No,' she whispered, shrinking from the cruelty of that reminder. 'It was real.'

'Then why should you find my attentions so unwelcome now?' he mocked.

'Because in Jamaica you wanted me with passion in your heart. And now you only want to hurt me!'

Kyle's face darkened. 'Yes,' he said thickly, 'I had passion in my heart, then. What a fool I must have been, mooning over you like a love-struck boy. How did you keep yourself from laughing out loud?'

'I didn't laugh because I felt the same way! Because it meant something to me, something wonderful!'

'Fabricator.' His voice was like tearing velvet, and Sophie felt his fingers bite into her arms. He stared down at the pale oval of her face, his eyes hot green slits. 'You played your part sublimely well. You're a talented actress. Your only trouble was that you didn't run far enough, or fast enough, to get away from me.'

'Kyle, *no*,' she begged, as he slowly bent to touch her breasts with his mouth.

'But then,' he murmured, his breath warm against her skin, 'you'd have had to run to the other side of the world to get away from me. And even then, I'd have come looking for you. How did you ever think you could get away from me?'

The touch of his lips was ruthlessly seductive, making her moan brokenly, her eyes closing.

'I've dreamed of these pale, sweet breasts,' he said raggedly, his lips trailing down the panting valley between them, savouring the taste of her skin. 'The only thing missing is that perfume, that intoxicating smell. Do you know what really hurt me in Jamaica?' He looked up at her, smouldering-eyed. 'You put some of your perfume on that letter. As soon as I opened it, you were there in the room with me. And I couldn't get the smell off my fingers for days...'

'Oh, Kyle,' she said unevenly, 'I'm so sorry.'

'Where is it?' He rose, and stalked over to her dressing-table, long brown fingers searching through the small collection of cosmetics. He found the Giorgio Armani bottle instinctively, and lifted it to his nose. 'Yes,' he said softly, 'this is it.'

He walked back over to where she lay defenceless on the bed. Holding her gaze, he sat beside her again, and took the little glass stopper from the bottle. She flinched as he touched the icy wet tip to her skin, drawing a delicate line of perfume slowly down between her breasts.

The mysteriously seductive smell touched her, flooding her mind with memories. Stronger than wine, it brought the remembrance of that night back into her mind with intoxicating force, reminding her of her own loss, of the paradise she had once lost, and could now have again—at a price.

Kyle smiled, eyes dark as he assessed the effect he'd had on her. He put the bottle down on her bedside table. Then, without further words, he bent to kiss her mouth, hard, crushing her soft lips with ruthless passion. His tongue thrust like a flame between her teeth, plundering the sweet, moist depths of her inner mouth.

Sophie couldn't stop her arms from drawing him close, from clinging to him with trembling passion. She was aching for his possession now, all the pain turning to need.

He was so good to hold, so strong and confident, his maleness filling her senses. She hardly realised that her own nails were biting into the muscles of his shoulders, rough spurs that answered his own igniting need.

She whispered his name, twice, her hands caressing languidly across his warm, naked skin. The third time, his name turned into a gasp that caught in her throat as he caressed the swollen curves of her breasts, then bent to kiss the taut pink tips, anointing them with his tongue, firming them to unbearable hardness in his mouth.

She cradled Kyle's head in her arms, pressing her mouth into the crisp, thick hair, inhaling the clean male scent of him. His hands moulded her hips, drawing her close as he kissed her flanks, the smooth skin of her ribs.

'I've missed you so much,' she whispered. 'I thought I would die without you——' She broke off, arching as his teeth punished her nipples for the tender words.

'No lies,' he rasped. 'Just touch me.' He pulled his belt loose, unfastening the brass button at the waist of his denims. 'Touch me,' he commanded roughly. 'Touch me the way you did before.'

It was if she had no will of her own any longer. Her trembling fingers obeyed, moving timidly down the flat, muscled belly, down the opened front of his denims. The heavy zip slid open, as if eager to admit her.

The delicate touch of her fingers made Kyle arch against her, crying out her name.

'Sophie . . . you drive me crazy.'

It didn't matter that she hardly knew what to do; she had merely to touch her fingertips against the hot, swollen manhood that stretched his briefs to make him shudder with pleasure. Her whole body was trembling now. She hated herself for the way she was responding to him, yet she could no longer stop herself. Kyle was too strong, his effect on her too potent for her to fight.

She lifted her hips unthinkingly as he unfastened her jeans and pulled them down, discarding them on the floor. She was wearing only plain cotton panties with a lace trim, her body tanned and slim against the coverlet.

Groaning her name again, Kyle bent to bury his face against her soft belly, his powerful arms embracing the delicate curve of her hips. He raised himself on his elbow, meeting Sophie's swimming eyes.

'Have you any idea how much I want you?' He caressed her thighs, his palms savouring the silky skin. 'I want you so much that it's a fever.' He lowered his head to kiss the smooth skin of her thighs, close to the lace border of her briefs.

Sophie tried to will her body not to respond, not to betray her, but his touch was so expert, so exquisitely erotic. She shuddered in despair as she felt his tongue trace teasing circles on her skin, his breath warm and quick against her inner thigh.

Shame and grief made a choking sob rise in her throat. Sophie forced it down, covering her eyes with one hand, but she couldn't stop the trembling that shook her whole body.

'What are you trembling for?' Kyle mocked, sliding his thumbs into the lace of her panties, as though he was about to pull them down and expose her nakedness to his kiss. 'Am I hurting you? Haven't you dreamed about me every night since you left Jamaica?'

He must be a sorcerer, to know her mind like that! 'Yes,' she whispered, lowering her hand to look at him with swimming grey eyes. 'But not like this, so cruel and mocking——'

'Sex without love often has both cruelty and mockery in it,' he said brutally. 'Sex is an odd thing, Sophie. A man can dislike a woman, almost hate her...' his teeth grazed her soft skin, making her gasp '...and yet he can also desire her body. In a way, the anger makes the desire all the stronger, all the more potent.'

'It's not a game any more,' Sophie pleaded quietly, knowing this was her last chance to save herself from the destruction of being seduced by a man who hated her. 'Maybe you were justified in thinking I did something really bad to you in Jamaica. Maybe you were even justified in wanting to . . . to punish me. But you can't justify this, Kyle.'

'Do I have to justify it?' But, as though her unquestionable emotion had touched him in some obscure way, Kyle's hands slowly slid away, releasing her briefs. He moved, freeing her from the weight of his body. Feeling utterly naked and vulnerable, Sophie rolled away from him and curled into a ball of misery, hiding her face in her arms.

'Why are you doing this to me?' she whimpered, desire and pain mingling sickly inside her. 'Have I ever done anything to you that made you feel half as wretched as I feel now?'

'I don't know,' he said in a sombre voice. He watched her in silence for a moment, then went on quietly. 'If I'm wrong about you, then I don't know how you'll ever forgive me. Or how I'll ever forgive myself. But if I'm right about you, then it's no more than you deserve.'

'You're wrong about me,' she said passionately, lifting her head to glare at him with blurred eyes. 'You've been wrong about me from the very start.'

'Have I?' he said with a slow smile.

'You bastard,' she told him shakily. 'I wish to God you'd never come into my life!'

'And that sounds like my cue to leave.' He rose with fluid grace, zipping his denims and clipping the heavy brass buckle of his belt.

'Where—where are you going?' she asked, her chestnut hair tumbled around her face.

'Out of your life,' Kyle said flatly. He reached for his shirt and pulled it on, muscles rippling for an instant before the black denim covered his torso. 'I don't think I need to pursue my vendetta any longer. I've just discovered something—that I can't hurt you without hurting myself. So it's over.'

Her mind tried to grapple with the realisation of what he was saying. She reached numbly for her own jeans. 'What about Jenny, what you said you'd do——?'

'I'm not interested in Jenny,' he said with contempt, tucking his shirt in. 'I never had any intention of taking her to bed. You were all I was interested in. As it turned out, you were too easy to fool. It would only have been fun if you'd shown some spirit.' He turned and watched her as she got into her jeans and pulled a T-shirt out of a drawer.

When she was dressed, Kyle took the key out of his pocket and unlocked Sophie's bedroom door. She followed him out on shaky legs.

'Kyle——'

'What?'

'Will—will I see you again?' she whispered.

'You and I are like oil and flame—a dangerous combination,' he replied. 'We're better apart. We do nothing but harm to each other. I think we've both driven each other a little crazy...'

She hugged her aching breasts, pale-faced. 'Then it's all over?'

'Yes,' he answered indifferently. He walked to the door, and opened it. If he noticed that she was crying, he gave no sign of it. 'Enjoy Pisa,' he said laconically. 'It's a beautiful city.'

'Kyle!'

But he was walking out of her life, just as he had promised. Sophie ran to the door, but he didn't look back. He climbed into the black XJS, switched on the ignition, and drove off down the street without a backward glance.

Sophie was still standing numbly at the doorway of the flat as Jenny came walking up the street from the direction of the tube station. She came up the stairs, lifting her sunglasses into her red-gold hair.

'I've just seen Kyle driving away,' she said suspiciously. 'What the hell is going on, Sophie? What was he doing here?' Jenny looked closer at her cousin. 'You look like a bus just ran over you. Come on, let's get inside.'

Once in the little living-room, Jenny looked around, seeing the bottle of wine, and Sophie's opened bedroom door, the rumpled bed visible inside, the torn blouse on the floor. She stared at Sophie's dazed face, and then grabbed her arm. 'Sophie!' she said in shock. 'Have—have the two of you been making love behind my back?'

Sophie shook her head mutely. Jenny released her arm, her cheeks suddenly pale with anger. 'You're lying! I always knew there was something going on between you and him!' Furiously, Jenny flung herself into the chair. 'I might have *known*!' she snapped. 'I might have bloody well *known*.'

'Jenny——'

'God, I've been such a fool! You were all he ever wanted to talk about. Sophie, Sophie, Sophie. Endless questions about *you*. The man was obsessed with you—and he never so much as wanted to kiss me!'

'We've all gone a little crazy,' Sophie said tiredly, echoing Kyle.

'He was just trying to get at you, wasn't he?' Jenny's blue eyes sparkled with indignation. 'Just wanted to make you jealous enough to get you into bed with him!'

'You don't understand,' Sophie said wearily.

'I understand only too damned well. I've been a patsy.' She glared up at her cousin. 'So you've lost that precious virginity of yours at last. I hope you realise it was thanks to *me*.' She gave Sophie a twisted smile. 'Cat got your tongue? The least you could do is tell me what it was like! Marvellous, I expect.'

'If I told you the truth, you wouldn't believe me,' Sophie said quietly. Tears were flooding her eyes, tears of finality and loss.

'Oh, don't be silly!' Jenny exclaimed. She jumped up and hugged Sophie. 'Losing your virginity isn't such a big deal! You're much better off without the damned thing.'

But Sophie was crying so brokenly that Jenny looked afraid. 'Don't cry like that,' she pleaded. 'I know I've been a bitch to you sometimes, but I really care about you, you know that, don't you?' She hugged her cousin tightly. 'I'm glad you've won for a change. I was starting to think you must be frigid or something.'

Sophie tried to fight back her tearing sobs. 'You don't understand,' she said. 'But it—doesn't matter—any more. It's all over. It's all—over—now.'

CHAPTER EIGHT

THE Leaning Tower of Pisa was something Sophie had seen in countless photographs. It was as familiar to her as Big Ben, or the Eiffel Tower. Yet nothing could have prepared her for the sheer, stunning beauty of the building, with its slender columns of white marble soaring upward, row upon row. Even if subsidence hadn't caused the tower to start leaning sideways, centuries ago, making it an object of wonder, it would still have been one of the great monuments of the world.

As it was, the soft evening sunlight gave the leaning tower a surreal quality, its unlikely profile dominating the other, no less beautiful buildings in the long, grassy quadrangle.

Sophie stared up at it with misty grey eyes as the continuity girl arranged the folds of her skirt. It seemed to her like a symbol of human hope, once tall and lovely, now sinking slowly into absurdity.

She was sitting on the grass, reading Dante, and waiting for her lover.

At least, that was what was written at the top of Scene 217, being shot for the fourth time that evening.

Her lover, at that moment, was sitting a few feet away with a much-stained paper towel round his neck, having his make-up adjusted by Angela, the make-up girl. He was trying to drink a Coke at the same time, and chattering volubly to Franco Luciani over Angela's lean brown arms.

It was hard to keep your romantic illusions about an actor, even one as handsome as Luigi Canotta, once you'd got used to seeing him in a bib stuffed with cotton wool, having greasepaint applied over his features.

Her own face felt slightly stiff under the layer of lightener that made her look so pale. She was now dying. Or meant to be. What would it feel like, she wondered absently, to be really dying, on this romantic evening in early autumn?

It was impossible to imagine. And yet the sadness of Marjorie had entered her soul over the past weeks of filming, making her feel at times infinitely depressed. She had never quite realised just what a tragic script *The First Day of Autumn* was. But then, she hadn't felt quite this sense of acute loneliness when she'd first read it . . .

The scene was about to be shot again. The sound crew had checked the little tape recorder concealed in the folds of her skirt, and were now crouching over the bigger machines, headphones on as they listened for any intrusive ambient noise. Angela, the make-up girl, finished with Luigi and picked up her kit, hurrying over to check Sophie's face. A little work with a big, soft brush had the make-up to her satisfaction, and she trotted back to the cameras, calling out. 'They're ready,' to Franco Luciani.

'OK,' Franco said, uncurling his tall frame from the director's chair, 'let's go.'

'Wait!' several people called. The continuity girl pointed upwards. A patch of cloud was moving across the sun, changing the scene.

Everyone waited patiently for the cloud to drift its slow way out of the sky, which was now a clear eggshell blue, fading to yellow near the horizon. A beautiful, Italian sky, Sophie reflected, like skies nowhere else in the world. It was five o'clock in the evening, almost the end of October. She had been in Italy for six weeks, and *The First Day of Autumn* was now nine-tenths in the can. Franco had been true to his word: filming had been swift and without hitches, and within a short while her own part in the film would be over. The crew would be disbanded, and filming would resume in Rome, at the vast complex of studios known as Cinecittá. Sophie herself would soon be going back to England.

As the cloud headed serenely northward, someone started shushing the chattering crowd of tourists who were watching from behind the rope barrier that had been erected around the set.

Something like silence gradually prevailed. Sophie caught Luigi Canotta's eye, and he grinned at her. Over the past six weeks they had struck up an excellent rapport. Apart from a general conviction that he was God's gift to women, he was a likeable, amusing boy. Only three or four years older than Sophie herself, he was also a talented actor with whom she'd enjoyed working.

'OK,' Franco called, finally satisfied that all was well. 'Ready, Sophie?'

She nodded. Everyone was speaking Italian, but she'd learned enough in the past month and a half to understand everything that was said to her. Or almost. There had been a few mix-ups, but luckily these had been comical rather than disastrous.

One of the sound men lowered a foam-wrapped microphone on a long boom until it was hovering over Sophie.

'Cameras . . . action!'

She was staring at the book as the scene began, reading the beautiful lines of poetry. There wasn't much dialogue in this scene, but the action had to be convincing. These were the scenes she hated most, the scenes in which she had to counterfeit physical passion. Sometimes it was only with an effort that she could get through them, and Luigi's easygoing sense of humour really helped.

Luigi Canotta walked across the grass towards her. As his shadow touched her she looked up, smiled, and held out her arms to him.

Laughing, he sat down beside her and embraced her. They kissed, mouths miming passion as Sophie slowly sank down on to her back, Luigi on top of her.

As had always happened, at moments like this Sophie's mind flooded with thoughts of Kyle. With memories of *his* kisses, *his* touch. The rush of emotion was intense, covering her skin with goose-flesh. She had to force her mind to forget Kyle, and to relinquish the shuddering remembrance of how it had been with him. This was here, now. This was fiction.

One of the cameras had dollied forward on its tracks, and was now zooming slowly in for a close-up over Luigi's shoulder. The kiss broke off.

'What are you reading?' Luigi asked. The script was all in English; an Italian version would later be dubbed for distribution on the Italian circuits.

'Dante,' she told him, looking up at him with adoring eyes.

'Dante?' he laughed. 'Why does an English girl read Dante?'

'Because he speaks of our love,' she replied. Had she really once thought this corny script so touching? Or was she just getting blasé about it?

They clinched again, lips meeting in kisses that grew longer and more passionate. Sophie's arms twined themselves around the young Italian's neck, her eyes closed as she feigned the abandon of a woman in love.

But she was not a woman in love. In the cinema, months away, it would seem like a highly emotional scene. But to Sophie, right now, it meant almost nothing. She was thinking how absurd kisses were when there was no emotion to give them a meaning: grinding contacts of lips and teeth, empty and uncomfortable.

The kiss went on for longer than in the first three takes. Franco must be pleased with the way this take was turning out. Imprisoned by Luigi's embrace, Sophie was growing self-consciously aware of his body on top of her own. She could hear his breathing, taste the sweet trace of Coca-Cola on his mouth. She waited tensely for the end of the take, her hands restlessly caressing Luigi's back.

At last, Franco's voice broke into the silence.

'Cut!' he called, and came over as Sophie and Luigi broke their clinch. She had to restrain herself from wiping her mouth in distaste. She didn't want to hurt Luigi's feelings.

The director was smiling broadly. 'Excellent,' he nodded. 'Just right. We'll stop there for tonight—the light's going. I'll check the rushes tomorrow, but I think that last take is going to be just perfect.'

Luigi was pulling grass out of his clothing. He grinned. 'Pity. I was just getting into that scene.'

Sophie smiled, getting to her feet. It was Luigi's usual joke. In fact, they had already played far more intimate scenes, in bed. Luigi had been completely naked for some of them, Sophie herself wearing only briefs. She just hadn't had the depth of professionalism to carry off those scenes without embarrassment. Somehow, pretending to make love to a strange man in front of a watchful crew of ten or fifteen technicians had always made her feel acutely uncomfortable. She suspected it always would. Just what kind of actress, she wondered, was she?

'Tomorrow afternoon,' Franco was saying to Sophie, 'we'll start working on the hospital scenes. I'd like to have a short script conference tomorrow morning, to discuss some aspects of your part. OK, Sophie?'

'Fine,' she nodded.

'I'll run you home as soon as you are ready. Be waiting for you in the car.'

'Thanks, Franco,' she smiled. She borrowed cleanser from Angela, sat down on one of the canvas chairs, and started taking off her make-up amid the general confusion of packing up.

The heavy canisters of film were being unloaded from the cameras, and the road crew had moved into action, dismantling the other equipment for the evening.

They were moving location tomorrow. With the illogicality of film-time, the sequel to scene 217 had already been shot, a few days ago. They'd come to the Leaning

Tower this evening because, it being a Wednesday afternoon, there would be the fewest tourists.

When she was ready, she gathered her belongings into her kitbag, said goodnight to Luigi and the crew, and walked over to Franco's big silver Mercedes-Benz. As he drove her through the busy centre of Pisa towards her hotel, which was out in the countryside, Franco was eagerly discussing the next phase of filming. The hospital scenes were the last in the film; Marjorie was to overdose on heroin and be rushed into a clinic, where she was destined to die.

The 'clinic' was actually a beautiful sixteenth-century *palazzo*, now an old-age home run by nuns, in which Franco had hired a floor for a week. He was very enthusiastic about the setting, which was admittedly beautiful.

But then, old buildings in this part of Italy had so much charm. Even her hotel was exquisite; it never failed to lift her heart to come back to the Pensione D'Este after a tiring day's filming. An old Tuscan farmhouse set among cypresses, it had immense charm.

She said goodnight to Franco and went up to her room, which overlooked a central courtyard. Just at the level of her windows a huge pergola supported a leafy vine, which was now heavy with dark grapes. If she'd wanted, she could have reached out and plucked one of the dusky fruits...

She showered, and got into a loose cotton dress, then went downstairs to the dining-room. There were no more than half a dozen guests, and it was a quiet evening. She ate a light supper of minestrone followed by fresh strawberries. Her appetite was practically non-existent these days, which was all to the good. The extra-slender pallor made her performance as Marjorie all the more convincing...

A week. Not much more than that, and she would be going back to England. Back to everything she had left behind her.

She didn't want to go home. Her memories were still acutely painful.

The weekend after that last scene with Kyle was still rather hazy in her mind. Jenny and she had hardly spoken. Still put out at having 'lost' Kyle to her cousin, Jenny had been offended that Sophie was unwilling to discuss what had happened. It was so natural for Jenny to boast about her conquests of men that she hadn't been able to comprehend that Sophie wanted to keep her experiences with Kyle private.

Eventually, they'd made it up, but by then Jenny's feelings had been hardly relevant any more. Sophie's sense of hurt and loss had been impossible to shed. More than ever, she had been overwhelmed by her sorrow, her incomprehension, and her hopeless love for Kyle.

It was now almost a whole year since they'd first met, in Brighton, and Sophie realised that for those twelve months he had hardly been out of her thoughts for a single day. He had haunted her from the first moment they'd met. In that long spell between Brighton and Jamaica, she had dreamed of him, and for three miraculous weeks in Jamaica he had been hers.

Even the savage period of his 'game' with Jenny had made her love him still further. She would rather have Kyle tormenting her than not have him at all. Than have this emptiness, this vacuum...

How had it all turned so sour? When she looked back at the decisions she had taken, at the way she had left him, with that cool little note, she found it almost impossible to explain her own behaviour. She'd treated it all like a game, but it hadn't ever been a game. Kyle's feelings for her had been deep and true, and she'd made a mockery of them.

The truly sad thing was that she knew in her heart that Kyle's feelings towards her were still profound. He would never have expended so much passion on trying to wound her if he hadn't really still cared, deep down. That Scorpio temper...what a tragic waste.

He was out of her life now, forever. She lived in dread that one day she would hear, or read, of his marriage. That was a blow that she truly dreaded. How could she not dread it? Kyle was the only man she had ever loved, and she would never stop loving him, not until the end of her days.

She tried not to think about Kyle at all, but the memories were obtrusive, and she had been in the habit of dreaming about him for so long that it was almost impossible to break. His loss made her whole future seem so dark, so without hope. What *was* her future? Where did the path forward lie? Sometimes she felt she could not see it at all...

These past weeks in Tuscany, she had been feeling more and more insecure as an actress. She had lost something vital, the will to impersonate someone else's feelings, and it astonished her sometimes that Franco and the others couldn't detect that. At times she felt utterly naked, the script empty words in her mouth, her actions mechanical and without life.

What was she going to do when she got back to London? Joey kept promising great things, but she felt so unprepared for any more work that she didn't know what she was going to say to him. Maybe she would go home.

It was months since she'd been with her parents. Maybe a few weeks in Scarborough, listening to that gravelly North Sea rhythm, would help clear her cloudy head. She was beginning to see why nervous breakdowns were so common in the acting profession. Once you began to doubt yourself, the strain on you became enormous...

She went up to her room after dinner, and stared at the pages of a book. As the Italian dusk deepened, the sweet trill of a nightingale sounded from the distant cypresses, to be answered by another, then another...

Enchanted by the exquisite song, she put down her unread book, and went to the window.

The evening sky was deep violet, streaked with gold and crimson. A soft, warm breeze was blowing, smelling of the distant Mediterranean.

While the twilight gathered, a deep peace stole all around. As she looked down into the courtyard, her heart faltered.

A tall figure was standing under the pergola, looking up at her window. A figure so like Kyle that she thought she must be dreaming. She laid a hand instinctively over her suddenly racing heart.

'Kyle?' Eyes wide with shock, she stared for a few seconds longer, then turned and ran to the stairs. She was praying that it wasn't a mirage as she raced down the tiled staircase, her breath fast and uneven. Would he be there when she got down? Had he been a figment of her grieving heart's imagination?

She pushed the door open, and stepped out into the twilit courtyard, her mind spinning. It hadn't been an illusion.

Kyle was standing where she had last seen him, motionless, a dark, tall figure that had haunted her mind for so long. They stared at each other tautly for a long moment. She couldn't speak for emotion.

Then he walked slowly over to her, those deep, beautiful eyes staring down into her face. 'God help me,' he said huskily. 'You're so very beautiful, Sophie.'

'Kyle, what——?' Her voice caught in her dry throat. 'What are you doing in Italy?'

'Looking for my salvation.' He looked tired, and his chin was dark with stubble. The jacket he was wearing was grey vicuña, soft as a cloud. He reached out to touch her face with gentle, almost hesitant fingers. 'Looking for forgiveness from a woman whom I've hurt beyond forgiving. Looking for you, Sophie.'

'Oh, darling,' she whimpered, melting into his arms, almost too stunned to take his presence in.

His arms wrapped around her, the way they'd done in countless dreams. Except that this was real.

'Can you forgive me for my stupidity and cruelty?' he asked huskily, his mouth pressed into the fragrant curls of her hair. 'Since you left, I've ached for you until I thought I'd go out of my mind...'

'There's nothing to forgive,' she whispered.

'I've been standing out here, trying to gather the courage to come in and see you.' His voice was strained. 'I—I didn't know how you'd receive me.'

Curious faces were peering at them from the windows. 'Come up to my room,' she begged shakily. 'We can't talk here!'

She took his hand, and led him up to her little room, now bathed in the crimson and gold of the sunset. As she shut the door behind them, Kyle took her in his arms with the urgency of a drowning man, and started covering her face with kisses. Sophie clung to him, gasping at the male passion she felt in the rigid muscles of his body.

'I love you,' he whispered, his mouth finding hers for a dizzyingly deep kiss. 'I've lain in bed dreaming of you beside me, and waking to loneliness and regret. I told myself to wait until you got back from Italy, but I couldn't stay away. I had to come and find you. I've been in Italy for two days.'

Her eyes were closed in bliss. She felt as though a pain of months had suddenly been taken away, to be replaced by a throbbing delight. 'Why didn't you come to me as soon as you got here?'

'I had to pluck up the courage.'

'Do you need courage to face me?'

'I need courage to face how much I need you, how much I adore you... I stood among the crowd watching you working yesterday and today. Watching that boy pretend to be your lover——' His arms tightened, their formidable strength almost crushing her. 'It tore me apart. I thought I'd die, standing there, seeing another man kissing you, holding you in his arms, making love to you——'

'Oh, Kyle! None of that is real!'

He cupped her face in his hands, kissing her mouth. 'I've thought so many times of that threat you made—that you'd have a love-affair with Luigi Canotta——'

'Of course I haven't done that,' she laughed unsteadily. 'It's all only fiction, my love,' she said, looking up at him with eyes that were filling with tears of unbearable emotion.

'With you, I can no longer distinguish between what is real and what is fiction,' he said quietly. 'All I know is that without you my life is a barren wilderness, without hope. I can't go on without you, Sophie. I love you, with all my heart and being. I want us to put the dark past behind us, and enter the future together.' He drew a deep, ragged breath. 'I want you to marry me.'

Joy filled her, making her legs weak. If this was a dream, and she woke up alone, she would kill herself.

'I'm yours, Kyle. I always have been! Oh, Kyle—you don't have to marry me. Just let me be close to you!'

'Close?' He touched her wet eyelashes with his lips. 'My love, I'm going to grapple you to my soul with hoops of steel. For God's sake, tell me you forgive me for the way I behaved in London!'

'I forgave you even before you hurt me,' she said softly.

'How much I must have made you suffer. I was half mad, my darling. During that bloody awful cruise with Emma, I just brooded and burned. I got no sleep, no peace. I swore I'd have a terrible revenge on you for doing that to me. When I got back to London, I wanted to come round to your flat and tell you exactly what I thought of you. But I didn't trust myself not to weaken and break down. I had this horrible vision of me making a fool of myself in front of you, telling you how much I loved you—and you laughing in my face!'

'How could you ever have had such an idea about me?' she asked numbly.

'My mind was distorted with pain and disappointment. It was that Scorpio need to strike back that you once spoke about. All I could think of was punishing you, even though somewhere, deep down beneath my anger and hurt, I knew that you really did care about me. When Hélène mentioned your cousin Jenny, I suddenly realised how I could get at you.'

Sophie shuddered. 'You chose a very cruel weapon. When I thought I'd lost you to Jenny, my heart almost broke.'

'God forgive me,' he whispered. 'As if I could ever have any serious feelings towards that feather-brained little flirt . . .' He drew her close, his lips closing on hers. 'I adore you. I can't live without you.'

'I'm the one who needs forgiveness,' Sophie whispered, a long while later. 'What I did in Jamaica was imbecilic. But I was so afraid, Kyle. So afraid of losing you that I had to run away. I didn't know how deep your feelings were. I didn't think they could possibly be as deep as mine!'

'Sophie . . .' They sank down on to the bed together, Kyle's magnificent face tight with emotion. 'That night in Ocho Rios, the night before you left . . . I was going to ask you to marry me.'

She felt the blood drain from her heart. 'Kyle!'

'I'd only known you three weeks—or so I thought. But I knew there would never be anyone like you again. I started to get terrified of losing you. I had this sort of nightmare that one day you would suddenly be gone.' He pulled a wry face. 'Little did I know how soon that nightmare was going to come true! I wanted to ask you to be my wife after we'd made love. But things didn't work out that way. I told myself I would ask you the next day. I spent hours lying awake, and rehearsing a stupid little speech. And I, too, was terribly afraid. I knew you wanted me, but it was so hard to tell how deeply you cared. If at all. You were so mysterious, so hard to fathom. You made me feel so uncertain, so clumsy——'

'My love,' she said brokenly, 'I had no idea. Oh, if I'd only known!'

'After you left, it was as though my soul had been poisoned,' he went on, shaking his dark head. 'I was so bitter, so desolate. I wanted to come racing after you, but my pride wouldn't let me. It took a long while for it to sink in. Sophie Aspen, not Sophie Webb. The Sophie I fell in love with in Jamaica was the same girl I'd once laughed at in Brighton.' His eyes were dark as they looked into hers. 'Well, I've paid for my folly, my darling. If I hurt you in Brighton, if I was stupid and blind and didn't look beyond appearances, you made me pay tenfold in Jamaica. I've never felt so crushed in my life.'

'I was afraid that once you knew who I really was you'd lose interest in me,' she said in a husky voice. 'I thought it might happen all over again—that you'd find me absurd and ridiculous——'

'Sophie.' He took her hands. 'When I met you in Brighton, you were an overweight girl in heavy spectacles, wearing shabby clothes, with lank black hair. You were a strange creature, then. So drab and plain. Even when you came off set, Maisie still seemed to hang over you. You were uncertain and shy, yet there was something about you that intrigued me. What I saw on that beach in Ocho Rios was an exciting, beautiful woman with a slender body and chestnut hair. Tanned, poised, graceful, hiding mysteriously behind dark glasses. It was nine months later, in another world. Do you find it so hard to understand how I didn't recognise you?'

'I was still the same person,' she smiled tremulously.

'Yes.' His expression was bitter. 'I've been so blind. When I first met you in Brighton, I should have seen beyond appearances. I should have listened to the voice in my heart that was telling me you were something special, something wonderful. But I let you slip through my fingers. I hurt you then, and I hurt you in London—but I swear I'll never hurt you again.' He paused, gathering his thoughts. 'Remember that I told you I hadn't watched *The Elmtree Road Murders*? Well, of course I did watch it. There was no ladyfriend. And while I watched, I had the weirdest feelings. I was remembering it all so clearly. Remembering you, in Brighton. There was something so familiar about you, when we next met in Jamaica. I was sure I knew you well, but I could never put my finger on it. You appearance had changed so much that it was impossible for me to recognise you as Sophie Aspen. And the longer I was with you, the harder it got for me to pin-point that mystery. I thought that this feeling that I knew you was natural, because we were so perfectly suited. I didn't realise that I was already in love with you.' His voice gentled. 'But I didn't fall in love with your face or your figure. I fell in love with *you*, with the woman you are inside. And I've realised something else over these past few weeks of misery—that if I'd only got to know you better in Brighton, I would have fallen in love with you then.'

She laughed quietly. 'The idea of magnificent, passionate Kyle Hart falling in love with ugly little Maisie Wilkin is crazy!'

'Not so crazy. You were in disguise, though. You fooled me, not once, but twice! Sophie, my sin lay in not looking beyond appearances. My only plea is that it's a very common male fault. We men are fools. We tend to judge women through our eyes, rather than through our reason. We're terrible blockheads that way. All I can say is that your appearance made it easy for me to get to know you in Jamaica. And to know you was to love you. I've learned my lesson. You're the only woman I have ever wanted to marry. The only woman who ever got through my defences far enough to make me feel an emotion I thought I could never feel, an emotion that I thought was beyond me...love.' He brushed his lips over her half-open mouth. 'I've never known love before. I never will again.' Their kiss deepened. She felt his hand cup her breast, caressing the soft curve with trembling hunger. 'I'm madly, irrevocably in love with you, Sophie,' he whispered. 'I want to spend the rest of my life proving it to you. And I'm not leaving here until you say you'll marry me.'

'You're not leaving me at all, not ever. Not ever again. And yes, I'll marry you, my love. Without you I'm nothing, you see. If I don't marry you, I'll just wither up and die, and blow away on the wind...'

She clung to him, arching her neck ecstatically as he kissed the hollow of her throat, that favourite place he so loved to kiss. She ran her fingers through the thick, crisp roots of his hair, just losing herself in the scent and the feel of him. Suddenly, they didn't need any more words. Clinging together, they sank back on to the bed, mouths seeking, kissing, adoring. The tension of long separation was starting to coil like a spring between them, making them ache for release.

'We'll marry as soon as we get back to London,' he was planning thoughtfully. 'How much longer must you stay here?'

'A week.'

'Just enough time to get a really big wedding on the go! But...does that boy have to kiss you again?' Kyle asked, dark eyes searching hers.

She smiled dreamily. 'Luigi? Hardly. There's only a week's filming left, and Marjorie has to die soon. Quite appropriate, really, when you think that Sophie is starting a new life.'

The emeralds of his eyes were bright with love and amusement. 'My little actress, how I love you!'

'I'm only an actress for one more week.' She was deadly serious as she looked into his eyes. 'I want nothing more than to be your wife, Kyle. I don't have any ambitions after that. This is the last film I'll ever make, Kyle. I'm never going to act again. From now on, I only want reality—the reality of our love.'

'Sophie, that isn't what I want,' he said gently, caressing her slim flanks.

'It's what I want,' she replied tenderly. 'I just can't do it any more. I was getting desperate. I don't want anything except truth from now on. I don't want anything that will take me away from you, not for so much as a day. I don't ever want to have to kiss another man, or to have to pretend another love. I'm going to take marriage to you very seriously, Kyle. I'm going to put every ounce of myself into it. Into loving you, loving our children, making sure nothing ever goes wrong again——'

'Nothing ever will,' Kyle vowed.

'Make love to me,' she whispered.

His eyes glittered. 'Here? Now?'

'Here and now. I've waited so long that if I have to wait any longer I'll go mad!'

He was kissing her throat, his fingers flicking open the buttons of her dress. 'Don't you want to be a virgin on your wedding-day?' he whispered.

'No,' she said simply, 'I want you, now!'

'Scorpios have stings, little virgin.'

'Go on,' she invited, her eyes dreamy as he started kissing her naked breasts. 'Sting me...'

The twilight had deepened into velvety darkness. In the deep blue sky, a golden moon slowly rose over the Italian cypresses until it was high enough to shine in at an open bedroom window, where two lovers were learning the old, secret, mysterious language of love. But the moon was too old to be shocked by anything it saw through open bedroom windows...and the lovers never even noticed.

Just answer these simple questions for your FREE book

1 Who is your favourite author? ____________________

2 The last romance you read *(apart from this one)* was? ____________________

3 How many Mills & Boon Romances have you bought in the last 6 months? ____________

4 How did you first hear about Mills & Boon? *(Tick one)*
❑ Friend ❑ Television ❑ Magazines or newspapers
❑ Saw them in the shops ❑ Received a mailing
❑ other *(please describe)* ____________________

5 Where did you get this book?

____

6 Which age group are you in? ❑ Under 24 ❑ 25-34 ❑ 35-44 ❑ 45-54 ❑ 55-64 ❑ Over 65

7 After you read your Mills & Boon novels, what do you do with them?
❑ Keep them ❑ Give them away ❑ Lend them to friends
❑ Other *(Please describe)* ____________________

____

8 What do you like about Mills & Boon Romances?

____

9 Are you a Mills & Boon subscriber? ❑ Yes ❑ No

Fill in your name and address, put this page in an envelope and post TODAY to: **Mills & Boon Reader Survey, FREEPOST, P.O. Box 236, Croydon, Surrey. CR9 9EL**

NO STAMP NEEDED

Name (Mrs. / Miss. / Ms. / Mr.) ____________________

Address ____________________

____

____________________ Postcode ____________

You may be mailed with offers as a result of this questionnaire

PWQ1

'Over the years I've learned that you have this endearing ability to spot a chance to make a profit further than a leopard can spot a limp,' Jake said.

'Why must you always believe the worst of me?' Shiona demanded.

'Perhaps because it's so easy to believe the worst of you.' Jake smiled a slow smile as his eyes swept over her, and one hand reached up suddenly to cup her chin.

'Look at that mouth.' His thumb brushed her lips, sending prickles of sensitivity quivering through her. 'That is the mouth of a temptress, a seductress. A mouth that was made for lies—and kissing.'

Books you will enjoy
by STEPHANIE HOWARD

ROMANTIC JOURNEY

Vittorio de Esquerez denigrated Kate's journalism and the serious magazine for which she worked; just because he was wealthy and successful, he thought he could walk over anyone who got in his way. But she'd show him—she desperately needed to get her story, and she intended to get it, no matter what!

KISS AND SAY GOODBYE

Eve Adams felt that at last everything was beginning to go right for her—she had the perfect country cottage, and even a charming, handsome neighbour. But then the arrogant Rodrigo Garcia Marquez came into her life—and everything became much more complicated!

A MATTER OF HONOUR

It was vital that Beth find her stepbrother, Giles—that was why she had come to Italy. The last thing she needed was to be haunted by Lorenzo dei Cesari. After all, she had been warned about him. So why should it hurt so much that he clearly despised her?

DANGEROUS INFATUATION

There were simply no words to describe adequately Angela's feelings about Sheikh Rashid al-Hazar. He thought he could do what he wanted, when he wanted and how he wanted. And he wanted her out of the country. But she had no intention of giving up her job on his paper—even if it meant putting up with his male arrogance!

BATTLE FOR LOVE

BY

STEPHANIE HOWARD

MILLS & BOON LIMITED
ETON HOUSE 18–24 PARADISE ROAD
RICHMOND SURREY TW9 1SR

All the characters in this book have no existence outside the imagination of the Author, and have no relation whatsoever to anyone bearing the same name or names. They are not even distantly inspired by any individual known or unknown to the Author, and all the incidents are pure invention.

First published in Great Britain 1991
by Mills & Boon Limited

This edition 1992

ISBN 0 263 77306 X

Set in 10 on 12 pt Linotron Palatino
91-9202-48628
Typeset in Great Britain by Centracet, Cambridge
Made and printed in Great Britain

CHAPTER ONE

SHIONA was watching from an upstairs window when the car appeared at the foot of the driveway.

Instantly, she felt herself tense and the butterflies in her stomach grow stronger, as the immaculately shiny black Mercedes headed swiftly for the forecourt below her and drew to a halt with a splutter of gravel.

She glanced at her watch. He was a few minutes early. Clearly, he was anxious to see her, and that, she sensed, could only mean trouble.

'Don't worry, I'll get it.' As she turned to leave the room, she caught sight of Inge hovering out on the landing.

'Thanks, Miss Fergusson. Is it OK if I leave now?' The plump au pair blushed a little coyly. 'I have an appointment in the village.'

'Of course it's OK.' Shiona smiled kindly. 'Just do me one favour before you go. Tell Nettie that Mr MacKay has arrived, and ask her to be good enough to bring us some tea.'

'Of course, Miss Fergusson.' The blonde girl nodded and headed swiftly for the stairs.

'Oh, and Inge. . .' Shiona stepped out on to the landing. 'Be sure to pick up Kirsty from school at four.'

'I won't forget.' As Inge plunged down the stairs

and headed for the kitchen at the back of the house, Shiona watched her go with an almost envious smile. If only I was as carefree right now, she was thinking.

Then, bracing herself, she strode to the top of the staircase and stood gazing down the wide, sweeping curve of it to the imposing hallway and the big front door. I shall wait until he rings before opening, she decided. No need for him to know that I was watching at the window.

She started down the stairs, her steps deliberately unhurried, breathing deeply to calm her twanging nerves, and paused for an instant to scrutinise her reflection in the massive gilt-framed mirror that hung above the banisters.

A pale oval face with wide hazel eyes and a halo of shoulder-length auburn hair, as bright as burnished copper, stared back serious and unblinking. She gave herself a shake. No need to look so anxious. Whatever he's come for, he's not going to eat you!

She pinched her cheeks quickly to add a little colour, and straightened the skirt of her plum-coloured sweater-dress before squaring her slim shoulders and resuming her descent.

Not only was he not going to eat her, she thought crisply, he would not even manage to unnerve her. These days she was more than a match for his bullying!

A few steps from the foot of the crimson-carpeted staircase Shiona paused, her eyes fixed on the front door. Any second now he would ring the doorbell in his usual autocratic, impatient manner. But she would wait a full minute at least before answering. She wasn't his little slave girl any longer.

But in that very same instant, momentarily demolishing her composure, the door burst open with the force of an explosion and a tall dark-haired figure in a charcoal-grey suit came striding purposefully into the hall.

He paused at the foot of the stairs to look up at her. 'How very thoughtful of you to hurry down to greet me. I hadn't expected so eager a welcome.'

Of course. He had a key. Stupidly, she had forgotten that. Her expression far from eager, Shiona looked back at him. 'Hello, Jake,' she offered. 'You made it, I see.'

'Of course I made it. Why wouldn't I have made it?' He had come to lean against the foot of the banisters, looking up at her with a spark of challenge in his eyes. 'Were you perhaps hoping that I might fail to keep our appointment?'

Shiona suppressed a mirthless smile. He had read her mind with perfect accuracy. When his solicitor had phoned to make the appointment, refusing to say why his client wished to see her, she had secretly prayed that fate might intervene and mercifully save her from this meeting.

She had seen him only once during the past three years—two bleak weeks ago at the funeral, when her grief had been so great that she had barely registered his presence. And she had sincerely hoped that that would be their last meeting ever.

Now she let her eyes travel over his arrogant face—the aquiline nose, the wide caustic mouth, the straight black eyebrows, the firm aggressive chin—and hated the way her heart quivered inside her. Once, she would have laid down her life for this man, and the memory of that devotion could still make her soul weep.

But as she shifted her gaze back to his eyes—eyes as brightly blue as the bluest summer sky and such a startling contrast with his almost-black hair—that momentary tremor inside her was extinguished. She remembered how cruelly those eyes could look at her, turning her blood to vinegar in her veins. And the memory strengthened the hatred within her.

In a cool voice she answered, 'I thought you might be late. You have come quite a distance, after all. New York isn't exactly just a few miles down the road.'

'I got back from New York late last night.' The blue eyes watched her from beneath long black lashes. 'It took me just over an hour to drive here from Edinburgh.'

'I'm surprised you found your way. You're such an infrequent visitor. These days you seem to spend most of your time in the States.'

He smiled at that. 'I spend a fair amount of time there.' Then the smile altered slightly. He raised one dark eyebrow. 'How very flattering, my dear Shiona, that you should keep such a careful check on my movements.'

Shiona grimaced in response. 'Please don't feel flattered.' How she hated the way he called her 'my dear Shiona'. The false endearment grated on her nerves. 'If I kept a careful check on your movements—which I don't—I can assure you it would not be for sentimental reasons.'

Jake held her eyes. 'Don't worry,' he parried. 'It would never for one moment cross my mind to accuse you of being a sentimentalist.' He stepped back from the banisters. 'But enough of these pleasantries. I suggest we make ourselves comfortable and get down to business.'

As he spoke, he had already turned abruptly on his heel and was leading her in swift strides across the wide hallway. Then he was sweeping through the doorway of the main reception-room, with Shiona having to hurry in order to keep pace with him.

She glared at his back, hating him warmly—the self-assured set of the broad, powerful shoulders, the unfaltering step of those lean athlete's legs. Everything he did seemed like a statement of his authority. Even the simple act of crossing a room.

But what was this business he had referred to? What was this meeting supposed to be about?

Before she could ask, he paused in mid-stride, so that she almost went crashing right into him. 'Shall we sit by the window?' he enquired, glancing down at her. Then, without bothering to wait for her answer, he had swung round again and was heading imperiously for the group of gold-brocade-covered armchairs that stood in the curve of the huge bay window, overlooking the sun-burnished waters of Loch Lomond.

'How beautiful it is at this time of the year.' He

paused for a moment to glance out of the window. Then he turned back to Shiona. 'But, I'm forgetting. . .' His eyes lit up with a mocking little smile. 'The rustic delights of a Scottish spring aren't really to your taste. You're a big-city girl. What you love are all those glitzy London shops where you can indulge your weakness for expensive baubles.'

The malice in his tone scraped at Shiona's nerve-ends. So, he was at it already, she thought, straightening her shoulders. The same old accusations, the same scathing comments. But he was mistaken if he thought that he could upset her. Nothing Jake might say could upset her any more.

Averting her gaze, Shiona sat down in one of the armchairs, smoothing the skirt of her dress over her knees. 'You're right, I enjoy my life in London. As a city it has a great deal to offer—especially to someone like myself who works in the rag trade. But I also love it here.' She swivelled her eyes round and paused for a moment as they meshed with Jake's. 'Why else would I have set up my workshop near Killearn?'

'Why else, indeed?' His tone was sharp with irony. 'I suggest *you* know the answer to that one.'

'And what are you implying?'

'Implying? Nothing. But let's just say it has crossed my mind to wonder why you were so keen to keep a foothold in this part of the world.'

'It used to be my home.'

'Only very briefly. You only lived here for a couple of years.'

'I lived here for three years, if you want to be

precise.' Shiona's tone was tight with resentment. She narrowed her eyes and added in clipped tones, 'I know you always thought of this as *your* home and that you never wanted me to be a part of it. But, like it or not, it became my home too, the moment your father married my mother.'

At the mention of her mother, her tone suddenly faltered and a pain like a lance went driving through her. It had still barely sunk in that just over two weeks ago her mother and her stepfather had been killed in an accident.

Her eyes dropped to her lap. She stared at her hands. 'Another reason for setting up my workshop near here was so that I wouldn't lose touch with my mother.'

'And my father. Let's not forget my father—the goose who laid the golden eggs.'

He was still standing over her, his back to the window, so that his features were shrouded in shadow. 'Well, your devotion paid off.' His tone was cynical. 'You now have a half-share in my father's house.'

What a foul suggestion! 'How dare you say that?' Quivering with anger, Shiona turned to glare at him. 'I happened to be extremely fond of your father!'

'Of course you were. And even fonder of his money. You were extremely fond of all the MacKay men—and they all let you wrap them round your little finger. With one significant exception, of course.' He paused and laughed roughly beneath his breath. 'But then, I, my dear Shiona, saw through you from the start.'

Jake had been hurling these same insults at her now for years, and by now she ought to be totally immune to them. But, ridiculously, they still hurt as much as ever. The poison in his words burned like gall through Shiona's veins. The only difference now was that she did not show it. She had failed to acquire immunity, but she had learned to fake it.

'You're wrong about one thing.' Shiona eyed him harshly. 'I was fond of your father and I was fond of your brother, but I can't say I was ever the least bit fond of you.'

'You cared about none of us!' He dashed her claim aside. 'All you ever cared about was what you could get out of us! Well, you've had all you're getting, my sweet little stepsister, and that's the reason I'm here today—to assure you that I intend to finally put an end to your grubby manoeuvres to extract money from my family!'

As her cheeks paled visibly, he went on without mercy, 'You may have succeeded in getting your greedy little hooks into my father and my brother, but you're never going to get them into my sister. So you can forget right now any ambitions you might have as far as Kirsty is concerned!'

'What sort of ambitions? What are you suggesting?' Suddenly Shiona was trembling with outrage, but her tone was as cool as tempered steel as she told him, 'The only ambition I have regarding Kirsty is to be appointed as her legal guardian!'

'That's what I mean.'

As his eyes drove into her, she had a sudden sharp insight in to what he was here for. She narrowed her eyes at him and warned him icily, 'If you've come here with some idea of trying to block my petition to become Kirsty's guardian, I warn you right now you're wasting your time!'

As she said it her heart tugged with emotion at the thought of her five-year-old little sister, the daughter of Jake's father and her own mother, so recently and so tragically orphaned.

She looked Jake in the eye and demanded flatly, '*Is* that the reason why you're here?'

But, alas, she was destined to have to wait for an answer, as Nettie, the housekeeper, chose that very moment to come into the room carrying a tea-tray.

Oblivious of the anger that crackled in the air, she cast a welcoming smile in Jake's direction. 'It's nice to see you again, Mr MacKay.'

'It's nice to be here,' he replied with a composed smile, seating himself at last in one of the armchairs, as the woman arranged the tea things on a small table in front of them. 'I was just saying to Miss Fergusson how very beautiful it is.'

Shiona darted him a quick look, her heart still pounding. Who would ever guess from the benign expression on his face that just a moment ago he had been exploding with anger? He was like a chameleon, she thought with wry admiration, able to adapt at will to any situation. Which was why, of course, no one else had ever guessed at just how much he had always loathed her. The expression of that loathing had been reserved exclusively for her.

And yet for years I adored him, she thought with horrified wonder. For years I allowed him to treat me like dirt. But he's wrong if he thinks he can push me around now. Those bad old days are gone for good.

She raised her eyes to Nettie, her composure equal to Jake's now. 'Don't worry, Nettie, I'll do the honours.' She reached for the teapot and poured without a tremor. 'Thanks,' she smiled, as the woman turned to leave.

When they were left alone, a silence descended, broken only by the click of silver against porcelain as Jake helped himself to sugar and stirred. Shiona picked up her own cup and sat back in her seat, eyeing Jake over the rim as she raised the cup and drank. Then she laid the cup down again and turned pointedly to look at him.

'We were talking about Kirsty,' she prompted in a cool tone. Yet her heart fluttered anxiously inside her as she said it. What exactly had he meant by that stupid, spiteful threat?

'That's right, we were.' His eyes slid round to look at her, but he did not pursue his earlier tirade. Instead, he cast his gaze round the room where they were sitting. 'Naturally,' he informed her, 'I intend to buy you out.'

That threw her totally. 'Buy me out of what?'

'The house, my dear Shiona. Your share of the house. As you are aware, my father left half of it to each of us.' He smiled without humour. 'A most unfortunate arrangement. Surely he can't have imagined that we would wish to live together?'

What an abominable prospect! Shiona pulled a face. Then she informed him crisply, 'But I don't intend to sell.'

Jake sighed a little impatiently. 'I'll pay you a good price. You don't have to haggle. I don't intend to cheat you.'

'I'm not interested in your price. I don't intend selling. In fact. . .' She paused. 'You've given me an idea. I would much prefer to buy your share from you.'

'What the devil for?' His impatience was growing. 'Stop playing silly games and just accept my offer. The house means nothing to you. I'm sure you'd much prefer the money.'

He really did believe that money was all she cared about! Shiona felt her hackles rise in anger. 'I don't want your damned money and I don't intend selling! You're wasting your time by trying to persuade me!'

'And why won't you sell?' Jake's tone had grown flinty. 'What good is half a house in the middle of Scotland to someone who spends all her time down in London?'

'I don't spend all my time down in London! That just shows how little you know about my affairs! I make frequent visits to the Killearn workshop and I need a base for when I'm in Scotland. In the past I've always stayed here at Lomond View, and that's precisely what I intend to carry on doing!'

Jake sat back in his chair. 'OK, so you need a base, but surely you don't need one quite as big as this?' As he spoke, with forced patience, he stabbed his fingers through his hair and narrowed his eyes at her in irritation. 'With the money I'm prepared to pay you for your half of the house you could buy a more than adequate little base for yourself—and still have change left to indulge in a few luxuries.'

He smiled condescendingly. 'Just think,' he told her, 'you could treat yourself to a trip down Bond Street and splurge on a few trinkets and some new clothes for your wardrobe.'

'How kind of you to be so preoccupied with my needs.' Shiona's tone was heavy with sarcasm. 'But I've already told you you're wasting your time. I haven't the remotest intention of selling.'

'And why would that be?' The blue eyes narrowed thoughtfully. 'Perhaps, after all, you really do secretly relish the thought of sharing a house with me.' He let his eyes travel over her, openly appraising, as his gaze took in the firm, high breasts, softly moulded by the cashmere of her sweater-dress, then drifted down to the dip of her waist and the womanly curves of her hips and thighs.

'Is that what's behind this strategy of yours? Are you hoping to get to know your stepbrother better?'

In spite of herself, Shiona was aware of a warming of her skin from her scalp to her toes, and her reaction both humiliated and angered her. It reminded her of the old days when just a passing glance of his could reduce her to a state of burning confusion.

She pulled herself together, swallowing hard, and forced herself to look him straight in the face. 'I already know you as well as I could ever want to. And besides, it would take a stronger stomach than mine to contemplate furthering our acquaintance.'

As he simply smiled at her reaction, she hurried

on to ask a question of her own. 'But surely you're not intending to move in here permanently? You already have a house in Edinburgh.'

'I already have several houses, my dear Shiona. And, no—I'm sorry if this disappoints you—I'm not planning to move in here on a permanent basis. But it would make rather a lovely weekend home.'

'A little large for one, surely,' she countered, taking pleasure in turning his own words against him. 'Wouldn't it be more sensible to sell your share to me and buy yourself a smaller place?' She fixed her hazel eyes on his and elaborated, smiling, 'You could treat yourself to a few trinkets with the change.'

He smiled back at her briefly, but his eyes remained hostile. 'It is you, not I, who have a penchant for trinkets. Particularly when you don't have to earn the money to pay for them.' Then, before she had a chance to rebut that accusation, he added, 'And besides, I really wasn't planning to spend my weekends here alone.'

I'll bet you weren't! Shiona smiled thinly, but refrained from voicing her suspicions out loud. What did it matter to her, after all, that he no doubt planned to entertain his ladyfriends here?

Instead, she assured him. 'Neither was I. The reason I intend to keep my stake in this house is so that Kirsty and I can use it when we come up to Scotland.' She paused. 'Which brings us back to what we were speaking about. . . Kirsty and my application for custody.'

She looked straight into his face. 'I asked you a

question and I'm still waiting for your answer. Do you intend to stand in my way?'

He smiled a veiled smile and sat back in his seat. 'Yes, as a matter of fact, I do.'

'You can't be serious!'

'I'm afraid I'm most serious.'

'But why?' Shiona frowned at him with irritation. 'Why on earth would you want to do that? Who do you expect to look after her if not me?'

His gaze never flickered. 'Me,' he answered.

But that was preposterous! 'You? You're joking! You're never in the country! How can you possibly look after her?'

Jake did not answer her question directly. He flicked imaginary dust from the sleeve of his jacket and informed her, 'As you must surely be aware, Kirsty has already been placed in my custody.'

'Temporarily,' Shiona hastened to remind him. 'Only an interim custody order has been granted. The court has still to make its final decision.'

'Which, in due course, it will make in favour of me.'

Shiona could scarcely believe what she was hearing. She swallowed. 'I find it hard to believe you're serious. I was surprised when I found out about the interim order, but I assumed that was only a convenience measure, because you're resident in Scotland and I'm not. It never occurred to me that you intended to apply for permanent custody.'

She cleared her throat. 'I don't know why you're doing it, but it strikes me as being quite inappropriate.'

Jake looked back at her levelly. 'I have many reasons for doing it, the principal among them quite simply being to ensure that you never get your hands on my sister. That would really be "inappropriate".'

So he was acting out of spite. Anger welled up in her. 'You're despicable! Would you really play around with a five-year-old's future just because you have a grudge against me?'

He was unrepentant. 'You, my dear Shiona, are the one who has plans to play around with her future. All I'm doing is protecting her—from you.'

She couldn't let that pass. Not a second time. Shiona thrust up her chin and looked straight at him. 'Kindly explain what you mean by that.'

Jake shook his head impatiently. 'Don't play the innocent. We both know exactly what I mean.'

'I'm afraid I don't.' That was not quite truthful. She had learned how to read Jake like a book. But she refused to let him off with insinuations. If he had something to say, let him come out and say it!

Relentlessly she pressed him. 'Kindly explain.'

With a sigh of impatience Jake leaned back in his seat and ran his fingers through his thick dark hair. 'OK, I'll spell it out to you, if that's what you want. My father left Kirsty a considerable amount of money to be held in trust until she reaches eighteen. . .' He paused. 'Do I really need to go any further?'

'I'm afraid you do.' She would not let him off the hook. 'I haven't the least idea what you're getting at.'

Jake shrugged. 'OK. If you insist.' He laid his arms along the arms of the chair, his long, tanned fingers cupping the curved ends. 'Let me put it as delicately as I can. I don't wish to offend you any more than I need to. . .'

Shiona smiled cynically. You had to hand it to him. He could play the good guy so convincingly. Little wonder that, once, she'd been totally taken in. Then she tensed as, after a brief pause, he continued.

'A girl of eighteen is highly impressionable, easily influenced by those who are close to her—particularly in matters relating to money. Few young people have much business sense. . .'

Shiona nodded. 'I would agree with that.' She lifted her eyebrows. 'So, what are you saying?'

'What I'm saying is this. . .' The blue eyes pierced through her with that cold, callous look that once was capable of breaking her heart. 'If you were, as you were hoping to be, her legal custodian, you would be in a very powerful position—and I have reason to fear that you might abuse that power.'

She had known he would say that, but still her heart was thundering. 'Abuse it in what manner?' she heard herself asking.

'Come, come, my dear Shiona. You know perfectly well what I'm talking about. We both know that if you were ever to find yourself in such an influential position, my sister's inheritance would not long remain her own.'

It took all of Shiona's strength to keep her body from trembling. She would not let him see how much he had offended her. That would only give him pleasure.

She counted to ten inwardly. 'You're so damned predictable. Don't you ever get tired of insulting me?'

'You demanded the truth and now you've got it. It's not my fault if the truth happens to be unpleasant.' He smiled a false smile. 'Believe me, my dear Shiona, if I could, I'd much prefer to say something pleasant.'

'*You* say something pleasant to *me*? I'm sure you'd sooner cut out your tongue!'

As he smiled with cool amusement—without denying it, she noted—Shiona added, 'However, what you said was not the truth. It was just a vicious slander, based on nothing more substantial than your obsessive dislike of me!'

'Oh, no, my dear Shiona, it's based on much more than that.' Jake leaned forward in his seat to fix her with a look. 'Over the years I've learned that you have this endearing ability to spot a chance to make a profit further than a leopard can spot a limp. You ruined my brother. You left him penniless. You won't get a chance to do that to Kirsty!'

'I did not ruin your brother!' That was a mean and vicious slander. 'All I did was try to help him!'

'Oh, sure, you helped him! You helped him to spend his money! As we both know, that's something you're exceedingly good at.' His blue eyes flayed her, as he demanded harshly, 'Do you deny that he died with barely a penny to his name?'

She could not deny that. Shiona shook her head stiffly.

'And do you deny that for the two years prior to

his death you'd been living with him in his flat in London?'

'We shared the same house, but we weren't living together. Not in the way you're trying to suggest.'

'Liar!' Impatiently, Jake sprang to his feet. 'I've heard all these pathetic lies of yours before—but the facts of the matter speak for themselves. When you moved in with Ryan he was a wealthy man. By the time he died he was financially ruined. Parties, holidays, trips abroad. . . God knows the ways you found to help him fritter away his fortune.'

He bent suddenly to imprison her, his hands gripping the arms of her chair, his face thrust forwards furiously, inches from hers. 'Where are all the presents he no doubt bought you? The jewels, the diamonds, the baubles you're so fond of? Do you have them locked away in a bank vault? Do you take them out from time to time and gloat?'

What he was saying was horrible, and miles from the truth. And it struck Shiona, not for the first time, as she looked into those blue, accusing eyes, how easy it would be for her to clear her name.

He was so sure he was right, so sure he knew everything, so absolutely certain she deserved his dislike. But if she'd wanted to she could easily have told him something that would have stopped him dead in his tracks. That she chose to remain silent was out of loyalty—just one of the many little attributes that, according to him, she did not possess.

She faced his dislike now without flinching, and answered in as calm a voice as she could manage, 'I can assure you Ryan never bought me anything—

certainly not all these diamonds you keep inventing.' Then, as he shook his head at her disbelievingly, she demanded, 'Why must you always believe the worst of me?'

'Perhaps because it's so easy to believe the worst of you.' He smiled a slow smile as his eyes swept over her, and one hand reached up suddenly to cup her chin.

'Look at that mouth.' His thumb brushed her lips, sending prickles of sensitivity quivering through her. 'That is the mouth of a temptress, a seductress. A mouth that was made for lies—and kissing.'

As he paused, Shiona felt a sudden rush of anxiety. Surely he wouldn't. . .? Her heart tightened within her.

But he made no move to close the gap between them, as his deep blue gaze continued to caress her.

'And this hair. . .' He let his fingers tangle in its brightness, sending jolts of electricity skittering across her scalp. 'This is the hair of a wild free spirit, full of secret, sensuous promise. A man might sell his soul just to bury his face in it.'

He lifted up a handful of burnished tawny curls and let them slide silkily through his fingers. 'The hair, too, you see, is the hair of a temptress.'

His eyes seemed to darken as his gaze slid lower. 'This body is the body of a temptress also.' And, as his hand moved downwards, Shiona shrank back in her chair, every muscle in her body tensing.

But he did not touch her, though it felt as though he had, as his hand curved round the outline of her breast. And to her shame and horror Shiona felt her nipples tighten and press hard against the softness of her dress.

This unfortunate development did not go unnoticed. A wolfish smile lit up his eyes.

'I see you also have the soul of a temptress. It is clearly something beyond your control.' He touched her mouth again with the flat of his thumb, making her heart thud strangely inside her. 'You make it very difficult for any man to resist you. No wonder my poor brother fell under your spell.'

'It wasn't like that.' At last she found her voice and struggled to sit upright in her chair. Just for a moment there he had seemed to hypnotise her. Even now she felt oddly drugged by her nearness to him.

Jake smiled disbelievingly. 'More lies, my sweet temptress? But your lies, alas, will get you nowhere with me.' He straightened suddenly and looked down at her coldly. 'Ryan was a good man, but he was easily influenced. You will not find it quite so easy to get round me.'

Then he smiled lazily, his eyes flitting over her. 'I have nothing against sampling what you have to offer, but I warn you you will gain nothing in return.'

'I'm offering you nothing and I want nothing from you!' A flash of belated anger brought her back to her senses. Shiona sprang to her feet to confront him furiously. 'You think you can intimidate me, but you're mistaken! I'm not scared of you, Jake MacKay! If you think you can claim custody of Kirsty, you're wrong. You'd ruin her life, and I won't let you!'

'You're the one who'd ruin her life. And take my word for it, you'll never have her!'

'Oh, but you're wrong! I love my sister. And I'll fight for her, if need be! What sort of home could you possibly give her—even if you were suitable as a parent, anyway? Would you have her dragged up by a succession of au pairs and housekeepers while you went gallivanting all over the world? Is that the sort of future you intend to provide for her?'

'And what sort of future would you provide, surrounded by your glitzy London friends? A future of wild parties and extravagant spending?' Jake laughed a hollow laugh and regarded her flintily. 'Perhaps you're hoping she'll end up like you? Poor Kirsty. That's the worst thing anyone could wish on her.'

The insult hurt. It made her catch her breath. But with an effort Shiona forced herself to swallow it. 'What I can provide for Kirsty is security and love. Financially, I have the wherewithall to give her a very good life. And since I'm my own boss, my hours are flexible. I can work while she's at school, and be at home when she needs me.

'What's more, I intend to hire a live-in nanny to give me a hand and to be there when I can't. And there's a very good school near where I live. Don't worry, I'll see that she has everything she needs.'

She paused for a moment before pointedly adding, 'As to your other point, I must confess I think it would be worse if she ended up like you.' She spoke the words softly, but with feeling. 'Anyone who's prepared to use a child as a pawn just to score points in some personal vendetta has to be just about the lowest form of life. You *know* that Kirsty would be better off with me. You know I love her. You know I'd look after her.'

'What a hypocrite you are!' Jake's tone was lethal as he looked down at her with eyes that had turned to blue ice. 'When did you ever look after anyone except yourself? The only reason you want custody of Kirsty is so you can get your hands on her inheritance. You're the one who's playing games with an innocent child's future!'

'I'm doing nothing of the sort. I wouldn't dream of doing that!'

'That's just as well, for you'll get nothing out of her. Not a single penny, I assure you. For if I have my way, when this custody suit is over you'll never set eyes on Kirsty again.'

Shiona could see from his eyes that he meant it. She felt her cheeks pale just at the thought of it. But even as she looked back at him, hating him, loathing him, a new thought suddenly popped into her head.

With new confidence she looked back at him. 'I think you're fooling yourself. What court is going to award custody of a five-year-old girl to a single man who's constantly overseas on business? Especially when she happens to have a half-sister who can provide her with a stable and secure home in London?' She allowed herself a thin smile of triumph. 'I think you'll agree your case is pretty hopeless?'

He did not answer immediately. He stuffed his hands in his trouser-pockets and regarded her with enigmatic eyes. Then, to her surprise, he conceded, 'You're absolutely right. Put like that, my case does sound pretty hopeless.'

'I'd go so far as to say that you're wasting your time even to think of applying for custody.'

'Yes,' it looks that way.' He glanced away for a moment, his gaze seeming to drift beyond the window to the loch and the granite peak of Ben Lomond beyond.

Shiona felt a shaft of sudden optimism. Perhaps he realised he'd been rash. Perhaps he wasn't going to fight her, after all.

But then he glanced back at her, and his expression had hardened. 'However, the situation is not quite as you've described it.'

Shiona felt herself tense. 'In what way?' she demanded.

'There is one small detail I have omitted to tell you, and that I feel will have a certain bearing on the judge's ruling.' He smiled a harsh smile and held her eyes as he told her, 'You may be able to offer Kirsty a comfortable single-parent home in London, but I can offer her a great deal more than that. . .'

'An ultra-luxurious single-parent home in Edinburgh, in which the parent is regularly absent?' Shiona threw him a hard look. 'You'll have to do better than that!'

Jake held her gaze. 'Then how about this. . .? What if I could offer her a proper home, a proper family, with *two* parents? What if I could offer her both a father and a mother?'

Shiona's stomach tightened. 'What are you saying?' She did not like the smile of relish that was suddenly creeping over his features.

'What I'm saying, my dear Shiona, is really very

simple. . .' Jake smiled sadistically as he prepared to drop his bombshell. 'What I'm saying is that I can provide something that you cannot—a proper family set-up for Kirsty to grow up in.

'You see, my very dear Shiona, I'm planning to get married in a couple of weeks' time.'

CHAPTER TWO

'MARRIED? *You*? In a couple of weeks' time?' Shiona gasped and blinked disbelievingly. 'You can't be serious! You're pulling my leg!'

'Absolutely not. I'm deadly serious. What's the matter? Did you think that no one would have me?'

Jake smiled as he said it, knowing perfectly well that no such thought had ever entered her head. After all, he was an eminently eligible man, attractive and immensely wealthy. There must be dozens of women who'd be only too happy to marry him.

She had dreamed of it herself once, Shiona thought with a painful flutter. But that was before she had taught herself to hate him.

'So, you see. . .' Jake was smiling down at her triumphantly '. . . I think you will agree this rather changes the situation. If you foolishly persist in pressing your claim for custody, you'll be wasting both your time and your money. And I know how much the latter means to you, my dear.'

For once, Shiona barely registered the insult. Her brain was spinning with the shock of his revelation. He was right, his getting married changed things dramatically. In any fight for Kirsty he would definitely have the edge.

She had a sudden dark suspicion that he was doing

this deliberately—cold-bloodedly engineering a convenient marriage just to do her out of custody. But almost in the same instant she rejected that idea. Surely no one, not even Jake, could be as calculating as that?

'So aren't you going to congratulate me?' His tone was taunting. 'Aren't you going to wish me every happiness for the future?'

No, she damned well wasn't! Shiona eyed him abrasively. 'Who is this woman you're planning to marry? Do I know her? Have we ever met?'

'I'm afraid you haven't yet had that pleasure.' With a smug smile, he reseated himself in his armchair and, lifting his cup, took a swig of his tea. 'She's a lovely person. She'll make an ideal wife—and a perfect mother for Kirsty, of course.'

'You're sure about that?' Shiona remained standing. 'You're quite sure she's a fit person to be a mother to my sister?'

'Oh, yes, my dear Shiona, I'm absolutely sure. She'll be a far better mother than you're capable of being.'

That hurt, but Shiona did not show it. 'You haven't told me yet who she is.' Her expression was impenetrable as she faced him. 'Is there some secrecy surrounding her identity, or does this fiancée of yours have a name?'

He smiled right through her. 'There's no secrecy, dear Shiona. Her name, since you're so curious, is Janice.'

'And does she do anything in particular, this

Janice? Does she work? Does she have a career of some description?'

'Yes, she works. She's an executive secretary.'

'Yours?'

'Not quite, but she works with my firm.'

'How very convenient. Once you're married, you'll be able to have her at your beck and call twenty-four hours a day.' She smiled at him acidly. 'That should suit you right down to the ground.'

Jake smiled, quite unperturbed by her sarcasm, and helped himself to a shortbread biscuit. He took a bite. 'I'm afraid not. Once we're married, she'll be leaving the company. Janice plans to stay at home and devote herself to looking after me and Kirsty.'

'Don't jump the gun!' He was being just a bit too sure of himself. 'You haven't been awarded custody yet!'

'But I will be. You'll see.' He took another bite of his shortbread. 'Face it, Shiona, you haven't a hope.'

She had to admit it looked that way. What judge would award custody of a five-year-old girl to a single working woman down in London when there was a proper home, with both a father and a mother, waiting for her right here in the country of her birth?

With a little inner sigh Shiona turned to the window and gazed out thoughtfully at the loch. As much as she wanted Kirsty to be with her, she could see that she might be better off with Jake. And little Kirsty's welfare was the only thing that mattered.

She turned round slowly and looked Jake in the eye. 'If you can convince me that you can make Kirsty happy, believe me, I won't stand in your way.'

Then, as he raised surprised eyebrows, she added a warning. 'What I decide, however, depends on what I think of Janice. I have to be convinced that she'll make a good mother.'

'I already told you. . .' Cruel blue eyes looked straight back at her. 'She'll make a far, far better mother than you ever could.'

'That's your opinion.'

'It'll also be the judge's—if you're so foolish as to go ahead and fight me.' Jake sat back in his seat and surveyed her critically. 'What kind of mother could you possibly be when you're working all day and out partying all night? Looking after a child is a full-time job, not something to be slotted in when you have a spare moment.'

Out partying all night! That would have been comical if it hadn't been so downright offensive.

But Shiona kept her cool, though her tone was contemptuous as she responded. 'Lots of mothers these days manage to work and look after their children perfectly well. And I've already explained to you how I would arrange things.'

'Ah, yes, of course, the live-in nanny to look after her while you're out enjoying the high life.'

'What high life are you talking about?' She breathed deeply with irritation. 'I spend most of my evenings, as it happens, at home.'

Jake laughed out loud. 'Pull the other one! Don't tell me you've lost your taste for nightclubs and fancy restaurants.'

'I never had any particular taste for nightclubs and

fancy restaurants. That's a fable you invented all by yourself.'

'Lord, but you're good!' Jake shook his head scornfully. 'If I didn't know better, I might almost believe you.' Then, as she skewered him with a look of pure detestation, he reached out suddenly and caught her by the wrists. 'But I know all about you, remember! Beneath that wholesome, respectable façade you put up, I know what you're really like!'

'I doubt that very much!' Shiona wriggled to be free of him. 'You may think you do, but you know nothing about me!'

'I don't *think* I do, I *know* I do!' He rose to his feet to hold her more firmly. 'And you know exactly how I came to know—and how you influenced and finally ruined my brother!'

Shiona felt her control desert her for a moment. 'How can you believe that?' Her heart twisted inside her. 'All I ever did was try to help Ryan.'

'You mean help yourself!' Jake would never believe her. His eyes were like splinters as he glowered down at her, yet in their depths she could see the pain that tormented him.

He had loved his younger brother with a fierce, protective love capable of showing no mercy to those who sought to harm him. That was why she knew he would always hate her. He believed she had brought about Ryan's downfall.

He shook her roughly. 'Ryan trusted you. He loved you, for pity's sake! How could you do what you did to him?'

His pain and anger were like a lance twisting

through her. Shiona could scarcely bear to look at him. And there was nothing she could say in her own defence. Her promise to Ryan had sealed her lips forever.

Almost to herself she murmured, 'I loved him, too. I promise you it wasn't like you think.'

But Jake wasn't listening. He wasn't interested in her denials. His eyes were hard as he tightened his grip on her.

'So, you see, I don't intend to let history repeat itself. There's no way I'll let you get your hands on Kirsty.' He narrowed his eyes at her. 'Don't waste your time here. Just pack your bags and get on back to London.'

'I'll pack my bags when I'm good and ready——' Shiona eyed him defiantly '—and not a moment before!'

'But you're wasting your time. You have nothing to stay for!'

'That may be, but *I'll* decide when I leave!'

'Unless, of course——' Jake's eyes glittered down at her. 'Unless your reason for hanging around here is simply to irritate me with your unwelcome presence.' As she tried to tug her hands free, he jerked her closer, so that her body was pressed against his. 'Is that what's behind this stubbornness of yours?'

'Don't be so stupid! Just let me go!' Shiona writhed against him as he simply held her tighter.

'First, answer my question,' he insisted. 'Do you secretly enjoy getting in my hair?'

She looked up into his face, anger seething through her, and was surprised to see that he was smiling.

Then as his hand released her wrist and slid round against her back, drawing her even closer so that the warmth of him burned through her, something very strange suddenly happened inside her.

In an instant the coldness of her fury evaporated and her heart was flooded with a tide of raw emotions—excitement, confusion and a desperate yearning that tore at her insides and left her breathless, as though she had been knocked to the ground and run over by a steam train.

Shiona struggled for breath, appalled that she should react like this. Surely all these emotions had died long ago?

'Answer me, my little temptress.' His eyes burned into her, so blue, like sapphires, and twice as brilliant. And the scent of him in her nostrils was dark and heady. 'You know the battle's already lost,' he was saying. 'There can be no other reason for wanting to stay on here.'

With an effort she struggled to the surface of the emotions that, like a bubbling maelstrom, threatened to pull her under. And, somehow, in a frail voice, she managed to tell him, 'The battle's not over. That's why I'm staying.'

'In that case, the next few weeks should be interesting.' The hand on her back had crept up to her neck, sending squiggles of sensation from her scalp to her toes. 'In fact, I reckon they should be very interesting indeed.'

'And why should they be interesting?' That was not a word she would have chosen. 'Fraught' and 'unpleasant' sprang more readily to mind.

'They will allow me to have a taste of what Ryan had the privilege of enjoying—albeit,' he added, smiling, 'with certain restrictions. I am, after all, soon to be married.'

He was talking in riddles. 'Restrictions? What restrictions?'

Jake laughed then. 'You're right. What need is there for restrictions? While I am still free, I am at liberty to take my pleasure when I choose. And you are, after all, such an irresistible little temptress.'

All at once Shiona didn't like the look in his eyes. The warmth of a moment ago that had so overwhelmed her had cooled to a more familiar glint of contempt. She tried to pull away from him. 'What the devil are you talking about? Let me go and kindly stop talking in riddles!'

He did not let her go, but his grip on her slackened. He took a step away and looked down into her face. 'For the next couple of weeks it looks as though we'll be living together. That is, if you seriously intend to stay on.'

'I most certainly do intend to stay on!' Shiona's hazel eyes flickered with resolve. 'But what makes you think we'll be living together? Your home is in Edinburgh, not here.'

'My home is where I choose.' Unexpectedly, he released her. 'And right now I choose to make my home here. Until the final custody proceedings are over, it is best for Kirsty that she remain here, where her friends are, where she feels most at home.'

Shiona couldn't have agreed more, but all the same

she felt her heart sink. 'But it's not necessary for you to be here if I'm here,' she protested.

She might have guessed at his answer. 'I would say it's *doubly* necessary. As we have already discussed, I don't want you influencing her. As it is, you've already had her to yourself for too long during my regrettable but unavoidable absence. I left her in the care of Nettie and Inge. I had no idea that you'd be coming here to spin your little web.'

Shiona felt like striking him. The man was intolerable. 'Kirsty's my sister,' she reminded him in a sharp tone. 'And if you have any intention of trying to keep her from me, I warn you, I won't stand for it!'

'And how will you stop me?' Jake regarded her arrogantly.

'I'll stop you. Don't worry.' Her eyes flashed a warning. 'That is something you can be very sure of.'

To her irritation, he smiled. 'Quite the little tiger, aren't you? I shall quite enjoy taming you over the next couple of weeks.' He reached out to cup her chin with his fingers. 'Yes, I think I shall enjoy that very much indeed.'

Her temper suddenly snapping, Shiona slapped his hand away. 'God, I hate you, Jake MacKay! You're the most contemptible individual I've ever encountered in my life!'

'So, at least we have something in common,' he countered. His eyes blazed through her, as though they would consume her. 'It has long been my opinion that you, my dear Shiona, are the most contemptible individual that *I* have ever encountered.'

He smiled a twisted smile. 'Two such contemptible individuals ought to prove an excellent match for one another. The more I think about it, I must say, the more I'm looking forward to our time together.'

That did not surprise her. Jake thrived on conflict. There was no one who enjoyed throwing his weight around more.

Shiona raised her head scornfully, about to voice that very notion, but at that very moment the sitting-room door burst open and a small excited figure burst into the room.

'Aunt Shiona! Aunt Shiona!' With a squeal of delight, Kirsty rushed into her arms.

Shiona held her for a moment, her anger instantly vanishing to be replaced by a warm, maternal well of love. Then, carefully stifling her own personal feelings, she took the little girl by the hand. 'Look who's come to see you. Uncle Jake. Aren't you going to say hello to him?'

'Uncle Jake! I didn't see you!' With another whoop of delight the child threw herself at Jake, flinging her arms around him as he bent down to scoop her up.

Shiona felt her heart tug as she watched them together, aware as always of how very alike they were. The same almost black hair, the same vivid blue eyes. There was no doubt that Kirsty was one hundred per cent MacKay.

She cleared her throat. 'Did you have a good day at school?'

The little girl turned round, nodding enthusiastically. 'We had sums, and I came top of the class!'

'Clever girl!' Jake ruffled her hair and kissed her. 'I think you deserve a treat for that.'

'What kind of treat?' The child's eyes widened. 'Can I have it now, Uncle Jake?'

'Of course you can. It's out in the car. Come on and help me look for it.'

As he set her on the floor again, Kirsty turned to Shiona. 'You come, too. Come and look for my treat.' Then she was bounding out of the room, heading for the front door and rushing outside into the garden.

Without a glance at one another the two adults followed, Jake stepping aside at the sitting-room door to allow Shiona to pass into the hall ahead of him. And in that instant he paused to look into her face, causing her to glance up automatically at him.

'She's a delightful child, isn't she?' he observed. Then, as Shiona nodded, he added a malicious warning. 'I would advise you to enjoy her while you can. You may not have very much longer.'

That night Shiona lay in bed, propped up against the pillows, trying to read. She had known she wouldn't sleep. Her brain was teeming with a whole tangle of emotions that she could barely sort out.

The remainder of the day had passed almost enjoyably, with Jake and Shiona and little Kirsty appearing to behave like a happy little family. For in the presence of Kirsty Jake behaved impeccably, with not the slightest hint of animosity towards Shiona, just as Shiona behaved towards him.

Yet Shiona could not quite drive his warning from her mind and the look of cold dislike that had accompanied it. She would never grow used to the way he hated her.

But on the surface, at least, all was sweetness and light, and there was no doubt that his affection for Kirsty was genuine. Shiona smiled to herself with an uneasy kind of pleasure. He might be all the rotters of the universe, but he had a gentle, magical touch with the child.

And it was equally obvious that Kirsty adored him. She seemed to beam with happiness in his presence and hang on every word he said.

Shiona sighed and leaned back against the pillows. How painfully that reminded her of herself.

Once, she, too, had hung on his every word and beamed with happiness just at the sight of him. Once, she had worshipped the ground he walked on. Once, she would have died just to hear a kind word.

Shiona had been sixteen when Jake entered her life. Innocent. Impressionable. Hopelessly unworldly. A beautiful child full of wild ambitions and a passion to taste all the good things in life. And Jake, at twenty-four, dark and dashing and handsome, had appeared to embody all the romance that she dreamed of. Her heart had been lost to him the first moment she had set eyes on him.

That first meeting had been shortly after she and her mother had moved into the house on the banks of Loch Lomond, and even now she remembered it as a magical time.

The house alone had been like a dream come true after the two-bedroomed flat on the outskirts of Stirling where she and her mother had lived in near penury for the past seven years since Shiona's father's death.

'So, how do you like it? Does it meet with your approval?'

She remembered how Douglas, her new step-father, had taken pleasure in showing her round Lomond View, pointing out the paintings, the antiques, the porcelain, the like of which she had never seen before.

'I think it's all gorgeous!' she had enthused with real feeling. 'It's the most wonderful place that anyone could live!'

He had ruffled her hair. 'I'm glad to hear you say that, because from now on this is your home.'

Shiona had looked into his face with a stab of emotion, and just for a moment had been unable to speak. This man, whom she had taken to immediately, had transformed the lives of herself and her mother.

Her mother had shed ten years since her marriage to Douglas, and after all the years of struggle had learned to laugh again. And Douglas had promised that Shiona's lifelong ambition—to study fashion design in London—was hers for the taking if she could make the grade. No longer would it be necessary for her to leave school early and find a job to help support the household. Thanks to Douglas, her future was rosy.

At last she had found her voice and managed to

tell him, 'Thank you. Thank you for everything, Douglas.'

'Don't be silly. It's my pleasure.' He had fished in the pocket of his grey wool cardigan and, with a broad smile, produced a small jeweller's box. He'd handed it to Shiona. 'This is for you. A little gift to welcome you to Lomond View.'

'You shouldn't, really. . .'

But he'd simply laughed at her protestations, the same way he always laughed when her mother protested at his seemingly endless generosity. 'Open it up. See if you like it.'

Shiona had opened the box and her heart leapt within her. 'It's absolutely beautiful! Oh, thank you, Douglas!'

'Put it on. Here, let me help you.' He had lifted the locket on its fine gold chain and deftly fastened it around her neck. Then he'd turned her round to admire her. 'You look terrific. Let's go downstairs and show it off to the others.'

Shiona would never forget the next few minutes when the two of them had arrived in the big sunny sitting-room.

Ryan had instantly jumped to his feet, beaming at her as he crossed the room towards her. 'It's the locket we saw in town the other day! The one in the window, the one you so admired!' He'd grinned from ear to ear, grey eyes dancing. 'It suits you perfectly. You couldn't have chosen better.'

'Thanks. I love it.' Shiona had smiled back at the fair-haired youth who had so recently become her brother. Already she had become exceedingly fond of him. Ryan had been as warm and as welcoming as his father.

And then, quite suddenly, over Ryan's shoulder, she had been aware of a tall dark figure watching her.

Ryan had seen her gaze shift. 'Let me introduce you. This is Jake, the big brother I'm forever telling you about.'

With barely a smile Jake had then stepped forward, and Shiona had felt her heart clench anxiously inside her as a pair of blue eyes, as bright as sapphires, just for a moment had seemed to pierce through her.

He'd held out his hand to her. 'Pleased to meet you.' And as his fingers clasped hers, a strange sensation had shot through her, as though with that handshake he had branded her forever. For she had known in that instant that this dark-haired man before her was destined to leave his mark on her soul.

'Pleased to meet you,' she had responded, for the very first time since her arrival at Loch Lomond feeling unaccountably awkward and strange.

With a veiled smile he had glanced down at the locket. 'My brother's right. You chose very well.'

Looking back on that moment, it had often occurred to Shiona that it had marked the path that their future relationship was to take. For in the softly spoken comment she had sensed condemnation. She had sensed that he believed she had asked for the locket, that she was guilty of abusing his father's generosity.

Perhaps she should have put him right there and

then, but at the time it had not seemed terribly important, for instantly, chameleon-like, his demeanour had altered. In the flicker of an eyelid the hostility had vanished and he had become a model of charm and smiling good humour, as he politely asked her all about herself and answered her questions in return. At the end of the day Shiona had innocently believed that her second new stepbrother was her friend.

That misconception had continued on and off over the following six or seven years. Six or seven years in the course of which her infatuation with him, in spite of the rare times she saw him, had grown increasingly severe.

It was that detached, aloof quality of his, she had often thought, that had originally attracted her so fatally to him. That strength of mind one could sense below the surface, that glow of authority that seemed to radiate from his skin.

'He's like our father,' Ryan had once told her. 'Not only in looks, but in character, too.'

And though Douglas on the surface was more generous, more giving than his sometimes taciturn elder son, Shiona recognised that what they shared in common was that fierce individuality and sense of purpose that had brought Douglas, through his own efforts, from rags to great riches. Jake, she had sensed, would be capable of the same.

'Me, I'm like our mother,' Ryan had gone on to enlighten her. 'You've seen photographs of our mother, haven't you?'

Shiona had nodded. 'She was very beautiful. And you are just like her, with the same blond hair.'

Certainly, two brothers could scarcely have been more different—and not only in looks, in temperament as well. Younger by four years than his go-getting elder brother, Ryan was basically easygoing, with no driving ambitions, content just to get by. Jake, by contrast, quite independently of his father, who had also made his fortune in the building industry, had set up as a building contractor on his own. And already, at twenty-four, he'd built up a formidable business, successfully fulfilling contracts all over the world.

'When our father retires, he'll take over his business, too. No wonder Dad's proud of him,' Ryan had told her.

'But what about you? Wouldn't you like to be a part of it?' Shiona had felt obliged to ask him.

He had shaken his head. 'That's not for me. And, anyway, how could I compete with a brother like Jake?'

Shiona sank against the pillows now and closed her eyes as a rush of sadness went washing through her. Poor Ryan, he had had a heart of gold. It was a tragedy that he should have died so young.

She bit her lip, remembering that awful time when the news had come that he had lost his life in the fire that had demolished his holiday hotel—and how the tragedy, for her, had turned into a nightmare. For it had been when Ryan had died, three years ago now, that the situation between her and Jake had come to a head.

The disapproval she had sometimes sensed from him, and that had bothered her fleetingly from time to time, had erupted into a torrent of burning hatred at the discovery that, in spite of the fortune his father had showered on him, Ryan had died in a state of virtual penury. To Shiona's absolute horror, Jake had blamed her.

Everyone knew she and Ryan had been living together, and it was easy to jump to the wrong conclusions. But things had not been at all what they'd seemed—though she was bound by her promise never to reveal the truth.

She'd paid bitterly and dearly for her unshakeable loyalty. For since that day when he had made his accusations, tearing her heart to shreds in the process, Jake had refused to have any more to do with her. For three years they had neither met nor spoken. The rift had been total and, she had believed, final.

At first the agony had been unbearable. She had loved him, almost obsessively, since the age of sixteen and, though he had never in any way encouraged her, over the years she had built all her dreams around him. He was the man she had prayed that one day she would marry. And now, to this man, she had ceased to exist.

But she had turned her agony into a blessing. Recognising the hopelessness of her situation, she had resolved to do what she ought to have done years ago, and systematically banished him from her heart.

It had not been easy, but she had succeeded—principally by concentrating on her career. Three years ago she had just recently left college, one of thousands of graduates looking for a job. Now she was running her own knitwear business with a design studio in London and a busy workshop here in Scotland. She'd had to work like a Trojan to achieve it, but it had been worth every drop of blood, sweat and tears.

And not only for the pleasure of running her own thriving business, but for the more fundamental change it had brought about in her. That impressionable child who had swooned and sighed and lain in bed dreaming of Jake MacKay had finally grown up with a vengeance. Her days of swooning and sighing were over. Professional success had knocked some sense into her, and she had taught herself to return hate with hate.

Furthermore, she had grown to be grateful for the fact that their lives had drifted irretrievably apart, and she had prayed that things might stay that way for ever. But now the tragedy that had killed her mother and Jake's father and made an orphan of little Kirsty had, cruelly, brought them together again.

She leaned back against the pillows and, sighing, closed her eyes. She had thought she was healed, beyond his reach forever, and in every real sense she knew that she was. But today she had felt old wounds being ripped open. Even as she lay there, she could feel them ache and throb.

She sighed again, and switched off the light and dropped her unread book on to the floor. But there was one thing she was sure of. He could torture her all he wanted, but he would not succeed in breaking her a second time.

Beneath the sheets she clenched her fists. She would die before she would let him do that.

CHAPTER THREE

'So, YOU'RE still here, are you? I thought you might have gone.'

Shiona glanced round, startled out of her reverie, as Jake appeared suddenly in the doorway of the breakfast-room. 'Of course I'm still here. Where else would I be?'

'When you didn't show up to see Kirsty off to school this morning, I thought you might have caught an early flight back to London.' He walked into the room, his eyes travelling over her, disapproval in every harsh line of his face. 'However, I see that you've only just got up.'

Seated at the breakfast table in her pink wool robe, Shiona felt a blush rise to her cheeks. It was after ten o'clock, and he would be quite right to disapprove, if it weren't for the fact that, in spite of appearances, she had slept for only a few hours last night. She'd heard the grandfather clock down in the hall chime every quarter-hour until three o'clock. No wonder she hadn't wakened till after half-past nine!

But she wasn't about to excuse herself to Jake. 'It's Inge's job to see Kirsty off to school.' Defiantly, Shiona tilted her chin at him. 'It really wasn't necessary for me to be here too.'

'That's what I thought you'd say. Leave it to the au pair. Let someone else look after your sister while you have a few hours' extra beauty sleep.' He came to stand before her. 'You don't change, do you? Still looking after number one, as ever.'

As his eyes, blue and flinty, held hers, Shiona was tempted to protest that that wasn't fair. Every morning since she'd been here, apart from today, she'd been up bright and early to see Kirsty off to school.

But she didn't say it. She didn't care what Jake thought of her. He already hated her, so what difference did it make?

'Still, never mind.' He drew back one of the chairs and proceeded to seat himself at the table opposite her. 'Your absence meant that I had her all to myself at breakfast—with the additional pleasure of escorting her personally to school.'

Shiona ignored his smug smile. 'How dutiful on your part. You're really putting on quite an impressive little show. I wonder how many times in the past, when you've been staying here, you've gone to the trouble of escorting Kirsty to school?'

His gaze never flickered. 'I'd say at least a dozen.'

It was probably true, but she responded scornfully, just as he always did to her. 'Sure,' she scoffed. 'I'll just bet you have!'

'Ask Kirsty, if you doubt it.' He regarded her smoothly. 'Believe me, I wouldn't go to the trouble of lying to you.'

Had he emphasised the 'you', implying that she wasn't worth lying to, or had she simply imagined the insult? Shiona looked back at him, hiding the flicker of hurt inside her. 'I think you'd lie to St

Peter,' she retorted evenly, 'if you thought you might get something out of it.'

He merely smiled. 'I think, my dear Shiona, you've rather got that the wrong way round. *You're* the opportunist around here, not me.'

'Of course. I was forgetting.' Shiona smiled at him sarcastically. 'And you're the one with a halo around his head!'

The blue eyes surveyed her face for a moment, their expression dark and oddly unreadable. Then, with a shrug, he let his gaze slide over to the coffee-pot. 'Is there any coffee left?' he enquired.

'I'm not sure. I think there ought to be.'

She was on the point of reaching over to pick up the coffee-pot and obligingly fill one of the spare cups for him. But, just in time, she managed to stop herself. She had reacted out of habit. It had been a kind of reflex action. But she wasn't Jake's little slave girl any more.

Deliberately, she pushed her hands into the pockets of her robe and sat back in her chair as he proceeded to serve himself. Once, she would not only have poured his coffee for him, she would have spooned in the sugar and stirred it for him, too. Then sat and gazed at him adoringly while he drank.

She felt a clench in her stomach of resentment and rage as she remembered just how pathetically servile she had once been. In those bad old days she would even shine his shoes for him, and beg for the privilege of hosing down his car. And he, of course, would accept her ministrations as though they were quite simply no more than his due.

Suddenly she felt deeply irritated by his presence. 'What are you doing here anyway at this hour of the day?' Her tone was barbed, unmistakably hostile. 'Shouldn't you be at your desk in Edinburgh, sorting out the world?'

He deliberately took a mouthful of his coffee before answering. 'Is that where you would like me to be, Shiona?'

She met his eyes. 'That wouldn't be my first choice. Personally, I'd choose somewhere a little further away.' Like Outer Mongolia, she added to herself, as she lifted up her own cup and drank. Then, as he simply smiled, she regarded him over the top of it. 'I thought you were a workaholic? I thought Jake MacKay Contracting couldn't operate without you?'

'What a flattering notion. So, you believe me indispensable? I had no idea you held me in such high regard.'

'Oh, believe me, I don't,' Shiona assured him quickly, irritated at herself for handing him that one on a plate. 'It's just that I know how all-controlling you are. How can you bear to relinquish the helm, even for a single minute?'

'And who says I have relinquished the helm?' Jake regarded her with superior amusement. 'If there are any important decisions to be made, I'm only a telephone call away.'

'Ah, but when the cat's away the mice will play. Someone might do something behind your back.'

'You're right.' He smiled a mirthless smile. 'And that's precisely why I'm here. The only one I'm worried about doing things behind my back, my dear

Shiona, is your sweet self.' As she glared at him, he continued, 'So get used to the fact that, if you plan on staying on here, you will unfortunately be seeing rather a lot of me. There's no way I intend leaving you alone here with Kirsty.'

Damn him! Shiona glowered across the table at him—so utterly poised, so hatefully sure of himself in his immaculate dark blue Savile Row suit. As always, he had that look of having the world on a string, everything indisputably under his control.

Shiona scowled into his face with its arrogant high cheekbones, self-satisfied mouth and eyes as hard as sapphires. How hateful he was. How could she ever have loved him?

She laid down her cup and leaned towards him across the table. 'And what exactly do you think I might do to Kirsty if you were rash enough to leave her alone with me?' She bit the words out at him, full of anger and resentment. 'You're not seriously suggesting I might do her some harm?'

'Not physical harm.'

'Then what kind of harm?'

'Emotional. Moral. Psychological. Who knows?'

'That's cruel and unfair! How can you say it?'

'Because I've learned from bitter experience precisely what you're capable of. I've told you that already. Why do you keep insisting?'

He was referring to Ryan again. She could see it in his eyes. That flicker of pain and anger that would never go away. And again she felt that helpless rush inside her, knowing that she would never be able to set the record straight.

She turned her eyes away, unable to answer him. It really did still hurt that he believed her capable of such evil. She had a feeling it probably always would. Without looking at him, she listened as Jake went on to say,

'I hate to keep repeating myself, but you really are wasting your time. Why don't you just give up and go back down to London? It can't be so easy for *you* to run your business from here.'

'I'll manage, thank you.' Her tone was curt. It was no affair of his that she had left the London studio in the capable hands of her assistant. It would tick over perfectly without her for a few weeks. She flicked Jake an openly sarcastic smile. 'There's really no need for you to be concerned.'

There was a momentary silence as she averted her gaze again, and she was aware of him picking up his coffee-cup and drinking.

Then he said conversationally, laying down his cup again, 'I hear your business is doing very well.'

'Is that what you hear?' Still she did not look at him.

'My congratulations. You've done very well. I hear you were even nominated for the Young Designer of the Year Award.'

There he went again, playing the good guy, pretending he was interested in her success! But she would not stand for his condescension. Shiona twisted round and pierced him with a look. 'No doubt that surprised you, even irritated you a little. I bet it really gets up your nose that my knitwear's proving so popular.'

'Why should you believe that?' One straight black eyebrow lifted. 'Why should I be anything but pleased at your success?'

Because you hate me! Because you despise me! Because you'd like to see me suffer for what you believe I did to Ryan!

How she would have loved to have yelled these words at him and finally have the whole thing out in the open. But she could not, so she simply told him in a flat tone, 'We've recently started exporting to Europe and Japan. I've had to take on more staff at the workshop in Killearn.'

'Again my congratulations.'

He was so damned convincing!

'You must have put in a lot of hard work.'

Of course, the irony of what he had just said escaped him, but it caused Shiona to smile a bitter inner smile. Often she had wondered if she would have been quite so successful if she hadn't thrown herself so totally into her work in a desperate attempt to mend her broken heart. Perhaps, to some extent, she thought with wry amusement, she owed her professional success to Jake.

She glanced across at him. 'Yes, it's been a lot of hard work. But, fortunately, hard work is something I enjoy.'

'Not all hard work, I hope?' He threw her a strange smile. 'I hope you've had time for other things as well?'

'Other things?' She feigned incomprehension. 'What sorts of other things do you mean?'

'The normal sorts of things that make up one's life. Friends. . .leisure interests. . . Hobbies, if you like.'

'You mean parties and fast living? Isn't that more my line?' Shiona regarded him harshly, tossing back her auburn hair. 'I admit I've had to cut back a little just recently, but I'm hoping to get back into my stride really soon.'

Jake shook his head as he continued to watch her, regarding her irritated face with a discreetly shuttered look. 'No doubt you are, but that's not what I was meaning. What I was wondering was if you have any serious boyfriend these days?'

'Serious boyfriend? I don't go in for serious boyfriends. I only take up with men for what I can get out of them.' Her hazel eyes glinted across the table at him. 'But surely you, of all people, don't need to be told that?'

Suddenly she was shimmering with anger as she faced him, yet not quite certain where her anger had sprung from. His conversation, though insincere, had not been unpleasant. She was the one who had initiated this skirmish.

She could see in his eyes that he was thinking the same, as in a flat tone he told her, 'Point taken. Let's drop the subject.'

But still her anger continued to bubble as a new suspicion came into her mind. 'What's the matter? Were you worried that I might be on the verge of getting married, too? Was that why you wanted to pry into my private life? After all, if I did have a fiancé tucked away, that would change the situation rather dramatically. I'd have as strong a claim for custody as you!'

'Indeed you would. But, take my word for it, the possibility had never for one moment occurred to me.'

Had it not, indeed? That was vaguely insulting.

But before she could react, Jake went on to assure her, 'What's more, you're wrong to believe I was prying. All I was doing was making conversation. I couldn't be less interested in your private life, as it happens.'

Another fleeting insult. Shiona straightened her shoulders, feeling jumpy and hopelessly out of control. 'That's just as well,' she told him evenly, 'because I don't intend discussing it with you.' Then she rose to her feet—she'd had enough of this conversation. 'If you don't mind, I think I'll go and get dressed.'

'I don't mind in the least.' He glanced at his watch. 'I'll be going to collect Kirsty from school in about an hour. If you like. . .'

He paused just long enough for her to wonder if he was about to do the decent thing and invite her to join him. Then he smiled into her face as he finished the sentence.

'If you like, I can drop you off at the travel agent's so that you can book your flight back down to London.'

Shiona eyed him coldly. 'That won't be necessary. I'll be booking my ticket when I'm ready.' Then she tilted her chin at him. 'However, I will come with you. I'd like to go and collect Kirsty, too.'

Jake simply smiled. 'You may as well while you

can. As I warned you already, you may not have very much longer.' Then, as Shiona started to turn away, her body stiff with loathing, he added calmly, 'Oh, by the way, I have a piece of news that I think will interest you. . .'

She half turned round. 'Yes? What is it?'

'You said you wanted to meet my fiancée so that you could judge her for yourself. Well, I'm happy to say, you'll soon have that opportunity. . .'

A smug smile curled around his lips. 'I've invited Janice to spend the weekend with us.'

Good. I'm glad the woman's coming. Shiona told herself with just a flicker of uncertainty, changing into second gear as she rounded a bend. It was important that she meet this fiancée as soon as possible, so that she could judge her suitability as a mother for Kirsty.

With a sigh now she took a turning off the narrow road into one of the summer picnic spots overlooking Loch Lomond. She drew the car to a halt and pulled on the handbrake. Once she'd met Janice and come to some conclusion, then she would know what she had to do next.

She stared at the still blue waters of the loch, overhung by weeping willows in their fresh spring greenery. A curlew called out as it rose above the waters, then came to rest alongside its mate among the rushes. Very likely there was a nest there, full of hungry little mouths waiting to be fed.

With another wistful sigh she sat back in her seat. More than anything she would love to be Kirsty's guardian and, in spite of the harsh things Jake had said to her, she knew, if that happened, she would do a good job.

But she also knew that if Jake and Janice could offer the happy home that Jake had promised she would give up her own claim in an instant. Though it would be a great personal sadness to have to do it, it would nevertheless give her the greatest satisfaction to see Kirsty settled in a warm and loving family. Having known the lack of that luxury herself, she was all too aware of how important it was.

She pursed her lips. Before the weekend was out she would know whether she should stay or go back to London. For her decision depended solely on her assessment of Janice.

As far as Jake was concerned, she had no doubts at all as to his suitability as a father. Sure, she had indulged in the occasional uncharitable observation that his affection for the child was no more than a front. But that didn't reflect her true opinion. It was merely an expression of her own personal dislike.

Jake loved Kirsty dearly. That was obvious to anyone. He seemed to love her as fiercely as he had once loved Ryan, Shiona thought to herself with a little inner shiver. And he had the makings of a strong, but kind and loving father, who would always have the little girl's best interests at heart.

But that wasn't enough, she reminded herself sharply, watching the male curlew as it waded out into the shallows, searching for food beneath the surface of the loch. Jake would be a good father when he was around. But he was away a lot, and then it would be up to Janice.

Janice. Just to think of her made Shiona anxious. Kirsty's entire happiness could depend on Janice.

There were other feelings, too, that the thought of Janice provoked. A sense of irritation. A sense of resentment. A sense that she had no right to intrude into their lives.

Ridiculous feelings, Shiona decided, rejecting them. It was perfectly natural that Jake should marry—and, apart from how it might affect Kirsty, it was not an event that interested her in the slightest.

Though she had found one small revelation of mild interest.

She and Jake had been driving back to Lomond View after accompanying Kirsty back to school when Jake had swivelled round in his seat to inform her,

'I've asked Nettie to prepare the rose room for Janice—that is, if you have no objections. . . You weren't planning to use it for any of your own guests, were you?'

Shiona had shaken her head. 'No, I wasn't.' And though she was not surprised that, for the sake of appearances, Jake's fiancée was to be installed in one of the guest-rooms, it did surprise her that he had chosen the rose room. It was the guest-room that was furthest away from his own room. He evidently wasn't planning any passionate trysts!

She'd had no time to examine her reaction to this revelation any further, however, for he had proceeded to cut across her thoughts.

'I understand you've never had a guest while

you've been here? You really ought to invite one of your boyfriends. I assure you I wouldn't mind in the least.'

It wasn't his place to mind, she'd felt like telling him. The house was as much hers as it was his. But she'd restricted herself to snapping, 'I'll bear that in mind,' and abruptly ending the conversation. For some reason his observation had niggled.

Now, a couple of soothing hours later—she'd spent most of that time at the Killearn workshop—she knew exactly why she'd reacted as she had. And why she'd reacted the same way yesterday evening when Jake had started questioning her about her private life.

On the subject of boyfriends Shiona was notoriously sensitive, and doubly so, it appeared, when Jake brought up the subject.

The curlew was still moving silently through the water, long, curved beak poised above the surface. Shiona watched it, reflecting that the reason for her sensitivity was that her private life was the only area of her existence that gave her absolutely no satisfaction at all. It remained empty, barren, a hopeless wasteland. Since that day when she had ruthlessly cut Jake from her heart there had been no one. No one who really mattered.

It wasn't that she hadn't tried to form relationships, but somehow they had just never amounted to anything significant.

'I don't think you really want a proper relationship,' one of her more recent boyfriends had told her. 'I don't think you're really interested in getting seriously involved.'

She'd tried to make a joke out of it. 'I'm just a slow starter! Don't worry, I'll get round to it eventually.' But in her heart she had felt a pang of unease. Was there something wrong with her that she seemed to shy away from commitment? After all, she was twenty-six years old. Why couldn't she, like other people, just fall in love?

Of course she *had* been in love, for years and years, and perhaps, she sometimes wondered, that experience had spoiled her. Perhaps all those years wasted mooning over Jake had somehow robbed her of the ability to give her love to someone more deserving.

For there had been no lack of men whom she had wished she could fall in love with, good men who would undoubtedly have made her happy. But, frustratingly, that vital spark had been missing.

Damn Jake! she thought for the hundred-millionth time. Damn him for ever coming into my life! And damn him for daring to pry into my affairs and for subtly mocking my singular state!

It was he who had tainted her! It was he who was to blame! He was a scourge on her life! How she hated him!

Shiona gripped the steering-wheel and squeezed her eyes shut and slowly counted up to ten. She was over-reacting. All this emotion was out of place. She had stopped giving a damn about Jake years ago.

She breathed in slowly, concentrating hard. It seemed that just being around him was starting to get to her. She bit her lip. She must be stronger than that.

She counted to ten, then opened her eyes again—to see the curlew suddenly emerge from the water with a fat, squirming fish held firmly in his beak.

Shiona smiled to herself. She must be like the curlew, and concentrate all her energy on those who needed her. She must think only of Kirsty and Kirsty's future. She must not think of Jake. Jake was the past.

She switched on the engine and headed back on to the road. The first part was easy. It was the second part that was hard.

'When are Uncle Jake and his friend Janice coming?' Kirsty was pressed against the drawing-room window, excitedly waiting for Jake's Mercedes to appear.

Shiona was seated on the sofa, her back to the window, leafing stiffly through a magazine. She glanced at her watch. 'Any minute now. If the train was on time, they should just about be here.'

'Here they are now! I can see the car!' With a whoop of pleasure Kirsty rushed across the room, heading for the door that led out into the hall. 'Come on, Aunt Shiona! Let's go and meet them!'

Shiona laid down her magazine. 'No, I'll wait here,' she smiled. 'You go and meet them, if you like.' Then she rose to her feet, as Kirsty scampered out i4to the hall, and, adjusting the collar of her cream silk blouse, walked on measured steps towards the window.

She stopped a few feet away, so that she was hidden by the curtains, and fixed her gaze unblinkingly on the long black Mercedes that was heading sedately up the driveway. She pushed back her hair, as bright as copper in the sunshine that slanted through the big bay window. This was it. The moment she'd been waiting for.

She breathed in deeply, seeking to allay her nervousness, eyes squinting impatiently to distinguish some shadow behind the infuriating smoked glass windows. What would she be like? Would she like her?

The car drew to a halt alongside the front door, and an instant later the driver's door swung open. Jake jumped out and strode round to the passenger door, but before he could open it Kirsty appeared, flinging herself at him and squealing, 'Uncle Jake! Uncle Jake!'

He paused to hug her and ruffle her hair, then at last the passenger door was swinging open and there was what seemed to Shiona an endless moment before Janice at last stepped into view.

Shiona stopped breathing, her heart pounding inside her. She looks all right, she assured herself warily. A little older and somewhat plainer than she'd expected, but the woman had a distinctly motherly look!

She felt elation and sadness all in the same instant. It looked as though she would lose Kirsty, after all. But how wonderful if this woman could give Kirsty a good home!

A moment later she had the opportunity for a

closer look, as the trio came trooping into the sitting-room, Jake in front, the two females right behind.

'Now meet Shiona,' Jake was saying, guiding his fiancée forwards with a hand at her waist. 'Shiona Fergusson, my stepsister.'

The smiling figure in the tan checked suit stepped forward with hand extended to greet her. 'Shiona, I'm delighted. I'm Janice MacGregor.' She shook hands warmly. 'I've heard so much about you.'

Shiona smiled back. 'Pleased to meet you, too.' And she was trying desperately not to be too obvious as her eyes scrutinised every line of the other woman's face.

Luckily, Janice had already glanced away, her eyes circling with interest the splendid sitting-room. And for an instant her expression seemed to alter subtly. A fleeting, hard look seemed to drift across her eyes. Almost as though, Shiona thought with a small shudder, she was mentally totting up the value of the contents of the room. But then an instant later she was wondering if she'd imagined it, as Janice turned to beam a warm, glowing smile at Jake.

'What a beautiful room! And what a splendid view you have! I had no idea it was so lovely here!'

Of course she'd imagined it, Shiona told herself firmly. Janice MacGregor was a perfectly nice person, and she, Shiona, in her hyped-up state, was simply looking for things to criticise.

'I'm glad you like it,' Jake was saying. 'You have almost as good a view from your bedroom.' He had stepped towards her, his hand on her waist again.

'I'll show it to you now. You can freshen up and change.'

'What a wonderful idea!' Janice beamed at him and slipped an arm through his before turning to Shiona. 'I hope you'll excuse me,' she apologised, smiling, 'but I really am desperate for a shower.'

'Of course I excuse you,' Shiona was quick to assure her. 'Take as long as you like. Dinner's not till eight.'

It was as the pair of them were passing through the doorway into the hall that Jake turned for a moment to catch Shiona's eye. He said not a word, but he didn't have to. The message in his eyes was loud and clear.

So, now that you've met her, you may go back to London just as soon as it's convenient.

Shiona dropped her gaze away. Yes, she was thinking, that's really all that's left for me to do.

'Can I go, too, and show Janice her room?' She glanced down suddenly to see Kirsty looking up at her.

She forced a smile. 'Of course you can, darling. Just make sure you don't get in her way.'

As the child bounded off, Shiona stood and watched the happy threesome cross the hallway and head for the stairs.

That was rich, she thought to herself wryly. I'm the one who's in the way!

CHAPTER FOUR

I'LL announce my departure over dinner, Shiona decided, as she slipped into a pretty blue dress in her room and combed back her mane of bright auburn hair. There was no point in her hanging around any longer. Kirsty, she was almost certain, would be in good hands with Janice.

Almost. . .

She frowned at her reflection in the mirror. Why did she say 'almost' and not 'entirely'? Almost, after all, wasn't nearly good enough. Kirsty's happiness was far too important to take a gamble with.

But then she thought again of that motherly, homely face that seemed to radiate a simple gentleness and warmth, and she felt sure that she was being over-cautious, perhaps even slightly prejudiced in her feelings about Janice. It wasn't an easy thing, after all, to approve of any fiancée of Jake's! Just by association, her sentiments tended towards the negative!

And you have no right to let such feelings affect your judgement, she rebuked herself sharply, slipping on her shoes. You have no right, out of prejudice, to stand in the way of Kirsty's chance to be a part of a proper family.

She sighed, and adjusted her pearl drop earrings

and the pretty gold locket at her throat. Help me to do the right thing, she prayed silently.

It was a quarter to eight when she stuck her head into the kitchen to have a quick word with Nettie before dinner.

'Is everything OK?' she enquired, smiling. 'Do you need a hand with anything?'

Pink-cheeked with her exertions, Nettie shook her head. 'Everything's fine, Miss Shiona,' she assured her, beaming happily, quite clearly in her element. 'Miss MacGregor is waiting in the drawing-room. As far as I know, Mr MacKay isn't down yet.'

Shiona nodded gratefully. 'I'll go and join her. Just give us a shout when you want us to move into the dining-room.'

Then, smiling to herself, she hurried along the corridor, rather looking forward to the opportunity to see Janice on her own.

But, as she reached the open door of the drawing-room and caught sight of Janice in the middle of the room, some instinct told her not to enter immediately. She took a step back into the shadows of the hallway and watched the other woman, her heart beating strangely. Playing the spy was not something that came naturally to her, but in this particular instance she sensed it was her duty.

Janice, needless to say, was quite unaware of her presence. Evidently, she believed herself to be quite unobserved.

She was circling the room with an almost predatory air, examining each painting, each piece of furniture, and it was not appreciation that was etched on her face. Her eyes were hard, her expression calculating. Pounds sterling, not aesthetics, were clearly on her mind.

Shiona felt a cold hand touch her heart. It was that same look she had caught a glimpse of earlier.

Then Shiona had preferred to deny the evidence of her eyes, but this time she could no longer do so. The woman was a gold-digger. In an instant she knew it. She felt her stomach squeeze sickly inside her.

'Good evening, Shiona. What are you waiting out here for?'

She spun round, startled, at the sound of Jake's voice, to find him standing at her elbow, blue eyes dark with condemnation as they looked down into her face.

'Don't you think you should be looking after our guest instead of prowling about out here in the corridor?'

'I was just going in.' She felt foolish and guilty, like a child caught with her fingers in the cake tin.

Jake pushed the door wider. 'Then what are you waiting for? I'm sure you've seen all there is to be seen.'

Shiona met his gaze then. 'Yes, I'm sure I have. I've certainly seen all I *need* to see.'

'There you are, the two of you!' They were interrupted at that moment as Janice came hurrying over to greet them. She kissed Jake's cheek and beamed at Shiona. 'I love your dress! That blue really suits you.'

'Thank you.' With an effort Shiona smiled back at

her. It was hard to believe that this generously smiling woman was the same predatory creature she'd been watching just a moment ago—but the image she had seen was seared in her brain, and suddenly she knew there was no way in the world that she could allow this woman to be a mother to Kirsty.

She turned away with mingled sadness and determination. 'I think we should go through to the dining-room now. Dinner must be nearly ready.'

Dinner itself was an uneasy experience. Like three actors in a play they each played their part, chatting inconsequentially about this and that, and pretending to be the best of friends. But, for her part, Shiona could barely wait for the iniquitous ordeal to come to an end. She desperately needed some time alone to think.

It was Janice who made the first move to end the evening. 'That was a fabulous meal,' she declared enthusiastically after the pudding plates had been cleared away. She stifled a yawn as she laid a hand on Jake's. 'But I suddenly feel totally exhausted. If you don't mind, darling, I think I'll skip coffee. All at once I feel a great need for bed.'

As Jake started to stand up, she shook her head and smiled. 'You stay where you are and finish dinner properly. Your bedtime isn't for hours yet!'

'Are you sure you'll be all right? You're feeling OK?' Suddenly he was frowning, his manner solicitous.

'I'm feeling fine. Just a little tired.' Janice patted his hand as she rose to her feet and turned to address

Shiona with one of her smiles. 'Goodnight, Shiona. I'll see you in the morning.'

Shiona nodded. 'Goodnight.' What an actress! she was thinking. From the look of her, butter wouldn't melt in her mouth!

A moment later, as the door closed behind Janice, Shiona toyed with the idea of making her own exit. But just then Nettie walked into the room, carrying a silver tray piled with coffee things.

'Only two for coffee?' she enquired with a slight frown. And as Jake nodded, Shiona reluctantly resigned herself to being trapped at the table with him for another little while. Nettie, after all, had gone to some trouble, with dishes of peppermint fondants and dark after-dinner chocolates, in addition to the steaming silver coffee-pot and the matching silver jug of thick fresh cream.

She laid the things out on the table, along with a decanter of brandy and some glasses, then took her leave as Jake told her, 'Thanks, Nettie. That'll be all. We can manage on our own.'

He picked up the silver coffee-pot as the door closed behind her, and poured the strong dark brew into the pretty Wedgwood cups. Then he reached for the brandy and tipped a measure into his own cup before offering to do the same with Shiona's.

But Shiona shook her head. 'No, thanks. I'll just have cream.'

'I like a nightcap after a busy day.' Jake took a mouthful of his coffee. 'I find it helps me to get a good night's sleep.'

Shiona glanced across at him, only half hearing

what he was saying. Has he any idea, she was wondering, that that woman is only marrying him for his money?

Then, as the blue eyes looked back at her with a flicker of curiosity, she responded automatically, 'So, you have trouble sleeping? I can't say that comes as any great surprise.'

He feigned incomprehension. 'Oh, and why would that be? Why would you suppose that I'm some kind of insomniac?'

Shiona shrugged, not needing to think about her answer. This sparring routine of theirs had grown so familiar that her brain had more or less switched to automatic.

'Something to do with the state of your conscience. I imagine you have a great deal to keep you awake at night.' As she spoke, her mind was still on Janice. How much would it hurt him, she was wondering, when he finally discovered the truth about his fiancée?

In the meantime, he was smiling. 'That's an interesting theory. I suppose you wouldn't care to elaborate further? I'd be most interested to know what you think keeps me awake.'

Shiona shrugged. 'Oh, I don't know the sordid details. And in a way I'm even a little surprised to hear that your conscience actually bothers you. I've always tended to think of you as rather lacking in conscience.'

'Like you, you mean?'

'No, not like me.'

'Is that why you sleep so soundly in your bed—

because you're conveniently incapable of suffering from guilt?'

'I have nothing to feel guilty about.'

'Yes, you would say that, wouldn't you?'

'And why would you deny that it's true?'

He did not answer her immediately, just continued to watch her across the table, his blue eyes suddenly as cold as ice. 'I think we both know the answer to that.'

'You mean Ryan, don't you?' She knew that look well. 'But I have nothing to feel guilty about, regarding Ryan.'

'So you've told me.'

'Then why won't you believe me?'

'Because the evidence speaks otherwise.' Jake's tone was bitter. That pain burned deep in his eyes again. 'You ruined my brother. My brother trusted you. And all you did was bleed him dry.'

Shiona's stomach clenched like a fist within her. That accusation was like a blow to the midriff, still as hurtful as ever, no matter how often she heard it. She was filled with an overwhelming desire to strike back at him, and suddenly she knew exactly how she could do it.

Are you aware that Janice doesn't really love you? Are you aware she's only marrying you for your money?

The words swarmed through her mind as she glared furiously back at him, but somehow she couldn't bring herself to say them. Instead, she said, 'I've decided to fight you. Over custody of Kirsty. I won't let you take her.'

There was a momentary pause at this sudden switch in the conversation. Jake drained his coffee-cup and laid it down on the saucer. 'Is this decision of yours just to try and thwart me, or do you have any particular reason?'

'I have a very good reason, as it happens.' She held his eyes. 'I don't like Janice. I don't believe she'd make a good mother for Kirsty.'

To her surprise, he laughed. 'You're so damned predictable. You just don't give up when there's a profit to be made.'

Again Shiona was filled with the urge to say it, to hurt him as he had so often hurt her. But he wouldn't believe it even if she said it, she decided. He'd simply accuse her of being spiteful.

He was still watching her across the table. 'So why don't you like Janice? Tell me. I'm interested.'

'Interested in my opinion? I sincerely doubt it.' Shiona sat back in her seat and narrowed her eyes at him. 'I just don't like her. I don't intend to elaborate.'

'Female intuition?' He was mocking.

'Something like that.'

'Is that why you were spying on her when I caught you out in the hallway? Were you hoping to catch her stealing the silver?'

He was closer than he thought, Shiona thought with a small shiver. She laid down her napkin. Suddenly she felt tired, and she had no desire to get into a harangue with him. 'If you don't mind, I think I'll go to bed.'

'I'll tell you something before you go. . .' Jake's eyes were on her, biting into her. 'In spite of your intuition, my dear Shiona, Janice is a much nicer person than you, and far more suited to be Kirsty's mother.'

He paused for an instant. 'And if you really are serious about pursuing your ridiculous claim for custody, I shall make damned sure that the court knows all about you. As beautiful and as wholesome as you may be on the outside, I shall reveal you for the black-hearted trickster that you are. The woman who exploited and ruined my brother will never be appointed guardian to my sister!'

Suddenly Shiona was trembling with anger. 'How dare you threaten me?' she spat out across the table at him. 'How dare you threaten to go to court and lie about me?'

She jumped to her feet, her stomach churning with emotion, and jarred one hip violently against the edge of the table, sending her untouched coffee-cup toppling sideways on its saucer.

'I won't have to lie. I shall simply tell the truth. That will be more than enough to put an end to your claims.'

It was that superior, malicious arrogance of his that triggered Shiona's reaction. As she reached for the coffee-cup, half of its contents now in the saucer, all she intended to do was right it. But as her trembling fingers closed around it, a more satisfying notion flew into her head.

'You wouldn't recognise the truth if you found it in your brandy glass!' Furiously, she hurled the accusation at him. Then, in the very same breath, she snatched up the toppled coffee-cup and flung the lukewarm contents in his face.

Then she was turning on her heel and heading for the door, anxious to make a speedy escape.

But as she reached the door, one hand on the door-handle, suddenly an iron band clamped round her arm. She was swung round forcefully, so that her breath gasped from her body, then with equal force she was flung against the door.

'And what was that meant to prove?' Steel fingers gripped her arm, while the fingers of his other hand closed tightly around her chin. He thrust a face dark with anger into hers. 'Was that meant to convince me what a sweet innocent you are?'

To her dismay Shiona saw that her aim had been off. The coffee had simply splattered across the front of his shirt. 'I wish I'd thrown the coffee-pot!' she seethed at him defiantly. 'I wish it had been boiling and I'd poured it over your damned head!'

'Yes, I'll bet you do.' He gave her a shake, forcing her chin up as he glared down into her face. 'A young woman with a nasty, vicious nature like yours is capable of wishing all sorts of evil things.'

'It would be no more than you deserve! And one day I'll do it! One day I'll get back at you, Jake MacKay!'

'Get back at me for what? For seeing right through you? For being the only male in my family to recognise you for what you are?'

'You really believe that, don't you? You think you're so clever! You're so damned self-righteous you make me sick!'

'So put me right, my dear, since you keep insisting I'm mistaken. Finally reveal the sweet-scented truth about yourself that has been so cruelly denied for all these years.' He smiled sarcastically. 'Believe me, I'm all ears!'

She was standing pinned against the door, her hands flattened against it, her escape entirely blocked by Jake's powerful form. As he spoke, he had deliberately moved even closer. She dared not flex a muscle or she would be pressed hard against him.

'I wouldn't waste my breath!' Her hazel eyes flayed him. 'So just kindly let me go, and stop playing the heavy.'

His fingers caressed her jaw. 'Don't be in such a hurry. I'm giving you a chance to convince me. Take it!'

'I don't want your chances! I don't want anything from you! Just do me a favour and let me go!' Suddenly she was almost suffocating from the oppressive agony of his nearness.

'You have nothing to say, do you? Just lies and more lies.' He took his hand from her arm and slid his fingers through her hair. 'And how well those temptress lips of yours know how to lie.' His eyes dropped to her mouth, causing her stomach to flip over. With that sensuous, slow gaze of his it was as though he had kissed her.

Shiona held her breath. 'Please let me go. Look, I'm sorry I threw the coffee at you.' Anything to make him release her!

His eyes slid back to hers. 'More lies,' he murmured. And as his hand caressed her scalp, his expression had subtly altered. 'I bet you tell some whoppers to all your lovers. I bet the poor devils don't know whether they're coming or going!'

He was driving her crazy the way he was holding her and the way he was looking down at her with smouldering blue eyes. She turned her face away. 'Let me go!' she croaked desperately. 'All I ask of you is that you please let me go.'

'Why, my dear Shiona? Am I hurting you?' There was amusement in Jake's voice, but there was something else as well.

'Yes,' she lied. 'And, what's more, you're suffocating me.' She took an elaborate deep breath. 'I can scarcely breathe.'

She felt him smile, but she did not look at him. And it was true, she was finding breathing increasingly difficult, thanks to the wild commotion in her heart.

Just as they had that other time when he had briefly held her, her senses were reacting with a will of their own. With her mind and her intellect Shiona knew that she hated him, yet, shamelessly, wantonly, her body still craved him. She could have wept for the agony of raw longing that burned through her.

She had never been kissed by him in all the years she had known him—apart from a brotherly peck on the cheek. But she had dreamed of it endlessly in those days when she had adored him. Her imagination had run wild as she had fantasised tirelessly about how it would feel to have him hold her, his mouth pressed in passion against her own.

Now suddenly she could feel the pleasure such imaginings had aroused uncurling in a warm spiral in the pit of her stomach. All at once a bright fire seemed to burn through her veins, making her skin glow and causing her limbs to tremble.

She shuddered helplessly and closed her eyes. 'Jake. . . Oh, Jake. . .' Her voice trailed off. She no longer had any idea what it was she wanted to say to him.

'Yes, my sweet temptress?' His warm breath fanned her face. She felt him move closer, his fingers tangling in her hair. 'I'm listening, my sweet temptress. Tell me what you want?'

I want nothing! Let me go! But she did not speak the words, only whispered them despairingly inside her head. She felt like that fish caught by the curlew, one part of her praying that he would spit her out again, the other, perversely, longing for him to swallow her up.

And then, to her astonishment, she heard herself say, 'Shouldn't you go upstairs and see how Janice is? I'm sure she's waiting for you to look in and say goodnight.'

'You think so, do you?' There was a harsh note in his voice.

'I also think you'd be better employed looking after your fiancée instead of bullying me.'

'Is that what I've been doing?'

'What else would you call it?' At last she dared to meet his eyes again. 'And you ought to know by now that it's a waste of time.'

There was a dark look in his eyes as he continued

to look down at her, but as she proceeded to wriggle away from him he made no move to stop her. 'You're right. Everything with you is a waste of time.' He smiled a harsh smile and stepped away from the door. 'Go on. Get out of my sight before I lose patience with you totally.'

Without a word, Shiona hastened to oblige, turning on her heel and snatching hold of the door-handle, then, with a final crushing glance at him, stepping out into the hall.

But as she hurried up the stairs to the sanctuary of her bedroom, what filled her mind was the stark, appalling thought of the treachery she had so nearly perpetrated on herself.

If, back there in the dining-room, he had tried to kiss her, she knew she would have made no effort to stop him. And worse. Even now the thought of that kiss, that for one moment had hovered so dangerously between them, writhed inside her like a bitter, cruel torment.

For she had longed for it desperately. And, to her shame, she did still.

It was the longest weekend Shiona had ever endured. A hundred miserable lifetimes condensed into two wretched days.

What made it even worse was that she had to pretend to enjoy it. For Kirsty's sake she had to put on a bright face.

Jake had organised a mass of entertainments—including a visit to Stirling Castle, a leisurely hill-walk over the Braes of Balquhidder, and a trip to the legendary Rob Roy's grave. And, although they were all enjoyable excursions, to Shiona they felt like a dose of purgatory. For they meant that she was forced to spend the entire weekend in Jake's company.

Of course, she had an option. She could have declined to accompany them. But even if Kirsty hadn't insisted, she would have taken part anyway. In spite of everything, being with Kirsty was fun, and, besides, she wanted to keep an eye on Janice, and perhaps gather more proof regarding her own 'intuition'.

This she did to her quiet satisfaction, thanks to a careless slip by Janice. After their walk across the Braes of Balquhidder, Shiona and Janice got back to the car first. Janice climbed into the leather-scented Mercedes and looked around her with a self-satisfied smile.

'Quite a car,' she murmured half to herself. 'I shall quite enjoy getting used to this lifestyle.'

'I'm sure you will.' Shiona spoke quietly. 'And, after all, if you haven't got it yourself, it's a pretty smart move to marry into money.'

'My philosophy precisely.' Janice had said it without thinking, but then an instant later she realised her lapse. 'Just my little joke.' She forced a sweet smile. 'I would never dream of marrying for anything less than love.'

'Of course you wouldn't.' Poor Jake, Shiona thought, the sentiment surprising her a little. Surely Jake deserved a wife precisely like Janice—the gold-digger he'd always accused Shiona of being.

But that was not what concerned her. What concerned her was Kirsty. And now she was doubly determined that Janice would never be her mother.

It was a relief when the weekend was finally over. On Sunday night Shiona got ready for bed, knowing that by next morning Janice would be gone. At least in the meantime there would be no more cosy threesomes to endure, and she could put her mind to deciding how to conduct her battle to save Kirsty.

But even more of a reprieve was lurking round the corner. As she was brushing her teeth, the phone in the hall began to ring—and was answered almost immediately, she guessed, by Jake. Then, a few minutes later, as she climbed beneath the bedovers, propping herself against the pillows to read a chapter of her book, she heard footsteps coming up the stairs. Jake, she thought idly, on his way to bed.

But, to her astonishment, a moment later there came a knock on her door. She pulled the covers up around her. 'Who is it?' she called, sensing that she knew.

'It's me. I have to talk to you. Can I come in?'

She pulled the covers higher. 'Of course. If you must.'

Jake smiled as he saw her. 'Quite the little virgin. You'd think no man had ever seen you in your nightgown before.'

No man ever had, she could truthfully have answered him. But she simply snapped instead, 'What do you want?'

As he stepped into the room, the door swung shut behind him, causing a skitter of claustrophobia to make Shiona catch her breath. Please open the door, she felt like telling him. But she knew he would only mock her, so with an effort she refrained.

'That was one of my senior managers on the phone.' Though still dressed, he had removed his jacket and tie, and the top few buttons of his shirt were undone. 'There's been a bit of a crisis over the weekend—some vital supplies have been held up—and, apparently, my presence is urgently required.'

Shiona raised her eyebrows. They're more than welcome to you, she was thinking. 'How unfortunate,' she observed with an insincere smile.

'Yes, I figured you'd probably be pretty broken up.' Jake stuffed his hands into the pockets of his trousers. 'This means I'll have to leave tomorrow morning with Janice. I hope to be back before the end of the week.'

'That serious?' She smiled again. 'Well, I won't try to stop you. And please feel free to stay away as long as you please.'

Jake laughed softly and shook his head at her. 'You're so damned predictable. I can always tell exactly what you're going to say next.'

'Then that makes two of us,' Shiona countered, meeting the blue eyes that suddenly seemed to have grown darker beneath the sweep of thick black lashes. 'I can always tell what's in *your* mind. All I have to do is think of the most unpleasant thing possible.'

'So, what's in my mind now?' He had taken a step towards her. Suddenly he seemed to be standing very close to the bed. He paused and looked down at her, a strange smile hovering on his lips. 'Go on, tell me, since you know me so well.'

Shiona shivered beneath the bedclothes, though her flesh was suddenly burning. And somehow she couldn't stop her gaze from straying to the triangle of naked chest where his shirt buttons were open. She longed to reach out and press her open palm against it.

She tried to cast the thought from her, but it stayed stubbornly with her as he took another small step towards her.

'Aren't you going to tell me?' He was smiling strangely. 'It's not like you to be so backward.' Then, to her horror, he reached out and touched her hair. 'How utterly tempting you look lying there.'

Shiona caught her breath. Her heart was suddenly pounding. She felt a twist of raw burning longing in her loins. 'When will you be leaving?' she enquired crassly, not quite daring to meet his eyes.

'Long before you're up, my sweet Shiona. Unless, of course, you particularly want to see me off. I can easily wake you, if you wish.'

'Please don't bother yourself.' She forced herself to speak calmly. 'It's quite enough for me just to know that you're going.'

'You'll be good while I'm gone?' His fingers touched her hair again, stroking the bright strands that fell against the pillow. 'You won't do anything I wouldn't approve of?'

'Like what, for example?' Her voice was husky. She longed to turn her cheek and press it against his palm.

'I mean you'll look after Kirsty?'

'Of course I'll look after Kirsty.'

'You won't go gallivanting about, looking for excitement, and forget where your first responsibility lies?'

Shiona managed a small laugh. 'I think I'd have a hard job trying to find the sort of excitement you're referring to here, around Loch Lomond.'

'Yes, I think you probably would.' Jake smiled in agreement. 'It's not the liveliest place in the world.'

That's why I like it. Shiona almost said it. Suddenly she desperately wanted him to know the truth. The sort of 'gallivanting about' that he seemed always to associate with her had never been a part of her life at all.

She looked into his face. But he would never believe her. And she already knew how much it hurt to keep trying and trying, only to fail.

'Goodnight, Shiona.'

As she continued to gaze up at him, a million thoughts writhing around in her head, all at once he bent towards her, making her heart stop, and planted a soft kiss on her cheek.

Then, almost in the same breath, he turned on his heel and strode out of the room without another word.

CHAPTER FIVE

IT APPEARED to be a week for crises.

On the Wednesday after Jake returned to Edinburgh to deal with the crisis at MacKay Contracting, Shiona received a frantic phone call from Desmond, her second-in-command in London.

'You've got to come down,' he urged her, close to panic. 'That big fashion gala we've got scheduled for Paris is going to fall through unless you have a word with the organisers. I've done my damnedest, but they insist on speaking to you.'

'Oh, lord!' Shiona wailed. 'Can't it wait till next week? There's no way I can manage to come down at the moment.' With perfect bad timing Inge, the au pair, had left that very morning on a few days' holiday, and tomorrow was Nettie the housekeeper's day off. Who would look after Kirsty if Shiona was to go dashing down to London?

'It's up to you, darling, but next week will be too late. If you want the Paris gala to go ahead, you'd be wise to get down here before the weekend.'

Shiona felt like weeping. She couldn't jeopardise the gala. She had been planning it for months now, and it was vitally important. Already her knitwear had gained a small foothold on the Continent. This gala could finally secure her position.

'OK, I'll do my best,' she promised Desmond. 'If

there's any way to fix it, I'll be there before the weekend.'

As she put down the phone, her brain was working overtime. How on earth could she possibly manage it? Then, in a flash, the perfect solution occurred to her. Instantly she rushed out into the garden to find Kirsty.

The little girl, newly returned from school, was playing with a ball beside the sundial. Shiona took her hands in hers and knelt down beside her. 'How would you like to go with Aunt Shiona down to London?'

The child's eyes widened. 'On the train? I've never been on a train before.'

'On the train, if you like,' Shiona nodded, quickly amending her original plan to fly. If they caught the Sleeper tonight instead of flying down tomorrow morning, it would work out equally convenient. 'Just for one day,' she told the bright-eyed Kirsty. 'We'll come back again tomorrow night.'

'On the train again?'

'On the train again.' Shiona gathered her up in her arms and kissed her. Then she held her at arm's length and frowned a little. 'But you must promise me not to tell Uncle Jake. You must promise me that this will be our little secret.'

'I promise.' Kirsty nodded. 'But what about Miss Brewster? We'll have to tell Miss Brewster that I won't be at school.'

'Don't you worry about Miss Brewster. Aunt Shiona will phone her and explain everything,' she promised. Thank heavens, she was thinking, that she was on good terms with Kirsty's teacher. Speaking to Miss Brewster wouldn't be a problem.

The next thing Shiona did was phone Glasgow Central Station and book two sleepers on the overnight train that left just before midnight. They would arrive in London just after six, giving her an entire day to sort out her problems.

As she quickly packed a bag before preparing dinner, it suddenly struck her what a risk she was taking. If Jake found out he would have her guts for garters!

She pursed her lips determinedly. But he wouldn't find out. How on earth could he? she reassured herself.

A couple of hours later she was bundling a sleepy but highly excited Kirsty into the back seat of the car, then heading towards Glasgow with a huge sigh of relief. Her worst fear had been that Jake would show up before they had even left Lomond View.

That was one hurdle passed, she thought, gripping the steering-wheel. But, all the same, she wouldn't feel safe until they were finally aboard the train and it was heading south out of Central Station. Only then could she really afford to relax.

Kirsty chattered excitedly throughout the journey, helping to keep Shiona's mind off her anxieties. By the time they'd parked the car and were hurrying towards the station platform, the little girl's enthusiasm had soothed her tattered nerves, and she was really looking forward to their day together in London.

Once inside the tiny sleeping compartment, Kirsty

changed quickly into her pyjamas. 'Can I have the top bunk, Aunt Shiona?' she wheedled.

Shiona rumpled her hair. 'If you promise not to fall out.'

'I won't fall out. I'm not a baby!' As the little girl clambered up, as agile as a monkey, Shiona started to pull her own pyjamas from the bag. But a moment later her heart stopped in her chest as a sharp tap sounded on the door.

Surely it couldn't be Jake? she thought in startled panic. Surely it wasn't possible that he had tracked them down?

She held her breath and opened the door a crack—then almost fainted with relief as the steward enquired politely, 'Will you be requiring tea or coffee in the morning?'

'Coffee, please,' she grinned, so relieved she could have hugged him.

He smiled in return. 'Sleep well,' he told her.

Shiona closed the door just as the train began to move, leaving Glasgow and the threat of Jake behind them. She turned to smile at Kirsty. 'We're on our way. When you wake up we'll be in London.'

Kirsty smiled at her drowsily. 'I like the train. I'd like to sleep on the train every night.'

Minutes later, feeling suddenly totally exhausted by all the nervous tension of the past few hours, Shiona kissed the already sleeping Kirsty goodnight, then climbed into her own bunk and closed her eyes.

I've done it! she thought with a sweet sense of triumph. For once, I've actually outwitted Jake!

Her only faint regret was that Jake would never know!

It seemed like only moments after Shiona had fallen asleep that the light snapped on in the compartment and a strong hand was dragging her from her bunk.

'Get dressed!' a voice snarled. 'In double-quick time!' The hand shook her violently. 'You deceitful little brat!'

Shiona blinked her eyes open, half wondering if this was a nightmare, her gaze flickering automatically to the upper bunk where Kirsty was still lying peacefully asleep. Then, still a little dopey, she glanced back with a frown at the dark, menacing figure standing over her.

'Jake?' she frowned. 'What are you doing here?'

'Don't waste time asking questions! Just get dressed!' he repeated. 'You and Kirsty are leaving the train!'

Shiona rubbed her eyes. 'Are we in London already?' She glanced quickly at her watch. 'We can't be. It's only half-past one.'

'I already told you not to waste time asking questions! I want the pair of you dressed and off this train in five minutes—or I swear I'll drag you off in your pyjamas!'

He snatched the trousers and sweater that hung from a hanger on the wall, and threw them at her, the gesture violent. 'I'm not joking, Shiona. You're in serious trouble. This time you've really gone too far!'

So saying he backed out into the corridor again,

where Shiona caught a glimpse of the frowning faces of a couple of uniformed railway officials. And suddenly she was wide awake. It looked as though she really was in serious trouble.

It took her less than a minute to pull on her clothes and a couple more to dress the still sleeping Kirsty. She gathered the little girl into her arms, grabbed her bag and headed for the door. Suddenly her stomach was churning with anxiety.

Gently but firmly, careful not to wake the child, Jake took Kirsty from her as she stepped out into the corridor. Then, with a nod in the direction of the railwaymen—'Thanks for your assistance, and for holding up the train'—he had grabbed Shiona unceremoniously by the wrist and was dragging her towards the door.

She half stumbled behind him, her anxiety growing. What was going on? Why had they held up the train?

From the signs on the station platform she could see now where they were. And they were nowhere near London. They were in Carlisle, just a few miles south of the Scottish-English border. She shivered in the hostile, cold night air. What was this melodramatic gesture of Jake's all about?

With Kirsty still sleeping soundly against his shoulder, Jake strode towards the exit of the deserted station and out to where his car was parked.

So he had driven down from Edinburgh to intercept the train. He must indeed have been utterly determined to thwart her—not to say very certain that she was on the train. Shiona wondered irritably how he had found out.

As he pulled open the passenger door for her, she scowled at him defiantly. 'Where are you taking us?' she demanded to know.

'Perhaps where I'm taking you is to the nearest police station. . .' His tone was harsh, his eyes like thunder. 'To turn you in for abducting a minor.'

Shiona's eyes shot wide open. 'To *what*?' she protested.

'You heard,' he cut back at her. 'As you're well aware, Kirsty happens to be in my interim custody. She may not be taken out of Scotland without special permission.'

Just for a moment the blood left Shiona's face. For some idiotic reason it had never crossed her mind that she might be doing something illegal. The only thing she'd been worried about was Jake finding out.

But, all the same, he was over-reacting. She turned to glare at him and made an effort to resist as he made to propel her into the passenger seat. 'You know perfectly well I wasn't trying to abduct her! I had to go to London and I couldn't leave her. And anyway, I was planning to bring her back tomorrow.'

But he was clearly in no mood for listening to her excuses. 'Just get in before I throw you in!' he commanded brusquely. 'I'm not interested in hearing what you were planning to do.'

No, she hadn't thought he would be! Shiona threw him a harsh look as, shrugging off his hand, she climbed into the passenger seat. When had he ever been interested in hearing her side of things?

He slammed the door shut, then with infinite care proceeded to lay Kirsty on the back seat. A moment later he was climbing into the driver's seat. 'What an irredeemably selfish person you are to do something like this to an innocent little girl.'

'Kirsty was enjoying herself!' Shiona instantly defended. 'I would never have taken her if I'd thought it would upset her.'

In response Jake gave an angry little laugh. 'Save it for the police. They might listen to your excuses.'

'Yes, I think they might.' Shiona was defiant. 'In fact I'm sure they'll be much more reasonable than you. At least they'll *listen* to what I have to say!' She sat back in her seat and kept her eyes fixed ahead of her. 'So by all means take me, and let's sort this whole thing out.'

If he thought he could scare her with his stupid little threats, he would soon find out that he was mistaken!

But, fifteen minutes later, it wasn't the police station, but one of the local hotels that they drew up in front of.

'Take your bag and get out,' Jake told her without looking at her. Then, as she obeyed, he was reaching into the back seat of the car and lifting out Kirsty, who had never once stirred.

'I thought you were taking me to the police station.' Shiona eyed him challengingly over the bonnet of the car. 'Don't tell me you've had a sudden change of heart?'

'Perhaps I've decided it can wait until tomorrow.'

His tone was as icy as a glacier. 'I think our first priority should be to get Kirsty to bed.'

Shiona couldn't have agreed more, but her tone was taunting as she told him, 'What a pity you'll have to wait until tomorrow to see me led away in chains.'

'For such a pleasing spectacle I don't mind waiting. It'll give me something to look forward to.' With a brief, mocking smile, he turned away and hurried up the steps to the hotel lobby, his back as hostile as a roll of barbed wire.

Once inside, he turned and handed her Kirsty. 'Perhaps you can look after her for five minutes while I go and book the rooms?' His gaze grazed hers. 'You'll manage that, will you?'

Shiona sliced him a look as she took the child to her bosom. 'I always look after her!' she snapped back.

A couple of minutes later he was snapping his fingers at her, inviting her to follow him to the lift. He took Kirsty again, and handed Shiona a key. 'Second floor. Room 207.'

The room was warm and comfortable, with a big double bed and its own adjoining little bathroom.

Jake laid Kirsty on the bed. 'You'd better get her into her pyjamas,' he told Shiona. Then he turned—so Shiona thought—to go off to his own room. But instead he headed for the bathroom. 'I'm going to have a very quick shower.'

What was he up to? Shiona frowned. 'Wouldn't you be better to have it in your own room?'

He turned then to look at her, his expression faintly mocking. 'This *is* my own room, my dear Shiona.'

'Then where is mine?'

'Yours is right here.'

'You mean to tell me we're sharing a room?'

He nodded. 'That's right. You've got it in one.'

Shiona took a deep breath. 'But that's out of the question. I have no intention of sharing a room with you.'

'Then you must sleep out in the corridor.' The blue eyes were shuttered. 'This is the only room they have.'

'And where are we all supposed to sleep? The three of us all together in one bed?' She shuddered pointedly. 'That may appeal to you, but there's no way I would consider it even for a moment.'

'I quite agree.' He was watching her closely, and she could not quite make out the expression in his eyes. 'Three in a bed would be something of a crush. However. . .' He paused. 'If you look over in the corner, there's a little ante-room with a single bed—intended, so I believe, to accommodate a child.'

Shiona followed his gaze and saw the ante-room door that had quite escaped her notice before. Then once more she snapped her eyes back to Jake. 'That's still not good enough,' she protested. 'I have no intention of sharing a bed with you!'

He smiled an amused smile. 'You needn't worry. I'm so damned tired after the drive down here that I doubt I'll have the energy for anything more than sleep.'

In spite of herself, at the way he looked at her,

Shiona felt a flutter in the pit of her stomach. Even in this far from congenial situation the thought of sharing a bed with Jake made her pulse beat faster and warmth rise to her cheeks.

Yet in the very same instant the warm flutter died away to be replaced by the weight of cold reality. How could she, even fleetingly, entertain such a thought for a man who despised her so deeply and so openly?

She glared across at him. 'I'd rather sleep on the floor than have to share a bed with you.'

The blue eyes narrowed as he regarded her for a moment. 'Don't worry, dear Shiona. For once, I share your view. I can think of nothing less appealing than climbing into bed with you—which is why I intend to sleep in the ante-room. You and Kirsty can share the bed in here.'

He turned away sharply. 'Now, if you don't mind, I'm going to have that shower and get my head down. I'd like to get a little sleep tonight.'

As the door of the bathroom closed behind him, Shiona picked up her travel bag with a flash of irritation. So, he had been winding her up about their sharing the same bed, amusing himself at her expense! She pulled out her own and Kirsty's pyjamas. Well, let him have his little joke! All that really mattered, after all, was that there would be a stout door to separate the two of them tonight!

It was just at that moment that Kirsty stirred. She blinked at Shiona and half sat up on the bed. 'Are we in London?' she wanted to know.

Shiona hugged her. 'No, we're not in London.

We're somewhere much nicer. We're in Carlisle.' She kissed the child warmly. 'And, what's more,' she told her, 'there's an extra-special surprise for you waiting behind that door. . .'

As she nodded towards the bathroom, right on cue it opened, and Jake, dressed in trousers with a towel slung round his neck, came walking with a broad smile into the room.

Kirsty grinned from ear to ear. 'Uncle Jake!' she squealed happily. Then she frowned a little. 'Why aren't we on the train?'

Jake perched on the edge of the bed beside her. 'I'm afraid that's my fault,' he confessed. 'I got Aunt Shiona to leave the train early so we could all spend the night together here.'

Shiona nodded in agreement. 'I hope you don't mind? We'll go on the train to London some other time.'

'OK.' The child nodded, apparently content with that promise. Then she rubbed her eyes. 'I'm sleepy,' she sighed.

Five minutes later she was tucked up in bed, sleeping happily once again, while Jake had retreated to his little ante-room. Shiona gathered up her pyjamas and headed for the bathroom, her mind retracing the events of the night.

Now that she had calmed down it was very clear to her that her actions had been rash, to say the least. She had broken the law unwittingly, but still she had broken it, and if Jake was really determined he could make her pay for it.

If he decided to report her, he could then use her

lapse against her when the custody case finally came to court. It would not be too difficult for his legal representative to brand her as rash and irresponsible—scarcely attributes the judge would be looking for in little Kirsty's potential guardian!

She washed quickly and undressed. Somehow she must convince Jake that it would be wrong to judge her harshly. She may have acted impetuously, but she'd intended no malice, and she'd always had Kirsty's best interests at heart.

And now would be a good time to talk to him, she decided, as she pulled on her pyjamas and brushed back her hair. His mood had softened after his little chat with Kirsty. And besides, she knew that if she waited till morning she would simply toss and turn all night.

As she stepped out of the bathroom she stole a quick glance at the bed, just to check that Kirsty was still sleeping. Then, taking a deep breath, she crossed to the little ante-room and tapped with her knuckles on the door.

'Jake, are you awake? I'd like to speak to you.'

There was no reply, just an impatient grunt that at least confirmed that he wasn't sleeping. Shiona pushed the door open and stepped inside, pulling it to again before she tiptoed towards the bed.

'I'm sorry to bother you,' she whispered. 'But I have to talk to you. I promise you it'll only take a minute.'

The only light was the crack of light down the side of the door. She could just make him out as he rolled over to face her. 'What the hell do you want? Can't you let a man sleep?'

'I'm sorry, Jake.' She squatted beside him, as he propped himself up on one elbow to scowl back at her. 'I can't sleep without telling you what really happened.'

He expelled his breath impatiently. 'What are you talking about? I already know exactly what happened.'

'No, you don't.' Shiona hurried on quickly. 'You seem to think I was planning to abduct Kirsty. I wasn't. I was merely taking her down to London for a day. I was planning to bring her back on the Sleeper tonight.'

'I'll bet you were.' He regarded her sceptically. 'And what made you think that poor little Kirsty was so desperately in need of a day-trip to London?'

Shiona shook her head. 'It wasn't a day-trip. I *had* to go to London. There's a crisis on at the studio. And, since Inge's on holiday and it's Nettie's day off, there was no way I could leave her at Lomond View.' She peered at him through the semi-darkness. 'That's the only reason I took her.'

Jake seemed unmoved by her explanation. 'So why couldn't this tale of yours have kept until morning?' In the half-light of the room his eyes were scornful, the set of his jaw mocking and hard. 'Do you perhaps believe a man is more susceptible to persuasion when he's lying in bed naked in the middle of the night?'

Shiona blinked, taken aback by his accusation. 'Of course not!' she protested. 'The thought never occurred to me!' Yet, though it was perfectly true, she backed away a little, for suddenly she was quite overpoweringly conscious of his virile naked form beneath the blankets.

He simply smiled, openly disbelieving, and raised himself a little higher on his elbow. His eyes seemed to darken as his gaze roved over her. 'Perhaps you also believe that a man is more easily persuaded by a beautiful, semi-naked girl.'

'I'm not semi-naked!' All at once Shiona's heart was pounding. The broad, sinewy shoulders and the powerfully muscled chest suddenly seemed to fill her vision. She swallowed drily, backing away another centimetre. 'I'm wearing a perfectly respectable pair of pyjamas!'

'Not from where I'm lying, you're not.'

As his eyes drifted pointedly downwards to her bosom, Shiona saw his free hand reach out towards her. She started to spring away—'What the devil do you think you're doing?'—and simultaneously glanced down at her pyjama-jacket. And to her horror she could see that in her haste to come and speak to him she had only buttoned the bottom two buttons, and the way she was sitting, crouching forward slightly, one smooth, firm breast was entirely exposed.

Colour flooded her face as she tried to struggle to her feet, desperate to evade the hand that was stretched towards her. But he was far too quick for her. As she staggered awkwardly, he grabbed firm hold of the sagging pyjama-jacket, arresting her flight as he held her there.

Her skin was burning as she thought he might

touch her. Any minute she expected to feel his hand on her breast.

But instead he pulled the jacket closed, the gesture deliberately rough and contemptuous. 'Cover yourself, Shiona,' he admonished her harshly. 'I'm not remotely interested in your crude efforts at seduction. You may have succeeded with my brother, but I've warned you before you're wasting your time with me!'

As he released her she stumbled to her feet, her face on fire, her heart thumping within her. 'Don't flatter yourself! I wasn't trying to seduce you!' She felt angry and hurt and deeply humiliated.

He regarded her coldly. 'I've told you, I'm not Ryan. You won't find it quite so easy to manipulate me.' Then, with a look that froze her, he turned away. 'Go now!' he commanded. 'Leave me in peace!'

Shiona bit her lip. Suddenly she felt like weeping. Then without another word she rose to her feet, hating the huddled figure lying with his back to her.

'My pleasure!' she muttered defiantly to herself, as she hurried from the ante-room, closed the door behind her, and headed for the sanctuary of her own bed.

'It's time to get up!' Kirsty was shaking her. 'Uncle Jake says we've to be down for breakfast in a quarter of an hour.'

Shiona struggled to consciousness and rubbed her eyes. 'What time is it?' she mumbled hoarsely. She felt as though she'd been asleep for about five minutes!

'It's eight o'clock. Uncle Jake says it's late. He says we've got to be on the road by nine o'clock at the latest.'

With a huge yawn Shiona pulled herself upright. Then she reached out and hugged little Kirsty tightly. 'How are you feeling? Did you sleep all right?'

Kirsty nodded. 'Yes, and I'm hungry. Can I have toast and honey for breakfast?'

'Of course you can. You can have anything you like.' Shiona swung her legs down on to the carpet. 'I'll race you. Let's see who's dressed and ready first!'

Just under twenty minutes later, with Kirsty having won the contest easily, the two of them were heading downstairs to the breakfast-room. And, as they walked through the doorway of the big, sunny room, the dark-haired man at the table by the window glanced up from his copy of *The Times*.

He looked immaculate and well rested, as though he had slept for twelve hours instead of a scanty, meagre five. She had circles like bicycle tyres under her eyes, but there was no sign of even the faintest shadow beneath his!

Damn him! Shiona thought. How does he do it?

As Kirsty scampered towards him, Jake laid down his newspaper, kissed her on the cheek, then glanced up at Shiona. 'So you made it, after all.' His tone was lightly sarcastic. 'You looked as though you were set to sleep all day.'

She probably would have done if she had been left to her own devices! But she feigned disdain as she sat down opposite him. 'I have far too busy a day planned for anything so self-indulgent.'

Before he could comment a waitress arrived to take her and Kirsty's order for bacon and eggs and toast and honey. But once the woman had gone, Jake raised one dark eyebrow. 'Perhaps you wouldn't mind enlightening me as to what you're planning?'

Shiona paused before answering to pour some orange juice for Kirsty. Then, her eyes on his face, she poured some for herself. 'Of course, it all rather depends,' she put to him in a wry tone, 'on the outcome of our visit to the police station. If they decide to arrest me and throw me in gaol, my plans will have to be drastically altered. . .'

She saw a flicker of something cross his eyes. Possibly amusement. Possibly something else. He topped up his coffee-cup before answering, 'And what do you plan to do if they don't?'

Shiona shrugged. 'Catch the first flight to London. As I told you, there's a crisis on at the studio. They need me there to sort it out.'

He took a mouthful of his coffee. 'So that story you told me. . . You mean to say it was true, after all?'

'Of course it was true. Why would I lie to you?'

That struck him as funny. He gave a small laugh. 'To save your hide, that's why you'd lie to me. And also because you're in the habit of doing so.'

Shiona sighed impatiently. 'Surely even you couldn't have seriously thought that I intended abducting Kirsty?' She cast a quick, cautious glance at the little girl, fearing that she might have over-heard, but Kirsty had slid down from her chair and was quite clearly totally absorbed in watching the antics of the hotel cat through the window. 'I would never subject Kirsty to that sort of tug-of-love.'

He regarded her for a moment as though considering what she'd told him. 'OK,' he said at last, 'I shan't turn you in. I've decided to let you off this time.'

As she smiled smugly—she'd suspected he wouldn't—he deliberately threw her a frosty glance.

'But don't ever try a trick like that again,' he warned. 'There was no excuse for it, whatever the circumstances. All you had to do was telephone me, and I would have come at once to look after Kirsty.'

'I didn't think of that.' It was true, she hadn't. 'I took her because there was no one else around to look after her.' She tilted her chin at him. 'No harm would have come to her. She would have enjoyed her little trip to London.'

'Perhaps she would.' Jake smiled enigmatically. 'But the law is the law. It's not there to be broken. So don't do it again.' He held her eyes a moment. 'Next time I really will turn you in.'

Shiona took a mouthful of her orange juice. 'I'm still curious about one thing. . . How did you know we were on that train?'

'An educated guess.' He sat back in his seat. 'I phoned Lomond View to say I was coming back tomorrow morning, and when no one answered I was immediately suspicious. I'm afraid I simply put two and two together.'

He gave her a shrewd smile. 'You see, I know you. I know the sort of devious little things you get up to.

So I got straight into the car and headed south, hoping I could reach Carlisle before the train did. I knew the train wouldn't stop again until it reached London.'

'What a pity you made it.' Shiona smiled unsympathetically. 'That would've been quite a drive for you all the way to London. I reckon it would've taken you most of the night.'

She laid down her orange juice. 'But I'm still curious. How did you manage to persuade British Rail to allow you on to the train so you could drag me off?'

'I didn't drag you off, I merely escorted you. I'm sure they wouldn't have stood for any rough stuff.' He paused and shrugged. 'I simply told them that you were my wife and that you had taken all our money and our little girl and were running off to London to be with your lover.' He smiled a smug smile. 'They were most sympathetic. But though I say it myself, I spun them a pretty good story.'

'You devious devil!' Shiona laughed in spite of herself. 'What on earth must those men at the station have thought of me?'

Jake laughed with her. 'Not a lot, I'm afraid. I really laid your crimes on with a trowel.'

'I'll bet you did!' Her tone was teasing. 'No wonder they were giving me funny looks!'

He continued to smile across at her. 'Let that be a lesson.' Then, as the waitress arrived with Kirsty's and Shiona's orders, he glanced at the slim gold watch at his wrist. 'If you don't mind, I'd like to be on my way pretty soon. I'm expecting a couple of overseas phone calls at the house.' He paused. 'I can drop you off at Glasgow airport, if you like, or you can take a train to Prestwick and catch a plane from there.'

Shiona thought for only a moment. 'I'll fly from Prestwick.' She suspected it might be marginally quicker.

'OK, then I'll drop you off at the station.' He called to Kirsty. 'Come and eat your toast. They've brought your favourite brand of honey.'

Twenty minutes later they were on their way, the three of them piling into the big black Mercedes and heading back to the railway station.

Shiona stole a secret glance at Jake's profile. In a strange sort of way things felt easier between them. The anger and the hostility had quite gone from his manner, as though some kind of tacit truce had been reached.

And she had to confess, much as she hated to, that it felt nice to be on amicable terms with Jake. Perhaps, now that the air had been cleared between them, they might be able to achieve a state of understanding. Perhaps when she got back to Loch Lomond tomorrow they could sit down and discuss things in a civilised fashion.

Jake started to slow down as the station came in sight, and Shiona turned to him, pulling a face. 'I hope the same guys aren't there who were on duty last night. I don't think I could bear to look them in the face.'

He pulled into the forecourt. 'Don't worry, they won't be there. Their shift will have ended long ago.'

Shiona smiled. 'I certainly hope so.' Then she leaned into the back of the car to kiss Kirsty. 'I'll see you soon. Probably tomorrow. In the meantime, be a good girl.'

'I will be. 'Bye, Aunt Shiona.' As Shiona grabbed her bag and bade farewell to Jake, then hurried round the front of the car to the station entrance, the little girl leaned against the window and waved.

As Shiona paused to wave back, Jake's window buzzed open and suddenly he was leaning out slightly towards her. 'I wouldn't bother coming back,' he told her in a detached voice. 'It's a waste of your time and an annoyance to me. Just accept that you're beaten and stay away.'

Before she could answer, the window buzzed closed again and the big car was moving away from the kerb. And suddenly, for no reason, a pain went through her, as though he had reached out and driven a stake through her heart.

And in that moment she wished with every fibre of her being that it really was possible for her to stay away. Out of his reach. Where he couldn't hurt her. Where she need never think of him again.

She turned away stiffly. But she had no choice. For Kirsty's sake, she had to return.

CHAPTER SIX

'THANK heavens you're here!'

As she walked into the studio, a beaming Desmond rushed up to greet her. 'I've just had Henri on the line again, still being as hopelessly impossible as ever. He's threatening to fly back to Paris this evening unless he can fix up a meeting with you.'

Shiona took his arm as they headed for her office. 'Well, I'm here now, so he can see me whenever he likes.' She laughed good-naturedly and squeezed his arm. 'Come and fill me in over a cup of coffee.'

Twenty minutes later, after a diplomatic phone call, Shiona had succeeded in smoothing some of Henri's ruffled feathers. As she made a quick tour of the studio before dashing out to meet him, she was aware of a great sense of personal satisfaction.

It was so good to be among people who respected and admired her, and whom she admired and respected in return. After the past week at Loch Lomond, with Jake forever finding fault with her, it was like a dose of summer sunshine just to be accepted for what she was.

For she was far from being the ruthlessly manipulative monster that Jake appeared to have convinced himself she was. All she was was an extremely hard-working girl whose dreams and aspirations had, miraculously, been achieved. And achieved, what was more, almost entirely by her own efforts—even her stepfather had granted her that. For, unlike Jake, Douglas had never accused her of having cheated Ryan out of his fortune—in spite of the fact that, like the rest of the family, he had never known the tragic truth about his son.

Perhaps her mother had convinced him that Shiona was incapable of such behaviour, or perhaps he hadn't needed any convincing. He had always been kindly disposed towards his stepdaughter. Perhaps he had simply given her the benefit of the doubt.

Unlike Jake, who had always done the opposite. But then Jake seemed to take pleasure in believing the worst of her.

Shiona cast these thoughts from her as she hurried out to grab a taxi. Ahead of her lay an important business meeting. She must not allow thoughts of Jake to disturb her and upset her precious peace of mind.

But even as she deliberately shut him from her thoughts, it struck her with an icy sense of unease that over the past week something rather worrying had happened.

She had thought the time had gone when thoughts of Jake could upset her. But that, quite simply, was no longer so.

The meeting with Henri was a resounding success. Back at the studio three hours later Shiona told Desmond, 'The Paris gala is on! Henri has promised his full co-operation!'

'Congratulations! I knew you'd do it!' Desmond

subjected her to a spectacular hug. He glanced at his watch. 'Let's go and have a drink, then you can treat me to a celebratory dinner!'

'So, what are your plans?' he asked her later, as the waiter served them gâteaus from a sumptuous dessert trolley. 'Will you be staying around for a while, or going straight back to bonny Scotland?'

Shiona shook her head. 'Going straight back, I'm afraid. The custody hearing could be called at any time. I have to be there. I have to be on hand.'

'Do you think you can win?' Desmond's tone was sympathetic. 'I know how much that little girl means to you.'

Shiona shook her head. 'She means the world to me. That's why I've got to try, even though it looks hopeless. I can't let her fall into the hands of that awful woman.'

Desmond eyed her anguished face with sympathy. Then he took a bite of his passion cake and asked, 'How come Jake's marrying her if she's so awful? From what you've told me, he doesn't sound like anybody's fool.'

'Believe me, he's not. Anything but. But he never sees the awful side of her. When he's around she's all sweetness and light.'

'Have you told him what you've seen?'

'He wouldn't believe me. He'd think I was saying it out of spite.' She sat back in her seat. 'But perhaps the judge will believe me—and he's the one I really have to convince.'

Desmond reached out and laid a sympathetic hand

on her arm. 'I'm sure you can do it. You're a winner, Shiona. Whatever happens, just remember that.'

Shiona's plane touched down at Glasgow airport just a few minutes before midday the following day. Remembering that her car was still abandoned at Central Station, she took a taxi to where she had left it, and was relieved to find it still waiting there.

But as she drove out of the city, heading for the road bridge and the Kilpatrick Hills on the north bank of the Clyde, she could feel the tension in her tightening. Usually the familiar beauty of this place had the very opposite effect on her, but today as she headed towards Loch Lomond she was filled with a terrible sense of doom. By the time she finally headed south again Kirsty's future would have been decided. The thought made her stomach shrink inside her.

Instantly she chided herself. Be a little more positive! Remember what Desmond said. Remember you're a winner!

Just that thought made the energy surge through her. However hard she had to fight, she would make certain that Janice never became Kirsty's mother!

It was a great relief when she arrived at Lomond View to discover that the only person there was Inge, looking rosy-cheeked and happy after her few days' holiday. The thought of an immediate confrontation with Jake was not one which Shiona had been particularly relishing.

But she was a little worried when Inge told her, 'They haven't been back here, as far as I know. Mr MacKay phoned last night, just after I got in, to say that he and Kirsty were in Edinburgh and that they'd be staying there until further notice.'

Shiona bit back her anger. What was he playing at? Was this his way of paying her back for trying to sneak Kirsty down to London?

She put on a calm face. 'Well, whatever he said, he can't keep her away indefinitely. He has to bring her back for school on Monday. She's already missed a couple of days.'

But by Sunday evening there was still no sign of him, and no telephone call to explain what was happening. With difficulty Shiona resisted the urge to phone him up at home and demand an explanation. After all, he might be planning to bring Kirsty back on Monday morning, and there was no point in antagonising him unnecessarily.

When by Monday lunchtime there was still no word from him, however, she tried phoning him up at MacKay Contracting—only to be told that he was unavailable. The story was similar when she tried calling the house in desperation later that evening. 'Sorry, Mr MacKay can't be disturbed. If you'd like to leave a message, he'll get back to you.'

Needless to say, he did not get back to her. When Tuesday arrived Shiona was still in the dark. But not for much longer, she decided, her anger growing by the minute. Since he refuses to talk to me over the phone, he'll have the pleasure of talking to me in person instead!

She drove to Edinburgh in just over two hours, and headed for Jake's office, just off Princes Street, in the shadow of the capital's ancient, brooding castle. She parked her car and strode through the grand, carved doorway, her heels clicking purposefully as she headed for the reception desk.

'I've come to see Jake MacKay,' she told the girl at the desk, tossing back her mane of bright auburn hair.

The girl looked her up and down with curiosity. 'Do you have an appointment?' she enquired politely. 'Mr MacKay never sees anyone without an appointment.'

'Oh, don't worry, he'll see me. I'm his sister. And I'm here on urgent family business.'

As the girl raised a surprised eyebrow, Shiona smiled to herself. She had also surprised herself a little with her claim. It was the first time she had ever referred to herself as Jake's sister. She had never even referred to herself as his *stepsister* before! But then, she had never thought of him in a sisterly fashion. Unlike her attitude towards Ryan. She had been a true sister to Ryan.

The receptionist, still watching her, was phoning up to Jake's office. 'Your sister's here on urgent family business. She wants to see you right away.'

After a moment she laid the receiver down again, her surprise now turned to total bafflement. 'I'm sorry, he says he's too busy to see you.'

Shiona clenched her jaw. 'Does he indeed?' Then she was marching swiftly past the reception desk, heading for the lifts at the back of the hall. 'Well, he'll see me anyway!' she muttered to herself.

She had only ever visited his office once before—as an awestruck teenager in the company of her stepfather—but she remembered precisely where it was. On the top floor of the building, with a fine view of the castle.

As the lift doors opened and she stepped out into the corridor, it occurred to her that she must strike a very different figure from the wide-eyed girl who had made that first visit. Though her heart was thumping as it had then, no one but herself would ever know it. This time she appeared outwardly to be perfectly in control.

She strode through the door to the outer office of his sanctum, past his personal secretary, who blinked in astonishment. Then, without pausing for breath or breaking her stride, she pushed open the door of his private office.

Chin up, shoulders squared, she stepped into the room, and in a cool tone accused him, 'You don't look busy in the least. I'm sure you can spare me a few moments of your time.'

He was seated at his desk, his back to the window, so she could not see his expression clearly. But she didn't need to see it to sense the burning anger that poured from his eyes as he looked up at her.

'How dare you come barging in here like this? Who the hell do you think you are?'

Shiona never faltered. Her nervousness had vanished. She felt suddenly bold, on an adrenalin 'high'. With a mocking smile she lifted one eyebrow. 'Have you forgotten? I'm your sister.'

Jake had risen from his seat and was standing to face her. 'I thought I told you to stay in London? You should have taken my advice. I really don't want you here.'

'That's just too bad. I don't take orders from you. And I don't give a damn if you want me here or not. What's more. . .' she seated herself in one of the button-back chairs '. . . I won't be leaving until you've told me what I want to know.'

There was a click behind her as the office door opened. Shiona heard a soft female voice say, 'I'm sorry, sir. . .' Then, apologetically, 'Shall I bring you some coffee?'

He was about to say no. Shiona could sense it. She turned round sharply and addressed the secretary. 'I'd love some coffee. Black, please. No sugar.'

As she turned back to face Jake, his anger was tangible. He nodded to the secretary. 'Black for me, too.' Then, as the secretary retreated, he sat down in his chair again, laying his hands along the green leather arms. 'Why have you come back?' he demanded, scowling.

'I have unfinished business here.' She looked straight back at him and, smoothing the skirt of her blue wool suit, crossed her legs elegantly at the ankles. 'Don't tell me you'd forgotten that as well?'

He narrowed his eyes at her, then surprised her by smiling. 'Why did you tell Doreen, the downstairs receptionist, that you were my sister?' he enquired.

'Why, isn't it true?'

'Fortunately, no.'

'Stepsister, then.'

'If you insist. Though I must confess I'm rather

surprised that you should wish to claim any relationship at all with me.'

Shiona smiled thinly. 'Yes, it went against the grain. However, my motives, I assure you, were purely practical. I figured it might be useful for gaining access.'

Jake shook his head at her. 'I'm sure no one believed you. No girl could look less like my sister than you do.'

'That doesn't mean anything. Siblings don't always look alike. There are plenty that you would never even guess were related.'

As soon as she'd said it, Shiona wished she hadn't. She felt a sudden uncomfortable twist in her stomach, and she could sense that Jake had felt the same. What two siblings could have been less alike than Jake and his very own brother, Ryan?

She bit her lip, watching his face for that familiar, fleeting shadow of pain, which mention of Ryan always brought to his features—and waiting, feeling suddenly tense, for the bitter attack on her that invariably followed it.

But just for once Jake refrained from attacking her, though he held her eyes for a long, dangerous moment. Then he lowered his gaze and observed with dark humour, 'The receptionist probably thought you were some irate girlfriend come to bring me to book about something or other.'

Shiona frowned at him. 'And you about to be married? Surely there are no irate girlfriends in your life any more?'

She had caught him unawares. He seemed to shift

slightly, and his gaze became shuttered as he answered quickly, 'Absolutely not. I was merely posing a hypothesis.' He reached for the Caithness paperweight on his desk and fiddled with it absently for a moment. Then, as the office door opened, he seized the diversion.

'Ah, here you are with our coffee already.' He smiled at the secretary. 'Just what I'm needing.'

From beneath lowered lashes Shiona watched him in silence, as the secretary set out their cups of coffee before them. What on earth, she was wondering, had caused that un-Jake-like reaction?

She could tell that his remark about 'some irate girlfriend' had been spoken quite spontaneously, without thinking, as a joke. And though it had struck her as a slightly odd remark for a man on the brink of marriage to make, she most probably wouldn't have thought any more about it if he had responded to the way she had light-heartedly picked up on it with his usual unassailable self-assurance.

But he most definitely hadn't. He had seemed thrown for a moment, as though it had genuinely slipped his mind that he was about to be married. Shiona frowned to herself. How very peculiar. Scarcely what one expected from a man who was deeply in love.

And he was in love, surely? she asked herself, frowning. Why else would he be marrying Janice?

She had a sudden sharp memory of the unexpected sleeping arrangements during the weekend when Janice had stayed at Loch Lomond. It had struck her as strange that he had put Janice in the rose room, at the opposite end of the house to where he himself slept. Though she had no personal experience, she had always assumed that Jake would be a man of vigorous sexual appetites. And quite clearly, at least for the duration of that weekend, there had been no sexual activity between himself and his fiancée.

Was it possible, she wondered with a secret lift inside her, that his relationship with Janice was not all it seemed?

She was snapped out of her reverie as the door clicked shut and the secretary left them alone again. Jake sat back in his chair, his fingers toying with the glass paperweight, yet looking totally composed again, back to his old self.

The blue eyes regarded her across the stretch of mahogany desk. 'So, now that you're here, you'd better tell me what you've come for.'

'I think you know what I've come for.' Shiona's eyes narrowed. 'I've come to find out what you've done with Kirsty—and when you intend returning her to Lomond View.'

Jake lifted up the paperweight and let it rest in his palm, his eyes seeming to examine it as he responded, 'The first part of your question is easy to answer. Kirsty is currently staying with me. As to the second part. . .' He shrugged and raised his eyes to meet Shiona's. 'I'm afraid it's impossible for me to give you a definite answer.' He smiled infuriatingly. 'Let's just say that Kirsty will be staying where she is until I see fit to return her.'

Shiona clenched her jaw, her irritation rising. 'How typically high-handed of you,' she replied, her tone glacial. 'Has it slipped your mind that the child has to go to school?'

'High-handed?' He smiled. 'That's good coming from you. At least my action is within the law.'

'I sincerely doubt that.' She let the rebuke slide over her. 'I think you'll find that it's a legal requirement in Scotland that a child be provided with an education.'

'There are schools in Edinburgh.' He regarded her harshly. 'And since she will eventually be coming to live here anyway, don't you think she may as well make the change-over now?'

'No, I'm afraid I don't!' Shiona's eyes were glittering. 'How can you be so utterly selfish as to uproot the child from her home and school at this stage, when nothing has been finally decided by the court? What if I win? Have you thought of that? What if she has to be uprooted all over again, just as she's getting used to her new school?'

She paused for breath as a sudden thought occurred to her, then leaned forward in her seat, her eyes accusing. 'Perhaps that's why you're doing it? To strengthen your case. You're going to present the court with a *fait accompli* to try and persuade them to rule in your favour!'

'They'll rule in my favour anyway.' Jake's tone was dismissive. 'I don't have to resort to such underhand tricks.'

'So you admit it's underhand? Underhand and selfish! I actually thought you cared about Kirsty. Now I know just how wrong I was!'

Jake watched her for a moment, then observed in

a soft voice, 'Of course, I care about Kirsty. I care very much.' Then, before she could answer, he leaned back in his chair and dropped the paper-weight on to the desk. 'That's why I'm keeping her at my place for the moment.' He raised his eyes sharply. 'Until she's recovered from her flu.'

Shiona felt momentarily stunned. She blinked at him owlishly. 'Flu?' she repeated. 'You mean Kirsty has flu?'

'That's what I said.' His tone was acid. 'She started shivering and sneezing soon after we left Carlisle. Considering there was no one to look after her at Lomond View, I decided that the best place for her was with me.'

Shiona swallowed. 'And who's looking after her at your place?'

'Me, when I'm there. But for the most part Mrs Aitken, my live-in housekeeper. Kirsty knows her well and they're very fond of each other. You don't have to worry, she's in excellent hands.'

Shiona glanced away, her eyes dropping to her lap. Suddenly she felt quite overcome with shame to think that Kirsty's illness might be all her fault. If she hadn't subjected her to that late-night journey, with all the upheavals that had accompanied it, perhaps the poor child would not have fallen ill.

'I imagine she caught the bug from someone in her class at school. I understand there's quite a bit of it going around.' Jake fingered the paperweight idly as he continued, 'It had probably been developing for a few days. I suspect that wherever she'd been—on a train to London or at home at Lomond View—it wouldn't have made the slightest bit of difference. It was bound to knock her under, sooner or later.'

It was as though he had read into her mind and gone out of his way to reassure her. Shiona looked across at him, touched by his kindness, and more than a little bewildered by it, too. It was so unexpected. So unlike him.

'I suppose you're right,' she answered gratefully.

He reached for the paperweight and weighed it in his hand again. 'She's already much better, I'm happy to tell you. She's a strong little character, and she's a fighter. In a couple of days she'll be up and about again, but I've been told by the doctor to keep her off school for a while longer. Not that she's complaining about that, of course.'

Shiona smiled. 'Yes, I'll bet.' And inwardly she thanked fate that, after all, Jake had stopped them on their flight to London. If Kirsty had fallen ill once they were down in London she would have been forced to stay there until she'd recovered—and then she would have been in serious trouble, not only with Jake but with the law as well.

She cleared her throat. 'Once she's recovered, you will be bringing her back to Lomond View?'

'Of course. For the moment that's her home. And, as you so responsibly pointed out just a moment ago, that is also where her school is. I'll be taking her back as soon as she's well.'

'I see.' Shiona hesitated for a moment. 'If you don't mind, I'd like to see her before then. Would you object to my paying her a visit?'

He did not answer immediately. Perhaps he would say no. Shiona steeled herself for disappointment.

But instead he answered, 'That would depend.'

'Depend on what?'

'On your intentions.'

'What do you mean?'

'I mean, my dear Shiona, that I must have your absolute assurance that you don't intend trying to spirit her away again.'

'Of course I don't! What do you take me for?' Shiona bit her lip. 'You have my assurance. Absolutely. Unconditionally. I wouldn't dream of doing such a thing.'

Jake dropped the heavy paperweight into the palm of his other hand, his eyes never leaving hers as he did so. 'OK, I'll believe you. For once, I'll trust you. But pity help you if you let me down.'

'I won't.' She felt a dart go through her. What an abysmally low opinion he had of her—and, unexpectedly, that reminder hurt. She held his eyes carefully. 'You can trust me.'

He nodded. 'We shall see.' Then he straightened suddenly and returned the paperweight to its place on his desk. 'You can see her this evening, since you've already made the journey. You can come with me when I leave the office.'

'That would be great! Thank you,' Shiona answered. Then a thought occurred to her. 'That's going to be rather late. By the time we get to your place it'll almost be Kirsty's bedtime. I'd like to spend a little more time with her than that.'

'So stay overnight and spend time with her

tomorrow. That's no problem. There's plenty of room.'

Shiona hesitated, surprised by the invitation, and for some reason assailed by an anxious tightening in her stomach at the thought of staying overnight at Jake's house.

How utterly ridiculous! she chided herself sharply. We've spent dozens of nights under the same roof in the past!

'OK,' she answered, not quite looking at him. Then, on a practical note, she enquired, 'What time do you leave the office?'

'Pretty late, usually. Never before six.' Then, as her face fell, he added, 'However, since Kirsty's been staying with me I've made a point of packing up just after five.' He glanced at his watch. 'It's just gone three now. Can you amuse yourself for a couple of hours?'

'Easily.' Shiona rose to her feet.

'Of course. I'd forgotten.' He deliberately met her eyes. 'You'll have no problem at all filling in a couple of hours with all the Princes Street shops to keep you occupied. Spending money, after all, is one of your favourite pastimes.'

It was yet another dig, and again Shiona felt it bruise her. As Jake started to come round the desk towards her, she turned away, averting her eyes. What was happening to her? Her immunity was crumbling. She was becoming almost as sensitive to him as she had been all those years ago.

On long strides he was leading her towards the door, oblivious to her inner anguish. 'Wait for me downstairs in Reception. I'll be there as soon after five as I can make it.'

He held the door open for her, and she stepped quickly through it. Then as she muttered, 'Goodbye,' he warned in a clipped tone,

'Make sure you're waiting. If you get carried away with your shopping and turn up late, I won't hang around, I'll just leave without you.'

'Thanks for the warning.' Shiona turned to meet his eyes, hating the way her heart was still beating so fast. Then she turned smartly on her heel and marched out of the door.

CHAPTER SEVEN

IN FACT, Shiona very nearly didn't make it in time. She'd been browsing in a bookshop after buying a bedtime book for Kirsty when she'd suddenly caught sight of the clock on the wall and seen, to her horror, that it was nearly five o'clock.

She smiled to herself now as she drove through the outskirts of Edinburgh, eyes fixed like limpets on the black Mercedes in front of her—if she lost sight of Jake now, she was done for! She would never find her way to his house on her own!—and recalled her headlong flight down Princes Street and her breathless arrival back at MacKay Contracting.

'Has Mr MacKay left yet?' she'd enquired of the startled receptionist. It wouldn't have surprised her in the slightest if he'd left a few minutes early, just for the pleasure of leaving her stranded.

But the girl had shaken her head. 'No, not yet.' And, with a thankful sigh, Shiona had sunk down on one of the sofas in the reception area. 'That was a close one!' she'd muttered to herself.

In fact, he didn't appear till almost twenty-past, by which time Shiona had managed to catch her breath and run a surreptitious comb through her wild mane of hair.

As he stepped out of the elevator and strode towards her, she felt her heartbeat do a funny little dance. He looked so tall, so strikingly handsome in the deep blue suit and immaculate white shirt. The hero of her dreams of all those years ago, those dreams that she had never quite forgotten.

She checked the thought instantly. She had taken leave of her senses! Of course she had forgotten them! They were dead and buried! Something must have short-circuited in her brain!

'So you made it.' He smiled a fleeting smile, carefully surveying her as she rose to her feet. 'But where are all your packages?' he asked. 'Have you hidden them in your car?'

Did he never grow tired of making these accusations?

'I don't have any packages,' she informed him tightly. 'All I've bought is a toothbrush for myself and a story book for Kirsty.' She paused an instant. 'You're forgetting,' she reminded him, 'it's only other people's money that I enjoy spending.'

'So it is.' His eyes surveyed her for a moment. Then, almost impatiently, he turned on his heel. 'Let's get moving before the traffic gets jammed up. It can be pretty horrendous at this time of the evening.'

He hadn't been joking, Shiona observed to herself now, as she followed his tail out on to the road to Balerno. The rush-hour traffic in the city centre had been as thick as a plate of home-made porridge! Yet Jake had negotiated it with skill and creativity, darting up side-roads to avoid the congestion and taking clever detours that saved both temper and time. It had felt like a game of hide-and-seek, and Shiona, though at times she had been terrified of losing him, had thoroughly enjoyed the drive.

And now they had left the city behind and were heading out into the open country. Shiona felt a tiny tremor of excitement. She had never visited Jake's home before.

It appeared quite suddenly as they turned a sharp bend, an imposing stone edifice with ivy-clad walls, set among tall poplars, well back from the road. And somehow she didn't need to be told they had arrived. It was precisely the sort of place where she had always imagined he would live.

They turned in through a pair of eagle-mounted gateposts, then at the end of a long driveway at last drew to a halt. Shiona climbed out on to the crunchy, gravelled forecourt and looked around her.

'It's beautiful,' she said.

He seemed not to have heard her, and in a way she was grateful. It had not been her intention to favour him with a compliment. The observation had simply slipped out.

'This way,' he was instructing, leading her on brisk strides up the double stone staircase that led to the front door. As they reached the top the door opened magically and a beaming, plump-faced woman was waiting to greet them.

'Welcome home, Mr MacKay.' The woman grinned at Shiona. 'I see you've got a visitor with you.'

As they stepped into the hallway, Jake introduced them. 'Shiona, this is Mrs Aitken, my most able and valued housekeeper. Mrs Aitken, meet Shiona

Fergusson, Kirsty's half-sister. She'll be spending the night here.'

Mrs Aitken beamed at her. 'So *you're* Aunt Shiona! I've heard so much about you, you wouldn't believe it. Kirsty will be fair delighted to see you!'

Shiona's cheeks turned pink with pleasure. 'How is she?' she asked, barely covering her delight.

'Much better today. She's got her appetite back.' The plump-faced woman turned to Jake now. 'I gave her some poached chicken breast at lunchtime and she even managed a couple of scones for tea.'

'Well done.' Jake smiled at her. 'You're doing a good job.' Then he glanced fleetingly at Shiona before heading for the staircase. 'I suggest we go up and see her now.'

They stayed with Kirsty for just under an hour, and it was a relief to Shiona to see how well she was looking. She had obviously been well cared for throughout her illness—but then, Shiona had never for one moment doubted that.

When it was time for 'lights out', she and Jake left the room together, and out in the corridor Jake told her, 'Mrs Aitken usually serves supper about eight, so if you want to freshen up you have a bit of time. I'm going to have a shower. I'll show you where your room is.'

'Thanks,' Shiona nodded, suddenly feeling awkward to be alone in his company without a third person. She shook herself mentally. What a silly thing to feel!

A moment later, with a curt 'Follow me', he was

leading her down to the end of the corridor, then along a short passageway off to the right.

'Here we are.' He pushed one of the doors open and invited her to enter the pretty pink and white room.

'You have your own bathroom.' He pointed vaguely. 'I think you should find everything you need. If there are any problems just call down to Mrs Aitken. There's an internal phone there by the bed.'

Once he had gone, Shiona sank down on to the bed and kicked off her shoes, glad to be alone for a few minutes. She leaned back against the pillows and looked around her. Here in Jake's splendid and tastefully furnished home was the very last place she had expected to be tonight. In fact, a lot of unexpected things had happened today.

She had a sudden sharp recall of that moment in Jake's office when he had revealed his strange lack of commitment to Janice. And the more she thought about it the more she felt certain that her instinctive deduction had been right. Whatever else he was, he was not in love with Janice—unless that moment in his office had been a mere innocent slip.

It could have been, she told herself doubtfully. These things could happen, after all—even to men as unprone to making slips as Jake! But something was telling her it was no slip—and then, in a blinding flash, she knew!

She sat up, her heart racing. He wasn't in love with Janice! He was, after all, simply marrying her in order to gain guardianship of Kirsty!

Suddenly she was assailed by a tangle of emotions,

not least among them a silly sense of relief that she knew was totally out of place. Why should she care whether he was in love or not?

She also felt shock that he should actually be capable of such an utterly cynical act. Would he have been prepared to marry anyone who would have him just to keep Kirsty out of her hands? Did he really know what type of woman Janice was? Didn't it matter to him that she was only after his money, that she was far from being the warm, motherly soul that she seemed?

But her instincts told her no. He adored little Kirsty. There was no way in the world that he would deliberately inflict on her a woman who was unsuitable to be her mother.

Shiona jumped to her feet, the adrenalin racing through her. She must waste no time in putting him right. At the first opportunity she must tell him what she knew. And, perhaps, since he was not blinded by love after all, he might be prepared to listen to her for once!

Fifteen minutes later, after a lightning shower, and dressed once more in her cream suit and silk blouse, Shiona hurried downstairs to join Jake in the drawing-room.

He was standing by the drinks table, pouring himself a measure of neat whisky, when she walked into the room. 'I was expecting to have dinner with a client this evening, but the appointment has been unexpectedly cancelled.' He flicked her a glance. 'So it looks, after all, as though you and I will be dining together.'

She couldn't resist it. 'You must be overjoyed.' Quite the opposite had been evident from his tone of voice.

He smiled a dry smile. 'I expect I'll survive it.' Then, watching her, he took a mouthful of his drink. 'Just so long as you're not planning any physical attacks on me this evening. . . I'd prefer not to have any cups of coffee thrown in my face.'

Shiona had almost forgotten that unfortunate incident. 'I shall try to control myself.' She met his mocking gaze, noting that in spite of the typical little dig there was less malice than usual in his manner. Perhaps he was trying to be hospitable—not an easy task for him when she was the guest!

At any rate, he was looking relaxed, dressed in beige trousers and a deep blue sweatshirt, and the informality of his attire suited him, Shiona thought. The soft lines of the sweatshirt that moulded the broad shoulders gave him an air of easy, masculine power, and the blue almost exactly matched the blue of his eyes.

Shiona stopped herself short. She was doing it again! Reacting to him physically, just as she used to all those years ago. And it really was quite out of place!

She drew herself up, stilling her racing pulses, as he asked her now with a wave at the drinks table, 'Would you care to indulge in a drink before dinner?'

'Yes, thanks. I'd like a Dubonnet.' She cleared her throat. 'With just a splash of lemonade.'

'Ice?' he enquired, as he reached for a glass and Shiona seated herself in one of the armchairs.

'Yes, please,' she nodded, taking care not to look at him. Even now she had not entirely recovered herself.

He came towards her and held out her glass to her, then seated himself in one of the armchairs opposite. 'Dinner will be ready in about fifteen minutes. I hope you're hungry?' he offered, watching her.

'I'm absolutely starving.' Though her voice sounded normal, Shiona was aware that she was feeling awkward again, just as she had when they were upstairs earlier. It was a new sensation, and she didn't like it in the slightest. She took a mouthful of her drink and pulled herself together. 'I haven't had a bite to eat since breakfast.'

'Mrs Aitken will be pleased.' Jake smiled fleetingly, an affectionate smile that softened his features. 'I got the impression that something major was happening in the kitchen. She appears to be going to a bit of trouble in your honour.'

'That's very kind of her, but quite unnecessary.' Shiona found herself watching his softened features with a feeling almost of secret envy. He was capable of such thoughtfulness and generosity towards others. It was only towards herself that she'd ever seen him act meanly.

She squashed the thought. It made her feel vulnerable, the way she always used to feel in the past. And she did not want to start feeling that way again.

Just concentrate on watching out for the right opportunity to broach the subject of Janice, she reminded herself. That's the only thought that need occupy you this evening!

She sat back in her seat and glanced around her. 'This is a very nice place you have here,' she told him. Perhaps flattery might please him and soften his mood further. The more malleable he was the better for her!

'I'm glad you like it.' He did not appear flattered. 'Personally, I find it very much to my taste.'

'I love all the little knick-knacks.' Shiona continued to glance round her. 'These beautiful lamps and lovely ornaments. . .' Her gaze fell on the Baccarat crystal pyramid on the glass-topped side table at her elbow. 'This is beautiful,' she enthused. 'So simple, yet so striking——' And then her breath caught in her throat as though someone had kicked her. Her voice trailed off. Her heart was pounding.

Although she did not look at Jake, she could feel he was watching her and that he knew what had stopped her dead in her tracks. And try as she might she could not detach her eyes from the object on the table that had so totally winded her.

Then she heard Jake speak. 'It's a good likeness, isn't it? It was taken just before his twenty-first birthday.'

'I know. I remember.' Shiona swallowed drily, her fingers clutched tightly around her glass as she continued to stare with unblinking, blurred vision at the photograph of Ryan in the big silver frame.

'But then, Ryan always did take a very good photograph.' There was an edge to Jake's voice now, an edge of hostility, that caused her to turn round and look him in the face.

But she could not say a word as he went on in that same tone.

'You say you can remember that photograph being taken. It was a very happy day, I seem to remember.' Then, as she nodded in agreement, he added viciously, 'Were you already planning, even as that photograph was being taken, how you were going to fleece him of every penny he possessed?'

Shiona felt her blood go cold. She felt like jumping from her seat and running from the room. She could not bear to listen to his accusations. But her limbs were paralysed. She was glued to the cushions. She stared back at him miserably. 'No,' she answered numbly.

'That came later, did it? Once you were down in London?' He leaned back in his armchair and regarded her harshly. 'I've always been curious to know how you did it. . . Did you have some master plan or did you just plan it bit by bit?'

The anger in his face was like a wall between them. A wall that bristled with bayonets and barbed wire.

Shiona took a deep breath. 'I don't blame you for being angry, believing what you do about me. I know you loved Ryan and that you always stood by him. But I loved him, too. I was never his enemy.'

'Then what were you?' Jake's blue eyes flayed her and she could sense the pain that shimmered in his voice. 'Most certainly you were not his friend. In my book friends don't rob one another.'

'Nor in mine. I never robbed your brother.'

'You mean what he gave he gave to you freely?' His tone was scathing. 'That makes all the difference! And in return, no doubt, you gave him a good time in bed!'

'I gave him nothing of the sort!'

'Oh, not even that? Poor Ryan!' His mouth twisted. 'He really got a rotten deal!'

To have to sit there and take his abuse was like being bound hand and foot to a torturer's chair. Shiona longed to yell, Stop!, and pour out the truth and see the rage and the pain and the hatred of her finally and forever erased from his face.

But she could not. All she could say was, 'You're horribly wrong. I loved your brother. I would never have harmed him.'

It was a relief when a couple of minutes later, amidst the deafening silence that had descended on the room, Mrs Aitken poked her head round the door. 'Dinner will be served whenever you're ready.'

'We're ready now.' Jake rose to his feet, smiling, throwing off his anger like a mantle. He even managed a civil glance at Shiona. 'Shall we go through? We don't want dinner to spoil.'

He'd been right about Mrs Aitken having gone to some trouble. That was evident the moment they stepped into the dining-room. The table was laid out fit for a king, all gleaming silver and twinkling crystal. And the meal that followed was a veritable banquet.

There was fresh salmon to start with, baked in a light-as-a-feather pastry, then duck cooked in a mouth-watering loganberry sauce, plus a couple of huge tureens of fresh vegetables and plenty of white wine to wash down each delicious mouthful.

And as the meal progressed the atmosphere between them lightened. The subject of Ryan was mercifully dropped, and for once Jake appeared to be as anxious as Shiona was to avoid any further confrontation.

They spoke of nothing in particular—holidays, films—and by the time Mrs Aitken appeared in the doorway, carrying aloft a flaming baked Alaska, the tension in Shiona had all but vanished. To her astonishment, she had almost enjoyed their conversation. Its very normality had been something of a novelty!

But what was still troubling her was the fact that she had still not broached the subject of Janice.

Surreptitiously now, she glanced across at his profile as Mrs Aitken piled baked Alaska on to each of their plates. Would he listen to her when she told him the truth about Janice? Would she be able to persuade him that he was making a mistake? One way or the other she would find out soon enough, for she must definitely speak up before the meal was over.

As Mrs Aitken left, Shiona braced herself. What she had to say must be handled with delicacy. She must tell him what she knew about Janice without alienating him. He must be made to realise that she was speaking up for Kirsty's sake, that she was not motivated by personal spite.

But how to begin? She eyed him cautiously. He

was like a tinder-box where she was concerned. One wrong move and he would be up in flames.

As though he were telepathic, he raised his eyes to look at her. Shiona sensed that he knew she had something on her mind. But he did not prompt her. On the contrary. He simply turned his attention back to his pudding.

She cleared her throat and took a deep breath. 'Jake, there's something I'd like to discuss with you.'

He took a mouthful of his pudding. 'And what might that be?'

She cleared her throat again. 'It's about Janice,' she said.

'Janice?'

'Yes, Janice. Your fiancée.'

He smiled. 'Yes, I do know who she is. What do you want to discuss about her?'

This was the hard part. Shiona laid down her spoon. 'I don't think she'd make a suitable mother for Kirsty.'

Blue eyes met hers candidly. 'Yes, I know,' he said.

'You mean you agree with me?' Shiona was astounded. 'Then why——?'

'What I mean is that you have already told me,' he cut in sharply. 'You need not repeat yourself.'

'But I haven't told you why. I have good reason. I believe you're making a terrible mistake.'

His eyes had grown ice-cold. 'Is that so? Well, perhaps I'm not interested in what you believe.'

'You ought to be!' Damn his arrogance! 'Our little sister's future is at stake!'

His eyes looked right through her. 'Don't you mean *your* future? That's the only future *you* care about!'

Shiona counted to ten. 'You're wrong about that! You're wrong about me and you're wrong about Janice!'

He shook his head. 'Oh, no, my dear Shiona, I fear I have never been wrong about you. Alas, over the years I have become far too familiar with your greedy, grasping little ways.'

'That's almost funny!' Shiona laughed harshly. 'But the one with the greedy, grasping little ways happens to be your fiancée, not me!'

It was his turn to laugh harshly. 'Go and tell that to Ryan! I'm sure, if he were alive, he'd find that most reassuring!'

The mention of Ryan almost silenced her. She felt that familiar wave of nausea wash through her. But as she looked into Jake's face and his condemning blue eyes she was overcome by a rush of indignation. He had hurt her enough with his false accusations. It was time she did a bit of hurting, too.

She narrowed her eyes and threw the cruel truth at him. 'I don't know why you think she's marrying you. Maybe you're fool enough to believe she loves you. But she doesn't love you. She doesn't even care for you. The only reason she's marrying you is to get her hands on your money!'

To her chagrin he did not look hurt in the slightest. His expression remained flinty and quite unreadable.

'No doubt you feel better now you've got that off your chest.'

Damn his composure! Shiona clenched her fists beneath the table and continued to glare across at him with ferociously narrowed eyes. 'But, of course, I'm forgetting. . .' Her tone was lethal. 'You don't care that she's not in love with you because you're not the least bit in love with her, either!'

'Is that what you think?'

'That's what I think!'

'Well, do you know what *I* think?' He leaned across the table towards her. 'I think that my relationship with Janice is really none of your damned business!'

'Oh, but you're wrong! Your relationship with Janice happens to be very much my damned business, particularly now that I understand the truth!'

'*You*, understand the truth? I very much doubt it. For you the truth is simply something you invent.'

Shiona shook her head. 'No, that's your game! *You're* the one who's inventing the truth!'

'And what am I inventing?' His tone was jagged. 'Please be so good as to enlighten me.'

'What you're inventing is a whole false little scenario of supposedly future wedded bliss, just so you can win custody of Kirsty. Well, I know what you're up to and I've tumbled to Janice. She's nothing but a mercenary little gold-digger, and I will not allow her to be a mother to my sister!'

Jake's eyes had narrowed to pinpoints. 'A gold-digger, is she? Well, I suppose it takes one to know one, as they say!' He pushed aside his plate. 'But don't think you can fool me. I know exactly what you're up to. . .' He held her eyes a moment. 'But you'll never win custody. That is something I can guarantee!'

'What a pity it's not for you to guarantee! The ultimate decision will be taken by the court—and, don't worry, I shall make very sure that they know precisely what type of person Janice really is. Not the type of person to be Kirsty's mother.' She glared across at him. 'And if you really loved Kirsty like you say you do, you would realise that for yourself!'

'Don't you worry about Kirsty!' He pushed back his chair, the gesture violent, making the chair topple. 'I shall see to it that she doesn't end up in the wrong hands. Never doubt that for a minute.'

As he rose to his feet, Shiona glanced up at him. 'You mean you'll reconsider your marriage to Janice?'

His eyes scowled down at her. 'I mean what I said. I will never allow Kirsty to fall into the wrong hands. And the worst possible hands she could fall into are yours!'

Then, with a final black glance at her, he stepped away from the table and swept like a tornado through the dining-room door.

Next morning Shiona remained in bed until she was certain that Jake had left for the office.

She stared at the ceiling. So, they had come to this. They were about to become locked in a bitter legal battle for the future of the child they both loved.

It was totally wrong. It mustn't happen. Kirsty's future mustn't be decided in such a way.

Through her anger and frustration there was another emotion, too. A sense of deep and profound disappointment. As long as she had believed that Jake had no suspicion of what type of woman Janice really was, she had been able to forgive his cynical marriage. But last night he had refused even to consider what she had told him, tossing it to one side as though it didn't matter.

Either he loved Kirsty less than she had given him credit for, or he hated Shiona even more fiercely than she had ever suspected.

She sensed the truth was undoubtedly the latter, and it was like a lance driving through her. If only he knew he had no cause to hate her. If only she could tell him the truth.

Could she? she wondered. And, more appropriately, *should* she?

She turned the possibility round and round in her head. If it might benefit Kirsty for him to know what had really happened between herself and Ryan, would she be justified in breaking her promise? For, once he knew the truth, he could no longer believe that she was the monster he had branded her, and that might lead him to abandon his marriage, whose only purpose, she was certain now, was to thwart her.

Surely, she reasoned, the future of a child was more important than a promise to a man who was now dead?

Yet it was a hard decision. She had promised Ryan faithfully. And yet the only alternative was to sacrifice Kirsty. Even Ryan, she felt certain, would not have wanted that.

But at last she came to a painful decision. She got

up, showered quickly, and pulled on her clothes. I shall go to his office and tell him, she decided. This afternoon. Before I change my mind.

Kirsty was still sound asleep, she discovered, when she poked her head round the little girl's door. So she hurried downstairs to fix herself some breakfast—and almost stopped in her tracks at the sight of the figure who was seated at the kitchen table.

'Janice?' She blinked. 'What are you doing here?'

Janice laid down her coffee-cup with equal surprise. 'I could ask the same thing of you,' she countered crisply.

Not much sign, Shiona observed, of the good-natured warmth and motherly charm that was so much in evidence when Jake was around!

'I was visiting Kirsty,' she answered flatly. Then she added, 'I spent the night here,' hoping to annoy her.

She sensed that she had. Janice's hard eyes glinted. Then she seemed to shrug as though it really didn't matter.

'I came to see Jake.' She picked up her cup again. 'But Mrs Aitken told me I'd just missed him, so I got her to make me a cup of coffee.'

I'll just bet you did! Shiona thought disapprovingly, as she crossed to the coffee-maker to switch it on for herself. I can just imagine you bossing poor Mrs Aitken around!

She glanced at Janice over her shoulder. 'How come you're not at work today?'

There was a momentary pause as Janice drank her coffee. Then she laid her cup down on her saucer with a click. 'I have the morning off.' She paused another moment, as though ensuring that she had Shiona's full attention. Then she added in an oddly tantalising tone, 'Today's my morning at the hospital.'

Shiona turned to look at her. 'Hospital?' she repeated. And, in spite of her dislike, her tone was sympathetic. In no way did she wish ill health on the woman.

'Hospital. That's right.' Janice smiled a strange smile. Then, feigning coyness, she fluttered her lashes. 'I suppose I can tell you. I was at the antenatal clinic. It's supposed to be a secret, but I'm pregnant.'

Shiona was unaware that her jaw had dropped open. 'Pregnant?' she repeated. 'Pregnant? You?'

Janice nodded. 'Rather silly of me, wasn't it, to go and make such a careless mistake?'

Shiona felt as though a bomb had gone off in her face. She swallowed drily. 'It can happen to anyone.' She was vaguely aware that she ought to offer congratulations, but for some reason she didn't feel in a congratulatory frame of mind.

Janice started to stand up. 'I'd better go now. My appointment at the hospital's in half an hour, and sometimes the traffic can be just deadly.'

Suddenly there was a triumphant little lift to her chin. She knew her news had left her audience speechless.

Out of politeness Shiona escorted Janice to the door, then stood in the doorway to watch her drive off. It was all clear now—why Jake was marrying Janice in spite of the lack of love between them. And it was such an obvious explanation that she ought to have thought of it herself, but for some reason it had never for one moment crossed her mind.

Naïve fool, she thought, staring into space, fighting back the emotions that threatened to swamp her. For all at once she could feel sweeping in on her a sense of utter desolation, the like of which she hadn't known for years.

CHAPTER EIGHT

AFTER Janice had gone Shiona went back inside and sat down at the kitchen table with a cup of strong black coffee.

What a mess, she was thinking. What a total jumble. With every corner she turned things seemed to grow more tangled. It would be futile now to think of trying to persuade Jake to rethink his intended marriage to Janice. How could he do that when she was carrying his child? He really had very little choice in the matter.

Carrying Jake's child.

The words seized her by the throat. She squeezed her eyes shut and clenched her fists tight. She was jealous, she realised. Bitterly jealous. Yet how could she possibly feel jealous over a man whom she had so long ago evicted from her heart?

As she took a mouthful of her coffee, her hands were shaking. What a fool she was. What a perfect idiot. She was feeling exactly as she had in the old days. Heartsore and vulnerable and sick with misery.

She gave herself a shake. Snap out of it! she commanded. It isn't really you who's feeling this way, it's the girl you used to be who's been somehow resurrected—brought back to life by all the memories that surround you. And you mustn't allow her to take over your emotions. You must put a stop to her before she destroys you.

Abruptly, she stood up. Nothing would destroy her—least of all these totally inappropriate emotions for a man who had brought her nothing but misery. Surely she had more pride than that?

She let out her breath, stilling the trembling within her. I shall go and get ready, then drive into Edinburgh and finally tell Jake the truth about Ryan. If he has to marry Janice, that's his misfortune, but I shall force him to see that if he really loves Kirsty he won't force her to share his fate. I shall convince him that Kirsty would be better off with me.

Steeled with resolve, Shiona felt much better. Head high, she hurried upstairs to change.

Alas, Shiona's plans were destined to be thwarted.

She arrived at Jake's office shortly after ten to be told by his secretary, 'He's not here, I'm afraid. He's gone to a meeting at Cambuslang. I don't expect him back until mid-afternoon.'

Shiona cursed her luck. 'Then I'll come back after lunch. In the meantime, if you hear from him, please tell him I need to see him urgently.'

The girl glanced up at her. 'You're his sister, is that right?'

'In a manner of speaking. We're not blood-related. Just tell him it's Miss Fergusson who needs to see him.'

As she turned away, she felt a small surge of triumph. Already she had put a little distance between them!

But the day dragged on with still no sign of Jake. She'd been waiting outside his office for the best part of three hours when his secretary came to tell her that he'd just phoned in.

'The meeting's been extended. He won't be back today—at least, not to the office; he'll be going straight home.'

'Did you tell him I was here?'

'I told him, Miss Fergusson. He said to please meet him back at the house this evening.'

Did he indeed? How uncommonly civil of him to make such a co-operative and hospitable offer! But though she was anxious to see him, Shiona had no desire to end up spending another night under his roof.

She rose to her feet. 'If he calls in again, please tell him I'll come back to the office tomorrow morning. I'm going back to Loch Lomond now. If he wants to, he can reach me there.'

Shiona took the long way back to Loch Lomond, via Perth and Comrie and Loch Earn, stopping for a meal at a wayside hotel, then heading south via Glen Dochart just after nine o'clock.

She felt edgy and unsettled, dreading tomorrow and the final show-down over Ryan—for the prospect of breaking her solemn promise to him still lay heavily on her mind.

But there was no other way, she kept reassuring herself. For Kirsty's sake, she had to clear her name.

The sitting-room light at Lomond View was on as usual as she turned into the darkened driveway. Nettie always left it on, even when no one was at home and she herself had retired to her own rooms for the evening and Inge was out, as was the case tonight.

Shiona parked at the front, instead of at the side of the house where everyone normally parked their cars, and, pushing back her hair, headed for the front door.

A quick bath and bed, she promised herself, sighing, as she stuck her key into the front door lock. All at once, she felt desperately tired.

But as she stepped into the hall she knew something was wrong. With all her instincts she could sense it.

She frowned and looked around her. 'Nettie?' she called out. 'Nettie! Are you there?'

'Nettie's gone to bed.'

Shiona jumped and spun round, startled, as a voice spoke from the drawing-room doorway behind her. Then, as she saw who it was, her stomach tightened.

'What the devil are *you* doing here?'

Jake leaned against the doorway, blue eyes narrowed, an inscrutable expression on his face. 'I thought my secretary told you to meet me at the house in Edinburgh? Why do you always force me to go chasing after you?'

What was he talking about? 'Chasing after me? I told your secretary I would see you tomorrow. What I wanted to see you about isn't *that* urgent.'

'I didn't get that message.' There was a troubled air about him. He had the look of a man who'd been pacing about restlessly, his tie loose about his throat, his shirt collar undone. Even his hair was distinctly ruffled, as though impatient fingers had been frequently run through it.

He let out his breath sharply. 'When you weren't at the house I came straight here.'He glanced at his watch. 'I've been waiting for two hours.'

She almost apologised, but in time she stopped herself. 'It really wasn't necessary for you to go to all that trouble. What I have to say to you could have waited till tomorrow.'

Besides, she was thinking, what on earth had possessed him to come rushing over here just because she wanted to see him? But then, in his next breath, he enlightened her.

'But I'm afraid what *I* have to say to *you* couldn't wait.' There was a grim expression about his mouth as he said it. The narrowed blue eyes seemed to pierce right through her. 'I've come to talk to you about Ryan.'

'Ryan?' Shiona blinked at him. Had the world gone crazy? 'I don't understand.' She frowned across the hall at him. 'It was precisely about Ryan that I wanted to talk to you.'

One cynical eyebrow lifted. 'What a coincidence.' Then he shifted impatiently and gestured to the drawing-room. 'I suggest we make ourselves comfortable before we start talking.'

In the drawing-room there was further evidence of his impatient vigil. A couple of cups and glasses, their contents half consumed. Newspapers and magazines impatiently tossed aside.

With a prickle of anxiety Shiona sat down. What the devil was going on?

Jake picked up his half-empty glass of whisky, knocked back the contents, and pulled off his tie, flinging it over the back of the sofa beside his discarded jacket.

'I'll go first,' he told her with a scathing smile. 'Since I've come all this way, I think I deserve that honour.'

Shiona could feel the tension in her growing, taut as the strings of a violin. He was acting so strangely. He seemed racked with emotion. She had never seen him like this before.

Then he floored her completely as, in a voice stiff with anger, he demanded, 'Why the hell didn't you tell me about Ryan?'

For a moment she simply stared at him. Then stupidly, she answered, 'Tell you what about Ryan?'

His eyes were like meat-hooks, tearing into her. 'The truth,' he said harshly. 'That would've done for a start.'

Shiona felt herself pale. Her skin was prickling uncomfortably. 'You mean you know the truth about Ryan?'

'Yes, finally I do.' His eyes drove into her. 'At least three years too late to be able to help him.' His tone was accusing, thick with emotion. 'What the hell made you think you had the right to keep the facts about my brother from me?'

Shiona swallowed, wishing she had a drink. She licked her lips. 'It wasn't my decision. Ryan made me promise never to tell you.'

'And you kept a promise—to a *junkie.*' He emphasised the word with hurt and loathing. 'You put a promise to a junkie before your duty to me?'

'What duty to you? I had no duty to you! Your brother may have been a junkie, but he was also my friend and I happened to love him! My duty was to honour the promise I made to him!'

'Your duty was to inform his family!' Overcome with anger, Jake sprang to his feet, looking as though he longed to demolish the room about him. 'If we'd known, my father and I might have been able to help him! Didn't you ever think of that?'

'Yes, I thought of that!' Shiona sprang to her feet, too, her emotions suddenly overwhelming her. 'But he didn't want you to know! He was desperately ashamed! The only one he wanted to help him was me!'

The pain in Jake's face was making her heart weep. She took a step towards him, her eyes beseeching. 'I was a stranger, remember, not really one of the family. It was easier for him to come to me.'

'A stranger. . .' He nodded. Then he turned away from her. She saw his shoulders lift and fall as he sought to gain control of himself. Then he said in a quiet voice, 'Some damned stranger. According to what I've been told, you were his saviour.'

He turned round slowly, his eyes burning into her. 'I've spoken to the doctors at the hospital where he was treated, and they've told me the whole long, miserable story. How you stood by him when he was at his very lowest, how you continued to believe in him when no one else did.'

He shook his head slowly, breathing in deeply. 'You were his "guiding light", his "will to survive". That was how one of the doctors described you. You were the one who never deserted him, in spite of the horrors he put you through. You took all of the abuse, the failures and disappointments, and kept on coming back for more. And you did all of this without a word to anyone. . .' His voice trailed to a halt. He closed his eyes.

Shiona was trembling uncontrollably. She longed to reach out a hand to comfort him, but her muscles refused to obey her brain.

'I only did what anyone else who loved him would have done. You would have done the same if you'd known.'

As he opened his eyes and smiled at her strangely, she added, 'And it was worth it in the end. He kicked the habit, as his doctors must have told you. He'd been off drugs for six months when he died in that fire.'

Jake nodded. 'I know.'

'And I'm sure he would have stayed off.'

'With you around to help him, I've no doubt he would.'

'Even without me. He'd grown much stronger. He was determined to make something decent out of his life.'

Jake was looking at her as though it was the first time he had really seen her. He took a step towards her and touched his hand to her cheek. Then he frowned, and there was a note of torment in his voice as he demanded roughly, shaking his head, 'For God's sake, Shiona, why didn't you tell me?'

'I couldn't. I told you, I promised Ryan.'

He took a deep breath. 'How can you forgive me?'

She felt his fingers tremble lightly against her cheek.

'All those things I've said to you. All those awful accusations. How could you go on letting me think that they were true?'

'It wasn't easy.' Her flesh was melting beneath his fingers. She looked into his eyes and felt herself drowning.

'My poor, dear Shiona.' He was stroking her hair, as though to stroke away all the hurt he had inflicted. 'All that money I thought he was spending on you, he was spending on drugs. I ought to have guessed.'

'How could you have guessed? You had no reason to believe it. Even I didn't believe what was going on at first. I knew that some of his friends were into drugs, but I didn't know Ryan was until he collapsed on me one day. That was when he begged me to move in with him to try and help him. He was desperately trying to kick the habit on his own, but he needed moral support and someone to keep an eye on him. A sort of policeman-cum-nursemaid, that's what I was really.'

'My dear Shiona, you were his saviour.' Jake continued to stroke her hair. 'He would never have made it if it hadn't been for you. And, as his brother, that puts me in your debt, too.'

Shiona smiled with sheer joy. It was the most wonderful thing to hear Jake finally say such things.

To know that he knew the truth at last. To feel him touching her, to see him looking at her with his heart washed clean of all the old hatred.

She looked into his face. 'But how did you find out? And on the very day I planned to tell you myself?'

'I found out by accident.' His eyes were hard again for an instant. 'If fate hadn't intervened, I might never have known.'

Then his expression softened once more. With both hands he framed her face. 'It was all thanks to a woman at the meeting today that I had my first inkling of what had really been going on.'

He had moved very close to her now, their bodies almost touching. Shiona swallowed hard. 'What woman? Who was she?'

'Her name's Marion Ritchie. She was a neighbour of yours and Ryan's in London. She's been back in Scotland for several years now, and she didn't know that Ryan was dead. But for some reason she knew he was my brother, and she asked me how he was keeping these days.'

His hands slipped to Shiona's shoulders. He made a face. 'There was something about the way she asked it that made me suspicious. When I probed a bit, rather reluctantly she told me that she understood he'd had an "illness", and was a regular out-patient at a local hospital.'

Shiona was frowning. 'I remember Marion Ritchie, but she was never a close friend. How could she have known anything about Ryan?'

'Alas, neighbours often know a great deal more

than we think they know. She knew he was an addict, I'm certain of that, though she didn't actually come out and say so to me. Still, I managed to get her to tell me the name of the hospital, and then I spent my entire lunchtime talking to the doctors there who treated Ryan.

'I'll tell you one thing.' He made a face. 'The afternoon meeting went right over my head. All I could think about was getting back to speak to you.' The fingers on her shoulders momentarily tightened. 'It was my intention, my dear Shiona, to tear you apart.'

He sighed and gathered her to him. She could feel his heart beating. 'Do you think you'll ever be able to forgive me?'

'I already have.' Her own heart was pounding. 'How could you judge? You didn't know the truth.'

'But I *did* judge,' he insisted. 'And I judged unfairly. I wouldn't blame you in the slightest if you never forgave me.'

'But I do forgive you. Absolutely.' She raised her eyes to him and smiled. 'Anyway, it was partly my fault. I could have told you if I'd wanted to. After all, you gave me endless opportunities.'

He sighed and let his hands slide round her shoulders, drawing her even closer towards him. 'I always sensed there was something you weren't telling me. That was why I kept pushing you and provoking you—to try and make you spit it out. But the more you refused to say anything, the more I began to believe that maybe there was nothing to tell, after all.'

'I longed to tell you.' Shiona shook her head. 'I could scarcely bear for you to believe what you did.'

'And yet, out of loyalty to Ryan, you let me.' Gentle fingers stroked her hair, sending helpless shivers across her scalp. 'I was also wrong about you and my father—though I had actually begun to suspect that years ago. I know how compulsively generous my father was. He was a man who wouldn't take no for an answer. But when all this business about you and Ryan cropped up, it sort of renewed all my earlier suspicions.'

He sighed a harsh sigh. 'What an idiot I've been!'

Shiona gazed with compassion into his face. 'We all make mistakes. I'm just glad it's straightened out.'

Jake drew back to look at her. 'You know, you're quite a girl.' Still watching her, he reached for one of her hands and pressed the warm palm against his lips. 'Quite a girl,' he repeated softly. 'And I was so blind I couldn't see it.'

Shiona felt her heart perform a triple somersault and lodge itself somewhere in the region of her throat. She swallowed and wondered if she should pull her hand away, but as Jake continued to hold it against his cheek, watching her with eyes that suddenly threatened to swallow her, she was aware that all at once her hand had become paralysed. In fact, every inch of her was quite incapable of movement.

With his free hand he was softly pushing back her hair, sending goosebumps scattering from Shiona's head to her toes. She shivered inwardly, a delicious sensation, and felt her heart break into a gallop.

Whatever was about to happen, she knew she could not stop it.

Jake stroked her hair. 'My flame-haired temptress.' There was a strange smile playing round his lips. 'My beautiful, unpredictable, flame-haired temptress. What a very special person you've turned out to be.'

Shiona found her voice. 'I'm not so special. I'm not special in the slightest, as a matter of fact.' Perhaps she could convince him to stop looking at her that way—though, in her heart, she did not want to stop him.

'Oh, yes, you are.' His fingers scorched her as they trailed through her hair, making her spine tingle. 'What you did for my brother was very special. I shall always be in your debt for that.'

His fingers stilled suddenly. He frowned for a moment. 'And the strength it took to keep your secret to yourself is the kind of strength that very few possess. Take my word for it. . .' he smiled unexpectedly, lighting her heart with an unspeakable pleasure '. . .you are a very special person indeed.'

I love you. The thought went exploding through Shiona's head, winding her, driving the strength from her body. I love you. I love you. The words kept repeating themselves until she was afraid he must be able to hear them.

Shiona closed her eyes and forced the thought from her. Where had such perfect madness come from?

When she opened her eyes again, Jake's were burning down at her. They seemed to pierce into her like rods of blue fire. She tried to move away, but still she was paralysed. And then she felt his arm slide round her waist.

'My dear Shiona. . . My sweet Shiona. . .'

The way he spoke her name twisted her stomach into knots. And the way his hand was pressed against her back was turning her limbs to pillars of sawdust.

As he drew her close to him, she let herself fall against him. And it was as though someone had peeled away the skin from her nerve-ends. Suddenly her senses were up in flames.

Just the touch of his chest pressing hard against her breasts, just the lightest fleeting brush of his thighs against hers, and suddenly her heart was weeping from the wanting of him. Her hands trembled as they fluttered to rest against his shoulders.

He murmured something, but she did not catch the words. The thundering in her heart had grown so enormous that she would not have heard a thing had there been an earthquake. But she saw his lips move and her eyes fixed on them, for suddenly she hadn't the courage to look into his eyes. There was something in their depths that seemed to devour her—and her own eyes, she feared, revealed the torment of her soul.

The hand in her hair was caressing her gently, and imperceptibly tilting her face towards his. She felt her head go back and her lips part with anticipation. Then, for one breathless moment, the whole world stood still.

'Shiona!'

She felt rather than heard him say her name. Then she died a thousand deaths and was born again instantly as at last his lips came down to cover hers.

It was just as she had dreamed in her dreams it would be—a blissful sensation that shot down to her toes and sent her blood, like fiery rapids, exploding through her veins. But she could never have imagined the bright colours that filled her brain—a vivid, intoxicating, shifting kaleidoscope of wonder and pleasure and excitement and joy.

I love you! I love you! Her arms circled his neck, as the words roared unstoppably inside her head. She caressed his hair and slid her hands along his shoulders, her heart threatening to burst from the ferocity of her emotions.

And his hunger, as he kissed her, seemed as powerful as her own. There was a passion in his lips and a fire in his caresses that filled her heart to overflowing. His desire for her was as real as her own. She could feel the power of it consume him.

As his lips moved against hers, burning, arousing, Jake's hands swept the warm, receptive curves of her body. And Shiona pressed herself against him, enthralled by the hard feel of him, her body responding to every little touch.

His hands brushed her breasts, already ripe beneath her blouse, sending shafts of electricity darting through her. With a sigh she slid her hands beneath the front of his jacket and let her own fingers graze the hard stubs of his nipples.

He groaned and drew her closer, one hand around her waist, while the other separated her blouse from the waistband of her skirt. Then his hand was slipping beneath the soft silk fabric, making her flesh jump excitedly as he touched her, and his fingers were reaching for the strap of her bra, dropping it loosely over her shoulder and peeling the cup of her bra away.

An instant later her breath caught in her throat and a hopeless shaft of longing went writhing through her loins, as he cupped the weight of her breast in his palm and strummed the burgeoning nipple, till it ached, with his thumb.

Shiona gasped from the sheer extravagance of the sensations shooting through her. It was almost too much pleasure to bear. And yet, if he were to stop, she would have to cry out in protest. The agony of such a torment would tear her to shreds.

Without even realising what she was doing, she had undone the buttons of his shirt and was sliding her hand now against his naked chest. She let her hands rove over the hard, smooth muscles with their central sprinkling of rough dark hairs, and as she breathed in she could smell the clean male scent of him. She shivered and pressed her lips against his skin. Warm and delicious. Utterly intoxicating.

He was kissing her hair, her brow, her ears, then bending to kiss the hollow of her neck, and she could feel the breathing in his throat growing harsher and his hunger thrusting hard between his legs.

Love me! Please love me!

She longed to say it. To fall down on the sofa and tear off her clothes and beg him to make wild, abandoned love to her. She longed to feel his nakedness pressing against her, to feel his strength as he entered her, to feel his power as he consumed her. And her heart was crying out, Oh, Jake, I love you!

It was as though he had sensed her unspoken pleading. He pulled her close, his arms tight around her, and buried his face for a moment in her hair.

'You know where this is leading?' His voice was a harsh murmur. 'You know what's going to happen if we continue with this?'

'I don't care.' Her face was pressed against him, so that the words were swallowed against his chest. She strained to look up at him. 'I don't care,' she repeated. 'I want it to happen. More than anything.'

He groaned and did not look at her. 'I want it, too.' Then he smiled lop-sidedly. 'But then, I scarcely have to tell you. I'm sure you're perfectly well aware of that.'

'Then there's nothing to stop us.' Her voice was a whisper. Her heart was pounding in her chest.

But he was shaking his head again, making her soul freeze. 'I wish that were true, but we both know it isn't.'

He didn't have to say why. Shiona knew. It was Janice. He couldn't be unfaithful to the mother of his child.

Her heart turned over sickly. 'Of course,' she conceded. 'I was being crazy. You're absolutely right.'

As his grip on her loosened, she took a step back, and it was as though a cold wind suddenly whistled all around her. Adjusting her blouse and dropping her eyes away, she wrapped her arms protectively around herself. Her soul ached. Suddenly they were on different planets.

Shiona felt him sigh as he laid his hands on her shoulders. 'I think it would be wise if I went straight back to Edinburgh. It would simply be asking for trouble for me to spend the night here.'

Shiona nodded in response. 'Absolutely.' Then her heart seemed to crack as his hands slipped away.

She looked up into his face, fighting back the urge to reach out her hand and stop him from going. Then she heard herself murmur, 'There are things I have to say. . .about Janice. . .about Kirsty. . . That was partly why I wanted to see you.'

But he was turning away. 'Not now, Shiona.' And suddenly there was a darkness about his demeanour. All at once he seemed terribly far away.

She started to protest. Her heart was crumbling.

But he cut in almost roughly, 'Goodnight, Shiona.' Then, on sharp, swift strides he was heading for the door, while Shiona continued to stand where she was, rock still, as though rooted to the floor.

She continued to stand there, eyes closed tightly, long after the front door had closed behind him and she had heard his car disappear down the drive.

And suddenly wolves were howling in her head.

All she could think was, I love you! I love you!

Over the next few days it became clear that Jake was avoiding her. Whenever Shiona phoned—at the office or at his home—she was told that he was unavailable. And when she tried several times to pin him down at the office, invariably, as if he were telepathically aware of her intentions, he was elsewhere.

What was he up to? Shiona wondered through the desperate sadness that consumed her. Was this perhaps his way of trying to tell her that he deeply regretted what had passed between them? Was he afraid she might try to push for more?

He needn't have feared, she thought to herself sadly. A single kiss never changed the world, and she was all too aware of the reality of the situation. Jake was tied to Janice by their unborn baby. He could never be Shiona's, even if he wanted her, and there was nothing to indicate that he really did.

So he had no need to hide. She would not have pushed him. Wasn't she used by now to disguising her love for him? She smiled to herself bitterly. She'd had years of practice. Years of pretending that her love had turned to hate.

But it had all been a bluff. She realised that finally. A bluff she had perpetrated mainly on herself to give herself the strength to go on living. But she had never really hated him, though she had sincerely wanted to. The only emotion she had ever truly felt for him was love.

So what would happen next? she wondered bleakly. Would she have to face him across a court and wrangle with him in public over custody of Kirsty? The thought appalled her more now than ever. But what choice did she have if he was determined to oppose her? And it seemed that he was. He would not even speak to her.

In the meantime Kirsty had made a full recovery. On her daily trips to Edinburgh to try to pin Jake down, Shiona made a point of seeing her little sister, and she was delighted at how well she was looking, even though, as yet, she wasn't back at school.

'Will I still be able to spend Easter at Carol's?' Kirsty enquired anxiously one day. Then she'd added swiftly, 'Dr Fraser says I'm well enough.'

'I'll have to check with him—and with Uncle Jake.' Shiona bent to kiss the anxious little brow. She had almost forgotten about the long-standing arrangement with Kirsty's best friend Carol's parents for Kirsty to spend a couple of weeks with them at Easter.

'I really want to go,' Kirsty assured her. 'I really like it on the farm.'

It turned out that Dr Fraser was in favour of the idea. 'A bit of country air will do her the world of good.'

And, according to Mrs Aitken, Jake had no objections, so arrangements were made for Carol's parents to pick up Kirsty on the appointed day.

And still Shiona had failed to pin down Jake, despite the fact that, out of desperation, she had taken up residence at his Edinburgh home. The latest development, according to his secretary, was that he was out of the country.

'He's gone to Holland on business for a few days.'

And then, out of the blue, as she was getting ready for bed on the evening before Kirsty was due to go off on holiday, Mrs Aitken tapped on Shiona's bedroom door.

'There's a call for you, Miss Fergusson. It's Mr MacKay.' She handed her the phone. 'You'd best take it in your room.'

For an instant Shiona was overcome by a sense of total confusion. Just the thought of talking to him, the thought of hearing his voice had caused her heart to leap to her throat.

But she managed a composed smile as she took the phone. 'Thank you.' She nodded and closed the door.

Then she seated herself on the edge of the bed and, breathing deeply, raised the phone up to her ear. 'Hello? This is Shiona. I'm glad you've phoned. As you know, I've been trying to get hold of you all week.'

'I'm sorry about that.'

He sounded far away—spiritually, as well as in terms of actual distance.

'I'm phoning to tell you something that should please you. . .' He paused for an instant before continuing, 'I won't be contesting your claim for custody.'

Shiona could not believe her ears. For a moment she was speechless, then she said, 'You mean you're happy for Kirsty to come and live with me?'

He gave a bitter laugh. 'I'd rather she lived with me. But yes, I'm happy for her to live with you. Now that I know the truth about everything. . .' there was a note of apology in his voice as he said it '. . . I'm convinced you'll make her an excellent mother.'

'But what about——?'

She had intended to say, 'What about you and

Janice?', but before she could finish the sentence he had cut in to tell her,

'I'm in London, at Heathrow Airport on a stop-over. But I expect to be back in Scotland within the next couple of weeks, so we can discuss whatever needs to be discussed then. I understand from my solicitor that the custody hearing won't be till after the Easter holidays, so we have plenty of time.

'But I have to go now. They're calling my flight. Give Kirsty my love.'

Then he hung up.

Shiona frowned at the phone in total bewilderment. What on earth had all that been about? she wondered. And what on earth had brought on his sudden change of heart?

She laid down the phone and leaned back against the pillows. She suspected she knew the answer to that second question. The reason Jake had had a change of heart was because he had finally realised for himself that Janice would not make a good mother for Kirsty, and that Shiona, on the other hand, would. He loved the child enough, after all, to give her up.

Warm pride surged through her. She smiled to herself. He had done what was right without having to be pushed. But then, hadn't she always known that he was a good and decent man?

She pushed the thought from her. Such thoughts were too painful. She must not dwell on his good points. She must simply forget him.

And the best place to do that, it suddenly struck her, was London. Back at work, in her studio, surrounded by all her friends and workmates. There was nothing to keep her here, after all, for the moment. Kirsty was going off tomorrow to Carol's and, as Jake had said, the custody hearing would not be scheduled till after Easter.

Shiona felt suddenly strengthened by her decision. It would do her psyche good to get away from here, even just for a couple of weeks. By the time she came back, with any luck, she would have emerged from her current emotional upheaval, able at least to *act* with indifference towards Jake.

He had said he'd be back within a couple of weeks. Where was he off to? she wondered briefly. No doubt on some other business assignment. But it wasn't important. All that was important was that she leave here immediately, as soon as Kirsty had gone to Carol's, and start working on driving him out of her heart.

She got up from the bed and started packing, throwing things haphazardly into her bag.

But all the will-power she could muster could not shut out the desolate sense of emptiness that had closed like a cold hand round her heart.

CHAPTER NINE

'HERE's to Paris!'

'And to the collection!' Desmond grinned across the restaurant table at Shiona as they clinked champagne glasses together. 'I just know it's going to knock these Parisians dead!'

Shiona laughed. 'It certainly ought to, considering all the work that we've put into it!'

'You mean all the skill and talent that *you've* put into it! *You're* the one who deserves the honours!'

Shiona smiled across at him. 'It's been a team effort. You know that.' But all the same she felt a flash of gratitude for the wonderful way Desmond had kept up her morale over the past ten emotionally tormented days. If it hadn't been for Desmond she would never have got through them.

On her first day back at the studio, he had taken one look at her, pulled a sympathetic frown, and told her sternly, 'What you need, my girl, is to get down to some hard work and chase from your head whatever it is that's bothering you.'

Then he had reached out and pulled her into his arms and held her tightly for a moment. 'Tell me about it, if you think it'll help you. You know I'm famous for being a good listener.'

Helplessly Shiona had wept against his shoulder, overcome by his simple kindness and concern. 'I'll tell you about it later,' she had promised. 'But right now, I think you're right. Work is what I need.'

In fact the Paris gala was weeks away and they needn't have rushed into finalising the preparations. But as Desmond had said, 'There's no harm in being ready early. It gives us the chance to change things if we decide to.'

And so, now, just ten days after her return from Loch Lomond, all the garments and accessories were miraculously ready, and Shiona and her number two were enjoying one of their celebratory dinners.

'Hard work agrees with you. You're looking terrific,' Desmond announced as he sipped his champagne. 'If you ask me, you look fit for anything—even a face to face with you-know-who!'

'Jake?' Shiona smiled and pulled a face. 'Yes, I'm feeling a whole lot better. I think I've finally managed to come to terms with that débâcle.' She took a mouthful of her drink. 'And then there's Kirsty. . . Thinking about her, making plans to be her mother. . .' Her face glowed with pleasure. 'That's a wonderful thing.'

She sighed an inward sigh. Her emotions were so confused. On the one hand she was filled with total elation at the prospect of soon having Kirsty with her. But at the same time that emptiness in her heart still haunted her, that emptiness that only Jake could fill. Perhaps, she had finally decided, I shall simply have to learn to live with it.

Desmond cut through her thoughts. 'If you ask me, that Jake of yours must be totally blind, not to say crazy. Fancy throwing up the chance of a girl like you! What he needs is his head examined!'

'It's me who needs my head examined!' Shiona frowned and stared down into her champagne glass. 'Fancy falling in love with the same man twice—when I knew he could never be interested in me!'

'He sounded interested enough from what you told me. Or at least not entirely indifferent, shall we say?'

Shiona shook her head. 'That was just one of these things.' She knew he was referring to her last meeting with Jake and that explosive love scene in the drawing-room, only the sketchiest version of which he'd been privy to. She herself had thought about it often throughout many a long and sleepless night, tormenting herself by reliving each sweet moment, yet knowing it would be wiser just to forget it.

She raised her eyes to Desmond's. 'It didn't mean anything. And besides,' she added, 'he's probably married by now.'

It had struck her that perhaps that was where Jake had been going that night he'd called her from Heathrow Airport—on a secret brief honeymoon with Janice after a quick, quiet register office wedding. In fact, the more she had thought about it the more convinced she had become.

As she bit her lip, Desmond recognised her pain, and reached out sympathetically to touch her hand. 'You'll forget him. You'll see,' he assured her, smiling gently. 'One day you'll fall in love again.'

Shiona nodded. 'Of course I'll fall in love again.' Though she didn't believe it for a moment. The only man she had ever loved was Jake. She suspected she was incapable of loving any other.

Her friend squeezed her arm and winked across at her. Then his expression brightened as he gently changed the subject. 'Let's talk a little more about the Paris gala. . .'

It was late—after eleven—when they left the restaurant, and they decided to share a taxi.

'We'll drop you off first,' Desmond suggested.

But Shiona insisted, 'Don't be silly. It makes much more sense to drop you off first.'

'But I prefer to see you safely to your flat. A young lady like yourself needs looking after.'

'I can look after myself.' Shiona wouldn't hear of it. 'Don't worry, I'll be perfectly OK on my own.'

Famous last words, she thought to herself, as she stepped out of the lift on to the second-floor landing of the luxury block of flats where she lived. Though the landing was empty and there wasn't a sound all around, she had the strangest sensation that someone was there.

The entrance to her own flat was down one of the narrow corridors that led off from the rectangular landing, and as she stepped towards it she noticed with sudden uneasiness that one of the wall lights halfway down the corridor had gone, plunging the passageway into semi-darkness. All at once she was wishing that Desmond was with her.

Don't be silly! she chided herself with impatience. You come home alone every night of your life! What are you suddenly so afraid of?

But she had barely gone two steps along the

corridor when something moved out of the shadows. The tall, threatening figure of a man. Her heart flew to her mouth as she yelped and turned tail.

'Stop! Come back!' a man's voice was calling. She could hear footsteps striding along the corridor behind her.

But she kept on running, as panic overtook her, and didn't stop until she was back at the lift.

'Shiona! It's me!' As her finger jabbed the button, suddenly a firm hand was on her sleeve. 'I'm sorry I scared you. I didn't mean to.' He swung her round. 'Shiona, it's me!'

Her heart was almost jumping out of her ribcage. She stared at him breathlessly, unable to speak. Then she sighed and swallowed. 'Jake!' she breathed.

He held her by the shoulders, his grip firm and comforting. 'I've been waiting for you for the past three hours, pacing the corridors, wearing out the carpet. I didn't mean to give you a fright like that.'

Shiona smiled shakily, as her shock turned to bewilderment. What on earth was Jake doing here?

He had dropped his hands down from her shoulders and slipped them into his trouser-pockets. 'I know it's late, but I want to talk to you.'

'What about?' Shiona was still standing by the elevator, watching him with suspicious hazel eyes. There was something odd about him, an air of uncertainty, a dark, worried look at the back of his eyes. Then a thought suddenly occurred to her. She felt a dart of panic. 'Is it something to do with Kirsty? Has something happened to her?'

'It's nothing to do with Kirsty. Kirsty's fine.' He

smiled reassuringly and for a moment his expression softened. Then once more the deep blue eyes grew serious. 'Do you think we can go to your flat now and talk?'

She wanted to say yes. She wanted to take hold of him and throw herself recklessly into his arms. But at the same time, for her sanity's sake, she knew she must say no while she still had the strength to do so.

She averted her gaze. 'I'd rather not. It's much too late and I'm extremely tired.'

'Please?'

Shiona blinked. Had she heard him say please? She swallowed awkwardly. 'Can't it wait until tomorrow?'

'It could, but I'd much rather talk to you now. I've come all the way from Loch Lomond just to see you. It won't take long. No more than half an hour.' He smiled persuasively. 'Then I promise I'll leave.'

Her will was broken. There was no way in the world she could deny that earnest, almost pleading look in his eyes.

Shiona sighed, defeated. 'OK, then. But remember you promised half an hour.'

Jake nodded. 'As soon as I've told you what I've come for, I promise you can throw me out.'

They walked down the corridor in single file, Shiona leading the way to her front door. Then, once inside the sitting-room, she bade him take a seat. 'I'm going to have a drink. What will you have?' she offered.

He nodded. 'I'll have a whisky with just a dash of water.' Then he sat down on the sofa and looked around him. 'This is a pretty nice place you've got here,' he told her.

'Thank you. I like it,' Shiona answered over her shoulder, as she poured a whisky for him and a brandy for herself. It wasn't like Jake to make small talk, she was thinking. What on earth was going on?

She crossed the carpet and handed him his whisky, then seated herself in the armchair opposite him, smoothing her slim skirt over her knees. And she found her eyes drifting to examine his left hand, noting that as usual he was wearing no rings, hating the way hope stirred foolishly for a moment.

Almost as though to punish herself for that foolishness, she forced herself to look him in the eye and enquire, 'So, how is Janice enjoying married life?'

He paused for only an instant. 'I can't really speak for her, but I would imagine she's enjoying it.'

His words were like a body-blow. Momentarily, Shiona felt winded. Suddenly she realised just how much she'd been hoping that Jake and Janice were still not married.

She swallowed the mountain that had lodged in her throat and asked with thin sarcasm, 'Why, hasn't she told you?'

'As a matter of fact, she hasn't. But then, she hasn't had an opportunity.' His eyes, as he spoke, were strangely shuttered. 'I haven't seen her since the wedding.'

'How very peculiar.' Shiona's breathing was ragged. She felt like jumping to her feet and asking him to leave instantly. This conversation was proving to be unbearably painful. Each word he uttered was a knife in her heart.

'What's the matter?' she enquired. 'Aren't you speaking?'

He shook his head. 'We haven't spoken since the wedding.'

Shiona frowned. He was starting to confuse her. Then he smiled lop-sidedly and confused her even further. 'She's currently in Mexico on her honeymoon.'

'Honeymoon?'

'Honeymoon.'

She was lost completely. 'So why aren't you with her?' Shiona peered across at him. 'Don't tell me she's honeymooning alone?'

'Absolutely not.' Jake sat forward in his seat. 'She's with her husband, just as she should be.'

Suddenly the room had become a total blur and Shiona's limbs felt as though they belonged to someone else. She laid down her glass before she dropped it. 'Would you kindly explain to me what you're talking about?'

'It's very easy.' Jake's eyes were on her. 'Janice has married someone else.'

'Someone else?' She could not believe it. 'But she told me she was pregnant with your baby!'

'Pregnant, yes, but not with *my* baby. I'm sure she never told you that. The father is the man who she's just married.'

Shiona sank back limply in her seat. 'You'll have to explain. I'm lost,' she told him.

'It sounds complicated, I know, but it's really

pretty simple.' Jake took a long swig from his glass. 'I agreed to marry Janice to get her out of a fix. This man she's married finally came to his senses, but he was refusing to marry her at one point. She was in a desperate state because of the baby. She's not the type to be an unmarried mother.'

'So you offered to marry her? That was pretty good of you.'

Suddenly the whole story was perfectly clear to her. Shiona's eyes narrowed as she elaborated tartly, 'But, of course, the arrangement was handy for you, too. It meant that you would gain custody of Kirsty!'

He was silent for a moment. Then he nodded his head. 'It sounds pretty cold-hearted when you put it like that, but I love that little girl. I wanted to be her father——'

'Even at the cost of marrying a woman you didn't love?'

'That was what I thought——'

'How could you? You're despicable! To go to such lengths to stop me gaining custody!'

At her words, for an instant his expression hardened. 'You're right; at that stage I would have done almost anything to stop Kirsty falling into your hands. And at that stage, when I entered into the agreement, I believed that a marriage to Janice could have worked.'

What he was saying hurt Shiona more than she could ever have believed possible. How could he have behaved so cynically? Did this man whom she loved have no heart at all? Had her love of all these years been thrown away on a man who was incapable of loving in return?

She reached for her brandy glass, her fingers tight around it. 'How could you even contemplate marrying a woman like that?'

'Because I was blind. Because I was desperate to save Kirsty—and because I didn't realise what type of woman Janice was. But I soon found out—even before you told me—and I was totally appalled at what I'd done. I knew I could never inflict her as a mother on Kirsty, but I was totally trapped by the promise I'd made. When I tried to get out of it, she threatened suicide. I was caught in a trap of my own foolish making.'

He sighed a harsh sigh and leaned back in his seat. 'I knew there was only one thing I could do—find the father of Janice's baby and persuade him to marry her in my place.' He shook his head and stabbed his fingers through his hair. 'It took me weeks, but I finally did it. I finally tracked him down to Antwerp.'

Shiona's eyes were wide, mesmerised by his story. 'So that was the business that took you to Holland?'

Jake nodded. 'That's right. But when I got there, he'd already moved on to the Middle East. That was when I phoned you. I thought I'd lost him forever. I thought I was going to have to end up marrying Janice, after all.'

'But you found him?'

'In the end, I found him. It wasn't easy, but I persuaded him to do the right thing. Let's just say there was a small exchange of money.'

Shiona shook her head. She could scarcely believe it all. 'And how about Janice? How did she react?'

'She was over the moon. She's really in love with this guy. As you yourself so candidly pointed out, she was only marrying me for my money—and, of course, to get out of a fix.'

Suddenly it was all clear—except for one thing. Shiona frowned. 'But why, once you'd found out the truth about Ryan and me, didn't you drop your custody claim immediately? Why did you wait until you were in Holland?'

'Because up until then I was absolutely positive that I would eventually manage to get out of the marriage, and it was my plan to seek custody as a single person. It was only when I was in Holland that I had my first serious doubts that I might actually fail and have to marry Janice—in which case there was no way I would wish to claim custody.'

'I see.' But there was still something else that bothered her. 'But what if you hadn't found out about me and Ryan? What if you'd gone on believing the worst of me and into the bargain you'd ended up having to marry Janice? What would you have done about Kirsty then?'

'Don't make me think of that.' A pained look crossed Jake's face. 'I would have had to have come to some arrangement with Janice—separate houses, separate lives—and taken on the job of looking after Kirsty myself, even if it had meant giving up my job.' His eyes were fierce. Shiona could see he was serious. 'Don't worry, there was no way in the world that I would ever have allowed Janice to get anywhere near her.'

That made Shiona feel better. But then a new thought occurred to her. She took a nervous mouthful from her glass. 'Have you come here to tell me that you're going to fight me after all, now that Janice is no longer around?'

He shook his head. 'No, that's not why I've come here. We've already done more than enough fighting, you and I.' There was a momentary pause. His eyes were on her. Then he rose to his feet suddenly, taking her by surprise. 'I suppose you know all of this is your fault?' he accused her.

Shiona blinked up at him, a sudden nervousness within her. 'I don't know what you're talking about,' she defended.

'What I'm talking about is that secret of yours and Ryan's.' Suddenly he had crossed the gap between them. 'If you'd told me the truth about that years ago, none of this wretched business would have happened.' Then, before she could answer, he had reached down to take hold of her and was drawing her firmly to her feet.

He looked down into her face. 'If only I'd known the truth about you, Shiona, there would have been no need for me to keep running away from my feelings for you. I could have told you years ago how I feel about you instead of trying to pretend to myself that I felt nothing.'

Suddenly Shiona could not look at him. She fixed her eyes on his tie, though she could barely focus. 'I've always known how you felt about me,' she mumbled. 'I've never had the smallest doubt that you hated me.'

He laughed a harsh laugh and shook her impatiently. 'Liar! You know I've never hated you—though for years I've been wishing that I could!'

Her eyes swivelled up then. Was he making fun of her? But as his gaze meshed with hers she knew that he wasn't. There was pain in his face, anguish shining from his eyes. Her heart stilled as suddenly his grip on her tightened.

'For pity's sake, Shiona, don't you know I've always loved you?'

Love?

For a moment the universe tilted. She had to hold on tight to him or else she might fall off. And suddenly that cold void deep within her was running over with warmth and happiness.

She leaned against him.

'Oh, Jake! Oh, Jake!'

Much later they lay in one another's arms, at peace amidst a frenzied tangle of bedclothes.

Shiona snuggled happily against Jake's broad, hard chest, listening to the steady sound of his heartbeat. 'I love you,' she whispered. It felt wonderful to say it.

'And I love you.'

He had said it a hundred times over the past blissful hour together, and each time the sound of it had been even sweeter. Then he sighed and ran his fingers through her hair.

'What fools we've been to waste so much precious

time. All those years when we could have been together.'

Shiona glanced up at him, at the head of thick hair, so dark and glossy against the creamy pillow, at the sculpted curved nose, the wide, mobile mouth and those eyes of deepest darkest sapphire. 'It's pointless to regret things,' she told him, smiling. 'And, besides, I wouldn't have missed this moment for the world.'

He tousled her hair that tumbled over her shoulders in a wild, bright mane of warmest auburn. 'My beautiful temptress.' He leaned and kissed her, letting his hand slide over her breast. Then, as she shuddered, he held her for a moment against him. 'There will be many more moments like this,' he promised her.

Shiona closed her eyes and drank in the scent of him, the virile, masculine scent of love. And her stomach twisted as she relived deliciously the moments of passion they had so recently shared.

She felt a shudder deep inside her. How well, how wonderfully he had loved her.

They had arrived in the bedroom without knowing how they had got there. As though their need for one another, so long denied, had demanded finally to be fulfilled. Then they had been sinking on to the bed and, between kisses and caresses, peeling the clothes hungrily from one another, until at last they lay naked, side by side.

Then with love they had explored one another's bodies with hands that were urgent, yet full of tenderness, each touch a declaration of the joy that possessed them, each kiss an unspoken protestation of love.

Shiona had never known such perfect happiness. To be kissed in such a way and caressed in such a way, with so much love, by a man she adored. And inside her an unbearable excitement was building as they had moved towards that luminous moment when the two of them would finally be one.

When at last he'd come to her, his manhood hard against her, she held her breath and looked into his eyes.

'I love you,' he'd whispered and her heart stood still within her. Then she had gasped as he entered her and her poor heart burst with joy.

Surely it cannot be possible, she was thinking, to love anyone as intensely as I love this man.

Jake was kissing her now and stroking her hair. 'There will be many more such moments,' he repeated, smiling down at her. Then he frowned at her suddenly. 'How on earth could I be so crazy?'

'Crazy, you?' Shiona was smiling at him. 'Crazy isn't something I've ever thought you were.'

'Yet I am, nevertheless.' He gathered her to him. 'All these years I denied my love. All these years I tried to kill it.' He frowned into her face. 'I was so desperately afraid that you would turn out to be the sort of person who cares only about money and possessions.' He shook his head wryly. 'Like Janice, in other words.'

As Shiona touched his cheek, he paused for a moment. 'Did Ryan ever tell you about our mother?'

'Only that she died and that he loved her. He never told me any details.'

'Then let me tell you. It might help to explain things.' He rested his dark head against the pillows and gazed up at the ceiling as he spoke. 'Unlike my father, who had to work for his money, my mother was born into a very wealthy family. She always had everything she wanted. She never had to work a day in her life.'

He sighed. 'Let me tell you, that's not good for anyone. By the time she was thirty she was a bored, disgruntled woman whose only interest in life was squandering money. But that didn't make her happy. She started drinking heavily. Eventually she became an alcoholic.' He flicked a pained look in Shiona's direction. 'You were probably told that she died of a heart attack—but she didn't. What she died of was acute liver failure.'

There was a momentary silence. Shiona stroked his furrowed brow. 'Just like Ryan with his drugs,' she said quietly. 'He went the same way as your mother.'

Jake drew in breath. 'I should have suspected, but I thought we'd both learned from the tragedy of our mother.' He exhaled impatiently. 'Poor Ryan. I wish I'd known. How I wish I could have helped him.'

Shiona touched his cheek. 'He wouldn't have let you. He would have hated it if you'd known he was an addict. He admired you so much.' She smiled gently. 'More than anything he wanted to be like you.'

'Like me?' Jake smiled wryly, disbelieving. 'Why on earth would he want to be like me?'

'Because you're so successful, so together. And because everything you've achieved, you've achieved on your own.'

Jake shook his head and smiled at her wryly. 'Yes, that was a bit of an obsession, I'm afraid. Right from the start I was utterly determined I wasn't going to fall into the trap of the idle, pampered, rich man's son. I would never have been able to respect myself if all I'd ever done was take from my father.'

Shiona sat up on her elbow and looked down into his face. 'Is that why you were so disapproving of my apparent readiness to exploit your father's generosity towards me?'

'I'm afraid it was.' He pulled a face. 'And I reckon it was all tied up with what happened to my mother.' He reached out to touch her hair, running his fingers through it. 'I should have recognised that you were a stronger character than that, and accepted your delight in the presents my father gave you for what it was—sheer, innocent pleasure.'

He leaned to kiss her face, his eyes dark and serious. 'Perhaps I also used these silly criticisms of mine as a kind of buffer against the way I was starting to feel about you. For even then I was falling in love with you, though you were little more than a child at the time.'

Shiona punched his arm playfully. 'I was sixteen! I hardly think you can call that a child!'

'Well, to me it seemed a child. I was twenty-four. I felt that falling in love with you at that stage would very definitely not be a good idea.' He turned away. 'And then, years later, when Ryan died with not a penny to his name, I jumped to all the wrong conclusions—and, of course, you let me. You never defended yourself.'

His voice caught in his throat as he turned to take hold of her and press her fiercely against his chest. 'You wonderful little fool. How much I love you. And how painful it's been at times to love you. I tried to stop, but I couldn't do it. You are etched in my heart. I couldn't erase you.'

Shiona hugged him and kissed him. 'I'm glad you couldn't. And I'm glad *I* couldn't. I'm glad I love you.'

'Thank heavens for Kirsty!' He smiled at her suddenly. 'If we hadn't got involved in fighting over Kirsty, we might never have found out how each of us really feels.'

Shiona made a face. 'I don't believe you. Surely you always knew that I was in love with you?'

'I swear I didn't. How could I have known it? After all, you never told me.'

'But it must have been obvious!' Shiona scowled at him. 'I used to behave like your adoring little slave girl!'

'Did you? I didn't notice.' He smiled at her roguishly. 'And do you plan on continuing to be my adoring little slave girl?'

'I'll think about it.' Shiona bit his ear. 'If you promise to be my slave in return.'

He laughed and kissed her. 'I can think of nothing

nicer. I shall be your slave, if you wish. And, of course, your husband.'

Shiona blinked at that.

'You have no choice but to marry me.' He smiled at her, teasing her. 'You owe it to Kirsty. She needs a mother *and* a father.' Then his expression sobered. 'Besides which, my dear Shiona, I've waited long enough for you, and I've just come all the way from Loch Lomond to propose to you. There's no way I intend to let you out of this bed until you've promised that you'll marry me.'

'Is that really what you came for?'

'That's really what I came for.' He kissed her face. 'And as I said, there's no way I'm going to let you out of this bed until I have your answer in the affirmative.'

'But I like this bed.' Deliberately, she teased him, though her heart was thundering with happiness inside her. 'I'm in no hurry to get out.'

'OK. Then let me put it another way.' Jake leaned across suddenly, pinning her arms against the mattress. 'I refuse to make love to you again until you've agreed to be my wife.'

'You heartless creature!' Shiona's eyes were shining. 'In that case, what choice do I have but to agree?' Then she stretched up to kiss him warmly on the lips. 'Besides, I love you. I want to be your wife.'

Jake gathered her to him and rolled over on his back, so that she was lying on her stomach on top of him. 'I've already made arrangements to cut down on my travelling, but what are we going to do about you? Will you commute or should I move my base down to London?'

Shiona shook her head. 'No, we all belong in Scotland. I'll commute when I need to, at most once or twice a week.' Then she laughed with sudden pleasure. 'It's all going to be perfect! I just know it! I can feel it in my bones!'

He was smiling up at her. 'It's going to be more than just perfect.' He stroked her hair and kissed her face, then rolled her over to lean over her once more. 'It's going to be the best damned marriage there ever was!'

And as she pressed against him and felt his passion stirring, and saw the depth of emotion that shone from his eyes, Shiona knew beyond a doubt that his promise was true.

The battle for love had been fought and won, and the prize, at last and forever, was theirs.

From the author of Mirrors comes an enchanting romance

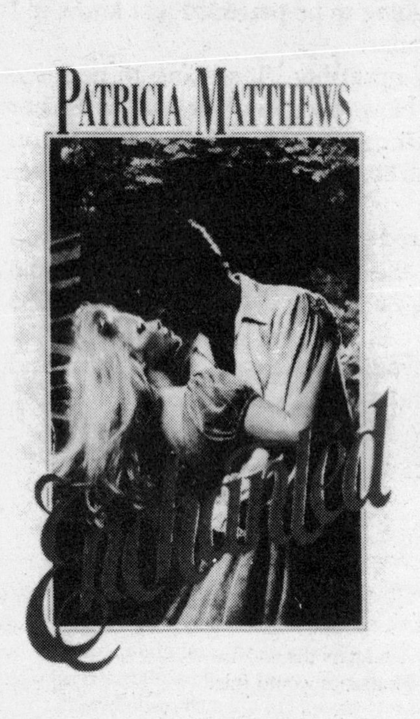

Caught in the steamy heat of America's New South, Rebecca Trenton finds herself torn between two brothers – she yearns for one, but a dark secret binds her to the other.

Off the coast of South Carolina lay Pirate's Bank – a small island as intriguing as the legendary family that lived there. As the mystery surrounding the island deepened, so Rebecca was drawn further into the family's dark secret – and only one man's love could save her from the treachery which now threatened her life.

WORLDWIDE

AVAILABLE IN JANUARY 1992 – PRICE: £3.99

Available from Boots, Martins, John Menzies, W.H. Smith, most supermarkets and other paperback stockists.
Also available from Mills & Boon Reader Service, PO Box 236, Thornton Road, Croydon, Surrey, CR9 3RU